Living to See You

LIVING TO SEE YOU

Geoff and Ro

with love

Maggie

BEE JOHNSTONE

Matador
9 Priory Business Park,
Wistow Road, Kibworth Beauchamp,
Leicestershire. LE8 0RX
Tel: 0116 279 2299
Email: books@troubador.co.uk
Web: www.troubador.co.uk/matador
Twitter: @matadorbooks

ISBN 978 1785898 884

British Library Cataloguing in Publication Data.
A catalogue record for this book is available from the British Library.

Printed and bound in the UK by TJ International, Padstow, Cornwall
Typeset in 11pt Aldine401 BT by Troubador Publishing Ltd, Leicester, UK

Matador is an imprint of Troubador Publishing Ltd

FSC www.fsc.org MIX Paper from responsible sources FSC® C013056

This book is dedicated to my parents, upon whose wartime lives it is based.

Acknowledgements

I am grateful to J.T. for her invaluable assistance with the manuscript; Gary West for his detailed advice on aviation and the RAF; Tony Cowland for his cover design; and Derek Robinson for encouraging me to self-publish. I would also like to thank RAF Shawbury and the archivists at RAF Boscombe Down, for their contribution and help.

The *Textbook of Medicine*, edited by J.J. Coneybeare, sixth edition, 1942, was on loan from the Royal Society of Medicine.

I would also like to thank my husband and my family for their patient support.

Author's Note

While many of the characters in this book are fictional, the story is based on true fact. When characters are named, it is intended as a tribute to their contribution to the war effort, for example, Vic Willis, who won the DFC for his part in Operation Jostle.

Contents

Autumn 1940

Part One:
Fever Ward

1

It was never really quiet on the ward at night, even when the children were asleep. Some small child would wake and cry; another might call out, such that a quiet orchestra of subtle sounds permeated the dim light. The ward was cold, despite the stove at one end, and the stark framed beds were lined up and down each side.

It was lonely, the long night stretching through from seven o'clock in the evening until eight o'clock the next morning, only interrupted by night sister on her rounds. Still, Honor was glad to be on the scarlet fever ward, where most of the children would recover and go home. Not so the diphtheria ward, which she had found the most difficult so far. There was so little antitoxin available and many of the worst cases presented too late. That smell on the breath of the sick children, the awful membrane which could fill the throat, the desperate attempts to ensure an airway… Honor had been night nursing on the diphtheria ward for three weeks and had no desire to go back. She had never thought to see children die in such a way, and was shocked at their quiet suffering: some, in particular, stuck in her mind, like grubby little Jamie, not four years old when he was admitted from his crowded back-to-back house in the slums. He had looked like a real fighter at the start, but had finally surrendered to the overwhelming consequences of the disease. She had watched by his bed in horror, holding his limp hand, while the doctor had tried to insert a tracheotomy needle into the gasping child's neck. It had not worked, and Jamie had died anyway, as she had informed his grief-stricken mother the following morning.

With none of the daytime bustle, there was more time to think, and try to study. Whatever the tribulations of the ward, it was nothing compared to the exams which lay ahead of her. There was always so much to learn, usually at the side of a more experienced nurse, watching and memorising procedures and routines: how to wash a bedpan, clean the sluice, take a throat swab, test urine, assist the doctors, sterilise the instruments, or worst of all, how to lay out the body of a child who had given up the unequal struggle to survive.

Honor was not troubled by her long hours, sparse time off and poor pay. Her training was not only stimulating and challenging, it was the key to a better life.

2

She had not planned to run away from home so precipitously. Suddenly, she could take no more: no more of her parents who rejected her because, as the middle of three girls, she should have been a boy, and thus represented a continuous disappointment. No more of her unsympathetic sisters and the drudgery in the vicarage where she had been sent as a kitchen maid after leaving school. No more of the unwanted attentions of the parson, who would appear silently and suddenly behind her as she blacked the grate. No one would listen to her plight, trapped as she was in her class and its prejudices.

'I'm sure the parson would never try and touch you, Honor!' Her mother cut her off in horror. 'He's a man of the cloth! And so respected in the village.' But Honor knew that the parson had tried to do much more than that, and would continue with increasing force until he had his way. So escape was her only recourse, and she fled to the City, friendless, nearly penniless, innocent and unworldly.

Her strong sense of self-preservation was her only guide, but could not protect her from some perilous encounters. She had finally found work as a ward maid in the Lambeth Hospital. It was bitterly hard, but safe, as she had accommodation in the maids' rooms and the protection of the institution. The nurses, especially the sisters, expected impossibly high standards of cleanliness on the wards. Each day she rose at dawn, and poured the freezing water from the jug into the basin to wash her hands and face before dressing in her austere uniform. Then it was straight to the wards to light the fires, followed by a regime of cleaning, scrubbing, damp dusting and polishing that seemed as though it would never end. She saw it as a haven, nonetheless, from the pitfalls outside; the horizons of her eighteen-year-old world had contracted to a safer place, she accepted the back-breaking work with dignity, and found herself on good terms with the nurses who noticed her assiduity.

It was Sister Martin who changed her life, in an act of Christian compassion that Honor had long since ceased to expect.

'Why are you doing this job?' Sister asked her late one autumn day, noticing the girl's fatigue and her chapped hands. She was a kindly, middle-aged Scottish nurse of strict values and undoubted vocation.

'I don't have much choice,' Honor answered stoically. 'It's a good deal better than some of the alternatives, I can tell you.'

'Have you got any family or friends?'

'None that are interested in me. I expect they were all glad to get rid of me.' A note of bitterness crept into Honor's voice.

'You seem bright enough to me,' the senior nurse persisted. 'You work hard too. Why don't you train as a nurse? We're bound to need more nurses in this war, you might stand a chance.'

'They'd never allow me! I left school at fourteen. That's why I'm a ward cleaner, and I expect that's what I'll stay.'

'Nonsense,' replied the older woman. Sister Martin was not accustomed to allowing small obstacles to stand in her way. 'I'm going to talk to Matron on your behalf.'

Honor had little hope for the outcome. Since when were girls from her background allowed to train as nurses? The rigid class systems of the country were as strong as ever, irrespective of intelligence or aptitude. Even the start of the war last year had done little to lift her aspirations, and merely helped to confirm the necessity of hard work and forbearance.

She had not reckoned with the determination of Sister Martin, who came to find her in the sluice the next day. Honor was mopping down the floor and wiping stains from the white tiled walls with Lysol.

'I told you so!' Sister's face was triumphant. 'Matron says you're to see her this afternoon!'

Honor looked at her with incredulity. 'What do you mean?'

'She's going to give you a chance!'

'Are you sure?'

'Yes, Honor, she wants to talk to you. Not everyone is against you in the world, you know. I know you've had some hard knocks, but don't stop trusting people altogether.'

'Sister, I don't know what to say.' Honor felt the tears rising, tears she had suppressed for so long in the grim struggle for safety and survival. 'You're a truly kind person.'

'There, my dear, no time to cry.' Sister put an arm around her slight shoulders. 'You and I will have a little cup of tea first.'

When it came to it, the encounter was better than Honor could have hoped. Matron could be a most forbidding personage, and Honor knew what fear she could strike into the heart of any inattentive member of staff. She had seen senior nursing sisters in tears after one of her unannounced ward visits. It was accepted that Matron's rule was absolute and no one, not even the doctors, would seek to defy her. She was, nonetheless, a serene-looking woman of late middle age, neat and precise in her matron's uniform, with a composed face that must have been attractive in her youth.

'Honor, I've heard good reports of you from Sister Martin, and others,' she began. 'Sister thinks that you're capable of nurse training. What do you have to say about it?'

Honor sat bolt upright on the hard wooden chair, looking Matron directly in the eyes, respectful but not in awe. 'I never thought I'd have the chance, Matron,' she replied steadily. 'I wasn't able to stay on at school, you know, but I always liked learning. I'd give everything to be a nurse – when I see those sick children in their beds, I want to help them, more than just by cleaning. I'd work my back off, honestly, I wouldn't let you down!'

Matron looked thoughtful. 'No, I don't believe you would. Do you think you have the strength, Honor?'

'I've certainly needed it so far, Matron. I wouldn't be here if I was one to give up easily.'

Matron looked at some papers on her desk. 'I've decided you will start as a probationer next week, after I've taken your case to the Hospital Board. Sister Hobbs is in charge of nurse training, and she will take over responsibility for your timetable. I warn you, it will be very tough, but I trust you to do your best and hope to see you as a state registered nurse one day.' She nodded at Honor, who rose to her feet.

'Thank you, Matron', she replied, and left the room feeling curiously disorientated, as she trod the dark wooden polished corridor back to her ward.

3

Honor found the training demanding, but not impossible. The hours, though long on a twelve-hour day shift, were no worse than she had experienced as a ward maid, and there was the constant stimulation of learning, rather than the plain drudgery which had preceded it. She was, if anything, more robust than her fellow students, most of whom had come from better-off homes. The majority were the same age, with a few older women prompted into nursing as part of the war effort. She tended to stay rather apart from the other girls, who seemed to her immature and occasionally silly. She liked Beatie, though. Beatie, short and slightly plump, had an infectious sense of humour.

'Are we cooped up in the hospital all the time?' Beatie asked on her first day. 'Do we never get to go out, you know, to dances or the pictures?'

Honor felt slightly disapproving. 'Oh dear me no, we hardly have any time off and I don't think we'll be allowed out to that sort of thing.' She had no desire to return to the dangers of the outside world.

Beatie rolled her eyes upwards. 'What are the doctors like? Any good-looking ones?'

'Oh, I really don't know,' replied Honor truthfully, for she had caught little more than glimpses of the medical staff when she was on her knees cleaning the ward.

'More like a nunnery than a hospital if you ask me.' Beatie tossed her fair, curly head, leaving the distinct impression that she would be seeking freedom sooner or later.

Honor smiled cautiously. She was now dressed in the regulation probationer's uniform, black stockings and flat shoes, but even the plain, dark dress could not hide her slim, upright figure. Her brown hair was severely pinned back, framing a face of character, but also beauty, in the dark wide-set eyes and determined full mouth.

Their conversation was interrupted by Sister Colville, one of the dragons of the higher nursing echelons. Sister Colville's compassion had long since seeped out of her thin, bony frame, and she peered at Beatie disapprovingly.

'Nurse Molesworth, your hair is not properly pinned back. Go straight to your room and put it right. Now, Nurse Newson,' she turned her attention to Honor, 'you and Nurse Molesworth will train here on the children's wards for the first month. You will both answer to me, as well as the other sisters. Your nurse tutor today is Sister Reardon, you must stay with her every moment of the day and do exactly as she tells you. Follow and watch extremely carefully, and when you are asked to perform a procedure, make sure you do it correctly. You will attend the classroom lessons even if these are in your off-duty time. Do you have any questions?' she concluded.

'No, Sister,' replied Honor.

Mercifully, Sister Reardon was a much less forbidding character. She smiled at Honor. 'No need to look so worried, you'll just be watching me at first.' She spoke with a soft Irish brogue, and had a pleasant, almost homely demeanour.

'Bed-making first,' Sister Reardon said. She stopped by a small girl in one of the heavy iron beds. 'Morning, Heather, how are we today?' She stroked the little forehead as she spoke.

'Bit better.' Heather, who could not have been more than six years old, looked flushed and anxious.

'Well, Heather, Nurse and I will tidy up your bed and then I'll check your temperature.' Sister motioned Honor to the other side of the bed. 'This has to be exactly right,' she added, then proceeded to show her a wonder of folding, turning and tucking of sheets that left Honor in a state of some confusion. Her face must have betrayed her. 'It's all right,' Sister said softly, 'I'll be showing you lots more before you have to do it by yourself.'

As the days passed, Honor began to accept some of the essential duties which would fall to her. She soon found she was able to take a swab, clean a bedpan, sponge a feverish child, all carefully watched and encouraged by her mentor. She kept a little notebook to help her memorise some of the important facts, and felt able to ask questions of Sister Reardon, which were succinctly and helpfully answered.

'Lucky you,' moaned Beatie one day as they walked over to the nurses' dining room for lunch. 'I'm absolutely terrified of my tutor, she's a real tartar, and every time she asks me to do anything you can be sure I'll get it completely wrong!'

Honor sympathised – she could never have coped with the likes of Sister Colville breathing down her neck. Beatie, her independent spirit not easily given over to the disciplines of nurse training, began to show signs of defeat.

'I can't take much more of her,' she confided to Honor at the end of the first month. They were due to have a preliminary exam the following day, and a pass mark would be essential if they were to continue. 'What say we skip out tonight, Honor?' Beatie suggested on their way back to the nurses' home. She pulled her hated cap from her head whilst warming to her theme. 'We can pop down the fire escape after lock-up, hop on a bus to the Palais, have a dance with some of the servicemen and be back before any of those shrivelled old nurses know anything about it!' The front door to the nurses' home was always locked by 10pm, but that did not stop the truly determined from trying to break out.

'Beatie, no! We've got an exam tomorrow,' Honor remonstrated. 'Besides, you'll get caught, then you'll be thrown out, and then what will happen? Just wait for a bit, it might get better soon.'

Beatie was not to be deterred. 'I'm sick of it all,' she replied hotly. 'If I can just get out for a bit of normal life, a bit of fun for a change, maybe I'll be able to put up with it tomorrow. Are you sure you don't fancy it? You're so strait-laced, it would do you good to let your hair down. Come on, what's stopping you?'

Honor shook her head. 'I couldn't,' she said quietly, 'I've got more to lose than you have.'

'Please yourself.' Beatie could see that she was a lost cause. 'I'll ask Nancy, she looks one for a bit of a lark.'

They arrived at the austere nurses' home with Beatie's resolve strengthened, rather than weakened, by her friend's refusal. Honor said no more but doubted that Beatie would have the nerve, especially tonight.

She had underestimated Beatie. After spending the evening washing her hair and trying to read and memorise her textbook, at midnight Honor finally turned the page on *The treatment of childhood tuberculosis* and began to prepare for bed. She was in her flannel nightgown, and intent on diving beneath the covers as soon as possible. She was settling down to sleep when she was disturbed by a gravelly sound at her first-floor window. Rising reluctantly from her bed, she lifted the curtain tentatively. There, in the middle of the flower border, were Beatie and Nancy, waving and signalling to her urgently and silently. Honor opened the window a crack.

'What's the matter?' she hissed at the two girls.

Beatie did not reply, but pointed up to the fire escape and grimaced, miming trying to open a locked door handle. Honor shook her head in despair, while Beatie held up her two hands in silent entreaty.

Honor sighed. What type of ridiculous mess was this? 'Stupid, stupid Beatie,' she muttered under her breath as she wrapped her rough dressing gown tightly around her. There was no choice really, she could not leave them standing there. Tiptoeing without her slippers, she left her room, remembering the little torch supplied for use in the blackout. Making her way quietly up the long polished staircase to the second, then third floor, the fire escape was in sight when she heard a door opening in the corridor behind her. Honor ducked into the bathroom and hid behind the door, scarcely daring to breathe. After a long time, the lavatory flushed and she glimpsed the retreating figure of Sister Colville. Retracing her steps, Honor tried the fire escape door gingerly. Beatie was right, it was locked, but all the domestics knew that the key was kept on top of a tiny cupboard beside it. Retrieving it, she unlocked the door, and left it ajar for the two shadowy figures on their way up.

The girls hurried in. Honor, with her finger to her lips, noticed that Nancy was slightly unsteady on her feet, and motioned them to remove their shoes. Beatie, mouthing, 'Thank you!' scurried off while Honor locked the door. The others had only one flight of stairs to reach their rooms, and they had disappeared by the time Honor took the final flight back to the safety of her own. She had nearly made it, when one of the sisters appeared in the corridor.

'Is there anything the matter, Nurse?' It was Sister Davies, a young, attractive woman, who still looked as though she might have a life other than nursing in front of her.

'Sorry, Sister,' Honor moved towards her door handle, 'I've just got a bit of a tummy ache and needed to go…' She pointed toward the lavatory.

'All right, Nurse,' Sister responded briskly, 'I expect you're worrying about tomorrow. Best go and get some sleep.'

'Thank you.' Honor was inside her room in a flash, sitting on the bed mutely until the danger was over. *That was close*, she thought to herself, *too close*, sobered by the possible implications of Beatie's rashness. *Next time*, she resolved, dropping off to sleep, *they'll have to take the consequences alone*.

4

Honor awoke to the alarm bell after a surprisingly heavy sleep, populated by dreams of pursuit involving Sister Colville, Matron and herself. After one last glance at her textbooks, she went down to the dining room for breakfast. It was the usual lumpy porridge and dry toast, but she ate it hungrily. Honor had always felt hungry since she was a child, remembering the sparse meals put together by her mother out of almost nothing. Some of them, on good days when her father had been paid for his endless labouring on the land, were still delicious in her mind, like the bacon dumplings. It would be a long time before rationing allowed her to have even such simple fare again.

Nancy looked blearily across the table at her.

'You all right, Nance?' Honor ventured, but Nancy merely shook her head in reply.

Moments later Beatie made a last-minute entrance to the dining room, looking pale but determined, and sat down to her cup of tea after surreptitiously squeezing Honor's hand under the table.

'Right, I'm off,' Honor rose as if to distance herself from them both, 'see you later.' She made her way quickly to the large, airy classroom on the ground floor where they were to sit their exam.

The next two hours required all of her concentration, as she tried to recall the information she had learnt so painstakingly both on the ward and from her textbooks. She had not reckoned with all of the questions, and found herself quite stumped by some, including: *Why is the diphtheria patient nursed flat and not allowed to move?* Also: *Explain the function of the iron lung*. How would she know, she thought, her brow furrowed; she had not yet nursed on the polio ward. She tried her hardest and was glad when the hand bell rang for the conclusion of the exam. As they trooped outside for some fresh air, there was a bite in the wind that cut through their thin probationers' uniforms. She sat on one of the benches, by herself under the furthest tree, and was joined by Beatie and Nancy.

'Honestly, you must be crazy!' Honor began. 'What on earth did you think you were doing?'

Beatie looked contrite. 'You're a real pal,' she said. 'We didn't think the door would be locked! You saved our skin, Honor, I'll never forget it. I thought you were going to leave us there!'

Honor looked at them sharply. 'Next time I will,' she replied, 'and I really mean that, Beatie. I can't afford to lose my place here, it's my only chance. I'm not like you, I haven't got a family who'll take me in when things go wrong!'

Beatie stood up and faced her. 'You're right – we nearly got you into trouble too. I wish I'd listened to you – it was a horrible evening!'

'Well, what do you expect? It's not a fairytale out there, you know. You can't trust men just because they're in uniform!'

Beatie sighed. 'I've worked that out.' She linked her arm with Honor's and the two girls returned to the grim Victorian building which was their home.

The results were posted on the noticeboard the following morning. Honor anxiously scanned the list, only allowing a moment's incredulity when she saw her surname, Newson, just above the pass line. She turned away in relief, then saw Nancy, looking utterly downcast, at her side.

'I failed!' moaned Nancy. 'They'll throw me out!'

Beatie interrupted them. 'I just made it!' she announced, then caught sight of Nancy's face. 'Oh, Nancy, didn't you get through?'

'No, I didn't,' she retorted, 'and no thanks to you, Beatie Molesworth! You can go by yourself next time you get some crazy idea for a late-night outing!' Nancy turned away, her eyes filling with tears. 'I'm off to see if I can talk to Matron, maybe get a second chance.'

Beatie looked crestfallen. 'That was all my fault. You don't think she'll tell?'

'No, she's not the sort to land you in it,' replied Honor. 'Although honestly, it's more than you deserve.'

Beatie looked at her in mute appeal and Honor put her hand on her arm.

'Come on, you chump, it's time for lunch.' Honor had done with recrimination, and felt a chink of hope about her own future. After all, she had passed, hadn't she, and managed to do as well as the others even though she had never finished her proper schooling!

5

Matron had not seen fit to give Nancy a second chance, for she was packing her bags when Honor returned to the nurses' home that evening.

'It's no good.' Nancy was utterly dejected. 'I'm not allowed to repeat the course or sit the exam again. I'm out – suppose I'll have to go home and make peace with my father. He's going to be mad at me!'

'At least you've got somewhere to go,' Honor said.

'Just because you've a family, doesn't mean they're going to be nice to you!' Nancy retorted.

It was no use prolonging the conversation, and Honor slipped off to her room.

The City was accustomed to air raids, but had not expected one on the scale that followed that night. Honor woke to the air raid siren, wailing in the pitch blackness. She remembered the drill, put on her coat and shoes, picked up her gas mask and torch, and joined the other nurses from her floor on the landing.

Sister Davies was supervising. 'Don't rush!' she commanded. 'Make your way slowly to the cellars!'

They trooped down the staircase, the night sky suddenly alight with flashes of brilliant yellow and white, and the all-too-close sound of bombs falling. Panes of glass were breaking on the floor below.

'Move!' shouted Sister, and they broke into a disorderly rabble, past the boardroom and on towards the cellars. Honor broke off from the crowd before she reached the door.

'I can't go down there!' she shouted at Sister Davies, who was herding the young women to safety.

'You must!' Sister tried to take her by the arm, but Honor broke free.

'It's OK, Sister, I'll take my chances up here!' She ran back, past the other girls, amongst the sound of plaster falling and dust in the air. The banging was becoming louder; this was her worst raid yet.

She pushed open the boardroom door. The room was lit up by nearby explosions and Honor dived under the stout oak table, covering her head with her hands and trying to shut out some of the terrible noise.

She lay crouched, semi-supine, for what seemed like an eternity of falling brickwork and shattering glass. The children! She hoped the night nurses had managed to get them out in time. She buried her head deeper in her arms. Perhaps this was it – what a way to die!

She was conscious of more loud flashes and falling plasterwork, then all went quiet. Half of the solid oak table was leaning at an angle, but it had protected her from the worst. She crept her way out, choking in the thick dust, and crawled over to the door, which had been blasted from its hinges. As she stood up to go through, she saw a scene of complete destruction. The nurses' home, her place of sanctuary, had been blown to bits. There was an ominous silence as she picked her way through the rubble towards the cellar door. It appeared to be jammed, and she tugged it towards her, whereupon the door opened only halfway before sticking in the warped door frame.

'Are you there?' she yelled down the dark staircase.

'We're here!' a frightened voice called back. 'Can we come up?'

'I don't know!' The sirens were still wailing. Suddenly there was a flash of light and Honor was thrown backwards into the corridor.

When she came to, she was sprawled out on the dust-covered parquet floor which she had once polished so assiduously. An air raid warden was helping her to her feet and the banging had stopped.

'Are you all right, miss?' The tall, heavily built man looked closely at her ghostlike figure.

'Yes, but what about the others?'

'Where are they?'

'In the cellar!' Honor stood dizzily against him and motioned to the door, now hanging from its panels amidst the broken masonry.

'Over here!' shouted the warden to his mates, who assembled and stood looking down into the cellar.

'I'm going down. Give me some light!' The big man descended into the smoky gloom of the cellar stairs, and the two others followed behind.

'Best sit down away from here.' Another warden led Honor to the kitchen. 'Sit there, ducks, we'll come back to you later, after we get those others out of there.'

He left her at the once-scrubbed kitchen table, surveying the desolation around her. Cupboards had been smashed; glass, cutlery and crockery strewn over the floor. She leant her head against the table, her ears still ringing from the blasts. Then there were ambulance sirens, more shouting and coming and goings with urgent footsteps along the corridors. She heard women's voices in the background, and forced herself to her feet.

Gazing out from the kitchen, she saw an unsteady group of her fellow nurses being led slowly down the corridor. Like her, they were covered in dust, some choking into handkerchiefs, others limping as they walked. There seemed so few of them; where were the rest? She went up to the ones at the front. One of them, Addie, nursed on the ward next to hers.

'What happened, Addie?'

Addie wiped her face, leaving a large, grimy streak across it. She looked almost too shocked for words. 'Cellar roof came down,' she replied softly. 'Some of them are trapped.'

Honor held her hand, which was cold and shaking. 'Oh, Addie,' she whispered. 'How many?'

'Don't know,' the stricken girl replied, taking a deep breath. 'Don't know, we were the lucky ones, near the stairs.'

A nurse came and ushered Addie toward the front door of the home. Honor intercepted an ARP warden on his way to the cellar.

'What's happening?' she asked. 'Can you get them out?'

'Can't say, miss. We're bringing stretchers up soon. You'd best join the others.' He motioned her out of the way.

In the breaking dawn at the front of the house stood a small group of women in their nightclothes, some weeping and supported by others. They were the 'walking wounded', apart from one or two propped on the cold, damp steps. Honor could recognise only Sister Colville, who had her arm around a crying girl.

'What happened, Sister?' Honor was desperate to find her friends. 'Where is everyone?'

Sister Colville looked at her steadily. She was not a woman to lose her dignity in a crisis. 'I'm afraid the ceiling didn't hold,' she answered.

'What do you mean? They'll get them out soon, won't they?'

'Even if they do, dear, I'm not sure that they'll be alive.' Sister Colville did not attempt false comfort. 'We'll have to wait and see.'

Honor sat on the steps with Addie until the wardens took a roll call and directed them over to the main hospital building for a cup of tea.

'Can't I go and get my things?' Honor was still in her nightdress and coat.

'No, duckie, it's not safe.' The tall warden who had first helped her to her feet ushered her to the door. 'You can't come back in yet.'

In the main hospital canteen, the women struck a forlorn picture, as the kitchen staff plied them with tea and biscuits. The nurses' home had taken a direct hit, whereas the rest of the hospital had escaped with relatively little damage. Honor was relieved to hear that the children on the wards had been evacuated, but there was no news yet of the other probationer nurses. Matron appeared in the canteen and came to join them, stopping to talk to each one. She looked shocked, but resolute, like Sister Colville.

'What's happened?' Honor asked as Matron drew up a chair beside them.

'Some of the girls were trapped when the ceiling collapsed,' she replied in a flat voice. 'We're not sure how many yet.'

'What do you mean?'

Matron sighed. 'They're bringing out some of the bodies now, as well as the severely injured.' She took Honor's hand in hers. 'They didn't stand a chance.'

Honor looked at her, seeing the grief in the older woman's face, and said no more. Matron motioned to Sister Colville, who came to join her and then stood to address the group.

'It's been a terrible night for us all, and I can only thank God that the children, at least, are safe. I don't know how many nurses we have lost, but you will have to be brave, and help each other through. It's obviously not safe for you to return to the home, so you will be taken to one of the empty wards where you can wash and rest for a while. I'll speak to you again in the hospital chapel later. Until then, stay strong and pray for those who are not with us.'

Matron turned to leave the canteen, with a straight-backed, if dishevelled Sister Colville in her wake.

Honor fell into a doze on the hard iron bed in the ward. It was a relief to lie down, and give in to the incessant dizziness and ringing in her ears. Someone must have tended to her, for when she awoke she was snug under a pile of blankets, feeling no desire to move or think. A nurse she did not recognise came to her with a cup of sweet tea, which she sipped slowly. Looking around she saw other figures huddled semi-sleeping in the beds, as though they too were trying to escape from the shock of the night's raid. Presently a senior sister, again not one of their usual staff, came to help her out of bed and into some borrowed clothes, a warm Fair Isle jumper and some slacks.

'Shouldn't I be in uniform?' Honor said.

'No, dear, you won't be working today. Matron is going to see you all in the chapel soon.'

Once they had washed and dressed, they went as a small, orderly group down the wide flight of stairs to the chapel. It was a vaulted, quiet place, framed with Victorian stained glass windows and a little altar at the front. Honor had swept the deep red carpets there but had never entered for any other reason. *It must be about two o'clock*, she mused, her watch opaque and broken.

Matron was standing by the front pew as they filed in, and she directed them to sit on the upright wooden rows close to her.

'I'm sorry, my dears, you have all had a terrible time.'

The unreality of their situation could not have been more closely brought home to them. Matron never called any nurse 'dear'. Whatever were they about to hear?

'I can't go into details as the next of kin have yet to be informed. As you all know by now, the cellar, which has proved a place of safety in previous raids, partially collapsed under the sheer force of the bombing.' She shook her head, eyes momentarily closed, before collecting herself to continue.

'There is a casualty list posted on the main corridor, and those listed are now patients in the Royal London. You'll be able to visit your friends in due course, but not until their conditions have stabilised. I'm afraid that's not all.' She paused, as though it was difficult for her to continue. 'Due to the high casualty rate, the authorities have decided that the probationers must be evacuated.'

Honor was shocked; surely she was not going to lose her coveted training place after all she had been through?

Matron continued, more steadily than before. 'The current group of students will continue their further training in Leicester. You'll all leave early next week. I'm sorry, girls, we can't keep you here, it's just not safe…' Her voice finally broke, worn with the strain.

The chapel door opened and one of the senior hospital administrators came in. He looked at Matron, and immediately took over, explaining to the probationers that they would be housed on the ward until their departure. Owing to severe staff shortages incurred during the raid, there would be no further ward training. They were to receive a morning classroom lecture for the time being, but otherwise their time was free and any nurse who wished to take a period of leave during the next few days would be at liberty to do so. There were a few questions from the group but Honor was no longer listening. All she could think about was Beatie and Nancy, both conspicuous by their absence.

She joined the gloomy procession to the main corridor, not wishing to be the first to read the list. She forced herself to scan the names – down to M, and yes, there was Molesworth, Beatie must be alive! Further on, though, looking for Summers… Nancy's name was missing.

'What does it mean, if they're not there?' She grabbed Addie urgently by the sleeve.

Addie shook her head. 'She was too far down the cellar, you know. Not with us, by the stairs…'

The two girls put their arms around each other.

'Oh, Addie, she can't be dead!'

Sister Reardon came up and led them both gently away. 'That's enough, girls, time for some rest. You can't bring any of them back.' Sister's voice was bleak, and her soft Irish tones had lost their lilt. 'It's a mercy you weren't down there yourself, Honor!'

6

The London bus edged its way slowly along the uneven streets of Whitechapel. It was not an area that Honor knew, being some way across the city from her own hospital. She looked out of the steamy window at the bomb-damaged buildings with incredulity. This was London, wasn't it? The capital city, where the king lived, reduced to rubble in one street after another. Still, somehow people were getting on with their everyday lives, walking to and from work, queuing for rations at the sparsely filled shops. It was early November 1940, and there seemed to be no let-up to the Blitz. When would it end, Honor wondered, more mindful of it now she was out of the confines of the hospital and able to see the devastation of the nightly bombing raids. The conductor nodded at her helpfully.

'This is your stop, Royal London.'

She thanked him as she climbed down the steps. There was no missing the hospital, an imposing Gothic building near the bus stop, and she walked in through the wide doors to the main entrance and the reception office beyond.

'Can I help you?' A well-dressed woman with a surprisingly upper-class accent was behind the desk. Honor drew herself up to enquire.

'Yes, I've come to see one of the patients, a nurse from the Lambeth. Name of Beatie Molesworth, please.'

The woman took a long list from the desk and ran down the names.

'Yes, here she is, James Ward. That's up the stairs to the second floor. It's directly on your right.'

Honor climbed the long, straight staircases to the second floor and walked through the glass doors on to James Ward. She saw Beatie straight away, lying quietly in a bed halfway down the ward. Well aware of the protocol, she found the ward sister first of all and asked her permission.

'Could I see Nurse Molesworth, Sister? I'm from the hospital.'

Sister looked her up and down. 'I hear you all had a bad time of it,' she said. 'Such a shocking raid, on defenceless nurses too! Where will they drop those bombs next? Of course you can see her, she's quite stable, has a broken tibia and fibula, but otherwise recovering well.'

As Honor approached Beatie's bed, her friend turned towards her. 'Honor!' she called in surprise.

Honor kissed her on the forehead and pulled up a chair beside her. 'You're alive!'

'Of course I am, it'll take more than a bomb to get rid of me!' The girls looked at each other, Beatie's eyes filling with tears.

'Sister says you've broken your leg!'

'A beam fell on it and jammed me underneath,' Beatie said. 'I've to be in plaster for six weeks so I don't know what'll happen to my training! It was terrible down there, Honor, I was one of the lucky ones, you know.' She paused. 'What about the others?'

'Don't let's go into all of that now! The main thing is you're going to be all right.'

'You've got to tell me!' Beatie said, as though not knowing carried a special pain of its own.

Honor looked steadily at her. 'Some of the girls were killed in the force of the blast, when the cellar didn't hold. Apparently it's usually safe down there, but it took a direct hit. Poor Sister Davies, she was doing her best and following instructions.'

'How many, Honor?'

'About twenty-five at the last count.' She took Beatie's hand, as Matron had taken hers.

Beatie's face went even paler, her curls lying limply on her forehead. They were still dusty, Honor noted, adding to her wraithlike appearance.

'Best not talk about it anymore,' Honor said.

Beatie started to cry, deep, convulsive sobs that seemed to come from somewhere down inside her. Sister hurried over to the bed.

'There, Beatie, hush, you're going to be fine.' She put an arm around the girl's shoulder. 'Maybe that's enough for today.' She motioned Honor to leave.

'I'll come back tomorrow.' Honor kissed Beatie's pale cheek and stroked her hair.

Sister caught up with her in the corridor.

'Sorry, Sister, I didn't mean to upset her, she just kept asking me things!'

'No, that's not why I want to speak to you. You have to tell her the truth. She knows anyway.' Sister bore the authority of years of experience, and had witnessed every type of sadness, grief and loss. 'She seems troubled about something, keeps asking about someone called Nancy.'

Honor straightened her back. 'You'd better tell her Nancy's dead if she asks again,' she replied bleakly. 'I'm not sure I have the heart. I'll come again tomorrow, Sister.' Without waiting for a reply, she turned to make her way down the echoing steps.

As she sat on the bus back to her hospital she found herself wondering what could be the meaning of it all. How come she hadn't been in the cellar, instead of Nancy? Why was she alive today when hundreds of other innocent people had died in that raid? As for God, where had He been? She had been brought up in strict observation of the faith, Sunday an endless day of sermons and Sunday school, but recent events, not least the vicar, had put paid to that. Honor shook her head; it was all senseless, from the death of a child with diphtheria to her friends buried in the cellar.

The days that followed brought an unexpected emptiness, giving her for once some space in her life. After the morning lesson, she would go and visit Beatie, who improved steadily each day. Then her time was her own, the first she could remember. Some of the girls had gone home, but that was not an option for Honor. She took buses around the city, wandering in places she had not seen before, acutely aware of the beautiful architecture and the damage that resulted from the nightly raids. She felt curiously unafraid of venturing out on her own. She knew she had a safe haven to return to, and could look at the world with raised eyes. Of course, it was an extraordinary place to be, war-torn London, and she only just past her nineteenth birthday.

The funerals were held at the end of the week, with a single service in their local church. A sombre group of nurses, in their strict uniforms and capes, sat in the back pews, behind the grieving families.

Honor had found Matron beforehand.

'You won't have to tell Nancy's father about her exam, will you?'

Matron had not yet recovered any semblance of composure. She had lost her own fiancé in the trenches at Ypres, twenty-six years ago come December.

'Of course not,' she replied. 'Nancy was a good girl, though she probably didn't quite have the brains for it. You do, though, don't you? You did well to pass that exam.'

'Thank you,' Honor said gravely. She had received so little approbation in her life before. 'I'll miss this hospital, and I'm grateful to you for giving me a chance, Matron.'

'On you go, and don't worry about Nancy's family. They have every right to be proud of her.' Matron returned to her ward rounds, her unmistakeable figure sweeping through the doors.

After the service, Honor caught sight of a sparse, upright figure, dressed in black and holding two little girls by the hand. The older child looked just like Nancy.

'Excuse me, is it Mr Summers? I'm Honor Newson, I was a friend of Nancy's.'

He shook her hand, but was beyond words. She stood awkwardly for a moment, smiling at the children.

'Are you her sisters?' she asked the tousled redhead with a freckly face. The child nodded, then pulled at her father's arm.

'Thank you, Honor.' He recovered himself sufficiently, before continuing. 'We can't believe she's gone, you see. Can't imagine life without her! She was all the world to us, you know, especially since we lost her mother.'

'Daddy, won't we see Nancy now she's dead?' the younger child interrupted.

'No, Ruthie, not any more, she's in Heaven,' he replied. He turned to Honor again. 'We were so proud of her, training to be a nurse.'

'She was one of the best.'

'I know,' he said, before making his way to the church aisle where Matron and the vicar were shaking hands with the mourners.

Honor watched them go, the two little ones clinging tightly to his hands. Nancy must have been braver than she had ever let on, bringing up two younger sisters like that. Why had she kept it to herself? They had all been so preoccupied with their own lives. Now Nancy was gone, and they would never be able to make up for it. Remorseful and bereft, she walked slowly down the stone steps of the small churchyard, and into the bustle of the city beyond.

She visited Beatie again for the last time before her departure. Beatie, looking better by the day, was becoming impatient with her confinement.

'I wish I could come too,' she said restlessly. 'Not much fun sitting here all the time, while you're all off to a new start.'

'Don't be silly,' Honor said. 'You'll be sent home to recuperate soon and then, in no time, you'll be joining us in Leicester.'

'Home? That's all I need! More fussing and fuddy-duddy old ladies round to see me every hour of the day! You can't imagine what it'll be like!'

Honor said nothing, and sat looking at her fingernails.

'Sorry,' said Beatie after a little while. 'I don't mean to be ungrateful, I know I could be buried in the cellar like the others. Sometimes I wish I was – I should have died instead of Nancy. It just makes me so cross! Who does God think He is anyway? What kind of compassion is that – burying a load of defenceless, frightened girls in a dark cellar? Thanks a lot – they can keep religion if that's how it ends!'

Honor rose to her feet. 'You'll feel better soon, honestly. I've got to go now, and get packed and sorted before tomorrow. I'll write to you once you're home and let you know what it's like.' She put her cheek to Beatie's, brushing her soft, fair curls.

'Honor!' Beatie called after her.

'What is it?' She paused at the door of the ward.

'Nothing. You be careful too, and I'll see you soon.'

Part Two:
Tiger Moths

1

The light was fading as the slow steam train drew into Desford Halt. The young man, who had been gazing out of the steam-filled window for most of the journey, rose to take his kitbag down from the luggage rack and nodded to the woman and child opposite as he left the carriage.

There was no one on the platform. He had expected as much, late as he now was after missed connections and crowded wartime trains. The stationmaster was making his way through the wicket gate as he caught up with him on the path.

'Where to, lad?' the stationmaster asked.

'The RAF base,' the young man replied. He drew his coat close around him, feeling the chill December air more acutely after the stuffy train.

'Thought so, that's why most of you get off here,' the railwayman commented, tucking his whistle into his pocket. 'It's up the hill, into the village, then take the left-hand road before the church. There's no sign to Peckleton anymore, but it's about a mile down there.'

The young man thanked him, and started walking in the gathering darkness along the road. There was little sign of life, even in the pub at the bottom of the hill. Since the blackout, the whole of Britain appeared to live in semi-darkness, chinks of light escaping from drawn curtains and blinds. If there was anyone in the pub, it would have been difficult to tell from the road. Anyway, he was late and there was no chance of stopping now, hungry and thirsty though he was.

Desford appeared to be a small hamlet, with a few houses, another pub and the church. He took the small left turn and continued his way, towards the windsock in the gloom of the airfield beyond.

He had spent much of the long day thinking about the sequence of events that had brought him to this point in his life. Just nineteen years old, he had managed to pass all of the medicals for entry to the service. His clear grey eyes were certified as visually normal, his hearing acute, his beating heart without defect, and his intelligence and character had been sorely tested during the last twelve weeks at his initial training wing in

Aberystwyth. He had jumped through all of the hoops they had set him so far, and now they were going to let him fly an aeroplane.

He had not initially intended to join up. He had a place at university, so when war was declared some fifteen months ago it had seemed reasonable to carry on according to plan. Ominously quiet at the beginning, the war had escalated so rapidly that the news of the retreat at Dunkirk last May had come as a shock. Those newsreels showing a fleeing British army wading through the surf on the beaches of Northern France, desperate to get across the Channel in any little boat the country could muster, had made his decision for him. Without discussing it with either family or friends, he found himself in an RAF recruiting office. He was still waiting for his final paperwork to come through when the Blitz started. It was unbelievable that the freedom of his country could be so suddenly challenged, with innocent civilians dying in bombed buildings in London, and the might of the German Reich seemingly held at bay by a few fighter pilots.

As soon as he received his confirmation letter, he had climbed the stairs to the professor's office and knocked at the door.

'Which service did you say, Fordham?' the professor enquired, as he sat down in front of him in his rambling office, shelves packed to capacity with volumes of books, most greying and dusty, a little like the man himself.

'RAF, sir,' he replied. 'I hope to train as a pilot.'

'How old are you?' the professor had asked quietly. He was a Great War veteran himself, and could see no point in any of it.

'Nineteen, sir.'

The older man had looked at the boy in front of him. He was a composed individual, probably a reasonable sportsman at school, he conjectured, not classically good-looking but a pleasing face with a firm, aquiline nose, brown hair and level eyes.

'Well, we'll be sorry to lose you, Fordham, but I won't try to make you change your mind. Your place will be here for you when it's over, and don't forget to let County Hall know that you're going down so they can hold on to your exhibition.' He knew the family; Fordham's uncle was a lecturer in the engineering faculty and had personally interceded to release the boy from the grim farming college where his father had placed him, and on to the agriculture course.

'Goodbye, sir, and thank you.'

'Good luck, my boy,' were the professor's parting words.

Leeds was now a rapidly distancing memory of freezing fogs, tall city buildings and dry lectures in uncomfortable theatres, which seemed completely irrelevant to his future.

'Name, rank and number.' The sentry at the gate looked cold, stamping his regulation boots on the ground, his breath visible in the night air.

'Leading Aircraftman Fordham 1108986,' he replied, handing over his documents and posting details.

'Through there, straight on and up to the administration block; the office on the left.'

The sentry opened the gate, allowing him to pass through.

Night was falling fast now, but the young man could still make out the airfield beyond. There were Tiger Moths inside and outside the large hangars, long grass runways and utilitarian, flat-topped buildings. He walked up to the main administration block, went inside and knocked at the door of the only lighted office.

'Come in.' The Warrant Officer looked up from his desk.

'LAC Fordham, sir, 1108986, reporting for training.' Will stood to attention.

'You're late, Fordham,' the officer replied, taking a sip from a cold cup of tea in front of him.

'Sorry sir, bad connections on the trains from Aberystwyth.'

'Well, you're the last to report in today, so you'd better be the first on parade ground tomorrow,' came the curt reply. 'You'll be in bungalow ten. The boys already there will show you the mess and get you orientated. Six am sharp start tomorrow.' With that, he returned his attention to the map upon his desk.

2

LAC Fordham opened the door to bungalow ten, which was warm and bright inside, though the usual blackout blinds were at the windows.

'Hello?' he called, although there was no one immediately visible.

A red-headed boy, about the same age and height as himself, peered around one of the bedroom doors. He was freckled with a long face, close-set eyes and small mouth, and smiled affably, screwing up his eyes as he did so.

'You're a bit late, where've you been?'

'On a slow train from Aberystwyth!'

'Initial training wing there?' The young man settled himself sideways on one of the armchairs in the small living area, his legs dangling over the side.

'Yes,' Fordham replied. 'Been there for the last twelve weeks. And you?'

'Oh, I've been holed up in Torquay, marching around the town, bored half to death. Can't wait for some action!' said the young man. 'I'm Richard Sinclair, most people call me Dick.' He stretched out his hand.

'Will Fordham.' He took it and returned a steady look.

'You'd better drop your stuff in your room, it's over there.' Dick gestured to the end of a small corridor. 'The others are already over in the mess, I'll take you over when you're ready.'

'How many of us are in here?' Will asked.

'Six in all.'

His room was much more habitable than his previous lodgings in Aberystwyth. He had been billeted in an old hotel there, sharing a room with three others. They had become friends but had each been posted to different flying schools, two of the boys as far as Canada for the next part of their training. He dropped his kitbag on the bed, took out most of his things and arranged them hastily.

'Where are you from?' asked Dick as they strolled slowly across the dark airfield towards the mess, another long, low building not far from where he had entered the camp.

'Yorkshire.'

'Thought so, I've got some relatives up in those parts,' said Dick companionably.

Will did not speak in the same flat, clipped tones as the boys who had been to public school. He had by now met a wide range of recruits. Some, but not all, were younger than him, having come straight into the air force from the sixth form. At least he had experienced something of university life – the camaraderie with other students, the dances and socialising, and Sybil. Sybil was a stenographer whose firm had been moved from London to Leeds after the outbreak of war. She was a watchful, rather shy brunette whom he had met at a dance and would take to the pictures at weekends, or to the pub with his friends. He liked her, and she him, in her undemanding way, although in reality their relationship had progressed little beyond holding hands and the occasional, slightly furtive kiss outside her YWCA hostel.

'What about you?' Will said.

'Oh, Home Counties, Hampshire.' Dick had no time to elaborate further before they arrived at the mess. Familiar sounds of conversation, laughter and animated voices met them as they opened the door.

'Ah, here they are!' announced a square-faced, rather thickset, dark young man near the entrance.

'This is Will Fordham.' Dick introduced him to the closest circle of individuals, all of whom, it transpired, were in his bungalow.

'Matt Brown, Jim Alderdice and Andrew Farrington,' said Dick, gesturing to the three young men. 'And this one is Guy,' he added, nodding at the dark one, who was lighting a cigarette.

'Clarkson,' added Guy, proffering his hand.

'We've all just met, same bungalow,' Dick added, as if to distance himself from any responsibility for the characters of the others. He wandered over to the bar, with Will and Guy alongside.

'So what's the gen?' asked Will.

'Don't really know,' said Guy. 'I think we'll have some sort of pep talk after dinner. That's the CO over there.' They looked at a middle-aged, straight-backed man of some bearing and authority, talking to a group of officers nearby. He had a typical RAF moustache, and on the chest of his blue uniform he wore the DFC.

Will had the distinct feeling that they were all back at school. The food was notably better and they were served a substantial meal, after which the squadron leader rose to his feet.

'Good evening, gentlemen,' he announced brusquely after silence had fallen. 'Please sit. For those of you who don't already know me, I'm Squadron Leader Wyatt-Hughes. Now, this base is dedicated to making pilots out of you, though we'll have our work cut out for us, if the last lot were anything to go by. Just to make it clear, I will tolerate no slacking or dodging of the rules. Learning to fly and serving your country in wartime is the most difficult challenge any of you will ever face. I can tell you right away you're not all going to make it, but there's no shame in that, we'll just deploy you to another role. What I do expect is self-discipline, commitment, and a clear head. That means not too much drinking in this mess or elsewhere,' he paused for effect, 'and no gallivanting. Some of you have come directly from school but I can promise you that it'll be no playground here at Desford. Make sure you report at 6am sharp tomorrow for PT.' With that he sat down, resuming his conversation with his neighbour.

The young men looked at each other across the table.

'Is that it?' said Dick as conversation resumed. 'Not giving much away, is he?'

'Well,' said Guy as the orderlies cleared away the dinner plates and the tables started to empty, 'I'm going back to number ten, bearing in mind that early start. Anyone coming with me?'

They all stood up except Jim. 'Don't you want another beer?' He had a wide mouth full of teeth, with short, dark, curly hair. He was one of the tallest there, and Will wondered how he could possibly fit into the cockpit of a Tiger Moth.

'No thanks, Alderdice,' said Guy. 'We'd better get back if we don't want black marks in the morning.'

Jim made a gesture of disappointment, the corners of his large mouth downturned. 'OK, chaps, I'll catch up with you in a little while.' He sauntered over to another group, all with full glasses of beer nearby.

'Is he a friend of yours?' Dick asked Guy on the way back.

'Not really,' replied Guy. 'We were in the same ITW.'

Guy Clarkson was, Will supposed, the oldest in the bungalow. He looked about twenty-four, a rather short, well-built young man who would fit in well on a rugby field, most likely a prop forward in the first fifteen. Guy was chartered to an accountancy firm in the Midlands from which he had been released, like the others, to embark upon his flying training. He was solid and responsible-looking, set in his opinions and not easily led.

'Looks like he's going to make a night of it!' said Matt. He smiled, eyes bright through a shock of fair hair. His nose looked as though it had been broken, which stopped him short of being handsome, but his demeanour was one of extreme affability. 'So what was that pub like on the way up here?' he teased Will.

'Never set a foot inside!'

They strolled companionably through the dark, discussing nothing more important than the possibility of finding pretty girls in the village.

'Where's Andrew?' said Dick as they opened the door to the bungalow.

The last of their number, who had lagged a little behind on the walk, made his way in. He was a shy, fair, fine-featured boy, trying hard not to look as sensitive as he really was. Miserable years at public school had exposed his every failing, especially upon the sports field. He should have been at Oxford this Michaelmas term, but had not taken up his Classics scholarship, surprising his masters and family alike by his sudden determination to join the RAF. Andrew did not believe in war, and had considered but rejected pacifism as a logical response to the unfolding events in Europe. He did not want to be a conscientious objector, even more outcast from society than he already felt.

'Sorry, lads, right with you,' he called. Then, 'Goodnight all' in a purposefully cheery voice.

With that, they all retired to their single rooms, a luxury they had not experienced since joining the service.

3

They woke to a cold, grey, frosty dawn. As predicted, Alderdice had returned to the bungalow noisily and irritatingly drunk in the early hours of the morning, stumbling as he wove his way to his own room having tried mistakenly to join Guy in his.

'Get out, you stupid bugger,' Guy had hollered, followed by a slurred 'Sorry, old chap' from the retreating, unsteady Jim.

'Find your own bloody bed, and leave me in peace!'

None of them were surprised when it proved impossible to rouse Alderdice for the mandatory PT.

'Get up, you'll be late.' Will shook him by the shoulder.

'Just leave him,' said Guy. 'It's nothing new, judging by his performance at the last place.' So they trooped out, leaving him, snoring and deeply comatose, to face a session of physical fitness testing in the biting wind, which seemed tantamount to torture.

'On the double!' barked Sergeant Jones, and they were out across the Leicestershire fields, jumping across muddy bridle paths and through fallen leaves. Will was more than able to outpace the others; he had been a keen tennis player at school and the hard work on his uncle's farm had made him even fitter.

'Come on, you lazy lot,' the sergeant shouted at the stragglers. 'Call yourselves fit?'

They were pink with cold on their return, but revived after showers and breakfast. Jim's absence had been noted at roll call, though when he casually ambled into the teaching room to join them it would have been difficult to tell that he was at fault.

'Thanks for waking me,' he mouthed at Andrew.

'We couldn't, you were out for the count.'

They were grouped together in the hall of the main teaching block.

'Right! ' A flight lieutenant called them to attention. 'You'll pick up your kit in the next room, where you will be assigned to an instructor. There are two groups: mornings and afternoons; you'll find out which you are in from the list on the board. It's a decent day, weather-wise, so you should all get on training flights today. You'll be training on the DH82s. You may think that because there are plenty of them around this airfield we might not miss one, but you'll be saying goodbye to Desford if you bugger one up.

'You can pick up your logbook from the table over there. You must fill it in, without fail, after each flight. It'll be countersigned at intervals by your senior officers. Hold on to it at all costs – it is your personal record of flying experience, and it'll take you all the way through the war. It's an official document, and as such, the property of His Majesty's Government.

'Any questions from now will be dealt with by your instructor, whose word is God as far as you're concerned, so make sure you do what he says!'

Searching out his name on the list, Will found he was in the morning group. He noticed, contrary to his first impressions, that a significant proportion of the trainees were older than him. He knew that the upper limit for recruiting pilots was twenty-six, but some appeared a little older, either with established careers or the true gentleman flyers, with double-barrelled names and racing pasts. He also detected some unusual accents, and was not able to place them all in their country of origin.

He filed up for his logbook, which he had to sign for. The blue Pilot's Flying Log Book, with *Royal Air Force* and a space for his name at the bottom, was a sizeable book, a bit like a ledger of accounts. He would have to fill in the date, aircraft, crew, flying hours and duty each time he went up.

There was a queue for his kit – a pair of gauntlets, overalls, a Sidcot suit, helmet and goggles. With his seat parachute, which was a bulky contraption, it was complete. The name of his flying instructor was on the board. Will found him at the corner of the teaching room.

'I'm Fordham, sir.'

'Flight Sergeant Hart.' He was middle-aged, of medium height, with a prominent forehead and dark, bushy eyebrows concealing two firm brown eyes. 'Right, you've got your kit, I need to check your parachute drill, then we'll go out to the plane.'

He was not about to waste time, as he helped Will into his parachute, reminding him how to pull the ring to open it, and 'count to three after jumping out'.

They walked across the grass to a line of Tiger Moths. It was a chilly, clear morning, with a bright sun and slight crosswinds, perfect conditions for the time of year. So this was it, Will thought to himself; at last, after weeks of anticipation and theory, poring over his *RAF Pilot's Notes*.

'Right,' said Hart, 'I'll be in the back seat. I want you to get the feel of the controls – it's a very sensitive stick, so you really only need to touch it lightly and the aircraft will respond. Don't yank at it, and try to relax. The main difficulty in these Moths is taking off and landing, they're very stable in the air. First of all, let's see what you know about the cockpit layout.'

He quizzed Will on the dials ahead of him, six in all: airspeed indicator, turn and slip, altimeter, oil pressure, engine speed and of course, the central compass. There were rudder pedals at his feet, and the control stick. Hart showed him how the speaking tube worked so that he could communicate with him in flight.

'What's the wingspan of this plane?' Hart asked.

'Twenty-nine feet and four inches, sir.'

'Fuel and oil capacity?' Hart followed.

'Nineteen gallons and two point one gallons.'

Hart seemed satisfied with Will's groundwork and showed him how to strap himself into the front seat of the aircraft. It was a tight fit, especially on top of his parachute.

Hart settled into the rear seat, checking the controls before the mechanic swung the two-bladed propeller until the engine fired.

'Off we go.'

They taxied over the grass, Hart explaining through the voice tube the weaving movements on take-off that would be necessary to obtain a clear view. The biplane seemed extraordinarily light and flimsy, and it was very difficult to see ahead out of the front cockpit. The Moth turned into wind and Hart opened the throttle, increasing speed until the Moth lifted and they were up in the cold air, quicker than Will had imagined, rising above the fields and houses. As the wind whistled in the wires, he was captivated by the unique sensation of flight.

'Now watch the horizon! You need to find out how to keep it level.' Hart's voice came through the earphones. 'And keep a good lookout all the time, around and behind you – it's the aviator's lookout, not like driving a car. I'm taking the controls, but keep your hand on the stick and your feet on the rudder bars, so you can follow me through.'

For Will, it was as though he was in communication with his instructor through the stick and rudder. Soon he knew from the subtle movements which way the plane would dip and turn. All the while the wind was rushing through the open cockpit, accentuating the impression of speed and height.

'Now it's your turn,' Hart said. 'Put your right hand on the stick, fingertips and thumb only, don't grip it, then move it slowly backwards and forwards.' Will felt the nose of the Moth go up and down as he did so.

'Fly it level,' ordered Hart, and Will kept the nose steady, trying very hard not to make sudden, jolting movements with the stick. The plane responded so quickly to the slightest touch. How would he ever learn to do this?

'It's not just about the stick,' Hart said, 'it's about the position of the nose. Try to concentrate on that.'

Gently moving the stick in response, Will worked out how to keep the nose close to the horizon.

'The wings have been level up to now,' Hart said. 'I want you to move the stick to the left and feel the plane bank into a left turn.'

Will made the manoeuvre, keeping the nose steady.

'And now to the right.'

The right wing dipped, initiating the turn.

'Gently does it, you can relax! It won't let you down,' his instructor said. Will stopped trying so hard, and began to enjoy the feel of this extraordinary plane. He looked around him at the long view, the horizon ahead and the patchwork of fields below. It was as though little was separating him from the clouds themselves.

He was still mesmerised by it all when the stick was being inched forward for the descent.

'I have control,' said Hart. 'You need to keep the nose high for this as you come in. Almost as though you're trying not to land.' The Tiger Moth glided along parallel to the grass before sitting down gently on it.

'That was amazing, sir!'

'Did you enjoy it?'

'I should say! Thank you, sir!'

'Don't thank me,' said Hart. 'I'll be making your life a bloody misery before your training's over. Don't forget to fill in your logbook!' He smiled nonetheless, eyebrows raised, and an amused look in his eyes.

So that was it, Will thought, his first flight. He went back to the classroom and filled in the first entry in his logbook in his legible and regular handwriting:

> *DEC 15th 1940 DH82 No. N6443 F/S Hart – pilot, pupil – self: 1. Air experience; 1A. Familiarity with cockpit layout; 2. Effect of controls: dual time 0015; 3. Taxiing; 4. Straight and level flight, dual time 0030.*

He flicked over the empty pages to the final two sheets: record of service and aircraft flown. He wrote, *DH82, Gypsy Major* on the first line of the last page, and waited for the ink to dry.

Promoted to the rear cockpit for the next flight, Will took the controls, using the rudder pedals and trying to work out the ailerons, which controlled the aircraft in roll. He had learned that the drag in the opposite direction of the roll would be counterbalanced by the rudder, but putting it all together was exquisitely difficult, and a matter of touch and feel. It was a world away from the manuals.

'I want you to do some more turns and take the nose up and down, so you can feel the speed change as you get to a stall,' said Hart. At first it seemed impossible; the slightest touch of the stick and the kite was all over the place, but eventually the dynamics between ailerons and rudder began to make sense.

His absorption with his task that first morning was absolute. Will was not conscious of time passing, so completely was he concentrating on how to control this plane, unlocking its hidden secrets and experiencing the sheer miracle of being airborne.

Fortunately he had started off with the assumption that he would be able to master it, like riding his motorcycle or driving a tractor on the farm. It was another man-made machine, after all, defying gravity by mathematical design. The de Havilland engineers knew how to make a plane, and if he stuck at it, he would soon know how to make it work.

Imagine being able to fly! Like most boys, he would have given anything for such a chance – it was just a pity that the war, that giver and taker-away of life and opportunities, should have been the reason for it all.

His group met again for the lunch break. Matt looked pleased with life.

'What a beaut!' he said.

'I suppose you're going to be a natural, aren't you?'

'I wouldn't like to say,' Matt replied modestly, although he seemed to be exactly that: at ease with himself and the world, not afraid, just joyous in the expectation of learning to fly. *A true Icarus*, thought Will, then immediately withdrew the comparison from his head, not wishing to foresee any future harm to the fair-haired, open-faced boy at his side.

'Oh my God.' Guy joined them both in the queue at the canteen. 'That was tough. I haven't a clue how I'll ever get the hang of it!' he said despairingly. 'I hope my instructor's a patient man, or I'll be for the chop.'

'Best not be thinking about that! He's bound to cut you a bit of slack.'

'I'm not so sure. How did you get on, anyway?'

'Oh, not so bad,' replied Matt nonchalantly, concentrating on an already fully laden plate of food.

'Is that all you're having, Guy?' Will said.

'Oh, I'm not too hungry right now, felt a bit dizzy as we came in to land.'

They politely ignored his indisposition, and continued with their lunch, comparing excited notes as they did so.

'What's it like?' Jim joined them with the classroom group. He looked eager and confident, not at all concerned by his early-morning lapse at PT.

'Ask Matt, he's going to be the golden boy at this one,' replied Will, smiling, but Matt had his mouth full and just shrugged his shoulders.

'You can take it from me, it's not easy!' said Guy. The colour was returning to his face, and he reached for a piece of bread.

'Nothing that's worth doing ever is!' Dick said, though his face betrayed a flicker of anxiety.

'Well, I can't wait to give it a go! What about you, Andrew?' said Jim.

Andrew did not answer, for at that precise moment he was more interested in his jam roly-poly pudding. It was a pointless question anyway – it had taken so much effort to make it this far; of course he wanted to fly the thing!

By the time they arrived back at the bungalow that evening, the light had faded and all the Tiger Moths were safely back on the ground.

Jim Alderdice was holding forth. 'Piece of cake, boys,' he said, wide mouth grinning. 'That's probably one of the best things I've ever done! Actually, I can't remember anything I've enjoyed more!'

'Not got a girlfriend then?' responded Guy swiftly. They all shared the joke, and further debate over whether or not sex might be preferable to flying, with no significant conclusion reached before it was time to wash, change and go to the mess. In fact, they were mostly innocents apart from Guy, who already had a fiancée, Marion, whose picture he had shown confidingly to Will. The black-and-white portrait showed a smiling, long-haired girl, looking expectantly at the camera, full of hope.

Alderdice would have been only too willing to share with them the range of his previous conquests, except that they all shouted him down with a 'Not very likely, Jim' or 'I doubt any girl would do that with you, old boy', leaving him unable to expand upon his prowess.

4

They soon settled into a regular pattern of training, which contrasted the tedium of duties like early morning PT or the drill ground with the absolute absorption of the flying lessons. The early December weather held good, if cold, so that they were able to fly on most scheduled days, and were not grounded by fog or rain.

Jim had prudently decided to turn up on time, if at all possible, though his inner arrogance took a beating on the parade ground.

'You don't know your bloody right foot from your left, Alderdice!' bellowed the drill sergeant when Jim's concentration lapsed during square bashing.

Their classroom course was exacting but not without interest, particularly the subjects that might be necessary to keep you alive, like navigation. Being able to route-find and get back to base safely was undoubtedly of use, no matter how boring the lesson might be, or how unfamiliar the P4 and P6 compasses. Will preferred the meteorology to anything else. The language of the weather was so whimsical, he thought, learning terms like 'cirrus', 'altostratus' and 'cumulus'. If only he had studied physics harder at school, perhaps the aneroid barometer would not be such a mystery.

However, it was the flying that engrossed them, with each lesson bringing new challenges. There was more climbing, gliding and turns, with Will now in the rear cockpit and his instructor up front.

'Taking off today,' Hart announced on the fourth day, after Will had satisfied him that he could master a stall. Will's heart sank, as taking off in a Tiger Moth was going to be tough.

To start with, it was almost impossible to see over the front of the cockpit, meaning that the plane had to be manoeuvred sideways to get a clear view. The plane jolted more to the right and left than he would have liked as it trundled along the grass, but he opened the throttle smoothly and felt the tail lift into the air. He checked that the engine was on full power and the oil pressure correct as he initiated the climb, hoping with a sudden surge of optimism that if he could do this, then maybe he could do the rest.

Once safely in level flight, Hart's voice came through. 'Not bad, Fordham, we'll have you landing tomorrow!'

And so it was, the following day, another cold and clear morning, that Hart made him take the controls. Will managed once more, miraculously, to get the plane off the ground, followed by some of the usual turns, then a powered approach to the landing, 'Hold it steady, now' from Hart as, and he was really not sure how, he managed to bring the Moth down on to the grass, bumping along into that sitting position before it drew to a merciful halt.

'Could be worse!' said Hart, by way of approval, as they strolled back to the classroom. 'It'll soon be second nature, you know!'

Each evening, the young men mulled over the day's events. Will said little, as he was ever conscious that a good day could be rapidly followed by a bad one. Matt was non-committal, although they were all aware that he was turning into a natural and faultless pilot. He made it look completely effortless, as any of them who watched him take off or land could testify. Matt's instructor already recognised his potential to become an ace fighter pilot, it was that combination of natural skill, alertness and poise without fear that singled him out. Despite the fact that he was such a promising pupil, Matt was never heard shooting the line.

In contrast, Jim reminded them frequently that he was 'the tops'. Jim's interpretation of his superior skills was not shared by his instructor.

'That young man will come to no good,' was his comment to Hart over a quiet beer in the corner of a local pub. 'Too cocky by half, not a bad pilot but nowhere near as good as he thinks.'

Meanwhile, Guy had been struggling from the start. He tensed up in the Tiger Moth, unable to relax and feel the plane as he must. He was not frightened in the air, more unsettled and bewildered by the complex nature of the tasks required. Fortunately, he had a tolerant, softly spoken instructor, who was inclined to give him the benefit of the doubt.

As for the others, Andrew Farrington, sensitive though he was, seemed unfazed by the flying lessons, enjoyed himself and quietly did as he was expected. In fact, he felt that at last he could do something that his peer group would respect and envy. Up there in the air, he was not a fair-haired pretty boy, a swot, or any of the other unmentionable names he had been called at school. He would like some of the school bullies to see him handling the Moth, and gave himself the satisfaction of thinking that they would not be brave enough to do it.

Dick Sinclair was having problems. He was brilliant in the classroom, absolutely gifted at maths and navigation. In the air, however, it was a different matter.

His instructor berated him: 'Concentrate, Sinclair, you're meant to be flying the ruddy thing, not frozen on the stick', but for Dick it was not just about concentration. After five hours' dual instruction he had not been able even to attempt take-off or landing. He sat despondent in the bungalow that night.

'It's no good, lads, I just don't think I'm going to make it.'

'No, you'll be fine,' encouraged Will, patting him on the shoulder. 'You just lack confidence, that's all. Look how good you are at the classroom stuff – nobody gets that maths and navigation like you do. Let's go to the pub for a bit, take your mind off it.'

The two of them left the base and walked into Desford where they found a pub in the middle of the village, The Bell. It was a low-beamed, typical Leicestershire pub and they both had to stoop to get into the bar.

'Two half-pints, please,' said Will to the landlady. They had already heard of Rose, who knew most of the young airmen at the base.

'Have you had a bad day, dearie?' Rose passed the amber beer to the troubled-looking young man.

'Pretty much,' replied Dick.

'Well, never you mind, you're all such nice boys, it can't be easy what you have to do. I bet your mother worries about you – I can't sleep for worry about my son Stan in the navy.' She polished the bar vigorously.

The two young men took their glasses to sit at one of the small round tables by the window.

'I've not got a cat in hell's chance!' Dick said. 'I should be getting on for my first solo, and I'm nowhere near the basics yet…'

'Dick, you'll be all right, just stop panicking. What's bothering you?'

Dick looked Will in the eye, as they did when talking to each other.

'I'm not sure I really like it up there,' Dick said, taking a deep draught of beer. Will understood him perfectly. It was a mystery to him that more of the would-be pilots did not feel the same. Perhaps they did, but were just better at concealing it.

'Maybe tomorrow will be a better day.'

'Yes, sure.' They drained their glasses, waved goodbye to Rose, and walked slowly back to the airfield.

'I'm worried what my family will say if I get thrown out,' Dick confessed. 'They were all so pleased when I got my place. My little sister, Anna, she worships me, thinks I'm some sort of god, can do anything…'

'They'll be proud of you, you'll see, whatever happens,' Will said.

The dark country lane back to the base was deserted. Few civilians were using cars now that petrol rationing was in force, and bicycling could be hazardous at night. An owl hooted in the trees above them.

'I should have joined the navy!' Dick continued glumly. 'Got an uncle in the fleet!'

'You'd get seasick! Mind you, those Wrens are a bit of all right!'

'That's a thought! Wonder if it's too late to change my mind?'

5

Eight days had passed since he arrived at Desford. Will's logbook recorded a total of five hours' dual flying by December 23rd. Lessons were to be suspended for two days, but none of them were allowed home, unless there were special mitigating circumstances.

So Will, along with his fellow pupils, was to spend Christmas 1940 on the base. He had written a short letter home, explaining that his flying training was going well, and that he could not get leave but would try and come home when he was next able. *Happy Christmas to all at home*, he had written in his firm, clear hand.

It did not turn out so badly after all. In any event, the sober and religious Yorkshire Christmas with his parents, brother and sister in Guisborough was no great loss. Will thought about his mother, cooking the cockerel with such care, the lack of over-indulgence and sobriety of their Christmas meal. His grandmother would be overseeing events as usual, her imperious presence making his mother's life harder than it should have been. He would have liked to have seen his mother, but could manage without the rest.

Christmas Eve in the mess was predictably merry. Their mess bills were just about covered by their fortnightly pay of two pounds and ten shillings, so there was plenty of beer and the food, as usual, was good. Alderdice became boisterously drunk as the evening drew on.

'What about a human pyramid, lads?' he suggested recklessly to the others at the table, his speech already indistinct.

'Sounds a stupid idea to me,' replied Guy, but the idea had already spread to the next table and suddenly a whole group of excitable and inebriated young men were keen to take part. Hugh Radley, one of the 'gentleman' flyers, who owned a large green Bentley, was particularly enthusiastic.

'Great show, old boy,' he encouraged Jim, and in no time they were all scrambling over each other trying to get a foothold on a shoulder. Will sensibly found himself on the first tier, ably supported and securely held by Dick, but as the others tried to climb ever higher the whole lot fell in a convulsive heap on the floor. Radley crawled out from underneath, cradling his left arm.

'Think I've bust it, boys,' he declared, seemingly unperturbed, although it did indeed prove to be the case. One of the officers was mustered to take him to the nearest hospital in Leicester, from which he returned many hours later, with his arm plastered and in a sling.

'Four weeks off flying for him, poor bugger,' said Jim at breakfast on Christmas morning.

'Now who would he have to thank for that?' retorted Guy.

Christmas settled down more quietly after that. They were all expected to attend morning service at Desford church, and they felt quieter and more contemplative in the solid Norman building. They attracted the attention of the usual congregation; looking smart and upright in their blue uniforms, caps under their arms.

'Wonder where we'll be singing carols next Christmas?' Guy muttered under his breath, as they broke into *Hark the Herald Angels Sing*. Will thought of his mother, and sang seriously and in tune. He wondered if Sybil was spending Christmas back at home in London with her parents. He had not managed to write to her since he arrived, but had received a little Christmas card from her, *with love from Squibs, Christmas 1940*.

He looked up at the stained glass windows, and across at the stone chancel. The candles were lit, creating a soft glow, and they could see their breath as they sang.

6

It was New Year's Day 1941, as Will and Hart walked out to the Moth, which was waiting for them on the grass. Hart looked up: the sky was clear.

'Now, you've not done any spins,' he said breezily. 'We've been over the technical side, so it's just a matter of getting on with it. Make sure you're properly strapped in, we don't want you to fall out, now, do we? Don't forget to lock the slats.'

Will's take-offs were improving and they were soon up, practising medium turns.

'Right, off you go,' said Hart, and Will took a deep breath, then started to raise the nose, cutting the throttle until the plane began to stall. He kicked on the rudder in the direction of spin and went into the first flat and slow turn, which rapidly speeded up into a steep rotational spin. Will felt a rush of adrenaline – that sudden confrontation with death unless he could pull the plane out. How long did he have before they hit the ground?

'Bring it out now!' shouted Hart, and Will closed the throttle, kicked on the opposite rudder and pressed the stick slightly forward, until the plane stopped spinning. His heart rate dropped back to normal and he went in to land, trying to gauge the drift as there was more of a crosswind today. With corrective manoeuvring of wings and rudder they were safely down, taxiing along the grass.

'Well, at least you didn't write us both off,' commented Hart cheerily as he hopped out of the plane. 'It'll be easier the second time round!'

Will extricated himself from his straps. 'Don't we ever frighten the living daylights out of you, sir?'

'Always, Fordham, always!'

Leading Aircraftman Fordham was no longer in his teens. His twentieth birthday dawned on the third of the month, and he had already received a card from his mother, enclosing a five-pound note and wishing him *Many happy returns from your loving parents*. It was much more than he would have normally expected, nearly a whole month's pay, and as his father was not prone to generosity, he surmised that his mother must have interceded on his behalf. *Better not blow it all in the mess*, he thought to himself; *might save it up for a nice little car*.

Home, and all to do with it, seemed very far away. He felt increasingly removed from real, everyday life.

He told Matt it was his birthday over breakfast. 'Hey, happy birthday!' Matt congratulated him. 'Lads, it's Will's birthday, so drinks are on him in the mess tonight!'

'Surely it's the other way round?' Will smiled, suddenly anticipating the rapid disappearance of his five-pound note.

'Not if you've got my mess bill,' responded Matt. 'Anyway, how old are you?'

'Twenty today,' replied Will.

'Twenty!' broke in Guy. 'I've got a few years on you.'

'I haven't,' said Andrew, 'I'm still nineteen.'

'Me too, not twenty till the summer,' said Matt.

'Older, and better, that's me!' Jim, as usual, had the final word.

Will had a good morning with Hart, though the weather was turning cooler and he often felt frozen in the cockpit of the Tiger Moth, no matter how many layers of clothing he was wearing. He consolidated some of his turns, taking off, and landing.

'You're making progress,' said Hart as they walked back over the grass. 'Did I hear it's your birthday?'

'Yes, sir.'

'God, what I wouldn't give to be your age!' There was a pause. 'But you'll need to be a damn good pilot to survive this war.'

'I know, sir.'

'Well, you've got what it takes, just keep your wits about you, and let's hope that luck is on your side!'

7

He was given little warning of his solo flight. It was a cold, clear day with an easterly wind, and Will was reminding himself to watch the drift when he saw Flight Lieutenant Lang standing by his plane. He was a tall, slightly tired-looking man, with prominent ears and a well-defined mouth.

'Right, Fordham, today's the day! I want you to show me what you can do, starting with the controls, then taxiing out to take off, a few turns, then put her into a spin before we come in to land,' he said brusquely.

'Right, sir,' replied the young man, as he climbed into the back seat while Lang manoeuvred his long legs, with some difficulty, into the front.

Will launched into the familiar drill of checks before priming the engine, and shouting, 'Contact' to the ground mechanic who swung the propeller. He taxied in the usual zigzag then took off into the prevailing wind, applying full power and keeping the plane straight, checking that he was at the proper climbing speed and altitude. He managed to maintain his height nicely in the turns, stalled the plane, then corrected by pushing the stick forward, then went into another stall to start a spin, from which he came out cleanly. Hart was right: it had never proved so difficult as the first time, and he felt in control during such manoeuvres now, not merely subject to the whim of fate. His concentration did not waver as he brought the Moth in to land, a little bumpy but nothing untoward.

'Right,' said Lang, climbing out of the front, 'if you want to kill yourself, I'm getting out! Off you go!' With that, he walked away to chat to Hart, who was waiting nearby.

'Is that it?' Will muttered, savouring his first taste of freedom. It was up to him now, and he would have to get on with it as best he could. As he took off steadily into the winter sky, the Moth seemed to know it too, that he no longer doubted his own competency, and could make the plane do as he wished. They were at one in this solo flight, and each part of the routine instilled an added confidence for the next. By the time he came out of his spin he had almost forgotten that his test was nearly over, and for a whimsical moment he fancied flying away and leaving them all behind. He returned to the business in hand, landed in perfect order, and taxied to a halt.

Will made a prayer of thanks to his mother's ever-present God, before extricating himself from the aircraft.

'Not bad, for a Yorkshireman,' Hart conceded, smiling, and Lang added, 'Yes, that'll do. Let's just have a shufti at your logbook.'

Andrew and Matt were waiting for him, having completed their first solos already.

'What's up with Dick?' Matt inclined his head towards a stationary Tiger Moth in the distance, where Dick and his instructor appeared to be in conversation.

'I'm not quite sure he's ready to go solo,' Will said.

'Well, ready or not, it looks as though he's about to have a try,' replied Matt, watching as Dick's instructor climbed out of the plane.

'Oh God, I hope he makes it!'

'Oh, he'll be fine,' Matt replied, but it was easy for Matt, he could have had a pair of wings sprouting out of his back.

The Tiger Moth, with Dick alone in the cockpit, weaved unsteadily across the grass and took off, flying too low over a hedge but correcting into a climbing position and up to level flight. All three boys were now outside watching the progress of the small plane intently.

Dick was trying to do a circuit and managed a few medium turns.

'He's getting there,' said Will, but no sooner had he spoken than the plane took up a shaky approach to landing. They watched mesmerised as the flimsy aeroplane hit the ground unevenly, clipping its left wing and careering into a hedge before it came to a halt. The main body of the Moth appeared intact as they all ran towards it, joined by Dick's instructor.

'Dick, are you all right? Dick!' shouted Will.

Dick's head was forward on the controls and he appeared to have been knocked out. Will and Matt extricated him from his seat, releasing the safety lock and unstrapping his parachute.

'What's going on?' he mumbled, and by the time they had lifted Dick on to the ground he was able to stand, unsteadily and looking dazed, but in one piece.

'Are you OK?' Dick's instructor checked the young man, who was pale beneath his freckles, before walking around the plane, from which had been smashed most of the left wing and the propeller. Fortunately the fuel tank appeared intact. The instructor was taciturn while Will and Matt took Dick safely inside to get him a cup of tea.

'Made a nasty mess of that plane!' said Hart, shaking his head.

Some two hours later, after he had been passed fit by a medical orderly, Dick found himself waiting outside the CO's room.

'Come in.' Both Wyatt-Hughes and his own instructor were seated at the desk, as Dick was motioned to a chair. He sat down, certain that he had guessed his fate before it was about to be meted out to him.

'Well, Sinclair,' said Wyatt-Hughes slowly, 'it's not to say that we don't let some pilots go on even after they've smashed up a plane, because we do. But in your case – well, I've been going over things with your instructor and we don't think that you've got what it takes.'

Dick looked at him in despair, hearing the words he had most feared.

'Look, Sinclair,' the CO went on, in a conciliatory voice, 'it's not your fault, we know you've been trying hard. Not everyone's cut out for it, that's all there is to it. I hear that you are a decent mathematician and should make a first-class navigator, so we're transferring you to air navigation school.'

'But I want to be a pilot, sir.' Dick's brow was furrowed in pain. 'Couldn't I have another chance?'

'No, Sinclair,' Wyatt-Hughes replied. 'I don't think that would be in your best interests, and anyway I need to keep my quota of Tiger Moths intact. You'll be going to Cranwell tomorrow. Good luck.' He extended his hand. Before Dick knew what had happened he was out of the room, feeling dazed not just by the morning's crash, but by this sudden turn of events. He felt a complete failure, and a deep sense of gloom overcame him as he walked back to the bungalow.

Will was the first back, a little after five o'clock.

'How did it go?' he asked breathlessly as he came into Dick's room, where he found him lying on his bed with his eyes closed.

'I've got the chop,' Dick replied dully. 'Off to navigation school tomorrow.'

8

By the time they awoke for drill the following morning, Dick's room was empty and he had gone. It was frosty and bitterly cold, so that their early morning exercises seemed even more punitive than usual. For the first time since coming to Desford, Will felt a sharp sense of loss. Suddenly the fun had been taken out of their training, and he had lost a potential ally and friend. Back at the mess for breakfast, the five of them looked at each other, silently raised their teacups and considered their situations. Guy spoke first.

'I expect I'll be the next,' he said in an utterly despondent voice.

'No you won't,' replied Matt. 'I've watched you flying, you're perfectly OK. You should just believe in yourself more.'

The others looked in surprise at Matt, who was not usually given to such observations. 'He's right,' said Jim, chewing his toast. 'I don't know what all the bloody fuss is about! You should just get on with it!'

'There you go, that's settled then,' said Will. 'We, the combined voice of bungalow ten, do solemnly believe that you, Guy Clarkson, are fit to become a not-very-good pilot in His Majesty's flying service.'

They raised their cups again, and Andrew clapped Guy on the back, which was the closest sign of affection that any of them could give. Guy looked around them.

'I liked Dick, he was a good man,' he said.

'We all did, Guy,' replied Jim, 'but he wouldn't want you to follow him to navigation school. Anyway, you'd be no bloody good at it.'

It was such a beautiful little contraption, the Tiger Moth, Will thought as he walked out to the plane with his instructor. Those steady parallel wings with the struts and wires between, such a forgiving machine of almost elemental design. Will took his aeroplane very seriously, carefully and almost obsessively performing all of the necessary checks prior to, during and after flying. The ground crew had him worked out as a young man who did the job properly and would not cut corners.

'Switches off, fuel on, throttle set.'

'Ready for start!' the fitter would reply.

'Switches on, contact!'

'Contact!'

Will felt safer adhering to the meticulous system of checks and counterchecks with the fitters, realising that his survival in the air was just as much a function of their skill as his own. He was intensely earnest about his flying training, not one of the carefree like Matt, who just seemed to clip on his aeroplane and fly.

'Low flying today,' announced Hart through the interconnecting voice tube as they strapped themselves in. 'You take off, then I'll show you how it's done so you can take over.'

The sky was beginning to look white and overcast as Will taxied over the grass, opened the throttle with the tail lifting as he took off into a reasonable climb before levelling out. He handed over to Hart, who brought the little plane down from its usual flying height of five thousand feet until they were almost skimming over the Leicestershire fields and hedges. *Just as well it's a flat county*, thought Will to himself as they lifted over a small copse, following the rolling countryside but staying clear of villages and farmhouses. Hart banked around another wood, and crested an apparently medieval hill fort, up and then down the other side.

'You take over,' he ordered Will, who, keeping the plane low and steady, continued to fly nearly parallel to a small railway line before banking to the left at a mossy railway bridge.

'That's good, keep going,' Hart encouraged, as Will experienced the sheer novelty of low flying, almost like a bee buzzing its way forward in search of honey. It seemed only a short time before he had to climb back to normal height, continue the exercise and return. Will put in a half-decent landing, made easier by a lack of stiff wind.

'Looks like snow,' Hart commented. 'I doubt we'll get up tomorrow, but let's wait and see.'

Hart's words proved correct, as Will and his fellow students sat watching heavy flakes of snow falling over the airfield that afternoon during their meteorology lesson.

Their instructor used the wintry weather as his example for the day: 'That's when you'll get real problems, at altitude, with wings icing up on, for example, a heavy bomber.'

'Sounds bloody marvellous, that does,' muttered Jim under his breath.

Guy, now temporarily grounded by the weather, had still not managed to complete his first solo, which threw him into a state of continued suspense. For the others, two days off in the snow proved to be a welcome distraction. It was impossible not to join in a good snowball fight, and they pelted each other in the fading light late that afternoon with endless snowballs, degenerating into a free-for-all spontaneous rugby tackling in the snow, fortunately to white and soft landings.

9

The bungalow was empty without Dick. His room had been cleared by the orderly the day he left so there was no trace of his occupancy, thus heightening their own sense of impermanence.

Will retired to his room one evening later that week to read a letter from home. His mother, whose strong Methodist faith made her seem closer to God than her own family, wrote in her usual measured way.

Guisborough, December 1940

My dear Will,

I hope you are keeping well and managing to stay warm in this bitter weather. I expect your training is progressing by now and I feel sure you are applying yourself wholeheartedly. Your father and I pray for your safety and ask the Lord to watch over you.

More of your school friends have 'joined up' since you left, so that Guisborough seems a quiet place without its young men. Your sister Grace is planning to join the Women's Royal Army Corps. Your brother will of course stay to help with the grocery, as his health does not allow him to enlist, and contribute to the war effort in that way.

Take care to lead a good life and remember the pledge.

Your loving

Mother

Fordham looked rather ruefully at the letter. He loved his gentle mother, even if she had been so much taken up with God during his life. He remembered being taken out with her as a child on endless visits to raise money for the Methodist missionaries. Indeed, his maternal grandfather had been such a missionary in China, and the nickname for his surviving grandmother was 'The Empress of China'. Imperious, she was, the old woman, and poor tired Hannah seemed to spend much of her day looking after her. Hannah's family had not approved of her marriage, as her mother was wont to remind her; she had married 'beneath her', yet they seemed to enjoy the fruits of their son-in-law's labours at the grocery shop and market garden.

Will felt closer to his mother than his father, whom he called 'the old man'. He did not underestimate him, though, acknowledging that he must possess a fair amount of nous to have become a successful businessman and county chess champion. Not given to showing emotion, the old man had grasped his hand and looked him straight in the eye as he left home for his initial training in Aberystwyth.

He thought of home and the framed announcement on the dining room wall: *Jesus is the head of this house. A silent listener to every conversation and a silent guest at every meal.*

The old man did not share Hannah's religious fervour, but tolerated it, just as he did the pervasive presence of his mother-in-law.

It was just as well Will's mother could not see him drinking in the mess, or the pub of an evening. He had signed the pledge to abstain from alcohol to please her, but life was turning out so differently to her expectations, and indeed, to his.

He folded the letter and put it into his top pocket. Alderdice strolled into the room, self-assured as usual.

'Letters from home?' he enquired. 'Got a nice little floozy tucked away there?'

'It's from my mother,' replied Will coldly. 'Just keeping me posted about things at home. My sister's going to join the WRACs.'

'Sister, eh?' Jim said. 'Nice-looking, is she? Got a beau? What say I meet her?'

Will rolled his eyes in despair. He could not imagine introducing any of his family to Alderdice, let alone his extremely plain schoolteacher sister Grace, who, to his knowledge, had never had a date with a man in her life. He was joined by Guy, who sensed his discomfiture.

'That's enough of your nonsense, Jim, family is off-limits.' Guy had reclaimed his role as older statesman, having managed to scrape through his solo test some days before. 'You really need to grow up!' he added.

Will was not the only one to have a letter that day. Andrew's news was far more interesting. 'My father's found me a little car, an Austin 7, says I can collect it when we're next on leave!'

'You jammy bugger!' Matt longed for a car, but was a long way from affording one, given that most of his pay went on beer.

'Yes, I can't wait,' said Andrew. 'We can go on some jaunts when we're off duty – might make it beyond the local pub, maybe to a dance in Leicester!'

Andrew's popularity saw a sudden rise as they all envisaged a rapid improvement in their social life, and a chance to meet some girls at last.

10

The January days that followed were cold and unusually clear, ideal for flying and with few breaks to their schedule. In each lesson they built upon their basic skills and tried, with help from their instructors, to master new ones. Instrument flying was, as Guy had grumbled, a difficult and counter-intuitive obstacle as it involved overcoming the inherent balance setting in flight, which is peculiar to the normal human inner ear. The Tiger Moths were fitted with a special hood for blind flying, which was clipped in place to cover the student and the instrument panel, thus allowing no other fix upon the outside world. Will had, like his fellow trainees, experienced several sessions under the hood before he was timetabled for his first night flying exercise, nearly two weeks after his first solo.

He walked out to his aircraft with Lang late that evening. Impassive as usual, Lang gave the impression he would rather be doing something more useful. The runway beacons were lit, and there was a half-moon shining, better than some of the pitch-black Leicestershire nights they had experienced in the cloud. Will reflected that the five of them sometimes had difficulty finding the mess at night, let alone making it across the night sky and back to base again.

'Remember the rules,' said Lang laconically as Will strapped himself in. 'I want you up in a circuit, in a north-easterly direction, then straight down again to land.'

Will nodded, gave a thumbs-up sign to the ground crew and taxied down the grass. He did not feel unduly apprehensive for he was becoming more used to his 'old kite', and he took off faultlessly into the dark sky. It was even colder than usual, despite his many layers of clothing and his silk undergloves. Clouds passed over the moon, taking away the comfort of its light, and leaving him alone in the inky darkness. He checked his instruments, took a north-easterly course as directed, flying at the correct speed and height and obsessively checking the dials. Noticing that he was dropping height without meaning to, he eased the stick to correct his position, keeping his plane steady on the long circular turn. As he came towards the end of it, he looked around for a familiar landmark. There was no sign of the runway lights – he must have overshot the circle, but how? And where the hell was he?

Instruments, Fordham, instruments. He calmed himself, checking the dials in front of him. Compass was reading wrong; he was surely north-east, not north-west? *Must be compass error.* He tapped it uncertainly with his finger. *Remember, Fordham, the instruments are always right.* It was as though Hart was sitting on his shoulder. Feeling as though the night sky had swallowed him up, Will slowly corrected his heading according to the compass reading until he was back in position. He glanced around, with little expectation of an improvement in his situation. *What a way to go*, he thought, *lost on my first night flight.* Suddenly he saw a glimmer in the distance, followed by another, and another until he gratefully concluded that it must be the flare path at Desford. He steadied out for the approach, taking great care as before, checking and cross-checking, until he could feel the Moth coming in safely through the lighted corridor, wheels down and bumping steadily along the grass. He taxied round to dispersal.

'Lost you for a while, did we?' Lang said.

'Just for a bit, sir.'

'Not easy, is it?'

'No, sir, it's not.'

'Never is, the first time, Fordham! We'll have a beer when the others are in,' said Lang as they walked through the dark to the hangars.

He waited there until the others had all returned safely. Guy, who was the last to do his circuit, looked tense but resolute, with a determined set to his shoulders as he had walked out to his plane. Will silently wished him good luck and watched as Guy disappeared from view into the night.

'It can be a bit tedious waiting for the last one to get back,' said Lang, lighting a cigarette and offering one to Will. He took one, still trying to accustom himself to the unpleasant taste. They strolled over to one of the night braziers where the fitters were warming their hands. The ground crew were chatting about their favourite wireless programme – *ITMA*; *It's That Man Again*, but Will was straining to hear the engines of the Moth returning. Five more minutes passed.

'He's taking his time.' Lang looked at his watch. 'Keeping me waiting for my beer.'

Will stood, back straight, craning to look into the black sky.

'You won't see him, matey,' interjected one of the fitters. 'Not before you hear him, anyway.'

All the same, it was difficult not to look expectantly upwards. Where was Guy? It was a reasonable night; conditions were pretty good now that the cloud had shifted a bit. Even Lang began to look discomfited. Guy's instructor joined them at the brazier, rubbing his hands in the warmth.

'So where's your boy?' Lang asked, but his colleague merely raised his eyebrows in reply.

'I thought he was up to it, actually,' he said. 'We'd been over it so many times. He can usually fly the bloody thing when he stops worrying.'

The night sky remained silent, with no comforting returning sound of the Tiger Moth engines.

'What do you think's happened, sir?' Will said.

'Not got a clue,' replied Lang dismissively. 'Perhaps he got lost and made a forced landing somewhere. Hope he hasn't buggered up a plane. We'll give it ten more minutes, then I'm going to sit in the mess for a bit. At least it's warm in there and we can get a drink. You coming, Fordham?'

'I don't think I will, sir, if you don't mind.'

Will walked slowly back to the empty bungalow. He laid down quietly on his bed and gazed at the ceiling, remembering that awful sense of disorientation in the dark sky. The stark truth hit him that Guy might already be dead. He thought of the photograph of Guy's fiancée with her eager, open face. Was this what would befall them all, by degrees? Picked off, one at a time?

11

Andrew had meanwhile become the proud owner of a blue Austin 7 two-seater car. His father and uncle had met him in the village the previous Sunday afternoon to hand it over. Dr Farrington had driven the Austin down from Cambridge in convoy with his brother in the solid black family Vauxhall J-type saloon. Andrew had time to join them in the tea room in Desford, but was too excited about his new car to answer any of his father's gentle questions about his flying training. He drove ecstatically back to the airfield, having already obtained the necessary permits for the car. His friends gathered round on his return.

'Look at her, what a beauty!' said Andrew, eyes gleaming. 'I can't wait to take her out for a spin!'

'That is one lovely car,' Matt said. 'Not much room for the rest of us though.'

'You can take it in turns!' replied Andrew, pleased with his new status as benefactor.

'How well can you drive?' asked Jim. He had been an apprentice engineer before the war.

'Oh, well enough! You can check her out if you want!'

'Should be pretty straightforward,' Jim said. 'Not much to go wrong with a model like that.' He walked round and raised the bonnet of the small car authoritatively.

'Spark plugs might need a bit of work soon,' was his verdict, followed by 'Come on, then, what are you waiting for?' Jim climbed into the passenger seat.

'Have we got time?' said Andrew, a note of anxiety creeping into his voice. 'I was only allowed a pass until five o'clock.'

'Sure, you'll be fine, it's only half past four, that gives us thirty minutes,' replied Jim impatiently. Andrew took his place in the driver's seat, Matt cranked the starter and they were off, driving sedately through the Desford gates.

'Lucky chap,' reflected Matt. 'I would give anything for a car like that.'

They strolled over to the mess for a cup of tea, Will having resolved to write to Sybil that afternoon in his free time. It had been some time since he had received a letter from her, but the correspondence had been for the most part one-sided, as he had only intermittently replied. He excused himself on the grounds of the constraints of his training, and was still in the mess writing a rather laborious letter when Matt appeared.

'I think they must have broken down, Will, they're not back yet.'

It was now 5.30. Will sighed.

'I'm getting fed up with everyone getting back late,' he pronounced. 'First there's Guy flying around Leicestershire airfields in the middle of the night, now Andrew and Jim, off on some joyride! I'll be old before my time!'

'I'm not sure that Jim's the best company for Andrew's first trip out,' said Matt.

Just as the clock struck six, the blue Austin 7 pulled into the base, Andrew negotiating entry with some difficulty with the sentry, for his pass had expired one hour since. Down the driver's side of the beautiful blue car was a large dent, not bad enough to make her unroadworthy, but serious enough to have spoilt the look, and value, of the car.

Andrew and Jim climbed sheepishly from the car, Jim looking amused but Andrew completely crestfallen.

'You were going too fast at the crossroads,' Jim said.

'But you told me to put my foot down!'

'Not so you shoot over a crossroads and get hit by another car!' Jim replied hotly. 'Anyway, the car's still all right, you can drive it, can't you?'

'Oh, you don't understand, it was just perfect and now it's buggered up.'

Will and Matt surveyed the damage, which was clearly the result of a side impact to the car.

'It could be repaired,' said Matt.

'At what price, and what's my father going to say?' Andrew looked close to tears.

'If that's the worst prang you're in, then I expect he'll be very relieved,' said Will. 'It's payday soon, so take the car to a local garage and get them to bash the dent out. A lick of paint, and you'd never know.'

'I suppose so,' replied Andrew, relaxing a little.

'What happened to the other car?' asked Matt.

'Hardly any damage at all, just a mark on the bumper. Big Ford van,' replied Andrew bitterly. 'Added to which, I'm in trouble with my late pass so I'd better go and make my peace with the duty officer.' He threw the car keys at Matt, who caught them neatly and put them in his pocket.

'Can you put it away for me?' he asked, and Matt nodded, only too pleased to be in the driving seat at last.

12

Guy Clarkson stood in front of the two men who were to decide his destiny.

'What went wrong, Clarkson?' The CO came straight to the point, sitting back in his chair with his fingertips touching.

'Well, sir,' Guy began slowly, as if mere words could not express the depths of his dilemma, 'I started off all right but then I lost my bearings in the dark. I kept trying to get back on course, but I just couldn't find the flare path. So I flew around for a bit keeping an eye on the fuel gauge, and looking for some lights, finally saw some and thought I'd better land. Sorry it was the wrong place.' He grimaced, the whole affair obviously intensely painful to him.

Wyatt-Hughes looked at Guy's instructor, then they both looked at Guy.

'Well, Clarkson, at least you're honest,' said the CO. 'God knows how you got the plane down at Braunstone, but you did. Let me make it entirely clear that members of the Royal Air Force are not expected to land in the "wrong place", as you so quaintly put it: one more trick like that and you're out, Clarkson. Get back to your classroom!'

'Certainly, sir, thank you.' Guy fled from the room before they could change their minds.

He found Will on his tea break. 'I'm pardoned! Dunno why they're letting me stay on, though!'

'Because you'll be a first-rate bomber pilot one day. They know it, and so do you.'

'Right,' said Hart to Will the following morning, 'another good day for flying. Are you on top of things?'

'Not too bad, sir. Not very keen on the navigation tests.'

Guy had been helping him of an evening, going over some of the more difficult aspects of the course. The others did not choose to join them, apart from the occasional appearance from Matt, who looked mystified and usually left for the mess as soon as he could. Guy was a patient teacher, and because of his accountancy training had a decent grasp of the mathematics.

'Good,' continued Hart. 'Then let's go over some more essentials today. I want a forced landing after engine cut-out, then we must go over the emergency drills.'

It was a bitterly cold day, but there was no time to dwell upon frozen hands and feet. Once Will had the Moth up in stable and level flight, Hart switched off both magnetos momentarily, thus effectively cutting out the engine.

'Over to you, Fordham,' he said, the plane suddenly gliding in mid-air. Will had been checking for a suitable place for a forced landing, and spotted a wide, flat field in a northerly position below. No cows, no farm buildings, no people… He used the rudder to slip height and glided noiselessly into the field. It was bumpier than he had expected, for the feudal ridge and furrow, or grassy undulations, made for a less than smooth landing.

'That's Leicestershire for you,' grumbled Hart as the Moth taxied to a stop. 'Right, now you're on fire, where's the extinguisher?'

Will put his hand on the fire extinguisher to the right side of his feet.

'How would you take it out?' Hart continued.

'Pull it forward from the clips and break the safety wire, sir,' Will replied.

'That's right. Now you're in mid-air, and you've got to get out. Show me how, and make it quick!'

'Sorry, sir, but to begin with, as you're the passenger, you should get out first,' Will recalled.

'Quite right, I have. Now what?'

Will opened the cockpit door, disconnected the intercommunication lead and undid his safety harness. He made as though to slide over the side, head foremost, facing the tail.

'OK, don't break your neck,' ordered Hart. 'That's enough realism, and I hope you didn't forget your parachute.'

'No, sir, wouldn't dream of it.'

'Well, you'll probably have to get out of other aircraft before too long,' reflected Hart. 'The most important thing you did then, and got exactly right, was telling me to go first. I'm afraid the pilot is always responsible for getting his crew out of a plane, Fordham. You'll be the last to go, you know, and in a bomber that can mean four or five members of your crew first.' Hart looked thoughtful. 'It's just the way it is, Fordham – many a good pilot has gone down with his plane to save the crew.'

'Actually, sir, I was hoping to fly Spitfires,' put in Will as Hart paused in his commentary.

'Were you, Fordham? Now, why would you want to do that? Some of the bombers are beautiful machines – take the Wellington, for example. Barnes Wallis at his best! I was second pilot in a Wellington in one of the early Berlin raids.'

'What happened, sir?'

'I was lucky,' replied Hart brusquely, declining to say more. Despite his silence, the flashback of the events of that night returned to him like an unwelcome guest. Ted Wilson had been a brilliant pilot, able to bring their stricken Wellington back in sight of the English coast before ditching it in the sea. All Hart could remember were his own frantic attempts to release Ted, who was badly concussed, from his harness as the plane filled with seawater.

'Ted, wake up, get out, we're going down!' he had shouted, but it was no good, and he was overtaken by events as the nose went down. He had barely clambered out on to the wing with the other crew before the whole bloody lot sank beneath them without a trace. They had hauled themselves into their rescue dinghy in their 'Mae Wests' and had floated until the early grey dawn brought them deliverance in the shape of a small fishing vessel. Poor Ted, he'd never known a pilot like him. Hart often wished he had been the one to drown, then Ted would have been around to look after Connie and the baby…

'Sir?' Fordham's enquiring voice broke into his reverie. 'What's next?'

'Back to base, Fordham,' he replied. 'That's enough for today.'

'Right, lads.' Andrew spoke with his mouth full over his shepherd's pie as they took their lunch break in the canteen. 'There's a dance on in Leicester this Saturday, anyone want to come?' Andrew had recovered his composure since the damage to his car, and was keen to maintain his popularity.

'I will.' Matt was the first to respond.

'How are the rest of us going to get there?' said Jim.

'What about Radley? He could take us in the Bentley,' suggested Guy.

'I'm not sure he can drive yet, with his broken arm,' Will reminded them, but Jim was already on his way to find Hugh Radley and see if he would step into the breach. It was more than four weeks since Radley's descent from the human pyramid, but his arm was still in a sling and he was not yet back to flying.

'Sure, boys, I'll come along, though one of you might have to help with the gears!' Hugh replied, always good for a challenge.

They reckoned that they should all be able to fit into the Bentley, so could make their way to the dance in two cars. Although it was more than three days away, the dance became a focus of pleasant anticipation. Andrew took it upon himself to obtain the necessary passes, anxious not to fall foul of the authorities again.

'It's two o'clock, back to classes.' Guy marshalled their collective thoughts and they rose from their table. 'I expect they'll have something else in store for us before then,' he added bitterly.

13

Will was the first to find out about the cross-country exercise. Lang forewarned him of his objective, as it meant combining his flying and navigational skills, and he was set to fly from Desford to Duxford the following morning.

'Right, Fordham, I want you to fly a direct course to Duxford, land there and get signed off before returning,' Lang instructed, in his usual 'take it or leave it' tone. 'Should take you about an hour each way.'

As always, the instructors made it sound easy, Will thought to himself. He reckoned that the flight to the base south of Cambridge should be relatively straightforward, but had heard tales of several other would-be pilots coming adrift on this one. He had carefully charted his route, south-easterly past Peterborough, then over the airfields around Huntingdon to Duxford, which was well south of Cambridge. Will was already familiar with some of the bases adjacent to Desford, including Cottesmore in the little county of Rutland, but had never flown solo this far before. At least there was a cathedral at Peterborough, he reminded himself; might be of help as a landmark. He was suddenly envious of the trainees in the British Empire Flying School, who had been sent to places like Canada or South Africa, where presumably you could fly cross-country for miles just by following the train tracks.

He would have to refuel at Duxford, and he checked his fuel gauge again before setting off. Some of the pre-flight procedures felt routine now, and he supposed that one day he would just get into some complex great plane and fly it with hardly a thought. Maybe some of the others, like Matt, felt like that already.

The sky was a little grey as he took off, but visibility was more than adequate as he followed his compass reading. He followed a course south over the city of Leicester, past the Leicester East airfield, one that he knew already, then onwards over the flat and tranquil Leicestershire countryside. He felt in control, calm and alert but not unduly concerned. In many ways, it was nice to have a bit of peace away from the base, all by himself. He soon made out the tall cathedral spire and realised he was well on course, then he distinguished a cluster of small airfields to the east of Huntingdon. *That must be Oakington*, he thought to himself, as he went over an RAF station that looked as though it was still partly under construction. It had been built for a bomber squadron, he remembered; No. 7 would be operating from there. There had been an article in the newspaper recently about King George VI visiting the newly commissioned airfield in mid-January, and it looked as if the Stirlings were going to have their work cut out for them over Holland and France. He was surprised to see no concrete runways, then recalled that even bombers were still taking off from grass airfields.

Then he was over Cambridge, home of No. 1 ITW, where Andrew had trained, and onwards south to Duxford, a large grassy landing field to the east of the Newmarket-to-Royston road. He had it right, he was sure, as he took a steady approach in to land.

His plane bounced neatly over the grass, and after checking all of his switches he hopped out and walked over to the control tower.

'Is this Duxford?' he asked a cheery-looking flight sergeant on his way in.

'Yes, you're in the right place, is it your first cross-country?' the young man replied.

'Yes, I've come over from Desford!' Will said.

'Good for you, it's all a bit of a struggle at first, isn't it?' The airman was ruddy-complexioned and round-cheeked, little older than Will himself, and with a soft West Country accent that made it easy to imagine him on a farm in Somerset, just the sort of lad Will would have enjoyed working alongside.

'Now, don't hang around before you get back,' the flight sergeant continued. 'The weather's looking dicey: grey skies, possibly rain, so you should get signed off and up again as soon as you've refuelled. I'm Arthur Wellesley, by the way. Want a cup of tea?'

'Sounds good,' Will replied, following Arthur to the mess. It was less well-appointed than Desford, but had the same familiar groups of animated young men taking a break from their training.

'What's Desford like?' Arthur asked.

'Good training school,' replied Will, his mouth full of rich tea biscuit. 'Nice flat countryside, like here.'

'You're not from this part of the world, are you?'

'No, I'm from Yorkshire, and I reckon you must be from the south-west,' answered Will. 'I've got some cousins there.'

'Great farming county, Somerset.'

'Oh, I don't know, I wouldn't mind a few hundred acres in Leicestershire,' replied Will, and having established a mutual interest they were still deep in conversation when Arthur looked at his watch.

'Off you go, Fordham – there's one of our officers over there. Get him to sign your logbook, make it to the petrol bowsers and get back to Desford before the heavens open.'

'Where are you off to?' one of the ground crew at the pump enquired.

'Back to Desford.'

'Get a move on, looks like there's a storm brewing.'

Will needed no further encouragement, taxiing out under the ever-darkening sky. He checked his bearings for the return leg, signalled for take-off to the ground crew and rose up and away from Duxford.

Once in the air, he followed a north-westerly course, repeatedly checking his compass reading. As the visibility worsened, it became increasingly difficult to fix on any landmarks. In addition, the wind into which he was flying was becoming stronger, buffeting the little Moth, which was lifting and dropping in the air. After ten minutes of flying, he felt the first drops of rain and hunched down in the cockpit.

'Damn and blast,' he muttered. 'Just when it was going so well.'

Dropping height, he searched in the worsening light for somewhere he could safely bring the plane down. After flying dismally low without success he suddenly spotted some lights in the distance, then, opening out before him like a miracle, an unbelievably long runway on which he very promptly landed before the wind could flip him right over.

He taxied over to a position close to one of the large hangars, and switched off his engine. The rain was still pelting down as he took a deep breath, composed himself, and climbed out. He had no idea which RAF base he was on, as he ran over to a low set of prefabricated buildings nearby.

'Hello,' said an adjutant on duty at the desk. 'What have we here?'

'Sorry, sir, Fordham 1108986, diverted by bad weather on the return leg of a cross-country flight, Desford to Duxford.'

'Well, you're dripping wet and making a mess of my floor,' the adjutant replied. 'I expect you're cold too, better get you sorted out before you expire on us. All our planes are safely on the ground, I needn't remind you.'

'Where am I, sir?' Will ventured.

'Warboys, Fordham, Warboys. That long runway is for bombers, not generally meant for stray Tiger Moths, but we'll pass on that one this time. We're an overflow unit for Upton, you know, and Wyton, so we're used to the unexpected. Still, there's plenty of gash crew around today to entertain you. There's no chance of you getting off the ground today, you'd better hole up here for the night and try again tomorrow. I'll ring through to Desford and let them know you're here.' He picked up the telephone and spoke briefly to one of his superiors, who soon appeared in person. The tall flight lieutenant spoke breezily.

'Well, at least you got her down, absolutely filthy weather. Why ever did they let you take off from Duxford? Don't they have any Met men there? I agree with the adjutant, let's get you dried off, then you'll just have to put up with the Warboys mess for the night. I warn you, it's a bit rowdy, bloody bomber crews can make a lot of noise.' With that, he led Will through the building to a small accommodation block where he showed him a single room.

'Perkins?' The flight lieutenant summoned a batman. 'Could you requisition some clothes for LAC Fordham before he freezes to death?'

'Certainly, sir. I'll look after him,' the batman replied. He had the appearance of an elderly valet, used to catering to the whims of an unpredictable gentry.

In no time Will was ushered into a tiled bathroom, with a warm bath already filled, into which he gratefully sank after divesting himself of his sodden Sidcot suit. He was soaked to the skin, and only started to relax a little as he warmed up in the hot water.

'Your tea will be in your room, sir,' Perkins announced.

Will lay back in the bath, momentarily overwhelmed by his sudden change of fortune. *One minute you think you're for the chop, the next you're luxuriating in a hot tub…* He closed his eyes and listened to the rain battering on the bathroom window.

Later, re-kitted in some spare uniform, he was directed by Perkins to the mess, which he entered without confidence.

There was a card game in full swing at one of the tables; looked like poker, with a surrounding group of hangers-on.

'Hey, old chap, have you come to join our little game of cards?' a moustached man, in his early thirties, with a very loud voice, boomed across the room. 'Hang on, you must be the Tiger Moth chappie.'

'I'm afraid so,' Will said. 'Got caught up in some nasty weather.'

'Quite so, best to land and sit it out here. Now, do you play poker? Got any cash on you? I suppose not – best have a beer while you warm up.'

Will began to feel more at ease. He rather liked the brash camaraderie of the pilots, who became increasingly combative over their cards. At that moment, they looked as though everything depended on the game, and nothing else in the world mattered.

'No bloody flying tonight, thank God.' A tall, well-built man was sitting reading in a comfortable armchair in the corner. 'We don't like going out in this stuff, do we, Leonard?' he enquired of the bespectacled man next to him. Will noted that Leonard wore the navigator's half brevet.

'No we don't,' agreed Leonard. 'We'd soon be up the spout, like this poor bugger here!'

The large, friendly base was populated by crews of Sterlings and Wellingtons. There was a contingent of Polish pilots there too, the first Will had met, determinedly hard drinkers with unfamiliar names like Stanislaw or Karol. Will turned in early to his crisp, white-sheeted bed, hoping that conditions would be better in the morning. He would have to face the music on his return, but at least he and his plane were still in one piece.

14

Perkins had magically dried all his clothes by the time he awoke. The day looked grey, but not so stormy, so after a brief breakfast in the mess he strode out to his plane.

'Bye, old fellow, hope you make it home today.' One of the poker players waved cheerily to him over his plate of toast.

The fitters had already checked his plane over. 'We don't see many of these DH82s here, more's the pity,' one of them volunteered. 'It's all those bloody great bombers, they just get bigger and bigger!'

Will nodded in agreement as he taxied past rows of huge aircraft. How on earth would you lift off the runway in one of those, especially with a full bomb load?

He had checked his course before leaving and thanked Perkins for his ministrations.

'It's my pleasure, sir,' Perkins had responded nobly, as though Will were a country house guest who had been riding to hounds on a particularly rough day.

Will took off into a leaden sky and steadily followed his course back to Desford. The wind had dropped considerably, so his passage was uneventful and dry, if cold. Passing over Leicester on the homeward leg he experienced a novel sensation of calm, as though he had gone to some precipice and peered over it, yet still survived.

He landed neatly at Desford and taxied to a halt. Lang was nearby, talking to a fellow trainee. He broke off his conversation:

'Fordham, how good of you to return!' he said. 'Enjoy your night away?'

'Made a nice change, thank you, sir.' Will suddenly felt tired of apologising all the time. Not everything that happened was his fault, he decided. 'Weather was pretty bad, sir.'

'Yes, I know, Fordham – unfortunately you were one of several not to return yesterday. To give you your due, you are the first back today with an intact plane.'

Will took this as a compliment, gathered up his parachute, and walked back to the teaching block with as much dignity as he could muster.

Matt was there, waiting to go back into class after the morning break.

'What happened?' he said.

'Oh, the usual cock-up with the weather, shouldn't really have taken off from Duxford. Got blown about a bit and came down at Warboys. Nice friendly mess!' Will added, smiling. 'If I'd had some money with me I could have joined a good game of poker. What about you?'

'Guy and I were flying west, where the weather wasn't so bad, so made it back yesterday, but Jim was last heard of at Cottesmore.'

'Did he have to land there?' asked Will.

'Yes, he's on the 185 squadron base there, had to spend the night, like you. There are four others out there somewhere. I think Andrew got caught out at Bourne.'

'That's not good,' commented Will. 'Why the hell did they let us all go in the first place? Don't these Met men get anything right?'

It seemed to Will that the boffins had not a clue what the weather would be like until it was right on top of them. He thought of the bomber pilots at Warboys, being sent out on some filthy night to bomb impossible targets across the Channel.

'I know what you mean,' agreed Matt. 'Anyway, I expect Jim'll be back soon, he's pretty indestructible.'

His prediction was correct, and Jim landed his Tiger Moth about an hour later. He was full of news and seemed to have enjoyed the diversion.

'Great place there, had a good time! Full of bombers, mostly Handley Page Hampdens, but the accident rate's a shocker!' The Hampdens were renowned for their high loss rate in bomber training, and Cottesmore had lost more aircraft than any other base in the county.

'Ruddy pilots are on their own in that training cockpit,' Jim added. 'I wouldn't want to be on one of those day raids either.'

During the course of the morning the remaining cross-country novices returned to find themselves summoned to a meeting at noon with the CO. They gathered uneasily in one of the training rooms, waiting to hear what he would say.

The CO sighed before addressing the group.

'I just need to make one thing clear, and I'll keep it brief. Under normal circumstances, if you fail your cross-country then you're out, as we clearly don't want pilots who can't get from A to B. However, on this occasion most of you seemed to get to B, but were unable to return to A. The truth is, none of you should have taken off at point B, because the weather was already starting to close in, but you did, and then ended up having to use your own initiative. That's what flying is all about of course, it doesn't always go according to plan. Wherever you finally chose to land, I hear that you acquitted yourselves well. Under the circumstances, I can confirm that your extended cross-country exercise will be recognised as completed, and you may proceed with your training. That is all, gentlemen.' He turned to leave the room.

Jim looked at Will, and as soon as Wyatt-Hughes had left said, 'I should bloody well hope so! I think we should be given more credit for getting ourselves out of a jam!'

'I don't think that that's the way his mind works,' replied Will. 'He sees that as a basic skill, which I suppose it is, if that's the way to stay alive.'

'Well, after Cottesmore I don't know which is more akin to committing suicide, fighters or bombers,' said Jim. 'Which way do you plan to go?' No answer was expected, or given, and they walked to the mess for lunch.

15

Will woke the next morning feeling decidedly unwell. He was feverish, and had an uncomfortably sore throat. He went for a glass of water, then sat down on the bed.

'I'm not going to make it to PE this morning, got some flu bug,' he told Matt, who was nearly dressed and ready to go.

'You'd better see the MO or they'll have you up for slacking,' Matt advised, leaving for the gruelling morning exercises.

The weather was bad again, more rain and freezing winds, so it seemed unlikely that there would be any flying today.

Will went straight to the sickbay, where he sat waiting to see the MO.

'Come in,' a voice called, and he followed it into one of the examination rooms.

'Fordham 1108986, sir,' he reported on entry.

'What's the trouble, Fordham?' the medical officer, Flight Lieutenant Hall, asked. He was in his white coat today, but Will had seen him flying and knew he had his wings. Dr Hall was a serious, active-looking man of middle age.

'I'm a bit shivery, sir, sore throat too.' In fact Will was feeling rather worse as time progressed, and his teeth were chattering as he spoke. The doctor took his temperature, pulse, examined his throat and ears and listened to his chest.

'Were you one of the chaps who got rained off on your cross-country?' he asked.

'Yes, sir, caught in a storm.'

'Well, you seem to be coming down with influenza,' the medical officer said. 'You'll have to come over to sickbay and we'll keep an eye on you there. Go and get a few things, then straight back here for at least twenty-four hours' rest, and aspirin.'

Will did as he was told, and soon found himself in one of the white-framed beds in the sickbay. He drifted in and out of sleep, sweaty and hot, rather losing track of the time. One of the orderlies brought him a cool drink, which he took eagerly. He was woken by the arrival of another patient in the opposite bed, and looked over to see a tall red-haired young man, one of the other trainee pilots, whose pale face was familiar but whose name he did not know. Will's eyes were hurting and his head began to ache; he was given more aspirin, then dozed again.

It must have been mid-afternoon when the doctor came to his bed again and examined him.

'I don't really like the look of this, Fordham,' he pronounced. 'I'm concerned you might have rheumatic fever, so I'm sending you, and Johnstone over there, into the fever unit at Groby Road Hospital in Leicester. You'll be properly looked after, and I expect you'll be back soon.'

'I'm not ill enough to go to hospital, sir,' Will remonstrated, but the unsmiling doctor was taking no risks.

One hour later, he and Johnstone were in the back of a forces ambulance, being driven by a pretty WAAF driver named Florence, on their way to Groby Road.

'Jesus Christ, it's bumpy,' said Johnstone cheerfully, by way of a conversational opening. He had a strong Scottish accent.

'Waste of time sending us to hospital,' replied Will; 'there's nothing that much the matter. Just got soaking wet on that cross-country.'

'Me too,' said Johnstone. 'It was a complete balls-up, sending us out in that weather. I reckon I was lucky to get back – had a nasty moment out in the Fens when I didn't give much for my chances. I'm Neil, by the way.'

'Nice to meet you,' Will replied. They were both lying uncomfortably, on opposite sides of the vehicle, though any more jolting would have propelled them to the floor.

'At least we'll have a few days off,' Neil said.

'I'd rather not miss any flying,' groaned Will. 'I'll be fine tomorrow. It's a lot of fuss about nothing.'

'Pity Florence doesn't know how to drive this thing!' Neil yelled as they hit a particularly bad pothole. 'Pretty lass, though.'

Will closed his eyes. That was the last thing on his mind at the moment. Why in heaven's name were they sending him to hospital, and how long would he be there? All he wanted was to get out of the ambulance and back to Desford, his aeroplane and his friends.

Part Three:
After the Blitz

1

The railway journey to Leicester had taken far longer than intended. The group of probationer nurses, overseen by Sister Colville, were in crowded compartments mostly populated by servicemen. It transpired that one of the army divisions was moving to a temporary base in the Midlands, their own unit in London having also suffered badly in the bombing. Sister Colville frowned at any attempt of fraternisation between the uniformed young men, keen to try their luck, and the young women she was escorting. Matters were not helped by protracted delays, thus offering more opportunities for random conversation and meetings in the corridor. Addie became quite flustered by the attentions of a young fusilier, who managed to extract her address during a furtive visit to the next carriage. He had been sitting in the corridor for hours, on his pack, looking singularly cheerful despite the obvious privations of the journey. It had been impossible for Addie to ignore him completely, especially since he was very good-looking and so polite.

'What should I say to him?' she whispered to Honor.

'For goodness' sake, don't ask me, how would I know?'

Sister Colville, who missed nothing, looked over at the two girls disapprovingly.

Honor smiled back at her, before telling Addie to stop encouraging the young man, who looked to her as though he was not to be trusted. 'Too handsome by half, you mark my words.'

Addie managed the small success of passing him her address without any help at all from her friend.

'He's called Ken,' she said to Honor on her return.

Honor shrugged and shook her head. 'Honestly, Addie, you should be more careful, you've just given your address to a perfect stranger!'

'Well, at least he's a handsome one,' her friend retorted. 'Sometimes I think you have no interest at all in the opposite sex. What would Beatie do if she was here?'

Honor thought she could guess, but refrained from replying.

Fortunately the next stop was Leicester and the young women descended in an orderly crocodile, Addie managing a restrained wave to her new friend.

'That's enough of that nonsense!' pronounced Sister Colville briskly. She was glad to get the girls off the train and would be even more relieved to deliver them safely to the hospital.

It was dark in the station, with all the same blackout procedures they were used to in London, and as they went out to the waiting bus they could see little of the city beyond the Victorian station facade. The bus bumped through the streets until they had almost reached open fields, and saw the dimly lit sign reading *Groby Road Hospital*, before rattling down the entrance road into the hospital site. The young women could just make out the rows of Nissen huts on each side.

'Looks more like a prison than a hospital,' breathed Addie.

They stood in the gloom of the dark winter evening, their spirits even more deflated by the drab hut which faced them.

'This will be your accommodation, I think,' said Sister Colville, looking anxiously around for a welcoming committee of any sort. A torch flashed at them from a distance, then drew closer, to reveal a woman of strong build with a jolly face.

'She looks like my school gym teacher,' one of them whispered, but she turned out to be their new matron.

'Sorry about the digs!' she said cheerfully, unlocking the door to the hut. 'We don't have a proper nursing home for probationers here, so you'll just have to make do until we can sort out something better. One of the porters is coming to get this stove lit, that'll cheer things up a bit. We had no idea when you would arrive! We'll get you a hot meal in the main block, then I'll be able to fill you in about tomorrow. In the meanwhile, make yourselves at home and welcome to Leicester!'

Matron withdrew to confer with Sister Colville while the girls looked around them. Anything less like home would be hard to imagine, with the stark beds and lockers lining the Nissen hut. Honor supposed it must be one of the old wards, and by the look of the peeling paintwork, it was certainly due for refurbishment. She would probably cope with it better than some of her peers, who were looking cold and miserable after the long day's journey. The stove, once lit, smoked badly, but at least there was some warmth generated, and Honor sat down on one of the beds feeling tired and in need of a cup of hot tea. She felt a pang of homesickness for their organised, tidy nurses' home in London, with the polished floors and the wide, airy rooms.

Addie was the first to rally. 'Come on, you lot,' she announced, 'we're lucky to be here at all really, so we'd better get on with it.' She resolutely put her bag beside the locker and started to unpack, with the others soon following suit. In half an hour, after they had washed in the primitive basins, they were summoned by one of the porters, who led them through the damp and chilly paths with his torch to the main block, where he left them. Once inside, the brighter lights and smell of cooking comforted them and they sat down to nourishing stew and potatoes.

'Tastes good,' Addie commented. 'Think it must be rabbit.' The shortage of food since rationing meant that the probationers were glad of every meal, and completely unconcerned as to its provenance. Except of course, with the notable exception of tripe, which Honor had to force herself to eat, swallowing it quickly and washing it down with plenty of water.

After their supper, which included the additional luxury of sultana sponge and custard, the company sat back while Matron rose to speak.

'I hope you all feel stronger after your supper.' She smiled warmly. 'We have managed to stretch to a better meal than usual for you, thanks to some of our generous local farmers. I know that your living quarters are not ideal, and I'm sure you must all be feeling rather like fish out of water. Our hospital board was very sorry to hear of your plight during the Blitz and when asked to help, we felt we could rise to the challenge of training you here. We are not normally a training hospital like the Lambeth, but we have many experienced sisters who have volunteered as tutors so you will be well looked after. As you know, this is a fever hospital, not a big general hospital like the Lambeth. Your fever training will be much the same as before except we have more adult patients, including those in iron lungs in two of our polio wards. There is a list assigning you to your wards on the main noticeboard in the hall. Please report at 7am sharp to the sister in charge and I hope you all have a decent night's sleep.'

Honor liked the friendly, enthusiastic matron. It all seemed less formal than in London, and she began to hope that she might fit in here.

'What do you make of it all?' said Addie on their way back to their hut. 'Not quite like the old place, is it?'

'No,' Honor replied, 'but then, as you said, we're lucky to be here and not buried under a pile of rubble in that cellar!'

'Yes, and the food's better too, at least for the first night.' Addie linked arms with her through the darkness to the unprepossessing entrance of their accommodation.

2

The next morning Honor was assigned to Ward 5, a children's rheumatic fever ward. She had little experience of rheumatic fever nursing in Lambeth, as it was due to be her next attachment, but had learnt the practical aspects for her recent examination. On her way to the ward that morning, she tried to recollect what she should know: that most young patients with this condition would be treated with complete bed rest, not allowed to walk to the bathroom, and would be confined to bed for washing and feeding. They had to be kept happy and warm, and entirely at rest, physically and emotionally. She remembered that shortage of the new antibiotics, which were reserved for those on active service, meant that early treatment of streptococcal disease was just not possible in many cases. Rheumatic fever usually followed on from a 'strep throat' or scarlet fever, and was commonest in children and adolescents, with a risk of long-term damage to the heart and joints.

Honor's first impression of Ward 5 on a morning shift was not exactly one of peace and quiet. A harassed-looking nurse was trying to respond to several children at once.

'Nurse, I need the pan!' a dark-haired, thin boy, probably about ten years old, was shouting as she closed the ward door behind her.

'Me too!' came a chorus of small voices.

Honor intercepted Sister, who was rushing from one end of the ward to the other.

'I'm Nurse Newson, the probationer,' she said.

The nurse hardly paused to respond. 'Yes, just give me a hand with these bedpans, the sluice is at the end of the ward', and Honor, pleased to be of immediate help and not to have to undergo a lecture, or detailed questions about her previous training, slipped off her cape, and went straight to the sluice. She found a fresh apron and equipped herself with as many bedpans as she could carry, which she promptly distributed to the noisiest children.

'Can't I just get out?' a tearful child requested.

'No, you know that's not allowed.' Honor paused by the little figure, and smiled at her in encouragement.

'I want my mum!' Her small lip was trembling in grief.

'When did you come in?' Honor asked softly, knowing that parents were not permitted on the children's wards.

'Yesterday,' the child replied. 'I want my mum and sisters! I want to go home!'

'Of course you do,' said Honor firmly, 'and you will, just as soon as you're better. Just try and do as you're told and then you'll get better quicker, won't you?'

The child looked unconvinced.

'What's your name?' Honor briefly held her hand.

'Maisie,' the child replied.

'Right, Maisie, hop up on this bedpan and then I'll come and take it away when you're finished.' Honor went on, deftly slipping the child on to the cold pan, giving her another smile and moving on quickly before Maisie had time to change her mind.

Even working side by side, the two nurses took some time to see to each child, and then continued in the sluice together, washing and emptying the pans.

'What did you say your name was?' Sister looked only a little older than Honor, and was trying to push back her spectacles, which had steamed up in the sluice.

'Newson,' Honor replied.

'No, what's your first name?'

'We weren't allowed to use our first names at the Lambeth.'

'Oh, for goodness' sake, it's only you and me on here and we'll be worked off our feet all day without any of that "Nurse Newson" stuff!' She looked indignant. 'Honestly, what do they expect? We have thirty sick children and we're not even allowed to use our first names! I'm Ann Blackwell, and this is my ward. I'm glad you're here, but I won't have much time for teaching. We'll just have to manage as best we can, won't we?'

'Yes, that's fine with me. I'm Honor and I'd much rather be getting on with some work!'

'There you go, that wasn't too bad. Now it's breakfasts,' said the forthright young woman, leading Honor back up the ward to the kitchen. 'I'm glad you got Maisie round, she's a bit distressed and keeps setting the others off. She'll settle in a few days, you'll see.'

Honor, looking at Maisie's tear-streaked face as she walked past, wondered how this would come to pass.

'Hey, you're new, aren't you?' One of the older boys cheekily surveyed Honor. 'Look, lads, they're sending us pretty ones now!' he said to his adolescent neighbour, who winked at her equally rudely.

'That's enough, Tom,' her senior colleague interrupted. 'We'll be sending you off to adult surgical if you don't behave!'

'I thought this was just a fever hospital?' Honor asked.

'Yes, it is,' Sister Blackwell replied, out of earshot. 'We haven't got a surgical ward, he's just getting too cocky by half. I hope Dr Simpson sends him home soon – he's so much better, and more troublesome by the day!'

Then it was breakfast for each child: porridge and bread spread with jam on each tray, with a cup of milk too. Honor thought it looked nourishing, and most of the children appeared hungry despite their illness. Little Maisie left hers untouched by the side of her bed.

'Come on, Maisie, eat up, it'll make you better.' Honor held the cup of milk to the child's lips.

'I'm not hungry,' she persisted, but took the milk eagerly, and then watched as Honor cut the bread into little slices.

'Just one or two.' Honor put a slice into the little hand, and waited while Maisie decided to eat it, very slowly, looking at Honor solemnly with dark eyes while she slowly chewed her way through one, then two slices of the sticky bread. 'Now the porridge,' she urged her, and proffered a spoonful, which the child took, surveying her with her direct gaze all the while. 'There now, try and have a few more.' Honor patiently helped the child through several more mouthfuls. She smiled at her. 'Good girl, Maisie, you can do that all by yourself now.'

Maisie wiped her fingers on the sheet, but Honor thought it best not to remonstrate. There was so much for a small child to cope with, unwell and cut off from family and home. Anyway, it would soon be time for washing, bed-changing, and temperatures before the doctor's ward round. She and Ann had better get a move on, she realised, looking at the clock. She caught Ann's glance, nodded and carried on with her duties as promptly and sensibly as she could.

By the time Dr Simpson and Matron arrived they had just finished the daily 'obs', and were completing the charts. Sister Blackwell brushed a stray hair into her cap and straightened her spectacles once again, as they came on to the ward.

'Morning, Sister.' Dr Simpson was a small, dark man in his early thirties. He was a man who liked things done quickly and well, and had a brusque manner that did not encourage prevarication. 'Shall we proceed?' he added, as Doctor, Matron and the two nurses stopped at each bed for a progress report on each child from Sister Blackwell. Honor listened carefully to the summaries, and watched the detailed examination of the children. Maisie hid under the bedclothes on their approach, but Matron, with extreme gentleness, seemed to know what to say to the child to allow Dr Simpson to examine her.

'Her temp's high,' he commented when he had finished. 'She will need aspirin four-hourly and tepid sponging if it goes any higher.'

They moved on to the end of the ward, stopping at Tom's bed.

'Can't I go home?' He grinned at Dr Simpson. 'See, my temperature's down and I'm feeling better. My legs don't hurt anywhere near so much as they did, I bet I'd be fine to walk now.'

Dr Simpson looked thoughtful. 'What do you think, Sister?' Ann frowned before replying.

'Well, I'd been thinking he was ready for bed rest at home, but his respiratory rate has gone up this morning. As you can see, he is as full of himself as ever.' She grinned at Tom as Dr Simpson put his stethoscope in his ears.

'Let's have a listen.'

The boy rolled up his eyes, but lay quietly while the doctor listened attentively.

'You're not going anywhere, young man,' he concluded, standing back.

They withdrew to the middle of the ward and Dr Simpson explained what was on his mind. 'He has a loud heart murmur and as you correctly say, Sister, his pulse and respiratory rate are both up. He will need maximum rest, no exertion at all and hourly obs. Call me back if there's any change – he could well be developing a carditis.'

Honor looked at Ann in dismay – what did he mean? Dr Simpson added, for her benefit, having noticed her confusion, 'That's when his heart muscles stop working properly, Nurse. Unfortunately, it's one of the common complications of rheumatic fever. We'll have to keep a very close eye on him!'

'Thank you, Doctor,' said Sister Blackwell, and Matron nodded as she left the ward.

'I thought you said he was ready to go home?' Honor asked as the doors swung shut.

'That was before I did his obs,' Sister replied. 'He was trying to be his usual chirpy self but his colour's poor and he's breathing rapidly. Children can go off more quickly than adults, you always need to remember that.'

Honor was impressed. She would have to listen hard to this young woman, if she was to become half as good a nurse as her.

3

Honor soon became used to the pace of the ward. Ann Blackwell proved to be a reliable and frank teacher, and Honor made rapid progress as she was inevitably given increasing responsibility on each busy shift. She came to know more about the children on the ward, and without meaning to, instinctively grew fond of little Maisie in particular. Tom's condition continued to concern Dr Simpson. He developed a refractory carditis during the first week and Honor was dismayed to see him lying pale and exhausted, no longer capable of his wicked jokes, which they would all have been glad to hear again. He was obviously struggling with his breathing as they drew up to his bed on the morning round some days later. Dr Simpson listened to his chest carefully, but the look in the lad's eyes now was one of fear.

'Take it easy, old chap,' Dr Simpson said gently.

'I can't breathe, doctor.' The boy's anxiety was palpable, and Honor glanced at Matron.

Ann moved to hold Tom's hand. 'It's all right, Tom, Dr Simpson'll sort you out.'

The doctor looked at Ann, but said nothing until the group withdrew from earshot.

'Can't you do something to help his breathing? I can't bear to see it!'

This was uncharacteristic of Ann, who usually remained composed on the ward round.

'I agree,' Matron said. 'We're just watching him deteriorate day by day.'

'He's in heart failure, that's the problem,' replied Dr Simpson. 'His lungs are filling with fluid because his heart's not able to beat properly. That's got fluid around it too, it's called a restrictive carditis.'

'I don't doubt the cause, Doctor,' Matron said, 'I just don't think we can continue with conservative management. The boy is going to die if we do nothing.'

Dr Simpson sighed. He had reckoned that one more day might see a spontaneous improvement in Tom's condition. He was not very keen on cardiocentesis, the drawing of fluid by needle from the pericardial space, as the last patient he had performed it upon had died shortly afterwards, though whether as a consequence of the procedure or the progression of the disease, he would never know.

'Aren't there any drugs which would work?' Honor felt able to ask questions now, and did not always stand mutely, as she had done at first.

'Well, we could try digitalis, but it doesn't usually help much in this type of heart failure,' responded Dr Simpson. He looked distracted, and had lost his usual confidence.

'You don't really have much to lose,' Matron put in quietly.

'All right, we'll give it a go for twenty-four hours, and if there's no improvement by tomorrow then I'll do a cardiocentesis after the morning round. Nurse Newson, I'll write this up, then please would you go straight to the pharmacy so we can start it as soon as possible?'

'Certainly, Doctor.' Honor, relieved to be doing something at last, put on her cape and walked over the frosty paths to the pharmacy. The chill late November weather was beginning to bite, and she felt her chilblains rubbing against her stiff black regulation shoes. The night temperatures had dropped, and most of the girls in her hut were suffering, despite the stove being on through the early hours. She arrived at the pharmacy and passed the chart to the bespectacled, over-worked pharmacist, who was the sole dispenser of medicines on the site.

He read it, and with an almost imperceptible shake of the head, disappeared around the back, amongst the rows of pots, potions and pills. He came back with a small packet neatly labelled with Tom's name, and the precise dose, in fine copperplate handwriting.

'You have to be careful with this one,' he advised Honor solemnly. 'Children can be very sensitive, even to a small dose, so watch carefully for side effects.'

'Like what?'

'Thready pulse, low blood pressure,' the pharmacist replied. 'Don't look so frightened, I'm sure the doctor knows what he's doing.'

Honor sighed, thanking him, and made her way back to the ward. She looked up at the clear, cold blue sky as she did so and wondered how low the temperature would drop tonight. She was used to the cold, her childhood home having offered little warmth apart from the kitchen stove, but still hated the bitter chill of winter, especially harsh for the under-nourished. She consoled herself with the realisation that at least she was better fed now.

'Thanks.' Ann took Tom's medication, read the instructions carefully, and went to give the boy his first dose, double-checking with Honor as she did so.

'That's good, well done.' She patted his hand as he swallowed the pills down slowly.

'Am I going to die, Nurse?' Tom asked disarmingly, between breaths. It was said in a perfectly straightforward way, without emotion, just a simple question that demanded an honest answer.

'I hope not,' Ann replied, equally solemn. 'Just keep breathing gently, and try not to panic. This new medicine should do the trick.'

'I hope so.' Tom rested back on his pillow, sapped by the effort.

When it came to the end of her shift, Honor did not want to leave the ward. The boy looked so weak, she could not see how he could possibly survive the night.

'Off you go,' Ann said brusquely, 'there's nothing more you can do now.'

Passing his bed on the pretext of collecting some instruments from the steriliser, Honor called softly, 'Night, Tom, see you tomorrow', but the boy, in a shallow sleep, did not answer her. Dr Simpson was entering the ward as she left, but as she looked back, Ann waved her away summarily, and she walked slowly out into the night air.

She went back to the probationers' hut, kicked off her shoes, and sat on the bed for a bit, rubbing her chilblained foot. Was it all going to be like this, she wondered? Perhaps Matron at the Lambeth had been right; maybe she was not really strong enough for it after all. She could hardly bear the fact that children could die so quickly, of these awful diseases. All of the nursing practices, which she had been trying so hard to learn, seemed suddenly pointless to her. She began to wonder if any of it made any difference: either the child was going to die, or not, just like the arbitrary toss of a coin.

Addie arrived to interrupt her thoughts.

'What's up? Trouble on the ward?'

'No,' said Honor quietly, 'but one of our boys isn't going to make it.'

Addie came to sit beside her. 'It won't help if I say that's part of the job, but it is, and you and I both know that. You knew it when you started, but it doesn't make it any easier.' She swallowed, and went on, 'My little sister died from diphtheria, she was six years old. I loved her so much, I couldn't believe that she'd be taken from us. I knew I wanted to be a nurse from that time on. It was a way of keeping her memory, by helping others who were ill. I don't suppose I make any difference really, but at least I'm trying, and so are you.' Addie stood up briskly and stretched out her hand. 'Come on, time for supper, you need something against the cold tonight.'

Honor took the slim hand between hers, drew on her cardigan, and rose to join her.

4

She heard Maisie crying as she entered the ward the next day, and went straight to her, although noticing that the curtains around Tom's bed were closed.

'I want Rabbit!' Maisie was inconsolable.

'Which rabbit?' Honor sat on her bed and stroked her cheek.

'Tilda's rabbit!' Maisie wailed, and Honor remembered that Tilda was one of Maisie's older sisters. Maisie looked very flushed, and Honor, checking her chart, noted that her fluctuating fever seemed to be responding to aspirin, but little else. It was unusual to see rheumatic fever in such a young child, though Maisie's little swollen joints added weight to the diagnosis. She must remember to ask Dr Simpson why Maisie was making such little improvement, next time he did the round. She gave Maisie some sips of milk and then went to distribute the bedpans. Peering through Tom's curtains, she saw Dr Simpson in white gown and gloves, assisted by Ann, who was assembling a small trolley of instruments next to him. It took only one glance at Tom, and at the absorption of her two colleagues, to realise that the boy's condition had become critical. Dr Simpson was about to perform a cardiocentesis, the procedure he had been trying to avoid. Tom was breathing in shallow, short breaths, and his face had taken on a bluish tinge. Honor slipped behind the curtain to join them, and went to take the pulse on Tom's responseless hand.

'Right, I'm going in,' the doctor announced firmly, inserting the needle, which was attached to a large glass syringe, into Tom's ribcage to the left of the breast bone. Tom gasped as, nothing having yet entered the syringe, Dr Simpson pushed a little further. There was a sudden give of the needle and yellowish clear fluid started to flow back into the syringe, filling it quickly to capacity. Dr Simpson, deftly replacing it with an empty syringe while the needle was still in place, drew up another full syringe before the pressure seemed to drop and the fluid stopped pushing at the circular glass walls. Honor, mute in attention, felt Tom's thready pulse falter, then pick up, and they all watched anxiously as Dr Simpson withdrew the syringe, and pressed down hard with a gauze swab at the entry point. Honor noted how steady his hands were, despite the fine sweat which had broken out upon his forehead.

'That's it,' he concluded, pulling off his gloves, all the time watching the boy. 'Tom, we've finished.'

Ann knelt by the boy's ear, counting his respirations with her watch as she did so.

'They're coming down,' she announced after a few minutes had passed. 'Thirty and falling!'

Dr Simpson wiped his forehead as he removed his gown. 'All right, keep up the observations, Sister, you had better stay with him for at least fifteen minutes to make sure he's stable. Nurse Newson can manage the rest of the ward. I'll be back for my ward round in an hour.'

Honor drew back the curtains around Tom's bed to see a worried face looking up at her from the neighbouring bed.

'He's going to be all right, Nurse, isn't he?' The boy was a little older than Tom, but they had been firm friends since they both came in, sharing the same jokes at the expense of everyone else on the ward.

'I think so,' replied Honor steadily. 'It looks as though he's going to pull through, but don't disturb him.'

'I won't, honest, Nurse, I just want him to get better, that's all.'

Honor resumed her usual morning duties – bedpans, washing, and breakfasts – in as quick a time as she could, by herself.

Tom's condition seemed to stabilise over the course of the day. Ann spent much of the morning shift attending to him, so that Honor only just managed to complete her tasks. The ward round started at the usual time, as they briskly passed from child to child before stopping at Tom's bed.

'Well, Sister, how is he doing?' Dr Simpson listened to Tom's chest once again.

'His respiratory rate and pulse are both steady.'

'Good, his lungs sound a bit less congested to me. Keep it up, old boy.' Dr Simpson patted Tom's arm, but the boy was too exhausted to manage anything other than a weak smile.

They moved on, finishing at Maisie's bed. She did not hide now when they approached, but just shut her eyes tightly, screwing them up as if that would make them all go away.

'I'm worried about Maisie, her temperature just keeps going up and down,' Honor said.

'How are her joints?' Dr Simpson asked.

'She says they still hurt, especially her knees.'

The doctor checked Maisie's chart, examined her and frowned slightly. 'Not sure why she's not responding better,' he muttered, partly to himself. 'Is she taking her aspirin?'

'Yes, Doctor,' Honor replied, remembering what a struggle it had been at first to coax the child to take it.

'She's young for rheumatic fever,' Matron observed. 'Do you suppose it could be something else?'

'Not much of a differential diagnosis in her case,' Dr Simpson returned peremptorily. 'Best carry on as we are and see how she goes.'

Maisie peeped from under her half-closed eyes. 'I want Rabbit,' she whispered to Honor.

'Yes, Maisie, I know.'

It was a long day, and by the end of her shift that evening Honor's feet were aching. She checked Tom once again before she left; all of his obs were steady, though he still lay back weakly on the pillows, as though it took all of his strength to survive.

She was ready for a break, and some respite from the ward. A small group of probationers were clustering around a crackling radio set, listening intently as she entered the hut.

'What's happened?' Honor asked one of the girls.

'Ssh,' she replied, finger at her lips, 'it's dreadful news – Coventry's been badly bombed!'

5

Tom did not look much stronger the following morning, but at least he was still in his bed and not the hospital mortuary. He managed a weak smile when Honor went to take his obs.

'You look a bit better today,' she commented. He did not answer, but let her lift him on the pillow for some sips of orange.

Making her way down the ward, she found Maisie asleep under her blankets, her little face barely visible under a comforting nest of bedclothes.

'Milk time, Maisie.' Honor gently touched the small figure, who peeped out at her. As the child reached out to take her drink, Honor noticed a little blood on her pillow.

'Where's that from?' Honor made a mental note to tell Dr Simpson, and continued with her morning tasks.

Dr Simpson seemed pleased with Tom's progress. He had privately shared Honor's dread of seeing an empty bed, and was heartened that the boy was still alive.

'Best keep him on the digitalis for the time being, but half the dose,' he said, altering his chart as he did so. They moved away to the other cases, one a young teenage girl who had developed distressing fidgety movements and facial grimacing.

'It's rheumatic chorea,' Matron said, explaining to Honor that it was yet another manifestation of the disease. Dr Simpson examined the girl, who seemed very tearful, with unusually slurred speech. She flexed her hands in an odd way when asked to hold them straight out in front of her.

'That's a "dinner fork" deformity,' the doctor continued. 'She must be kept very quiet, aspirin as usual, and absolutely no exertion.'

At Maisie's bed, Honor remembered the blood on the pillow that morning.

'Where's it coming from?' Dr Simpson asked.

'I'm afraid I don't know, I couldn't see anything when I gave her a bed bath,' Honor replied.

'Well, let's take a look.' He was briskly efficient as usual, but took a long time to examine the child's mouth.

'What is it?' Matron asked when he had finished and they had drawn back to the middle of the ward.

'She's got bleeding gums,' he replied slowly, 'and I think that might be the focus of infection. She needs an X-ray of those swollen knees – I'll pop down to radiology on my way back and sort it out.'

Matron and Sister Blackwell looked at each other, before they all broke away from the round to continue their work.

Maisie was wheeled to X-ray by one of the porters early that afternoon.

'You'd better go with her,' Ann said as Maisie became increasingly tearful at this disruption to her normal routine. Honor bundled her up with blankets against the cold and walked alongside the porter to the old radiology wing.

'Terrible business, this Coventry bombing,' he chatted as they went along the frozen paths. 'Death toll rising every day!'

'How many?' Honor did not really want to know, but it was all anyone talked about at the moment, and there was no escaping the grim details.

'Five hundred so far,' he replied, shaking his head. 'I hope our RAF boys go over there now and give them what for!'

Maisie tolerated her X-ray and was soon back in bed, but Honor was surprised to see Dr Simpson and Matron back on the ward later that afternoon. The doctor was carrying a brown X-ray envelope and he slipped the films on to the screen at the end of the ward. Ann joined them, and they stood looking at the images, with Honor wondering what on earth she was supposed to see.

'There they are – see them, the transverse bands?' Dr Simpson was pointing to some horizontal bands just above the knee joint, shaking his head as he did so.

'What does it mean?' Honor said.

Dr Simpson's voice was dry and hard.

'It means, Nurse Newson, that Maisie has leukaemia.'

6

It was Honor's afternoon off. A month had passed since Maisie's departure for the Infirmary, and there had been little encouraging news since. Honor missed the little rumpled face each morning when she went on to the ward, and found herself dwelling on the child, and her prognosis. Ann could not bear to talk about it, so she had gone that same day to look it up in the nurses' training room, hauling down a large tome entitled *Diseases of Childhood and Infancy*. It made grim reading, and as Honor scanned through the *Clinical Manifestations and Course*, she realised that Maisie was not going to survive. Worse still, the complications seemed to be dreadful, and she could find little solace in the dreary script.

She trudged along the Groby Road towards the city, looking for a bus, but eventually giving up and determining to walk the distance. She was young after all, and despite the physical exhaustion that followed each shift, she still found her spirits lifting with the thought of a long walk away from the claustrophobic atmosphere of the hospital. It was beginning to snow lightly, but not settling, so she set her face toward the buildings of the city and increased her pace. *What an ugly city*, she thought to herself, comparing these flat, utilitarian dwellings with the grandeur of the London architecture. She stopped once or twice to ask directions, and in her nurse's uniform was met with polite assistance.

'Just along there, miss, then right at the crossing. Don't keep going to the railway station, you'll have gone too far.' A stocky driver of a brewer's dray reined in his horse to help her.

When she found herself at the entrance of the Infirmary she paused, uncertain of the location of the children's wing. With the aid of further directions from a porter, she made her way to a two-storey building, standing a little away from the main block, with the sign *Children's Hospital*. Maisie's ward turned out to be on the first floor, and as she climbed the stairs she felt apprehensive about what she would find.

Entering the familiar environment of neat beds and high ceilings, she was struck by the sense of order and discipline on the ward. She could smell the polish on the shiny floor, and there was nothing out of place, exactly as it had been in the Lambeth hospital. She had almost forgotten what a traditional ward would look like, and it gave her a sense of confidence. She introduced herself to the ward sister before attempting to find Maisie. She had hoped she would be sitting up in bed, maybe wanting one of her rabbit stories. Sister looked thoughtful.

'She's not too good today,' she answered carefully. 'You'd better just come into the office.'

Honor followed the tall, upright figure into the small room at the end of the ward. Sister motioned her to a chair, and let her sit down before continuing.

'I'm afraid she's developed meningeal leukaemia. We're just trying to keep her comfortable. Her parents have been informed, but we're not expecting them until later.' She took pity on Honor's obvious confusion. 'I'm sorry, it's such an awful disease, and there's so little we can do. You know how it is – fever nursing is much the same when you run out of treatments. Do you want to sit with her for a bit? She won't recognise you, I'm afraid, we've had to give her some morphine for her cerebral irritation.'

Honor walked slowly into Maisie's cubicle, took off her cape and gloves, and sat by her bed. The child was sleeping deeply, unaware of anything around her. Honor stroked her soft head and started to talk.

'I know you can't hear me, Maisie, but it's Honor, your nurse, and I've come to tell you a story about the brown rabbit.' She took a deep breath. Maisie's eyelids did not even flicker, but Honor continued resolutely. 'Once upon a time there was a brown rabbit. He belonged to Tilda but loved Maisie very much. One day, Maisie had to go on a special journey, and when Rabbit heard about it he decided to run away so he could go with Maisie. So he jumped out of the window to find her. It was snowing, and he left little paw-prints in the snow.

'"Maisie! Where are you?" Rabbit called.

'"Here, Rabbit, nice and warm in bed," Maisie called back, so Rabbit could find her, and he came jumping in through the window of her room and hid under the bedclothes, so he could be with her forever and always.'

Honor held the child's hand to her own wet cheek, and reached in her bag for a scruffy parcel, tied in brown paper and string.

'It's Rabbit, darling. I'll unwrap him for you because you're not very well today.'

She carefully took off the paper to reveal a brown knitted rabbit, slightly misshapen. Addie had knitted it, painstakingly, after admitting to Honor that she wanted to do something, no matter what, for the child. Honor knew that toys were not allowed on the fever wards, but had already decided not to enquire about the protocol here.

Having finished her story, she sat by the child, holding her small hand. It was quiet in the cubicle, and Honor lost track of time, listening to the slow, shallow breathing and watching as the little chest rose and fell.

Eventually Sister looked around the door.

'I'll just do her obs.'

Honor rose to go.

'It's all right, you can stay.' Sister added the readings to Maisie's chart.

Honor shook her head. She tucked the rabbit under Maisie's lifeless little arm and kissed her on the forehead.

'Goodbye, darling.'

Honor drew her cape around herself, then walked out into the darkening shadows and the snowy streets beyond.

7

Honor was seized with a great inertia in the days and weeks that followed. She had run out of steam, and the world had become a flatter place. Despite carrying on with her duties as usual, she found herself cutting off emotionally from the children on the ward. Even the return of Tom's health and cheekiness failed to lift her spirits, and he started to tease her less, not more, with each passing day of his recovery, concentrating his efforts on easier targets. Ann took her aside during her break.

'Honor, are you all right? You seem so distant nowadays. I know you're upset about Maisie, but the others need you too, and I mean all of you, not just the sad bit left behind.'

Honor looked back at her unrepentantly. 'Why did she have to die? I just don't understand it. What had Maisie done to deserve that?'

Ann put her arm around her shoulders. 'It's just the way it is, you can't change that, and never will. We're not just here to make sick people better, you know. We have to learn to care for the ones who aren't going to make it, no matter what we do. Look, I'm going to change the rota and put you on night shift for the next few weeks. It'll give you a bit of breathing space. I'm sorry, because it will mean you are on nights over Christmas, but unless you had any pressing plans, I think it'll be for the best. You're quite capable of managing a ward on your own at night now, and the extra responsibility will do you good.'

Honor could hardly disagree. She had nowhere to go, anyway, so she might as well work on through and hope that her mood would lift.

She tried to make an effort with her fellow probationers that evening, despite feeling deeply uninterested in their chatter. Addie was excited, having received another letter from the young soldier she had met on the train.

'He wants us to meet on his next leave!'

'Just you be careful!' Honor warned, immediately feeling disappointed with herself for dampening her friend's joy.

She sat on her bed and opened a thick handwritten letter. It was from Beatie. Honor had kept her word and written regularly to her, updating her about their new hospital. Beatie replied infrequently, and generally sounded fed up with her protracted convalescence. This letter, however, bore some news: she was due to return to her training in early January, so at last could escape the stifling atmosphere of home. Honor showed Addie the letter, rightly anticipating her pleasure, though not exactly sharing in it. Life was always more complicated when Beatie was around, and as she remembered from one of her much-used schoolbooks, leopards never changed their spots.

As Christmas approached, some of the probationers were looking forward to a spell of leave. Addie was returning to her home in Oxfordshire.

'Poor you, having to stay here on night duty all the way through Christmas!' she commiserated while packing her case.

'Oh, it's not so bad,' Honor replied. 'I wouldn't be wanted at home, so it's just as well I can be useful here.'

In fact, she did not mind the nights. If anything, they had become a source of solace to her. It was easier to hide your emotions on the long, lonely shift, and she did not have to make an effort to interact with others any more than her immediate nursing duties required. Generally, if the children were asleep, she might find a moment to catch up with her studies or just allow herself a period of quiet reflection. She found as time passed that she thought of Maisie less concertedly, and that the child's loss did not inhabit her waking moments to quite the same extent. At first, she had felt a little frightened on the long, dark ward by herself, the shift only punctuated by the night sister's round, but she grew accustomed to it as December drew on.

She arrived on shift on Christmas Eve, and was pleased to see that the day staff had put up simple decorations. Coloured paper chains festooned the ceiling, and there was a little spruce tree with a star. Some of the younger children were talking in whispers.

'Does Father Christmas come to hospitals?' a tousled red-headed child, pale under her freckles, enquired hopefully of her neighbour.

'Of course he does, Jenny,' a little boy replied. 'Father Christmas can go anywhere!'

'Well, let's wait and see what tomorrow brings!' Honor paused at the end of Jenny's bed. 'But try not to get too excited, because he can't come unless you're all asleep.' Jenny screwed up her eyes tightly, and Honor smiled and continued down the ward.

Tom's recovery had so far been uncomplicated. He was still on a small dose of digitalis but his pulse was steady and his lungs were now clear of the fluid which had so nearly taken his life. He smiled conspiratorially at Honor.

'It's not true,' he whispered, 'but it's nice they think so. I saw the day staff bring in a sack of presents earlier – they've hidden it in the office. One for each child, Sister Blackwell told me – can't I help to give them out?'

'Certainly not! You're still on strict bed rest!'

Honor was secretly charmed by the atmosphere on the ward that night. She carried on with her duties as usual, finally taking round the night-time drinks of hot milk or Horlicks. Later, she would be able to have her own cup of Horlicks, which she savoured, despite its tendency to make her eyes close in the early hours. She was in the sluice when she heard the sound of carols, and came out to see the children, turned towards the door of the ward, which opened to let in the sound. A small group of nurses, warmly wrapped against the lightly falling snow, were singing *Silent Night*, and suddenly there was nothing but the sound of the carol on the still ward.

Honor listened, as transfixed as her charges, to the timeless refrain. She closed her eyes and turned her head away to hide her tears.

'Say thank you, children.' She recovered herself as the carol ended. The nurses waved goodbye, and the ward was quiet again. 'Now, what about these drinks?' Honor busied herself and the night marched on.

8

With the New Year 1941 came Beatie. She arrived in the late evening, having motored down with a family friend, so that Honor was already on the ward and did not see her until the following morning. The two girls embraced, and Honor stood back to look at her friend.

'Beatie, you look so much better!' She noticed that Beatie's cheeks looked fuller and she had lost her pallor. 'How's your broken leg?'

'Much better, thanks. I'm so glad to be back with you all! It was absolutely dreary lying around at home with nothing to do, surrounded by irritating relatives. But what a place – it's a bit grim here, isn't it?' Beatie looked up and down the hut as though to make her point.

'Oh, you'll get used to it, it's not that bad, and the nursing is good.' Honor felt a new sense of loyalty to the hospital.

'What's night duty like? I won't get a chance to see much of you, just crossing paths as we swap shifts,' Beatie said.

'Oh, you'll be fine, Addie will show you all the ropes and I think you've been attached to a decent nurse tutor,' Honor replied, 'I'll see you tonight. Maybe we'll have more time then, I don't want you to be late for your first day!' she added, seeing that the other probationers were ready to leave.

'OK, I'm coming,' Beatie said, and went with them, leaving Honor to her daytime sleep.

It was so difficult to sleep in the day, the drawn curtains still allowing enough light through to disturb her diurnal rhythms. She mulled over the day's events, not least the return of her friend, before finally dropping off.

She was already awake and dressed for her night duty when the girls returned. Addie and Beatie were chatting as they came in.

'She's been really nice to me all day!' Beatie was discussing the sister on her ward, with some incredulity, as her previous teachers at the Lambeth had been far from forgiving.

'I told you so,' Honor said, and the two girls perched on her bed while Honor attached her watch to her white starched apron in readiness for her shift. 'So, is your leg completely better?' Honor enquired. 'How did you manage the work?'

'Oh, it's not too bad, aches a bit.' Beatie looked tired. 'Sister let me sit down for a while this afternoon, sorting out some linen, she said I shouldn't overdo it.' She paused. 'I'm perfectly all right, you know.'

Honor stood up. 'I've got to go, I'll be late, so catch up tomorrow?'

'Yes, sure,' replied Beatie, taking off her cap so her curls could finally make their escape. 'See you tomorrow.'

Their paths crossed only fleetingly in the days that followed, and there was no time for a proper talk in the brief minutes each side of the shifts. More than a week had passed when Honor, alone with a late afternoon cup of tea, was surprised to see Beatie rushing into the hut. Her entrance was followed by the sound of vomiting in the bare, cold bathroom. Honor went in to find Beatie crouched over the pan, her head resting on the wooden seat, and a sweaty pallor on her face.

'Beatie, what is it? Have you got a tummy bug? Or did you eat something…'

Honor's voice tailed off as Beatie slowly shook her head. 'No, it's not that,' she replied shakily, wiping her mouth on the towel. 'Some people are sick in the morning, but I just get it in the afternoon.'

'What do you mean, Beatie?'

'I'm pregnant.' Beatie's answer was flat, and she looked at Honor impassively, not even trying to gauge her reaction. Honor moved swiftly to her side and took her hand, which was clammy and cold.

'Let's get you out of here,' she said firmly, lifting Beatie to her feet.

'But I might be sick again!' Beatie protested, finally agreeing to be led to Honor's bed where she sat, clutching her towel as though it was the only hope of her salvation.

'You can't be pregnant!' Honor said. 'You've been in plaster at home for weeks!'

Beatie smiled wanly. 'Sorry, old thing, it was before that.'

'When before?' Honor could not work it out – what was the girl talking about? 'You've got to tell me, I can't help unless I know what's going on.'

'You won't want to know this one,' Beatie replied bitterly. 'No enduring love or anything like that, just in case you might think there was!'

'What happened?' Honor asked.

Beatie sighed. She had to tell someone sooner or later; she could not keep the awful secret to herself any longer. Those months at home, watching and waiting for the period which never came, her well-meaning family hovering around until she thought she would go mad with despair…

'It was that night we skipped out, me and Nancy. We went to a dance and got talking to a couple of lads, army boys up in town. Nancy was managing all right on the dance floor, then my chap asked me to go out for a walk. He seemed OK, I didn't think much of it, but when we were outside he kept steering me away from the hall, towards the darkness. "Hey, what's up, matey?" I says, nicely at first, then he makes a grab for me, pushes me into the bushes and…' She stopped, tears filling her eyes.

'No, Beatie, no!' Honor was shocked, holding the cold hand tightly.

'I couldn't stop him, honestly, he was a strong man. I tried to scream but he had his hand over my face. Then, suddenly, it was over. Afterwards, he pulled me to my feet, said I'd been asking for it all along, but it's not true, Honor, I didn't!' Beatie began to cry, choking back sobs while Honor took her in her arms and stroked her hair.

'You should have gone to the police, Beatie!'

Beatie shook her head slowly. 'I was in enough trouble as it was, likely to be hauled up in front of Matron for being out at all. Then there was Nancy – it wasn't fair, I made her come with me that night, she didn't really want to. All I could think was, if we can get back, I'll think about what to do later, just get Nancy back safely first. So I did, and there you were, putting yourself on the line for both of us.' Her head dropped into her hands. 'I'm so sorry. You see, when the bombs started to fall I wanted to die anyway. It should have been me, not Nancy,' she concluded dully, mopping her face with the towel.

'Look, the others will be back soon. Just trust me, Beatie, there must be a way through!'

'Don't you think that's all I've been thinking of, all those weeks, lying, waiting and knowing what was going on inside me?' Beatie said. 'I'm going to get rid of it, I've made up my mind!'

9

Honor could think of nothing but Beatie's predicament as she walked over to the ward. It was another bitterly cold night; though the recent snows had thawed during the day, each night brought further freezing temperatures and it was icy underfoot. What was she to do?

The thought of Beatie procuring an abortion filled her with horror. She knew, from the Lambeth hospital, what fate befell girls who had been to backstreet abortionists, hearing of women brought in by ambulance, bleeding to death from botched procedures. These illegal practices had not been stamped out, and women still risked dreadful complications to avoid the shame of an illegitimate baby. The names of people providing such services would be normally passed covertly, whispered mouth to mouth; it was hardly a service you could advertise in the paper. And even Beatie, ever resourceful, would be hard put to find an abortionist in a city she did not know.

Honor was glad to arrive on the ward and resume her normal duties. The pattern of the solitary night shift had instilled in her a renewed energy for her work, and she was busy enough for thoughts of Beatie to recede. Tom stopped her as she went past his bed.

'Don't you ever get a night off, Nurse? Bet there's lots of lads who'd like to take you out!' He looked better each day, and being one of the oldest on the ward, felt it his duty to entertain her during the evening.

'Tom, you never stop!' she remonstrated.

'They were cleaning up two of the cubicles today, looks like we might have some company tomorrow. Not the usual sort, either!' he added mysteriously.

'What are you talking about? Honestly Tom, I've got work to do,' she replied brusquely, taking out the thermometer by his bed and wiping it on some gauze. She popped it under his tongue, effectively silencing him for a moment, but he continued to look at her with mischievous eyes.

'Just you wait till tomorrow night, then, you'll see!' were his final words as she completed his chart.

The night passed uneventfully, though she noted, as Tom had said, that two of the cubicles at the end of the ward had been thoroughly scrubbed and disinfected for new admissions. She gave her report to the day sister and made her way back to the hut. Beatie had already gone, leaving her bed tidy and neat. Honor shook her head – how did Beatie manage to get away with concealing the early stages of her pregnancy? She wondered what excuse Beatie had given for bolting from the ward the day before, but then somehow, Beatie could always come up with a plausible explanation.

She settled down to her morning sleep, wishing she could lead a straightforward life and not become involved in other people's problems. Perhaps she should ask Dr Simpson's advice on Beatie's behalf? She pictured the scenario if she did – he would assume it was her in the club, not Beatie, and then where would she be? She crept closer down the bedclothes, wishing her feet were not so cold, then fell asleep.

Beatie was not back before she left for her shift, but she was waiting for her on the dark path to her ward.

'Honor, I'm here,' Beatie whispered. 'I can't talk to you in there, someone will hear. I've got a name, someone in Leicester.'

'How, Beatie, who did you ask?'

'The ward cleaner found me in the sluice when I was being sick,' Beatie continued breathlessly. 'She cottoned on straight away. I was crying again, it makes you feel so wretched, having to hide all the time. She says did I want to get rid of it; "You bet I do," I said, then she wrote me down an address. I'm going there on Friday, I've asked for an afternoon off. Told Sister I've got to have my leg checked. I'm going ahead with it, Honor, you can't stop me now!'

'I'm not trying to stop you, I couldn't anyway. It's just that it's so dangerous, Beatie, you never know what might happen to you! I don't want you to die!' Did Beatie not understand what the procedure involved: the lack of cleanliness, the gruesome instruments? Honor put her arm around her friend. 'Do you want me to come with you?'

'No, Honor, you can't. It's not fair, look what happened to Nancy through my own stupidity. I've learnt my lesson, and I'm not going to put anyone else through this, it's my own problem!' Beatie said emphatically.

'But you can't go by yourself!'

'Can't I?' Beatie replied, her strong voice now carrying through the night air. 'Just you wait and see if I can't!'

10

'We have two new admissions, over from men's medical, suspected rheumatic fever,' the day sister concluded at the end of the handover.

'Adults?' Honor asked in surprise, her eyebrows lifting. 'On a children's ward?'

'Yes, it's a bit of a botch-up – adult medical is full and they need isolating. They're in the two cubicles, RAF chappies, quite young, and not looking particularly ill.'

Honor took this information in her stride, but could not avoid Tom's cocky face. 'Told you so, Nurse, got some real company now!' He winked at her as she went past.

She saw the tall redhead through the glass cubicle windows, but went in to see the other patient first. He turned towards her as she entered.

'Who are you?' he asked quickly, looking her up and down.

'Nurse Newson, on nights,' she replied, reaching for his chart in a sudden fit of embarrassment. She perused it studiously. 'So how are we today? You're Fordham, aren't you?'

'That's me,' he replied airily. 'Sorry to land on a children's ward like this, but the chap next door,' he said, waving towards his colleague, 'has never really grown up anyway.' He smiled at her, sensing her discomfiture. 'Don't suppose you were expecting the likes of us this evening?'

'Not exactly.' She allowed herself to smile back, taking in his face properly for the first time; the slightly earnest look in his wide-set eyes, and the strong, almost Roman nose. 'I've got to take your temperature and check your pulse,' she continued formally, wishing to keep the professional boundary lines clear.

'Fine by me,' he replied amiably, holding out his arm. His pulse and temp were both up, she noted, and she checked to see when he had last been given aspirin.

'You've got to drink plenty, and I'm going to get your tablets.'

He nodded, and lay back on the pillow as she left the cubicle. What a good-looking girl! Hiding away on the children's ward! He wished that he felt better, and that his head did not ache so. At least there were some compensations, he mused, for this hospitalisation, even if it was quite unnecessary as far as he was concerned. He would have liked to chat to Johnstone about her, but like even the smallest child on the ward, they had both been confined to strict bed rest, doctor's orders as of the morning ward round.

He did not see her again for much of the evening. As far as his view from the cubicle windows allowed, she seemed very busy, working efficiently by herself along the rows of children who inhabited the ward. She seemed to know most of them well, and he wondered how long she had been here. He heard the lad, Tom, further down the ward, ribbing her about something and almost anticipated her serious reply. She did not look the sort to let the barriers down, that girl – much too careful for that.

She brought him his milky drink after lights were out and removed his full urine bottle. It was his turn to feel embarrassed.

'Sorry, I wish I could take it myself,' he said.

'Don't be silly, it's my job. I have to do much worse things than that,' she reassured him, meeting his eyes once more. 'Goodnight, I hope you get some sleep. The children can be a bit noisy at night.'

'Not a bit of it, I shall sleep like a log,' he replied confidently, and as she walked up the ward in the cold, dark hours of the morning, she saw he had done just that.

He was just waking as she sorted out the ward the next morning prior to her departure. He looked flushed and was still feverish, unlike Johnstone, whose temperature had settled overnight.

'Can't I get out and go to the bathroom?' he asked her pleadingly.

'That's what all the children ask, even when they know the answer,' she replied, handing him a bedpan.

He sighed. 'I expect you're going to be telling me it's time for a bed bath.'

'Don't be silly, the day staff will do that.' Honor allowed herself to tease him gently. There was something about him that made her want to smile.

'So I'll see you tonight?' he added hopefully.

She shook her head. 'No, it's my night off, I'll be back tomorrow.'

'Going out on a date, I suppose. Pretty girl like you, must have lots of admirers!' He looked momentarily disconsolate.

She had a sudden desire to reassure him, to tell him that no such thing was possible, and that she would spend the evening washing her hair and sorting her clothes, but she thought better of it, smiled at him encouragingly and called, 'See you tomorrow', as she left the ward.

She did not mean to keep thinking about William Fordham as she walked back for breakfast. She decided not to hurry, but to go to the canteen and sit down for a while, gathering her own thoughts against the day. There was a glimpse of early morning sunshine through the trees, and she thought she could hear the first birdsong of the year.

11

Honor was drying her hair before bed, having given up any chance of talking to Beatie alone, when she finally appeared, with her sponge bag, on her way to the bathroom.

'Beatie…' Honor intercepted her.

'What?' Beatie's chin was set forward in determination.

'Let me come with you. How will you get back?'

'I'll get a taxi. I'll be all right. Just stop worrying about me, I don't want you there.' Beatie paused, taking momentary pity on her friend, and her voice softened. 'I'm sorry, I just know I have to go it alone.' She touched Honor on the arm as she left her.

Honor tried to concentrate on her nursing textbook, but found herself unable to think straight. She had classroom sessions all day tomorrow, as so often during her time off. She knew she should be revising, given the question-and-answer sessions that would be an inevitable part of the day, but she fell asleep over the dry pages and only roused to the sound of the morning alarm.

Her first thought on waking was of her new patient. Would his temperature be down today? She shook her head briefly – what was all this about? Back to priorities, she told herself strictly, washing her face with cold, soapy water as if to take a grip of the day. She glanced at Beatie, who happened to be looking into the mirror at the same time.

'Good luck,' she whispered.

The day seemed endless. Anatomy was the most difficult subject for her; she hated having to memorise all those bones and organs. The skeleton in the teaching room dangled meaninglessly before her, as though a premonition of her own and others' mortality. The tutor was a strict one, expecting constant and unwavering attention from her pupils, many of whom were struggling to stay awake, particularly in the session after lunch.

'Nurse Newson!' Sister's voice interrupted her thoughts, which were far away with Beatie in some awful upstairs bedroom with the curtains closed.

Honor shuddered. 'Yes, Sister?'

'What is the artery that runs down the leg?'

Honor tried not to panic; she had hardly been attending at all. She hazarded a wild guess. 'Femoral artery?'

'Correct,' the tutor replied succinctly. 'At least someone's listening.'

Addie nudged her. 'Where did you get that from?' she whispered.

Honor did not try to reply, conscious of Sister's gaze and the ever-present chance of another impossible question.

They were having their afternoon break, prior to the last lesson, more interestingly entitled *Ward hygiene and common pathogens*, when Addie brought her a cup of tea.

'What's up? You look miles away,' she said.

'Oh, nothing, just sleepy after being on nights.'

'I wonder how Beatie's getting on,' Addie continued. Honor looked at her in surprise – surely Beatie had not shared her secret with anyone else?

Their teaching day concluded with an endless list of bacteria that constituted an ever-present threat to health. The probationers were becoming used to the daily scrubbing, disinfecting and sterilisation of their equipment, without always understanding the bacteria involved. Honor listened aghast to details of such organisms as the staphylococcus, which could be carried harmlessly on the skin, before gaining entry through a wound site, to cause serious complications. By the end of the day her notebook was full of strange-sounding names like salmonella, clostridium and mycobacterium, with hurried annotations about the diseases they could cause. There would be enough studying to last her a lifetime, she reflected, thinking back, as she did so often, to Matron's words before she accepted her for training at the Lambeth.

She walked back to their hut with Addie, feeling slightly sick at the prospect of seeing Beatie.

They found Beatie lying on her bed, with her legs drawn up, under her blankets. She looked washed out, and as the two girls approached, did not attempt to sit up.

'How are you?' Honor could not wait to ask, even in front of Addie.

'Not too bad,' Beatie replied, looking back at her in warning. 'Just this wretched leg as usual.'

Addie clearly thought it best to leave her in peace, but Honor stayed at her side and held her hand.

'How did it go?' she said, under her voice.

'You don't want to know. Nobody wants to go through that, not even in their mind,' Beatie whispered back, though her hand held Honor's tightly. 'But it's done, Honor, I'm shot of it! I said I could do it and I have, just got these awful period pains and feel a bit sick.'

'Shall I help you to the bathroom?' Honor offered.

'No, best not make a fuss,' said Beatie. 'But could you stay with me until you go on duty? Just while the others go for tea?'

'Of course. I'll get Addie to bring you something back.'

'She doesn't know, does she?' Beatie looked as though she was about to cry.

'No, don't be silly, it's only me that knows anything. Addie thinks it's your bad leg. I'm just going to get you some water.' She released Beatie's hand and went to find Addie.

'I'm going to sit with Beatie for a bit,' she said. 'Could you bring her back something from the canteen?'

Addie looked puzzled and not a little anxious. 'She's OK, isn't she?'

Honor looked away. 'Yes, of course she is.'

During the next hour, Beatie began to pick up. While the others were gone Honor took her to the bathroom, Beatie leaning heavily on her all the way. She found her some more sanitary pads, and noticed, with relief, that the girl was not bleeding excessively. After giving her some aspirin for her cramps she settled her back into bed. Beatie took some sips of water and her colour started to improve.

'There, I told you I'd get away with it. I always do!'

12

Honor made it for her shift, just in time. Sister was looking out anxiously for her as she ran down the icy path.

'Steady on, you'll fall! Where have you been?'

'Sorry, Sister! Didn't see the time.'

The day report was uneventful: both the airmen were making progress and the young Scotsman was to be discharged tomorrow. Fordham had to remain, as his temperature was still elevated. Honor listened quietly; she had not supposed that either of them would be sent back to their base so soon. She was used to the children spending a protracted amount of time on bed rest, it never occurred to her that the men's stay might be brief.

Her time was immediately taken up with another new admission, a small boy with a reddened rash (erythema marginatum – she remembered the proper name) on his trunk and limbs. He had very swollen joints and was clearly in pain. Honor looked at his chart to see that he had only recently been given aspirin, so would not be due more medication before the late night round.

'Cheer up, Freddie,' she said, 'the tablets should start to work soon.'

'But it hurts so,' he pleaded.

'Just try and lie still,' Honor replied. 'I'll come back and check on you soon.'

The evening wore on, and she still had to make time to see her adult charges. Johnstone's cubicle door was open and she went inside.

'I hear you're leaving us.'

'Aye, that poor boy Fordham will be at your mercy now, Nurse.' He winked broadly at her. 'You take good care of him, they'll want him back flying his aeroplane, not living it up in here!'

She had heard from the day staff that they were both trainee pilots, but was determined not to appear impressed. To hear some of the nurses talk, you would think they were gods, which she was quite sure they were not. Just boys really, and probably quite foolhardy ones at that.

She moved on to the adjacent cubicle. Fordham's eyes were shut as she entered, but he opened them and looked at her attentively.

'Hello,' he said pleasantly, 'I've been waiting for you to get back! Did you have a nice night out?'

'What makes you think I went out anywhere?' She had decided to put him out of his misery. After all, she might not have time to indulge in teasing, if he were suddenly discharged.

'I stayed in, as it happened,' she replied truthfully. 'Had some studying to do, there's a lot to learn.'

'I know how you feel!' he commiserated. 'You should try navigation!'

She smiled. 'Are you any better?'

'I think so, I certainly don't feel so bad, it's just that I keep getting these hot sweats and the shivers.'

'Well, you're probably in the right place,' she said.

He looked at her again, a long look, holding her eyes for just a second longer than he should, then said cheerfully, 'I can't think of anywhere I'd rather be, except in my plane.'

'When I'm not so busy, you can tell me what it's like.'

'What, flying, or being stuck in here?' He could not be quite serious with this girl, however solemn she might appear to be. 'Why don't you come back later, when the little ones are asleep, then we can have a chat over my cocoa?' he ventured, conscious that he might be moving too fast for her. Not seeing her last night had made him restless. How had she made a little place in his head already, he wondered; hang it, he had only just met her!

'Well, I'll see how things go.' She hesitated, not wishing to give him the wrong impression.

'You'll be quite safe, I can't even get out of bed.' It was his turn to tease. 'Now if that was Johnstone asking you, you'd be well advised to say no! I just fancied a bit of company, and you'll have to sit down sometime!'

By the time she came back, he was just dropping off to sleep, having given up hope of her escaping her duties, even for a moment. She drew up a chair by his bed, and handed him a mug of the Horlicks she had made for them both.

'I thought you weren't going to make it,' he said quietly, as she sipped her drink.

'One of the new admissions, Freddie, he's a bit restless. I couldn't just leave him,' she explained.

'Of course you couldn't.' His voice was firm. He felt sorry for the little kids, away from home and family. His only experience of medicine so far was having his tonsils removed on the kitchen table when he was five, an operation skilfully performed by his family doctor. This was his first time on a hospital ward, and he felt lucky to have escaped what these children were going through.

'So, I still don't know your name,' he said gently. Her brown hair was framed by her white cap, which in this dim light looked like a halo on the figure of a medieval icon.

'Honor,' she replied, equally quietly. 'Does everyone call you William?'

'No, there are several versions! Mostly Will in the mess, or Bert to my family.'

'I think I'll stick with the proper version,' she said, and he nodded.

'Yes, best get it right from the start.'

It was easy to talk in the dim, quiet room, in which they shared a privacy peculiar to those who are awake when all the rest of the world is sleeping. He told her about his childhood, describing the Yorkshire moors and dales, his face animated by his description of the local river where his father had taught him to fish for salmon; the secret pools and runs where the fish were most likely to rise. She talked fleetingly of her childhood, glossing over parts she would rather not share, and always keeping her reserve. He wondered about her reasons, and whether she would eventually tell him more.

She rose and took his cup. 'I must go, no more slacking!'

'Thanks for coming.'

He stretched comfortably in the bed after she had gone, and turned on his side with nothing but her in his mind as he fell asleep.

She was scrubbing a rubber sheet in the sluice the following morning when Ann Blackwell came in.

'You still here?' she exclaimed. 'Time you were off, Honor.'

'Yes, I know, just a bit behind. Little Freddie wet his bed, and I promised him we'd get him changed before the others woke up. He's had a disturbed night, poor little thing.'

'I'll see to him,' Ann replied. 'You look in control – how's the shift going?'

'Much better,' Honor said gratefully.

'Good, that's what I was hoping to hear. I think I'll leave you on nights for the rest of the month, then we'll see how you feel.'

'Thanks,' Honor said. Just at the moment, she had no desire to return to day duty.

She left the ward, hoping she would be in time to see Beatie, who was dressed and ready to go, her head held up, her chin forward.

'Are you all right ?' Honor asked, the anxiety creeping into her voice as soon as she saw her.

'Right as rain! Now stop fussing! I'll see you this evening, you get some sleep and stop worrying about me.' She picked up her cape and left, looking for all the world like the old Beatie, her natural confidence almost restored. Honor shook her head; she would never understand that girl! Still, you had to hand it to her for sheer, downright pluck.

She slept soundly through the day, helped by the dark grey winter skies, which threw little light into her sleeping quarters. The stove was on, and whilst she was not exactly snug, at least her chilblains had stopped hurting for a bit. She had been awake for some time before the girls came back. She noticed Beatie looked very tired, and that her colour was not as good as this morning. Still, she knew not to fuss, and passed by with a smile and a brief pat on Beatie's arm.

'OK?' she ventured.

'Exhausted!' Beatie smiled wanly back. 'Sister seems to have forgotten about my leg today.'

Addie joined them. 'I'll look after her,' she volunteered. 'And yes, I know, Beatie, you don't need it, but just humour me, there's a girl. Let's get you into bed and try and rest for a while.'

13

The children were asleep by the time she managed to check on her one remaining adult patient that night. He looked so pleased to see her when she came into his cubicle that she could not help but smile.

'Hey, Nurse Newson, I'm all by myself now, so don't forget to come and keep me company!' The young airman looked rather better, less flushed, and his face full of optimism.

'Did your friend get off all right?' she asked, holding his wrist to take his pulse.

'Yes, he couldn't wait to get back to the base,' Will replied, with a little note of envy in his voice.

'While you, LAC Fordham, are stuck here.' She finished the sentence for him, writing in his chart at the same time.

'Oh, it's not all that bad, there are compensations, particularly the night staff. You'll come back later, Honor, won't you? It's been a long day, and I can't even talk to the kids from here.'

'Of course I will.' She replaced the chart at the end of his bed. 'Your temperature is coming down, that's good.'

'Not sure about my pulse rate though,' he ventured, attempting to tease a reply out of her which he did not get, though he noticed the fleeting look of pleasure in her eyes.

'See you later, William,' she said, and he watched her as she walked away.

Later, in the dim light, in quiet conversation over their hot drinks, she asked him about his flying.

'Don't you feel frightened up there?' she wanted to know. He decided it was no time for bravado.

'Well, yes, sometimes, if you want the honest truth. But at least you're free to make your own decisions, get yourself out of a mess if you can, and take your own chances. I couldn't bear to be with the Army, stuck in the trenches like the last war, just waiting to be shot at.'

'My father was in the cavalry,' she volunteered. He looked at her in surprise; she proffered so little information about her family.

'Really, what regiment?'

'Ox and Bucks,' she replied. 'He was very lucky to come back, most of them didn't. Anyway, I wouldn't be here if he hadn't. He never likes to talk about it, so I don't really know much more. Maybe if I had been a boy he would have told me more.'

'Well, it wasn't the war to end all wars, as they said it would be,' Will said. His own father had not seen active service during the Great War, having helped the war effort through his market gardening and food production. Nonetheless, Will felt it was right to volunteer. No able-bodied man wished to be thought of as a coward. 'What did your father do in the war?' was an ever-present question to his generation and those that followed.

'Was that what they wanted, then, your parents – for you to be a boy?' He had picked up the note of resignation in her voice.

'Oh, yes, I was a great disappointment to them. Still am, I suppose,' she concluded, without obvious emotion.

'Honor!' He looked at her in disbelief. 'How could you possibly be a disappointment to anyone?'

She did not have time to reply, as the sound of Freddie's voice carried down the ward.

'Nurse!'

She rose to his summons. 'I'd better see what's the matter.'

'You can always come back again,' he pleaded.

But with a firm 'You need your sleep, William', she left the cubicle.

When she looked by an hour later he was, once more, soundly asleep. She paused to look at his face in repose, wondering why he had already aroused such feelings in her, and wishing she knew what was going on in his sleeping mind.

She hardly had time to say goodbye in the usual morning rush, having less time than usual for her handover to Ann, who had uncharacteristically arrived late. She looked distracted, prompting Honor to ask what was wrong.

'There's been a dreadful blitz in Portsmouth. I've got relatives there on my mother's side: my aunt and her family. I just don't know if they're all right.' Ann pushed her glasses straight. 'It's been such a bad raid, because of the port, I suppose. Nowhere's safe nowadays! Best get on with the report, there's nothing I can do, I just wish there was!'

14

Honor walked back down the frozen path in the early morning to her hut, and opened the door. She had expected it to be empty by now, but was immediately alerted by the sight of Addie sitting on Beatie's bed, holding her hand.

'What's the matter?' Honor said. Beatie looked ashen, lying almost motionless in bed, grey-faced, with dull eyes, and Addie beside her, distraught.

'Honor, help me with her, I don't know what's wrong! She doesn't want to wake up! She was all right last night – a bit washed out and shivery, she said – didn't have much supper, then went to bed. But this morning, she's out for the count, won't even take a drink of water!'

Honor, panic-stricken, had no idea what could have gone wrong. 'Beatie!' She rubbed her friend's hand. 'Beatie, wake up!'

Beatie turned on her side, moaning quietly, but not replying. Honor took her pulse. It was rapid and weak.

'Have you got a thermometer?' she asked Addie quickly.

'No, but I'll go and get one from the ward!' Addie looked relieved to have something to do, and rushed away.

Left to herself, all the alarm bells that Honor had learned in her training started to ring. She lifted the bedcover to see if Beatie had been bleeding. There was little obvious sign of blood, and she checked the back of Beatie's nightie as she lay on her side, just to make sure. So it wasn't a haemorrhage, then, she reasoned, her breathing slowing slightly. Nonetheless Beatie's nightie felt damp, as though she had been drenched in sweat.

Addie returned out of breath with the thermometer, which they put under Beatie's tongue. Her temperature was very high. Honor remembered the bacteria lecture – Beatie must have got an infection from the instruments! It was bound to be a serious one to make her that ill so quickly.

'Honor, what is it? You're keeping something from me!' Addie said urgently.

'I promised her I wouldn't tell anyone!'

'You have to! She looks terrible! What's going on?' Addie was trembling, as Honor sank down on to the next bed, putting her head into her hands.

'She had an abortion,' she said bluntly, after a long pause. 'I think she's been infected by the instruments. I told her not to do it, Addie! I told her it was dangerous! She wouldn't listen, she never does!'

Addie breathed deeply. 'Look, Honor, it's not your fault – Beatie never listens to anyone! We've got to get help! She looks like death!'

It was that final word which roused Honor from her indecision. 'You stay with her!' she shouted. 'I'm going to get Matron!' She ran from the hut, sprinting up the icy paths to the main block where Matron's office was located. She had never been in it before, and was breathless by the time she had scaled the long flight of stairs and knocked at the door.

'Come in.' Matron's composure left her when she saw the agitated girl. 'Good heavens, what's the matter, Nurse Newson?'

'You must come quick, one of the nurses has collapsed! In our hut!' Honor was pulling Matron by the arm as she reached for her cape.

'I'm coming, I'm coming, tell me on the way!' The two women, one hardly beyond girlhood and fleet of foot, and one more maturely rounded, but moving surprisingly fast, rushed down the stairs and out towards the hut.

'What's happened to her?'

But if Matron was breathless, Honor could hardly speak as they opened the door to the hut. Addie was still sitting beside Beatie, who if anything, looked slightly worse.

Matron had come to a halt, surveying the girl, and took charge immediately, dropping to her knees to take Beatie's pulse, which was by now thready.

'Come on, Newson, what's the history? Tell me, quickly, I need to know the facts!'

Honor closed her eyes, swallowed, and realising that there could be no escape – not for Beatie, nor for her either – clenched her hands.

'Hurry, Newson, we've got a sick girl here!' Matron's voice was imperative.

Honor replied equally steadily, surprising even herself, as though she had jumped into an icy pool and just had to keep swimming. 'I'm sorry, Matron, she had a backstreet abortion two days ago! Beatie had been raped, you see, there was no way out! I tried to stop her, but I couldn't, she wouldn't let me go with her, and I promised not to tell. She seemed all right when she got back, not much bleeding, then she was very tired last night, and this morning… I think she's septic, Matron!'

'That's more like it, Newson,' Matron said. 'I daresay it's not your fault, but I'll need to talk to you later. I'm going to call an ambulance, we'll get her to the women's hospital as soon as possible, and she needs a drip up right now, and intravenous fluids. Stay with her, you two!' Matron ran out of the hut as swiftly as she had entered it.

The two girls looked at each other in disbelief, and Addie put her arm around Honor.

'You had to tell her,' she said softly, but Honor shook her head and went back to Beatie's side.

Suddenly, they were both superfluous, as the clanging ambulance could be heard drawing up, and one of the doctors, summoned by Matron, pushed them aside, rapidly trying to insert a drip into Beatie's arm. He was sweating.

'Christ, I can hardly get in,' he muttered. 'What's her BP? You there, hold the bag, higher.'

Matron, on the other arm, was inflating the cuff, then listening over the brachial artery 'Seventy-five over fifty,' she responded quickly. 'At least, I think so, certainly no more.'

'It's all right, I'm in.' He attached the saline solution to the cannula. 'Let's get her out of here!' The ambulance men deftly lifted the barely conscious girl on to the red stretcher.

'Can I go with her?' Honor moved alongside.

'No, I'll be going. She's one of my girls, whatever's happened to her, I'm responsible for her now,' Matron said firmly, and suddenly the crew departed, the door slammed, and they were gone, to the sound of the urgent, ringing bell.

15

Honor lay on her bed after Addie had gone to report for duty, just gazing at the ceiling, and not even bothering to undress or wash. She must have dozed in the early afternoon, for she was roused by a knock at the door. It was the hospital almoner, Mrs Josephs. Honor knew her from one of the lectures about the social work they performed with the patients and their families. She was a kindly woman, softly spoken and quietly competent.

'Matron asked me to come and see if you are all right,' she said, sitting on Honor's bed and registering the despair in her pretty face.

'Is there any news?'

'Not that I know,' Mrs Josephs replied, 'but you're to go and see Matron at five.'

Honor felt a wave of panic. What would be her fate, let alone Beatie's? She was an accomplice to an illegal act, after all; she would be thrown off the course and back on the streets again. Lose her future and her livelihood, just when she had thought that at last things might work out.

'Can I get you a cup of tea? Have you had anything to eat?'

'Thank you, I'm not hungry,' Honor said. 'But tea would be nice,' she added, allowing Mrs Josephs to leave her in search of some. When she returned with the hot, sweet tea, Honor sipped it and felt slightly stronger.

'What will happen to me, do you think?' she ventured.

Mrs Josephs looked steadily at her. 'I really don't know the details, my dear, but you can take it from me that Matron is a fair and compassionate woman.'

She went soon after Honor had finished her tea, leaving her alone to wash and change, ready for her fate, and dreading the news about Beatie. She looked sadly around the hut before she left. Perhaps this was it: no more hospital, nursing, patients or friends, and no night duty ever again.

'Come in!' Matron had regained some of her composure, but showed none of the usual jolliness which was her hallmark.

'What's happened to Beatie?' Honor asked, unable to wait any longer. Matron folded her hands.

'She's still alive, Nurse Newson, thanks to an immediate response to M and B. Fortunately, the women's hospital had a stock in the pharmacy and they were able to get it in the drip straight away. It was touch and go, but the organism, probably a strep haemolyticus, is clearly sensitive to it, and her blood pressure is steadying.'

Honor looked at her in amazement. She was so sure that Beatie had died. Then she remembered M and B, the sulphonamide wonder drug, the antibiotic that was in such short supply and usually reserved for the troops. They had saved Beatie with that!

Matron continued. 'She's not out of the woods yet, you know – it looks as though they were in the nick of time.'

Another silence followed.

'So she stands a chance?' Honor said.

'Hopefully, she'll continue to improve, and with any luck, recover –

at least her health. Whether or not she'll ever be able to have children is another matter, but at the moment, that's the least of her problems.'

'And the abortion?'

'Well, personally I don't believe that young women should be penalised for something that's not their fault. If what you told me is true, then there is a much more guilty man out there somewhere. Nurse Molesworth will have suffered enough as it is, and so, no doubt, have you. If I can keep the authorities out of it, then I will. She will have to leave nursing, I'm afraid.'

'And me, will I have to leave too?' The girl's soft voice was anguished. She might as well know sooner than later.

'I don't see why.' Matron's voice was firm and matter-of-fact. She had been considering the matter all day, and had finally made up her mind. Newson had acted decisively and honestly, undoubtedly saving her friend's life. She respected qualities like that, which were just what you needed in a competent nurse. As for her getting mixed up in an illegal abortion, Matron did not really see what else the young probationer could have done, short of reporting Molesworth straight away, which would hardly have been honourable.

'You helped her as much as you could, after all,' Matron continued. 'Saved her life, in fact. It's not your fault she committed an illegal act, and you were not, as far as I am aware, an accomplice to it, nor did you procure it for her.'

'No, Matron, I did not.' Honor raised her eyes, too overwrought for tears. 'Will I be able to see her?'

'Not for a few days. Quite honestly, I want you back on that ward getting on with your job. That's quite enough heroics for one day, for both of us.'

Matron stood up, and smiled at Honor. 'Come on, Newson, you've got work to do.'

16

'Are you all right, Honor? You look awful. Has something happened? Not bad news, I hope?' Will looked up immediately from his book.

In wartime, one never knew when the axe would fall. Even an innocent civilian, minding his own business and trying to carry on as normally as possible, could be annihilated by a bombing raid. They all lived with the background uncertainty of survival, and where and whom the raids would strike. Fordham assumed that someone in her family had been injured, perhaps killed, maybe one of her two sisters or her parents. However distant from them she might profess to be, death was a final and irreconcilable event, and even worse for those who were divided.

She moved closer to his bed and he put his hand upon her arm.

'Sit down for a bit, tell me about it,' he urged, concern in his honest face. 'The others can wait.'

'No, I'm all right really, just had a dreadful day. One of our nurses is very ill, had to go to hospital. Can't tell you much more than that, I'm afraid.'

'And how is she?' he followed steadily, his grey eyes searching her face.

'I think she'll live.' Honor was grave. There was a momentary gulf between them, and he knew instinctively that she was not going to tell him any more, certainly not now, maybe never.

'OK, well don't overdo it. Just try and get through the night. Will you drop by later?'

'I'll try,' she said, the first faint smile lightening her face. 'I'll see how things go. Don't mind if I can't, will you?' The last was added almost plaintively, as though she could not take much more.

'Of course I won't, just look after yourself. Where would I be without you?' He released her, thus hoping he could seal her part in his life, whatever might befall them.

Will lay back on the bed after she had gone. Whatever could have happened to her today? He knew it must be bad for her to look like that, and he doubted she had managed to get any sleep all day. Despite her obvious exhaustion, he hoped she would be back later. The truth was that he longed for the evening, for her to come in on night duty, so that he might spend a little time with her after the long, tedious day. He was beginning to feel better, and realised that as his temperature fell, so did his chance of staying on the ward. Each day now he was conscious that the doctor might send him back to his base. How awful if he had to leave without having had the chance to tell her how he felt!

He was still musing upon his predicament when Honor popped her head round the door.

'I'm not going to make it later, there's heaps to do and I'm so slow tonight,' she said.

'Never you mind, you look whacked. But Honor, just one thing,' he added, and she came closer to his bed. 'If by any chance I get sent out of here, I want to see you again. You know that, don't you?' It was his turn to look earnest, suddenly anxious that time might run out for them. She nodded at him in response, emboldening him to continue. 'Tell me how I can write to you, then you can let me know when you'll be off duty, and we can arrange to meet.'

She said nothing, but went over to his bedside table where she picked up a pencil and some paper and wrote down her contact address at the hospital. She tore off the piece of paper and gave it to him.

'There you are, now you don't have to worry.'

He looked at her, folding the slip of paper she had torn off, and placed it carefully in his pyjama pocket. He patted it and smiled at her, his honest, open smile, and without meaning to, she reached out to touch his thick brown hair, turned and left.

17

'He's gone!' Tom said. 'They let him out this morning. You'll miss him, won't you?' he added, without his usual cheekiness. 'It's a shame, I bet it was nice for you to have a bit of company of an evening. I wish I could join the RAF. When I get out of here I'm off to enlist!'

'Don't be silly!' Honor had already seen that the cubicle was empty. 'You're much too young.'

'Nah,' Tom insisted. 'I'll lie about my age, he didn't look very much older than me anyway. He's only twenty, you know. Anyway, he asked me to give you this.' He handed Honor an envelope. She tucked it in her apron and hurried down the ward for Ann's report.

'So,' Ann concluded, 'two discharges, one of them Fordham, back to his base. His temperature has been normal for four days, no other symptoms, and Dr Simpson doesn't think he had rheumatic fever at all, more likely a severe chill. So that's good, he can get back to his flying and save us all from Hitler!'

Honor kept quiet. She had no desire to draw attention to her evolving feelings for the young man.

It was not until much later that she found a moment in the sluice to open his letter.

Dear Honor,
I'm sorry to have left without a chance to say goodbye, and glad I took your address just in case. I will write as soon as I can when I know my timetable and then we can meet on your afternoon or evening off. I should be able to get into Leicester as I can borrow a friend's car.

Don't work too hard, and don't worry about me – I'm glad to be given a clean bill of health and I suppose I had to go back some time!

Love
William

She leant against the sink. So that was it: no more pleasant anticipation of seeing him each night, and spending some time together, no matter how short, during her busy shift. Still, she did not feel as though she had lost him, as this was just the beginning, and her young heart was not downcast as she set about her duties; just held in a momentary lull.

18

Florence had arrived to take him back in the ambulance in the early afternoon. He had known from the look on Dr Simpson's face during the ward round that as far as his inpatient stay went, he was for the chop. Sister Blackwell, her usual brisk self, had been through the charts with the doctor, who had looked at them carefully, then thoroughly examined Will.

'How are you feeling now? Any aching or joint pain?' Dr Simpson asked, feeling the lymph nodes in his neck.

'Much better,' Will replied. 'The pains have gone, and I don't feel shivery any more.' It was no use saying anything else; he really felt pretty normal now, just a little weak. 'I'm probably ready to go back to my flying, if you have no objections, Doctor,' he concluded honestly.

Dr Simpson finished his examination silently, then nodded in assent. 'I think we can let you go.'

Will politely thanked them both as they left to inform Desford of his return. He eased himself out of bed for the first time, feeling decidedly wobbly before finding his feet. His primary thought, of course, was for Honor. What would she think when she came on to the ward tonight and found he was gone? At least she seemed to want to see him again, that was the main thing. Once he was out of here, and back to normal, he could get to know her on more equal terms. It was not easy to embark upon a relationship while confined to bed, in your pyjamas, on a children's ward! He wanted to show her the other side of him, the fit young trainee pilot, not dependent upon her ministrations. He hoped he had not been misreading her, and like all who are parted at an early stage, sought more reassurance from their brief interlude that it could reasonably provide.

He had soon put together his few belongings, and wandered down the ward.

'I hear you're off!' Tom waylaid him. 'Lucky you, I'd give anything to get out of here and go and fly an aeroplane!'

'How long have you got to stay?' Will asked the lad. He had heard Tom's voice down the ward, and was amused at the outspoken personage whose character seemed to dominate the scene.

'Oh, too long, I sometimes think I'll be here forever!' Tom rolled his eyes melodramatically. He liked the look of this RAF man, who did not seem that much older than himself. 'Anyway,' he continued conspiratorially, 'she's going to miss you!'

'Who is?'

'You know – Honor, Nurse Newson, that's who! I told her she needed some proper company, when the kids are asleep! Except not all of us are!' He winked at Will, who grinned back.

'Could you give her a letter?' Will said. 'It's just that—'

'Yes, I know, you didn't get a chance to say goodbye!' Tom interrupted him. ''Course I will, and if I were you, I should get in there quick. Pretty girl like that, knocks spots off all the other nurses round here. Nice with it, too!'

'Thanks. You're right, I plan to,' Will said, and returned to his room to write a scribbled note to her, which he then deposited with Tom.

'It's safe with me, I won't tell anyone,' the boy remarked. 'Just you make sure you do as I say!'

Will felt emotional as he left the children on the ward. He was a kind-hearted young man, and the sight of the little ones confined to bed was almost too much for him. He said his goodbyes to Sister Blackwell, waved at Tom, and was out, in the fresh air at last, to the waiting forces ambulance.

The afternoon lessons were finishing as he joined the back of the room. The instructor was concluding a lecture on bailing out over occupied territory. He had various items on display: the silk map of France and Spain ('Looks like a tart's headscarf,' Jim whispered) that should give them their bearings, the small square survival pack, and curiously, a fishing kit. On the blackboard was written the only information that they should divulge to the enemy if captured. *Name, rank, and serial number*. The audience was particularly attentive, given that they all had a vested interest in escaping from such a predicament. The instructor regaled them with tales of those who made it home, aided by the French resistance, along the mountain ranges of the Pyrenees to freedom in Spain. Suddenly, his secluded stay in hospital, and all that went with it, was out of Will's mind. It was back to the grim business of survival again.

'Any questions?' asked the instructor.

One hand went up – it was Guy's. 'Will we really have time for fishing, sir?' he asked innocently.

'Oh, bugger off, all of you!' came the weary reply.

Matt caught sight of Will first, rushed over and clapped him on the back.

'You're back, old boy!' He greeted him as cheerily as ever. 'We've missed you, hiding away in there! Are you better?'

'Yes, right as rain, just saw the MO. Not allowed to fly until next week, and no early morning drill for a bit, otherwise A-OK.'

'Lucky you! Sounds bit of all right, this hospital!' Guy had joined them, and looked equally pleased to see him. 'What's the gen? Johnstone says there were some pretty nurses in there!'

'I wouldn't have a clue,' replied Will. 'Have I missed much?'

'Not really, I expect you'll soon catch up. I've kept proper notes for you from all the classroom teaching.' Solid, dependable Guy could be relied upon to think of him and plan accordingly. 'I think you'll have a new instructor, though. Hart's off ill, left the base shortly after you did.'

'Oh.' Will was disappointed. He trusted his instructor implicitly, and had assumed he would be with him for the duration. 'What's the matter with him?'

Guy shrugged. 'We don't know for sure, but the word is he had some sort of breakdown, poor bugger!'

'Have you been faking it all just for a rest?' Andrew appeared at his side. He seemed to have grown in confidence, no doubt because of his undeniable progress with his flying. It looked as though he and Jim had arrived at some sort of truce.

'I wasn't, I was ill!' Will protested, to no avail.

'Oh, yes.' The wide-mouthed Alderdice grinned suggestively. 'Those little nurses been mopping your fevered brow? No wonder your temperature was up!'

19

Will's new instructor was a man of few words, older than Hart, with the usual handlebar moustache and a clipped accent.

'Sir.' Will stood to attention as he approached.

'Right, Fordham, I hear you've been languishing on the wards,' said Baker, without a smile. 'Never a good thing, breaking off your training, but I suppose it wasn't your fault.'

'No, sir,' replied Will, already missing Hart's friendly face. 'I'm ready to get back.'

'We'll see about that, shall we? Let's play it straight – taking off into wind, medium turns and a gliding approach to landing. I'll do it first, then it's over to you to see if you've still got the hang of things. All right?' Baker turned and took his place in the front cockpit.

Will lowered himself into the plane, feeling the cold air brushing his cheeks as they bumped across the grass. Then they were up, clearing the trees, and once more he could hear the wires hum and feel the flimsy wings take the strain. His hands and feet were on the controls while Baker talked him through on the Gosport tube. Suddenly, he forgot his nerves, and wanted to take the controls, and after the first circuit Baker let him go solo. He flew without thinking, back in the rhythm of it, his brain, hands and feet making the right connections, mercifully plugged in again as though he had never been away. After a passable series of manoeuvres, Will brought the Moth in to land, a perfect three-pointer with wheels and tail hitting the ground at the same moment.

He hopped out, his confidence much improved.

'Not bad, Fordham!' Baker said. 'But you've a lot to catch up on – the others have been at it solidly since you left. I'm putting you on extra flying time, but it won't all be with me. Sergeant Chadwick will take over when I'm satisfied that you're back up to scratch, but don't expect any favours!'

Will walked back to the plane, vowing that when he became an instructor one day he would not make the lives of his students a complete misery. What was the point in it? Much better to give encouragement and support, than bawl out trainees who were only trying to do their best. Still, it was the RAF, and this was wartime, so there would be a lot worse to come.

2nd February 1941
Desford
Dear You,
It seems funny being back at the base after my pleasant interlude on the ward. I am back to flying now. It took me a little while to get used to my plane again, but I won't bore you with the details! Except to say it's good to be up in the air again. I am writing this during a quiet break in my studies – remember how we decided we both have too much to learn? I hope all is well on the ward and give my regards to Tom! Or on second thoughts, maybe not!

You can write to me: LAC WR Fordham, No. 7 EFTS Desford, Nr Leicester, or you could even ring up Desford 215 between 1pm and 1.45, any day.

I could come into Leicester next Thursday 13th at about half past seven, if that is still your night off. Just let me know what suits.

I'm missing seeing you and hope you feel the same.

From Me

20

Honor read and reread this letter, written in black ink on thick paper with a firm, neat hand. She saw the man as she read the words – and echoed his feelings, for it seemed to her that a little light had clicked out when he left. Her anticipation heightened as she realised that, yes, Thursday would be her night off next week so she would be able to see him again, sooner than she had thought.

Addie came into the hut and sat down on the bed next to her. 'What's this, Honor? You're very secretive. Have you got an admirer?'

'Just someone I met,' Honor replied evasively.

'What, like Ken?'

'I didn't pick him up on a train, if that's what you mean!' Honor said, then seeing Addie's face, continued more gently. 'You should be careful. Look what happened to Beatie, taking up with someone she didn't know!'

'That's different, I didn't meet him at a dance, late at night,' Addie said, 'and he writes such nice letters. There can't be any harm in that, surely?'

'Well, I hope not.' Honor wondered if she was being a bit hard on Addie. How did she know if William was to be trusted? Yet she was surely planning to meet him too. 'Have you been to see Beatie today?' It had been Addie's afternoon off.

'Yes, I have, but I can't say she looked a lot better. She seems so slow to pick up. It's nearly three weeks, she's still on the sulphonamides and feels really weak. I'd like to talk to one of the doctors but they never seem to be around, and Sister rather ignored me today.'

'Do you think Matron would let me come with you next time?' Honor said.

'She won't, Honor, I'm sure of it, but perhaps she'll go herself, just to make sure everything's all right. In fact, I think I'll pop over to her office now, no time like the present.' Her mind made up, Addie left for Matron's office.

She returned just as Honor was leaving. 'What happened?' Honor asked, gathering her cape.

'Well, I told her I was worried about Beatie, and she listened carefully and said she'd go and see her tomorrow. She'll be able to get much more out of that ward sister than I can!'

'Oh, good. Keep me posted!' Honor waved at Addie and sped to the ward.

She had a relatively peaceful evening, but was surprised when Night Sister finished her midnight round by saying, 'Matron wants you to pop into her office when you go off shift in the morning.'

'Did she say why?' Honor asked, immediately discomfited.

'No, sorry, I haven't a clue,' Sister said breezily, on her way out.

So she had little option but to wait, through the early dawn hours, until she had handed over to Ann and could report to Matron.

'Come in, sit down.' Matron seemed less stern than at their last meeting. Honor took her seat and waited, while Matron looked enquiringly at her.

'How are you getting on now, Nurse Newson?'

'Much better, thank you, Matron. But I'm still worried about Beatie!'

'Yes, one of your colleagues came to see me last night. I gather all may not be well, and I'm going to check for myself. I think you should come with me, Molesworth will respond better to your presence than mine. I'll be able to get more of a measure of things.'

Honor started to mutter her thanks, but Matron forestalled her. 'Come on, we're going now, the hospital car is waiting and the sooner the better, so I can get on with my day!'

Matron sat in the front of the car, next to the driver. 'Did you hear Churchill's broadcast?' he asked as they wove through the early morning traffic of bicycles, cars and horse-drawn carts, against a backdrop of pedestrians warmly wrapped in drab clothes, each clutching their regulation gas mask.

'I did,' Matron said. 'What a man! "Give us the tools and we will finish the job!" He always strikes the right note, somehow.'

'Yes, he's the best wartime leader we could have,' the man agreed. 'If Churchill can't give them a run for their money, then no one can!'

Honor followed Matron on to the ward, noticing that Sister immediately responded to her obvious seniority, accompanying them both to Beatie's bed. Matron looked at the girl, then turned quickly to Sister.

'So, how is your patient?' she asked authoritatively.

Beatie had not really stirred with their approach, but Honor, unable to stop herself, kneeled by her bedside and took her hand.

Beatie half-opened her eyes. Her mouth looked dry and her once-pretty hair lay limply over her brow. 'Honor!' Beatie said weakly. Matron looked with open displeasure at Sister.

'Well,' Sister said, 'the doctors haven't been round yet this morning, but…'

'Yes?' Matron added drily.

'Well, she's had some gastric problems with the M and B, so we're keeping her on IV fluids.'

'And what dose of M and B is she on?' Matron enquired.

'Four grams daily now,' Sister said, checking the drug chart. 'She was started on nine grams per day, as an initial dose of two grams followed by one gram four-hourly, then decreasing to six grams for three days.'

'What's her white count?'

'Er, I'm not sure when it was last done, I'll need to ask the doctor when he comes round.'

'I should hope so!' Matron took the chart from her and looked at the line of figures. 'She's had more than twenty grams of sulphapyridine – you should be checking it on alternate days, and looking at the result too, you know!'

Sister was saved by the doctor's appearance. 'Dr Leather, Matron would like to know about this patient's white count.'

Honor noticed him look at Matron, then his back straightened. 'Could you bring her records, please, Sister?' he asked, then took a little while reading them, flipping over the pages and checking the back panel before replying.

'It doesn't seem to have been done for a few days,' he prevaricated. 'I'll take a sample now so we can have an up-to-date result.'

'Might I suggest,' Matron said, 'that you examine your patient with Sister while we wait outside? Then I want a full report of her condition. I'll be in the office.' She touched Honor on the shoulder, who squeezed Beatie's hand gently before following.

They sat in the austere office, on upright chairs by Sister's desk, waiting for the doctor to return. Matron did not speak, and Honor felt she had little to contribute. She did not really understand what Matron was on about – what was all this business about Beatie's white count? She only knew that her friend looked very ill, when she had hoped she would be better by now. She wished she had been allowed to come before.

Dr Leather reappeared with Sister in his wake. They both looked uncomfortable, and were talking in low voices as they entered the office.

'Well?' Matron asked, after a pause.

'She has an ulceration of the mouth and throat, and her temperature is raised,' he replied. We'll see what her blood result is, then if necessary we can transfuse her.'

'So, as I thought, she might have an agranulocytosis?' Matron said.

'Yes, it's looking that way,' Dr Leather agreed reluctantly.

'The complications of heavy sulphonamide dosage are well known, and you, Dr Leather, should have been on top of it before! I hope you haven't been ignoring her because of the circumstances of her admission! She needs your compassion, not your contempt! I'll telephone this afternoon to find out what is being done for her, and I don't intend to let it stop there! Follow me, Nurse Newson!' Matron turned, and swept off the ward.

7th February 1941

Groby Road Hospital

Dear You,

Thank you for your letter and I am glad you are back to your flying again. It seems very quiet on the ward now you are gone. Tom keeps asking after you, teasing me as usual!

Thursday is my night off so I will be able to come out with you for a while. Please could you pick me up at the main hospital entrance at 7.30? I will wait there for you.

From Me

PS: I will need to be back by ten.

21

He tucked the letter in his pocket and whistled to himself as he pulled on his gauntlets. So, she was going to see him again, and not too long to wait! He must be sure to get there on time; he would need to talk to Andrew about borrowing the car, which might blow his cover. Still, it could not be helped – he supposed it was bound to come out sooner or later, and he would just have to ignore the endless banter. Then there was Sybil. He had not been writing very regularly but she had still been his girl. He had no wish to 'two-time' her, so decided he had better break it off, even before he knew the outcome of his relationship with Honor. It was only fair, after all.

He stopped to chat to the fitters before climbing into the cockpit. 'Everything OK?' he asked.

The lead mechanic nodded, his face a grimy smear of grease and oil. He wiped his hands on a rag. 'Just keep an eye on the oil pressure,' he said briefly. 'It should be all right but the dial has been playing up a bit.'

The Moth took off smoothly into a clear, cold sky. Sometimes there was a hint of light now, presaging the spring and the end of the dreary grey days that had comprised most of his flying experience to date. It would be wonderful to fly with the sun on your shoulders, Will thought, climbing to altitude before settling out to complete his turns.

He had been checking the oil pressure gauge as he climbed; it had risen steadily to 30psig, the correct level for the climb. Concentrating on the 'turn and slip' indicator as he banked the plane into a turn, he tried to keep the top needle in the middle of the little circle. Coming correctly out of his first turn, he noticed with consternation that the oil pressure was beginning to fall. What the hell was happening? He tried to think logically, remembering what the fitters had said. There was no evidence of an oil leak – he could not see or smell oil, and there was none coming from the engine on to the wings or the cockpit, a perilous situation which could rapidly end in fire. The needle dropped inexorably; it was no good, whatever the cause, the engine would seize up in moments. He had to get her down! He started his descent, looking for a flat, empty field and trying to remember his forced landing drill. There were too many houses; he must be over a village, but as he searched, his engine predictably cut out, leaving him gliding low over a road and towards a low farm building. He just had enough lift to make it to the next field, into which he drifted, scattering sheep before landing perilously close to a small wood at the end.

Will jumped rapidly out of the cockpit. It was not a good idea to hang around in a plane which could be leaking oil. He was still puzzling as to the cause, none being immediately apparent, when an irate farmer came across the field towards him, waving a gun. Will sighed – it was clearly going to be one of those days! He raised his hands to placate him.

'What the hell do you think you're doing?' the farmer shouted, then noticing the RAF uniform, he paused.

'Sorry, sir, my engine cut out, oil pressure problems. I didn't come down there on purpose, events beyond my control!' He looked pleadingly at the farmer, who lowered his gun slowly.

'All right, son,' the man replied, 'it's just that we have a lot of your planes in the sky around here and it's not good for my livestock, especially these ewes, you know, being buzzed in their field.'

'I quite understand, sir,' Will continued contritely. 'I'm from a farming family, up north, myself. Hope to go back to it when this is all over.'

The farmer moved closer, uncocking his gun. He was a broad-faced, well-built man, weather-beaten and wearing worn moleskin trousers and a jacket that had seen better days. 'So what's up with your engine?' he asked, a note of interest in his voice.

Will knew that farmers had a major stake in their farm equipment and making it run. Many of them were experienced mechanics when it came to getting a tractor or car to go. Will's uncle had a love of engines that surpassed his own, frequently salvaging an old engine from one piece of equipment and putting it to work in another.

'Well, it's not been leaking oil that I can see or smell, but that's why I got out a bit sharpish,' Will continued. 'The fitters said the gauge was dicky but it's worse than that.' They both looked towards the Moth.

'Old plane, is it?' the farmer asked. 'Maybe a bit too much wear and tear in your engine. Needs stripping down properly, I should think.'

'Certainly does,' Will agreed. 'My name's Fordham – do you mind if I make a phone call to Desford from your house?'

'No, of course, laddie. I'm Bradley, by the way.' He stretched out his hand, calloused and rough as Will knew it would be.

They walked companionably back to the house. 'How many acres have you got, sir?' Will asked the question that all farmers expect.

'No need to call me sir, I'm not going to shoot you now!' The man smiled. 'Two hundred and fifty acres, used to be mostly sheep and arable, but now we're having to put more down to arable to get the country fed. Not really got enough help though: two of my own lads have joined up, so the missus and I are dependent on the Land Army girls now. Nice lasses, though, don't get me wrong, they just need a bit of training and of course they're not as strong as the men.'

'No, of course not,' Will agreed. He remembered that Honor had told him that her sister Ruth was in the Land Army. Tough work, but essential for the country's survival. 'How many have you got?'

'Six, all billeted with us. One of them's a dab hand at driving a tractor, I can tell you that!' he said as they entered the low-beamed farmhouse.

Will felt a rush of nostalgia; he could have been back on the farm at home: that same smell of wheat, curing hams and honey that combined into a sort of spiritual elixir of the land. The farmer's wife turned from the kitchen range as they came in, rubbing her hands on her apron. She was in the middle of her baking, and Will observed with pleasure the loaves proving on the wide, scrubbed table. She shook his hand, and he could feel the dust of flour on her palms.

'Has he been giving you a hard time?' She had a lovely face, wrinkles at the corners of her eyes and mouth, and clear eyes that seemed to sum up the young man at once. 'He gets in such a state about things nowadays, it's the war – too much to worry about at his age. Anyway, are you all right? You don't look any older than our own two lads – they're in the Army, both of them, now.' She swallowed, like all mothers who recall the whereabouts of their children, of whatever age, when their lives are uncertain.

'I'm fine, thank you, engine problems!' Will looked at her appreciatively.

'Sit yourself down, I expect you could do with a cup of tea.' She took the kettle from the range to make a new pot for him.

He sipped it, even happier when she cut him a thick slice of bread from one of her still-warm loaves and spread it with butter and honey.

'This lad's from a farming family, too,' Mr Bradley informed her. 'Up north, a Yorkshireman, I'll be bound.'

The couple were both interested in the connection, such that Will, in explaining it, almost forgot to ring the base to explain his whereabouts. The duty sergeant was brusque.

'Any damage to the plane?'

'None, sir, not apart from the fault with the oil pressure.'

'OK, stay where you are, someone will be along to get you in about two hours.'

Will returned to his cup of tea at the table.

'Don't they want you back?' the farmer enquired, his eyes alert and amused.

'Well, they certainly want the plane,' Will replied, 'but they won't be here for a couple of hours yet, I'm afraid.'

'Tell you what,' said Mr Bradley, 'I'll take you round the farm while you're waiting, we can go and get some feed to the sheep in the far fields.'

Will was up in the front of the tractor with him before he could change his mind. The trailer was already loaded with hay and they drove across the wide, flat fields, past the little wood, Will hopping down to open gates as required.

'It's very different land,' he commented. 'Your hedges are very neat, and your woods look tidy. Not like our moorland.'

'Well, it's laid out that way for the hunt, of course,' Bradley said. 'Prime hunting here – the Quorn help with the fencing and upkeep, to be fair to them. See that hunt jump at the far corner?'

Will looked over to the low, flat fence, the thick round top bar perfect for taking a hunter over. He did not ride himself, apart from the carthorses sometimes, but he liked the hunt, its traditions and close links with the land.

'Where are your sons serving?' Will knew what a loss that was to a farming family. Such boys could avoid the draft because of the obvious importance of agricultural work, but many chose not to.

The farmer raised his eyebrows. 'Oh, hecky me, don't get the missus on to that! They're both with the Desert Army, North Africa of all places! Worse thing is, it always seems to be one step forward, one step backward out there. At least they're giving the Eyeties what for! All I want is them back safely here, out of harm's way – just like your mother and father feel about you, I expect.'

Will nodded, seeing the cloud across the man's face. 'Your land is looking good,' he said, changing the subject. 'You must all be putting in the extra, you and those girls!'

Bradley drew the tractor to a halt and Will climbed down to help him with the bales. Even the hay smelt good to him – what would he give to be back doing this every day! The sheep gathered in anticipation, their solid forms setting the backdrop for the countryside beyond. Once they had spread the hay around, Will took his place in the tractor.

'Better get you back, I suppose.' The farmer cranked the gears as they went.

The RAF lorry had arrived at the farm, with a couple of fitters who were looking over the plane. The farmer's wife had already given them a cup of tea, and they winked at Will appreciatively.

'Fancied a bit of a break, sir?' The older mechanic was known for his dry sense of humour.

Will stood by as they tinkered with the engine. 'The whole thing cut out on me, and the oil pressure just started to fall for no apparent reason. I couldn't see or smell any leaks. What do you reckon?'

'This gauge needs to come off, but we'll get another on in no time. Looks like it was faulty – we weren't 100% sure about it when you took her up. Anyway, give us another half an hour, then you can be up and off again.'

'Thanks, lads, I'll wait in the farmhouse.' Will was quite happy to have another cup of tea, and perhaps Mrs Bradley might see her way to that second slice of bread.

The farmer had already returned to work, but she sat down at the table with him while he ate.

'You should pop back and see us sometime,' she said. 'Not in your plane, silly!' she added, seeing his puzzled look. 'Seriously, it'll do the old man good – you could drop by on your day off, maybe give him a little hand and take his mind off things. I can see he likes your company, and some days he does nothing but dwell on our boys. You can't help thinking about them all the time, and he worries about the farm so, without them here.'

Will finished his tea and looked at her. 'Of course I will,' he replied, without a second thought. 'It's been lovely to spend the morning here, especially after he put down his gun!'

Part Four:
Dear You, from Me

1

There was no doubt about it; the Austin was a terrific little car. The dent down the side had been repaired and as he drove out from Desford that Thursday evening, Will could hardly believe his luck. He felt indebted to Andrew, who, true to form, had shared his secret and covered up the fact that he was borrowing the car. He glanced at his watch: plenty of time to make it to Groby Road by half past seven. It had been a slightly warmer day but the light had gone by the time he motored down the dark country lanes to Leicester. Not much traffic around, and he kept his headlights dimmed according to the blackout rules.

He had checked the route before setting off, wishing to leave nothing to chance, although he was pretty certain he could remember the way that Florence had driven him back to base. He felt a mixture of apprehension and longing, such was his desire to see Honor again. He hoped nothing would go wrong, and most particularly had decided not to alarm her in any way, by 'getting fresh' too early on. He knew Honor would never trust him if he behaved badly, she was a girl who looked as though she might have had to protect herself in the past.

He settled himself down for the drive, savouring the handling of the car. He had never driven such a lovely model before; although he was an experienced driver it was more likely to have been the tractors on the farm, or his uncle's old Humber. His father did not drive, though his brother had the grocery van, which he was used to taking out and about. He glanced at the petrol gauge, reassured by Andrew that there was plenty of petrol to get there and back. It was strictly forbidden to take petrol from the aerodrome bowsers, but all the same, if no one was around, a little drop might be had from time to time. Otherwise, rationing being in full force, it could be difficult to source petrol even with the requisite coupons.

Passing through the village of Glenfield, he was soon in the city outskirts and turned off the main road into the hospital drive. He was early; it was only twenty past, so he parked at the entrance as Honor had said, switched off the engine and lights, and settled down to wait. It was chilly in the open-topped car, so he drew his warm flying jacket collar around his neck and sat back. There were few lights over the city, even less the hospital, and he reckoned it would have been quite difficult for a German bomber to make it out. Leicester had not been subject to quite so many raids as the nearby cities of Coventry or Birmingham, as it lacked the large munitions or engineering factories which made them both prime targets. It was a miracle how these bombed cities had managed to resume war work, he thought; an extraordinary testament to working people and their courage in adversity.

He sensed, rather than exactly saw, a figure coming towards the car. It was not Honor, though his heart had missed a beat in so believing, but the hospital night porter.

'Evening, sir, can I help you?' the man enquired deferentially, shining a small torch towards him. Will thought it better to stand up, in order not to be mistaken for a fifth columnist. The country was full of posters warning of the presence of German spies at every corner, but as he politely opened the car door, any concerns that the porter might have had were allayed by the sight of his RAF uniform.

'I'm just waiting to meet someone,' Will was beginning to explain, when she came walking fast out of the darkness towards them. She was not in her nurse's uniform, but a soft sweater and full skirt with a light coat, all of which somehow seemed to accentuate her slim figure rather than hide it.

He took her hand, gently, 'Hello, you', and walked round to open the car door.

The porter, of whose presence they seemed oblivious, ventured a cheery 'Evening, miss', and Honor gave him a little wave as she sat rather self-consciously in the seat and Will closed the door.

'Thank you, I'll have her back by ten.' Will nodded to the porter, as he started the car and they drove towards the entrance.

'Where to, and what would you like to do?'

She looked at him, and smiled. 'I'm rather hungry,' she replied, and so, of course, was he.

He parked outside the Grand Hotel. They had not talked much in the car, with the wind whistling around their ears, though he had made sure she was warm enough and tucked a plaid blanket around her knees before setting off. He opened the car door for her once again, and followed her through the hotel foyer and past the bellboy into the restaurant. He noticed her shapely legs for the first time, no longer in flat black shoes, but dressed up in stockings and heels.

'Yes, sir?' the maître d'hôtel was a tall, imposing man who was begrudgingly respectful of Will's uniform. It was a great advantage; that blue suit could open doors, Will thought, wondering how he would have been treated in civvy clothes. Still, the Grand's dining room was two thirds empty, as presumably most of the citizens of Leicester lacked the means to dine out there. It was one of the few places they could find a meal on a Thursday night, and he wanted to make it special for her. Fortunately he had not long been paid, and managed to salvage some cash in anticipation. Andrew had kindly lent him a fiver in case he did not have quite enough.

'Table for two, please,' he replied, as though he was used to such establishments.

Honor looked at him, her eyes alight, even more so when they were seated at the table and the waiter had spread a starched white napkin over her lap and handed them both the menu. Honor read it with some confusion. She had never been in a place like this before, and had no idea what she should order from the long list of French names. She shot a quick glance at Will, who came to her rescue.

'Do you like beef?' he asked. She responded with a willing nod. The truth was she would have eaten anything, such was her perpetual state of hunger with rationing and her physically demanding work. She could never really have enough to eat, she reckoned, and could not imagine a day when there would be surplus food on the table.

Will looked at the menu. 'We'll have two steak *haché* with pommes frites,' he said breezily.

'And how do you like your steak, sir?'

Will looked at Honor. 'Both well done, please,' he replied, not wanting to discomfit her with underdone beef, which he actually preferred.

'And to drink, sir?'

Will looked at the wine list and frowned. He had only heard of two French wines; one was Graves, and one Sauternes. His French teacher had talked about them during a long and tedious French lesson once, hoping to capture some spark of interest from the boys. He made up his mind on this basis, having no desire to ask the waiter's advice.

'A bottle of Graves, please.'

Honor hesitated. 'Could I have some water too, please?' she asked.

'Certainly, mademoiselle.' The waiter smiled back at the pretty girl. Lucky chap, bringing her out for the evening. The waiter realised that she was in unfamiliar territory, but liked her all the more for that. Better than some of those ghastly old harridans who came in here sometimes, ordering them all about. He would make sure the kitchen gave them a nice meal.

'So.' Will settled back in his seat once the waiter had gone and they had both crossed that particular hurdle.

'I don't really drink wine,' she said shyly.

'No, but I thought you might like to try a little,' he reassured her, smiling. She folded her hands in her lap; she was sitting very upright, as though at school or in an examination, though she was clearly suppressing a childish excitement at being there.

'Is it all right here?' he asked.

'Oh, yes, very nice, thank you.'

'How is the ward? Are you busy?' He decided to move on to familiar territory.

'I should say so!' She grinned at him. 'We've had lots of new patients, all children. You two seem to be the last adults we'll get! Some of the little ones are quite poorly, need a bit of looking after. Then I've got exams coming up next month so I keep trying to work in between. I never knew there were so many infectious diseases in the world!'

'How long are you staying on night shift for?' he continued. She was beginning to look more relaxed.

'Not sure,' she replied. 'I think Ann might move me to days next month.'

'Will you like that?' He guessed she valued her own little world at night, in the seclusion of the ward.

'I'm not sure,' she replied thoughtfully. 'I've rather got used to it now.'

'And Tom?'

She shook her head. 'Just the same as ever! But guess what: he might be going home next week! I don't know how we'll survive without him, he can certainly brighten your day! He says he's going to enlist, join the RAF like you, but he's only sixteen!'

'I'm not sure that'll stop him,' Will replied. He knew several lads who had lied about their age in order to join up. Still, in Tom's case his slight physique and recent illness would mitigate against him hoodwinking the authorities.

They were interrupted by the waiter bringing their wine. He opened it with a flourish, and poured a small amount for Will to try. He sipped it and nodded authoritatively, glad that he had seen David Niven doing just that in a film at the cinema recently.

Honor looked teasingly at him. 'Anyone would think you are always in places like this!'

He said nothing, but winked in reply, to her obvious amusement. She had been enjoying herself ever since she got into the lovely blue car; it was all so different to her normal life.

The waiter poured a little wine in her glass, but she put her hand up to stop him. She had no intention of becoming woozy on wine, to which she was not accustomed. Actually she did not like the taste, and anyway she knew of many girls who had done things they regretted after a drink or two. She certainly was not going to let that happen to her. She was rewarded by a discreet smile from the waiter as he poured some water into her other glass instead.

'It's all right, I'm not going to get you squiffy!' Will said.

'No, you're not!' she replied firmly.

'How's your friend?'

Honor looked momentarily crestfallen, and he wished he had not asked.

'Still not better, I'm afraid. She's had a blood transfusion but she's still very weak. I haven't been allowed to visit her lately – she's not in our hospital, you see.'

Her voice tailed off. Will wondered why she should need permission to visit a sick friend, but judged it wise to say no more.

'And you?' She recovered her composure. 'Are you glad to be back in your plane?'

'Too right I am! Except,' and he paused, 'I miss seeing you, Honor.'

She raised her eyes to his, shyly. He thought she had never looked so lovely, that he had never met a girl quite like her in his life. It was such a revelation, seeing her off the ward, in her soft, feminine clothes, her personality not defined by her occupation or responsibilities… He waited for her reply.

'Me too,' she replied, just managing to hold his gaze. 'It's not quite the same on night duty without you.' She was conscious that she was meeting a different boy from the patient on the ward. He seemed to have grown in stature, and however hard she tried not to, she had to admit that he looked handsome in his uniform, the mark of a man who was among the cream of their generation.

He took a deep breath. 'I should hope not!' He raised his eyebrows. 'Though I seem to remember I was asleep most of the time. I wish I'd stayed awake all night now, then I'd know a bit more about you!'

'You might not, William Fordham!' she returned, with a little shake of her head. 'I'm really pleased you're better though. It's lovely to see you up and about, back to normal, in your uniform. Had you missed much flying while you were away?'

He leant towards her. 'It was a bit tricky on my first flight back,' he admitted. 'I lost a bit of confidence, you see. It's not all like they make it out to be in the films. We all know that a silly mistake can take you out, you're being assessed all the time. The powers that be can chuck you off the course as soon as look at you! You just have to keep your head down and hope for the best. Anyway, it was all worth it because I met you, didn't I?' He took her hand across the starched white tablecloth, and she did not pull it back, so spontaneous was his gesture, but looked up tentatively at him again.

She withdrew her hand as the waiter appeared, placing white china plates with neatly arranged food in front of them both. Honor sat up; it looked so special and she could hardly believe that she deserved such a treat.

'Would you like to try a little wine now?' the waiter asked solicitously, so she took a small sip and swallowed it slowly, not liking the taste at all. She suppressed a grimace, noticing that Will seemed to be drinking his quite happily, and took up her knife and fork to eat, after a moment's indecision about which one to use.

The beef was delicious, a soft minced type of steak, with crisp fried potatoes and a green salad at the side. She did not think that the greens were as good as those her father grew, but otherwise it was perfect. They both ate silently at first, for good food was too important to overlook.

'Is it all right?' he asked her again. She nodded happily, and went on eating. He was pleased to see that she liked her food, though she was so slender that she looked as though she could do with a few more hot meals. He did not like girls who were picky about their food; it was such a stupid affectation.

The waiter was hovering. 'Everything to your satisfaction, sir?'

Will was studiously polite. 'Very nice, thank you,' before resuming their conversation.

'I might be able to fly over the hospital one day when I'm practising solo, so you'd better look out for me. Do you know what a Tiger Moth looks like, Honor?'

'Of course I do, silly, everyone does,' she replied. Honor had no wish to encourage acts of foolhardiness; she seemed to become more sensible with every passing day. Life was too serious to play around. 'You be careful though, I don't want you getting into any trouble or putting yourself in danger.'

He smiled gently at her. 'I'm not sure I'll be able to stay out of danger for the entire war, you know.'

'I wish you could!' she said. 'Please take care of yourself, won't you?'

'I think I'd probably do just about anything you asked me, but I'll certainly do that,' he replied solemnly, then noticing she had finished her beef, asked, 'What about an ice cream?'

Later as they drove back, Will having paid the bill, and left a tip for the waiter, all of which cleared him out of funds, including Andrew's fiver, he felt an overwhelming sense of happiness. He had her by his side, she was going to be his girl, no matter what, and life was ahead of them. He revved the Austin up into fourth gear as they drove down the Groby Road, then drew in at the gates.

'When will I see you again?' he asked quietly, as she was untucking the blanket from her knees. He put his arm around her shoulders and she leant towards his brief kiss.

'Soon,' she replied, rising into the dark night and waving goodbye. 'Thank you for a lovely time!'

2

'How did it go?' Addie was in her nightie, ready for bed. She was almost as excited as her friend.

'Oh, Addie!' Honor sat down beside her, looking curiously out of place in her smart clothes. 'It was such a special evening, I don't know where to begin.'

One of the other nurses came over to join them and perched on the bed, which was now becoming slightly crowded. 'Start at the beginning,' June said.

Honor sat back, took off the shoes, and handed them to her. 'Thank you, they're beautiful shoes. I'm going to save up for some. It's just as well you all dressed me up, he took me to the Grand Hotel for dinner! It was so smart there, I've never been anywhere like that before! Anyway, he's really thoughtful, picked me up in his friend's car, drove me there and back, didn't make a pass at me, bought me supper…'

Addie stared. 'You ate dinner there?' She was incredulous. 'It must have cost him a fortune!'

'Oh, I know!' Honor winced. 'He ordered wine too!'

'What was that like?' June was interested. In common with most girls of her generation and class, such a beverage was unknown to her. Beer or cider, possibly, or port and lemon, maybe even gin, but wine! That was something else!

'Actually, I thought it tasted horrible, and I didn't want to drink much anyway. Still, he seemed to like it.' Honor pulled the sweater over her head and relinquished it to Addie with a smile.

'And?' began Addie. 'And…?'

'And,' said Honor firmly and without artifice, 'I like him and I'm going to marry him one day.'

'Has he asked you?' June was amazed at the speed of this relationship. There was hope for them all if things could move this fast.

'No,' Honor admitted solemnly. 'But he will, I just know it, one day.'

3

'You're never leaving us! What will we do without you?'

Tom grinned back at his favourite nurse. 'Oh, you'll be fine! I'm off to join up as soon as I can, just you wait! Then I can be in the Air Force like your handsome boyfriend!'

'Tom! How do you know he's my boyfriend?' Despite herself, Honor blushed.

''Cause you're blushing, that's how! Anyway, I told him you were the prettiest nurse in the hospital and he'd better get in there sharpish! He's just doing what I told him to!' Tom was triumphant; his best matchmaking so far.

'You are the end!' She pointed a mock-stern finger at him, and checked the chart at the end of his bed. All of his obs were resolutely normal, had been for days, and he was off medication. 'We'll be sorry to lose you,' she concluded.

'No you won't, you'll all manage to get some work done without me larking about!' He settled down behind a dog-eared comic, resuming his read.

Honor was not entirely certain where to start that evening. As usual, it would have to be the child who was crying loudest, otherwise the whole ward would come out in sympathy.

At the far end was a child whose bedclothes were in disarray, some falling over the side, calling with a little constant refrain, 'Nurse, Nurse', as though she had almost given up hope of one appearing.

'Oh, my goodness, you're in a tangle.' Honor stepped authoritatively to the child's side. She was a child of about seven, whose little face reminded her suddenly of Maisie. Perhaps it was those big eyes fixed upon her, expressing the absolute shock at having been taken from her family to this strange place, where you were not allowed even to get out of bed. 'Let me sort you out.'

Honor was by now experienced in bed-making, one of the hallowed rituals of nursing. It was altogether more difficult with a small, hot child in the bed, but she smoothed the rubber mackintosh and draw-sheet before achieving some tight corners with the sheets that would even have met Ann's approval.

'What's your name?' she asked, gently moving the little girl from one side of the bed to the other.

'Audrey,' came the flat reply, eyes still following her. Honor realised it would take more than the brief time available to her to comfort the child, and gain her confidence. She would have to leave that until later, or another day. She took her small, sweaty hand.

'I'm really busy tonight, Audrey, but I'll try and come back.' She checked the child's last aspirin dose, reminding herself that this one would definitely need some more when Night Sister came round.

By the early morning, Honor, exhausted, sat at the desk, trying to catch up on her reports. Ann must have left her newspaper behind and Honor glanced desultorily at the headlines. *London latest, Café de Paris bombed!* There had been another particularly heavy raid the night before. The king and queen were visiting the East End to assess the damage and give encouragement to their subjects. Honor looked at the photograph of the monarch, with his slight build and harrowed face. The queen looked a bit jollier, she thought, but it was apparent even to Honor, far from the epicentre of things, that the war must be taking a huge toll upon George VI. Poor chap, she thought, never even wanted to be king, or so they had said in the days leading up to the shocking abdication of his brother. That Wallis Simpson! As if the country did not have enough problems without some American schemer on the make trying to become queen! The country would rather have the comfortable Bowes-Lyon girl, with her two pretty daughters, than an upstart divorcee any day!

She sighed, and roused herself: there were some urine samples in the sluice to test. There would be no quiet break for studying tonight, and later, as dawn broke over the sleeping ward, she pushed back the blackout curtains to see the misty light over the city, the searchlights now switched off, and the beginning of another day.

Ann stopped her as soon as she came on the ward. 'You're being transferred, Honor! I'm sorry, it was nothing to do with me, I'd rather you stayed here! But there's a bit of a panic in the diphtheria wards, one of the nurses has gone sick, and they want you as replacement. You're to start there on days tomorrow!' It was clear from Ann's face that she was upset.

'It's not your fault! It was bound to happen sooner or later,' Honor said, 'you've been a first-rate tutor and I'll never forget how you've helped me.'

Ann looked flustered, and pushed back her glasses, as she did in moments of confusion. 'Oh, tosh!' she replied. 'You're going to be a good nurse, and don't you ever forget it!'

4

'Beatie, it's us!' The two girls stood by her bedside, immediately taking stock of her state. There was a drip stand by her bed; she must have been transfused again, but still looked very pale. Beatie tried to sit up, and they each gave her an arm to help her.

'You're early!' Beatie looked confused. 'Did I know you were coming? Sometimes I just forget what's happening in here, can't even remember how long I've been in.' She looked abstractedly over to the wide window. 'What time is it?'

There was a quick glance between the two girls. 'It's about nine o'clock,' Honor replied. 'We just wanted to check that you're getting better.'

Beatie had taken on the same quiet look of resignation as the children on Honor's ward. 'Well, I think I'm going to die, aren't I? Nobody's said I'm not. It's all my fault anyway, isn't it?' Her voice betrayed no note of distress, just a simple acceptance of the facts as she saw them.

'Beatie, don't be silly!' Addie was shocked. She caught sight of the blue-uniformed sister and hurried down the ward for help.

Honor sat on the bed. 'Why do you think you're going to die?'

Beatie looked her straight in the eyes, quite rational again. 'Of course I am, Honor. I've been having blood transfusion after blood transfusion. Am I getting better? No, I think not. Why do they need to keep topping me up, like a leaky old bottle or something? I'm not bleeding, it's not that. Doctor says my bone marrow has been knocked by the M and B, but they stopped that after you and Matron came, so it should be picking up now. I'm not stupid, you know – I might be dying, but I'm not stupid. I expect the Almighty doesn't think I deserve to live, after what I've done.' She settled back in her bed, gazing once more at the sky beyond the confines of the window frame, as though there might be an answer out there for her.

'None of it was your fault, and you are not going to die, I won't let you!'

Beatie smiled again. 'And how precisely are you going to stop me? If my number's up, it's up. Should never have come out of that cellar. I wish I'd died with Nancy, saved all this trouble to no good end!'

Honor was at a loss for words, so compelling was Beatie's argument, and was rescued only by the arrival of Sister and Addie at the bedside. Sister looked more authoritative than ever.

'What's all this I hear, Beatie?' She sounded almost cross. 'I'll have no talk of dying on my ward!'

Beatie shrugged her shoulders.

Honor motioned Sister to one side, out of earshot. 'Could I have a word? It can't be doing her any good to be thinking like this. It's as if she's giving up the struggle! What do her parents say?'

'They've not been visiting much,' Sister admitted. 'I mean, not since her father found out the circumstances of her admission. I think her mother wants to see her, but I get the feeling he's washed his hands of her.' Sister tried not to judge girls like Beatie, but in her heart she disapproved strongly of what she had done, and did not identify her as a victim, rather a perpetrator.

Honor realised all of this, without being told. Such views were common among the nursing hierarchy, who could be harsh to such girls even when they were at death's door. She continued gently, hoping that Sister would not flounce off.

'Do you think there's any way of clarifying her prognosis?' She was pleased with her choice of words, 'prognosis' being one she had been learning on the wards recently.

Sister paused; this patient had been nothing but trouble so far. 'We'll ask Dr Leather, he's just coming down the ward.'

The medical man looked even more tired than usual. He had passed a wakeful night with two difficult deliveries, one of which, a breech, had ended up in the operating theatre as an emergency section. At least mother and baby had both survived.

'I suppose you've got a point,' he conceded. 'This has been dragging on for some time. Her blood count isn't really picking up, but it's difficult to interpret the results, after all the transfusions. I think it might help if I were to do a bone marrow trephine, then we can see what's really going on. I'll get that done early this afternoon, Sister.'

Honor returned to Beatie's side.

'I've talked to the doctor,' she said comfortingly. 'He's going to do a special test this afternoon, get some bone marrow, see if it's recovering. Then you can stop worrying!'

'Unless it isn't,' Beatie replied flatly.

'Well, let's cross that bridge when we come to it!' Addie interrupted breezily. 'Do try and buck up, it's not good for you. You'll not get better thinking that way!'

Beatie sighed and closed her eyes, as a signal for both girls to take their departure. 'Just a minute!' She roused herself in query. 'How precisely will Doctor get this sample of bone marrow?'

Both girls were nonplussed. 'I'll look it up, promise,' Honor replied, having no desire to question Sister on the point. 'I'm sure it won't be too bad! We'll be back soon!'

They went silently down the stairs, and it was not until they were back in the cold morning air that Honor took Addie's arm, and pronounced, 'We've done all we can, you know, we'll just have to hope for the best.'

Addie was not to be reassured. 'What if she's right? Don't you remember, Beatie always does what she says!'

5

'I was hoping they might do better than send me another probationer,' Sister pronounced unkindly. 'I need an experienced nurse on this ward, haven't got time to be training the likes of you!'

Honor was not sure what she had done to merit such disapprobation so soon after her arrival on Ward 10, but said in her defence, 'I've had a fair amount of experience on the rheumatic fever ward, Sister. I've been on nights, you see, so I'm used to working by myself.'

'Well, I doubt you'll be competent enough to work by yourself on my ward for a very long time!' Sister retorted. 'You'll be with Nurse Wilson, in the far corner. She'll keep you in your place, she's one of my best nurses so don't get in her way!'

With such an introduction to the ward Honor began to sense defeat. There were plenty of sisters like this one, she had heard all about them from the other probationers. It was just that she had been lucky enough to avoid them so far.

Nurse Wilson was setting up a steam kettle by the side of a small boy. He was coughing intermittently and there was a little trickle of saliva from the corner of his mouth. She looked warningly at Honor, who watched as she completed the task, then they withdrew to the end of his bed.

'He's got a pharyngeal paralysis coming on.' Nurse Wilson shook her head. 'I hope it doesn't get worse.' She was very tall, with large hands and feet, which might have been ungainly, but she had handled the child with much gentleness. Her brown hair was plaited under her cap. 'So, you're with me, are you? Don't worry about Sister, she runs one of the best wards in this entire place, so it doesn't matter if she's a bit sharp sometimes. Keeps us all on our toes, and so she should! Have you nursed diphtheria before?'

Honor went on to explain her previous training at the Lambeth, prompting the usual response from Nurse Wilson. She brushed it all aside airily: 'I expect we do things differently here anyway, so why don't we just start at the beginning, and I'll assume you don't know anything? Come along then, we've got to get some antitoxin drawn up for one of the new admissions. It's lucky we've just got a new supply in today, can't usually come by it for love of God nor money!'

Honor listened as Nurse explained that the dosage of antitoxin, which had to be administered as soon as the disease was suspected, was calculated on the extent of the membrane covering the back of the throat, and the number of hours it had been present. More antitoxin was given if the membrane covered both tonsils and pharynx. There was a chart to help calculation, and as this patient, a girl, had only tonsillar membrane, Sister drew up a thousand units in the sterilised syringe and they went together to the child's bed. Honor checked the drug chart; this was Rose King, was it not? Rose was less than keen on the idea of a large intramuscular injection, and she watched the two nurses preparing with horror in her eyes.

'Hold her hand, would you?' Nurse Wilson checked the syringe, while Honor sat beside her.

'Hold on, just a little needle prick.' She felt the child shudder and utter a muffled 'Ow' as the syringe slowly discharged its contents into her slim buttock.

'There, all done for today.' Nurse Wilson patted the child's head. 'You've been very brave. Before we go, would you just mind letting our new nurse look in the back of your throat?'

Rose obligingly opened her mouth. Honor remembered the smell of that membrane, or *foetor* as it said in the books, and experienced a familiar sense of revulsion at the life-threatening, tenacious grey membrane covering the child's tonsils.

'See, it's not extending down into the pharynx yet,' Nurse Wilson pointed out helpfully. Honor looked more closely, trying to define the edge of the membrane. There had been little antitoxin in the Lambeth wards, so she was unfamiliar with this dosage regime.

'Thank you.' She nodded at Rose, who closed her mouth and lay flat in bed while Honor felt her rapid pulse and noted that her temperature was only slightly raised.

The two nurses moved down the ward to one of the cubicles at the end. This was one of the children with a glucose drip, and the foot of his bed was raised. He looked exhausted, pale and listless. He was around nine years old, Honor surmised.

'We're treating for cardiac failure,' Nurse Wilson explained. 'It's one of the complications of diphtheria, affects the muscles. He's on a drug called Coramine, it's new. We don't know how well it works yet though.' She took the child's hand. 'How are you today, Simon?' Her voice was soft, almost as though she did not want to disturb him.

He whispered in reply, 'Bit better?', but there was a note of enquiry, almost uttered more in hope than fact.

By the time they had bed-bathed the next child Honor was beginning to feel more confident, though she was glad of Nurse Wilson's expertise, as the child had a tracheotomy tube in her neck, strapped tightly in with white gauze and a collar-like liniment bandage. She was not able to speak or drink, and Nurse put up a new bag of glucose for her drip, showing Honor exactly how to do it. Nurse Wilson carefully described the sequence of events that had led to the child requiring such intervention: her deteriorating condition, and spread of the deadly membrane to obstruct breathing, leaving the child choking for breath. Fortunately, the doctors had been able to intervene in good time and the patient had so far survived, unlike others that Honor could remember.

'Go on, time for your break!' She was finally allowed a pause just after midday and gratefully left the ward for the nurses' dining room, glad to be in the fresh air for a while.

June was waiting next to her in the queue. 'How's your boyfriend?' she asked interestedly.

'Oh, gosh, June, I've hardly had time to think about him!' Honor said. 'There's never a moment on that diphtheria ward!'

'So when are you going to see him again?' June persisted. She was incurably romantic, and loved the thought of the handsome pilot and her pretty friend. Some girls had all the luck!

'Do you know, I'm not sure,' Honor replied. 'All I can concentrate on is getting through the afternoon! Sister terrifies me to death!'

As she walked back to the ward she heard a low, buzzing engine noise, and looking up, saw a lone Tiger Moth flying low over the hospital. It was gone as soon as it had come and she thought for a brief moment that she had imagined it. She had not taken his remark seriously, but as she gazed upwards it dawned upon her that this must be him. She drew her cape around her and hurried onwards, fearful that anyone might have seen him, and almost shutting out the engine drone fading away into the distance.

No. 7 EFTS Desford
20th February 1941
Dear You,
I'm sorry, I couldn't resist it! Just happened to be doing some aerobatics nearby, so put in a little diversion of my own. Next time I come, I'll give you a few loops or a spin!

I know you don't approve of such antics but it will be ages until I get an evening off again, so just staying in touch.

Hope you are well and will write again when next week's exams are over.
From Me

6

It was late evening, and they were all gathered round a small table in bungalow ten trying to revise their navigation for the forthcoming test. Jim groaned.

'I can't take much more of this, I'm off to the mess for a beer. Anyone coming?'

Guy shook his head. 'Quite honestly, Alderdice, you're nowhere near up to scratch and I don't reckon a few pints of beer will help you much. I'm staying put until the others have got it sorted.'

Solid, dependable Guy was the self-appointed mentor for the group. Since Dick had left, he was their best hope at navigation, and he certainly tried hard to explain the principles to the others. Matt looked distracted, and he ran a hand through his mop of fair hair. He had the appearance of someone who was completely out of his depth, and resigned to that state.

'I think I'll join you.' He nodded at Jim, ignoring Guy's warning look. Will looked enviously after them, but felt he should in all conscience stick with it for a bit. Not that any of it was making much sense, this late at night.

'Come on, you lot, we'll have another go at position fixing,' Guy encouraged them, 'and remember, a fix must be as accurate as possible, and you'll need three PLs crossing for that three-point fix.' Will looked down at the charts and tried to concentrate. 'When we've done this, we'll finish up with a bit on the Lorenz beam,' Guy added helpfully, as though to spur them on.

Andrew glanced at Will and winked. They had become closer now Andrew knew about Honor, a secret that he had resolutely kept to himself. He hoped he would meet her one day; she sounded a nice girl. He had never had a girlfriend, living in the exclusively male environment of a boys' public school. Subject to endless ragging about his 'pretty boy' appearance, he had become truly confused about his orientation. Did he like girls, or was it just boys who liked him? He tried to block out some of the more unpleasant experiences that he had endured at school and was relieved that here, at least, the only thing that really mattered was whether you could fly a plane.

After correcting their work, Guy seemed satisfied. 'Let's call it a day!' he announced. 'I think we deserve that beer now.' Andrew fell in alongside Will as they walked to the mess.

'When are you seeing her again?' he asked.

'Oh, not sure, I'll have to save up for the next outing! I still owe you a fiver. It was worth it though,' he replied, remembering the look of joyful excitement on Honor's face. 'I flew over her hospital today, just after I finished aerobatics, but I don't suppose she saw me!'

'Watch it, old boy, you'll get into trouble if you go joyriding!' Andrew warned. He was secretly surprised; Fordham was such a careful chap, and it was quite out of character. He assumed it was the foolhardiness of love, and decided to keep a closer eye on his friend from now on.

'Well, I think it's time we had a little light entertainment!' Jim announced at the bar. 'What about a little trip to a dance in Leicester on Friday? Come on, boys, you're wasting your youth cooped up here!'

Andrew looked uncertain. He was perpetually distrustful of Jim's ideas. Matt's face lit up – at last, a chance to do something other than flying or revision!

'Oh, go on,' he urged Andrew. 'Let's go in your car – we can squeeze in, have a bit of fun for a change!'

Andrew finally bowed to the inevitable. 'Oh, all right, but you can't all fit in, you know that! It's a two-seater, unless that had escaped your notice.'

They gathered closer together, intent upon their plan.

'You coming?' Matt said.

'Oh, not me, I'm stony broke!' Will replied, glad of an excuse. He was much too taken up with Honor to wish to spend an evening on any dance floor that did not include her.

'Nonsense,' Matt returned stoutly, 'I'll lend you some. You're getting much too serious, you've been a bit of a dark horse ever since you got back from hospital!'

'Perhaps he's hiding something!' Jim said. 'Maybe he's met a little floozy, a bit on the side!'

'Don't be ridiculous,' Will countered quickly, glancing across at Andrew. 'I suppose I'll come if there's another car going.'

He was thinking about her, as usual, when he set off for his routine 'circuits and bumps' the next day. Flight Lieutenant Baker seemed to have become bored with him, from which he assumed his progress to be tolerable, and most of his tuition had fallen to Sergeant Davies, a short, muscular man with a Welsh accent who was rumoured to be one of the best rugby players in the RAF.

'Get it up, Fordham, nice and easy, then round she goes, you know how, don't you, boyo, then bring her back. Always keep on top of her, like you would a woman, don't let her be havin' any ideas of her own!'

Will's flying was improving, there was no doubt about that. He had almost recovered from the interruption to his training, and often found that he knew what to do instinctively. The March weather would soon be upon them, and he longed for the first signs of spring, if only to feel a bit warmer in the air. He finished his flight, and came into land, taxiing to dispersal to be met by Matt, who was waiting for him by his own plane.

'Good news, old boy, we've got you a lift! Florence thinks she can borrow one of the NAAFI vans tomorrow night so we'll all go to Leicester together to celebrate! I'll lend you a fiver, there you go.'

Will smiled back, caught up with his enthusiasm. 'What exactly are we celebrating?'

Matt was quick to answer. 'Life, that's what! And the end of that ruddy test next week!'

7

It was cramped and uncomfortable in the back of the van, which was intended more for the transportation of beverages than the young airmen who were squashed inside. Florence's driving had not improved and the van lurched uncertainly around corners and further into the ditch than was strictly necessary.

'Won't she get into trouble for taking the van for the night?' Guy said.

'I think Florence can get away with most things!' Jim replied. 'With that face and those legs, even the CO would be a sitting duck!'

They half-fell out of the back of the van when Florence opened the door to release them into night-time Leicester, and more significantly, the Trocadero dance hall. It was filling up quickly, as they stood waiting in the entrance queue. There were plenty of pretty girls around – 'glammed up' as far as was possible with clothes rationing – and an air of pleasant anticipation. Even Will was glad he had come, especially since their uniform clearly singled them out for special recognition in the eyes of the opposite sex.

Once inside, they took up the familiar dance hall positions, with the girls lining the walls waiting for the boys to ask for a dance, or failing that, to dance with each other. The band was good, playing the first of the Glenn Miller tunes from across 'the pond'. England had yet to encounter American servicemen, but some of the music had already arrived and sounded lush and smooth. Matt had lined a pint of beer up for Will, determined that he would have a good time.

'Do you think Florence fancies you?' he asked, looking across at the pert figure who was on the dance floor with Jim.

'Who, me?' Will said, surprised.

'Well, she keeps looking at you!' Matt rejoined. 'I'm sure she does, old thing, maybe you should ask her for a dance!'

Will looked awkwardly across the room. Beyond Florence, he saw a group of girls, one of whom he vaguely recognised. He thought for a brief, agonising moment that Honor might be there, maybe with some nurses from Groby Road! He scanned the far wall, but there was no sign of her.

'So, don't you think you owe me a dance?' Florence was back, her face lifted attractively to his. 'Especially after I saved you from the hospital and drove you home!'

'And half-near killed me on the way!' Will took her arm and led her on to the dance floor, where she put her hand on his shoulder for the waltz.

'You're not a bad dancer!' Florence commented. 'And don't you dare say I can dance better than I can drive, or I'll hit you!'

Will noticed that she moved a little closer to him, and he put his arm more firmly around her waist. Gliding past the group of girls he had seen earlier, he noticed one of them looking intently at him, but try as he might, he could not place her. He steered Florence back to the waiting group.

'Oh, you make a lovely pair!' Matt teased him loudly. 'I suppose that's it for the rest of us, eh, Florence?'

Andrew came to the rescue. 'Nonsense, I'm sure Florence will do me the honour of a dance!' he said, leading her back to the floor.

Will drew his breath.

'What's up?' Matt said.

'I'll tell you later.'

Matt, laughing, clapped him on the back and said, 'Well, I've been wondering when you would!'

Andrew returned with a now-breathless Florence, who looked over at Will. 'I'm boiling!' she announced. 'Time to stand down and have a drink. Might even go for a breath of fresh air, if anyone would like to take me?'

In the moment's pause that followed, it was Matt who took the initiative. 'Oh, come on, old thing.' He put a hand under her elbow and guided her to the bar. 'You're not safe with either of those two, you know.'

Andrew watched them depart. 'That was close.'

'It's worse than you think,' Will added. 'I'm sure some of Honor's friends are here. I hope I haven't been spotted!'

'Well, I can't say you were egging her on, but Florence does tend to snuggle up a bit!' Andrew said.

'I don't think that will help in my defence!' The concern was evident in Will's face. 'What if Honor hears I'm larking around with another girl? Honestly, Andrew, she's not the sort to take it lightly.'

'Time to cut and run, old chap?'

8

It was Matt who was the last to return, waking Will, who was always the lightest sleeper in the bungalow, as he did so.

'What's up, you're late! What time is it?' Will opened his eyes cautiously.

'I've been with Florence,' Matt replied, a blank expression on his face.

Will, making a conscious effort to wake up, sat up in bed. 'And...?'

'And?' echoed Matt. 'And,' he repeated with emphasis, 'she's a bit of a corker. You missed out there, I can tell you.' He lapsed into his reverie, leaving Will to conclude that there had been a certain momentum to events for which Matt had been unprepared.

'Was it good?' Will could not resist a smile. Matt blew out his cheeks expressively and raised his eyebrows in response.

There was a pause, one of those shared by friends who understand that not all emotions require words. Matt shook his head, like a shaggy dog who has jumped out of a river and needs to dry off.

'What was it you were going to tell me, earlier on?' he asked.

Will pulled the covers up under his chin. 'I've met a girl,' he said, before turning over to go back to sleep.

'Oh, is that all?' Matt replied. 'That makes us quits!'

They had not been celebrating after the event, but before it, as their exam was on the following Monday morning. Fortunately this gave them time to recover from the excesses of the evening, though Will began to wonder if Matt would ever be quite the same again. He seemed to have a permanently vacant smile upon his face, as though he was deep in a pleasant and engrossing reverie. Even the thought of the forthcoming test did not appear to threaten his bonhomie. However, after two hours of gruelling and occasionally mystifying exam questions, particularly in the navigation paper, none of them felt there was anything to smile about, and even Matt looked downcast.

'Oh my God, that was awful!' Guy said. He was reckoned to be the most intelligent of their group since Dick had left, so the others held out little hope that they could have passed. Will had tried his best to wrestle with the set problems and had at least been studying hard, but Jim, for once, was silent as they filed out of the examination room.

'I can't see how I could possibly have got through!' Andrew said. 'Do you think we'll have a chance to resit?'

There was a collective sense of despair, which continued through the afternoon. Will's instructor was far from sympathetic.

'What's up, boyo, brassed off about the test? Well, get this bloody machine up and see if you can stroke some life out of her! No good moping, now, is it? You're not going to die, are you? If you think that's stressful you should try having a bloody Messerschmitt up your arse! Now get out there and do some climbing turns for me!'

An unaccustomed patch of spring sunlight lit up the Leicestershire fields and neat hedges. Will put in the turns, pulling the plane level before it stalled, then banking steeply up into the next one. The air felt light and unsubstantial; he was, after all, just a boy in a flying machine, and for a moment, the perils of the war, the exams and all that went with it, seemed far away.

Guy was immersed in the newspaper when he returned to the mess.

'What's the latest?'

'Not good,' Guy said. 'Deutsches Afrika Korps moving into pole position in the desert.'

'I thought that was an Italian show?' Will asked. It was tricky to understand the war in North Africa; he had assumed the Italians to be in retreat after the Allied successes at Tobruk and Benghazi.

'Not any longer, they've called in the German tank corps to get themselves out of trouble,' Guy replied succinctly. 'Chap called Rommel pulling all the punches now, God help us!'

Desford

3rd March 1941

Dear You,

I had a horrible exam today and expect I've well and truly failed! We'll get the results tomorrow so thought I'd write while I am still a serving member of His Majesty's forces!

When is your next day off? I'd like to take you out into the countryside, to visit a farm. What do you say? It would do you good to get some fresh air. Andrew will lend me the car, like last time.

I hope you are getting used to the new ward, and not minding being on days.

From Me

9

Honor looked at the letter briefly and stuffed it in the pocket of her starched white apron. She had just come from the ward having finished a gruelling day shift, during which nothing seemed to go right. It had all started with Simon. He had been vomiting because of his heart failure, and the Coramine appeared to be of little beneficial effect. She had been struggling to tidy him up before the ward round, but what with the raised foot of the bed, his frightened eyes, and the vomit that had soaked through everything, progress was slow. Before she was anywhere near ready, they had arrived at the foot of his bed and she could feel the wave of disapproval before Sister's wrath descended upon her.

'Haven't you learnt anything yet?' Sister pushed her roughly aside and motioned Nurse Wilson to take the other side of the bed. The two women competently removed, folded and tucked the clean sheets, hardly seeming to touch the troubled child as they did so.

'Lambeth, that's where you came from?' Sister could barely conceal her contempt. 'You wouldn't have lasted long changing sheets on my ward, I can tell you!'

Honor stood chastened, unaware of the young doctor who was looking at her with sympathy in his eyes. The round moved on, leaving Honor to bundle up the soiled linen and take it to the sluice. She vowed not to cry, whatever Sister might throw at her. Any expression of weakness would be further exploited. Taking a deep breath, she plunged the sheets in to soak, and ventured out on to the ward again. Mercifully they were all busy with the child with pharyngeal paralysis, but from the looks on their faces all was not going well there either. Honor knew that once the diaphragm became involved, there would be nothing that could be done to save the boy, as he would not be able to breathe. There were worse things in life than being shouted at by Sister.

The child's condition deteriorated during the day and it looked as though he would not have long to live. Why had she ever thought she could make a good nurse? She began to wish she was in the Land Army, like her sister; at least she would be out in the fresh air, growing food for a hungry nation and not having to watch children suffer and die.

Nurse Wilson appeared by her side as she was setting up a glucose drip. 'Are you managing that?'

'I think so,' Honor replied hesitantly, looking up as Nurse Wilson checked the bag.

'Yes, that's good,' she said, in an undertone. 'Don't take what Sister says too much to heart. Her bark is worse than her bite, you know.'

After a dispiriting shift, Honor walked slowly back to the hut.

Addie was already there, deep in conversation with June. They stopped talking as soon as she came in.

'Hello,' said Addie, in that peculiar tone reserved for those who are pretending not to have been discussing another. 'You look tired, had a bad day?'

'Awful!' Honor kicked off her regulation black shoes and rubbed her feet. 'What are you two talking about? Not me, I hope!'

'Oh, nothing,' June responded, too quickly for truth.

'Go on, you'd better tell me,' Honor sighed. 'I can see there's something up, I'd rather know what it is. It's not Beatie, is it? I was going to try and see Matron later, have you heard anything?'

'No, it's not Beatie.' Addie spoke reluctantly. 'Look, you'd better know – one of the probationers went out to a dance in Leicester the other night. Says she saw your beau.'

'Oh,' replied Honor. 'How did she know it was him?'

'She'd been on a shift on men's medical, when he was first admitted. She's pally with June, you see, they were chatting, and she said she'd seen him at the dance.' Addie paused. 'He was with another girl.' She looked uncomfortable, not wishing to be the bearer of bad news.

Honor took off her apron, feeling the letter inside as she did so. 'Are you sure?' she asked.

'I hear they looked pretty cosy on the dance floor,' June chipped in. 'More than that, I wouldn't like to say! Gosh, is that the time?' she exclaimed, looking briefly at her watch. 'I must dash, promised to meet Jenny in the canteen!'

There was silence between the two girls after she had left.

'Look, I'm sorry,' Addie ventured. 'Maybe it's nothing, but we didn't want you to get led up the garden path.' It had been June's idea, telling Honor, but Addie could not bear to see her stricken face.

Honor shook her head. She had been so worried about losing Will to the war, it had never occurred to her that she could lose him to another woman.

'Well, I was bound to find out sometime. Now, are you coming with me to Matron's office or not?'

9th March 1941
Groby Road Hospital
Dear You,
I would have enjoyed a day in the countryside but are you sure you can fit it in between going to dances in Leicester?

Thank you for enquiring about my new ward. I am managing perfectly well.

From Me

10

Will soon located the flat, regular Nissen huts and began with an initial circuit, not too low. He had planned to keep it simple, but thought he might just put in a spin for effect. He levelled out high and straight, executed a beautiful left spin over the morning city, pulling out quickly as before, two turns only, regaining the lift with his anti-spin manoeuvres after about half a turn. He was out and level, and feeling calmer.

There was little time to think about her that afternoon as he stood in front of the noticeboard, anxiously scanning the pass list. His eye scrolled downwards – Dixey, Evans, Ewebank – his heart lurching until he found Fordham, on the next line, the comforting typescript of a survivor, in black letters, so small as to seem insignificant, so important as to hold the key to the next stage of his life. Such was his sense of relief that he moved away without registering more. He was joined by Guy.

'That was too close by half!' Guy said. 'Did you see the pass rate? Only about a third of us made it!'

'What about the others?'

'Matt and Jim both failed, Andrew got through! Looks like our late-night tutorials were of some use after all.'

'Oh God!' Matt groaned, walking towards them. 'What the hell will happen to me now? I just love flying, I can't live without it!'

Jim came up, looking equally appalled. It had never occurred to this cocky young man that he might meet any serious obstacles.

'We've got to go to the tutorial room, you and me, find out our fate. I hope they don't send me off to be a bomb-aimer or gunner, I'm not having that!' Jim was rapidly switching into confrontational mood.

Guy did not like to point out that Jim might have little choice in the matter, as the two young men left together for the teaching rooms.

'Good luck!' shouted Will after them, and Matt waved his hand without looking back.

'Well, they can't throw two thirds of the group off the course, they'll have no bloody pilots left!'

Andrew's loyalty was one of his great strengths. The following day, after classes, he handed Will a small brown paper package.

'What is it?'

'Oh, you know Radley – he has friends in high places! I'm afraid I had to tell him about your little problem, but he was very kind. He remembered Florence's overtures at the dance, you see. Said she was like a bitch in full heat, but I wouldn't dream of being so rude! Anyway we've all got to be careful now she and Matt are an item. Hugh said the stockings are on him, just make sure you use them to full advantage!'

Will raised his eyebrows, conscious that even a pair of silk stockings might not bring Honor round, but it would be worth a try.

'You're a real pal!' He clapped Andrew on the back. 'Thanks for that, and tell Hugh I owe him a pint! I'll borrow the car tonight, if that's all right, drop them by to her straight away!'

Desford

14th March 1941

Dear You,

Just dropped these off for you at the porter's lodge; thought they might come in handy!

Please don't draw the wrong conclusions about the dance – I was dragged along against my better judgement. As it happens, I left early with Andrew, the one who lends me the car, so nothing went on that you need to worry about, whatever your friend might have thought.

What about that day out in the country? I would love to see you. Please ring Desford 215, any time after four, and we can sort things out.

Looking forward to hearing from you.

From Me

11

Honor arrived on the ward the next morning to find the curtains closed around Simon's bed. Nurse Wilson touched her gently on the sleeve as she walked past.

'He didn't make it, I'm afraid. His heart failure just got worse, the Coramine couldn't hold it.'

Honor looked silently back at her. She had known that it would be like this on a diphtheria ward, one sad death after another. It was such a waste of a young life – what had Simon done to deserve it, any more than Maisie?

'Did his parents get here?'

Nurse Wilson shook her head. 'They were too late,' she replied. 'Not their fault, we should have contacted them earlier. They had problems getting in at the last minute, something to do with the other children.' Both nurses knew that bedside vigils were not a part of a fever ward, for relatives could only gaze helplessly from the glass window at the end of the ward, not much solace for a dying child.

'Sister's a bit edgy again,' Nurse Wilson murmured, hardly moving her lips. 'I'll try and keep you away from her – may be best if you go straight to the sluice and start to sterilise the instruments for the day. You'll be safer out of the way for a bit.'

Honor needed no further encouragement and scuttled off down the ward.

She was still busy in the sluice, fully gowned and removing the scalding instruments with a pair of tongs, when one of the junior doctors came quietly in. He was the same young man who had looked upon her with sympathy the day before, unnoticed by her or anyone else. A shy young man with a very fair complexion and straw-coloured hair, he had a gentle, almost vulnerable face.

'I just wondered if you were all right?' he said very softly, surprising her so that she nearly dropped the tongs. She looked up, frowning.

'I thought Sister gave you a rough time yesterday.' He was anxious to explain himself.

'I probably deserved it,' Honor replied resignedly. 'Couldn't even make Simon comfortable without messing him about. Not that it makes much difference now, poor little chap.' She turned her face away, gazing intently at the instruments. There was a pause.

'Well, you tried your best,' the young man said. 'I'm always getting bawled out for something or another. Some days I just can't put a foot right!' There was a momentary conspiratorial smile between them, after which he gave the briefest of fleeting winks, and walked off, leaving Honor in some doubt as to the purpose of his conversation. Still, at least he was trying to be kind, which was more than she could reasonably expect from Sister.

Hurrying late to her midday break, she was stopped by one of the porters.

'There's a package for you, miss,' he said in a confidential tone, 'at the porter's lodge, left by that RAF chap. Dropped it in himself, he did, said I was to make sure you got it today.'

Honor stood still for a moment, flushed with uncertainty. A package, for her, from him?

'Oh, thank you, I'll come after my shift.'

'You do that, miss, it'll be safe with me,' the porter replied. Her startled look had not escaped him. The porters knew everything that was going on in the hospital, watching as they did the comings and goings, admissions, discharges, the undertaker's van – there was very little that they missed. He had taken a personal shine to Honor, remembering her excited face the night the airman brought her back. He hoped that nothing was amiss – those boys, flying for king and country, were some of the best. Not that they could all to be trusted with girls, though he would lay a fiver on this one being the right sort.

The afternoon and evening on the ward seemed endless. Even with the best efforts of Nurse Wilson, Honor could no longer avoid Sister, who looked sharply at her at every opportunity, even when they were tending to the child whose breathing had become so critical.

'What will happen to her?' Honor asked her mentor, as they drew away from the end of the bed.

Nurse Wilson looked resigned. She had seen it all before, every complication of diphtheria that there could be had manifested itself to her over the years. She no longer railed against it like Honor did. That would just consume valuable energy, for there was little she could do to change the inexorable course of the disease. Either a child was going to make it, or not, and it was her duty to be as good and competent a nurse as she could be, to cherish the child in its last moments, or in its recovery.

'Well, you can't really treat respiratory paralysis unless you ventilate mechanically,' she answered.

'What does that mean?'

'You have to push air in and out of their lungs until they are able to do it for themselves again,' Nurse Wilson elaborated. 'That means either a bag and mask with someone inflating it for every breath, or a contraption like an iron lung.'

'So will she go in an iron lung?' Honor said.

'No, we reserve them for the polio cases,' Nurse Wilson replied. 'There are so few of them, they can really only be used for that. It's certain death for them otherwise, and once the paralysis subsides they can breathe for themselves again. Some of them make a good recovery. But diphtheria is usually much more complicated. You can't put a diphtheria case in an iron lung.'

Honor had not yet nursed on a polio ward, or seen an iron lung in action, apart from cleaning round one once in the Lambeth hospital. She was about to ask more when Sister came up.

'Nurse Newson, Matron wishes to see you in her office,' she barked. 'You're to go now, and I doubt you'll be back before your shift ends. I'm sure we can manage without you!' She dismissed her with a peremptory wave of her hand.

'Come in!'

Matron surveyed the young woman in front of her. Newson looked tired, no doubt about that. She was bound to respect her steadfastness, not giving up on her friend, and wondered how she would take the news.

'I've heard from the hospital about Nurse Molesworth.'

Honor looked up, prepared for the worst.

'Her bone marrow biopsy,' Matron continued, 'shows that there is some recovery of immature blast forms.'

'What does that mean?' Honor asked. It was the second time today that people were speaking in words she did not understand. It was like a foreign language all of its own.

'It means,' Matron said, 'that she will probably live.'

Groby Road Hospital
20th March 1941
Dear You,
Thank you for the silk stockings, where ever did you get them?

I must say that a day out in the fresh air sounds nice. I am off duty all next Friday, what about you?

It will be a good chance to talk.

From Me

12

For late March, it was an extraordinarily warm day. For the first time, Honor did not need to draw the rug around her as they motored through the quiet country lanes to the farm. She had been overwhelmingly relieved to see him, and he had stood back, holding her hand, as though to make sure that she was really there. They had spoken little in the car, but once out in the open countryside he pulled in at farm gate and switched off the engine. He turned to face her.

'I need to talk to you before we get to the farm.' His voice was earnest and she listened, her solemn eyes following him. 'I don't know what you heard about the dance,' he continued, 'and I'm not really sure I want to. You'll have to trust me, Honor, I'm just not that sort!'

She sighed and looked at him. 'I didn't think you were.'

'Right, that's settled then.' He leant across to take her in their first real embrace.

It was some time before she disentangled herself, painfully aware for the first time of the strength of her feelings for this boy. She had never really wanted anyone before; in fact most of her encounters had been quite the opposite. Yet this one, this one… what was it about his soft lips and gentle touch that could make her feel so alive?

'That's enough, we've got a farm to visit, haven't we?'

He had telephoned Mr Bradley the day before, and as he drove up into the farmyard he saw the tractor waiting outside. Will politely opened the car door for Honor and she stepped down. She still looked lovely, more simply dressed on this occasion in sweater, slacks, and sensible shoes, her usual off-duty clothes. He knocked at the open farmhouse door.

'Come in, lad.' Mr Bradley was washing his hands at the sink. 'I could have done with you ten minutes ago, one of my best cows in calf and not a soul in the place!' He reached out his hand and shook Will's warmly. 'So this is the lass, is it?'

'Yes, this is Honor. She's a nurse at Groby Road Hospital,' Will replied, noticing how shy Honor looked in these unfamiliar surroundings.

'A nurse, eh? Very nice too, me duck, and pleased to meet you.' He was joined by Mrs Bradley, her kind, creased face drawn into a wide smile.

'Hello, my dears, I've got the kettle on waiting, would you like a cup of tea?'

They sat round the scrubbed kitchen table, sipping sweet tea and eating Mrs Bradley's shortbread. Honor thought it was the most delicious combination, crumbly, sweet biscuit and strong, proper tea. Much better than the awful brew they served up in the hospital canteen.

'How are things on the farm?' Will enquired, taking his second piece from the proffered plate.

'Oh, can't grumble, nice to see some decent weather at last, get the growing season underway. We're a bit low on help – one of the girls had to leave, crisis in the family – so we're down to five. Still, they're hard workers, I'll give them that. I've got some overalls ready for you – it's going to be a busy day and I can't afford to waste a strong young man around the place!' Mr Bradley smiled and winked at Honor.

'Sounds good to me!' Will said. Then, turning purposefully to Mrs Bradley, 'Any news of your sons?'

She shook her head. 'Only what we hear on the newsreels,' she replied. 'That Rommel seems to be making life very difficult for them all: once he's on the attack, they just lose all the ground they've made. It's so difficult not to think about them all the time. I keep wondering about the heat – it must be hard for all our boys, stuck out there in the dust and the flies…' Her voice tailed off and she looked across to her husband. 'Alf says not to worry, don't you, dear? That they'll be right as rain, the two of them.'

'That I do,' said Mr Bradley forcefully. 'Good strong boys like that, take more than a few panzer tanks to stop them! Still, all folks will worry, that's only natural till they're home safe and sound. Have you got any brothers, Honor?'

It was a question she had been asked before. 'No, I'm one of three girls,' she replied, already anticipating the answer.

'Your poor father!' Mr Bradley clapped the table with his hand, only to be interrupted by his wife.

'There, don't take any notice of him. I wish I could have had three daughters as well as my boys, I'd be in seventh heaven! Would you like to help me with the cheesemaking while they're in the fields, my dear? I need to skim the whey this morning, it's for our Red Leicester cheese.'

Honor was delighted to be involved with anything to do with food. Will gave her a little kiss on the cheek and squeezed her hand – 'See you later' – and left, pulling on some capacious overalls.

Mrs Bradley watched them go. 'It's kind of him to come back, it'll take the old man's mind off his troubles,' she confided in Honor. 'Such a nice young man, and what a pair you make! He looks awfully fond of you, dear.'

'Oh, do you think so?' Honor was surprised. She had become so unsure about his feelings over the business of the dance, and even though it was bliss to be with him again and see his honest face, her habitual guard was up. 'I expect there's lots of girls after him,' she added doubtfully.

Mrs Bradley looked at the girl's young face, remembering as though it was yesterday all of her own longings for Alf, when he was only just out of his teens, and she a new milkmaid on the farm. One of several, and to her eyes, all the others were more beautiful than her.

'Oh, I shouldn't worry about that,' she replied authoritatively. 'Sometimes you just find the right person, don't you, and that's that. He doesn't look the sort to play around, and remember, he's lucky to have found a nice girl like you. Now, if one of my sons was to bring you home, wouldn't I be pleased!'

Honor smiled. 'You're very kind,' she said shyly.

'Nonsense, anyone can see you're in love with each other. I don't think you need to doubt him, dear, that's just losing valuable time. I wish you both happiness!' She paused, her eyes suddenly filling with tears. 'Just don't let this wretched war get in the way! Now, time for the dairy!'

Honor was so engrossed with her morning's task that she hardly noticed when Will came in, well past noon. She was dressed in a large white apron, methodically skimming the whey from the vats before separating it into the cloth-lined strainers. It was such soothing work, no one to shout at you or frighten you into making mistakes. If only every morning could be like this, she mused, as she felt him touch her on the sleeve. She looked up quickly to meet his eyes.

'So what have I got now, milkmaid or nurse?' he teased her gently.

She put her head on one side. 'I don't know, which do you prefer?'

'Do you know, I'd take you in any mortal shape or form!' he returned, to be rewarded with a dab of cheese curd on his nose. He ducked. 'Enough! You win!'

Mrs Bradley joined them. 'Come on, time for dinner. Let's hear what you think of the farm.'

13

'It's a complete balls-up!' Guy said, hardly lifting his eyes from the *Daily Mail*.

'What is?'

'Greece, of course!'

Will was not entirely clear about unfolding events in the Mediterranean. There was just so much to do, learning to fly and passing exams, that it seemed as though the war was a separate existence, running along in parallel to his own.

'The Italians are the root of the problem.' Guy warmed to the theme. 'Mussolini is set upon creating his own empire, mad fascist that he is, so first he invades Abyssinia, then moves on to Egypt last September, and into Greece from Albania in October.'

Will nodded, trying to give the impression that he had some idea where all these countries were. Actually, he was quite good at geography at school;

it was just that he could find himself a bit hazy over all those little countries of Europe. Now, where exactly was Albania? Must be somewhere between Italy and Greece, he supposed.

'Look, here's the map.' Guy pushed the open newspaper towards him. Will looked, as if comprehending for the first time, at the dotted lines showing the sphere of Italian influence, across the Mediterranean Sea to Greece, downwards past Crete to Northern Africa: Egypt and Libya, noticing the strategic cities, Athens, Cairo, Tripoli, Tunis, and the island of Malta.

'Go on,' said Will.

'Then, just when we should be booting him out of Libya once and for all, we decide to pull some troops out of North Africa into Greece, so we can help the Greeks get rid of him. Meanwhile, he calls on his nasty friends in Germany who send Rommel in to back him up in Libya, and then look what happens! Bloody mayhem! Next thing we know we're on the defensive, having to give up all we've gained!'

'Sounds a bit of a mess!'

'Too right, it is – Rommel's unstoppable, and now God knows what's going to happen to our blokes in Greece!'

'What a bloody way to spend a morning,' Matt said as he and Jim came out of the resit. 'I'm off to meet my instructor and get some decent flying in. If I've failed again, I'm going to kill myself!'

Jim shook his head, and tried to put it to the back of his mind. He, too, was at his best flying, though he was a different pilot to Matt, less natural, but more aggressive. He flew his plane as one would an unbroken horse, stretching it to submission by sheer force of will. He revelled in the gunnery training, and was a good shot, having been a clay pigeon enthusiast prior to joining up. Of them all, only Jim was able to strip down a machine gun in the dark and name all the parts. There was no streak of pacifism in his nature; unlike the gentle Andrew, he would happily strafe his way through as many Germans as he could. He longed to be in the cockpit of a fighter plane, pursuing the enemy until he could put a round of bullets 'up their arse', and was quite frankly fed up with all the barriers that the RAF seemed to have in place to stop him doing precisely that.

One other point of dissatisfaction for Jim was his failure to find a girl. He had tried his luck on various fronts: there were some lookers amongst the WAAF girls, and the dance had been promising. He just kept being rebuffed, though he had no idea why. Damn it, all the others seemed to be hitched up, apart from Andrew, and he did not count! Clearly Fordham had seized his opportunities on the fever ward, and even Matt, who appeared to him to be completely clueless, had nabbed Florence. What he wouldn't give for a slice of action like that! Perhaps Fordham could fix him up with one of the other nurses; he'd be more than willing to go on a blind date, especially if it led to some proper sex, not just lovey-dovey kisses and longing. The last thing he wanted was love, or anything to do with it; in fact, sometimes he was not even sure what it was.

The airfield was full of activity. An improving weather situation, with some warm spring days, meant that every possible hour could be given to flying. Most of the trainees were becoming competent Tiger Moth pilots, able to handle the flimsy machines, throw them around the sky when asked to, and return them safely to base. It would soon be time for decisions about the next stage of their training.

Much of this was done informally in The Bell of an evening, when the instructors would sit over a pint or two of beer, and discuss their charges. The key question at this point was whether a given pilot would go on to single or twin-engine training. Single engines meant the pilot would be destined for fighters; twin engines for bombers. Once the decision was taken, there would be no going back, nor did the trainees themselves play any part in the process. Some of the outcomes were predictable, for example, Matt's instructor had no doubts that he should go on to fighter training.

Andrew's instructor felt the same. The flight sergeant was an experienced man, and had long ceased to notice Andrew's Byronic demeanour, once he had realised how well he could handle the DH82 in the air.

'Are you sure he's tough enough?' one of his colleagues asked meaningfully.

'Yes, I've no problems with him, he handles the plane beautifully, should be able to fly himself in and out of trouble without thinking about it.'

'And Alderdice?' They all looked at one another and his instructor raised his eyebrows.

'What can I say? He's such a cocky bugger, but he's tough and decisive. Just the sort of bastard the Air Force needs on a bad day. He'll be for single engines.'

They supped their beer, silent in their agreement.

'So, what about Fordham?' It was Davies' turn to ask, in his lilting Welsh accent.

'He's a steady, responsible young man. Good pilot, thoughtful and measured, gets respect from the other men. I'm for putting him on to twin engines.'

There was a murmur of assent.

'And Clarkson?' Guy's fate was on the line. How would the young men have felt, had they known that their futures were being thus decided?

His instructor spoke up. 'More of the same,' he pronounced. 'A good, mature pilot, got over a bad start, gradually built up confidence. He's a sticker, and he'll carry a crew through a long raid. He's for bombers, I think we'd all agree.'

'That's it then, gentlemen, time for another round, I reckon.' With which the flight sergeant broke off, and went to the bar to ask Rose to fill up their glasses, for they were thirsty men, and it was going to be a long war.

14

Two large forces buses were waiting to transport them to the municipal swimming pool in Leicester.

'Got your togs, everyone?' Flight Lieutenant Lang called down the bus, to which there was a shout of general assent.

'Pity it's not mixed bathing today, sir!' someone piped up, amongst the general excitement.

The buses made their way through the open countryside. There was no doubt about it, spring was on the way and the April fields were becoming greener by the day. The recent showers had abated and the roads were drying in the clear air. Once in the city, apart from a brief halt at a roadblock, they soon disembarked outside St Margaret's baths.

'Right, you lot, straight in and line up at the poolside.'

The instructors had spent some time outlining the dinghy drill to the group: it would involve getting the lads into the water in their life jackets, or 'Mae Wests', fully clothed, then dinghy inflation and paddling it around the pool. It was nothing like real life: in the North Sea, many of the blokes died of hypothermia once they ditched, unless they could get into a dinghy pretty sharpish. One of the requirements for entry to training was an ability to swim, but of course this varied hugely from boy to boy – some were school swimming champions and others barely able to make it to the end of the pool. The instructors knew from previous experience that the whole exercise would be likely to degenerate into a soggy free-for-all, and could not easily contain the high spirits of their charges. Still, it had to be done, and if it had the potential to save a life or two, then it was worth it. Of course it was one thing being adrift in a dinghy, and quite another to get picked up. At that stage of the war, this would depend upon some passing vessel as there was no air-sea rescue in place. There was a limit to how long a frozen, exhausted airman, with nothing but emergency rations, could float about in a small dinghy and still survive.

They lined up at the poolside, shoes off but otherwise in light clothing and life jackets. The water looked uninviting and the pool was lined with stark white Victorian tiles.

'Off you go!'

Will looked at the others, some of whom were already shivering in anticipation. Will had been a good swimmer at school, and was used to the bracing temperature of the open-air baths. In the summer, he would swim in the sea, where the dramatic North Yorkshire coastline permitted, and had favourite spots, like Robin Hood's Bay, where he and a few chums would bicycle miles to spend a day in summer tousling with the waves in a churning sea.

He took a deep breath, and jumped. It was cold, and he felt weighed down by his clothes, but he had passed his lifesaving tests at school, so was not unfamiliar with the sensation. He struck out to one of the dinghies, which had already been inflated by the first boy to reach it, and hauled himself in.

'Christ, that was cold.' Guy came alongside, and he reached out a friendly hand to pull him in. They sat dripping in the dinghy, while the other swimmers tugged on the ropes. Andrew was next, then Johnstone and some other lads from his group.

'Hey, room for me?' The burley Radley approached, swimming unsteadily with an uneven stroke. He looked uncertain, a shadow of his usual jocular self, gulping mouthfuls of water unintentionally as he came towards them.

'Get him in!' Andrew's voice was urgent. 'He doesn't like water, can't swim that well!'

Will and Guy leant over the side to pull him in but Hugh's dead weight was more than they anticipated, and before they knew it, the whole dinghy had capsized and its occupants were either underneath, or swimming to the surface. Will, close to the side, came up for air and surveyed the scene. He had better make sure they were all safe, despite the shouts and laughter. His wretched lifejacket was in his way, slowing his progress, so he wrenched it off and surface-dived below the dinghy to investigate. He was right! Radley was spread-eagled, motionless, with the dinghy on top of him. Will tried to push the dinghy away, but it was too heavy, and he was beginning to despair before another strong swimmer was at his side. It was Guy, and together they flipped the dinghy over, turned Radley, and started to pull him to safety.

'Hugh!' Andrew leapt back into the water.

The three of them managed to manoeuvre him to the edge. By now the instructors were running round to help, and he was manhandled on to the side.

'Hugh!' Andrew was beside himself. 'Help him, someone, help him, he's not breathing!'

Guy and one of the instructors pushed Radley over on to his front and started to pump the water from his lungs.

'Oh my God, he's dead!'

'Shut up, Farrington, he'll be fine.' Lang was curt, and true to his word, Hugh coughed and groaned, coughed some more, spluttered and started to breathe. They let him recover a little before shifting him on to his side. Andrew retreated to the wooden bench at the poolside, where he sat with his head in his hands, then, collecting himself, began vigorously to towel his hair, as though to deflect unwanted attention.

The instructor shook his head. 'Well, lads, that's not quite what I had in mind, but hats off for getting him out. Take him over to the changing room and get him dried off, once he's OK to walk.'

He returned to his colleagues. 'I thought they were all able to swim!' he said crossly. 'How did that happen?'

'Someone slipped up on his entry papers?'

'Slipped up? More likely one of Daddy's friends circumvented the process! Best get the whole lot back to base, before we have any more disasters! If this is what it's like in the swimming pool, God help them when they get into the North Sea!'

15

The chief flying instructor, Flight Lieutenant Howes, took Will's logbook and checked through all of the entries. They had just spent more than two hours together in the air, during which Will had to demonstrate every manoeuvre he had so far mastered in the DH82, from take-off to forced landings, low flying, aerobatics and spinning. Will's aptitude and skills during the appraisal were noted by Howes, as were his total flying hours to date, thirty-two hours dual and thirty-four solo. It was April 8th, and an unusually sunny, if cold, spring day.

The blue ink from Howes' pen underscored his above average proficiency as a pilot, followed by the signature that would be the key to Will's future.

Howes closed the log. 'How do you feel about going on to the Oxford?'

'To be honest, sir, I was hoping for single engines. I wanted to be a fighter pilot, you see, not a bomber pilot.'

The chief flying instructor looked at him. The conversation was familiar to him, for all the men wanted to fly fighters, so romanticised had been the image portrayed during the Battle of Britain. Generally speaking, the best fighter pilots possessed a streak of recklessness which was not apparent in this young man. Fordham looked sensible enough to take responsibility for a crew of five men, with any luck he would be able to keep his head and bring them home when things became tricky. Howes felt that the other instructors had made the right decision.

'I don't know, Fordham, there's a lot to be said for flying bombers, you know. It takes just as much courage as the fighters, more if you think about it, because it's your duty to keep the blokes in your plane out of harm's way. You need to be the right material for that, and we reckon that's what you're best suited for. You'll have to keep your head through some tricky missions, the Germans will hardly be welcoming you lot with open arms!'

'I know, sir,' Will said.

'Well, you won't have too much time to dwell on it, you'll be off to Shawbury next week! Then hopefully by the summer you'll have your wings!'

The coveted wings! Nothing could be more important than that badge, the emblem on your chest that showed you were a pilot, serving in the RAF, in wartime! The very thought of it was enough to concentrate all of their minds.

Events were moving faster than Will had expected. Sometimes it had seemed to him that Desford had become a fixed place in his life, close to friends, familiar locations, and of course, Honor. He had not really thought seriously about having to leave her. Now everything was set to change again, and there would be another unfamiliar set of skills to master, with another band of brothers.

'You can cut back to the teaching block now, get the latest gen on your transfer,' Howes said. 'Good luck, Fordham.'

'Thank you, sir, I'll do my best.'

'I'm sure you will, Fordham. Off you go!' The chief flying instructor watched him leave. Thirty-four hours' solo flying was not really sufficient preparation for conversion to the Oxford twin engine, but there was a war on. Bit of a conveyer belt, he mused, remembering the good old days when the RAF could take its time with novice pilots. There would be no going back to that, or to the gentleman flyers who were looked after in comfortable quarters by old-fashioned mess servants. It was a shifting and evolving era, these keen grammar school lads coming in at one end of their training, then out again in no time.

Howes, like others of his age, had joined the newly formed service between the wars. He had never thought it would all kick off again so soon – so much for the Treaty of Versailles! Meanwhile, the Germans were going from strength to strength, invading Yugoslavia just the day before yesterday! Britain would need all the pilots she could muster, for despite Churchill's rousing words there could be no doubt the odds were against them, on land, sea and sky. How many of these young chaps were going to make it through? He only hoped to God that some of the things they had learnt here would help them survive, for survival would be the name of the game.

Nos morituri te salutamus. The Latin phrase kept creeping unbidden into Will's head as he walked slowly away from his beloved Tiger Moth. It was the Roman gladiators' greeting to Caesar, as he recalled from his Latin primer. *We who are about to die salute you!* It was a step up from the mock Latin phrase invented by the mess: *Nili illegitime carborundum*, or loosely translated, *Don't let the bastards grind you down*!

'Well?' Guy said.

'Oxford twin engines, Shawbury.'

Guy did not attempt to hide his pleasure. 'Great news, old chap, me too! At least there'll be someone there I know!'

'What about the others?'

'Fighters. Different stations, though, can't remember exactly who is going where,' Guy said.

'Looks like it'll be a heavy night in the mess!' Matt joined them. 'I never thought we'd do it! How did I pass that navigation test? If it wasn't for you, Guy, I wouldn't still be here!'

'Nonsense!' Guy smiled back at him. 'Where's your posting, golden boy?'

'Little Rissington, number 6 FTS,' replied Matt proudly. 'Somewhere in Gloucestershire, I think. What about you?'

'Shawbury, up in Shropshire,' Guy replied. 'Will and I have got the same posting, Group 2 training.'

'Lucky devils!' Matt was genuinely envious. 'I wish I had a mate to go with. We've all been split up: Jim is off to South Cerney, which if I remember rightly, is number 3 FTS, but Andrew, of all things, has been posted overseas for the next stage. How the hell did he pull that one off? He says he's off to South Africa!'

'Seriously?' Guy was surprised. 'They don't usually ship us out at this stage, do they?'

Matt shrugged. 'Don't ask me, old chap! I'd give my eye teeth for some nice South African sun. Those Empire training schools sound a bit of all right! Jim will be eating his heart out!'

'So will Radley,' said Guy, sotto voce. 'Speak of the devil, here they come!'

Radley looked solidly pleased with himself, and announced he had been posted to number 8 FTS, Montrose. 'That's a hell of a way off!' he added loudly. 'But not half as far as Cape Town!'

There was a cloud over Andrew's sensitive face. He could never hide his emotions, Will thought. The irony of it all was that he had the most coveted destination, learning to fly in the glorious open veld, following the drifting patterns of the continent and no doubt seeing a host of wonderful new sights. Not that Will was envious, for like Guy, he would rather not leave his girl at the moment, and was content to be posted within reach of her.

'Twin engines for me!' Radley said. 'Then I'll be off to bomb the hell out of the Reich!' Then after a pause, 'Sorry, I know it goes against the grain, Andrew, but there's really no place for pacifism now!'

'Just as long as there's no civilian targets,' replied Andrew, unintentionally taking up the gauntlet. He was relieved he had not been assigned to twin engines, as he was not sure he could square it with his conscience. Killing one armed Luftwaffe pilot was one thing, but innocent women and children would be quite another.

'Seems to me we have to use whatever means we can to stop Hitler in his tracks,' Guy put in seriously. For his part, he deemed it best not to think about the consequences; just to get on with the job in hand. Anyway, it was not as if they would be setting upon these tasks unbidden, and their lords and masters, Trenchard and Harris, would surely take their decisions responsibly, with the ultimate sanction of Churchill himself.

Jim arrived, the last of the group. 'Told you it would be all right!' he declared, uncharacteristically shaking Matt by the hand. Jim looked at Andrew with ill-concealed resentment. 'I hear you've got the jammiest posting of all! What have you done to deserve that?'

Andrew swallowed. 'No idea! All I know is I've got my embarkation papers from Liverpool in two weeks' time, and a whole lot of rotten inoculations lined up first! Not going to be much of a leave, but I should get back to see the folks for a few days.'

'Yes, maybe time for a bit of hunting too!' Hugh added. 'We'll soon fix something up, won't we?'

Will caught Guy's glance, and returned it, like a soft volley over the net in an undemanding match of tennis.

'See you in the bar tonight!' Matt turned to leave. 'I'm off to find Florence first!'

7EFTS Desford
10th April 1941
Dear You,
The good news is I passed all my tests and have been signed off for the next stage of my training!

The bad news is I've been posted to RAF Shawbury, which is in Shropshire, so it won't be so easy for us to meet. Still, it could be worse – one of our lot has been sent to South Africa!

I have a few days' leave and should go back and see the folks up north, but I wondered if there was any chance of seeing you before I go? I could work round your off-duty times, just ring me on Desford 215 as soon as you know.

Hope to see you very soon, then can fill you in on all the details.

From Me

16

He held her hand shyly in the quiet corner of the pub. It was not his local, The Bell, and he would not have wanted to share her with any passing aircrew, no matter how proud of her he might be. He had motored in the other direction from Groby Road, and found a little place in a village nearby. There were very few people in the bar, which suited them both.

'So how's the ward?'

Honor sipped her lemonade shandy. 'I'm getting a bit more used to it,' she admitted, 'but diphtheria is such a dreadful disease, you know. Sometimes we just seem to be watching and waiting while nature takes its course. I wish there was more we could do for them, the little ones are so brave.'

'Yes, I remember those kids on the rheumatic fever ward,' he said. 'It must break your heart when things go wrong.'

'Well, you're meant to be able to stand back from it, but I never can! I get much too involved, then it's even harder in the end…' Her voice faltered, as she remembered Maisie's face.

'And what about your friend?' he ventured.

Honor's face lightened. 'She's getting better!' she replied, as if she could hardly believe it herself. It was true: Beatie had rallied and there was even talk of her being sent home to convalesce next week. For all that Beatie would be thrown off the nursing course, Honor felt sure that she would pick up her life.

'That's good news! You've been worrying about her for ages! What happened to her?' Then he added quickly, 'It's OK, I expect you'd rather not go into it.'

'Can't really. I had a little chat with your friend Andrew on the phone, before he passed you on to me.'

'Oh, did you?' Will was interested. 'What did he say?'

'Just talking about this and that,' she replied. 'Said he was off to South Africa, but didn't sound very keen. He sounds a nice chap.'

'He is,' Will said. 'If it wasn't for lending me his car, I'd have hardly seen you!'

'Why doesn't he want to go?' Honor asked. She could not imagine why a young man would not seize the chance to leave war-torn Britain, to get to a country where there was no rationing, no dark skies, and no ever-present threat of invasion.

'I don't really know. Best not go into it!'

Honor always looked so pretty on their dates, he thought distractedly, though as far as he was concerned it did not matter what she wore. Sometimes he thought she was at her most beautiful in her plain uniform in the dim light of the ward at night, just as he had first seen her.

It was to be their last evening together for some time, but this seemed to inhibit rather than encourage their conversation. He had so many important things to say, but suddenly felt at a loss for words. He took another mouthful of beer, and looked around the bar. The pub was called The Cricketers, and there were faded photographs of the village team in victory over other local sides. It was so quintessentially English, he thought; the teams would be out again playing soon, while lads like him were up in some aeroplane over the night skies, or, like the Bradley boys, trying to survive in hostile arenas miles from home.

She took the initiative. 'I'm going to miss you, you know.'

'Well, it's deeper than that for me, old thing – I'm afraid I'm going to pine! You'll be carrying on as usual, busy and efficient on your ward, forgetting all about me, while there I am, heartbroken in my new aeroplane!'

She nudged him in the ribs. 'Not heartbroken, more ecstatic, I should think! What will it be like to fly?'

'The Oxford, you mean? Well, I don't really know, it's a twin-engine trainer. I expect it'll be just as much trouble as the Tiger Moth was at first.' Now that he was accustomed to the idea, he was looking forward to the next stage, even if it did mean he would end up flying bombers. Better not discuss that one with Honor though, she looked worried enough about him as it was.

As though to read his thoughts, she said, 'Be careful! I don't like to think of it! You're at the top of my worry list now, you know.'

'You'll always be at the top of mine, Honor!' He looked at her, serious now and full of conviction. 'There's nothing more important to me than you in the whole world, you know.'

Her eyes were gentle, almost velvety in return. 'Are you sure?' she asked softly.

'Oh, yes, I'm sure,' he replied, and later in the dark, cold night as he took her in his arms, she knew that he was telling the truth.

Part Five:
Oxford Twin Engines

1

'Bert!' Will's mother turned round rapidly from the pantry as he pushed open the kitchen door. 'You're back! And looking so smart in your uniform!' She stepped forward to take him in her arms, and kiss his shaven cheek. She could hardly believe the transformation of her beloved son into this blue-clad airman, cap on his head at exactly the right angle.

'You look taller!' she exclaimed, standing back to drink him in.

'No, I'm not!' he said. 'I think you've shrunk since I left!'

It was true, his mother looked even more diminutive than ever, her face careworn, but full of pleasure at his presence.

'There, Bert, how could I possibly shrink?' She smiled at her handsome son with pride.

'You work too hard, that's why.' Will sat down at the kitchen table while she made him a cup of tea.

'Have you eaten?' Her question was superfluous in wartime Britain, and he shook his head.

'Not since breakfast.' She brought out one of her soft teacakes and proceeded to cut it into thick slices. He sipped his tea and spread the fruited bread with jam.

He took a large mouthful. 'By, it's good to be home,' he pronounced, lapsing into Yorkshire dialect almost imperceptibly.

'How long have you got?' Her eager face anticipated the heart-wrenching truth that for her, the visit was bound to be too short. Such was the fate of all mothers in her situation, the timeless role of watching and waiting for a safe return. Would she ever be able to stop worrying about him?

'Two days, that's all,' he said. 'I've been posted to Shawbury, so I reckoned I'd better come and see you first.'

'Thank the Lord that you're here and I can look after you! How are you getting on? I worry about you in those planes! Your father'll be interested to hear.'

Will rather doubted that he would, but smiled at his mother affectionately.

'Where is the old man?' he asked.

'Up on the moors, checking his hives. He'll be back soon. John's in the shop. He's on new tablets, extract of thyroid, seems to be doing him good.'

Will recalled how his goitrous brother had suffered so badly with his thyroid gland since he was a child, his prominent eyes a consequence of the hormonal imbalance. There would have been no question of him joining up, with his state of health, and thus he kept the grocery in steady hands, with his father's help.

Will smelt the cured bacon frying in the pan. 'You're spoiling me!' he said. 'Don't use up all your rations!'

'If we can't spare you a couple of rashers of bacon and a fried egg, where would we be?' She would have given him her last morsel, but thanks to the shop and the market garden they were rarely as short of food as some folk. 'Your grandmother will be pleased to see you too,' she added.

'No, she won't,' he said good-humouredly, 'I'll just be a nuisance, as far as she's concerned! I expect she's in her room?'

'Yes, I must take her a cup of tea, it's past her time.' Hannah made up a small tray with great care, ready to climb the stairs with it before the imperious bell would ring. 'I'll tell her you're back, I expect she'll be down later.'

Will rose to open the kitchen door for her, then sat down to finish off his bacon and eggs. He looked around the familiar kitchen as he did so: the white curtains at the lattice windows, immaculately scrubbed kitchen table, and the same smell of honey and frying bacon. It was very good to be home.

The back door opened to reveal his father. 'By, lad, you back already?' The old man looked pleased to see him, for a change. He deposited his wide canvas bag, full of beekeeping equipment, on the floor. 'You look a right RAF type!' he said. They shook hands, further intimacy precluded by the customs of the day.

'Soon be trying for my wings, Father.'

'I should hope so, you've been at it long enough! Your mother misses you, always fretting…' The old man poured himself a cup of tea.

'Grace is in the WRACS, you know, gone training in Aldershot.' His father was devoted to Will's sister. Perhaps it was because she had become a schoolteacher, this plain Yorkshire girl, and was unlikely to find a mate and leave home.

'Yes, I know, Mother wrote to me,' Will said. 'I hope she's getting on all right.'

In fact he hardly gave his sister a second thought, for they had never been close and she seemed to disapprove of what she took to be his general foolhardiness and joie de vivre.

'Aye, she is,' the old man replied, 'and you're getting by, from the looks of it?'

Will anticipated that his father would question him no more, and he was right. The subject was rapidly changed.

'Will you have some time for fishing?'

Now there was a subject that united them, their love of the river. The Esk, a brown, tumbling river, carried some of the best salmon and his father knew all the pools like the back of his hand. Together, they would spend endless hours fishing silently, watching the fish rise, selecting the flies, and helping gaff one another's catch. The old man had passed on to his youngest son all his river lore, and he cherished it, as he did his rod and fishing tackle, given to him whilst still a comparative youngster.

'Yes, Father, if you like, we should be able to get a day in before I go back.'

His mother reappeared, bearing the empty tray. 'She says she'll be down later.'

'Eh, gracing us with her presence, is she?' His father caught his eye and winked. 'I expect she'll want to know you're keeping the pledge, Bert.'

Will felt uncomfortable, particularly in front of his gentle mother. He had never been very good at lying, so ignored the question and took another sip of tea. 'That was a grand egg and bacon.' He kissed his mother's cheek. 'I'll just go and put my bag upstairs, then I suppose I should walk down to the shop, say hello to John.'

'Aye, he'll be pleased to see you,' his father replied. 'Been very busy there, despite the shortages. He's doing a good job.'

'I'm sure he is.' Will picked up his kitbag. 'How's he getting on with that girl of his?'

'He'd best tell you himself,' his mother said, by which Will assumed that his brother's relationship with the solid Mary had progressed in his absence. He thought how little in common Honor would have with Mary – for a start, his girl was so good-looking, and almost worldly, in comparison, and then she had her own nursing career, unlike Mary, who was still at home with her parents.

The shop door jangled as he opened it. His brother was behind the counter, in a brown overall, weighing out rice from a large hessian sack.

'Bert, you're back! Ee, you look different in that uniform!' He came round from behind the counter. 'Excuse me, Mrs Preston, I'll just be a moment,' he added to his waiting customer as he shook his brother by the hand.

'Ay up, the Air Force is here!' Mrs Preston announced. 'My daughter Maureen will be down to see you if I let on you're back, and looking like that!'

'Now don't give her any ideas!' John said. 'I expect he's spoken for long since.'

'Aye, like you,' she replied. 'I hear you're engaged to that Mary Braithwaite.'

Will added his congratulations, though it had to be said that Mrs Preston looked far from pleased. Her unmarried daughter Maureen was headed for a life on the shelf despite her mother's many attempts to marry her off. Mrs Preston would have been content to see her with either of the Fordham lads. Maureen could have helped John in the shop, though Bert was a better catch even if that RAF uniform might put him out of her league. Her daughter should have enlisted, like Grace, plenty of men in the armed forces, and it would have been an easier job than the munitions factory, where she worked long shifts handling hazardous materials.

'Right. I'm off, I'll leave you two to yourselves,' she said, taking the brown paper bags and proffering the correct change. 'Nice to see you, Bert, you're looking well.'

'Half of Guisborough will know you're back by the time she gets home!' John shook his head. 'And that Maureen would be knocking at the door too, if I hadn't said you were spoken for!'

'Well, I am in a way,' Will confided, but they were not close, these two, so he was not pressed to go into further details. John could not help but be jealous of his athletic younger brother: he had excelled at sports while John was often too ill to play. Will might be in the RAF, but that place at university would be waiting for him when he came back. There would be no university for John; it would be the shop that would define his existence in this small Yorkshire market town. Still, there was always the compensation of Mary – she might be homely, but she suited him well.

'How long are you back for?' John said.

'Just a couple of days,' Will replied, 'and I've promised the old man I'll go fishing tomorrow.'

'No chance of you helping out in the shop, then?'

Will shook his head. If he had any precious moments on leave, he meant to spend them up on the moors or over at Robin Hood's Bay. Much as he respected his brother's work, he had no desire to stand in for him. After all, John was not risking his neck in some flimsy aeroplane every day!

At supper that evening he remembered why he had wanted to leave home in the first place. They were round the dining room table, in the dark room lined with sombre furniture. His mother had said grace, giving thanks for his safe return, and reminding them of all the starving people in the world. The 'Empress', his grandmother, sat in her black dress at the table looking for all the world like Queen Victoria, and sounding a little like her as well. She was holding forth about the new Methodist parson.

'He looks very young, Janey, I hope he knows what he's doing.'

'I'm sure he does, Mother', Hannah replied, helping her to potatoes and spring cabbage. Janey had been her family name, but the Empress was the only one still using it.

'How long did you boil the cabbage for?' this august personage enquired of her daughter. It would have been out of the question for the older woman to offer to help in the kitchen: that was Hannah's responsibility, which she shouldered single-handedly.

'Usual time, Mother,' she replied dutifully.

'Well it's a little underdone. Did you put in soda bic?'

'Of course, Mother.' Hannah caught her son's sympathetic eye and smiled at him, wishing he could be with her all the time. His father carved the cold mutton, and put it sparingly on their plates. Not that Will would have wanted any more; cold mutton seemed an endless repast in their house. He resolved, when he had a house of his own, never to eat cold mutton again. He poured himself a glass of water from the jug. John appeared to be enjoying his food.

'That Mrs Horrocks was in today, Father, complaining as usual.'

'What about, son?'

'She said there were mouse droppings in the rice!' John was suitably indignant.

'I hope you put her right,' his father rejoined.

'I did that!' John replied. 'There's never been a mouse anywhere near our shop!'

Will looked up at the ceiling. Yugoslavia might be on the point of surrender but the conversation around this table would never change. He wondered if he might pop out after the meal, and see if any of his friends were around. The clock ticked slowly, in time with his sense of imprisonment.

'What about a game of chess?' the old man said. Will knew he would have to acquiesce, though his father always ran rings around him on the chessboard.

'That'd be nice, Father.' Will glimpsed the look of pleasure in his mother's eyes. He would do anything to please her.

'I'm going to a church meeting tonight,' Hannah said, 'so you and your father can have a quiet game by yourselves.'

'And I'm off courting.' John rose, wiping his mouth on his napkin.

'Don't you want any rice pudding?' his mother asked. She had made an especially good one for Will, with a thick caramel skin on it.

'Sorry, Mother, Mary will be waiting.'

'My, I should think folks would stay until the end of the meal!' the Empress said after he had gone. 'I don't know what the world's coming to – there's Bert off flying aeroplanes, now John out canoodling – they're never at home when they should be!'

'It's all right, Grandmother,' Will said, 'I'm sure John wouldn't know how to canoodle, and anyway, aren't they engaged?'

He was rewarded with a 'humph' from the Empress, as he finished off his rice pudding and settled in for a long evening, moving the cherished wooden pieces around the board until the inevitable checkmate from his father.

14th April 1941

Dear You,

I am on my way to Stoke on a most uncomfortable train. Guisborough was a bit quiet, though it was good to see my mother. I wanted to tell her about you but there was never the right moment. Next time, I'll take you with me so that you can meet them all, if you can bear it!

Andrew wanted me to have his car while he's away, so I am the proud guardian of the Austin. At least it might mean I can get to see you, leave permitting.

Bad news about Belgrade in the paper today. You get the feeling that we are the only country still standing!

Anyway, it seems ages since I saw you, even though it's only a few days! I miss you and hope all is going well. I will write again when I have settled in.

From Me

2

'What do you think about this tongue?'

Honor groaned inwardly. Ever since she had been transferred to the scarlet fever ward two weeks ago, it seemed to her that the doctors and nurses discussed nothing else. She listed them in her mind – there was the 'white strawberry' tongue, which was covered with a creamy white fur; then the 'red strawberry' tongue, which was clean, red and congested; then on top of all of that was the 'raspberry' tongue, darker and redder as its name suggested.

She could only assume that the doctors who first described this disease had been keen fruit-growers, and it all seemed to her to be very contrived. Then there was the rash – why was this blotchy red rash called a 'punctate erythema'? The mantra of its progression was carefully observed: neck first, then trunk and limbs, but not on the face, which was brightly flushed with 'circumoral pallor'. She had already gathered that meant a pale appearance around the mouth, but such terms added to her general sense of confusion. Each rash had its own nature but there was so much to learn. Added to which, nothing in real life was exactly like its description in the textbook, and a sick and restless child could rarely bear such intense scrutiny.

'Well?' The young doctor looked as confused as Honor felt, but the spotlight of the ward round was upon him, and Dr Shepherd was waiting for his reply. Honor smiled encouragingly at him.

The child held her mouth obligingly open while he looked again. 'I'd say it was a raspberry tongue,' he uttered finally, without conviction.

'Well, let us see,' replied Dr Shepherd thoughtfully, then to Honor, 'What do you think, Nurse?'

'Me?' Honor was surprised. Probationers were not usually addressed on ward rounds.

'Yes, you, what do you think? You look sharp enough to know the answer,' Dr Shepherd persisted.

'I think it's a strawberry tongue,' she answered, no more certain than the young man had been.

'So,' said Dr Shepherd, 'we have one strawberry and one raspberry.' He was enjoying himself, protracting the agony. 'And what do you think, Sister?'

The child, Queenie, closed her mouth. She had a sore throat and felt very hot and shivery. She did not want to play this game anymore, and put her hands over her eyes.

Sister declined to answer his question. 'I just think we should get some antitoxin into her, before she becomes any worse!' she replied.

'Of course, Sister, we'll get on with it right away, but which type of tongue is it?'

'Strawberry, Dr Shepherd,' she replied wearily. 'Do you think we could get a swab done now?'

'Of course it's a strawberry tongue!' Dr Shepherd said. 'Now if you, and our probationer here, both know that, why don't you, Dr Donaldson?'

The young man looked full of confusion and blushed deeply. He did not attempt an answer, and Honor felt sorry for him, remembering her ritual humiliation at the hands of Sister on the diphtheria ward. His blue eyes were fixed upon the child.

'Nothing to say, eh?' Dr Shepherd had not quite finished. 'Well, you'd better come up with the right answer next time, and for now, kindly do as Sister suggests: take a swab and administer the antitoxin. Nurse will help you while Sister and I carry on with the round.'

They withdrew, to Honor's distinct relief. 'I'll get the swab tray,' she said, hurrying off to the sluice. When she returned to Queenie's bed, the curtains were drawn and he had already drawn up three thousand units into the glass syringe. She checked it, then held the little girl's hand while he injected it into her thigh. The small hand gripped hers tightly but she did not cry out. 'Good girl, Queenie,' Honor said. 'Could you just open your mouth once more, for a tiny swab?'

Dr Donaldson deftly took a swab from the back of the throat, causing the poor child to gag, then Honor gave her a little drink of lemonade before smoothing her sheets. She gathered up the tray and followed him to the sluice. He was studiously labelling the specimen before taking it to the laboratory.

'That was bad luck!' Honor commiserated.

'It's nothing new!' he replied good-humouredly. They had not seen each other since the incident on the diphtheria ward. 'I always seem to cop it when Dr Shepherd's around, I don't think he likes me much.'

'Oh, I shouldn't take it to heart,' Honor said. 'I try not to.'

'Hmm, that's easier said than done,' he replied. 'What's your name? I'd better know if we're going to be partners in crime!'

'Honor,' she answered, 'and you?'

'Peter,' he added. 'I'll look out for you from now on.'

They were interrupted by Sister. 'Nurse Newson, we need a urine sample!'

She shot him a quick, shy smile and fled from the sluice.

3

The evenings were becoming lighter and each day held the hope of warmth, after the long, gloomy winter. Honor was walking slowly down the path from the ward, when Addie hailed her. She was clutching a letter.

'We're going to meet this weekend! He's managed to get a pass to Leicester!' Addie was overjoyed, having maintained a long correspondence with the young soldier.

'You be careful!'

'I will, I'm not that wet behind the ears!' Addie said, though for the moment she looked flushed with such a youthful enthusiasm that it was hard to take her seriously. 'He's going to be here tomorrow, for my day off on Saturday! What shall I wear?'

'Where's he going to stay?'

Addie was excited beyond recognition. 'Oh, the best of luck! His uncle lives in Melton Mowbray, so he'll be able to stay there, and come in on the train!'

Honor relented and offered to lend her some clothes. Not that she had many, for her meagre salary of twenty-five shillings a month did not allow for a comprehensive wardrobe, rationing or no.

'You can borrow my new skirt,' she said.

'Oh, are you sure? The lovely navy and white one?'

Honor nodded. She had fallen in love with the smart skirt, which she saw in the window of the department store. It was navy and beautifully tailored, with white buttons and edging. It was her prized possession; she had worn it the last time she saw Will, but that was all the more reason to share it.

'Yes, and we'll do your hair, what about a perm?'

'I'm not sure, maybe I'll stay with my usual style at first.' Addie had lovely long red hair, which spent most of its time ruthlessly stuffed into her nurse's cap. She would wash it the night before, the girls decided, then sleep in rag curlers to give it a little wave the next day. They were happily planning the rest of her wardrobe as they passed the porter's lodge. Honor looked inside.

'Hello!' she called.

'How are you, miss? Not seen you for a bit. How's that young man of yours?'

'Well, he's been posted to another station so I won't see him for a bit.'

'What's he flying, miss?' The porter was full of respect for those RAF boys, putting their lives on the line – they seemed to be the only force that could keep the Nazis at bay.

A small frown crossed Honor's face. 'I probably shouldn't say.' There were so many warnings: – *Careless talk costs lives!* – and she knew better than to repeat any details.

'Of course not, miss, sorry I asked! It was just a slip, don't you go telling anyone what those lads are up to! I'm sure we're very proud of them all. Anyway, there's a letter for you.'

The large handwriting was immediately obvious as Beatie's, posted from her home.

'It's from Beatie,' she announced to Addie, and the two young women hurried back to their hut.

Skimming through quickly, she gathered that Beatie had been sent home last week, having been reconciled with her family. Her anaemia was not yet resolved, and she still felt weak, but for the first time she was talking about the future again. Honor handed the letter to Addie.

'What will she do, do you suppose?' Addie said after reading it.

'I don't know. I expect she'll hatch up some plan soon, knowing Beatie!'

'Well it won't be what we're expecting, it never is!' Addie replied. 'Now can I try on that skirt of yours?'

19th April 1941
Groby Road Hospital
Dear You,
I keep wondering how you're getting on at your new base. I bet you're enjoying your new plane and I hope you're taking care of yourself.

I've switched to the scarlet fever ward – it's always difficult starting again but I'm trying not to make a complete fool of myself!

I was thinking of the Bradley boys this week when I heard about the British withdrawal from Benghazi. Their poor mother must be worried stiff! I thought we only just took it back!

Anyway, I miss you too, can't wait to see you again.

From Me

4

It was tricky, that runway. Running as it did from north to south, the early morning sun could still dazzle you on take-off. Will had yet to feel fully confident in the Oxford, though his progress had been rapid, his first solo only five days after his induction flight. There was an imperative to complete this part of their training as soon as possible: they were needed on active service. With any luck he would have his wings by the end of June, then it would be on to the next posting.

It was all so very different to the Tiger Moth. The Oxford was much bigger, a twin-engine trainer in which he and his instructor, Flight Sergeant Owen, sat side by side. There was a wealth of dials on the instrument panel. The undercarriage indicator was on the centre of the instrument panel, red lights for travelling, green for down.

'Two lights is locked,' Owen had reminded him, showing him how to use the hand pump in an emergency. The two fuel cocks and the fuel gauge were on the left-hand side of the panel. 'One main tank, fuel pump feeds each engine, no cross-feed to the auxiliary system.' Owen was succinct and clear, knowing his trainee should have been checking up on his *Pilot's Notes* in advance. Still, no amount of reading could prepare you for the reality of flying a more complex plane; the pathways your brain would have to imprint before it became second nature and you could be deemed safe to fly.

Will liked the snub-nosed plane; it had a look of reassuring solidity, and with about six times as much engine power as the Moth, a rewarding acceleration during take-off. There would be more gadgets to play with during bomb training, with the bomb selector switches below the main panel presaging a whole new set of skills, and a constant reminder as to the ultimate purpose of his training.

He liked Shawbury too, apart from the fact that it was further from Honor. He had motored down the last leg of the journey, overjoyed to have the Austin to himself, with just enough petrol to reach his destination. It had been a clear day, and he could see the Welsh mountains in the distance as the car threaded through the country roads towards Shrewsbury. *Another green and pleasant county to fly over*, he thought, as he drew into the small village with its Norman church. The entrance to the base was set off one of the side roads, and he could see it was a more substantial affair than Desford, with attractive creeper-clad brick buildings. Like his new plane, it had an appearance that inspired confidence, as though it had been built to survive this war and others that might come after. The accommodation blocks were spacious, uniformly constructed single rooms with wide windows that looked out on to the Shropshire fields beyond. It was comforting to have proper accommodation and mess facilities; indeed the latter was a beautiful neo-Georgian building with a sweeping drive. He had entered it self-consciously that first night, looking around for a familiar face but failing to see Guy. Curiously, there was a look of recognition in one of the other faces, and he smiled in return. It was Edward, one of the lads in his year at Guisborough grammar school.

'Hey, Bert, what are you doing here?' Ed greeted him warmly.

'Same as you, I reckon,' Will replied. 'I didn't even know you were in the RAF, let alone pitching up here!'

'What a coincidence!' Ed said. He had found himself in a room of complete strangers, and then who should walk in but someone from school! They were soon comparing notes about their postings so far: Ed had been at a No. 2, ITW in Cambridge, then 22 EFTS just outside the city. He, like Will, was relieved to have made it through but, in common with just about everyone they knew, would rather have been selected for fighter training.

'Oh well, I expect they know what they're doing,' Will said. 'Anyway, it's a good posting!' He looked around the large, light room again, and across to the sweeping bar at the end, before catching a glimpse of Guy partially hidden there, with a beer in his hand.

'Come with me.' He put a hand on Ed's shoulder to guide him in the direction of the bar. 'I've got a friend I'd like you to meet, one of our lot at Desford.'

'Will! You daft thing, I nearly dropped my beer!' Guy beamed. 'Great to see you, how was your leave?'

'Oh, not too bad, went home to see the folks. How's Marion?'

'Just fine, didn't want to leave her really, but then we never do, do we?' Guy looked at Ed and held out his hand. 'I'm Guy Clarkson, by the way.'

'Pleased to meet you. Ed Bowen, friend of Bert's from school.'

'Never thought of him as a Bert!' said Guy.

'Well, that's Yorkshire for you,' Will said. 'Christened one name, known by many others! How about a beer, Ed?' They all slipped into the easy conversation of those who have interwoven pasts, if not necessarily futures.

In such a way he had come to know others in his group. There was the tall, impeccably spoken Dougdale, from one of the nobler families in Derbyshire, the oldest son and therefore set to inherit the country estate. At the other end of the social spectrum was Alf Wiggins, who joined the RAF as a fitter at the age of sixteen and, having worked his way diligently up the ranks, was now embarking on his twin-engine training. They could soon see why: Alf was an incredibly competent and measured pilot, who knew every engine back to front. He would definitely be able to extricate himself from trouble, and was worth two of those from more privileged backgrounds.

They spent most of their time in the air. Though the classroom lessons were regular, their theory sessions took second place to the concentrated flying training. A combination of fast thinking, and rapid reaction times, was the expected norm. One of the first exercises that Owen had demonstrated, just two days into Will's training, was flying on one engine.

'You'll need to get this one perfect, it's got to be just right,' he said. Will could feel the slew of the aircraft as the balance between the engines went.

'You'll need to apply opposite rudder to keep her straight,' Owen explained, as they descended to eight thousand feet and he put the fuel mixture lever on 'take-off' to boost the power. Despite careful use of the rudder, Will could feel on the dual controls the tendency to overbank, causing further loss of height.

'What's the optimum speed on one engine?' Owen enquired, once they were back in steady flight, and Will promptly responded 'Ninety-five miles per hour, sir.'

Not that any of the trainees thought that such emergency drill would be a waste of their time. Only a few months previously, Amy Johnson had disappeared in the Thames Estuary flying an Oxford. She was one of a select group of women pilots, the Air Transport Auxiliary, based at White Waltham, whose job it was to deliver planes to bases up and down the country. The loss of the famous pilot had been a shock to the country, and was emblazoned in headlines across the world.

Nearer to home, there were numerous flying accidents on the base itself, often during landing and take-off. The Accident Investigation Board, or AIB, would sift through the wreckage but the ensuing report would dwell little on the tragic loss of life.

The instructors were under no illusions about the task they faced. The young pilots might have been able to get safely home in a DH82, in which they stood some chance of survival. However, the twin-engine planes, like the Oxford, required a degree of finesse that the trainee might just not possess, however hard they tried to instil it into him. One small miscalculation on the runway could be all it would take.

Guy felt it more deeply than the others. He was older than many of the trainees, and with a secure job and a fiancée, might in better circumstances have considered his future secure. He was shocked by the accident rate and the imperviousness of the authorities to yet another death. He shook his head with despair after three consecutive days of landing accidents, though fortunately the young pilots had survived.

'What the bloody hell's going on here?' he enquired irritably of Will on their way to the mess for lunch. 'They don't seem to give a damn how many of us go for a burton.'

Will tried hard not to listen. You just needed to keep your confidence, and your head. He missed Matt, whose carefree approach to flying could be a real tonic.

'Just get on with it, don't think about it so much – that's what Matt would have said.' He wondered how Matt was faring at Little Rissington, and whether the Magisters were any easier to fly.

'Right,' said Owen. It was a light April morning, good visibility and not much wind. 'Pilot Officer Blezard will take you through your solo test, then it's up to you. Don't forget your final checks for take-off and landing – he'll be quizzing you on them first off. You should be A-OK, just carry on what you've been doing so far.'

Will knew the final checks by heart – trim, mixture, fuel and flaps. He had rehearsed it so many times in his head, and had a diagram of the fuel system pasted into his logbook with a signed entry to certify that he understood the petrol system, brakes, use of hydraulic system and manipulation of the throttle controls. The truth was, he did understand it all; that was the great advantage of his time on the farm, poring over how the engine worked on any available piece of machinery, learning to drive anything from a motorbike to a tractor and knowing how to put it right when it went wrong. It was that engine sense which gave the likes of Alf Wiggins and him the edge – they were not just flying the plane, they understood how it worked. Consequently, when the inevitable problem occurred, he would have a mental diagram of cause and effect, which might allow for a solution.

Blezard seemed cheery enough, and not that much older than Guy. Unlike some of the instructors, he had not yet lost his enthusiasm for the job. His relative youth, unaltered by an embryonic moustache, startled Will almost as much as his strange accent. It was a moment before he could place it, but Blezard's South African Air Force badge soon provided the answer.

'God, what I wouldn't give to be flying down the Cape in the spring sunshine,' he announced. 'Never mind, we'll just have to put up with old Blighty, so show me what you can do on this old tub, then I can go and read the papers and have a cup of tea!'

Will managed a decent take-off, opening the throttles slowly to check the tendency to swing to the right, and not attempting to get the tail up too early. Braking the wheels as soon as he was airborne, he retracted the undercarriage, and before climbing, increased the speed to a hundred miles an hour. Turning the fuel mixture control to normal, he was conscious of Blezard's apparent composure. He was whistling a tune to himself, jotting a few notes down on his sheet of paper.

'OK, take her through some climbing turns.'

Will did so, reducing his speed after 6,500 feet. After the mandatory spell on one engine, followed by a decent stall, he was soon performing his final checks for landing: the contents of the fuel tanks, brake pressures, and locking the wheels down for a powered approach.

'OK, your turn now.' Blezard signed the paper as he rose from the instructor's seat. 'Take it easy, and do exactly the same thing without me sitting next to you getting on your nerves!' He hopped out before Will had any time for further questions.

So here he was, April 17th 1941, his first solo in the Oxford. So much had happened since he joined up: first his ITW in Aberystwyth, then the EFTS in Desford, and now a twin-engine plane that would enable him to progress to bombers, if he could just do it properly. He thought of Honor, and how she would tell him to be careful. *Not really that sort of occupation*, he reflected, as he checked the fuel pressure gauge and opened the twin throttles. Taxiing down the runway, he felt a sense of responsibility rather than apprehension. Responsibility to the RAF for letting him fly the plane, and thinking he was good enough to do so; to his parents and Honor, to return safely from his solo; and to himself, to do as well as he could. That satisfying acceleration from the Armstrong Siddeley engines lifted him up into a stable take-off, apart from a bit of buffeting which ceased as he increased speed. Soon he was on a clear climb, and up into level flight. He could see Hawkestone Ridge directly north ahead of him, then he veered east on a climbing turn towards the Wrekin. Executing a stall, the left wing dropped and he relaxed the pressure on the control column, recovering as he had been taught. After that, it was the single-engine challenge, but he felt by now that he would be able to master this, using the ailerons and rudder effectively to stabilise the plane. He finished with a careful landing, remembering all the vital final checks: correct fuel tank, brakes off, wheels locked down, and then he was down again, taxiing along the runway to his waiting instructors.

'OK, Fordham!' Blezard looked satisfied. He would be unlikely to dispense any further praise, but Will was elated to have passed yet another hurdle. 'I'm off for my cuppa, but let me just see your logbook later,' Blezard said.

Will stood for a moment, looking at the sun on the church in the distance, and thinking of the other young men who had not made it thus far, then took off his gloves and strolled into the hangars to chat to the ground crew.

'Managed it, did you, sir?' One of the old hands looked up from oiling the pistons.

'Just about, Garnett, just about,' he said, as he bent enquiringly to see what the man was doing.

'That's the ticket.' Garnett was always pleased when the lads could fly his beloved planes properly. He was never more upset than when they crashed them unnecessarily. *Ruddy waste of a good plane!* This lad looked like a careful sort of chap; just what they needed, not taking any silly risks. *They'll have him on something bigger before the summer's out*, he conjectured. *Let's just hope he can stay in one piece, touch down on that home runway, and bring it back to the hangars*; Garnett's own domain.

5

For Guy, it was still the enemy within that he had to conquer rather than the one on the other side of the Channel. He had overcome his fears successfully in the Tiger Moth, but now it was all starting again. The Oxfords seemed downright dangerous to him. There had been another night landing crash the evening before, which did little to lift his spirits. He began to wonder if he would ever see Marion again, so inevitable did his own ever-beckoning accident become. Perhaps he should not have tried so hard to fly the Moth, for by now he would surely be in navigation school along with the likes of Dick. Not that the future would be any more comforting if he had, for it would still mean crewing up in some enormous bomber and entrusting his life to the pilot.

He despaired of the war. Every time he looked at a paper the situation was worsening: the Germans were now crossing the Yugoslavian border into Macedonia and would no doubt finish off Greece in the same way as almost every other European country. Heavens alone knew what would happen to the British army there, but Guy, with his usual scepticism, had a hunch that it would end no better than Dunkirk.

Guy's instructor knew about his inner fears but was determined to ignore them. A sizeable proportion of the trainees suffered from nerves, but some could be coaxed into reasonable pilots, and turned out to be more sensible than the ones who could not see danger even when it was staring them in the face.

'Now don't balls it up! Just remember what I've said!'

Guy swallowed and took his place at Blezard's side for his test. Fortified by his cup of tea, the blithe South African appeared totally unconcerned, though stopped whistling as Guy opened the throttles. Clarkson was rushing it, then struggling to gain sufficient speed before easing up the tail. Blezard sat up, discomfited. You could never rule out the possibility that one of these blokes would take you to Kingdom Come, even with the dual controls.

'Steady, old chum,' Blezard said, his hands instinctively moving to the control panel. Guy managed a shaky take-off, going into a climb before rapidly switching the fuel mixture control to normal, causing the engine to surge. Blezard raised a hand, and Guy tried resolutely to regain composure, and levelled out into steady flight.

Blezard had to endure a less than smooth single-engine exercise, in which Guy side-slipped and lost height before regaining adequate control. He was looking forward to terra firma, this instructor, and hoped that Guy's landing might prove more adequate than his take-off.

Guy was also longing for the flight to end, so appalling had been his unforced errors. He pushed the undercarriage lever to select the 'down' position, but the green lights did not show. Cursing under his breath, he repeated the manoeuvre without success. Blezard offered him no assistance, and for once Guy had to think for himself. What the hell was wrong? Guy knew the sequence: 'red lights – travelling', and 'green – down', but there was no light shining at all. He went into another circuit, giving himself more time. *The horn, you idiot!* he remembered, and closed one throttle to a third. The sound of the horn confirmed that the undercarriage was not locked down. How the hell was he to land? Not even glancing at Blezard, he pushed the emergency knob down and operated the hand pump. That was it; the green lights shone out on the instrument panel, as he lowered the flaps and took up the recommended approach speed, following with a passable landing. As they taxied to the hangars, Blezard was busy writing on his sheet of paper.

'Sorry, sir, that was a botch!'

'You got yourself out of it, that can't be bad! Not sure what's up with the undercarriage but you did well to get her down. And for Christ's sake stop thinking you can't fly the ruddy crate – if you couldn't, we'd both be dead by now!'

Guy was ready for a stiff drink in the mess that evening as he knocked on Will's door.

'How did it go?' Will looked up. He was reading a copy of *The Rubaiyat of Omar Khayyam*.

'Given to me by my English teacher at school,' Will explained, handing him the small red volume with its dark leather cover. Guy glanced at the verses, reading aloud the evocative words:

'Awake! for morning in the bowl of Night
Has flung the stone that puts the stars to Flight:
And lo! The Hunter of the East has caught
The Sultan's Turret in a Noose of Light.'

Will took it back, and followed on:

'Come, fill the Cup, and in the Fire of Spring
The Winter Garment of Repentance fling:
The Bird of Time has but a little way
To fly – and Lo! The Bird is on the Wing.'

6

'So what'll be next, I wonder?' Dougdale's usually crystal-clear upper-class accent was becoming a little slurred. They had all had too much to drink, buoyed up by their solo successes. Not that all the flights had been without mishap – one of the trainees had abandoned a take-off, supposedly because of air leaks around the panels, and another had been failed for inadequate final checks before landing.

'More instrument flying, I suppose,' Alf replied. With no problems at all during his solo, he was regarded as one of the most promising pilots in the group. Dougdale, in contrast, could be a little more erratic. He had been keen to fly fighters, and tended to treat the sturdy Oxford as though more could be coaxed from it.

'No, Dougdale, you may not spin an Oxford, not now, not ever,' his instructor had replied firmly to his enquiry as to when this manoeuvre would be possible.

'Never, sir?'

'Not unless you have a death wish,' was the curt rejoinder. 'And if you do, please commit suicide in a less expensive way.'

Dougdale had taken the reproof in his stride, but longed to be in a more exciting plane. However, no amount of string-pulling from his wealthy, aristocratic relatives had succeeded in a transfer to single engines thus far, so he was coming near to accepting his fate. Still, without anyone to supervise him, there might be a little more fun to be had, and he lived in hope.

'Dropping bombs, I s'pose,' Guy said. He put his empty glass down on the bar. 'I wonder how the Desford lot are getting on?'

'Haven't a clue, but I bet Matt's in his element in a Magister!' Will said.

'Magisters! That's what I want to fly!' Dougdale protested, taking another long draught of beer.

'We know you do, old chum, but it's not going to happen, is it?' Guy said.

'Damn shame!' Dougdale said. 'Can't get that old Ox-Box to do anything remotely exciting!'

'I should just try and stay alive if I were you,' Alf put in quietly.

'So where's your friend?' Dougdale asked.

'Little Rissington, No. 2 EFTS.'

'Some buggers get all the luck! Anyone for more beer?'

He was interrupted by some loud voices at the entrance to the bar. There was clearly an argument going on, but none of them recognised the protagonists.

'Joseph, you talk about my girl one more time, I kill you!' A scuffle broke out between two tall, dark-haired men, and the mess orderlies moved to intervene.

'You hear me, I get you by the throat and squeeze out your life!' One of the assailants was gasping as the men were pulled apart.

'Who the hell are they?' Dougdale looked on in interest.

'It's the Poles, sir,' said the bar attendant in a matter-of-fact voice. 'Just joined us, I believe. Renowned for their fights, the Poles are, sir.' He continued to pull a pint with his eye on the melee to see if his colleagues needed assistance.

The larger of the two men broke away, muttering in Polish under his breath, and made his way to the bar. He threw back his proud face.

'One pint your English beer,' he announced imperiously.

'Certainly, sir,' the barman answered with aplomb, as though nothing untoward had happened. 'And for your friend?'

'Friend?!' the man replied in a thick accent. 'He is very rude man, sod-awful pilot too!'

It appeared that the Polishman's command of the English language did not extend much beyond obscenities, and Will wondered where they had been learning it. He had heard about the Polish Air Force, refugees of their own broken state, some having made it to England to continue their fight against Hitler. He remembered them on the base at Warboys, heavy drinkers to a man.

'So,' the Pole continued, 'I am Count Edek Bronowski, Polish Air Force. We come to show you how to fly. Do not take notice of the other, he is only liar and damn drunkard!'

'Pleased to meet you,' Guy said, and his hand was firmly grasped in return.

'So, you've come to teach us how to fly?' Dougdale enquired, the cynicism in his voice not apparent to the foreigner.

'Why, of course!' the count replied. 'The Polish Air Force is finest in the world!' His attention was drawn to the figure of his ex-fighting partner, now approaching the bar.

'Ah, Joseph!' he greeted the man, as though nothing had passed between them. 'You want drink?'

'Not pissing English beer!' Joseph's language was no improvement on the count's. 'Why they drink such bad stuff?'

'Try again, maybe you like this time?'

Joseph begrudgingly took the proffered drink and sipped it suspiciously.

'So what you fly here?' the count asked, looking around the assembled company.

'Well, we're on twin-engine trainers, Oxfords actually,' Guy replied.

The count looked at him in disgust. 'You not flying Spitfires here?'

'Not exactly,' Will said. 'This is a bomber training station. When did you arrive?'

The question was ignored.

'So, you fly bombers here? No Spitfires?'

'Sorry, old chap.' Dougdale was beginning to feel he had something in common with these two. 'Didn't they tell you where you were coming?'

'They tell us damn all!' Edek almost spat out the words. He turned to his companion. 'Joseph, is mistake. We are on wrong place. I, one of best fighter pilots in Poland, am sent on a bomber. Tomorrow, I go to top brass, get us out!'

Joseph nodded. He seemed to be developing more of a taste for the beer, or at least was able to swallow it without an expression of disgust.

'Any chance I could join you?' Dougdale seized his unlikely moment, but was immediately stopped by a chorus of disapproval.

'Oh, give it a break!' Guy said, but Dougdale, undeterred, turned to his new acquaintances.

'Now, gentlemen, another drink? Then you can tell us how you got here and why you speak such godawful English!'

7

'I'm sorry, Count Bronowski.' The station commander, Squadron Leader Flynn, felt slightly out of his depth. There could be no doubt that the airman in front of him was an experienced pilot, but HQ Flight Training Command had posted him here, with his colleague Joseph Krause, with express instructions that they were both to be trained in Oxfords before posting to the HCU. This command was not negotiable, a fact which seemed completely lost upon the irate Pole in front of him.

'What you mean, you can't do nothing?' The count's voice was starting to rise. 'I am top fighter pilot, not fly bombers.' (He pronounced the second 'b' emphatically, for greater effect.) 'For what I fly this plane? You British want win war? Then give us Spitfires, Joseph and I can do it for you!'

'It's not quite that simple.' Flynn began a long, tedious preamble about the workings of FT command and the integration of the Polish Air Force. He was not allowed to finish.

'Not simple! Is simple: get me to top brass, I tell them if you not understand!'

Flynn sighed. He had tried to be patient but he too had his limits.

'Look, Count, you're posted here – you fly bombers. You don't like it? That's fine, I take you off active service. That means, in case you don't understand me, that you spend the rest of the ruddy war behind a desk in an office somewhere, counting how many Polish airmen we have in this country and looking after them. Perhaps you might like to start by teaching them some basic English so they don't have to eff and blind their way around the sky!

'You don't like that idea? Well, learn to live with it, like everyone else in this godforsaken war. I want you reporting for flying training immediately, or you're off the course!' He rose and showed the astonished count to the door, closing it quickly behind him before he had time to think up a response. He leant against the door, listening to the count's expletives as he made his way down the corridor.

Later, looking out of his wide first-floor window, he could see the figures of the two Polishmen heading sullenly to their planes. He smiled, remembering a military quote: *Orders are not a basis for discussion*, and resolved to see neither of the two men again unless it was absolutely necessary.

He turned his attention to the papers on his desk. There were still far too many accidents, and he for one was not yet sure if it was the quality of the pilot trainees or their instructors. Added to which, the use of the Relief Landing Grounds at Bridleway Gate and Bratton had failed to relieve the congestion, and he would have to look further afield. He had at his disposal sixty-six Oxfords, twenty-three Battles, and forty Harts, but at the rate these trainees were going, half of them would be unserviceable soon. It was a thankless task, even before the Poles had been sent to haunt him. What contribution they would make to the morale of the mess, he did not like to conjecture.

'Bloody bad luck, you two!' Dougdale said as he lined them up a couple of pints that evening. 'You don't like bombers? Neither do I! Still, if we don't blot our copybooks perhaps they'll let us move over one day!'

'What is this, blotting copybook?' Joseph wiped the froth from his moustache.

Guy came to the rescue. 'He means, he's going to toe the line,' he added, helpfully.

Edek frowned. 'Toe a line, why he want toe a line?' He still looked surly, but the truth was he had enjoyed flying the Oxford that afternoon. It was such a relief to be in the air again, after the humiliating loss of his country and his air force. He would drop bombs on the Nazis wherever they wanted. Edek and Joseph had soon mastered the twin throttles, finessing between the two engines, rudder and ailerons without a thought. Between them, they had flown most types of aircraft in their homeland, though few as serviceable as the ones they encountered here.

'So, how did it go?' Will thought some plain English was called for.

'It went good!' Edek responded, sipping his beer. 'Piece of bloody cake, old boy!'

8

Ed Bowen had never liked instrument flying. The boy from Guisborough grammar school could manage anything else, but that ominous practice flying under the hood in the DH82, then the fear of the dark night around him in a flimsy aeroplane, had made him wish he had never joined up.

Still, he would have to conquer such emotions. None of them wanted to be labelled 'LMF', or 'lack of moral fibre.' It meant dismissal from the forces and an ignominious end to one's flying career. It was probably better to keep quiet and take what fate had in store for you, as long as you could steel your nerve and brazen it out. Like the others, he found release in a welcoming pint of beer, though he had touched alcohol little before now. At least with a pint or two beneath your belt you could stop thinking about what you would have to do tomorrow.

He had hoped that the more solid plane might give him confidence, and once he had mastered the trick of the dual throttles, it seemed to be the case. However, he felt a growing sense of apprehension as his instructor took him through the instrument flying exercise for the first time.

'It's just the same principle as the Tiger.' The flight sergeant was matter-of-fact. He reckoned the young Yorkshire lad would make a half-reasonable pilot one day. 'I'll put on the hood, then you can fly her by the instruments. Just concentrate on your artificial horizon, that's the bit of kit that matters most.'

Bowen breathed deeply. He found the loss of spatial orientation almost distressing. He kept thinking his ears could tell him if he was straight and level, but he knew as a result of constant badgering from his previous instructor that this was not the case. He experienced once again the claustrophobia of the hood, and tried to concentrate.

The effort exhausted him, as though his whole being was focussed on the instruments in front of him. It was hot under the hood, and Ed was dripping sweat. As far as he was concerned, the whole exercise was torture.

'OK, we'll head back now,' his instructor said, after what seemed like an eternity. 'I want you to get into a descending left turn for the approach to the runway.'

As he made the manoeuvre, Ed became convinced that the aircraft was turning right. He checked the instruments again. The artificial horizon told him he was turning left, but panicking, he followed his senses and instinctively banked the wrong way. They were losing height rapidly, and gaining speed.

'Christ almighty!' the flight sergeant shouted, grabbing the controls, but it was too late. The Oxford stalled and plunged upside down into the ground.

'What do you mean, they're both dead?!' Will shouted. How could Ed have got himself killed? He had been talking to him earlier, at breakfast; he and Ed were going to meet up this afternoon!

He looked at Guy in disbelief, then strode from the hangar, still in flying suit and gloves, and scanned the horizon. Guy caught up with him and stood at his side, as they both looked at the plume of smoke curling into the sky.

'I'm sorry, old chap,' Guy said.

Will turned away, silently putting his face in his leather-gloved hands.

The spring sunshine was on their backs as the older man put an arm around his shoulder.

'He didn't stand a bloody chance!' Will finally raised his face.

'I know, we're all for the chop sooner or later.' Guy shook his head, as they turned, and walked slowly back the way they had come.

RAF Shawbury
30th April 1941
Dear You,
I am sorry I haven't written before but life is pretty hectic here – the flying takes up nearly all our time, and there's a lot to learn. It is a very reasonable base here and a first-rate bunch of people.

I have been given two days' leave to go to Yorkshire for a funeral, but have to be back here in good time otherwise I would have tried to see you. I think of you all the time.

I hope you are enjoying your new ward. I will write soon.

From Me

9

'Can I have a drink?' Alfie turned his puffy face towards Honor, and took a few sips of his lemonade. He was only allowed a pint of fluid a day, which under normal circumstances would have brought forth a storm of protest, but he was too ill to care. He had been like this for three weeks now, swelling up with fluid as his kidneys failed. Honor recognised in him the grim single-mindedness of a child who is struggling to survive. She had seen it before, different wards, different conditions, but the same desperate will to live, conserving every ounce of energy to that end.

'Can you hold out your arm?' she asked, so she could wrap the blood pressure cuff around it.

'When can I see my mum?'

Honor was watching the column of mercury fall gently down the narrow vertical tube, and the little beat of the oscillating meniscus as it did so.

'Not today, Alfie. When you're better, you know.'

Alfie lay back on his pillow. They always said that. He wished he could see his mother and brothers today. Why did they always talk about waiting till he was better?

Honor frowned. The child's blood pressure was elevated, unless she had taken the reading wrong. After a moment's indecision, she was relieved to see Dr Donaldson coming down the ward.

'Hullo, what's up?' Peter smiled at her. She had become his most important ally against the world, and in particular, Dr Shepherd. There was something about her; he always felt better when she was on the ward.

'I think his blood pressure's up, will you check it for me?'

Nodding, he repeated the measurement, Alfie lying quietly as he did so.

Dr Donaldson took the chart from her and countersigned her entry: 130 over 90. It was significantly elevated from the last reading. They looked at each other, saying nothing until they had both moved away from the child's bed.

'What does it mean?' she asked.

'He's developing hypertension,' the young doctor replied softly.

'That's not good, is it?' She knew the answer already. The outcome of acute nephritis was variable: some went into kidney failure while most progressed to a more chronic disease. Basically, the more complicated the initial attack, the worse for the child.

'Don't look so worried. It might settle, sometimes does,' he said.

He touched her gently on the arm before she set off down the ward.

Scabies was an unpleasant infestation, sadly not uncommon among the children from disadvantaged backgrounds. The nurses would check each admission for the telltale scratch marks and linear burrows between the fingers. It usually meant that the whole family would have it, but their only concern was to treat the child before it could spread on the ward.

A small, grubby girl was sitting on a chair by her bed, dressed in the threadbare clothes in which she had been brought in. She was carrying a small cardboard box.

'You must be Lily.' Honor took the small, grimy hand. 'I'm going to give you a bath, Lily, so you're nice and clean, then we'll put some special stuff on your skin before you pop into bed.'

The child said nothing, but meekly rose and allowed herself to be led down the ward to the bathroom. The soft soap and benzyl benzoate were on the shelf, ready for application. As Lily took off her clothes the scratches were evident all over her chest and abdomen. Honor chatted quietly to her as she washed her hair, covered her with soft soap, washed and dried her before brushing on the benzyl benzoate. The child winced.

'It stings!' She uttered her first and last words for the morning, so set was her little mouth.

'Nearly finished,' Honor said encouragingly, but she had still to apply the ointment to Lily's hair. All the children hated the smell, which seemed to permeate the whole ward, but Lily stood silent as Honor wrapped a towel round her head.

'There, that wasn't too bad.' She led the unresisting Lily back to her bed, and tucked her in. Lily reached for her box.

'What's in it, Lily, is it your gas mask? I'll take it for you.'

Lily shook her head and grasped the box more tightly. Honor sighed. It was going to be a long morning.

'You'll have to let me have it, sweetie. Then I can get you a nice drink of milk, and maybe there's a biscuit in the kitchen.' Honor usually found that the offer of food or drink would appease the most recalcitrant of children.

Lily gazed at her, then reluctantly handed her the box. Untying the string and lifting the lid, Honor found it contained the dirtiest rag doll she had ever seen. The hand-knitted brown toy could never have been beautiful, even in her prime, and it was all Honor could do not to comply with the rule to burn all such items from infested houses.

'It's all right, Lily, I'll give her a nice bath too, then you can have her back.' She hurried to the sluice to immerse the cherished dolly in a bucket of dilute Lysol, before Lily had time to complain.

Peter caught up with her there.

'Whatever are you doing?' He watched her in amusement as she energetically doused the doll in a bucket of disinfectant.

'It's Lily's doll,' she answered, pushing back a lock of escaping hair into her cap.

'Are you sure it's worth saving?'

She smiled, despite herself, and wrung the water out from the dripping wool.

'Definitely! You haven't met Lily.' She poured the grey water down the sink and dried her hands. He looked at her quizzically.

'Are you all right, Honor? You look worried today.' He was sensitive to the slightest change in her mood. 'It's not just about Alfie, is it?'

'Not really.'

'What is it then?' His voice was soft and seemed to coax a response.

She sighed. 'I don't really know. I've got a friend in the RAF, learning to fly, he's on a new base. I think something's happened, but I don't know what. His letter didn't quite say…' Her voice tailed off. What was she doing telling this young man about Will? It was none of his business, and made her feel curiously exposed.

Peter fell silent. He was equally confused. Did this mean she had a boyfriend? He realised that imperceptibly, he had grown to want her for himself, safe in the easy certainty that he could see her each day.

There was a further pause.

'I expect he'll let you know soon,' was all his response, when it finally came.

Honor looked back at him, conscious that something had changed between them. 'Yes, I expect so,' she replied briskly, busying herself with the thermometers on the shelf, as he put both hands in the pockets of his white coat and, whistling softly to himself, walked back on to the ward.

4th May 1941
Groby Road Hospital
Dear You,
Is everything all right? I wish I could telephone you so we could have a real conversation. I know that your letters can't tell me what's really happening there. I just get so worried when I don't know what's going on!

It's hard being parted when we were just getting to know each other. I'm sure you feel it too.

From Me

10

The forces van was making slow progress along the narrow roads. Will looked at his watch. It would be hours before they reached Doncaster. His driver had his eyes fixed to the road. It was not his first such errand, and was unlikely to be his last.

'Stop for a break soon, shall we?'

It was nearly three hours since they had left Shawbury. Will had stood, straight-backed, as the men loaded the coffin into the van and slammed the twin doors shut. It would be his responsibility to take Ed home, back to Guisborough, and to his grieving parents whose lives had been changed forever by the telegram boy at the door.

'Yes, I'm ready to stretch my legs.'

The driver looked for a suitable stopping place, and pulled up by a farm track leading up to a stone smallholding in the distance.

They both stood by the van, drinking tea from the thermos that the NAAFI had provided, and eating the corned beef sandwiches.

'First one of these outings, is it?' the driver asked, chewing steadily.

'Yes.' Will took another sip of tea, strong and milky.

'I'm afraid it'll not be the last.' The man was matter-of-fact. This was his second war and he had no illusions. He flung the tea leaves from his empty cup, a streak of brown across the grass.

'At least he'll be having a decent burial, not like the lads in 14-18,' he added tersely. 'Half of my mates ended up in unmarked graves, you know, "unknown soldier". Not enough left of them to identify. You can thank God you're not going to be buried in one of those trenches. Better falling out of the sky, any day, if you ask me.'

'Yes, I think you're probably right.' Will screwed the top slowly back on to the thermos. 'Let's get on, shall we?'

Ed's home was on a wide terraced street not far from the church. The net curtains twitched as the van drew up, and the front door was opened before he had time to knock.

'Bert!' Ed's mother was already dressed in black, but had her usual apron on top. She had spent so long scrubbing the step that morning that her husband had come to fetch her in.

'It won't make it any better, Mother,' he had said, as he wrapped her in his arms, his muscled shoulders enveloping her weeping frame.

'We should never have let him go!' Her anguish was more than he could bear.

'Don't take on, Mother, we had to! They all have to go, you'd not have wanted a conchie in the family!'

She stood tall, and faced him, wiping the tears from her face. 'I'd rather have a conchie than a dead son!' Her voice was fierce and strong, the animal mother trying impotently to guard her young. It was too late, they had taken him from her, killed him in a plane before he had even taken up arms. How could she ever go on living, carrying this searing pain of loss?

'I'm so sorry, Mrs Bowen,' Will said.

'Ee, lad, I never thought you'd be bringing him home like this!' The sight of Will in his blue uniform seemed to give her strength. 'Come in, and bring your friend, I'll make a cup of tea. The undertaker's men will be right here, Vic's gone for them.'

Later, in the parlour, where they had placed the coffin so that others could pay their last respects, Ed's father took Will aside.

'What happened, lad?' He was a coalman, Vic Bowen, strong and burly, always one to see his wife and children right. Losing his oldest son, the one they were so proud of with his place at the grammar school, had come to him as a complete shock. He had anticipated the dangers of active service, but to die on a training exercise!

Will followed him into the kitchen where they sat together at the table.

'We don't really know, Mr Bowen. He was learning how to fly the plane on instruments. You know,' he added, seeing Mr Bowen's frown, 'flying blind, with an instructor. For some reason, as they were coming in to land, the whole plane just ploughed into the ground. They were both killed instantly.' He paused. 'I'm sorry, I don't know more. The accident investigation board will look into it, and there'll be a report in due course. That's when the accidents usually happen, you know, in take-off and landing. Things can just go suddenly wrong.'

The coalman looked at the troubled face in front of him. How must he feel, young Fordham? He and Ed had been friends since primary school. After the funeral, he, poor boy, would have to go back to training and fly the bloody planes again!

He put his calloused grey hand over Will's. 'Thanks, lad, especially for bringing our Ed home. Your folks will be proud of you, just like we are of him.'

11

There was no ignoring the commanding knock at the door, which had opened almost before Squadron Leader Flynn's invitation to enter.

'Ah, Count! What can I do for you? I trust the Oxfords are to your satisfaction now?' Flynn deemed it best to humour Bronowski. After all, both the Poles were reported to be brilliant airmen, and could soon move to their next posting.

'The planes are not a problem. We would rather fly Spitfires, or something with real bombs. That is not why I am here. Squadron Leader, you are in charge, I think?' The count was proceeding with his usual hauteur.

'Of course.' What was the man leading up to?

'So. Why does man in charge let young men die?' Bronowski looked him straight in the eyes.

'Oh, the accident, you mean? Well, the board have looked into it, and we're waiting for the report. There are a great many trainees here, you know. We are bound to have the odd prang.' Flynn looked ill at ease. He was not expecting this – what right did the Polish chappie have to question him?

Bronowski's head was high. 'A prang is what you call it? That is not prang, that is murder. Joseph and I, we are not afraid, the Germans took our country and our heart! But every boy that dies here, his mother will come to you in your dreams. "Why did my son die? He did not even get to fight!" That is all I want to say to you, sir, and you know I am right!'

He marched out, slamming the door behind him.

Flynn looked disconsolately at his desk. Bronowski was right, damn him. It was a disaster to lose a chap like young Bowen, his instructor, and a perfectly serviceable Oxford. Flynn had done his best, opening the relief landing grounds, but they had become muddy and dangerous during the winter months. What he really needed was more slack on the programmes, to give these lads and their instructors, neither of whom were really up to the grade, more time to learn. In his heart he felt responsible for every one of the deaths, and hoped that tonight would not bring the spectre of Bowen's mother to haunt his dreams.

It was not the vision that startled Flynn from his slumber, but the sound of explosions. He leapt from his narrow bed, pulling aside the blackout curtain to see the station illuminated by exploding bombs. The Luftwaffe had found them again, and though the sirens were now wailing there had been no preliminary warning of the raid. Pulling on his trousers and jacket, and clapping a helmet on his head, he rushed out into the night.

The fire engines were already mobilised, bells clanging, with hoses unrolled and aimed towards the huge hangars. As far as he could see much of the activity was on the perimeter of the field. The brick airmen's barracks seemed to be unscathed, thank God, and he could already see the young men running out into the bunkers, according to their well-rehearsed drill. One of the staff cars drew up, with his WAAF driver, Claire, at the wheel. She looked far from her normal immaculately presented self, having thrown on her uniform over her nightie when she heard the sirens.

'Hop in, sir!' She leant over to open the door and he scrambled in.

'Good girl.' All formalities were gone. 'Just take me down the runway so we can see what the buggers have done this time! And get your helmet on!'

She pushed the tin cap over a mass of tangled curls and cranked the car into a higher gear.

'I don't think it's that bad, sir,' she said. 'It looks as though they might have overshot.' As they drove around the site, amongst the fire engines, trucks and ambulances, it appeared that she was right. Only one of the hangars, used for the overhaul of Whitleys and Lysanders, appeared to have taken a direct hit. There were a few men from the hangar being lifted on stretchers, but mercifully, only the night shift had been in there. He started to breathe more easily, conscious once again of Bronowski's words. Was he running a bad base? Should they have been more prepared?

Claire sat waiting, with the engine idling over. 'Where to now, sir?' She glanced solicitously at him. Flynn was looking drained, far from his usual ebullient self.

He took a deep breath. 'Over to the hangar, Claire, let's see how many we've lost tonight.'

She drove her way past the now familiar tableau of dousing flames, damaged buildings and general mayhem that formed the common backdrop of a country at war.

12

'Ruddy Krauts!' Owen muttered as he strode out to the Oxford the next day. 'I wish we had a few fighters here, then at least we could have gone after the bastards! Someone in the Observer Corps must have been asleep at their post! Two men killed, four seriously injured!'

'It could have been worse, sir,' Will said. 'At least we can still use the runway and the planes.'

'True, Fordham, let's get on with it!' Owen walked around the Oxford as they went through the external checks, working clockwise around the aircraft.

'What do you reckon to the tail wheel tyre?' he added as they stopped by it.

Will thought it looked serviceable, no cuts or creep. 'Should do.'

They continued with all the internal checks once inside the cockpit, then, satisfied as to the airworthiness of their plane, prepared for take-off. Their gaze was drawn to the damaged airfield around them as they taxied along the runway, but concentration was essential, especially with the extra debris around the place.

'Low flying!' Owen announced once they were safely in the air. 'Let's take a little trip to Staverton, as we planned.'

Will had been over the maps and navigation yesterday, but Owen took over for the first part of the exercise. It was not quite as much fun as in the Tiger Moth, Will thought, remembering the keen sensation of skimming in the fresh air just above the trees. In the Oxford, you felt as though you were low-flying as preparation for a fight, hence those bomb selector switches below the instrument panel. That would be the next step, learning how to use them and practise aiming.

Still, it was good to be away from the airfield and to see the Welsh countryside unfolding beneath him. It looked as though the farmers had been hard at work here, following the War Ag's instructions. The wheat and barley were coming up in solid patches of colour, interspersed by the neat hedges and winding roads. They flew over a tractor making its hardy progress through a tilled field, scattering flax seeds as it went, then flew higher so as not to frighten the two sturdy carthorses turning the earth over the seeds behind. Will had liked the carthorses on his uncle's farm, gentle Berrichons who seemed to respond to the very sound of his voice.

Staverton was one of the relief landing grounds, but as they came in to land, Will could see that it was far from dry and flat, causing a bumpy touchdown as the wheels slowed in the mud.

'Bloody hell, they need to tidy that up a bit! How the devil are we going to get airborne again?' Owen had avoided Staverton for a while, and thought he just might not bother to come back until the summer had dried it up. There was another Oxford at dispersal and Dougdale waved cheerfully to them as they drew close.

'Bit of a quagmire, old boys!' he shouted. 'More of a pigsty than a runway, if you ask me! The only thing in its favour is that the Hun has yet to bomb it!' Dougdale was flying solo. Owen frowned; he thought he remembered a directive that students should not fly solo from this RLG, in view of its 'undulating' condition. Still, it was too late now; Dougdale was already racketing along the grass. Will saw Owen's look of alarm and froze, momentarily transfixed by the sight of the uneven wobble of the plane. Dougdale was going to crash, he was sure, another senseless casualty!

They both watched in complete silence as the Oxford tipped a little to the left, but Dougdale must have righted the roll as he skimmed over the nearest hedge to the safety of the skies.

9th May 1941
RAF Shawbury
Dear You,
I didn't mean to worry you, and I can't give you a telephone number here. I'm not able to go into any details, but I know you understand that. I lost one of my old school friends from Guisborough, which was a terrible shock for his family, who I know well. He was only nineteen, and such a nice bloke – none of it makes any sense really.

Not that any of us have any choice, looking at what's happening in Greece and North Africa.

Anyway, I am back on base now, and I am getting better at flying the Oxfords. Can't wait to have my wings!

I hope you are well and not too exhausted by the new ward. My next leave will be in the middle of June, just in case there's any chance of you having a day off too then.

Thinking of you as ever,
From Me

13

'How long has he been like this?' Dr Donaldson's controlled voice showed no evidence of the near-panic which had gripped Honor when she found the convulsing child. She had shouted for help, bringing both Sister and Peter to Alfie's bedside to witness, as she had, the slow rhythmic jerks which seemed to encompass his swollen body. He was no longer conscious, despite his open eyes above the grey pallor of his face. Honor felt for his pulse.

'His blood pressure was still up this morning, and he said he felt tired, but drank a little orange juice. Then I was walking down the ward and saw him…'

She dropped her head, trying to concentrate on the elusive pulse. His wrist was so puffy she could hardly locate it.

'Could you get Dr Shepherd, please, Sister?' Peter said. Sister rushed from the bedside at his bidding, pushing the hastily closed curtains aside. There was no questioning his authority now.

'Can't you do something?!' Honor said.

'Have another go at his blood pressure.'

Honor was still taking the reading when the two superiors arrived. Dr Shepherd took one look at the child, and the young doctor at the head of the bed, and moved quickly to join him.

'The fits have only just started, Dr Shepherd,' Peter said. 'His blood pressure has been up but his urine output was improving a little. He's been on a very restricted fluid intake.'

'What's his reading now?'

Sister touched Honor on the arm and she took the stethoscope off. 'A hundred and thirty over eighty,' she said.

Dr Shepherd swiftly and efficiently examined the child, checking his heart and lungs, feeling his abdomen and then pressing with his index finger the pitting oedema at his ankles.

'What was his last urine result?' He proceeded brusquely. There was no time for cat-and-mouse today; he just wanted to satisfy himself as to the child's diagnosis. He had learnt long ago never to rush to conclusions, to evaluate the evidence systematically and always to rely on his own assessment of the clinical signs. It was what made him such a good consultant physician, however bombastic his ways.

'Positive for albumin, but no blood today,' Honor replied. She was terrified that she might have missed something. What if it was her fault that Alfie was fitting like this?

Dr Shepherd pursed his lips, and there was a moment's silence.

'I'm afraid it's a hypertensive encephalopathy,' he said. 'I doubt it will respond but we should try immediate venesection. Can I leave that in your hands, Dr Donaldson?'

'Of course,' Peter said. 'How much blood should I remove?'

'I should say at least ten ounces.' Dr Shepherd looked thoughtful. 'If it really has no effect you could do a lumbar puncture. I'll come back later, see how he is. You'd better let the boy's parents know, Sister.'

After they had gone, Honor whispered, 'What is a hypertensive encef…?', but was unable to pronounce the word.

'It's an encephalopathy, that means a brain swelling caused by his high blood pressure. We need to get on, prepare a venesection set.' Peter's voice was still calm, for he knew, unlike Honor, that the prognosis was hopeless. They could go through the motions, but it would be unlikely to make any difference to the poor little chap.

Honor left for the sluice, where she was joined by Sister.

'Do you know exactly what you need?'

'Two sets, Sister, one for venesection, and one for a lumbar puncture.'

'That's right, get a move on with it. You can assist Dr Donaldson.' Sister hurried from the sluice, satisfied that the task was within the capabilities of the young probationer. In fact, she secretly thought that Newson might make a half-reasonable nurse one day.

'You'll need to hold his arm for me,' Peter said, when she had laid out the set. The slow trickle of blood made its way from the child's elbow vein into the large syringe, Peter applying a vacuum by pulling back on it. Drip by precious drip, Honor began to wonder if the tube would ever fill.

'Dr Donaldson?' she began tentatively.

'Yes, Nurse?' He was concentrating on the venous line, jiggling it a little to augment the flow of blood.

'Was it my fault?'

He smiled in spite of himself. 'Do you think Dr Shepherd would have let you get away with it if it was?'

'But I should have realised his BP was too high!'

'Look, Honor.' Peter sounded more authoritative than ever. She was glad at least that he had stopped calling her 'Nurse'. 'You've done nothing wrong. This is a known complication, just very difficult to treat. Here, hold his arm just here, and try squeezing it, see if we can get a bit more before he starts to fit again.'

She did as she was told, and later, holding the child curled up in the foetal position, watched as Peter slid the fine spinal needle into the space between the vertebrae in his lower back. He was still fitting, but the jerks were less strong, and she could hold him still for just long enough. The straw-coloured fluid filled the tube in a rush, and Peter quickly withdrew the needle and pressed a compress on the puncture mark.

'You can turn him over now,' he said, but as she moved him she felt the child's respirations falter.

'Go and get Sister,' he said quietly and she did, but when they both came back, the child was dead and the young doctor was cradling him in his arms.

14

Addie was looking jubilant. Her meeting with Ken had exceeded her wildest dreams; he was, she told Honor, the most handsome, kind and loving man she had ever encountered. Whether it was the pretty outfit, or the fact that they had waited so long to see each other again, it was clear that events were proceeding apace.

She looked shyly across at her friend.

'He's asked me to marry him!'

'Addie, you've only just started going out with him!'

'Oh, yes, Honor Newson, don't think I can't remember what you said when you came back from your first date with Will!'

It was true, of course. In wartime, the momentum behind such relationships was intense, as was the air of heightened sexual awareness: it was difficult to say no to a young man who might be going to his death. Many couples circumvented the uncertainty by a whirlwind romance and hastily planned wedding, to fit in with an unexpected few days' leave, before a return to the harsh realities of service life.

'What did you say?'

'Yes, of course! I'm going to meet his parents at his next leave, then we'll probably just go right ahead!' There would be no stopping Addie, her mind was made up. Honor had never thought of her as an impulsive girl; it was just the war, yet again, shaping all of their lives.

'What about your folks? Won't they mind a shotgun wedding?'

'Honor, it's not like that! We wouldn't, not till we're married! No, my parents will like him just as much as I do, you'll see. Will you be my bridesmaid?'

Honor smiled. What could be the point in dampening Addie's enthusiasm?

'Of course.' Honor took her hand. 'I'm sure you've both thought it through. Don't forget Beatie, she won't want to be left out!'

Honor took off her shoes and stockings. Her feet ached.

'How was your day?' Addie said.

Honor swallowed. 'Alfie died,' she replied, her eyes filling with tears. She would have to stop this, she thought, she simply could not go on grieving every casualty, or it would extinguish her.

'Oh, Honor, I'm so sorry!' Addie put her arm around her and fished for a hankie. 'There's me, going on about my wedding!'

'It's just as well you did, Addie, at least it gives us something else to think about.' Honor wiped her nose, handed the hankie back and started to fold up her clothes. 'Let's write to Beatie, tell her your news, that'll cheer her up!'

Later, having finished Beatie's letter, she gazed at the next blank sheet of paper in front of her. She should write to Will, let him know her news. Not that she could tell him the most unwelcome bit, that without any encouragement from her, someone else had fallen in love with her, and that he was right there with her, every day, on the scarlet fever ward.

15

The chapter on enteric diseases lay open before her. The notion of polluted water supplies was familiar to Honor – the only tap in her family home was to be found in the kitchen and the privy lacked running water. She remembered bath night, the weekly immersion in the hip bath that was kept in the scullery. The three sisters were never allowed as long as they would have liked: she went in after Ruth, but before Audrey, only to give way to their father whose long, thin body they never saw unclothed, but could imagine it would fit into the small bath with extreme difficulty. The fire in the grate helped keep away the worst of the chill in the rapidly cooling water, and the soap never really lathered adequately. Still, there could be no subsequent sensation quite like that lovely feeling of clean skin and hair on a Sunday night…

She tried to stop daydreaming and concentrate on the book. There was only a week to go until the exams. She had not realised that typhoid fever could be contracted from milk, or that there could be so many complications. Her pencilled notes, with headings entitled *bacteriology* and *incubation period*, or *clinical signs*, were not helping it to sink in.

She flicked over the page to poliomyelitis, or 'infantile paralysis' as it was widely known. There had been a child in her village, Bet, who had one leg permanently shorter than the other as a consequence of the disease. Bet walked on crutches, but nothing could dampen her irrepressible spirit as she tried to keep up with the best of them. If you teased Bet, next thing you knew you would be flat on your face after she tripped you up with one of her crutches. Bet must be living out her days in Edgcott, denied the freedoms of war work which were liberating so many of her sex from a narrow world.

Honor read on, mesmerised by the description of the paralysis that followed the fever and muscle pain. Imagine ending up in an iron lung, unable to breathe without it? Like most probationer nurses, it was the disease she most feared catching. It was as unacceptable to discuss this anxiety, as it was for the student pilots to reveal their fear of dying. Besides, nurses were meant to be selfless, not interested in their own welfare.

Her thoughts drifted to the previous night. She should never have agreed to go to the pub with Peter, but he looked so crestfallen. It was stupid of her, thinking he only wanted to talk about Alfie – it was never going to be just that. Why had he switched so rapidly to talk of love?

'Quite honestly, Honor, I'm amazed you hadn't worked it out already!' His words hit a nerve: how could she have ignored the obvious truth? The conversation had deteriorated from then.

'What's he flying?'

'Oxfords, twin engines,' she had replied.

'Lucky chap!'

'If you really think that, then I'd better leave!' She had risen to go, but he grasped her hand.

'Lucky to have you, Honor, that's what I meant, and don't pretend you don't know!'

Reaching for her notebook, she tore out a sheet of paper.

14th May 1941
Groby Road Hospital
Dear You,
I am sitting in the library trying to work for my exam next week, but I can't concentrate! I hope you are well, and doing better than me in your swotting!

The latest news doesn't help – I never thought Greece would fall so quickly! Those poor soldiers stuck in Crete, it's just like last year all over again, but at least they stood a chance in Dunkirk. Maybe you know more about it than I do but I can't see how they can get them all out this time.

I think I should be able to manage some off-duty in June, but please would you let me know the exact dates? It will be lovely to see you again.

From Me

16

Will tucked the letter in his chest pocket and went to join his bombing class. The instructor was standing at the blackboard, in front of a chalk diagram of the operational bomb controls in the Oxford.

There was a hum of expectation in the room. Up to now, it had all been about trying to fly the plane, let alone managing anything else at the same time. Now they had arrived at the next phase, which would transform them from aviators to fighters.

'Right, let's have a bit of peace!' The instructor had plenty to cover this morning, and wanted their complete attention. 'This,' he continued, indicating with his wooden pointer, 'is the set-up for the bomb release equipment. You have the master switch, here, wired in the "on" position, then the selector switches here, at the bottom of the port instrument panel. When a bomb has been selected, the warning light will come on. The pilot's release button is here, on the port side of the control box, and this is the bomb jettison button, for releasing all the bombs. Any questions so far?' His tone did not invite interruption.

'There's a bombing steering indicator here, to the left of the blind flying panel. Now, you should all be competent at solo flying by now, but for bomb practice training, you'll go up in pairs, taking it in turn as pilots and bomb-aimers. Of course you won't be dropping the real thing.' He paused for effect. 'It'll be a simulated bombing, with the camera focused on a ground target. It's up to the pilot to bring the plane accurately into position, so that the bomb-aimer can press the tit.' Having already anticipated their response, he continued blithely. 'As I was saying, you press the tit when the sights are correctly aligned on the target, and not before, no matter how tempting. You'll have one practice run with your instructors this morning, then it's over to you for the afternoon session. The list at the back will tell you who you're paired up with, so just try and stay alert – that includes you, Dougdale. Just because you're the pilot doesn't mean you won't have to learn how to aim correctly. Your photographic test results will be logged and may be used in evidence against you! And that, gentleman, is that.'

Joseph raised his hand. 'Sorry, sir, my English is not good, what is "tit"?' He looked around the room innocently.

'A tit,' the instructor replied witheringly, 'is a small knob. Is that familiar to you, Krause?' He gathered his lecture notes before leaving.

When the laughter died down they made for the list. Will found that that he was partnered with Higgins, which suited him nicely. If there was a man who could be relied upon to do things properly, it was Higgins.

The two of them passed a pleasant afternoon aiming at targets on the ground. By the time he and Alf finished, they were making a passable success of the exercise. It was energising to be doing something other than purely concentrating on flying, and trying to hit a target accurately was merely an adult construction of most of their childhood games.

That evening, clustered around the wireless in the mess, brought with it an abrupt reminder of events in Europe.

'I knew it!' said Guy, looking shocked, as though even he had not believed his own predictions. Crete was under bomb attack by wave after wave of Luftwaffe planes. 'They'll be annihilated!'

'Surely the Navy can get them out? Look at Dunkirk,' Dougdale said.

Guy shook his head. 'Just you wait and see, those destroyers will be sitting ducks. They're surrounded there, you see there's no little fleet of ships to ferry them back over the Channel! Why the hell,' he added, 'if I can see these things coming, can't the powers that be? Don't they care what happens to their army?'

'You'd better go and join old Winston, give him a hand!'

'Oh, do shut up, Dougdale,' Guy replied. 'Don't you see there's nothing stopping them now?'

'Pity the old Russkies aren't on our side!'

'Haven't you heard of the German-Soviet pact?' Guy said.

'Well,' retorted Dougdale, with a characteristic non sequitur, 'what about this Hess chappie parachuting on to a Scottish moor? Now that's a turn-up for the book, isn't it?'

Dougdale, in common with most of the adult population of the country, had been following this event with interest. The news had broken a few days ago of the flight of Hitler's deputy, Rudolf Hess, parachuting on to Scottish soil, purportedly on a peace mission. The government had interned him immediately, and he would no doubt languish in jail for the rest of the war. Hess' motives were the subject of many a pub discussion up and down the land.

'Sorry, old chap, I'm not following your line of thought,' Guy said.

'That is because he does not have one!' Count Bronowski interrupted. 'Would you mind if we hear what it say on the wireless? I think it is all over for your men on that island!'

17

Joseph gazed in disbelief at the letter. His sister's normally neat writing, so rigidly drummed into her at school, looked shaky and indistinct. How had her letter managed to find its way out of the Warsaw ghetto? He had no idea, but its contents filled him with foreboding.

The language and prose pulled at his heartstrings like a refrain. There was no address or date, nor had he expected any.

> *Mój drogi Joseph,* the letter began,
> *We have to leave here and I am writing before we go. Our parents were taken last week and Ludmila and I must go before the Nazis come back for us. We are planning to follow the rivers and make our way to safety in Switzerland. Try not to worry. I pray we will be reunited with you in England one day. I can say no more but God bless you, my darling brother.*
> *Your loving sister Mira*

The young officer, with the insignia of the Polish Air Force carried so proudly on his epaulettes, looked around him in despair. Mira was only fourteen, and little Ludmila the baby of the family at nine. His parents had both worked at the university in Warsaw, where his father, an engineer, had met and married his mother when they were both students. Their son Joseph was their hero in uniform, but with the collapse of Poland to the German invasion, he and many other pilots had left them for the only country in Europe that was still standing.

The pain of deserting his family remained with him like an open sore. He had received no news of them since his departure, but had always hoped that they had stayed together, protected by his father's occupation. Until this letter! Now he could have no illusions about their fate. How could two young girls make their way across war-torn Europe? They could have no idea of the distances involved, or would not have left the comparative safety of the ghetto. There remained the agonising question of his parents' whereabouts, for he had already heard shocking rumours of the camps that were their destination.

The effort of staying strong during the gradual disintegration of his family proved too much for him, and he bowed his head, biting his hand and crying soundlessly on his taut knuckles.

Edek came into the room. 'Why you hide in here?' he began cheerily, then seeing Joseph's face, moved to his side. 'What news, Joseph?' His voice was low and urgent. The death of one Pole was a shared tragedy for them all.

Joseph shook his head, unable to speak, and handed him the letter. Edek scanned it quickly, then took the young man's wet hand in his.

'Look at me, Joseph!' he commanded, a man used to obedience. 'Look at me! You must keep hope, Joseph! They may still be alive. Mira is clever, careful too. Maybe she can get them out!'

The blank face stared back at him. 'They will all be dead by now!'

'Joseph, listen! What does your mother say to you? Does she say, "Give up, Joseph, is no point anymore"? She never says that, never does a Polish mother say that to her son! You owe her to keep fighting, not give up! Never! One day our nation will return, we will go back, find family and friends, live again. You must believe it!'

'And you, you believe it too? Sure my mother and father not gassed in a camp, my sisters not shot by the Nazis? Sure we will go back?' His eyes were angry with tears.

'We have to fight the war for them! There is no choice, Joseph!'

The young man wiped his nose on the back of his hand. 'As soon as RAF give me plane, I go back to Poland, find them!'

'I will never allow it under my command! Come now, we try main office, get in touch with Red Cross.'

18

Taking one look at the young pilot's stricken face, and the tall Polish airman supporting him at his side, the young WAAF officer rapidly drew up two chairs for them in front of her desk.

'Let me get you a cup of tea.' She looked at the older man for assurance. He nodded briefly at her and she rang a small bell to summon a tray.

Before the count could begin to explain, Joseph was seized with another fit of sobbing, and the woman rose to her feet, moved swiftly round the desk, and instinctively put her arms around his shoulders. He turned his face in to her and she could feel his tears damp upon the pocket of her regulation blue shirt. It was Alice's first day on duty in the office, having only been posted to Shawbury the week before. Not knowing what the work would entail, she was certainly not prepared for this. As the sobs subsided, she listened to the story of the Warsaw ghetto, her heart sinking all the time.

The one introducing himself as the count asked if she could contact the Red Cross, and opening a capacious filing cabinet in front of her, she hoped for inspiration. The frown that crossed her pretty face did little to spoil it, and Edek, who rarely found Englishwomen attractive, felt momentarily discomfited. Not only was she good-looking, a great deal of trouble had gone into her toilette, from her neat uniform to the waves of her short fair hair, and her well-lipsticked rosebud mouth.

She scanned the sections. Nothing under 'R', but trying another approach, she looked under 'I' for 'international agencies' and there it was. She drew out a long form with the characteristic insignia upon the letterhead.

'Look, Joseph, you can stop now, she will write to Red Cross!' Count Bronowski said.

Joseph blew his nose, as the young woman painstakingly took the details of his displaced relatives. It was a long form to fill in, but tea had arrived. Edek sipped from his cup and took the opportunity to observe her as she struggled with the complexities of the Polish names. She glanced up, feeling his gaze upon her, but he did not look away, merely smiled encouragingly. Her name badge read *Sergeant Alice Foulkes*, so that was good; at least he knew who she was, and where to find her. He thought of his last love affair at home, another beautiful girl whom he had left behind, along with everything else that mattered. What would have become of Agnieszka? He shook his head.

'Did I get something wrong?' Alice mistook his gesture as intended for her.

'You, Sergeant Alice? Not at all, you have been most kind!' He rose to his feet and, standing to attention, took her hand. 'We shall not forget, Joseph and I, how you help us! I must leave, but please to finish the writing and send to Red Cross for him.' He turned away, adding in a whispered tone, 'It gives him hope, you know!', then pressed her hand to his mouth in a gesture of courtly gallantry before leaving the room.

Alice gazed after him. What a funny chap, but so handsome, even if she could barely understand what he was saying! She turned her attention back to the form and the distraught young man in front of her.

'So how do you spell that first line of your address in Warsaw?' she asked patiently, pen hovered above the page.

19

'Not more bloody navigation exercises!' Guy looked up from his toast and marmalade. 'You'd think we'd have done enough by now!'

'Where's Joseph?' Will said.

It was unusual for the count to breakfast alone. Edek put down his cup.

'He got bad news from home.'

Will and Guy looked at each other. The Poles were so mercurial, one minute in drunken good spirits in the mess, the next lapsing into a profound melancholy from which they could not be roused.

'What happened?' Will asked.

'He got two sisters in Warsaw, Mira and Ludmila.' Edek shook his head.

'Are they all right?' Guy knew it was hardly likely, but what else could he say? Edek did not reply.

Later, when Will bumped into Joseph on their way to the hangars, Will gently touched his arm.

'I'm sorry to hear about your sisters,' he said.

Joseph took a deep breath, struggling with his emotions afresh. He nodded his head, unable to reply, and pulled on his gauntlets as he walked to his plane.

In the cockpit during pre-flight checks, Alf asked what had befallen the girls.

'Don't know, something bad,' Will said. That would be the fate of his own country's women and children if they could not win this war.

'Poor buggers,' Alf said, mirroring his thoughts. 'Let's get this damned wireless going properly for a change,' he continued, as Will pushed forward the throttle to taxi to the runway.

20th May 1941

RAF Shawbury

Dear You,

A long morning of navigation exercises and I'm glad it's time for a break! I keep thinking about my leave and hoping to see you. How does June 18th sound? I should have three days off, time enough to come over and back in the Austin.

I hope your swotting has picked up. Personally, I never want to sit another exam but that doesn't seem very likely!

Good luck anyway and remember to read the questions properly! At least, that's what they always used to say at school.

From Me

20

At least she knew the answer to the first question: *Describe the skin findings in acute rheumatic fever.* Honor was on safe ground, remembering vividly the rheumatic nodules, about the size of a pea, around the wrists and elbows. She wondered whether she should start answering this one straight away, before a look at the other questions took her confidence away, but then, mindful of the need to pace herself, she glanced down to the bottom of the paper. Frowning slightly, in anticipation of some doubt about the incubation period of measles, she settled down to write in her rounded hand. The examination room was noiseless, while they all concentrated on the examination as though their very lives depended on it.

Her hand was beginning to ache. Accurately recalling the antitoxin dosages in diphtheria did not present a problem, but she was having trouble with the three phases of poliomyelitis. She glanced up at the clock: only another ten minutes, and trying to stay calm, she scribbled assiduously until the bell went and they were all released from their labours.

For once she found herself agreeing with June, who looked ashen. 'What a filthy paper!' June said as they filed out of the room. 'How can you possibly answer all those questions on diseases you haven't even nursed?'

Addie was more phlegmatic. 'I'm sure it'll be all right.' She seemed to have gained a new confidence with her forthcoming nuptials. Spending most of their off-duty planning the event was beginning to wear a little on the other girls, some of whom, like June, did not even have a boyfriend to their name.

Beatie's last letter had made a welcome change:

Dear Addie,

Congratulations and I'm sure you'll make a lovely bride! I hope he's good enough for you, and that you aren't rushing into it. Still, I expect Honor is keeping you on the straight and narrow – make sure you listen to her!

I'd love to be a bridesmaid but not sure I can as I've just joined the FANYs! I am due to start my ten-week driver training course with the ATS soon, but at least I can already drive the family Rover so I am not a complete novice!

Keep me posted about your plans. I will write again when I know where I'm going to be posted.

Love to all.

Beatie

The girls looked at one another in disbelief. 'Just how does she do it?' June asked.

'She must be better, or they wouldn't have accepted her,' Addie said.

'It rather depends what she told them!' Honor added. 'Anyway, things are looking up if Beatie's back in business! It sounds quite fun, being an ATS driver!'

In the aftermath of their exam, it dawned upon them that Beatie might have the better option. The FANYs, whose name derived from the First Aid Nursing Yeomanry, were responsible for the driving side of the Auxiliary Territorial Service. Women were trained in vehicle maintenance as well as driving and could anticipate a variety of jobs, from driving staff cars and ambulances to lorries and motorcycles.

'Lucky devil!' June looked envious. 'I might just join her if I fail this wretched test!'

'You'll be perfectly all right! It's much better to be a nurse,' Addie said. The truth was that in wartime, women had a multiplicity of jobs open to them which would have been hitherto unthinkable. In their smart service uniforms, they presented a model of efficiency and determination, capable of rising to any challenge. No longer confined to rigid professions or defined by their class, the liberation of their generation was tangible.

'Whatever she does, we'll all hear about it sooner or later,' Honor concluded. 'I'm off to my shift, see you later.' Gathering up her cape, she walked to the ward. It was early summer, her favourite season, and the buds were just breaking in the hedgerows.

The ward was unusually quiet, for the ward round was over and Sister nowhere to be found. She eventually located an unfamiliar nurse attending to a young teenager with erysipelas in one of the cubicles. She was applying a boracic fomentation to the girl's swollen, inflamed arm.

'Where is everyone?' Honor asked.

The nurse looked up, as did the girl, who looked most unwell, causing Honor to reach instinctively for her chart. 'Her temp's very high.'

'I know.' The nurse finished her application. 'She's on sulphonamides, apparently they managed to get some specially for you, didn't they, Jenny?' She turned to Honor. 'I'm Molly Storey, standing in for Sister today. How was your exam?'

'I'd rather not think about it,' Honor replied, as she helped her tidy up. 'Where have they all gone?'

Molly raised her eyebrows. 'There, Jenny, that should be more comfortable. We'll be back later, try to drink as much as you can!'

'They've gone to a funeral,' Molly told her in the sluice, and Honor realised it must be Alfie. She fell silent. Probationers did not attend patients' funerals as a rule, for they could not have the time off, but she was glad that Sister had gone to pay their respects.

'Peter went too,' Molly added. 'He seemed pretty cut up about it.' She went on disposing of the soiled dressings.

'Dr Donaldson?' Honor said.

'Peter? Yes, he's a friend of mine from home. Our parents live in the same town. Though how he manages to stick this training is more than I can understand! He wanted to join the army, you know, but his parents kicked up such a fuss.' She paused. 'I don't know why I'm telling you all this.'

'It's all right,' Honor replied, 'I know him – we've been working on the same ward.'

'Oh, have you?' Molly looked at her with interest. 'You're not the one, are you?'

'What one?' Honor reddened imperceptibly.

'Well, somebody's been upsetting him lately, not that he'd tell me. I hope he's not being led up the garden path by some minx or another. He's honestly the nicest boy…'

'Let's get the bedpans done, shall we?' Honor reached for the stack of freshly cleaned pans on the shelf.

'So what's your name?' Molly said.

'Honor Newson.'

'Mm, Honor, I'll remember that. Now, what do you know about the child with otitis media in the first bed? He's very unsettled this morning.'

Once the ground rules had been set, the two girls started to work together surprisingly well. The ward could be like that: sometimes there was a synchronicity with a colleague that resulted in a simple, rhythmic division of labours, rather than an abrupt to and fro.

'Which ward are you normally on?' Honor asked as they were making the final bed, moving the feverish child effortlessly between the clean sheets until they were firmly tucked at precisely the right angle.

'Polio, Ward 17,' Molly replied, smoothing down the corner.

'What's it like?'

'Grim.'

25th May 1941
Groby Road Hospital
Dear You,
I have checked my on-duty and it looks as though I should be free on 18th. It's not long to wait!

Please keep me posted about your plans – where are you going to stay?

What dreadful news about HMS Hood! I knew one of the lads on the ship – he came from my village. I can't believe so many lives were lost.

My exam was horrible, just hope I haven't failed.

I'll save all my other news for when we are together again.

From Me

21

'What's she say?' Alf asked. His co-pilot had not yet told him he had a girl, but looking at his face as he scanned the letter left Alf in little doubt.

Will smiled and leant forward to flick the bomb switch on. 'How do you know it's from a girl?'

'Well, if it's from a boy I'll be needing to revise my opinions, Fordham!' Alf was checking the oil pressure prior to take-off. 'Is she pretty, this one?'

'She's more than pretty,' Will replied. 'Can't really describe her, she's just got what it takes!'

'Lucky you!' Alf meant it. He had yet to meet his ideal woman, and sometimes wondered if he ever would, at least not this side of active service. Despite all the good-natured joshing in the mess, many of the boys were sexually inexperienced, having joined up at a tender age, often straight from school. The clock seemed to be ticking against them in terms of matters outside the cockpit of an aeroplane: it was as though all of their youthful energies were harnessed to that one end. Very few had been as fortunate as Matt to meet a willing young WAAF officer.

'Fuel on, flaps twenty, checks complete,' Alf continued, as the Oxford in front of them on the grass runway trundled into the sky. 'Too many bloody aircraft around today,' he grumbled. 'Why aren't we at one of the RLGs?'

Alf had a point, but they had soon navigated away from the airfield to concentrate on the morning bomb-aiming exercises. As the camera clicked over the target, Will reckoned that their practice sessions were beginning to pay off. He wondered how their results were comparing to the others'.

'Time to get back.' They had completed the runs and were soon back in sight of the Shawbury runway.

'Still looks like Piccadilly Circus.' Alf's voice took on a note of alarm. 'Hold back, hold back, don't go in!' Will had already put the undercarriage down but immediately retracted it and opened the throttles to put them into a climb.

'What the hell's happening?' he asked, at the same moment as Alf's expletive burst forth.

'Christ Almighty! Stay up, Fordham, divert to Bridleway Gate!'

Pulling into a wide circle, Will was able to make out for himself the sight on the runway. One of the Oxfords was directly slewed into a Battle, both appearing to be completely wrecked. Smoke was already pouring from the engine of the Battle and debris was strewn around.

'Jesus Christ!' Alf looked shaken. 'What the bloody hell happened there? I doubt either of those two will get out alive!'

The office was due to close when Alice Foulkes looked up, hearing the knock on her door.

'Come in.'

The man in front of her seemed to have lost some of his confidence. She motioned the count to a chair.

'I'm sorry, sir, I've heard nothing back from the Red Cross yet. I think it'll take quite a while…'

Edek Bronowski looked despondent, but no less attractive than she had first found him.

'I know.' He waved his hand expressively. 'They will not write for many months. Is just… that boy, Joseph, he has lost hope. What can I do? It is not true to say they will be found, Alice!' He gazed blankly at the polished brown wood of the desk between them.

It was not the time to draw attention to his use of her first name.

'I know, sir, I understand,' she replied patiently. 'Look, I finish here in five minutes, why don't we take a little walk to the village, get off the base, and take your mind off it for a while?'

'We will take a walk, Alice?' He looked up at her concerned face.

'Yes, Count, we will take a walk.'

22

As they came down the dark lane back to the base, he stopped to face her. There was no preamble to his urgent embrace, gripped as she soon was in his uniformed arms. She felt no wish to resist, and raised her mouth to his kiss. Steadying herself against the intensity of the moment, she drew back, and stood with her hands on his shoulders.

'Does that make you feel better?' Her voice was soft, acquiescent in its tone.

'Alice, you will always make me feel better.' He kissed her again, slowly, savouring the moment. Neither was in doubt of their sudden and mutual longing, as he drew her towards the old oak tree in the hedge.

She heard the sound of the approaching staff car before he did, and pulled quickly apart from him as the headlights drew close. The car stopped and she was hailed by the driver.

'Alice! What are you doing out here in the dark?' Then a pause. 'Oh, evening, Count.' It was Pilot Officer Blezard, on his way back from the pub.

'Hop in, you two, I'll give you a lift back.' He opened the passenger door.

Alice struggled to regain her composure, but took her place in the seat.

'Is all right, I need the fresh air,' Edek said, closing the door for her.

'OK, if you're sure, see you in the mess,' Blezard said, then 'Having a nice walk, Alice?' as he changed into first gear.

She was glad it was dark in the car, for he would surely have seen her blush. She smoothed down her jacket.

'Yes, thanks,' she answered steadily. 'His friend is terribly upset about his sisters in Warsaw. I've been trying to help them contact the Red Cross.'

'Don't get too involved, old girl,' Blezard cautioned. 'Those Polish chappies are a law unto themselves. I don't think they really understand this country, or its customs. But it's nice of you to try to help.'

'It's my job, isn't it? They're fighting for us too! We can't just wash our hands of them!'

''Course not, Alice.' Perhaps he had gone too far. He liked the attractive young sergeant and had been planning to ask her to the cinema soon. 'Don't you worry your pretty little head about it. I'll take you for a drink in the mess!'

Edek walked slowly up the lane, enjoying the dark moment of solitude, and marvelling that in the midst of such unhappiness, he could suddenly experience such joy.

He did not see her again until much later that evening. She was surrounded by a group of noisy officers, including Blezard, who was standing possessively at her side. She looked up as soon as Edek drew near to their circle, giving him a shy smile that she hoped might pass unnoticed by all but him. Edek's confidence appeared to have returned, as he looked loftily at the young men.

'Ah, Count!' Blezard finally acknowledged his presence. 'Would you like a drink? I hear young Alice has been helping you two chaps find some lost relatives. Don't suppose it'll be much use, though, will it? I mean, in a country like yours there must be thousands of homeless people!'

The group fell suddenly silent, sensing animosity between the two men.

'So you think it not worth to try?'

'Oh well, she can try, old man, as long as she doesn't waste too much RAF time on a wild goose chase. I'm not sure that's what our sergeants are for!'

Joseph had detached himself from the bar and was moving to join his friend.

'Wasting time, is it,' Bronowski said, 'to look for lost children? Is not proper business of RAF?'

Alice moved forward and put her hand on his arm. 'Edek...' she began, but he shook her aside and squared up to his adversary, the others instinctively moving back.

'There's no need to take on!' Blezard said. 'You Polish chappies—'

He had no opportunity to finish the sentence as he was floored by the count's right hook. Staggering back, he rallied and tried to plant a punch on his opponent, but the count was sparring like a traditional boxer, just as he had been trained to do at military academy. Dodging the blow, he planted another one upon the pilot officer, which laid him out cold. He looked across at Alice, who had instinctively moved to Blezard's aid, then wiped the corner of his mouth, and strode from the room.

30th May 1941

RAF Shawbury

Dear You,

It's never a dull moment here! Still, I can't wait to see you again!

It's fixed: I will be arriving in Leicester on the 18th, late afternoon. How much time can you take?

I have two days altogether, but I haven't worked out where to stay. I thought I might put up in a local pub, if it's all the same to you.

I've managed to cadge some extra petrol so we could take in a little trip.

Only two weeks to go!

From Me

23

The girl on Ward 3 could not have been much older than herself. She was so pretty, Honor thought, as she placed the breakfast tray in front of her. Two wide eyes, framed by a mass of black hair, looked back at her from a face that was unnaturally pale.

'Hello, you're new,' she said sweetly, sitting up on her pillows. Honor noticed the effort that it took her, and put a supporting arm behind her back.

'Yes, my first day,' Honor said.

'Well, you'll soon get used to us, not much happens here!' the girl replied, then shyly, 'What's your name?'

'Nurse Newson,' she replied, looking at the chart, 'and you must be Vera.'

There was a nod for a reply, as the girl sipped her milk. 'I'll never get through all of this!' She motioned at the tray.

'You'd better try, or I'll be in trouble! How long have you been on the ward?'

'This one? About a month. Then before that,' Vera looked thoughtful, 'there was the time in Switzerland – you know, mountain air, my parents thought it might cure me…'

Honor thought it best not to question her further, for she could see that her breathing was becoming more laboured.

'Well,' she said with a brightness she did not really feel, 'you have your breakfast, then I'll be back to help you wash. Maybe we can have you out on the terrace today.'

Vera took a mouthful of porridge, very slowly and without relish.

'Nurse Newson!' Sister was calling from the other end of the ward.

The trouble was, Honor mused as she made her way down the ward, that you never knew what to expect with a new ward sister. Some of them seemed grim at first, then turned out to be reasonable and fair, while others could dupe you into a false sense of security, only to make your life a misery with each succeeding day. Which one would this be? She began to wish she was driving a truck like Beatie, her foot pressed down hard on the accelerator to freedom.

The woman in charge turned out to be neither of these two types: she was young and fair-faced, reminding Honor of Sister Davies at the Lambeth. She seemed particularly open-minded in her approach. Sister Hastings was that rare nurse who believed in students learning without oppression or fear. She positively encouraged intelligent questions and, through kindness and patient mentoring, did more for her probationers than many an autocratic despot. The nurses had heard gossip that she was engaged to be married to a naval officer, and perhaps it was her anticipation of a normal life that allowed her to treat her charges with respect.

'Right!' she said briskly as Honor stood in front of her. 'What do you know about tuberculosis?'

'Very little, Sister,' Honor replied, 'apart from what I've read in the textbooks or seen in the past.'

'It's your first TB ward?'

'Yes, Sister.'

'I like honesty, Nurse, you're here to learn, that's why you've come. You'll be working with Nurse Freeman, she'll see you right, just take it slowly and carefully at first. Which patients have you been looking after so far?'

'I've just given Vera her breakfast.'

'She won't eat it, poor thing. She has an open focus in her right lung, we can't get it to seal off. She knows it, too.'

Honor looked down at her polished black shoes.

'That's it, then, go and find Freeman.' She was dismissed, but not unkindly. So far, so good.

Nurse Freeman was gathering up the breakfast trays as Honor drew near; stacking the plates, most of which seemed as untouched as Vera's. The senior nurse appraised her rapidly. So many probationers had passed through her hands that she reckoned she could get a measure of them in the first five minutes.

'Sister told me to find you. I'm Nurse Newson,' Honor said.

'Do you know anything about TB?' the grey-haired woman asked.

'Not really.'

'Of course you don't. It's a condition that can surprise even the old hands like myself. Never think you know everything about a disease, or it will come back and bite you.'

Honor thought of Maisie and nodded.

'Our first job today will be to collect the sputum pots,' Freeman informed her, as she followed her to the sluice. 'We'll give out these clean ones. We have all ages here on the women's ward, mostly young adults, but as you can see, there are some older patients as well.'

In the first bed was a woman of early middle age. 'Morning, Ada,' Nurse Freeman said. 'Anything for me today?'

'No, same as usual.' Ada noticed Honor. 'Got an apprentice today? She'll want to know why I don't cough anything up, like all the rest do, won't she?' She clearly enjoyed her shared secret with Freeman, and had rehearsed the scenario many times before.

'Are you going to tell her, or shall I?' Ada said confidently.

'Show her your arms,' Nurse Freeman said, as Ada drew back the sleeves of her dressing gown to reveal a reddish raised, nodular patch extending down each arm. Part of it was ulcerated, and Honor drew forward to look more closely. She had never seen a lesion like that before; it was quite unlike the other rashes.

As she frowned at the unfamiliar skin signs, Ada looked triumphant.

'There, you don't know what it is, do you?'

'No, I'm afraid I don't.'

'It's lupus!' Ada said. 'I'm rare, aren't I, Nurse Freeman? All the doctors get it wrong, because I'm a bit too old for it! Just goes to show,' she added confidingly, 'you never can tell.'

'You are absolutely right!' Nurse Freeman said. 'And we're going to put you under the lamp again today.' She turned to Honor. 'It's the latest treatment, ultraviolet light. In Switzerland they're using heliotherapy but we don't have that here.' She paused. 'It's a great mistake to think of TB as a disease of the lungs only. It can be on the skin, like this, in the bloodstream, in the intestines and bones as well.'

They moved on to the next patient. 'This one is more classical.' Freeman took the chart, and showed Honor the temperature variation, low in the morning, raised in the afternoon, and the quickened pulse rate. 'This is pulmonary TB,' she added, counting on her fingers the symptoms: 'fatigue, weight loss, lack of appetite, night sweats', then taking the brimming sputum pot from the woman. 'The most important part of the diagnosis is to look for the bacilli under the microscope.' Then, seeing Honor's look of dismay, 'It's all right, the doctors do that.' She covered and labelled the pot and they continued down the ward until Honor began to doubt that any more sputum could be forthcoming.

Vera obediently gave a little cough as her pot was still empty, but this precipitated a fit of uncontrollable coughing. Freeman quickly drew the curtains round the bed and the two nurses supported the frail young woman, who, to Honor's alarm, began to cough copious quantities of blood.

'Pass me her towel,' Freeman directed, as she let the girl finish her spasm, the blood clots gathering on the white towel as she held it in front of her. She wiped her mouth as the fit subsided. Vera took a shallow breath, her eyes wet from the coughing.

'I'm so sorry,' she said weakly.

'You've nothing to be sorry about, Vera.' Nurse Freeman gathered the towel, and motioned to Honor to fetch a bowl of water. 'We'll soon put you right again.'

Vera slumped back on the pillow, her young eyes dull and resigned. 'It'll get me next time,' she said. 'Just you wait and see.'

For once, the senior nurse did not contradict her. Many years on the TB ward had taught her to allow people to accept their fate. The treatments had changed little since Victorian times: plenty of air, good food and adequate rest seemed a thin armamentarium against an overwhelming disease. Sometimes the doctors would decide to collapse a lung artificially, in order to rest it, but this had already been tried without success in Vera's case.

'She had adhesions, that's why,' Nurse Freeman said, then went on to explain that the pleural surfaces of the lung lining had become stuck together as a consequence of the disease.

In the earlier days of her training, Honor would have had two questions: what treatment was there, and what was the prognosis? She decided to ask neither, anticipating the silent look she would receive by way of an answer.

Nurse Freeman was not one to duck the issue. 'Sometimes patients get more hopeful when they're near to death,' she continued in a quiet tone in the sluice, stacking the sputum pots in neat rows. 'It's called *spes phthisica.*'

'Whatever does that mean?' Honor said.

'It's Latin,' replied her tutor. '"*Spes*" means "hope", phthisis, as you know, is what we call pulmonary TB.'

Some of the patients were already ambulant, in the recovery stages, and were allowed to take short walks. The more adventurous would try and find walking partners from men's medical, with all the added complications that might arise. Inevitable scandals would ensue.

'Did you hear about Dolly?'

Honor overheard peals of laughter from the bathroom, and when she saw Dolly sitting in the day room, looking even more breathless and flushed than usual, she thought she could guess her fate.

24

'So what do you think is the matter with this little lady?'

The chest physician on the morning ward round appeared to Honor to be the kindest doctor she had ever met. He was grey and portly, immaculately dressed with a smart bow tie, waistcoat and pocket watch. Not deeming it necessary to strike fear into the hearts of either the patients or the staff, he would stand discussing chest X-rays as though he really valued their opinion. Honor had not a clue what the shadowy black and grey images portended. Dr Jackson would try and point out the cardinal features to the surrounding nurses, who would nod in assent. There was just one junior doctor working on this ward, and to everyone's surprise, she was a young woman. There were so few girls making their way through medical school that such women were still regarded as a curiosity. Some of the patients simply could not accept that a female doctor might know what she was doing, and the nurses could be equally unkind, sensing unfair competition. This one, fortunately for her own self-preservation, was not pretty, so escaped more lightly.

Dr Sarah West was plainly dressed in a sensible tweed skirt, her white coat covering her shirt and cardigan. She wore thick lisle stockings and flat brown lace-up shoes. She peered at the patient through thick-rimmed glasses, as lost for an answer as the rest of the audience.

'Come and examine her, then,' the consultant encouraged her, as she took her stethoscope out of her pocket, and stooped over the girl, who could not have been above sixteen years of age.

'Use your eyes first,' he added gently, as she proceeded with her examination.

The girl, whose name was Hilda, timidly raised her nightgown on request to reveal a large, swelling abdomen. Honor was surprised – surely they would not have a pregnant girl on this ward?

The young doctor slowly and methodically continued, taking her time to feel the belly, touching it and tipping it from side to side, listening for bowel sounds and concluding with a detailed examination of the chest and back. She neatly replaced Hilda's nightgown.

'Have you any questions for her?' the physician prompted.

'How did it start, Hilda?' The young doctor's voice was beautifully spoken, and almost as gentle as her superior.

Hilda flushed, but looked steadily back at her. 'If you're going to ask me when it's due, I'm off!' she retorted. She was so tired of the incessant questions, as if her family had not been bad enough when she started to feel sick and get tummy pains. They all thought the same thing, which was a bit thick, considering she had never been with a boy and her periods were as regular as clockwork.

'That wasn't what I said,' Dr West replied. Hilda, emboldened, took a deep breath.

'I been sick a lot,' she went on. 'Tummy pains, then I can't go, you know, then I swells up like this. It's not my fault,' she added, 'I ain't done nothing!'

'I never said you had.' Dr West turned to Dr Jackson, and said, 'It's the ascitic type of tuberculous peritonitis, sir.'

Honor, who did not understand the words, waited for the reaction from on high, then Dr Jackson rubbed his hands and smiled, saying, 'Just the ticket, my dear, indeed it is.' The group gave an imperceptible sigh of relief.

'Would you like to explain to the nurses what that means?' he went on, and Dr West lucidly outlined the portal of infection to the peritoneum, via the lymph or blood supply, and the fluid, or ascites, which developed as an exudate in the abdominal cavity. Honor thought she understood, though would have to go and check some anatomy textbooks later just to make sure.

'So you don't think I'm in the family way?' Hilda said.

'Of course not.' Dr West was emphatic. 'Whoever said you were?'

Hilda, who did not like to recount the number of times this had been suggested, even by members of the nursing and medical professions, lay back on her pillows with relief.

'And the treatment?' the consultant continued.

'She'll need paracentesis.'

'I agree, what else?'

'Liquid paraffin for her constipation, then the usual TB regime. I can't find another active lesion, but we'll do a chest X-ray and sputum cultures.'

'Very good, my dear, I will leave her in your safe hands.' He patted her on the back before they all moved on to the next patient. Sister Hastings motioned to Nurse Freeman to assist the doctor, and Honor obediently followed her to the sluice, where she started to lay up a tray.

'What's a paracentesis?' she asked.

Freeman picked up the sterilised instruments with the tongs and transferred them to the tray. 'She'll draw off the fluid through a needle into the tummy wall.'

Later, standing by the competently gowned doctor, who introduced the needle gently into Hilda's protuberant abdomen, followed by a gush of yellow fluid that seemed to fill up syringe after syringe, Honor was relieved to see Hilda's response.

'That's better!' Hilda exclaimed, though her abdomen still looked swollen. 'I can breathe a bit now!'

Honor watched as Dr West completed the procedure. Imagine being a woman doctor! Now that was something for those old fuddy-duddies to think about!

The more she saw of tuberculosis, the less she felt she knew. She had been summoned to help Freeman with a dressing later on that day, and stood watching as she peeled off the old dressings to reveal a curved red scar along the patient's side, extending from under her ribs to her loin. The woman, fair-haired and in her late twenties, winced as the last gauze was removed.

'Sorry,' said Freeman abstractedly, inspecting the wound. 'Good granulation tissue, looks healthy,' she added, then proceeded to dab iodine tincture along the reddened edges. Honor moved to hold the woman's hand, noticing her biting her lips. There was the answering grip, extracting that primeval comfort that one being can give to another. How many such interlockings have carried the human race through the pains of birth, life and death?

'Done now.' Freeman began to apply fresh dressings to the wound and the woman relaxed. She smiled at Honor. 'You're new, aren't you?'

Returning her smile, Honor assured her that she was, indeed, the latest probationer on the ward.

'She's very good, is Nurse Freeman,' the woman told her. 'I don't know how I'd have got through my op otherwise.'

'Nonsense, Muriel, you've been a model patient,' Freeman said.

'I hope it works, do you think I'll get better now?'

'I think you should. They made the diagnosis early – it looks as though only one kidney was affected so now that's out…' Freeman wrapped a long bandage around her slim frame.

'I hope so,' Muriel reflected. 'I wouldn't want to go through that again!'

'What happened?' Honor said.

'Terrible waterworks!' Muriel screwed up her eyes with the memory. 'I was passing blood, and the pain! Nothing seemed to stop it, especially at night. I really didn't care if I lived or died, that pain was so bad! The doctor thought I just had cystitis, but I knew it was worse than that.'

'Well, you should start to mend now,' Freeman said encouragingly, 'and we'll need to get you moving today, you're three days post-op. Can't just have you lying around there, can we?'

'Slave drivers, that's what you are!' But Muriel looked relieved, as though that must mean she was improving at last.

Honor helped tidy up the dressings tray and wheeled it back down the ward. As she passed her bed, she noticed that Vera was still looking pale and listless. Perhaps there would be time to wheel her out into the sun, for who knew how many more days of precious sunshine would be hers?

Ratby House
June 8th 1941
Dear You,
I am working in the TB sanatorium here for the next eight weeks. It's a very stately house in the countryside, in beautiful grounds, and the food is such a treat! I miss the other girls, but it won't be long and I'm lucky to be here in this lovely summer weather. Sometimes I can almost forget there is a war on!

You'll need to drive to the village, then past the church and out towards Markfield; you can't miss the house.

I only have one day off, and will need to be back at ten in the evening.

From Me

25

Edek was waiting for Alice in their usual place after the midday break. She found him sitting back on the bench under the ash tree, his eyes closed under the warmth of the early summer sun. Sensing her approach, he rose to his feet and took her hand. They sat together for a little while, saying nothing, just enjoying the proximity to each other and the dappled light.

He broke the silence first.

'Is quite beautiful, your country, Alice. I thought it do nothing but rain and wind.'

She smiled softly at him. 'Yes, it's at its best today.' She held his hand within hers. 'I've had a letter from the Red Cross.'

'What it say?' he answered quickly.

'It says there is no trace of them,' she replied quietly. It was such a shame to cast a dark shadow on the summer's day.

He sighed. 'Is as I thought. But Joseph, what will he do? He looks bad, Alice, spend all the time in his room, not talking, not in the mess. I try to bring him round, is no good!'

'I'm going to have to tell him.'

'I know, of course.' Edek shook his head. 'I just hope he can bear it, that's all.'

Looking around to make sure no one could see, he kissed her softly on the lips.

'I bring him to your office at five,' he said, then kissed her again, until she extricated herself unwillingly from his embrace. As she walked back along the grassy path to her office, she could only think of him.

'What's that mean, no trace?' Joseph's eyes were fixed upon Alice as she read the letter.

Edek came to her aid. 'It means they cannot be found.'

'I told you they were dead!'

'But the letter doesn't say that!' Alice said, unable to bear his anguish.

'For certain they are dead! They are just little girls, Mira and Ludmila! If they are not dead, then even worse…' Joseph buried his face in his hands.

Alice put her arm around him.

The young pilot looked back at her, tears in his eyes. 'Day after day I think of them! The girls, and my mother and father. I fly the plane and think of them. I wake up, I think of them. I sleep, they are in my dreams! There is no peace, don't you see?!' He ran wildly from the room.

In the silence that followed, Edek rose to comfort Alice, whose reserve was gone.

'You'd better find him,' she said, and he stroked her wet cheek gently before he left.

Will heard him, in the distance, calling for his friend.

He had just come in from a difficult day, practising a forced landing at Staverton with Alf. Although the weather was clear, the conditions on the runways were far from perfect.

'Flaps down, eighty mph, undercarriage down.' The Oxford bounced badly as Will landed and he thought for an awful moment that he had damaged the undercarriage. 'Jesus Christ, that was close!' He was glad that it was Alf's turn to bring the plane back to base.

'What's up, Bronowski?' Will said, walking over the grass towards him.

Edek looked distracted. 'I cannot find Joseph. I try his room, the mess, all places!'

'Perhaps he's left the base, gone for a breather,' Will suggested. 'Why don't we go down to the pub, see if he's there?'

'I'll go with Fordham.' Alf joined them. He had been checking the undercarriage on the Oxford. His friend had been lucky; it had been one hell of a bounce, but there was no damage that he could see.

'That'll be our job, then, looking for Krause in the pub!' Alf smiled, for it was hardly onerous.

'Thank you, please to look in village and then bring him back!' Edek could not rest. He and Joseph had been together since their journey began. First travelling to France, before they realised with dismay that the French were not able to put up a creditable defence against the German advance, thence making their way to England by boat. Far from being welcomed with open arms, they had experienced obstacle after obstacle before they were allowed to fly again. Even then, it would be on bombers, not the Spitfires they had set their hearts on. From their very first stark encounter, surveying the wreckage of the devastated Polish airfield, Edek had taken charge.

'We have to leave!' He had dragged Joseph away from the damaged planes. 'We must get out!' He remembered the look of disbelief in the boy's eyes, his stunned denial of defeat.

'Let me kill them, I want to kill them!' Krause had muttered again and again.

'Another day, you will. Now come, or we both die together here.'

The flashback passed, and Edek was back in the present. He watched the two young men departing for the village, then resumed his tour of the perimeter fence, calling as he went.

They never made it to the pub. There was no reason for Alf to look inside the disused barn by the side of the road; he was just trying to be helpful. For his part, he was looking forward to a pint in the hostelry, where he was sure they would find Joseph propping up the bar.

From the stout oak beam, the lifeless figure swung, silhouetted against the crumbling grey stone walls, as the swallows swooped and dived about the eaves.

26

Dr Sarah West frowned. She did not like the look of Vera today: her pallor was increasing and she had suffered another haemoptysis, coughing profuse quantities of blood, the night before.

'I'm going to write her up for a blood transfusion. She's been cross-matched already, can you organise transport from Groby Road? Bring me a drip set and I'll get it up ready.'

Honor exchanged a glance with Nurse Freeman. It was more palliative care than curative, but they were all duty bound to go through the motions. Later, as the nurses monitored the slow drops of blood through the giving set, Vera must have read their thoughts.

'I think my parents should visit, don't you, Nurse Freeman?' she suggested softly.

'Yes, I think that would be very nice,' Freeman said levelly. 'I'll give them a ring and let them know.'

'That's it then, Vera, you'll feel better for that!' Honor said as she tidied up her bed.

'Will I?' The beautiful face did not appear troubled, as it had before. She smiled patiently at the two of them, and settled back against the pillows. 'Can I talk to Nurse Newson for a little bit?' she asked.

'Of course, but don't go tiring yourself.' Freeman nodded at Honor. 'You stay here, I'll carry on with the drug round.'

Honor brought up a chair to sit at Vera's side. 'Shall I brush your hair?' she offered, then with Vera's silent assent, began to brush the long tresses rhythmically.

'I'm going to die, you know,' Vera said. 'But it won't be too bad, not after all of this.'

Honor kept on brushing.

'Will you do something for me?'

'Of course.'

'There's a boy I know.' Vera was becoming breathless. 'My parents didn't approve. But if anything happens to me, you'll tell him, won't you?'

'I'll do whatever you want, but you must try to get better, Vera!'

'I can't.' The girl was serene. 'Pass me my diary.'

Honor found the little leather-bound book in her bedside locker.

'He's on the last page, see.' Vera showed Honor the name, exhausted with the effort of such a confidence, and let her tired eyes close, breathing shallowly. Honor put the hairbrush on the locker and held her hand until Freeman came to tell her that Vera's parents would be coming that night.

'I'm not sure she'll make it till then,' Honor whispered.

'I know. You stay with her, she shouldn't be alone.'

Much later, when the two figures arrived, Honor was still there, but the girl was already at peace.

27

Will had checked the route to Ratby on the map before he left, for without road signs it could be difficult to find his way. Still, it should not be too far, and as the Austin motored through the shady evening lanes, he experienced a sense of both longing and apprehension. What if she did not like him anymore? Maybe she had found someone else? He was still trying to banish such thoughts from his head when he spotted the imposing Victorian building at the top of the hill. That must be it. Glancing at his watch, he realised he was just a little early, but drew up the long driveway and parked by the house. He was just thinking what a pleasant place it must be to work when he saw a middle-aged couple, both dressed in black, coming out through the front door. The man seemed to be supporting the woman as she walked unsteadily to their parked dark saloon car.

His attention momentarily averted, he did not at first notice the small figure standing at the door. She must have been behind them – it was her! He climbed quickly out of the car, but she was down the stairs before him, and in his arms.

'Will, you made it!' She looked up at him, tenderly.

'Of course I did! Where do you want to go?'

'Oh, anywhere!' she replied. 'Anywhere with you!'

By the time they returned, the streaked pink sunset had been overtaken by a clear moon.

'I'll be right here, in the morning.' Honor extricated herself from his embrace. 'Sleep tight.' And she kissed him once more, a slow, indulgent kiss, before she watched the car make its way slowly down the moonlit drive.

Feeling almost light-headed as she climbed the stairs to her room, she wondered how she could ever bear to lose him. He was so excited about his forthcoming wings, but they both knew what that would bring – active duty, heaven knows where!

28

'Alf, look who's here!' Mrs Bradley ran out into the farmyard, wiping her hands on her floury apron. She had not recognised the sound of the motor as it drew up, little expecting Will to walk in through the kitchen door with Honor at his side. 'He'll be so pleased to see you!' She kissed them both warmly.

The low-raftered kitchen smelt as good as ever, the dough rising in cloth-covered bowls ready for the oven. Will smiled at Honor, who squeezed his hand. She had not known they would be coming here today; he had kept it a surprise for her, deciding to turn up unannounced.

Mr Bradley caught sight of the car as he left the barn. 'I'll be blowed, lad!' he said, shaking Will by the hand. 'Where've you both sprung from?'

'I've just had a couple of days' leave, thought we'd pop by and see how you are.' Will noticed the farmer looked worried, and guessed the reason before they had sat down for a cup of tea at the oak table.

'Any news of the boys?' he asked, glancing at Mrs Bradley.

'We haven't heard anything, just what we read in the papers,' she answered, her voice strained.

'And that's an almighty mess, from the look of it,' her husband added. 'They're never going to let Rommel take Tobruk again, surely? That siege, I mean, how long will it take? Where are our boys and our tanks? If I had my way, we'd beat the hell out of Rommel and finish him off! Some general out there doesn't know their job, you mark my words!'

He would have continued, but Mrs Bradley intervened. 'It's so hard, not knowing if they're all right! It's worst when you wake at night, wondering where they are, then you lie awake, waiting for the dawn...'

'We've driven them back before, maybe the latest push will do the trick,' Will said, with a confidence he did not feel. The truth was, Rommel was becoming invincible in North Africa, and it was difficult to see how the tide could turn in their favour again.

'Sure, lad, we've got to trust someone.' Mr Bradley beckoned to Will. 'Come over to the fields with me, see what you think of my wheat and barley. I'm hoping for a decent crop, and so are the War Ag!' They left the kitchen together, discussing yields and weather.

Taking another cup of tea, Honor asked about the land girls.

'Still got five,' Mrs Bradley replied. 'One short, but could be worse!'

'My sister's in the Land Army,' Honor volunteered.

'Is she, dear? You never said. Where's she working?'

'Buckinghamshire,' Honor said. She had rather lost contact with Ruth – her thoughts were so taken up with Will.

'How's your nursing going?' Mrs Bradley asked.

'Not so bad, in the TB sanatorium now. It's a nice change to be out in the open, at Ratby.'

'Well, you're always best off in the country air if you ask me,' the farmer's wife replied. 'Now what about helping me knock down this dough for the oven?'

When Will returned, she was up to her elbows in flour, and looking proudly at the neat loaves that were proving by the range. He watched her, transfixed by the thought that one day, life might be like this, Honor at his side in a farmyard kitchen, peaceful fields outside, and the war a distant memory.

29

At least flying conditions were good, the early July sun high in the sky. The chief flying instructor was carrying a clipboard, walking in long strides towards the Oxford where Will was waiting, trying to keep calm. He already completed the requisite checks inside and out, and had received a reassuring 'thumbs up' sign from Owen.

'Don't you go cocking it up, just remember everything I've told you!' were his final words.

'Right, Fordham, all set?' The CFI was a reasonable enough sort. He was known for his scrupulous fairness – he would only pass those whom he considered to be both competent and unflappable, and could spot a pilot who had what it took.

'OK, I want you to take off, and climb due west to seven thousand feet.' His instructions were succinct. Will had been over the drill with Owen many times, so when, as anticipated, he had to demonstrate flying on one engine, steep turns, and a high-speed stall, all went without a hitch. As it should do, he reasoned, having clocked up forty-nine hours solo in the Oxford now, as well as twenty-eight dual, covering everything from cross-country, instrument and night flying, and endless navigation tests.

Still jotting notes at his side, the CFI glanced at his watch. He judged Fordham to be confident and able; nearly time to draw it to a close. Perhaps he would just stretch him a little first.

'I want a single-engine landing, Fordham.'

Will groaned inwardly – that really was not fair! He had been coached through the emergency drills but had not expected this particular one during his wings test. He assumed the CFI must be having a bit of fun. Still, there was nothing else for it; he hoped the runway was not as clogged up as usual in case something went wrong.

Putting in a left-hand circuit, he kept his speed above ninety-five miles an hour and left the operation of the undercarriage until the last possible moment, locking it down just before his final straight approach. It required finesse, keeping up the speed in that one engine, then regulating the rate of descent. He hoped to God he could manage it, forgetting with the level of effort required, that the CFI was at his side. Suddenly, he was down, near perfect, though there were beads of sweat across his face.

If he thought he would receive any praise for his manoeuvre, he was wrong. The CFI was giving nothing away, just making a final entry to his notes.

'Righto, Fordham,' he said, as he stepped out, leaving Will perplexed as to the outcome.

His doubts were dispelled the following week, when after a gruelling set of exams, he finally made his way to the front of the throng at the noticeboard, and found his name on the list. Scrutinising it, he was sure there must be some mistake, but there it was, in black and white: *Fordham WR 1108986*. He still could not believe it, up until the moment when he carefully sewed the soft blue wings badge above his left chest pocket, each stitch sealing his future as a pilot. Where would he be sent next? And with what objective in mind? Picking up his jacket, looking proudly once again at the badge, he slipped it on and made his way, back straight and shoulders set, to the mess for what promised to be a rowdy celebration.

30

15th July 1941

Ratby House, Leics.

Dear Beatie

I am working at the TB san here, so thought I'd drop you a quick line. I hope you are getting on well in the FANYs and enjoying your training. Some of us were a little bit envious! Makes a change from being a probationer and the lowest of the low, I should think.

I quite like it here but TB nursing can be hard. I will be moving on next month, back to Groby Road again.

I saw Will last month, he has got his wings now! I hope he'll be careful.

Must go, Beatie, stay in touch and good news that you're up and about again!

Love Honor

She lifted the bonnet of the lorry and stood for a while, hands on hips, trying to work out what was wrong. It was hot, and Beatie wiped her hand across her forehead, leaving a greasy smudge under her cap. She should be able to fix it; that was all part of her training during the ten weeks at Camberley. Trouble was, when you were on your own in the middle of nowhere it was never quite so easy. She had not been long in the job, and had no wish to make a fool of herself in front of all those RAF types. The ground crew seemed to be perfectly reasonable chaps, her usual task being the collection and delivery of aircraft parts. They treated her with respect and she was starting to feel like one of the team. On the other hand, she had no desire to get mixed up with any of the airmen, who seemed to horse around like a group of schoolboys whenever they were off duty.

Her posting to South Cerney, No. 3 FTS, in Gloucestershire, had followed directly upon completion of her training. Her parents were against her joining the FANYs so soon after her illness, but she had been determined, and as always with Beatie, her resolve carried her through. In fact, she felt cheered by the prospect of working again: it was such a relief after the endless days of guilt-ridden convalescence.

'But darling, you look so thin!' her mother had protested.

'Nonsense, everyone looks thin nowadays,' she retorted. 'There's not enough food to go around. Besides, I'll be perfectly well looked after by the FANYs, and at least I'll be doing something useful.'

Unconvinced, her mother conceded the point, helping her pack and arrange her journey. She could not stop one final entreaty: 'But you will be careful this time, darling?'

Beatie left the house, tossing her curls in irritation at the remark.

Her thoughts returned to the job in hand and she started to clean the spark plugs, one by one, with an oily rag, absorbed in her task and hardly noticing when the motorcycle drew up.

'Hello, having a spot of bother?' The driver, a young RAF man, dismounted and pulled off his gloves. 'Want any help?'

'I should be all right.' Beatie's response was ungrateful. She did not want some smart alec bloke showing off in front of her.

'What's the problem?' He was undeterred by her tone and started rolling up his sleeves. She looked directly at him, her guard raised. Tall, with a wide mouth and large hands and feet, he had an air of self-assurance which made her immediately distrustful.

'I could give you a hand with those plugs,' he suggested, 'but I bet it's the radiator, playing up on a hot day.'

'It's not the radiator.' She was defensive. 'I filled it before I left.'

He took the rag from her and methodically checked the engine. 'Now go and turn her over,' he commanded. 'I think I might have it.'

It was the final straw.

'Look, whatever your name is, I didn't ask for your help and I don't need it. I know how to look after this lorry, and I don't need a man like you to do it for me!'

He stepped back, raising his hands. 'OK, keep your hair on! You're the boss, I'll just jump back on my bike and carry on!'

His goggles were down over his eyes and he was drawing off before she had time to interrupt. 'See you later,' he called good-humouredly.

Beatie muttered to herself. 'What does he mean, see me later? Who does he think he is?' It was becoming hotter by the moment, the sun now full in a cloudless sky. She could feel the perspiration dripping down her back to meet the prickly belt of her uniform trousers.

Wondering if he might be right, she climbed into the driving seat and turned the ignition, but there was no response.

'Damn!' she swore under her breath, and leant across for her thermos and NAAFI Spam sandwich, taking them to sit under the shade of a nearby tree. She lay back momentarily under the gentle light and closed her eyes. In normal circumstances, the flies, bees and prickly grass conspire against such outdoor naps, but not so for Beatie that day. Despite her protestation to the contrary, she had been weakened by her prolonged hospitalisation and might never recapture the robust good health of her youth.

Her eyes opened to the sound of the returning motorbike, and she sat up abruptly to see him dismounting once more.

'Had a nice snooze?' he enquired, and sat down uninvited on the grass to join her.

'I only shut my eyes for a minute!'

'No you haven't, it's half past four. Now shall we get on with fixing this lorry of yours before nightfall? Or perhaps you're planning a night under the stars?' He shook the thermos flask to see if there was any tea left.

A shadow of a smile crossed Beatie's face. 'Oh, all right, if you must.'

Stretching out his hand, he pulled her to her feet and they walked over to the lorry.

'What's your name?'

'Me? Oh, Beatie.'

'I'm Jim, now where's that spanner?'

31

20th July 1941

RAF Shawbury

Dear You,

Just a few more days here now before my next posting. I'll let you know when I've arrived there. Pity there's no leave first, but then I suppose we only saw each other last month. It seems an age away already!

I still can't quite believe I've got my wings. Most of the lads made it here, but I haven't heard anything from Matt yet, though I'm sure he'll have passed. I have no idea what's become of the others, but I expect I will find out sooner or later.

Anyway, I hope your last few weeks in the san go reasonably, and write to me soon.

From Me

He licked the envelope and popped the letter in his pocket, ready to post later. There was one more responsibility to undertake first, and he walked swiftly to the Austin, which he had left ready and waiting outside. He looked up at the open window to see Edek waving at him.

'Come on, old chap, we'll be late!'

The window closed and the Pole arrived a few minutes later, spruce in his uniform, sporting his Polish Air Force badge above his newly earned wings. Even Will had to admit that Edek looked the part today, from his neatly trimmed moustache to his freshly polished shoes.

'Is all right?' he asked anxiously, throwing his holdall in the back of the car.

'You look good,' Will reassured him. 'It's going to be a lovely day once the rain clears.' Edek took his place in the passenger seat.

'Before we go, this I must ask: is not too soon after Joseph?' His voice was earnest.

Will looked steadily across at him. 'Joseph would want you to be happy,' he said slowly. 'What's past is past. You know the lines: *the moving finger writes; and having writ—*'

'...*Moves on*,' Edek interrupted.

'Where did you get that from, old boy?'

'Ah, you think us Poles are ignorant, Fordham? We have soul, learn poetry like you!'

Will shook his head. He was such a cultured chap, Bronowski, he and Alice would make a good pair. Their love for each other was beyond doubt, and unlike some of his friends, Will did not frown upon the precipitancy of their marriage. Despite his surprise at being asked to be the best man at the ceremony, he was ready with the ring in his pocket as he started up the car for the short drive to the village church.

It was a relief not to be there for another funeral, and just on cue, the light drizzle lifted as they drew up. There would be only a handful of them in the front pews, not like the sea of blue at Joseph's wake. Edek, at the front of the church, began to pace up and down, suddenly stopping as the church door opened and Alice appeared, looking like a model out of *Vogue* magazine in a cream costume and pillbox hat. Wondering how she managed to look quite so elegant on her clothes ration, Will steered Edek into place, waiting as Alice walked steadily at her father's side to join them.

Lifting her veil, she smiled serenely at Edek as the minister stepped forward.

'Dearly beloved...'

Musing as the familiar words intoned, Will wondered whether he should be marrying Honor like this, quickly and without fuss. Guy was thinking the same. He had been engaged to Marion for some time; what would happen to her if he was killed in action? Worse still, supposing she fell pregnant despite his careful precautions and was left an unmarried mother, cast out by society? It would be far safer to tie the knot, like Edek was doing.

'Who giveth this woman...?'

None of them had met Alice's father before, and as the major stepped forward, an imposing presence in full military dress, stiffly upright, Will wondered how the impetuous Pole and traditional Army man would settle their differences down the years. Unlike his wife, a pretty, ageing English rose, he was not about to betray any emotion. She had her handkerchief at her eyes, and gazed at Alice, who made her vows in a clear and distinct voice.

'I now pronounce you man and wife. You may kiss the bride.'

Edek looked tenderly at Alice, before a long embrace in which they seemed unaware of the congregation, then walked hand in hand past the empty pews and out into the sunlight beyond.

Will shook the major's hand. 'Nice to meet you, sir, I think that went off very well,' then guided Alice's mother toward the church door.

'We'll be going to the Prince Rupert hotel in Shrewsbury for a wedding breakfast. I hope you'll come?'

'Of course, I'd be delighted.' Will was watching the couple, Edek with his arm around Alice's narrow waist, as they stood under the rose bower for the solitary wartime wedding photograph that would one day, fading but no less cherished, look out from its silver frame upon their unfolding lives.

Part Six: Wellington Bombers

1

The Anson headed down the grass runway, taking off surprisingly gracefully over Salisbury Plain. Flying Officer Grant, to whom Will was 'second dickey', pointed out the spire of the cathedral to the east as they levelled out.

'It's like the Oxfords to fly,' he added of the plane. 'Just a bit bigger with a few more gadgets. This one's been specially adapted to pick up the enemy beams.'

Will gazed at the downland falling away to the west, reflecting what a perfect high vantage point it was. At five hundred feet above sea level, it commanded an extensive view, with wide horizons all around. He had arrived at Boscombe Down the day before, to join 109 Squadron.

'Good posting that, Fordham,' the chief flying instructor said in farewell, 'All a bit hush-hush, you know.'

As it happened, he did not know, but was rapidly finding out. In the mess that first evening, there were no familiar faces. They had all gone their separate ways – Guy to Syerston, where he would fly Halifaxes, Edek and Alf to Scampton, lifting off from the flat Lincolnshire fens to take their bombs into the heart of the Ruhr.

'Aren't you going to put the undercarriage up?' Will said. It would be a retractable one on this Anson.

'Lord, no, not for a short flight. Do you know how many times I would have to crank it?'

Will watched Grant carefully and checked the cockpit layout.

'You'll be on Wellingtons tomorrow,' Grant said. 'See what you reckon to that.' His right hand adjusted the mixture control lever as the Anson climbed. 'Most of our flights are checking something out for the WIDU, you know.'

'What came first, the Wireless Intelligence Development Unit or the squadron?' Will asked.

'Well, they were merged into one over a year ago. It started with "flying down the beam", or what we used to call blind approach training,' Grant said. 'Now it's radio countermeasures, you know, trying to bugger up the Germans' attempts to do the same.'

The Lorenz beam was a concept that Will understood. Developed by the Germans in the 1930s, it relied upon a radio signal coming from a pair of transmitters that could guide the pilot according to the Morse code dots and dashes. In his headphones, the pilot would hear dots in his left earpiece, and dashes in his right, and would know the aircraft was on the right line when the two sounds merged into a single tone. This 'blind beam' approach allowed for accuracy in location-finding in poor visibility or at night. As far as he could see, the Luftwaffe had been a bit quicker off the mark with its development than had the RAF.

'It took us a while to realise they'd crisscrossed the country with enemy beams,' continued Grant, 'and there were plenty of people who didn't believe it! Mind you, they've had to eat their words!'

'How did you find them?' Will asked, still struggling to conceive that the Germans, operating from Cherbourg, at quite some distance, could have so thoroughly sewn up the country.

'Trial and error, old chap,' Grant replied. 'Just flew around a bit with the wireless operator and navigator, fiddling with the frequencies they might use. Got them at 31.5 megacycles. Trouble is, they're not all switched on at once.'

'So now you've found them, what next?'

'Well, you can either jam them, or send them back, rerouting them through another transmitter at a different location.'

'Oh, I get it! Leading their bomber stream off course!'

'That's the plan,' Grant said. 'Some of the top brains, you know, in WIDU. Can't understand what they're on about half the time, but they're backed all the way to the top!'

He made a 'V' sign, to show what he meant. Churchill's emblematic gesture was now enshrined in the very essence of the nation, embodying dogged survival against the odds.

In that summer of 1941, it was not just the British who had their backs to the wall. German troops were pushing deeper and deeper into Russian territory, their clear objective being Moscow. Taking the Soviet army by surprise from the very beginning, Operation Barbarossa cut swiftly through the Soviet Union before it was even able to engage its forces in retaliation. One by one, the Russian cities with historic names from Leningrad to Stalingrad were coming under siege from the fast-moving

German infantry, encircled in pincer movements which cut them off from supplies and reinforcements.

'So does the jamming work?' Will could not see how they could take out enough beams. 'Why don't we just ride the beam back to where it comes from and bomb the transmitters in France?'

'Oh, you mean the BBC,' Grant replied, then seeing Will's look of bewilderment, added, 'Blind Bombing of Cherbourg, that is. We've been at it since the end of last year, but it's not as easy as it sounds. We call the stations Ruffians, but there's more than one, as you might have guessed. Accuracy, you see, Fordham, that's the most important thing: getting the bomb directly on target. However well you made out in the Oxfords, I can promise it won't be like that dodging flak in some ruddy great bomber, high up in the sky on a winter night. That's why we're all here, testing out the latest gadgets!'

'Oboe, you mean?'

'That's it, old boy, and the rest. Who's taking the session this afternoon?'

'Chap called Reeves.'

'Yep, he's one of the TRE – Telecommunications Research Establishment, from Worth Matravers. He's a good lecturer, not quite so dotty as some of them!'

Will was becoming confused by the jargon – it seemed to be a hidden and secret world here on 109 Squadron. One thing was for sure: he would never be able to share any of this with Honor.

When it came to the Oboe teaching, he had to concentrate for all he was worth. The scientist stood in front of a small group of pilots, navigators and wireless operators, with some drawings on the blackboard in front of him.

'So this is the principle, gentlemen.' He pointed at the board. 'Two ground stations in Britain, let's say, one in Norfolk, called Mouse, one in Kent, called Cat. Signals from Cat keep the aircraft flying along the arc of a circle over German territory, aircraft maintains set height and speed, then signal from Mouse tells the navigator when to press the button and release the bombs. It's calculated to one hundredth of a mile,' he added casually, his wooden pointer showing the intersection on the arc where the bombs would fall. 'That's it in a nutshell – the Oboe precision ground-controlled blind bombing system. Any questions?'

They were all momentarily silent, not wishing to say anything too stupid or obvious. Then, one of the pilots was the first to venture.

'What about the range limitation, sir? Surely the curvature of the earth…'

Followed by, 'What about the wind?' from one of the navigators, then Will's contribution.

'Won't we be sitting ducks, flying straight and level like that?' This drew a general murmur of assent.

'Well, I can't say it's all entirely perfect yet, gentlemen – that's why you're all here, to try it out, modify and improve. We're not about to release it for general consumption, there's a lot of work to do on it first. Most importantly, we need to maintain good Morse contact between ground and aircraft at critical stages – the IFF equipment wasn't up to it at first.'

'Sorry to state the obvious, sir,' a voice with a soft West Country accent piped up from the back of the room, 'but won't the Germans simply jam our frequencies in retaliation, and put us all out of business before we've even started?'

Will looked round at the speaker, whose voice he recognised. It took him a moment to place him, then he remembered: it was the chap he had met at Duxford on his first solo cross-country in the Tiger Moth. What was his name? Wellesley, that was it; farming background, like himself.

Reeves nodded. 'Of course they might – they haven't yet, and it's why everything that goes on here is so top-secret. We just have to keep outwitting them, be one step ahead.' He took off his glasses and cleaned them carefully. 'Any more questions before I move on to GEE?'

As they filed out of the room an hour later, Will caught up with Wellesley. 'I think we've met.'

Looking at him for a moment, Wellesley's expression cleared. 'Duxford,' he answered, 'you were in a Tiger Moth, bad weather closing in, I remember! Did you get back all right?' He smiled before adding, 'I suppose you must have done! I'm sorry, I can't remember your name?'

'Will Fordham.'

'Arthur Wellesley.'

They shook hands. 'It all seems a hell of a long time ago! How are you? I haven't seen you in the mess.'

'Had to take some leave, my mother was in hospital, just got back.' A shadow crossed Arthur's face. 'Anyway, what do you think to the set-up here? I've been with 109 for a couple of months, converting to Wimpys. Just getting the hang of them, really.'

'What are they like to fly?'

'Pretty forgiving, I'd say. Swings to starboard on take-off, but it's better than the Hampdens I was on. Can feel a bit twitchy, in flight, but that's the frame, you know. Odd to think that it's covered with fabric, they say you can get shot up and still get home. Not had that pleasure yet!'

Will had studied the geodetic frame of the Wellington. It was an innovative design by Barnes Wallis, a duralumin lattice framework over which the fabric was stretched. It made for a remarkably resilient and powerful machine with the Pegasus 1050hp twin engines, now in major production for Bomber Command.

'Some decent blokes around too,' Arthur continued. 'My instructor, Willis, is a good sort. They expect you to pick it up quickly, but you'll have a go in the Link Trainer first. I think I must have had about seven hours' dual before soloing, but it seemed about right. Do you fancy a beer? Then you can tell me more about that flight back from Duxford!'

It was a balmy July evening as they walked over to the mess. The camouflaged brick buildings were not dissimilar to those at Shawbury, recently built and spacious, as were the accommodation blocks, laid out in a quadrangle.

'Great view from up here,' Will commented. He could see for miles, the green high plain stretching out to the wooded horizons beyond.

'Yes, it's quite a special place.' Arthur pointed west. 'Stonehenge is over there, you know, just a couple of miles away. You can see it clearly on some of the circuits. I was flying over it at dawn on the summer solstice, now what would the Druids have made of that?'

Will followed Arthur into the mess where they lined up their beers.

'Evening, squire.' A short, dark-haired figure came to join them, draining his glass as he did so.

'Ready for another? This is Fordham, just joined us, the thirsty chap is my navigator, Fred Ellis. He's our resident Aussie.' Arthur looked at him benignly.

'Pleased to meet you.' Will took a sip of his beer. They all tasted different, these local beers, whatever part of the country you found yourself in.

'So, you've come to join the Pathfinders?' Fred said.

The 109 Squadron badge was above them on the wall. The black panther in the centre had fire coming out of its mouth, and the Latin motto beneath, *Primi Hastati*, meant 'First of the Legion', as Arthur pointed out.

'Not sure I fancy being first,' Fred said, 'unless that means first getting home!' He looked over his beer at Will. 'Now, I've been trying to persuade old Art to come out to the George in Amesbury. He says he doesn't want a heavy night, got a big day tomorrow.' He winked at Wellesley.

'Another night, Fred! You never know when to stop!'

'Too right! 'Bout time you got some nice little English sheilas lined up for me,' Fred said. 'Why did I ever think it would be easy to pick up a girl in Blighty? Back where I come from, on the sheep station, we don't see a girl for miles, now here, they're all around, but, no, no,' he lapsed into a falsetto voice, '"Nothing doing, old chap, I've got to get home and wash my hair!" It never looks like it needs washing to me.'

'Perhaps they don't trust you, Fred,' Arthur continued, in a rerun of a conversation that they must have had countless times.

'Why ever not?!' Fred was indignant. 'Let's hope this new fella can open a few doors. You married, Fordham?'

'Who, me?'

'Yes, you, buddy, are you hitched up?'

'Sorry to let you down, Fred, but I'm not a free agent like you!'

Fred clapped him on the back. 'Fordham, my boy! You are always a free agent, unless she's right by your side! You're far too young to settle down. Now listen to me…'

Catching Arthur's eye, Will raised his eyebrows and smiled.

'What did you think of the briefing?' he said, in an attempt to change the subject.

'Oh my God, we've got a serious one! You don't need to worry about all that stuff!' Fred was in his element, his Australian accent ringing out over the mess. 'Just pretend you know what they're talking about, even if you haven't got a clue. I promise, it'll make no bloody difference in the end – they just get a kick out of asking us to do damn fool things! All that matters is that you can fly the bloody plane!'

2

Of course, Fred was right, that was all that mattered, he thought as he walked out to the Wellington the next morning in his sheepskin-lined Irvin flying jacket, leather helmet, trousers and boots. He was the second pilot in a five-man crew, and the first pilot today would be none other than the squadron leader himself. Hal Bufton was a tall, confident man, having been given command of the newly formed squadron last year. The higher echelons of the RAF were respectful of his intelligence, ability to command, and outspoken nature. They trusted his opinion, in particular as to whether the numerous bits of kit that WIDU dreamed up would work in the cockpit of a bomber, under extreme flying conditions. He was also renowned for his bravery, having led some of the blind bombing raids on Cherbourg earlier that year.

The other crew members, navigator, bomb-aimer, wireless operator and rear gunner, were chatting animatedly as they made their way up the ladder.

'Did you hear what the bloke did?' The rear gunner, Ted Baines, was incredulous. 'Just climbed out of the astro-hatch, and across the starboard wing to put out a fire from a fractured fuel line!' he continued. 'Only trouble was, they were airborne at the time, over Germany, shot up by a Me 109! Bloody lunatic, if you ask me, that's New Zealanders for you. Anyway, it worked, enough for the captain to land at Newmarket. They say he kicked footholds in the fabric as he went along the wing holding on to a rope, can you credit it?! Apparently he's about to get the VC.'

Up the ladder under the nose and through the main hatch, the conversation continued as they took their places, Will assessing the sheer size of the aircraft. He looked back along the walkway leading to the rear gunner's turret, past the suspended oxygen cylinders, rest couch and Elsan: Ted's was not a job he would have fancied, cut off from the rest of the crew like that. They were encircled by the geodesic framework, uncovered in the interior so that every element of the design was laid bare. The overall impression was that of a huge metal exoskeleton, fitted out with as many gadgets as it could carry from its blunt-nosed front, to the lattice bomb bays and the Vickers guns in the tail.

How the hell was he ever going to fly this hulk? He hoped his face did not betray his apprehension, as he made his way down the short corridor connecting the wireless operator and navigator sections. The fair-haired W/op broke off from fiddling with an array of dials to raise his hand in salutation, and Will took some comfort from the fact that at least he could identify the Morse key and transmitter unit. He resolved to familiarise himself with the rest of the equipment later on, as he would the navigator's station which was just behind. The navigator slid his seat out from under the table, revealing the stored maps below and the lamp and map-plotting arm on the table ready for use.

Then it was on, into the cockpit where, Bufton already installed in the pilot's seat, Will put down the folding second pilot's seat to sit close beside him. It was cramped in the cockpit, much smaller than he had expected in a plane of that size. He looked down at the bomb-aimer's compartment, directly below – how exposed would you feel, lying on your stomach down there, waiting to press the release tit?

Bufton's oxygen mask was off, and he was surveying the instrument panel with an easy familiarity.

'Bit baffling the first time you clap eyes on it!' he said encouragingly, 'but you'll soon get the hang of it.' He showed Will the controls to the left of the pilot's seat: throttle control levers, airscrew pitch and aileron trim tab control.

Bufton then turned his attention to the main instrument panel. 'It's much the same as the Anson.' He pointed to the airspeed indicator, artificial horizon, vertical speed indicator, altimeter and turn and slip indicator. *Safe ground here, at least*, Will thought as he tried to stay abreast of the functions and position of the other dials, and the stout control column in front. At least the familiar rudder bar was at his feet.

'That's your beam approach system,' Bufton added. 'Just started fitting them as a routine to the Mark Ics. And another thing, these Pegasus engines, the 1050hp, can heat up when you're on full power, especially on a single engine. What's the maximum speed of this kite?'

Having memorised it in advance, Will was quick to reply: 'Two hundred and thirty-five mph at fifteen thousand five hundred feet, sir.'

'And the bomb load?'

'Four thousand five hundred pounds, sir.' There was not much Will had not learnt about the Wellington, not least its impressive range – 2,550 miles, enough to get you to Berlin and back!

Bufton had started on his pre-flight checks. 'Main tank cocks are on, check all flying controls, brakes on, ignition switches off, undercarriage selector down, check all the indicator lights are green.' He was briskly efficient, waiting for the ground crew to turn each propeller manually to free it from oil. Satisfied, he switched on the ignition and pressed the starter, the Pegasus engines roaring into life as the oil pressure rose.

'Don't let it go above 140.' Bufton pointed at the dial, before starting the second engine, checking the fuel tank contents once more and showing Will how the supercharger worked. Bufton waved away the chocks, opened the throttles to taxi from dispersal, down the grass runway, where after satisfying himself with the take-off checks, he throttled back, released the brakes and turned into the wind.

'Raise the tail wheel early,' he added, finessing the throttles as he eased the thundering aircraft off the runway. Will could feel the thrust of the engines as Bufton, having braked the wheels to stop them spinning and retracted the undercarriage, increased speed before climbing to four hundred feet, raising the flaps as he did so.

'There we are, piece of cake, your turn next!' Bufton strapped on his oxygen mask. 'We'll change over, you can keep her in a climb at 135 mph.'

The noise and the thrum from the engines was deafening; they could only communicate with each other through the radio intercom, flicking it on or off for contact.

'You're lucky, it's not as cold in here today as it is in the winter. Heating system never really works properly, and as for the poor chap in the tail – it's bloody freezing, even in his special suit!'

The main engine controls were on the left-hand side, and Will closed his hand over the throttles, taking the control column in his right. He watched the altimeter as the plane continued to climb.

'Keep her steady,' Bufton said. 'She's a beaut, isn't she? The retractable undercarriage – that's Vickers hydraulics for you! In my opinion Barnes Wallis is a genius. Still, even he couldn't have imagined some of the tricks the WIDU want us to pull off! You should chat to the wireless operator, he's the poor bugger who's always trying to fiddle around for some frequency or another. I truly don't know how he does it, must have the hearing of a bat!'

'Are you talking about me, sir?' the wireless operator's voice interrupted. 'My station's fitted with sound insulation, remember!'

Bufton reminded Will of the fuel system as part of their pre-flight checks: two light alloy tanks in each outer wing, carrying a total of 634 gallons, then the two emergency tanks with another fifty-eight gallons, enough for an hour's flying time.

'By the time you're loaded up with all of that and a couple of two thousand-pound bombs, I can tell you it's best not to make any mistakes on take-off! Now, have a go at the flying controls.' Bufton pointed to the ailerons, elevator and trimming tabs.

Will tested them, feeling the giant bomber turn, rise and fall in response.

'That's the ticket, now let's decrease our altitude.'

The navigator's voice came over the intercom. 'Are you following this course or just fannying around, sir?'

'Wash your mouth out, Navigator, it's the second pilot's first day!'

'Even so, sir…'

Bufton smiled. He liked the banter with his crew; it kept them on their toes. 'What say we let him have another circuit?'

'OK, sir, but we'd advise you not to use the Elsan!'

Will did not attempt to join in. His whole being was focused on mastering the controls, and getting the feel of the Wellington. Gradually, he started to relax, trusting to the power and responsiveness of the plane. The bewildering array of dials began to make sense, and so it should; it was the best operational bomber of the day. Bufton sat back, silently assessing his second pilot's competence. The squadron leader knew when he had a decent airman on his hands, and reckoned this one would make the grade.

'OK, I'm going to take over for a bit,' Bufton said. 'I want to show you the auto controls.'

They changed places again, Will relinquishing the leather pilot's seat to his boss.

'So, the automatic pilot is mounted beneath the cockpit floor – and the gyroscope provides aileron and elevator control,' Bufton said.

Will listened intently throughout. He had never flown a plane with automatic controls before. Bufton was a pro, there was no doubt about that – the only trouble was, he made it look so damn easy!

'How are we doing, Navigator?'

'Well, Skip, that's Stonehenge down there, in case you hadn't noticed.'

'Right, it's time we came in to land.'

Looking down at the timeless stone circle, Will wondered what it signified. It was primeval in its simplicity, utterly arresting as it must always have been. He had never imagined that his first glimpse of it would be from the air, yet perhaps that was the best vantage point, flying free above it, unencumbered by the centuries that had passed since the early Druids somehow dragged the enormous boulders into place.

'Check brake pressure, air intake, trimming tabs, reduce to 140 mph.' Bufton switched the undercarriage down and locked. 'Set the mixture control to normal, flaps at twenty degrees, then take her down to a hundred and twenty.' He lowered the flaps for the final approach.

The massive Dunlop tyres hit the runway smoothly, and Bufton taxied over the grass, putting in his final checks before completing the cooling procedure, closing the throttles, and switching off the ignition. He took off his mask.

'That's it, Fordham, piece of cake! Go and let the rear gunner out, would you?'

Making his way down the main fuselage, Will undid the bulkhead door. The turret doors opened and Ted swung himself out backwards, holding on to the handrail as he came.

'Want a shufti?'

It was claustrophobic in there, exposed behind the Perspex shield.

'Frazer-Nash turret, two Browning .303 machine guns,' Ted said. 'It's bloody cold in here, ammo tends to jam, difficult to operate the doors, and my parachute's kept in the main fuselage. Apart from that, it's all tickety-boo. Fancy a beer?'

3

Flight Lieutenant Willis had been with the squadron from the beginning, nearly a year ago.

'Used to fly Sunderlands at Sullom Voe,' he told Will as they made their way to the Wellington two days later. 'Chaps used to tease me, made out I wouldn't know how to use a grass runway! Mind you, I loved those flying boats – there's nothing like the sensation of taking off from water. Still, I'm not complaining – the Wimpy is a viceless plane. How did you find it the other day? I expect Hal was showing you the ropes?'

'All a bit daunting, sir,' Will said. 'There's a lot to remember.'

'You'll get the hang of it soon,' Willis replied. 'We've got to do some trials for the TRE today, checking contact distances for the signal from Worth Matravers. Dr Jeffreys wants to know how far away we can pick it up at fifteen thousand feet, so we'll take a course out over the Channel and see how it goes. You've done the ditching drill, haven't you?'

Will nodded. One of the flight sergeants had rehearsed it the day before until it was imprinted on his memory.

'You've got three minutes, Fordham,' the sergeant had informed him. 'You'll have jettisoned bombs and fuel, then close bomb doors and inflate flotation bags. Remove the astro-hatch inwards – that's how you're going to get out! Pilot and rear gunner stay at their stations, other crew seated with their backs to the cabin rear step. Most ditching injuries are because the crew are in the wrong place, remember that! Slow approach to the water, as slow and horizontal as you can make it, thirty degrees of flap. Then get the buggers out and hope the ruddy dinghy's inflated!'

It was no use pretending it was not going to happen to someone, sooner or later. Will remembered his first instructor at Desford; lost his best mate in the cockpit when the plane went down. He thought of the rear gunner – imagine having to stay in that turret when a plane was ditching!

'Let's take it from the top, shall we?' Willis took Will slowly and carefully through all of the manoeuvres, swapping places with him so that Will could take the controls once airborne. The checks were beginning to embed in his brain and Will no longer felt overwhelmed by the flying panel in front of him. He reflected on his good fortune to have Willis as an instructor. Arthur had been right: if ever a man could show you how to fly an aircraft, then this was he.

The wireless operator and navigator were conferring over the exercise. 'We're 150 miles from base, Skipper.' Griff's voice came over the intercom.

'How's the signal holding up, Don?' Willis enquired.

A Scottish brogue came back in reply, 'Good so far, Skip', as they flew on, the engines thundering across the flat sea. 'Damn, lost it!' followed shortly after. 'Keep at fifteen thousand, Skip.'

'How far are we from base, Navigator?' Willis said.

'Around 173 miles, Skip, but it's no use, Don says it's gone.'

'What say we fly higher?' Vic Willis was determined. He was just the right man for this kind of exercise, not prepared to call it a day and give up. The Wellington ascended through the clouds, the altimeter dial moving slowly in response.

'Got it again, Skip!' Don said. 'Keep at this height!'

Cruising at twenty thousand feet, they continued a little further until 'Lost it again!' from the wireless operator.

'I think that's it, we'll not squeeze any more range than that. What are we at, Navigator?'

'Two hundred miles from base,' Griff replied. 'We're near Lorient, Skip, likely to meet flak soon.'

'OK, I'm turning back, I think that's what Jeffreys wants to know.' Willis skilfully took the plane on a wide arc over the French coast until they were heading for home. In occupied territory for the first time, Will felt less apprehensive than he would have anticipated. The skipper made it all seem such a routine job, just a calibration exercise, after all.

Except, of course, nothing was straightforward in this war, as they found out once again on their return to Boscombe Down. Squadron Leader Hal Bufton had been shot down in a raid with Number 9 Squadron, on Cologne, and the six-man crew was posted as missing.

'Christ Almighty!' Vic Willis was shocked. He admired Bufton, and was used to serving under his command. 'It was his first trip to Germany, and he wasn't even on the beam!'

'If the squadron leader can go for a burton, anyone can!' Don said. 'It's all about luck, nothing to do with experience! I hope to God they managed to bail out!'

'And spend the rest of the war as POWs! Still, at least they'd be alive.' Griff was stoical, starting to hum a song to the refrain of *My Bonnie Lies Over the Ocean*. They all knew the words:

'Two valve springs you'll find in my stomach
Three spark plugs are safe in my lungs
The prop is in splinters inside me
To my fingers the joystick has clung
Take the cylinders out of my kidney
The connecting rod out of my brain
From the small of my back get the crankshaft
And assemble the engine again.'

'Let's hope it's not that bad, chaps, Bufton is made of strong stuff,' Willis said. 'I'm off to let Jeffreys know how we got on, see you chaps later.' He departed, leaving the others in the crew room.

'Watch out your stuff isn't borrowed,' warned Don as they stowed their gear in the lockers. 'Someone's always pinching my boots!'

4

In the warm summer days that followed, Will became more familiar with the bomber; its cigar-shaped fuselage and wide, tapering wings became oddly comforting. He began to think of it as his plane, the iconic Wellington, so easily recognised in the air from its characteristic shape: the deep, rounded belly, flat top and tall tail fin. He was also learning to appreciate the special mix of skills – each member of the crew highly trained and functioning independently as part of the team. Some jobs seemed worse than others – he could never have countenanced the rear gunner's lot, nor felt he could have had the navigator's precision. Still, they were all no doubt relieved that he, as the pilot, would one day take responsibility for them all.

'Meaconing today,' Vic announced in the briefing room. 'Now Dr Jeffreys is going to take you through it first, then we'll give it a go in the air.'

As second in command to Reeves, Jeffreys was nothing if not intellectual. Tall, and with a slightly stooped frame, he pushed a lock of stray hair back from his broad forehead before beginning.

'Now, gentlemen, as you know, the Germans have criss-crossed the country with Lorenz beams to help guide them to their targets. Fortunately, we've managed to intercept the frequency, so now we have to neutralise them. It has not proved possible to take out the transmitters despite considerable effort by our bombers to that end, so we are left with several options. First, and most intuitively, we can jam them. The German Knickebein beam, transmitted from high-powered beacons – we call them "headaches" – transmit a dot-dash signal. So if our transmitters, called the "aspirins", transmit the dash, it will overlap and give the impression the pilot is flying off course. Problem is, their navigators can still reorient the plane once they lose the beam if they're sharp enough. So we've spent time on a plan to reroute the beams, thus causing maximum confusion. We call it Meaconing, from "masking beacon".'

He turned to the blackboard, writing the points as he made them.

'One: find the beam, usually around 31.5 megacycles. Our location here, Beacon Hill, is fortunately right on the flight path that most enemy bombers would take from occupied France to the industrial heartlands of the Midlands. That's one of the reasons we're all here, in case you hadn't worked it out already.'

He paused to draw a diagram on the board, wiping chalky fingers as he did so.

'Two: having picked up the signal from German aircraft calling their direction finding, DF, stations for a fix, pass the signal to one of our transmitters at a receiving site.

'Three: using our special phasing equipment, we eliminate the local transmitter signal, leaving only the aircraft signal in control. So the end result is that the enemy aircraft signal drives our transmitters, meaning the Hun end up in all sorts of surprising places, but thanks to our ingenuity, not at their target. Any questions so far?'

Don was the only one to respond, puffing on his pipe as he did so.

'So the transmitters at our end can be mobile, presumably?'

'Some, of course, will be fixed. We have a big one at Alexandra Palace, but yes, we have that capacity.' Jeffreys nodded. He was a concise lecturer, and Will felt he was starting to grasp what might be required.

'How long do we have to transmit the signal for?' one of the other wireless operators enquired.

'Ah, that might be the tricky bit, we're not quite sure yet. It depends a bit on the sensitivity of the vertical antennas that we've put up, that's why we need you lads to get the trial runs in.' He looked around the room steadily. 'I don't need to add that this is one of the most secret operations of the war. TRE have tried to come up with radio-countermeasures for every little scheme the Luftwaffe might dream up, and we certainly don't want them getting a notion of what we're up to!'

Was it Will's imagination, or did the Wellington handle like a dream today? Each time he and Vic changed places, squeezing round the cramped cabin to relinquish his flip-up seat for the solid, leather-covered pilot seat, he felt less apprehensive and more competent. The control column seemed to respond to his every movement, and the once-confusing array of dials were at last falling into place. The throttles, so responsive under his left hand, moved smoothly: it was all so perfectly designed.

'You'd better see if you can land her today,' Vic said. ''Bout time you gave it a go.'

The Meaconing exercise was more time-consuming than they had anticipated. Don's voice over the intercom sounded weary: 'Every time I think I've got it, it dies on me! No, hang on, keep this course, Skip, that's a strong enough signal to pass on!'

Will flew the lumbering aircraft just above the clouds on a steady course, watching the flight instruments as he did so. Then, passing over to Vic, he went to see what the 'Scotchman', as Vic liked to call his wireless operator, was doing, stopping by Griff's maps and sextant on the way.

'Know where we are, Griff?'

'Haven't a bloody clue.' Griff winked at him. 'If you know how to make these things work, you could give me a hand!' He stared out of his Perspex window, looking for a sighting. 'Just as well it's not a bombing run, Will, we've been flying on a straight line for far too long!'

Don's whole attention was focused on his exercise. Gently fiddling with the knobs and listening for signals, he was too immersed in his task even to notice Will standing by him.

'Bullseye! Relayed to receiver station! Let's hope the bloody aerials there hold up, I'm not sure I could find it again! Steady as she goes, Skip.'

Later, in the mess, Will took a satisfying draught of ale. He had landed the plane, and that was worth celebrating. Admittedly, Vic had been at his side, talking him through, and in no time, he had lowered the flaps on the final approach, and thundered in at about eighty-five miles an hour to touch down on his sturdy Dunlop wheels.

He would dream about that for the rest of his life, he reflected: the fact that he, William Fordham, could fly such a plane. Life would never be quite the same.

'What's up, Arthur? Can I get you a beer?'

'Thanks.' Arthur nodded, before they retreated to a quiet corner.

'Is your mother out of hospital yet?' Will asked.

'I'm afraid not, she's got TB.' Arthur looked grim. Will, remembering Honor's descriptions of the san, was not sure what to say.

'My girlfriend's been nursing TB,' he ventured.

'Oh, has she?' Arthur looked suddenly relieved, as though he now had a reason to share his problems. 'I didn't know she was a nurse. It's such an awful disease, I mean, when it gets to your lungs like that.'

'I know,' Will said. 'Still, Honor says there's lots of new treatments now – what did she call one of them, "heliotherapy"? Maybe something like that will do the trick.' He wanted to give Arthur some hope, however unfounded.

'Do you think?' Arthur's face brightened. 'I just wish they could make her better. My poor dad, he's so worried about her that he can't really manage the farm. If only I could get home to help him! I can't bear to think of him struggling on by himself, with just the land girls, and the ruddy War Ag down his neck half the time!'

Will thought of the Bradleys: how many farming sons were serving at the front while their parents tried to hang on? Knowing, even worse, that they might never come back and keep the land in the family, father to son in the centuries-old tradition.

'Anyway,' continued Arthur, changing tack as Fred came to join them, 'what's the latest on the Russian front?'

'I can tell you that, cobber, but it won't cheer you up any! Ruddy Hun are at Smolensk, reckon it'll be Moscow next!'

20th July 1941

RAF Boscombe Down

Dear You,

It's a whole new world here, but some things don't change! First, I am missing you as much as ever, and I hope all is well and you're ready to go back to Groby Road soon.

Secondly, I am learning to fly yet another aeroplane, it's just that this one is a bit bigger and there's more to get wrong! Still, there are plenty of old hands to show me how it's done.

Pretty countryside around here, and I hope I can show you Stonehenge one day – have you ever been? How the ancients pulled those stones into place is beyond me, but it's quite something to fly over.

Write soon and let me know how you're keeping.

From Me

5

'Won't you come with me, Molly? I don't want to go by myself.'

Honor looked across at her friend, who was lounging on her bed reading *Woman's Weekly*. She put the magazine down.

'I don't want to go either! Whatever will you say?'

'I don't know,' Honor said. 'It's just that I promised Vera, so I have to. I wrote to him, and he says he'll be coming tomorrow. Sister says I can have half an hour out of the afternoon shift; I'm sure she'd let you come too.'

'I bet she wouldn't,' Molly returned stoutly. 'Just say whatever you have to, then it's done.'

There was little point pursuing it further. Molly, to whom she had become closer over the last month, was not one to change her mind. Anyway, it was she, Honor, who had given Vera her word. She would just have to see it through.

'Fancy the cinema this Friday?' They would both have the same evening off, and with Will away, there was little point in saving all her off-duty.

'What's on?' Molly threw aside her magazine. She was tired of reading about the Women's Institute recipes for rosehip jelly. 'If you mean the latest Humphrey Bogart, then I'm on!'

The following afternoon, the ward bell rung on time. She checked with Sister, who nodded in assent, before gathering up her cape.

A tall, handsome lad in naval uniform stood shyly outside.

'Mr Clark?' Honor enquired.

'Yes, that's me. Will I be able to see Vera or do I have to talk to you first?' He looked eager, in anticipation of his visit.

Honor closed the door behind her, wishing she had told him the truth in the letter. Just what had she let herself in for?

'Let's go outside for a bit.' Honor led him through the tall conservatory windows on to the terrace beyond, over to a small seat away from the usual group of reclining patients. The sun was bright, though never hot enough to dry up the secretions that clung so tenaciously to their lungs.

'What's up, Nurse Newson? Your letter didn't make it entirely clear.' He was so polite, taking off his cap as they sat down in the shade of the ash tree.

'I'm sorry.' She watched the dawning realisation in his face. Vera...'

'What's happened?'

'She died last month. I'm sorry, I thought you knew.'

He blanched, and put his hand to his mouth.

'Oh, my poor Vera! I didn't know! Why didn't anyone tell me?'

'She was very ill,' Honor said softly. 'We couldn't save her – it was in her lungs, she kept coughing up blood…'

'Did she suffer much?' The tears were in his eyes and he made no attempt to brush them away.

'No, she was peaceful at the end. She asked me to see you, she wanted me to tell you…'

'Tell me what?' His face was agonised.

'That she loved you,' Honor replied. What else could she say?

It seemed a long time that they sat in silence under the tree, the sun high above them.

'I know.' He was the first to speak. 'I know she did. It would have been different if her parents had approved of me, but they didn't. NQOC, you know: "not quite our class". Just because I was from the wrong end of town, no prospects, or so they said, it didn't mean I couldn't love her! And I would have married her, just as soon as I made good in the Navy, and she got better. We've loved each other for years, even before her TB.' He looked at the ground in despair. 'Would you believe it, they didn't even tell me she was gone! I could at least have paid my respects, gone to her funeral…'

In the distance on the terrace, the nurses were coming to accompany some of the patients inside. He rose, and took Honor's hand.

'Thank you for being there for her.' He turned to walk alone down the long drive, under the line of trees, to the road beyond.

6

'Look, there's still a queue, even though we're early!' Molly and Honor took their places at the end of the line which extended from the Odeon Cinema to the blacked-out buildings round the block. The posters for the film, *The Maltese Falcon*, showed a suave Bogart, pistol in hand, and a reclining woman in an orange dress.

'I 'ope it's not about Malta, and those dreadful bombs!' a woman in front of them commented as they filed slowly forwards. 'I could do wiv cheering up a bit!'

As they neared the ticket office, the girls were hailed by a familiar voice.

'It's Peter!' shouted Molly.

'What's he doing here?'

'I never thought he'd make it!' Molly said. 'You don't mind, do you?'

Peter gave Molly a quick kiss on the cheek, then turned awkwardly to Honor, lacking an appropriate means of greeting.

'Hello, Dr Donaldson.'

'Evening, Nurse Newson.'

'Crikey, that's all a bit formal, do you mind!' Molly said. 'Peter, I think you know Honor already.'

'Of course.' Peter inclined his head. 'Have I jumped the queue?'

Somehow, when they came to take their seats in the dimly lit cinema, he was between them. Honor felt acutely aware of his presence throughout the Pathé newsreels about the king and queen visiting an aircraft factory, and during the film that followed. Molly looked rapt with the plot, upon which Honor could scarcely concentrate. Later, as they walked down the steep cinema steps into the dusk beyond, she found herself hoping that she would soon be on the bus back to Ratby. Peter had other plans.

'Just a swift half!' he said, outside the entrance to the Kings Head. Following him into the smoky bar, the girls waited at the table while he bought some drinks.

'Look, I can catch the bus back, you stay here with Peter,' Honor whispered.

'No, we'll go together, we won't be long!' Molly looked animated. 'Thanks, Peter,' she added, taking a sip of her port and lemon, and smiling at them both. 'Only another two weeks!'

'Before you're both back?' Peter said. 'Which ward will you be going to, Honor? The children on the scarlet fever ward have been asking after you. Do you remember the one with scabies, and that awful doll?'

'Lily!' Honor's face lit up. 'What happened to her?'

'Went home yesterday, back to the bedbugs, no doubt! She still had her little doll with her, and went off happy as Larry.'

Suddenly, they were both immersed in conversation. Honor had not realised how much she had missed the children, and wanted news of them all. Molly, looking a little put out, finished her drink and rose.

'Well, we'd best be off, or we'll miss the bus. Thanks for coming with us, Peter.'

'My pleasure, I'll walk you to the stop.'

It was always difficult to negotiate three people on a pavement: one would inevitably slip off the edge or take a unilateral decision to walk in front. Thus, as they neared the stop, Honor found Peter by her side and Molly ahead of them.

'I hope you get a good ward,' he said softly.

She looked at him, his sensitive face alert and caring. 'I expect it'll be polio next, not sure I'm looking forward to it though.' Leaving him with her friend, she turned to board the waiting bus.

It was the last one to Ratby, carrying few passengers other than themselves, once they had deposited the shift workers at the city stops. Molly was not in a talkative mood, though Honor ventured several questions about the film. Eventually, after a period of resolute silence, she broke.

'I'm sure he likes you, Honor.' Her voice was flat, accepting.

'Don't be silly! We just worked together, that's all we have in common. Anyway, in case it had escaped your notice, I've got a boyfriend already. You know how I feel about Will.'

Molly did know, having watched the penumbra of love surrounding the girl when Will was on leave. Her heart was obviously accounted for, as certainly as any could be in this war.

'Yes, I know that, but it doesn't stop Peter falling for you. Are you sure there isn't something you haven't told me?'

'Look, Molly, there's nothing to tell. He's a good doctor, I work with him sometimes, that's it and all about it! Now what did you really make of old Bogie in that film?'

28th August 1941
Ratby House
Dear You,
I passed my exam! It took ages to hear, they posted the results at Groby Road so Addie had to let me know. Anyway, I can't quite believe it and keep expecting to be thrown out – do you think they made a mistake? I'm sure I got most of the answers wrong.

Only another couple of days before I leave here. I'll miss the country air, though I'm probably ready to see the others again. I'm not sure what ward I'm going to, but I'll let you know.

I know you can't tell me anything about what you are doing but I worry about you all the time. Please stay safe and try not to take any risks, at least not more than necessary.

Thinking of you as always.

From Me

7

'So what happened in the pub last night?' Vic said at breakfast. The crew were in various states of readiness for the day. Don spread some more marmalade on his toast and took a mouthful of tea.

'He never gives up, that Aussie! It must be all those years on the sheep station, if you ask me!'

'You know the blonde barmaid?' Griff continued.

'He didn't!' Vic replied.

Griff nodded. 'She looks more than a match for him! I hope he knows what he's taking on!'

'I don't think that Fred's approach to life, or love.' Vic finished his coffee. 'Time for off, lads!'

In the briefing room a short time later, they learnt that they were on special duty, an Oboe test over the Channel. Dr Jeffreys was planning to accompany them, as was common practice among the TRE scientists.

'Just fancies a day out, if you ask me,' Ted muttered.

'Have you got a question, Baines?' the flight lieutenant on ops asked. 'If not, I'll pass on to Dr Jeffreys.'

The scientist was to provide them with a résumé of the exercise, which was to take place at a bombing range off the coast of South Wales.

'Right, you all know the principles and now we've established the range. Worth Matravers in Dorset will be the transmitting station, or "Cat", and West Prawle in Devon, "Mouse", the one sending the bomb release signal. The target is ninety-seven miles distant from the Cat station and eighty-seven miles distant from the Mouse station, the two points producing an angle of forty-nine degrees over the target, which is at a bombing range in the sea off Stormy Down. The Wellington you're flying carries the Oboe repeater and pulse communication system, we just need to test for accuracy and consistency. The pilots and wireless operator will be listening for the signals – either dot-dot, or the more familiar dash-dash of Morse, to keep them on course. The Mouse station will give the bomb release order, the pilot having maintained the final true course to that point. Let's see how it goes, gentlemen!' He gathered a sheaf of papers together and left the room with Willis.

Griff picked up the maps and followed them to the crew room. 'At least we're not over France or Holland today.'

'Soon will be, if the boss has his way,' Don replied.

Dr Jeffreys had obviously flown with the squadron before, and even had his own locker in the crew room. He looked perfectly happy in his flying jacket and boots, holding a long and erudite conversation with Vic all the while.

'You'd better try and keep me on track with those signals, Fordham,' Vic said as they climbed up the ladder into the cockpit. 'We'll need all the concentration we can get.'

As Jeffreys conferred with Don, the wireless operator, the Wellington took off from the grass runway and followed a north-westerly course for the South Wales coast. Will listened intently for the signals, hearing first the dots which signified they had yet to reach the track line. The normal Morse code dashes followed once they were on it.

'You're drifting, Skipper, too far to the left', as the dashes became longer than normal, followed by a righting action from Vic.

'Yes, got it, Fordham.'

Then, as Will heard dots again, 'You're too far to the right now, Skip!'

'Mouse requesting ground speed, Skip.' Don's voice came through the intercom, and Dr Jeffreys nodded in assent, as Willis relayed the information back.

'You need to hold the final true course from Mouse now.' Griff was already in the bomb-aimer's station, waiting for the signal, gazing through the Perspex panel at the sea below.

'That's it, let them go!' said Vic, as he received the split-second go-ahead from West Prawle, Griff simultaneously pressing the tit for bomb release.

'There she goes!' They watched the practice missile splash into the sea.

'Let's hope it's a good one,' Jeffreys put in, clustering into the front and looking pleased. 'If that was Cologne, it should be spot on!'

'I'm not sure I like being told what to do by a bombardier in Devon,' Griff grumbled. 'They'll be flying the bloody plane from there soon, you mark my words!'

8

Salisbury was a beautiful city, or so it seemed to Will, who had gone there for his day off with Arthur. They wandered round the cloisters of the cathedral, pleasantly cool after the scorching heat, and looked back at the magnificent west front.

'I'll show you the medieval clock.' Arthur led him to a curious contraption in the north aisle, a concentric series of cogwheels without a face. 'It strikes the hours, dates back to 1386, oldest clock in Europe, you know.' They wandered up and down, gazing at the architecture, classical columns and vaulted spire. 'They've removed Magna Carta from the chapter house while the war's on,' Arthur added, 'but fortunately the city's been relatively untouched so far.'

Will thought he would like to bring Honor here, and wondered what she would be doing at this precise moment. His life was changing so quickly, and he could not share it with her. It was probably just as well she did not know what his daily tasks comprised, not least the supreme challenge of keeping that Wellington at the right place in the sky.

Both men were in uniform, and could not escape the notice of those about them. The young waitress in the tea shop, smart in her black frock and white cuffs and apron, looked positively flustered when they sat down, and nearly spilt their tea in her desire to please.

'Just as well Fred's not with us,' Arthur said. 'Now, what else would you like to do while we're here?'

'I thought I might have a photograph taken, you know, one for Honor and my mother. Is there a reasonable photographer around?'

Arthur took a bite of the dry seed cake, which the waitress had apologetically left. 'Yes, we can go past one on the way back to the car,' he said, his mouth full of crumbs.

So it was that the young pilot sat in front of the photographer's flash, rather self-consciously, wings upon his uniformed chest, for a likeness that he could leave behind. He could not help but contemplate his future, as his present self was imprinted thus. Suppose it would be his last one? He did not like to think of the endless sepia photographs of those who had failed to survive the Great War: all their homes were littered with such brief reminders of wasted young lives.

'Aren't you going to have one done, too?' Will said, but Arthur shook his head.

'I've not got a girl.'

'But what about your mother, she'd want one, surely?' Will persisted, until Arthur unwillingly sat for a portrait.

'I don't think she's well enough to appreciate it,' he commented as they left the studio, having been informed that they could collect the photographs the following week.

'Nonsense.' Will's reply was brusque. 'All mothers want photos of their sons in uniform. Anyway, I expect you'll meet a girl soon, then she'll want one too.'

'Fat hope! I don't want to end up desperate, like Fred!'

They retraced their steps back to the Austin, but were hailed by a familiar voice. Dr Jeffreys was coming towards them, a remarkably pretty girl by his side. Both men instinctively stood a little straighter.

'Hello, chaps.' The scientist was in a friendly mood, though looking no less dishevelled than usual. Will supposed that the blokes in TRE were too busy thinking to bother to dress properly. How on earth had he come by such a good-looking girl?

'Can I introduce my sister, Phyllis?' Dr Jeffreys dispelled the mystery, as the girl shook hands with them both. 'We're just going to the tea room, would you care to join us?'

Arthur could hardly bear to look at the girl, so attractive did he find her. She was slim, carefully dressed in a grey silk dress with little apricot roses. Her blonde hair was equally neat, encircling a delicately featured face.

'We'd be delighted,' Will replied. 'At least, Arthur would, I've just got a few errands to run. I'll see you back at the car in an hour, old chap.'

He looked back to see the three of them setting off towards the same tea shop, and wondered what the waitress would think to Arthur's reappearance.

He was sitting reading a newspaper in the car when Arthur climbed into the passenger seat, but was glad to be diverted from the latest news, which was uniformly bad. The Russians seemed unable to halt the German advance, and had been able to do little more than dig in at defensive positions in an effort to hold them back. A siege had started in Leningrad and there was no knowing when it would end.

'Well?' he asked. Arthur's expression was almost exactly the same as Matt's had been, after his first foray with Florence. 'Don't tell me, she's the most beautiful girl you've ever met and you think you're in love!'

'How do you know?' Arthur said.

'I just do. Now the important thing is, have you arranged to see her again?'

'No, I haven't!' Arthur's face fell. 'I just didn't know how to!'

Will shook his head in mock despair. 'You should have fixed something!'

'How could I, she's only here for the weekend, going back to Oxford on Monday. She must be as clever as her brother – do you know she's at the university, reading maths?' Arthur said.

'That doesn't stop you asking her out, you silly chump. Do you know where she's staying?'

'In a hotel, I think, don't know which one though.'

'You'll have to move a bit quicker than that, old chum, or you'll be single for the rest of your life!' Will started the car, the mission having proved hopeless, as far as he could see, but found himself thinking what a nice pair they would have made, the girl in the grey tea rose frock, and the diffident young man in blue.

10th August 1941
RAF Boscombe Down
Dear You,
Not much to report at this end, spend most of my time learning to fly properly! There is a nice bunch of people here to help me along. I keep wondering how you are?

I went to Salisbury with one of the other pilots last week – it's a lovely city and I can't wait to show you all the sights. Unfortunately, there's no knowing when I will get leave as things are pretty busy here.

Good luck with your new ward and write soon. I enclose a recent photograph that I had done for you. Hope you like it! Can you do one for me?

From Me

9

'This is the third phase of polio, the paralysis.' The nurse, her grey hair tightly in a bun, pulled back the covers from the bed, the child watching her all the time. 'We're just checking you're comfy, Ida,' she said, demonstrating to Honor the pillows and sandbags supporting the small legs in a frog's-leg position, with the feet turned in. 'She hasn't needed splinting, but some do.'

Honor smiled at the child, who did not respond. 'They have to be nursed flat if the sacrospinalis muscle is involved,' the nurse added, 'but Ida's lucky, it's only her lower limbs affected. Her hands are good, look.' She gave the child a small beaker to hold. 'Take some sips, Ida, you know we like you to keep drinking.'

Ida sipped compliantly but said nothing, merely observing them both as they moved to the foot of the bed.

'How long will it last?' Honor said, but Nurse Robinson could not give an accurate reply, unable to foretell the course of the disease.

'It all depends,' she answered. 'Some recover quickly, some gradually, and some not at all. They can be permanently paralysed, you know. Ida is fortunate in that her back and thoracic muscles are spared, otherwise she would have had trouble breathing, and you know what that means.'

Honor did know, having passed the iron lungs at the end of the ward. All were occupied, their rhythmic swishing the only way of knowing that the patients were still alive. She had learnt about the two types of iron lung for her exam; this one was the Drinker box respirator in which the patient was enclosed, his head protruding at one end through a rubber collar around the neck. A motor produced the positive and negative pressures in the respirator and the chest was passively moved. All of the nursing duties had to be performed through small portholes at the side, so it was not going to be easy. She could not help but imagine how frightening it must be inside, but the patients did not look afraid. In fact, some of them, particularly the younger ones, looked quite cheery.

At the next bed, the young woman was lying flat. 'Can I have the bedpan, Nurse?' They drew the curtains around and Honor was despatched for the sluice.

'You'll need to put a gown on, barrier nursing, you know, like typhoid. The stools can stay infectious for some time.'

Honor needed no encouragement to follow these instructions to the letter. The thought of contracting polio was still in her mind, but as they gently moved and eased the paralysed woman on to the pan, she felt nothing but compassion.

'There we go,' she said softly as she covered the pan and took it away. On her return, Nurse Robinson showed her the flaccid muscles of left arm and leg.

'She can still feel, though, can't you, Peggy?'

Peggy sighed. 'When am I going to get better? It doesn't seem to be improving at all.'

'Nonsense, Peg, it's early days. You know there's lots of time yet,' Nurse Robinson said. 'Let's just get you settled again, put the pillows and sandbags back. I think a splint on that leg might be a good idea tomorrow.' She repositioned the limbs, keeping the hand in mid-position and away from the woman's sides. 'We need to keep the shoulder abducted when the deltoid's involved,' she explained.

'So I just have to go on waiting?' Peggy's voice sounded weary.

'Yes, but in a little while we'll be able to start the exercises and massage,' Nurse Robinson said. 'There's no call to lose heart.'

The young woman gazed upwards, a small tremble at the corner of her mouth. Honor squeezed her good hand. 'Be back later.'

Once out of earshot, she asked, 'How do they keep going?'

'They just hope, Nurse Newson, like we all do when faced with impossible odds. They hope against hope that they will recover, walk and breathe again, use the hand like they did before, leave here in one piece, and pick up their lives. What else can they do? That's why the Almighty gave us hope, so we could use it when the chips are down. It's one of the most powerful emotions known to man.'

As they entered one of the cubicles, Honor could see that the boy in the bed was very ill. He must have been about twelve years old, and was holding one of his hands in front of his eyes.

'It hurts so, Nurse,' he said.

Nurse Robinson took his pulse and temperature. 'Where does it hurt, Sammy?'

'My neck's so stiff, and my legs ache.' Sammy screwed up his eyes.

'I think we're going need a lumbar puncture,' Nurse Robinson said. 'The CSF will be full of cells, I don't doubt. You stay here with him, I'll go and ring for Dr Donaldson.'

Honor took the child's hand, trying not to think about Peter showing up. She had hoped they would be working on different wards. If only he had enlisted, as he had threatened, then their paths might never cross again.

'My eyes hurt! I want to see my mum!'

She was giving the child some sips of water when Nurse Robinson reappeared. 'Go and prepare the tray, would you? Have you assisted at a lumbar puncture before?'

Honor nodded. How could she forget little Alfie? She hoped this child would not die in the same way, and steeling herself, went to the sluice to check the sterilised instruments were complete. On her return with the trolley, she caught sight of Peter. He stopped abruptly.

'Are you assisting, Nurse Newson?' he asked formally.

She nodded. 'Yes, Dr Donaldson.'

'You don't need to look so worried,' Peter murmured when Nurse Robinson had gone. 'Not all of my LPs turn out badly, you know.' He smiled at her, despite himself. Why did her very presence always lighten his day?

'I never said they did.' Her voice was as low as his. They had both gowned up, and he motioned her towards the child.

'Now, Sammy, you've got to be very good. We're going to curl you up into a little ball, on your side, like this, and Nurse is going to hold you tight.'

'My neck!' the child protested, as they did so, then gave up the struggle and lay quietly in the foetal position in Honor's arms.

'Just some cold fluid, then a little tiny prick.' Peter was slick and professional, seeming to have gained confidence since Honor had last worked with him. She hardly felt the child recoil before the syringe attached to the needle in his lower spine filled up with turbid fluid. Peter grimaced; there was not much doubt of the abnormal result that would follow from the lab.

'All done.' He labelled the two specimen bottles, stopped pressing on the swab over the entry site and placed a small plaster on it.

'You can turn over now, but take it slowly.' Honor helped Sammy on to his back. 'That wasn't too bad, was it?'

The child looked apprehensive, even though the procedure was over. 'I want to go home.' His hands were over his eyes again.

'It's photophobia, you know,' Peter explained gently. 'He doesn't like the light, it's a symptom of meningeal irritation.' Honor gathered up the instruments on the tray as he turned to leave the cubicle. 'See you around,' he added, picking up the specimens, and before she had time to reply, he was gone. She had wanted to ask him about the treatment, especially in the early stages like this, for surely something could be done?

Knowing none of the other nurses on the ward, she was enjoying a solitary walk to the dining room during her lunchtime break when the porter hailed her. 'You've a letter in the lodge, miss, I'm on my way there now.' Following him to his office, she was handed the envelope with a smile, and little wink.

It was such a relief to be sitting in the warm sunshine at last, after the endless months of winter. Honor carefully opened the envelope and a small photograph, enclosed in the letter, fluttered on to the grass.

'Enjoying the sunshine?' June sat down, uninvited, beside her. Honor hastily picked up the photograph and tucked it away in her pocket.

'I'm glad you're back!' June said. 'Addie spends all her time going on about her wedding! It's only two weeks away, but I think I'll be ready to murder her by then!'

'So, are we to be dressed up as bridesmaids?' Honor said.

'No, that's one good thing about clothes rationing! We haven't got the coupons and of course, Addie wants to use hers on her dress. I promise, in the unlikely event of my ever getting married, I'll just go off quietly with the lucky bloke by myself! Cross my heart and hope to die!'

Later that evening, looking at the solemn-faced young pilot in the photograph, self-conscious in his uniform and wings, Honor smiled. Of course she liked it, even though it made her heart constrict in an uncomfortable way. Whenever would she see him again? Time was passing so fast, it would not be long until her finals in October, and then it would be on to another hospital as a state registered nurse, if she was lucky. Where might he be then: in one of those bombers over the night sky of Germany?

Bracing herself for another bout of Addie's preparations, she made her way back through the tranquil evening light to her hut.

10

By the next day, poor little Sammy could not move and his paralysis was rapidly spreading.

'It's the ascending type,' Nurse Robinson said as they turned the child to wash him. His breathing was worryingly shallow and she had already asked the doctor to take a look at him before he became any worse.

The ward was in a state of readiness for the morning round, Sister having completed her scrupulous checks when the door opened to reveal the familiar procession, headed by the senior consultant, Dr Shepherd, flanked by Peter and another doctor whom Honor did not recognise. He was short and sandy-haired with an affable smile which Dr Shepherd could wipe from his face with one or two choice words. Sister must have asked them to begin with Sammy for they were soon in the cubicle, where the open windows were allowing the cool breeze over the child's inert body.

'Dr Donaldson, if you please.' Dr Shepherd motioned to him and Peter examined the boy thoroughly.

'I think he needs to go in the respirator, sir,' he said.

'You do, do you?' Honor braced herself, expecting the ritual humiliation, and was surprised to hear the consultant add, 'So do I, get on with it, Sister, while there's still time.'

'What's happening?' asked Sammy, as they prepared him for the move. Honor, noticing a bluish tinge around his lips, was relieved to see that one of the respirators was ready, disinfected thoroughly, its previous occupant having been weaned off respiratory support the previous day.

Putting a patient into an iron lung could best be likened to opening the drawer of a long cylindrical filing cabinet, and sliding him across from the trolley on to the tray contained within the drawer. The next important stage would be to ease the head into the rubber diaphragm, zipping it tightly to ensure no air could escape, before pushing it closed, thus encapsulating the patient inside.

As they moved the child across into the unwieldy contraption, Nurse Robinson, realising that they had run out of time, pressed the red alarm button at the side. Running on the ward was only allowed under exceptional circumstances, but Peter sprinted to their side, helping them manoeuvre the child's neck into the collar. Sammy's body was becoming increasingly limp as they tightened the locking mechanisms, an essential prerequisite to starting the motor. It seemed an age before they heard the welcome sound of the large pump moving up and down, each rhythmical movement causing the paralysed chest to lift and take in air. They stood back, watching and waiting for the child to pink up. He looked half-dead, and Honor thought he was lost, but with each mechanical breath his cyanosis lifted a little and he appeared to be regaining consciousness.

'Sammy, wake up!' Peter rubbed his cheek and the child's eyelids flickered. The three attendants exhaled in unison.

'That was close!' Peter said, wiping the slightest trace of sweat from his brow.

Not that Dr Shepherd was likely to show them any approval on his way out. 'Next time, don't leave it so long!' His entourage, weaving around him, followed in his steps.

'Can you manage him?' Peter said.

'Yes, Doctor, he should be out of danger now.' Sister had joined them to confer. She did not like patients dying on her ward, especially during a ward round. At an earlier stage in her career she might have considered it tragic, now it seemed merely untidy. Cleanliness and order, above all, must prevail, for what other defences did they have?

11

Addie was trying on her wedding dress.

'Are you sure it's not bad luck?' June said. It had been a long day and they were not really in the mood. Honor, for her part, wanted to join Molly for an evening walk in the fresh air.

'Don't be silly!' Nothing could dim Addie's enthusiasm. 'What do you think, it's not too short, is it?'

The crepe white dress fell just below her knees, revealing her shapely legs, flat-footed and bare though they were. 'I wish I had some silk stockings. Do you think that boyfriend of yours could get me some?'

Honor was not attending to proceedings at all. 'It's only a week away!' Addie continued. 'Ken's leave will start on Thursday, you know, then we've just one day before I'll be walking down the aisle!'

June sighed. 'Where's he stationed?'

'Somewhere called Stanford.' Addie did a small pirouette, testing the feel of her hem as it lifted around her. 'He's on tank exercises with his regiment, the Royal Norfolks. He's in command of a Valentine tank,' she added proudly. 'I don't know where they'll be posted after that.'

Honor hoped for her sake that they would not be off to join the Eighth Army in the deserts of North Africa, but said nothing.

'If you two don't mind, I'm off for a little breather.' She slowly rose from her bed. 'Molly and I might just go out for a bit, it's such a lovely evening.'

'Oh, I thought you might help me take the hem down a little!' Addie said.

'Nonsense, it looks lovely just as it is, he'll be mad for you when he sees it!' Honor pinched her gently on the cheek. 'It's so stuffy in here, I won't be long.'

Molly was waiting for her at the entrance. 'There you are, I was beginning to give up hope! Do you want to go into town?'

'No, I'd rather wander around in the fresh air a bit. Sometimes I wish we were still at Ratby, it was lovely up there.'

They made their way towards Glenfield, enjoying the evening air while children played on the streets.

'Wish I could join them! Didn't you love playing tig?' Molly said. 'How's your new ward, anyway?'

'I don't like it much,' Honor confessed. 'It's the thought of being paralysed like that, not knowing when…'

'Peter's on your ward, isn't he?'

'Yes, he was in today, on the round, then helped us put a child in a respirator,' Honor said. 'Have you got the fair-haired chap on your ward?'

'Yes we have, poor sweet boy! He has a rotten time from old Shepherd,' Molly replied, 'looks more and more harassed with each passing day. Why can't they just leave him alone?'

Dusk was falling as they retraced their steps. By dint of studious avoidance of Peter's name, they had passed a pleasant evening, and discussed Addie's wedding instead, which was to be held in the church in Melton Mowbray, where Ken's uncle lived.

'Just as well I'm not coming,' Molly said stoutly. 'I've had enough of wartime romances, they're all doomed to failure if you ask me!'

12

As the summer days passed, Honor became more accustomed to the work. She was now adept at nursing a patient in an iron lung, and once realising that many patients could tolerate brief periods while they were disconnected from the ventilator, became efficient and quick at washing and toileting them. It was so much simpler if you could slide the patient out, and not have to do it all through the portholes. Working in unison with Nurse Robinson, she learnt how to put greased cotton strips around the patients' necks to stop chafing of the rubber collar. She recognised the importance of massage of the affected muscles, which could be acutely tender at first. Then, more importantly from a psychological point of view, she was able to follow patients through the slow process of remobilisation.

Watching little Ida trying to take her first tentative steps, swinging her legs while supporting herself on the two parallel bars, closely supervised by the physical therapist, Honor began to believe that for some patients, at least, there might be a future.

Weaning patients off ventilation could be as complex. For a start, they would be fearful about breathing unassisted, and only gradually build up confidence with increasing periods outside the respirator. Nurse Robinson taught her by example all the while, showing her how to assess the respiratory status, and when the patient would need to go back.

She was leaving the ward after a better day: Sammy was stable, and had smiled again for the first time. It was good to be outside, even though there was plenty of fresh air on the ward, given the policy of keeping all the windows open whatever the weather. Not expecting company, she was humming a tune, Vera Lynn's *We'll Meet Again*, when Peter appeared in front of her on the path.

'Honor, I was hoping I might see you! Would you like to come for a drink in the pub? It's such a nice evening, I could do with getting out for a while!'

Her face expressed her disquiet. 'Peter, I shouldn't, it's not fair on you.'

'Don't be silly, I only want to have a drink together! It's not a date, now, is it? I just feel like some company, that's all.'

She hesitated a moment too long, and he could see that he had won.

'OK, if you're sure.'

He waited for her while she changed out of her uniform, relieved that no one was there to ask her where she was going, and they strolled out of the hospital grounds unobserved.

'What'll it be?' The pub was half empty, and she sat at a small wooden table. He came back with her lemonade shandy and she smiled at him. She missed his company and disliked the constraint that had grown between them. She glanced at a newspaper left on the chair. There was a picture of Roosevelt and Churchill, the latter in naval uniform, seated in front of a bevy of generals from both sides. Winston looked as implacable as ever, puffing on his beloved Havana cigar.

'So what is this Atlantic Charter?'

'Well,' Peter warmed to the theme, 'Winston knows we can't win the war by ourselves. Do you remember what he said last year? "There is only one thing worse than fighting with allies, and that is fighting without them." He's been hoping the Yanks will help but they are still playing hard to get. Meanwhile, the Soviets are now on the same side as us, Hitler having invaded Russia in June. Winston has been meeting FDR in Newfoundland, on *HMS Prince of Wales*, I think it says. They're signing some charter, even though the Americans aren't in the war yet. It's about what should happen after the war, you know, no annexing of territories, and the rights of freedom. Unfortunately, Stalin isn't there to sign it too, he's too busy trying to stop the Nazis from beating the hell out of them. If you go back in history, most victors will claim the spoils of war, so it doesn't seem very likely that this treaty will stop it. Anyway, we're a long way from the end, if you ask me, even if the Yanks do join in.'

Honor was fascinated. Not having had the opportunity to study history before, she thought how interesting it must be to have such a perspective. She wished she were better educated, like Peter.

'Do you think Russia will fall?' she asked quietly. She much preferred conversations with Peter that were not about love and loss.

'I wouldn't like to say,' he replied honestly. 'Napoleon couldn't conquer it! But the trouble with the Nazis is that their army seems to have this extraordinary momentum that takes countries by surprise, overwhelming them before they've put up a proper show. Look at France – that was over in no time. One good thing about the Russians – they're fierce fighters and it's an enormous country. I hope to God they hold on!'

'Tell me about Napoleon,' she prompted, and he looked at her in surprise.

'Do you really want to know? I don't mean to hold forth, it's just that I loved history at school, and it seems to me that there are so many parallels with the past. We can learn so much from it.' He sipped his beer, as though he had resolved to stop talking for a bit.

'Go on, tell me!' she urged. 'I never had the benefit of a proper education so the least you can do is fill in the gaps!'

They stayed in the pub longer than intended. Honor looked at her watch.

'Is that the time?!'

She anticipated a barrage of questions from her friends about where she had been, but she need not have worried. Addie was in a state of shock, holding a crumpled telegram which told her that Ken had died in a training accident on the artillery range the day before.

13

'How can they call it "killed in action" when he wasn't even fighting the enemy?' June said. The date set for Addie's wedding had passed them by, its unremitting rain a backdrop to the senseless vacuum of the day. Addie had gone home to her parents during her leave, but returned surprisingly quickly to the wards, saying she could not bear it there and at least she would be useful back at work.

They had pored over the letter, which she had held out to them in mute entreaty. It was from his supervising officer, sent first to his parents. Unable to understand the terminology (after all, what exactly was a 'PIAT'?), they pieced together the story – that Ken had been killed while attempting to fire a handheld anti-tank missile. He had been on live exercises in the Stanford Principal Training Area, a part of rural Norfolk annexed by the military. The weapon had exploded, and only one of the two casualties had survived. Addie, yet to marry, had no legal rights in terms of information and would receive no widow's pension. At least his parents, who had grown fond of her even in such a short space of time, were supportive, but for Addie, it was almost as though he had never existed.

'I wish I hadn't held out until we were married!' she had mourned. 'I might have had his baby, then I'd have something to remember him by!'

Honor forbore to point out that a pregnant, unmarried nurse was not a role to aspire to, for she understood her friend's longing, and sudden emptiness. She tried to stifle the deep fear about her own fate with Will: was this what was in store for her too?

Of all of those around them, it was Peter who came to the fore, able to comfort Addie when others failed. He gave credence and longevity to her mourning, refusing to believe that she should just 'try and forget him'.

'You can't hurry grief,' he told Honor, 'it just takes its own time to pass, in phases of resolution. It'll work itself through in the end, but it can be a long haul.'

The loss of Addie's joyous enthusiasm took its toll upon them all. It seemed wrong to be planning their own futures when hers had been so rapidly cut short. A sense of gloom prevailed in their hut, until one particularly dismal evening when they were trying, and failing, to find a neutral subject for discussion, the door flung open to reveal Beatie.

'I came as soon as I could!' she announced, running to Addie's side, thus provoking a fresh bout of tears. Pulling an oil-stained hanky from her trousers, she surveyed the room.

'Not much's changed here then, girls! Poor Addie, how dreadful for you! To have found the right bloke, only to lose him!'

Beatie looked good, even in her FANY uniform. In fact, she looked better than she ever had in her nurse's pinafore and starched cap. It was as though she had been liberated from all the constraints that surrounded them. Although still very thin, and lacking her previous curvaceous figure, she was an arresting sight.

'Beatie! Thank goodness you're here!' Honor said.

'Well, I can't stay long, only got a pass for one night, but I borrowed a motorbike so at least I don't have to go on those beastly trains.'

'Borrowed a motorbike!' June looked incredulous.

'Yes, lots of the FANYs ride them, usually the despatch riders, which I am not! Merely a lorry driver, me!' She looked cheerful enough at the thought.

'Where is it?' June asked, as though it had to be seen to be believed.

'At the porter's lodge, he's going to keep an eye on it for me. God! I haven't thought about where I'm going to sleep! Can I stay here?'

She sat with her arm around Addie, who seemed to derive great comfort from her presence, and rested her head on Beatie's uniformed shoulder. When it came to information about how Ken had met his death, the others filled it in for her.

Beatie looked indignant. 'Well, I know the pilots on our base have accidents,' she said, 'but you'd almost expect that, they're flying dangerous planes. Surely Ken shouldn't have been killed firing an anti-tank gun! Looks like someone's not doing their job properly, if you ask me! Anyway, we never hear anything about it in the newspapers, do we? I wonder how many of our boys are written off before they ever get near the enemy!'

During the course of the evening, they learnt little more about Beatie's life. She seemed disinclined to talk about it: 'Just driving lorries, you know.'

'Have you got a boyfriend, Beatie?' Addie looked up at her, her tears dry at last.

'Who, me? Nothing worth telling you about, Addie dearest. Now listen, I'm starving, where can we get some food?'

24th August 1941
Groby Road Hospital
Dear You,
I am getting by on the polio ward, though it's not my favourite place! I'm learning every day, and seem to be doing OK, so I can't complain. I hope you

are all right and being careful, I was so pleased to have your photograph! I'll go and have one done for you on my next day off.

We have had a bit of a shock here, as Addie's fiancé Ken was killed in action two days before their wedding. It was a training accident and she is finding it hard to bear.

Do you think you might have any leave next month? It seems ages since June, and I miss you terribly.

From Me

14

'Now, gentlemen, tonight's exercise is extremely hush-hush,' the duty officer said. 'I don't need to remind any of you of the secrecy that surrounds all our operations. We have to stay one step ahead of the Hun, and it's proving damn difficult, I can tell you.'

The room was full of smoke as the crews casually passed around cigarettes. Arthur was puffing on his new pipe, settling back in his seat.

'Intelligence sources suggest that two of Germany's biggest warships, the *Scharnhorst* and the *Gneisenau*, are heading for the dry dock at Brest,' the officer continued. 'We want to be ready for them, so the mission tonight is Oboe-controlled, that is to say, riding a beam to Brest and testing our system of bomb release. This means we might get the chance to sink the two battle cruisers when they are installed. I don't need to tell you, gentlemen, that these two ships cause havoc to our convoys, and they are a major strategic target. I will pass over to Dr Cummings.'

Cummings stood up, polishing his pebble spectacles as he did so.

'Thank you, gentlemen, for your attention. If I may refer to the blackboard,' he took a pointer and continued, 'the track beam from Helston, the station we call the Broody Hen, is a narrow Lorenz-type Baillie beam. The signal has been tested already, and should come through loud and clear, though can fall off after 180 miles. In the run-up to target, the final two minutes are critical. The warning signal from West Prawle will comprise twelve dots, meaning the pilot must be prepared to keep to the course dictated by the beam from Helston. The final warning will take the form of a one-second pause in the transmission from West Prawle. At this point, the Broody Hen operator will light a red lamp situated in front of the bomb release operator – that's your visual failsafe indicator in case of equipment failure. Following the one-second pause, there will be a further transmission from West Prawle, between ten and thirty seconds, depending on the speed of the aircraft. Cessation of West Prawle's signal marks the exact release point.'

'Thank you, Cummings,' the CO said. 'Now, the tricky bit is the teamwork: the captain co-ordinates the signals, while the second pilot holds the beam at six thousand feet. When the ground signal is received, he opens the bomb doors. The navigator takes up the bomb-aimer's position, plugs into the Broody Hen, watches for the red light, hears the release signal, and lets them go. Now let's just take a good look at the landmarks at Brest.'

The room went dark as a photographic slide of the area was projected, clearly showing the location of the docks relative to the railway, river and bridges nearby. The duty officer reminded them that, contrary to their usual bombing raids, they would not be relying on navigation or visual fixes but using the Oboe system, both Wellingtons carrying the Hallicrafter S27 receivers.

There was a murmur of discussion among the audience.

'Any questions?'

'What are the anti-aircraft defences like over there?' Arthur asked, still enveloped in a cloud of smoke.

'Pretty tight, the rear gunners will need to be on their toes. You're bound to encounter considerable flak. Remember, you're not dropping real bombs this time, it's just a test run to see if the system works. We want both Wellingtons home, especially with all that kit in, so don't take unnecessary risks. There will be photographic backup, of course.'

Don let out a low whistle. 'Don't give much for our chances if they catch us over Brest,' he muttered to Griff.

'Let's give you the weather briefing.' They were informed it would be a cloudless night, with a full moon.

'Great!' put in Fred under his voice. 'The Luftwaffe will be pleased!'

'Look, chaps, it won't be easy,' the CO continued in his clipped, upper-class voice, 'but we don't have much time to test this equipment before the ships arrive. It could save countless lives if we can take them out, and change the outcome of the war. Good luck, gentlemen!'

They rose from their seats.

'I'm going to look at the maps with Griff,' Vic said. 'See you in the crew room.'

Arthur turned to Will as they left. 'I'm really not sure I fancy that bacon and eggs.'

'Come on.' Fred had overheard. 'I'll eat yours, don't waste it!'

There was the usual curious sense of isolation in the Wellington at night, it was as though the crew only existed in their own geodetic world. As long as the plane flew, they shared the same entombed fate, wound closer by the black skies around them.

'C for Charlie request take-off?' Vic opened the throttles until they were rumbling down between the lights, up over a dark Salisbury Plain, and headed for France.

Checking all the crew on the intercom – 'Is the receiver working, Don?' – Vic held them on steady course over the sea. 'How's the course, Navigator?'

'OK, Skip, should be another half an hour till we pick up the beam.'

'Well, we'll have to see if we can hold it.' Vic appeared unruffled by the prospect of snooping over a heavily fortified enemy port. 'Ted, the natives might be restless tonight, just keep a good eye out, will you?' he said to the rear gunner, alone in his turret.

'Sure thing, Skip!'

Ted swivelled round in his turret, surveying the dark skies as the bomber ploughed steadily on over the sea.

'Picking up the beam, Skip!' The wireless operator's voice came over the intercom.

'Right, this is it, there's the ground signal – you take over, Will, and hold the beam!'

'OK, Skip.' Will listened intently to the now-familiar mix of dots and dashes, holding the exact course. 'Altitude 6,500 feet.'

Far from enveloping them, the night sky was now full of flashes.

'Flak, Skip, plenty of it, I'm letting them have a few rounds,' said Ted, as the explosions, first visible as tracer bullets only, came closer. The Wellington began to rock and Will steadied the control column.

'OK, everyone?'

Will could see the river and bridges below – they must be nearing the dockyard. Where was the signal? Trying to dispel the uncomfortable notion that they were easy prey, he heard the twelve dots, and reminded himself to hold steady.

It seemed like an eternity before 'Bomb doors open!' from Vic, as the red light came on. The signal stopped, Griff pressed the button and the camera flashed in place of the 250-pounders.

'Let's get out of here, too much flak for comfort!' Will was already turning the bomber into its homeward course. There was another loud flash, juddering the plane again, and Vic was at his side.

'Have we taken a hit?'

'Don't think so, sir, I'll check with the crew.' Heartened to hear them all respond, he changed places with Vic. 'That was close, Skip!'

'Yes, pity it was a trial run! I can't wait to go back for those ships, now that's what I call proper action!'

Once over the Channel, they counted themselves lucky not to be pursued by enemy fighters, for which Ted kept up a ceaseless watch.

Will checked the gauges: 'We're losing fuel in the port wing tank, Skip!'

Vic swore under his breath, as the needle on the fuel gauge supplying the port engine continued inexorably to fall.

'Must have taken a hit! See if you can switch to the nacelle tank.'

The fuel system on the Wellington comprised a front and rear tank in both wings for each engine, with a back-up tank – the nacelle – holding fifty-eight gallons, enough for about an hour's running time. Unlike the trusty Oxfords, a Wimpy could not be flown on one engine, hence the complex backup system of fuel pipes that operated between the two sides. Will clambered back into the fuselage and pulled the nacelle cables adjacent to the main tank cock cables, to activate the tank.

Vic looked relieved as he came back to his folding seat beside him. 'We're in business, Will, should get us home!'

Later when the engineers showed them the ragged hole through the wing, Will marvelled that they had made it back at all.

'Seen them come in worse than that,' one of the erks added. 'Strewth, do you remember that one that went right through the fuselage? It's the fabric-covered frame, you know, takes a hit and just goes right on flying!'

Arthur's crew had already been through debriefing by the time they arrived. It was always difficult to concentrate on the minutiae after a sortie, but the intelligence officer wanted every detail.

'We'll see what the aerial photography shows, chaps, you can go now,' were his final words, as with a mixture of fatigue and elation, they finally made for their beds in the breaking dawn.

15

Cummings was pleased with the results of the Oboe raid, despite the fact that the West Prawle signal to the other Wellington had faded at a critical time. He had since worked out some modifications to the Broody Hen equipment, which he hoped would do the trick. He stood up in front of the group of airmen.

'Good work, chaps, all we have to do now is wait until the battleships are in the dock at Brest, then we should be able to repeat the Oboe exercise exactly, this time, of course, with bombs. I've read all of your reports, just wanted to know if there's anything else I should be aware of?'

Vic raised a hand. 'Are you fellows certain it's superior to our previous methods? I mean, we used to hit our targets before, and we're pretty vulnerable sitting on the beam like that. I reckon it's why we got shot up: we're dead meat flying straight and level, there's no room for evasive action when all hell breaks loose.'

Each Wellington pilot had, or would develop, methods of avoiding enemy attack, if he and his crew were to survive. One of the most hallowed manoeuvres was 'corkscrewing', putting the plane into a complex dive to shake off an enemy fighter. There would be no chance of such action while holding tightly to a beam.

Will remembered how it felt to count the seconds before the signal came, and Fred had spoken for them all: 'It's all right for the buggers on the ground!'

'May I?' Cummings looked across at the squadron leader, who nodded in assent. 'The problem is, you haven't been bombing the targets as accurately as you think. We have some recent data which shows that a significant proportion of a bomber stream miss it. In fact, only a third of you come within five miles of the aiming point.' He raised both hands in his defence, as the murmur of disapproval became louder.

'Look, chaps, it's no one's fault, but that's why the work of the Pathfinder Squadron is so important. You can be pretty sure that these new methods, Oboe, Gee, and others yet to be dreamed up, will be in general use in the near future. We have to improve our precision bombing, or the Hun will win the day.'

The room went quiet, for there was no more to be said. As they were leaving, Arthur looked even more distracted than usual.

'I wonder how many of us they expect to lose?'

'Best not think about it.' Will put a hand on his shoulder. 'Any news of your mother?'

Arthur brightened. 'Yes, I had a letter today. The doctors have collapsed one of her lungs, and it seems to be helping, so I'm just hoping for the best.'

'There, what did I tell you? The treatments are improving all the time, anyway that's what Honor told me.'

The mere use of her name evoked in him a sense of longing. When would he see her again? Any prospect of leave seemed unlikely under the circumstances. He hoped she would send him her photograph soon; he could put it in his pocket, for good luck, when he went on the next trip.

'Anyway, have you seen Jeffreys again? What's the gen on his sister?' Will continued.

'I've chatted to him, but how could I possibly ask? I've only met her once! Look, I'll meet you in the mess later, after firing practice in Lyme Bay.'

As Will walked into the canteen for a cup of tea later that afternoon, he spotted Jeffreys reading a newspaper. 'Can I sit down?'

'Please do.' Jeffreys motioned him to a chair. He folded the paper.

'Not looking good for the Russians, I'm afraid.'

'I don't expect they'll give up without a struggle,' Will replied. 'By the way, it was nice to meet your sister in Salisbury. I'm sorry I couldn't join you for tea.'

'That's all right, Fordham, she and Wellesley seemed to find plenty to talk about.'

'Did they now?' Will decided to take the plunge, knowing Arthur would never take the initiative. 'Just between you and me, I think he's a bit sweet on her!'

Jeffreys smiled. 'She's really only interested in her work, you know. She's frightfully clever, much brighter than me. They say she's going to get a first at Oxford.'

'Is she planning to visit again?' Will said.

'Funny you should ask, she's back in Salisbury next weekend. Something about an old school friend she wanted to meet.' Jeffreys stood up. 'I expect I'll be having dinner with her at her hotel, you can join us if you'd like.' He left the canteen before Will had a chance to reply.

Arthur's Wellington was late back from firing exercises, such that the air traffic controller stood looking at the empty space on the blackboard, where their return should have been logged by now. That was the trouble with routine trips: a safe return was subject to chance, no matter how mundane the duty. In fact, firing practice could be tricky, especially close to the water; the wing of the large bomber could clip the waves with disastrous results.

He was relieved to hear F for Freddie asking for permission to land, and soon the distinctive aircraft touched down on the grass runway.

'What kept you, Freddie?'

'Got mistaken for the enemy as we came back over the coast!' Arthur said contemptuously. 'It's bad enough fighting off the Hun, without being shot up by our own lads! Wretched Hurricane came at me straight on, firing his machine guns if you please! It's a miracle we weren't all killed. Can't you do something about them?'

The controller shook his head. Only last week anti-aircraft shells had gone off a couple of hundred yards behind another Wellington over Portsmouth. The crew were not amused when the senior naval officer subsequently telephoned to enquire about the accuracy of his gunfire.

'That beer tastes good!' Arthur said in the mess that evening. 'I wouldn't mind sampling some of the local ales, do you fancy a trip to Salisbury this weekend?'

Will saw his chance. 'I've been meaning to talk to you about this, old boy. As good luck would have it, I saw Jeffreys today.'

'And?' Arthur took another deep sip of his beer.

'And his sister is coming down again this weekend, he's asked me to join them for dinner.'

'What bloody good is that going to be? You've got a girlfriend already, surely you don't need two!'

16

The dining room of the Falcon Hotel was nearly full. Catching sight of Will, Jeffreys beckoned him to their table, where Phyllis greeted him.

She looked even prettier than before, this time in a lavender dress that set off her lovely hair. Will stood beside her, conscious that his plan might be about to backfire.

'Would you mind terribly if my friend Wellesley joins us? He happened to be giving me a lift to Salisbury and he'll have rather a long wait otherwise!' Will hoped they had not witnessed him driving up in his Austin.

Phyllis looked quickly across at her brother. 'Is that the chap I met before? He's so sweet, Roger, do let him join us!'

Jeffreys nodded begrudgingly and Will made for the lounge, where he found Arthur disconsolately puffing on his pipe. He rose to his feet, emptied his pipe, and followed Will into the dining room without a word. However, his face lit up at the sight of the girl, with whom he shook hands awkwardly before sitting down.

There was a moment's silence, which Will took it upon himself to fill.

'Arthur's from the West Country, you know.'

'I thought so,' Phyllis said. 'Whereabouts?'

In the stilted conversation that followed Will began to wish he had left well alone. Arthur was much too shy to take a lead, even if the poor girl did fancy him. He sat back and let them get on with it, preferring to read the menu instead. He would have to be careful as the place was not cheap and he had no wish to squander his pay.

'Right!' said Arthur, suddenly enthusiastic. 'What about a bottle of wine? My treat!'

'Good idea.' Jeffreys summoned the waiter, with whom he spent some time discussing the list. The food, when it arrived, was as disappointing as the wine but Arthur's enthusiasm was undimmed. Will had never seen him so animated, and wondered if the girl had any idea of the effect she was having.

The evening lagged. Jeffreys was obviously out of humour, but Phyllis seemed oblivious to her brother's mood. She encouraged Arthur's attempts at conversation and helped to fill in the gaps, smiling all the while.

'Your brother tells me you're a bluestocking,' Will said. It was time to change the subject, which had veered to farming again.

She blushed. 'I'm not sure that's a compliment, I always think of bluestockings as shrivelled spinsters who are stuck in a book!'

Arthur gazed at her longer than he should. 'You're most definitely not that.'

Phyllis looked back into his eyes, and for a brief moment it appeared to Will that Arthur might have pulled it off.

Jeffreys had obviously arrived at the same conclusion, for he wiped his mouth with his napkin. 'Right, chaps, we'd better not keep Phyllis up too late, she needs her beauty sleep! Good of you to join us.' He motioned to the waiter.

'Let me,' offered Arthur, but Jeffreys dismissed him.

'We'll split it.'

There followed a formal shaking of hands before the girl was ushered from the room by her brother. Arthur sat down again, transfixed by her departing figure.

'I don't know about you, but I could do with a brandy,' he said. Then in uncharacteristic expression of rapture, 'That was the nicest evening I've ever had!'

17

The red ink writing was scrawled across his logbook:

4/9/41 Certified that Sgt W. R. Fordham has qualified first pilot on Wellington A/craft.

Signed by Wing Commander Hebden, the entry confirmed his proficiency at day and night flying, in which he had gained the necessary experience.

He looked at it, scanning his experience in the Wellington to date. In all, he must have clocked up nearly twenty hours of night flying as first pilot, but nearly four times as much in the day. It was all becoming second nature to him now: the feel of the big aircraft, how it handled in the air, and the strategies for completing each duty carefully and completely. He had always been a meticulous pilot, and such attention to detail definitely paid off in the bomber. The crew were not yet a fixed entity, as they would be when he was on regular ops, but he was committed to his responsibility for their welfare, both on and off the aircraft. Mature beyond his twenty years, like many of his generation, he was focused on the business in hand and the strict discipline that underpinned it. In truth, all he really wanted to do was survive the war, and the better a pilot he was, the more likely that would be.

There was no time to keep up with his friends from Desford. Matt, flying Hurricanes with 229 Squadron at Northolt, was hardly likely to write regular letters, and though he had received a short missive from Guy, it had told him little of their nightly sorties over the North Sea to bomb the industrial heartland of Germany.

There was little cause for optimism in the progress of the war. Leningrad was now completely cut off, and Germany had occupied Estonia. Despite all of Winston's hopes, the Americans had yet to declare themselves, Roosevelt having committed himself to neutrality. It looked as though Britain was the only one to hold the line against an implacable force. Even more disquieting were the rumours about treatment of the Jews in the labour camps of Poland, though few could believe that crimes against humanity would be committed by the Nazis on a large scale.

Since Edek and Alice's wedding, his thoughts about marriage to Honor had altered subtly. Perhaps they should tie the knot sooner rather than later? He wanted to propose during his next leave, but the nickname of his bomber said it all: 'Widow Maker'. Was it fair to her? Look what had happened to her friend Addie! On the other hand, he recalled Alice's radiant face on her wedding day, taking on the odds with the man she loved.

Meanwhile, it was back to today's duty: a cross-country to White Waltham, then Aberdovey and Lundy before returning to base. His crew were ready and waiting as he donned his Irvin jacket, flying helmet and oxygen mask and picked up his parachute harness.

'C'mon, boss!' Fred was his navigator today. 'You don't normally keep us waiting! Where've you been?'

'Just getting signed off.' Will pulled on his flying boots.

'Well, get a move on, I'm looking forward to dropping in at White Waltham!' Fred winked, for this was the home of the Air Transport Auxiliary. 'Beautiful sheilas ferrying planes around – I can't wait!'

'Fred, you think of nothing else!'

It was a clear day and a straightforward exercise, making a pleasant change from fiddling with radio receivers or practising some abstruse jamming procedure for the TRE. As his experience grew, Will could revel in the joy of flight again, of moving the control column, his feet on the rudder bar where they wanted to be.

'C for Charlie, request permission to land?' He brought the Wellington neatly down and taxied to dispersal.

'Good-oh!' Fred was raring to go, swinging out of the hatch. 'Ladies, here I come!'

He did not have to wait long. The ATA woman strolling out to the Whitley was in full flying kit, but she had not neglected to put on her make-up. Fred could not resist a wolf-whistle, which she ignored, as she was reading her ferry pilot's notes.

She levered her small frame into the cockpit as the crew watched in awe, then a few minutes later, the bomber was thundering down the runway without so much as a wave from its diminutive pilot.

'Bloody hell, I've seen it all now,' Fred said.

'Little slip of a thing like that, flying that ruddy great plane all by herself!' the wireless operator added. 'That takes guts, you've got to hand it to them!'

Sitting in deckchairs in the sun outside the main building, two more women were sipping mugs of tea, the ATA badges on their smart uniforms reflecting their extreme professionalism. They looked up at the approach of the Wellington crew, but their attention was soon diverted by their own adjutant arriving with the day's orders.

One of them gave a barely suppressed shout: 'At last, Lettie! I'm taking the Spitfire!'

'Some people get all the luck!' Lettie replied. 'I can't wait to get my hands on one!' She shook out her fair curls before donning her flying hat. 'All I get is the Fairey Battle!' They took no more notice of the crew as they wandered towards the runway.

Minutes later, the Spitfire, the plane any pilot would give his eye teeth to fly, took off effortlessly to the skies.

'Well, I'm jiggered!' Don said. 'Are they all women, the pilots here?'

They found out later in the small mess, where an airman with a patch over one eye put them right.

'No, chaps, some of us are blokes! We're called the Ancient and Tattered! Lost my eye in a scrap in France, but I can still move these old crates around.'

'What a job!' Fred said. 'When can I sign up?'

'Sorry, old chap, I don't think the ATA need navigators! Anyway most of the girls are pretty stand-offish – usually off to London as soon as they get some leave, hitting the high spots. They're not interested in the likes of us!'

Fred chewed his sandwich reflectively. 'I'd be happy to give it a go!'

'Of course you would, Fred, it's just as well the Air Ministry are unlikely to agree! And would you mind concentrating on the next leg of our cross-country?' Will leaned across the table. 'Aberdovey, please, Fred, we can't stay here all day!'

8th September 1941

RAF Boscombe Down

Dear You,

I wish I had more time to write! Things are hotting up here and it is all work and no play! Still no news about leave.

Anyway, you will be pleased to hear that yours truly has been certified as fit to fly a Wimpy! I trust they haven't made an awful mistake! Still, the way things are looking on the Russian front, the Soviets are going to need all the help we can give, even from pilots like me!

I hope your patients are behaving themselves, and you are not worked off your feet. Infantile paralysis must be an awful disease!

I'm sorry to hear about Addie. It's somehow worse when lads never even make it to the front. It happened to a friend of mine – do you remember?

I'm still waiting for that photograph, and miss you all the time.

From Me

18

'What if I can't breathe?' Sammy did not want to come out of the iron lung. 'What will you do then?' His anxious eyes were watching both nurses as they began to slide him out.

'It's all right, Sammy, we'll just put you straight back! It's only for a little while,' Honor said.

Nurse Robinson took his hand gently. 'Look, Sammy, I want you to calm down and breathe very slowly. We won't leave you, Nurse will sit with you all the time. The doctors are so pleased with you, just try it for a little while. We don't want you to stay in there forever, now do we?'

Sammy screwed up his eyes. 'Just for a bit then. You promise you won't leave me?'

'Promise. Now I'm going to get you washed and comfy first, then I'll just rub some liniment on your back.' Honor talked quietly to him all the time. 'Wiggle your toes for me, Sammy,' she asked, but the child could not move his legs at all.

'I can move my fingers! Look.' Sammy was pleased to comply, the faint muscular contractions moving down his thin, wasted arms.

'Well done! The doctors know you're getting better, you see.' Honor massaged his flaccid calf muscles. If they could wean him out of the respirator then he could start his physical therapy, though given the severity of his attack, there was little cause for optimism about the prognosis.

She gave him a sip of lemonade, and checked his lips and tongue for signs of cyanosis. There were none; he continued to stay pink and increasingly confident.

'It's funny being out, Nurse, I feel like I've been in there forever!' He experimented with moving his hands again.

'Well, not forever, Sammy, but quite a few weeks all the same.' She squeezed out the flannel in the bowl. It seemed a long time to her too, since his urgent transfer from the main ward, with so many unwelcome events in between, not least the tragic death of Ken.

Addie had surprised them all by throwing herself into her work. Resolutely swotting for their forthcoming SRN exams, she was often to be found in the library, poring over some huge medical tome. Honor and the others tried to persuade her to take a break, but to no avail.

'I have to study!' she had replied, as though their suggestions were frivolous in the extreme.

Even her closest ally, June, began to lose patience. 'She'll end up a nun if she goes on like this! She can't throw away the rest of her life on a memory!'

Remembering Peter's words, Honor said, 'I expect she'll pick up soon, it's early days. If only Beatie were here!'

Beatie's sudden reappearance in their lives had concluded with her departure on the motorbike the following morning.

'Bye, all!' She had waved cheerfully before revving up and out of the hospital gates. At that precise moment in time, they would all gladly have changed places with her. What a life!

'Lucky thing!' June waved back. 'The open road!'

After Sammy had tolerated his prescribed period outside the iron lung, she slid him back inside again and started the motor.

'There, that wasn't so bad, was it? We'll do it again tomorrow.' Honor stroked his head before she moved on.

In a calliper to support her left leg, Peggy had started to walk unsteadily around the ward. Honor made up her bed while Peggy stood watching, holding on to the bed rail.

'You're coming on well, Peggy,' Honor said, changing the pillowcase for a starched, fresh one.

'It takes so long! Some days I can't see any improvement at all!'

'Well I can. When I started on this ward you couldn't get out of bed!'

'I suppose so,' Peggy admitted, 'but I still can't walk!' There was a pause. 'Nurse, do you think I'll ever ride again?'

'Does that matter to you?'

'Oh, yes, more than anything! I love horses – I work in a stable, or did, anyway. I couldn't bear to end up a cripple!' Her eyes filled with tears. She would have been a strong, athletic girl before the illness hit her.

Honor looked up from finishing the tight corner of the sheets. The girl could not have been much older than her.

'You must keep on trying, Peggy, the doctors say there's still time for improvement. You might still get better!'

'But what if I don't? It's all right for you, you're not having to drag yourself around with a piece of metal on your leg and a useless arm! I'm tired of being brave.' She wiped her nose on the sleeve of her dressing gown. 'I just want to go home.'

'Ida's going today,' Honor replied, to spur her on.

Later as she prepared the child to leave, Ida's excitement was as infectious as the disease that had claimed her.

'My dad'll be here soon, he's bringing the van!' The little girl would be leaving in a wheelchair – but at least she was with her family once more.

Honor bathed her, noticing how much more strength the child had built up in her legs. Not yet having made a complete recovery, Ida was lucky in that the doctors reckoned she would learn to walk again in time. Dressed and ready, her short hair held back in a kirby grip, Ida settled into her chair, her face lighting up as she saw the familiar figure through the glass in the ward door.

'Dad!'

19

There was a touch of autumn in the air: even though days were still warm they were preceded by misty nights, presaging another change of season and the coming winter. Honor hoped she would not have to endure the freezing Nissen hut, as she would probably be changing hospitals soon. She was not deterred by the thought of a move: her young wartime generation was learning to live with instability.

The hospital finals had to be passed first, and although she did not share Addie's single-mindedness, Honor managed to keep studying steadily. She had gained experience of so many more diseases, and recalling patients she had nursed herself made it so much easier.

Addie looked up as she came in from her shift. Honor's feet ached, and she took off her shoes to lie for a quiet moment on her bed. She was hungry too, ready for her supper, no matter how meagre. As long as it wasn't tripe – she could still hardly bear to swallow it!

'Honor?' Addie said softly, putting a bookmark in her book and closing it.

'Yes, Ad? How are you today?'

'I'm fine.' Addie's face was set. 'I want to tell you something.'

'What?' Honor sat up.

'I'm going to join the QAs when I've passed my exam.'

The QAs, or Queen Alexandra nurses, were military and service nurses, who volunteered to tend the sick and wounded in the theatre of war. The postings abroad could be dangerous, as they were often near the front line. The QAs were renowned for their discipline and fortitude, often having to cope with extreme conditions abroad.

'Oh, Addie, are you sure? It's not just because of Ken? It might be dangerous, what will your parents say?'

'They know already. I just can't stop thinking about him! If I can nurse soldiers, I'll be closer to him, helping lads who need me.' Her mind was clearly made up. 'I have to pass this exam, they won't take me otherwise. I'll go mad if I stay here, thinking about what might have been!'

'You must be careful.' Honor hugged her.

'You understand, don't you?' Addie said.

'Of course I do, you chump. I think you're very brave and Ken would have been proud of you.' As the tears gathered in Addie's eyes, Honor reached for the book. 'Come on, old thing, no time for that, let's do a bit of work together before supper. What d' you say we start on whooping cough?'

There was still a month to go, so on her next free afternoon Honor resolved to go into town directly after her shift. She was on her way through the main gates when she heard someone calling her name.

'Honor, wait for me! Where are you going?'

'Into town.' She folded her cape around her and glanced at her watch.

'Hang on, I'm coming too!' Peter ran to catch up as the bus drew in. 'That was a stroke of luck!' His face was animated. 'Where are you off to?'

She thought for a little before replying, 'I'm going to have my picture taken.'

'Are you?' Then with dawning realisation, 'Oh, I suppose it's for him.'

Honor nodded. 'He sent me one, you see…'

'Of course.' Peter's voice became curter. They both looked out of the window for a while. 'I'm sorry, Honor, I still feel so jealous! I know, I know,' Peter raised his hands, 'it's my own stupid fault! Look, there's a good photographer in Granby Street, would you like me to take you?'

Honor hesitated.

'Come on,' Peter said, 'it'll save you all the trouble of finding one!'

There was an air of normality about the city, as though it had become used to its wartime lot. Some of the bomb-damaged buildings were boarded up, but most of the shops were trading, and Leicester's large open market was still holding its own. He guided her to a small studio off the market square.

'This is it, I'll just come up and make sure you're all right.'

Peter automatically took charge, discussing her portrait with the photographer before sitting down with her in the waiting room.

'You don't have to wait!'

'Of course I will!'

She sat upright in her nurse's uniform and cape, under the lights, a small smile playing around her mouth as she thought of Will looking at the picture. With a flash, it was done.

'Come on, time for tea.' Peter took her arm as she folded the collection slip into her purse.

The market traders were clearing their stalls, and Honor stopped to buy some apples, Cox's Pippins, the recent harvest free from rationing. Oranges were never to be seen in a greengrocer now, and bananas were a luxury. She offered him one and they both bit into the firm fruit as they walked.

'Where would you like…?' His words were drowned out by the slow crescendo of a siren. They looked at each other in dismay. All around them, people were slinging their gas masks over their arms and making for the nearest shelters, some indignant at the interruption. Late afternoon was not the time for a raid.

'Where shall we go?' Honor shouted. Peter pulled her hand and they started to run in the same direction as the others, intuitively following the crowd. The streets changed from normality to organised evacuation in a matter of minutes.

'Come with me!' A middle-aged woman bearing the green armband of the WVS directed them towards an imposing set of Georgian buildings on New Walk. 'Come on!' She led them through the front door, sirens wailing behind, into an elegant hallway. 'This way,' she announced, before disappearing through another door and down the dark cellar stairs.

'I can't, you go! Leave me, Peter, I can't go down there!' Honor stood transfixed.

Peter took both her hands, his voice urgent. 'You must, you might be killed!'

'I'll take my chances! You go!' Honor was immovable, frozen in remembrance.

The woman's voice was hailing them from the cellar. 'Come on, you two, we need to close the door!' Honor shook her head as the sirens wailed on.

'I'm staying up here with her!' Peter shouted back, then in a harsh whisper, 'Don't you see, I love you, Honor!'

They were sitting at the bottom of the stairs when the all-clear came through. Hearing a solitary bomber, its engines whining, in the air above them, they had anticipated the worst, then all had gone quiet. The woman emerged from the cellar, and he let go of Honor's unwilling hand.

'Whatever was all that about? We haven't had a bomb scare for months! You two looked as if you hadn't a clue what to do!'

Afterwards they shared a cup of tea at her kitchen table. 'I'm so sorry, it's the maid's day off,' she apologised as she fussed with the cups and saucers. After a weak and lukewarm drink, they thanked her and made their escape.

'What happened?' Peter asked an ARP warden, manning the streets around.

'We think it was a Heinkel 111, sir, but God knows what it was doing here! It's a mercy it didn't drop a load of bombs on us – it must have got lost on its way home! Crash-landed in a field near Hinckley, they say!'

21st September 1941
Groby Road Hospital
Dear You,
Here it is! I hope you like it. I had it taken in uniform, firstly to remind you of when we first met, and secondly because clothes rationing is so tight that it's hard to look smart anymore. Sixty-six coupons a year doesn't go very far, bearing in mind that a new dress would take at least eleven! Most of my time is taken up studying for my finals – not long now, but I still don't give much for my chances.

The news from Moscow is more terrible each day. It is heartbreaking to think of the Germans at the gates of their city – imagine if that was London, and us building the barricades!

I'm just starting night shift, and not looking forward to it. Please take care of yourself and let's hope you can get some leave soon. I'll try my hardest to make it if you can.

Missing you as always.

From Me

20

'Why are we having leave at such short notice?' Arthur said.

'Your guess is as good as mine!' They were in the crew room kitting up for a consumption test – a three-hour flight to Cornwall, checking the air miles that could be squeezed out of the fuel tanks.

'I hope they're not planning to make it Berlin next time,' Will said. He had the distinct feeling that something was up.

'Still,' Arthur was pulling on his gauntlets, 'can't look a gift horse in the mouth! At least I'll get to see how my mother is. Will you be going up north?'

Will shook his head. 'No, I must see Honor, if she can manage it!'

The Cornish coast looked beautiful in the September sunshine. The early morning mist had lifted and they had a clear view of the sea, dotted with small fishing vessels. Their course after Ilfracombe took them over Padstow, which Will thought was one of the prettiest harbours he had ever seen, almost as good as their trip to the Shetlands earlier in the month. He resolved to visit all these places with Honor when the war was over.

Griff plotted the distances and they took meticulous readings of the fuel tanks. 'I'm sure they know all of this already,' he grumbled.

Back in the mess, Fred was planning his leave.

'The Windmill Theatre, blokes, that's where I'm off to! There're some beauties there, I'll be bound!'

'Fred, you must be careful,' Don said. 'Were you listening to the MO's talk about the clap, or did you sleep through it? It's the scourge of the forces, according to his reliable information.' He picked up their empty glasses and headed for the bar.

'Listen, cobber, I wasn't born yesterday, I'm not going with any old tart, you know!'

Despite the heightened sex drive which the war had brought in its wake, there could be little doubt of the MO's advice. There was no treatment for venereal disease as yet: penicillin had only just come into use, and was in short supply. The dreaded signs of a sexually transmitted disease would blight many a serviceman's life before the war was out, no matter what dire warnings they had received.

'Chap up at the bar was in the Berlin raid last week!' Don reappeared with their beer, providing them all with an excuse to change the subject. 'Says it was a dodgy show – ten of the Wellingtons didn't make it back!'

'Strewth!' Griff whistled. 'That's not how they made it look in the newspapers! Do you think they ever tell the truth nowadays? What's he doing here, anyway?'

'He's a Mosquito pilot. Been sent to gen up on his beam approach. It's all hush-hush, as usual. If I were the powers that be, I'd get the Mosquitoes to pick out the target, and drop the markers, then let the rest of the bombing stream follow. I mean, look how long it took to set us up on an Oboe raid – they couldn't do that with every bomber in the Beehive, could they?'

'You think they'll be that accurate?' Arthur sucked on his pipe, which seemed to be perpetually going out. He tried emptying it in the ashtray and starting again, causing the rest of the group to move away from the noxious smoke.

'What the hell does he put in there? Cow dung?' Fred said. 'You'll never pull a woman with that, old boy!'

21

Anxiously scanning the people leaving the train, Will began to wonder if Honor had missed her connection from Birmingham. He had been waiting on Salisbury station most of the long afternoon, eating into his cherished leave. What if she was not going to make it at all?

Suddenly he caught sight of her small figure making its way down the platform, in a light jacket and carrying a small bag. She walked straight ahead determinedly, unable to hear him calling through the crowd. He ran down towards her and took her in his arms.

'You made it! I'd nearly given up hope!' They kissed, oblivious to those around them, to whom they were just another meeting, or just another goodbye.

He took her bag. 'Thank you for coming so far! Were the trains awful?'

Her hand was tightly held in his as they walked briskly to the exit. 'There was a bomb scare at Birmingham,' she replied. 'I was worried they'd stop running completely!'

'I'm so glad to see you!' He kissed her again, opening the car door for her. She settled in beside him, looking as though she had overcome a myriad of obstacles in so doing. 'I've booked you in at the Falcon Hotel.' Then, sensing her confusion, he added, 'It's all right, a single room only!'

He waited for her in the hotel lounge while she washed and changed. As she came down the stairs into the lobby he could hardly believe that she was real, so much had he longed for her. If only his leave could last forever, and he would not have to face another parting.

She smiled at him and sipped her tea, looking more composed and beautiful than he could remember. Did she just grow more attractive, or was it him? Dressed in a simple white blouse and navy skirt, with heeled court shoes, she was as neat and smart as clothes rationing would allow.

'Don't just gaze at me like that!' she teased, finishing her cup.

'How can I help it? I can't believe you're really here.'

'Well, neither can I, but we'd better make the most of it.' She reached out and held his hand. 'What are you going to show me first?'

Of course she wanted to see Stonehenge, and he drove the Austin to the site. She climbed out, overawed just as he had been. Together, they stood in the shadow of the huge stones, the autumn light reflected on the granite.

'However did they get here?' she asked, as they began to walk around the circle. There was no one in sight, no one guarding this relic of an earlier age. For a moment, it felt as though it existed only for the two of them, as though the intervening centuries had been of no consequence.

'It's even better when you fly over it in the dawn,' he said, and she stopped to face him.

'Promise me you'll come back.' Her voice was insistent. 'You will, won't you?'

He cupped her face in his hands. 'I don't know where from yet, but I can certainly promise I'll try! There's no one else I want to be with, you know, it's only you.'

'I know.' She looked seriously into those grey eyes. 'It's always been only you.'

Later, she rested her head on his shoulder as they gazed up at the cathedral spire, looming above them in the dark. They had dined quietly in the hotel, enjoying each other's presence without constraint. There had been a subliminal shift in their relationship, a tacit understanding, giving them the security they would need to move on to the next phase of their wartime lives.

The hours counted down far too quickly; every time he looked at his watch he was nearer losing her. All too soon, they were on the platform again, breathless and late, she running for her train, he watching her waving from the carriage until the train was out of sight, both with the uneasy despair of separating lovers, for whom no follow-up assignation has been made.

22

'What the hell are they doing to my plane?' Arthur looked across at a group of fitters who appeared to be cutting a hole in the bottom of the fuselage. 'Hey! What's going on?'

'Orders, sir, we're only doing what we've been told. I expect you'll hear about it soon enough!'

Retreating to the briefing room, Arthur was not in sanguine mood. Far from buoying him up, his leave had served to depress his spirits unutterably. His mother, contrary to the optimistic note of her letters, appeared to be in decline and his father's air of complete confusion caused him great consternation. How would his dad manage without her? It was difficult enough running a farm in wartime without losing the one you counted on the most. Arthur began to wonder if he should ask for some compassionate leave to try and sort out the situation – not that such a request was likely to be well received.

The CO rose in front of a crowded briefing room, which hushed immediately. He had presence, this man, accentuated by his immaculate RAF uniform and the medals on his chest.

'The reputation of this squadron, and your hard work to date, is a credit to you all, gentlemen. There can be no clearer a signal of our importance to Bomber Command than the fact that a detachment of 109 Squadron has been singled out for special duties in the Middle East.' He waited for the reaction to die down.

'As I speak, six Wellingtons are being fitted with jamming equipment for the operation, codename Jostle; three will be crewed up from this squadron and three from Bomber Command. We have a very limited time for preparation, but I can tell you now that the first three Wellingtons will be leaving here for Egypt within eight days. The 109 personnel selected for the first detachment are as follows – Willis, Fordham, Griffiths, MacDonald, Baines, Wellesley and Ellis. If the trials go according to plan, your departure date will be October 15th. The next two Wellingtons will also be crewed up from this squadron, and those of you selected will be informed tomorrow. The three other Wellingtons, once fitted, will have new crews from Bomber Command, so it isn't just our show.

'No leave will be permitted to aircrew from now on, and the utmost secrecy surrounds this operation. I'm afraid you will only be able to communicate your posting by censored mail. It's tough on you, I know, but at least you've all had some time off recently.'

So that was it! Will's fate was sealed. Thank goodness he had managed to see Honor first – what if he had been sent abroad without the chance to say goodbye?

There was a buzz from the floor and the CO lifted his hand.

'I wish I could give you all some question time, but I'm simply not permitted to. This is highly privileged information, and there must be no leaks. I can tell you this – the jammers will work over the whole band, not just the ones you've been using so far. And of course, as is the case with TRE,' he smiled in anticipation of his joke, 'they'll be making it up as they go along!'

The audience smiled with him, though perhaps not quite so roundly.

'Tropical kit will be issued to all those in the first wave and you'll need to be vetted by the MO. And that, gentlemen, for today, is that. Once the Wellingtons have been fitted up, you will be putting in a few practice runs to Harwell, from there you will make the first leg of your journey to Gibraltar. I don't need to say it, but good luck!'

Gibraltar, Egypt… places they had only seen on the map. Eight days! They had been expecting Berlin, perhaps, but not this! They must be supporting the Eighth Army in some capacity, but Will had lost touch with the latest situation in North Africa, apart from the odd newspaper article or jingoistic newsreel item.

Arthur fell in alongside as they left. 'At least we're going together!'

Vic Willis joined them. 'You'll have your own planes and crew once we're in the desert,' he said. 'Now let's go and see what those fitters have really been up to!'

To Will, the jamming equipment looked like a truncated iron bedstead being lowered from the bottom of the fuselage on steel rollers.

'I've seen some weird contraptions in my time, but that about takes the biscuit!' Arthur said. It was just as well that Vic was first pilot on the inaugural test flight for, in a fit of infectious laughter, both the second pilots saw the absurdity of flying at low altitude with the thing dangling below.

'Shut up, you two, I expect the TRE know what they're doing!' Vic said.

'I'm sure they do, Skip.' Will wiped the tears from his eyes. 'At least I hope so, or we'll be the laughing stock of the Eighth Army!'

'Let's have a go at the jamming now, Don,' Vic continued.

'How long will we be keeping this up for, Skip?' the Scot said when he had run out of expletives before the equipment would work.

'Too bloody long, I should guess!' Griff answered for him. 'I expect we'll be sitting ducks, as usual, just this time it'll be in broad daylight over the desert! Keep on this course, Skip, steady as she goes or that contraption will shear right off!'

'You take over, Will.' Vic vacated his seat. 'Let me know what you think of the performance of the engine – it's been tweaked for desert conditions.'

'They must know what we're going to be jamming, what do you reckon?' Arthur joined him in the dickey seat.

Will was keeping a close eye on the dials. As far as he could see the plane was handling, for the most part, as usual, and he assumed the performance enhancement would only come into play at higher ambient temperatures. After all, it was going to be stiflingly hot out there.

'Haven't a clue, what's your money on?'

'My money, old chap,' Arthur replied slowly and deliberately, 'is on tanks.'

23

'Telephone call for you, Fordham.' One of the orderlies in the mess held out the black receiver. His heart skipped – could it be Honor? He had only just let her know about his posting, a brief missive scrutinised by the censor, which could not yet have arrived.

His voice was unsteady as he answered, 'Hello?'

'Will? Is that you?' It was Matt at the other end of the crackly line, sounding equally uncertain.

'Yes, it's me. What's up, everything OK?'

'Not exactly.' There was an unusually serious note in Matt's reply.

'Tell me,' Will said, catching his breath.

'I'm in hospital, place called East Grinstead. Had to get out of my plane in a hurry!'

'What happened?' Will felt sick, remembering the Hurricane's reputation when under attack.

'Bloody fuel tanks got shot up, nearly took me out! You won't believe how lucky I've been – you should see some of the blokes here!'

What was he trying to say? Will was struggling to work out how serious it was, for he could hardly bear to think of Matt as a burns victim, the end they all feared the most.

'How bad is it?' He had to ask, though did not expect an unequivocal reply, and did not receive one.

'Oh, should be all right once the boss here has sorted me out! My hands are worse than my face…' Matt's voice tailed off.

'Look, Matt, I've just been posted overseas,' Will said. 'You know how it is, precious little warning and we're off! There's not a remote chance of me coming over to see you – we're stuck on base until we go.'

'Don't worry, old chap, I'm going to be here for a bit! Just thought I'd let you know. Florence has been down already, she should be back soon.' Matt tried, and failed, to disguise his disappointment.

'I'll tell Honor, she'll be able to drop down, I reckon,' Will said, thinking fast. 'Then she can keep me posted on how you are. I'm really sorry, I don't like to think of you sitting in hospital with no one to cheer you up!'

'Oh, you haven't met some of the blokes here! I'm a member of the guinea pig club, you know!' Matt's voice sounded steadier as he went on. 'Honor will know about the set-up here, so tell her to come if she hasn't got anything better to do! And for God's sake take care of yourself – wherever you're going! I won't ask, because you can't tell me, but make bloody sure you come and see me when you get back, and don't forget the grapes!'

The receiver was back in place before Will had time to take it all in. What the hell did Matt mean, 'hands worse than face'? No one came out of a burning Hurricane intact; they all dreaded the horrific disfigurement from the burns and the eye injuries. It was the worst fighter plane in which to take a hit, with the petrol tanks sitting right in front of the pilot, not to mention the problems opening the cockpit hood before bailing out of the inferno. He sat down next to the phone and tried to collect his thoughts. At least Matt was alive, but his open, friendly face! What would have become of it?

Fred, passing by with the newspaper, stopped at the sight of him. 'Crikey, cobber, you look like you've seen a ghost!'

'Not a ghost, Fred.'

'Nah? What then?' He sat down next to him. 'You can tell me, old chap, girl trouble is it? Sheila playing up because you're going away?'

Fred was unusually solicitous, and though he would normally have been the last person to confide in, Will told him what Matt had said. Fred whistled in response.

'Jesus Christ, cobber, that's not so good. How bad is he burnt?'

'I wish I knew! Not a hope of going to find out, I'll just have to wait to hear from him again – or see if Honor can go.'

Fred rose. 'I'll get you a cuppa, mate, that's downright awful.' As he returned bearing a mug of steaming tea, Will wondered if they had all underestimated Fred.

'Thanks, old chap.' He sipped it gratefully, before leaving the mess for the momentary seclusion of his room. There was no time to dwell on Matt's misfortune; he had a letter to his parents to finish. He hoped that his mother would take his posting with fortitude, as she did all of life's crosses, looking to the Almighty to protect and succour her beloved son. For once, he had to accept that her religious conviction might be more comforting than the usual recourse of airmen, that of blind hope.

5th October 1941
RAF Boscombe Down
Dear You,
I know this letter will come as a shock but I will be leaving for the Middle East within the week. I have been posted as part of a detachment of 109 Squadron, but we are all in the dark about the details.

The holding address for letters is RAF Heliopolis, Cairo, Egypt, and the letter should be marked 'To await collection'. I may be able to send you a cable on arrival, and of course, aerographs once we are in camp.

Anyway, thank heavens we just had some time together as it looks as though it might be a long time before I see you again. I want you to know that I will always be thinking of you, the fun we have had together, and intend and hope to have when all this is over.

I had hoped to find you a little something for your birthday but we are confined to camp, and I cannot get to Salisbury, so wish you the very best on the day and send my fondest love with those wishes.

From Me

24

'So that was it. Honor's hands trembled as she reread the letter. Surely they would not make him go away so soon, with no time to say a proper goodbye? Why Egypt? She had assumed he would be on nightly bomber raids over Germany, stationed on some base in East Anglia, where she could see him between ops. It had never occurred to her that he might be sent so far away, to such a strange land. All she could remember about the desert was the Bradley boys in the Eighth Army, with their poor mother fretting after them night and day. That would be her lot now, waiting and hoping, but all the time dreading the worst, with no clear knowledge of when she would see him again.

She drew her cape about her and hurried to the ward. There was no option for her other than to hope that he would return safely, as he had pledged, for prayer was not in her nature or inclination. After all, she reasoned logically, God was killing as many mothers' sons in Germany, and they would be no less loved than he.

Sister looked up as she came in and then glanced pointedly at her watch.

'Sorry, Sister.'

Waved impatiently on, she gathered pace down the ward to the relative safety of Nurse Freeman, who was in the process of feeding breakfast to a little girl.

'Come on, Minty, just a little more.' She was trying to coax another mouthful into the child, who lay motionless, her arms and legs carefully positioned on the pillows, but mercifully breathing well.

'You're late.'

'I know, I'm sorry.' Honor busied herself with the breakfasts. Despite two new admissions to be dealt with, at no point during the morning did she stop thinking of Will. Ploughing automatically through her work, she wondered how she could adapt to such a gulf of separation, when he had become so much a part of her life.

'That's the wrong leg,' Peggy said as Honor started the stretching exercise upon her limb. 'You look miles away!'

'Sorry!' Honor moved to the other side of the bed. She must pull herself together before she made a serious mistake.

'Something up?'

'My boyfriend's been posted abroad,' Honor said, her guard momentarily down. Though not permitted to share one's private life with a patient, her reserve was faltering, and Peggy recognised the turmoil, close to it as she was herself.

She reached across with her good hand and took Honor's. 'I'm sorry, where to?'

Shaking her head, Honor tried to compose herself. 'I can't say.'

'Oh, Nurse, I am sorry, all I do is think about myself!' Peggy was contrite. 'You must be feeling awful! What does he do?'

'He's a pilot, Wellingtons.' Honor went back to the regular stretching of Peggy's calf and foot, trying to ease the muscles from their contracted state. She had given away too much already; she must try and regain her professionalism.

However, her confession had evoked a positive response in Peggy. 'There, it's time I stopped feeling so sorry for myself! There's lots worse off than me, look at what those boys are going through! Now don't you worry, I expect he'll come back safe, just you wait and see!'

'Oh, Peggy, do you really think so?'

'Of course I do. Like you said to me, you should never give up hope. It's all we've got, isn't it?'

9th October 1941
Groby Road Hospital
Dear You,
I don't know if this letter will arrive before you go but I just wanted to say I will miss you all the time you are away. You are always in my thoughts, wherever you are, and I will be waiting for you.

I promise to write whenever I can, and please keep your letters coming too, no matter how short, and how little you can really tell me about what you are doing. It is enough to see your handwriting and know that you are still with me.

I never imagined you would be posted so far away, but of course it was always on the cards – I just couldn't bring myself to think about it.

My life has changed so much since we met, and all for the better! I trust and believe you will come back to me, and we will never be parted again.

From Me

25

'Ouch.' He winced as the MO jabbed a needle into his arm. 'What's that for?'

'Diphtheria.' The doctor put the syringe carefully back on the tray.

'Bit old for that, aren't I?' Will rolled down his sleeve.

'Well, strictly speaking, yes, but it's the only one in current use apart from smallpox and I can see from your arm that you've already had that.' He motioned to the healed inoculation scar. 'Unfortunately we can't cover the tropical diseases, so you'll just have to be careful. Watch out for insect bites and try to keep your hands clean, especially before eating. I'm afraid that hygiene might be a problem in Africa, but you'll find that out soon enough.'

'I'm usually pretty healthy, sir.' Will stood up to leave.

'I know, but this is a different environment, with diseases you might not have been exposed to before. Each Wellington will carry a modified medical kit, some of the usual stuff, like morphine, disinfectants, and a new burns cream that's just come out. Chap called McIndoe recommends it – he's the guru for burns, down at East Grinstead.'

'Did you say East Grinstead?' Will paused at the door.

'Yes, that's it, foremost burns unit in the country. They say the chap who runs it is a brilliant plastic surgeon, which is just as well if you look at some of the repair jobs he has to do!'

So that must be the 'boss' who Matt had mentioned. No chance that his injuries could be mild, if he had ended up there. Will continued down the corridor to pick up his tropical kit, short-sleeved shirts, shorts and lightweight boots. Arthur was in front of him in the queue, looking unimpressed by the regulation shorts.

'Look at those, it's worse than prep school!'

As they came out into the October sunshine, they were met by the curious sight of a camouflaged Wellington. It was the first time they had seen the desert colours on the upper surface of the broad wings, and azure blue underneath, with the two red and blue roundels in their usual place.

'Daytime flying then,' Arthur said. 'Just as I thought!'

Will did not pursue Arthur's conjectures, for they would know soon enough.

'How are things back home?' he said instead.

Arthur shook his head in reply. 'I just wish I could have got down to see my mother again before we leave. It's like being under lock and key here.'

Arthur did not add, though he might have done, his fears that his mother would not be there when he came back – if he came back. That other lingering doubt in his subconscious, to which he never added probability by articulating.

Aircrews were superstitious to a man. They would individually carry good-luck charms or talismans that shielded them from harm, never flying without them if they could help it. For Will, it would be Honor's photograph; Arthur a crucifix given to him by his mother; Fred a small nugget of dirty gold dug from the mud of Kimberly. If a crew were lucky together, they did not want to part. Trusting the judgement of a pilot who had flown them out of scrapes before, they dreaded having to crew up with strangers.

The atmosphere in the crew room was subdued at the start, and even Fred did not indulge in his usual banter. At briefing, they learned the names of the second crew – Will rated all of the ten men in the two bombers staffed from 109, and felt he could rely on each one.

'Harwell and back today, chaps.' The flying officer took them through the duty for the day, which was further familiarisation with the jamming kit, on what was to be the first leg of their journey overseas in four days' time.

October 10th – it was Honor's birthday today, he realised, as he looked up at the board. He wondered how she would be spending it, then remembering she was on night duty, imagined her asleep, trying to catch some rest in the daylight hours. Would she be dreaming of him, as he dreamt of her? He was jolted from his reverie by the familiar sound of Jeffreys' voice.

'Right, gentlemen, just a few words from me. You've had a go with the aerials, I know you think they look bizarre but it's the best we can do with this deadline. Today we want you to try the transmitters that have been fitted to your planes. We've managed to convert them with a Hoover motor to emit musical jamming tones over 28-34 MCS wavebands, the power will come from an ASV alternator specially fitted into the aircraft.'

Fred raised his hand. 'Excuse me, sir, did you say a Hoover motor?'

'I did, Ellis.' Jeffreys was unruffled. 'We've hardly had a moment to turn this one round, it's the nearest thing to hand that'll do the job.'

'So,' Fred continued, 'you mean we'll be moseying around the Western Desert emitting vacuum cleaner sounds to all and sundry? I bet Rommel's quaking in his boots!'

The room collapsed into general laughter and for once, no one made any attempt to call order. Even Jeffreys seemed to see the humorous side. Eventually he found his voice.

'It's not quite that crude, you know!' he protested, which resulted in further hilarity, at which Fred thought he had the last word.

'In all the time I've been with 109, you've asked us to do some pretty damn fool things, but this one takes the biscuit! Who the hell thought that would be a good idea?'

The CO stood, with a final comment of his own, as silence descended. 'Actually, old boy, Winston did, and your kites have already been dubbed "Winston's Wellingtons".'

26

'So, lads, are we all set for the first leg?' Vic surveyed his crew, who nodded in assent. The five of them would be setting off from Harwell today for the nine-hour flight to Gibraltar. He would split the journey with Will, four or so hours each as first pilot. Griff had been poring over the maps until he knew them like the back of his hand, and for once Don would not be carrying out complex radio countermeasures. Vic hoped that Ted, his rear gunner, would have an easy time too, for they were not expecting enemy action. This part of the Mediterranean still belonged to the British, at least, even though the Luftwaffe were increasing their efforts against Malta, where the next lap of the journey would take them. Their kitbags were at their side, and their Wellington Z8948, or R for Robert, would be fully loaded with fuel enough for the journey and all their radio equipment besides. Vic, like the rest of them, was new to the Middle East, though he had heard about the Western Desert and the terrible toll it could take upon a man. Not a place to get shot down, he pondered; less chance of surviving there than in occupied Europe.

They had spent the last five days trying to perfect the techniques dreamt up by the TRE, and were ready to depart on schedule on October 15th. As Vic had quietly suggested to his crew in the days leading up to departure, if there remained any unfinished 'personal stuff', they had best sort it out soon for it would rapidly become an irrelevance. Apart from Arthur, who painstakingly penned a long epistle to Phyllis, for the rest it was more of a matter of counting down the hours.

'Would you read it before I send it?' Arthur said.

'Best not, old chap, you just write what you want to, she'll understand. Why don't you put in that photo you had done?'

The meteorologists informed them that the outlook was fine, no October storms anticipated, with a balmy route through to the Med.

'Any last questions?' The CO was there to see them off. 'I know I can rely upon you gentlemen to put up a good show for the squadron. I can't pretend it's going to be easy, but you've already worked that out for yourselves. Good luck with Operation Jostle, gentlemen, I just wish I could join you!'

'I'll swap places with him,' Fred whispered to Arthur. Theirs would be the second Wellington to leave. 'The more pep talks we get, the less I like the sound of it!' It was not in Fred's nature to respond to the patriotic rallying call; for him it was just a job, and a bloody awful one at that!

They filed out of the crew room, slinging their kitbags over their shoulders. At least the desert uniform was light, and they would soon be baking in their cockpits rather than freezing. For this leg of the journey, though, they were in standard heavy-duty sheepskin and fur-lined boots. It was going to be a long flight, and they would need the double rations of egg and bacon they had been given at breakfast to sustain them.

Will looked down over the neat English tapestry of fields as they took off, the Wellington lumbering to height under his hands. Vic had asked him to take the first shift, sitting by him in the second pilot's seat, ever watchful, and like the rest of his crew, wondering when he would see that vista beneath him again. As they levelled out through the light autumnal clouds, Will's thoughts were with Honor, to whom he said a silent goodbye as they crossed the English coast. He had dropped a final letter to her in the post before he left, for heaven knows when he would have time to write another.

'How's our course, Griff?' Vic's voice on the intercom broke through all their thoughts.

'Spot on, Skip,' came the reply, as the distinctive bomber powered its way steadily south across the sea.

14th October 1941

RAF Boscombe Down

Dear You,

This is it, old thing, we're off tomorrow and I'll be thinking of you all the time. Make sure you pass those exams for me, and keep writing to yours truly.

Can't say more at this precise moment, so cheerio for now!

From Me

Part Seven:
The Desert Air Force

1

Jutting out into a promontory on to the Great Bitter Lake, the airfield at Kabrit came into view.

'That's it, see how it links into the last stretch of the Suez Canal,' Vic said, scanning the landmarks. 'Looks like a decent airfield this time.'

Will drew a long breath before lining the Wellington up for the final approach. It had fallen to Vic to take off from Luqa; the runway on the island of Malta, that strategic foothold in the Mediterranean, was perilously short with only nine hundred yards before the grass overrun, the memorial chapel at the end and the steep valley beyond. Even Vic, experienced pilot as he was, had cursed as they cleared the hill on the right turn, and there had been one heart-stopping moment when it seemed they might not make it at all, heavily loaded as they were.

Kabrit looked a positively pleasant prospect in comparison; the flat, sandy terrain and the azure lake beyond induced a momentary sense of optimism amongst the crew.

As the wheels touched the tarmac, Vic's voice came over the intercom: 'We've made it, chaps!'

They had been nearly eight hours in the air on this last leg, and were all aching to disembark, have some breakfast and rest.

Although it was still early morning, the heat hit them as they climbed out. The light was new to them, bright and unyielding, making them squint after the dark belly of the Wellington. As they walked towards the untidy sprawl of low buildings, they could make out the desert tents beyond, which in some shape or form, were to become their home for the foreseeable future.

'God, it's going to be hot!' Don wiped his forehead, as the flies, their new and constant enemy, started to congregate.

'109 Squadron Detachment?' The adjutant looked puzzled as Vic stood before him, and rifled through the many pieces of paper adorning his desk. 'We weren't expecting you today!'

'Do you suggest we come back tomorrow?' Vic's tone was acid. He was hot and tired, having been on almost constant watch since they left Harwell. They had been fortunate to encounter no enemy fighters around Malta, but he, like all the crew, was conscious of the ever-present danger.

'No, sir, sorry, I didn't mean—'

'Just forget it,' Vic cut in. 'If you could direct us to the mess tent while you sort out the paperwork then my crew can have some breakfast.'

The ever-present NAAFI was operating a decent mess tent, and they lined up for a breakfast which seemed remarkably familiar, apart from the absence of bacon but with the welcome addition of fruit: bananas and melons, which they had almost forgotten existed. They were starting on their fried eggs when they were joined by a tall flight lieutenant with a shock of fair hair that matched the desert sand. He was casually dressed in shorts, an open-necked shirt, and comfortable-looking suede boots, and was suitably apologetic.

'Sorry about the welcoming committee, chaps. I'm Ferguson, in charge of ops – we did know you were coming, actually. Bloody adjutant doesn't know his arse from his elbow. We're expecting two Wimpys though, any news of your pals?'

Vic looked across at Will and raised his eyebrows, then took a sip of sweet tea before answering. 'They took off from Luqa after we'd left, or we assume they did. They certainly made it to Malta.'

'Hmm, we'll check with Luqa.' Ferguson appeared efficient, not one to waste time. He checked each crew member off on the list he had brought, putting firm ticks against their names.

'I expect you'll want to rest up today – the orderlies will show you the tents. First time in the desert?' He looked around, and receiving nods by way of answer, continued, 'It takes a bit of getting used to. We're relatively well set up here compared to some of the landing grounds further west, now they can be a tad primitive. The chaps around here are mostly from 70 Squadron, night bombers out on the Benghazi mail run. They'll no doubt tell you all about it in the mess: their main objective is to bugger up the port and Rommel's supply lines. You blokes from 109 have a different task, as I understand it, but we'll be going into that at briefing tomorrow. Any questions so far?'

'How many squadrons have we got out here?' Vic was still eating his toast, spread thickly with a curious-tasting, but not unpleasant, local jam.

'Five Wellington Squadrons in Egypt altogether,' Ferguson said; '37 and 38 at Shallufa, 108 and 148 at Fayid, and 70 Squadron here. We could do with some decent planes, Group Captain Maclean keeps asking for Mark II Wellingtons, but we're still waiting! Most of the time we just have to patch up what we've got, and I must say the ground crew are bloody brilliant at it, considering the conditions they're working in. Bloody sand gets in just about everything, as you're shortly to find out.'

'Who's winning?' Will asked, but did not receive the answer they might have hoped for. Ferguson wiped his hand over a sweaty brow.

'We never really know from one day to the next. All I can say is the pongos have got their work cut out – Rommel's no fool, as I'm sure you know. We could have kicked the Italians out of North Africa in February if O'Connor had been given his head. As it was, some of our brigades here, plus a sizeable RAF contingent, were sent to Greece instead and we all know where that got us! Then Rommel broke through in April, taking back most of the ground we'd made, and our counter-stroke, Operation Battleaxe in June, to relieve Tobruk, had to be called off after losing nearly half our tanks. So now, our ground forces are keen to seize the initiative, but waiting for the right moment. Our job will be to soften up the enemy in advance, or so they reckon, but I, for one, don't underestimate the opposition. The truth is things have been going rapidly downhill since Rommel pitched up. Anyway, we've got a new C-in-C now, Ritchie's apparently taken over command of the Eighth Army from Cunningham, so let's hope he can turn things around. Rumour is there'll be a push in a few weeks, but I wouldn't like to say.'

Vic reached for another slice of toast. 'What about our general housekeeping stuff, water rations and so on?'

'Two pints a day, that's one for drinking, one for washing. Still, at least you can swim in the lake here, rather than having to wash in a paltry cupful of the stuff. It doesn't taste too good, and your food will get worse the further up the landing grounds you go. You're pretty well sorted on the base, but watch yourselves outside, especially in the fleshpots of Cairo. Wops'll sell you anything, including their sisters, never leave you alone. But still, there are one or two decent bars we hang around in, unless they're full of Tank Corps squaddies drowning their sorrows. And the beer's cheap! Anyway, the orderly will give you the gen when he takes you to your quarters, and I'm around if you need me, just sorting out tonight's ops for the lads.'

'Keep me posted about the others, won't you?' Vic was trying not to look worried, but they all sensed it. What if Arthur had not been able to pull the Wellington out at the end of that damned runway in Luqa?

As it happened, it had not been Arthur's plane that crashed, but the one behind him. He had managed to unstick the plane from the runway with just six feet's worth of clearance of the chapel, whereas the next Wellington to take off crashed into a hill, with a full load of petrol and bombs aboard. There were no survivors, as Ferguson was later informed.

Meanwhile, they all looked up as one to the sound of the approaching engines, left the mess tent, and watched through the trembling heat as the bomber came in to land.

'That's him,' Will commented, catching sight of the camouflage which was identical to their own.

''Bout bloody time!' Griff said. 'Can I finish my breakfast now?'

2

The raucous voices sang as one in the cool of the Egyptian night. The tune was *Clementine*, but the words were hallowed to the crews on the mail run:

'Down the flights each bloody morning
Sitting waiting for a clue
Same old notice on the flight board
Maximum effort – guess where to.'

Followed by the chorus:

'70 Squadron, 70 Squadron
Though we say it with a sigh
We must do the bloody mail run
Every night until we die.'

Arthur raised his glass to Will's. At least they had both survived that appalling runway in Luqa, and now, after a day spent familiarising themselves with the intense heat, and their sparse tented accommodation, where everything had an air of impermanence, including their own futures, they were at last relaxing in the mess tent. As usual, the resident aircrews were drinking themselves to oblivion.

'Have you lost us, Navigator?
Come up here and have a look
Someone's shot our starboard wing off!
We're all right then, that's Tobruk.'

The voices increased in volume until the end:

'Oh, to be in Piccadilly
Selling matches by the score
Then I shouldn't have to do that
Ruddy mail run anymore.'

The chorus congratulated themselves with another round of drinks, whereupon a square-faced pilot, slightly older than the rest, detached himself from the group and came over to join them. Like Ferguson, he was dressed for comfort and deeply tanned, extending a welcoming hand as he introduced himself.

'Max Norton, you must be the chappies from 109. Hope you liked our little ditty?' He smiled widely and benignly at them. 'It's all we ever do, you see, the mail run: take off, bomb Benghazi, land at a desert landing strip if you can find it, refuel from four-gallon drums, and return to base. Piece of cake apart from the flak and general disagreeableness of the Hun! Still, word is you chaps have got other fish to fry! Anyone for a beer?'

'What's that? Got something better to do?' The diminutive navigator who had followed him unsteadily across the rush matting floor swayed as he surveyed them through round, thick-rimmed spectacles. He wore the emblem of the New Zealand Air Force, his accent slightly less abrasive than Fred's, who answered him.

'Where you from, mate?'

'Wellington, my old friend, prettiest place in the world! Better than this old dump, anyway. Sand in every orifice, that's the long and short of it. You wait until the ruddy khamsin blows, it's worse than a London fog!'

They had already heard of the desert sandstorms that could bring even the tanks to a standstill, and after their first day in the tents had discovered the impossibility of keeping the sand out of their kit, even on a clear day. Arthur was unperturbed, experiencing a curious sense of release in this new environment. Freed from the pressing anxieties about his mother, whom he could not be expected to help at such a distance, he found to his surprise that he could forget about her and Phyllis, for most of the day.

More conscious of his separation from Honor, Will experienced no such calm. They were now protagonists in a struggle to the death between the opposing forces in this barren, unpopulated land and he began to doubt his chances of survival. After all, what sort of mission would theirs be? If Arthur's original predictions were correct, then the German fighters would hone in on them like angry hornets.

Fred, as usual, had other thoughts on his mind.

'So you don't rate it much here? Any sheilas around?'

The navigator raised his eyebrows. 'Not unless you want a dose of the clap! Wait till you've been into Cairo, you'll see what I mean. Seeing as we're compatriots, we should stick together,' he added with the enthusiastic warmth of the intoxicated, 'but first you've got to tell me what you're doing here?'

'Oh, shut up Titch! I don't expect they've got a clue, any more than we have.' Max put in. 'Whatever our lords and masters decree!'

Vic nodded at him in support. This was neither the time nor the place for speculation, and they would find out in the briefing tomorrow what lay ahead.

Unlike the boys from 70 Squadron, they were sober by the time they left the mess tent.

'What a sky!' Ted Baines, not normally one for hyperbole, gazed up at the arc of stars above them in the dome of ebony sky, and Will remembered the words of Omar Khayyam, his small copy of the ancient verses in his kitbag, wrapped in brown paper to keep the sand from seeping between its flimsy pages.

3

The cold of the desert night had surprised them all, with a swing of temperature for which they had been unprepared. Will woke in the dawn light to hear Arthur's shouts.

'Bloody scorpion! It was in my boots!'

'Just kill it, for God's sake!' But the scorpion had already scuttled across the tent, and would no doubt return in its own good time.

The calm that Arthur had experienced the previous day seemed to have evaporated. 'There are rats in the latrines!' he said. 'Bloody great ones! I'm taking a stick next time, whack 'em away before they bite me!'

'Don't make such a fuss! Surely you've had rats on the farm?' Will crawled out of bed, reaching for his water and more than ready for his morning cup of tea. The sun was already warm on his body, providing welcome respite from the chill that had enveloped him. He resolved to wear more clothes in bed tonight, having resorted to his flying jacket in the small hours.

'Not like those brutes!' Arthur persisted. 'Anyway, the cats usually made short work of ours!'

Mindful of his rations, Will splashed a little water over his face and brushed his teeth in a teacupful. The rest could wait until his swim in the lake. They would have to be early at briefings, and he chivvied Arthur over to the mess tent for the reviving tea, fried bread and eggs.

'It's like being on a bloody scout camp!' Arthur muttered, as they walked through the sand.

Vic had breakfasted already, and was sitting back savouring a cigarette.

'Decent night, chaps?'

Arthur was now too intent upon his breakfast to grumble.

'Briefing at 0700,' Vic reminded them, but they were all ready and waiting to be given an accurate picture of their role, after days of uncertainty.

An air of gravity prevailed in the briefing tent that morning. All but one of the five Wellingtons had arrived at Kabrit the day before, so they were now joined by unfamiliar crews. The importance of their mission was underlined by the man in front of them, Group Captain Maclean himself, overall controller of the five Wellington squadrons in Egypt. In his middle fifties, and well-built, Maclean had a manner which the crews could immediately warm to, straightforward and to the point, without the clipped upper-class vowels of many of his contemporaries.

'Right, chaps, we'd better get on. We're still waiting for the last Wimpy, should be with us soon, but I don't want any further delay. Yours is a difficult task, and the sooner you know what it involves, the better. You've been hand-picked for this job, and the powers that be think you're up to it, every man of you.' He paused and looked around.

'To date, our opposing armies have been swinging backwards and forwards across Egypt and Libya like yo-yos – we make ground, then lose it. Basically, we're no further on than we were this time last year, and the army needs all the help it can get. Your task in the forthcoming campaign is to jam radio communications on the twenty-eight to thirty-four-megacycle waveband used by the enemy armoured columns. We hope that this will seriously disorganise the activities of the panzers.'

He waited for the information to sink in, and Arthur nudged Will with a whispered, 'Told you so!'

'I'll now pass you over to Squadron Leader Simpson, who's in charge of this show, and I'll take questions with him at the end.'

In front of Simpson was a map of the airfields in the Western Desert, along with the key ports, Tobruk, Benghazi, Sollum and Bardia. The names were mystifying, such as Gambut Main, Fuka, or more simply, LG121, denoting one of the many advanced landing grounds. The whole of the coastline of the Mediterranean across Libya and Egypt was littered with airfields, following the strategic army campaigns.

Simpson stood up, and perused the group of young men in front of him. Despite the hazards of their mission, he would have to put it to them honestly, or they would not trust him next time.

'Well, lads, I hope you're managing to acclimatise and get your bearings. It's a challenging place, the desert, but in many ways it's the cleanest theatre of war as there are so few civilians about. We have a formidable enemy in Rommel and Winston wants us to help our chaps put an end to him once and for all. Up to now, the RAF has been largely tasked with bombing his supply lines, cutting off his main arteries from the ports for supplies and petrol. Your job will be different, and, I have to admit, more dangerous. When the army re-engage on the next push, you will be flying over enemy lines, jamming their tanks.'

Fred's low whistle of dismay was not the only noise from the audience. They would be sitting ducks, no doubt about it. There was a collective drawing-in of breath.

'Christ,' muttered Ted. It was all set to be the rear gunner's nightmare, surrounded by enemy fighters in the full light of day.

'Fortunately for us,' Simpson continued levelly, 'we have some unexpected breathing space first, giving you chaps more time to try out your equipment, make sure it's all A1, and generally ease you into the pattern of life here. After some local flying tomorrow, we'll be sending you to Heliopolis the next day and thence to Palestine on special duty for a day or so. When the action starts in earnest you'll be mostly based at LGs 104 and 75.' He pointed to the map. 'The camps are a bit basic but you'll soon get used to it – as you can see, you'll be right where you're needed. All five Wellingtons will operate from there, taking it in turns to do the job. Right,' he added briskly, 'any questions so far?'

'Do we get fighter escort from our side?' Vic said, for surely this would be integral to the plan.

'Ah, yes.' Simpson's tone was, for the first time, equivocal. 'In an ideal world, of course that's what we'd provide. It's just that we don't have that many fighter planes in the Middle East, and they're never in the right place at the right time.'

The crews in front of him fell quiet. Will broke the silence.

'And what will be the opposition, sir?'

Simpson came straight to the point. 'Macchi 200s, I'm afraid, the Italians are better at flying than holding their own on the ground!'

The reputation of the Italian forces in North Africa was well known. Their ground forces were apt to surrender abruptly, and the stories of the lavish supplies discovered by the Tommies were legend. It was rumoured that they even had their own mobile brothels, quite apart from the wine, spaghetti and sundry luxuries that they left behind in their rush to escape, or give themselves up. The Italians did not attempt to adapt to life in the desert; rather they reinvented it, surrounding themselves with their own creature comforts.

Unfortunately the arrival of the panzers had stiffened the Italian morale and Rommel had cleverly interspersed his troops among them. The Italian Air Force was a different matter altogether, especially under German control, so the Wellingtons could expect no respite from attack.

'What sort of range are we looking at?' Arthur had forgotten his gripes about the local flora and fauna.

'Over the tanks, you mean?' Simpson replied. 'We're hoping for a range of about twenty to thirty miles between the armoured units.'

'So we'll just be flying back and forth?'

There was a complete hush in the room.

'Exactly,' came the sober answer, and to a collective silence, Simpson took his seat.

Maclean resumed his place in front of them. 'It's going to be a tough one, but we know you'll give it 100%. I don't know how long it will be before the show starts, but you'll need all the time you've got to prepare yourselves. And that, gentlemen, is it for today from me, apart from wishing you all good luck. The planning officer will take you through today's briefing.'

So engrossed were they with proceedings that it took them some time to notice that they had been joined by the final crew. Will, on his way out and deep in conversation with Vic, finally caught sight of the tall figure with a shock of ginger hair. He stopped short in disbelief.

'Oh my God…' Then they were shaking hands, laughing, clapping each other on the back while Vic looked on.

'Who the hell is this, your long-lost brother?'

Will shook his head, smiling widely. 'Vic, allow me introduce my old buddy and drinking partner: Dick Sinclair.'

4

They talked late into the night, the peace of the darkening desert around them. Dick, sitting back in his camp chair, drew a rough blanket around his shoulders as the chill descended.

'I never thought I'd get over it, you know, being thrown off the flying course. The worst bit was having to tell my folks, especially my little sister Anna. Curiously, none of them seemed to mind, my father just commented that the RAF knew what they were doing, and if they thought I was cut out to be a navigator, then so be it. "You have to trust these blokes, Dick", those were his words, and he turned out to be right. Cranwell was a doddle in comparison, and I got through navigation school with a minimum of effort. Spent most of the time in the bar, actually!'

'I bet you passed out with flying colours,' Will said, but Dick shook his head and laughed.

'What difference does it all make now, anyway? We're all in it together, however good or bad we might be! Still, I always hoped I'd get you as a pilot, but never imagined this!'

'So what happened after Cranwell?'

'I was posted to 161 Squadron at Tempsford. We're not really meant to let on what happens there, but I can't see that it matters telling you now in the middle of the desert! Best not let it go any further, though; 161 is a special duties squadron, supporting resistance movements in France and the occupied countries. Navigation is pretty much the key to operations there, and has to be spot on. I was in Handley Page Halifaxes – you know, the four-engine jobs, they'd taken out the lower gun turrets so we could use them to parachute agents, stores and ammo into Normandy, the Loire and Rhone valleys. The other flights – Hudson and Lysanders – landed in France, dropping off and picking up passengers. We used to spend hours poring over the photographs of the landing fields, checking them out and preparing maps and reference points. Some of those pilots had to do their own navigation and fly the plane at the same time!'

'Sounds very cloak-and-dagger,' Arthur put in. He was immediately drawn to Will's old friend, and the three of them passed round a whisky bottle in a spirit of comradeship.

'I should say so! Those agents had some guts, I can tell you, piled into the back of the bomber while we flew low over the coast in moonlight, then dropped them from six hundred feet to the reception committee below. I'll never forget their bravery, some of them were just slips of girls...' He paused, as though struggling with the memory.

'Did you get to know them?' Will said.

'Some of them, but only by sight, while they were doing parachute training. We never knew who they really were.' Dick took a small sip of whisky before continuing. The dark night enveloped them, as though meant for confidences and reconciliation.

'Then just when I think I'm doing a really useful job, they call me in to see the wingco, who tells me I've been selected for an important op in Bomber Command, and next thing I know I'm in a Wimpy with a load of blokes who seem intent on jamming every radio signal known to man! Thank God I'm just the navigator! I feel sorry for our wireless operator, I really do. Anyway, our skipper, Screwball – he's Canadian, a bit of a wild card but seems to have what it takes – got us out of a tricky hole in Malta!'

'What happened?' Arthur said.

'Ruddy Luftwaffe picked us up just as we'd taken off from Luqa. Me-109 gets up – sun above us, before the pounce. Johnny, our rear gunner, spots him first, yells at Skip who starts to throw the plane all over the shop, trying to give him the slip. He's hanging on like a limpet, and we're all waiting for the bullets when Screwball goes into this screaming dive. Christ, I thought we were for it, he'd never pull her out before we hit the waves. Just at the last minute, he eases her up, but the 109 ploughs on, straight into the drink! God only knows why, maybe we ran him out of juice, maybe he just miscalculated. Anyway, we circled to see if he got out of the plane, but there was no sign of him. Screwball was going to throw him the dinghy, he's that sort of chap!'

'I think I'd just want to get the hell out of it! Why were you flying in daylight?'

'Oh, there'd been an accident on the runway, couldn't get off the night before. Poor blokes before us copped it!'

Will glanced at Arthur, who was taking another tot, as if to blot the memory of his own close shave. 'Best not have any more, we're off to Heliopolis tomorrow,' he reminded him. They would need all their concentration the next day.

'So what about you?' Dick said, and they both filled him in on the details of their training since December, touching little on their private lives.

'Is that it?' he asked at the end, finishing his drink. 'Not hitched up, yet, Will? I thought you knew a girl in Leeds?'

'Ah, yes.' Will realised how long it had been since Sybil had crossed his mind. 'Well, the truth is, I met someone else—'

'Love of his life!' Arthur interrupted. 'He's mad about her, I can't think why they're not married already!'

'You're a dark horse! Why haven't you told me?' Dick said.

'He keeps her a secret, that's why!' Arthur answered for him, until, forced to respond, Will took her photo from his breast pocket, where it always lay, and handed it across.

Dick whistled. 'Nice looker! What's she called?'

'Honor.' It seemed to Will that she came closer across the bowl of stars as he uttered her name.

5

If he were to remember Lydda for any reason, he mused, flying low over the airfield as they checked and rechecked their jamming equipment, it would be for the oranges. They had spied the fruit groves as they came in to land from Heliopolis, but had not expected quite so many in the mess tent. He had held the warm fruit in his hand, marvelling at the abundance and the taste. So this was Palestine, the biblical land of milk and honey; his mother would be interested to know he was there, even if only for a short time.

They had been beset with complications from the early morning. First to succumb to a local illness, Griff had gone down with 'gyppy tummy', and was rushing to the latrines at dawn. Warned of such ailments in advance, along with others including dysentery, sandfly fever, malaria and sunstroke, they all assumed it was only a matter of time until they would be stricken. Griff's indisposition called for a replacement navigator at short notice, and they had kicked their heels on the hot tarmac waiting for one to be mustered. Fortunately Heliopolis was an established RAF base, and when the chap appeared, somewhat reluctantly from his day off, he was competent and surprisingly knowledgeable.

'Nice base, Lydda.' He had navigated effortlessly for them, having flown there many times before. 'We won't get shot at, for a change!' Reggie was less assured about their radio countermeasures. 'Is that really what you're going to do? Trail that aerial around the desert? Rather you than me! Are you sure it works?'

Don's dry Scottish accent summed it up: 'It's no well designed, but surprisingly functional, like a few girls I know!'

Despite's Griff's absence, they finished a successful set of manoeuvres before a welcome rest in the mess. Indulgently peeling his second orange, Ted summed up the situation.

'What say we stay here, lads, let the other blokes have a go with the panzers, see how they get on with it?'

Vic aimed another one at his head, but he ducked neatly. 'Only joking, Skip, I'm sure we're going to have a great time out there!'

The ground crew were playing bowls with grapefruit as they left, imbuing the whole place with an air of surreality.

Will shook his head. 'Just as well we're on our way, Skip!'

After refuelling they returned to Heliopolis as night fell, their new navigator guiding them to the flare path on the darkening runway. They found Griff still curled up on his camp bed, groaning gently.

'Are you all right, old chap? You look awfully pale!' Vic wanted all his crew on board and had not anticipated losing one to illness so soon.

Griff winced, and sipped the water Don proffered him. 'You must drink, you'll get dehydrated!' he insisted, ignoring Griff's protests that it would come straight out the other end. Half a cup later, he motioned Vic outside the tent.

'I don't like the look of him, Skip.' Don was Griff's oldest friend, watching out for him through all their flying so far.

'Neither do I.' Vic needed no encouragement to send Will in search of the MO. It was just as well the base was big enough to have one, and he was soon tracked down enjoying a beer in his tent.

'Oh God, everyone gets a tummy bug, it's a rite of passage. Welcome to Egypt!' The medic chatted as they made their way back to Griff's tent.

He was less than sanguine after he had examined the stricken navigator, and blew out his cheeks in response.

'Sorry, old chap, we're going to have to get you to the medical tent, I'm not happy about you!' In no time two orderlies appeared to carry him away on a stretcher while the crew looked on in consternation.

'What the hell are we going to do now?' Ted asked.

'Don't worry, I'm sure he'll be right as rain in the morning!' Why did Vic's words, hoping to raise morale, have the opposite effect?

The beer failed to lift their spirits that evening, and they turned in early with a collective sense of disquiet.

A light rain had fallen in the night, and the clear day that followed seemed to bring a different sense of colour to the arid landscape. The sand was never just one uniform colour, it shifted like the weather, and that morning had an almost rosy hue.

'Have you heard anything?' Don asked Vic at breakfast.

Moodily stirring his tea, Vic shook his head. 'I'm going to find out as soon as I've finished this.' Don wolfed down his plate of eggs so he could accompany him.

The news was not good. Griff had been transferred to hospital in Cairo, his condition having deteriorated further in the night.

'Christ,' put in Ted, 'we've only just got here! He can't get sick that quickly, surely?'

'Perhaps it's not gyppy tummy,' Will said. 'I mean, everyone gets that, don't they – the RAF would be completely grounded if they all ended up in hospital.'

After briefing, they learnt that Reggie would accompany them back to Kabrit, then no doubt hitch a lift from the next plane bound for Heliopolis. It was only a short hop, and Vic had protested that they were quite capable of managing without a navigator, but to no avail.

Reggie was equable about this turn of events. 'No bother, old chaps, I'm sorry about your chum. I expect he'll be right as rain soon, you'll just have to make do with me until he is!' Crewing up with strangers was always disconcerting, but airmen learnt rapidly to assess each other's skills. There would be no problems with Reggie, who already had ten months of desert navigation under his belt, and was used to the subtle landmarks.

He regaled them with stories on the way back. Tobruk, for example: 'Bloody lethal when your own side shoot you up!' When questioned as to the reason: 'Oh, the Jerries captured some of our aircraft, so the Tommies take a crack at anything now!' Then there was the lowdown on Benghazi harbour: 'It's got these Moles, you know, there's Giuliana, then the Outer, and the Cathedral, and in between them are the jetties – George, Johnny, Harry, Ink and Beer…'

None of the crew had the faintest idea what he was talking about, but his light-hearted chat was heartening for them all. He reminded Will a little of Matt; he did not seem to have a care in the world. Except, of course, that was the old Matt, before he had bailed out of a burning plane. How would he find him now?

He made a mental note to ask Honor to visit his friend when he next wrote. Now that they looked set for a quiet afternoon in Kabrit, he would have a swim in the lake, cool off, and write to her when the sun was beginning to set.

27th October 1941
109 Squadron, RAF Kabrit
Middle East
Dear You,
At last a moment's peace to write a letter. I hope you have already received the

aerograph I sent to let you know we arrived. I will be moving between airfields but you can write to me c/o above.

Life out here takes a bit of getting used to. My tan is coming on nicely, though we have to stay out of the sun in the extreme heat. At least the nights are cooler!

I'm afraid my letters might be a little tedious, as there's so little I can tell you about. Except I miss you all the time and can't wait to see you again.

Would you be able to go and see Matt? I don't know all the details, but he is a patient in East Grinstead hospital, Surrey. I'm afraid he was burnt bailing out of his Hurricane, and is having treatment there. It would mean the world to him if you could visit, and as you are a nurse you won't mind if he's in a bit of a mess. Also you'll have more of a clue what's going on. I know it's a long way for you to go, but perhaps on your next bit of off-duty?

It's difficult to write in the heat, my sweaty fingers keep smudging the ink! And the flies never let up!

Keep safe, darling, and write to me soon.

From Me

6

It was a miracle that she had missed none of her connections, expecting as she did the journey to be fraught with complications. The hospital seemed to be in the most inaccessible part of the Home Counties, and as she gazed out of a succession of train windows she wondered what she would find on arrival.

She had not been able to act upon Will's request at once, for the dreaded finals had taken precedence. Even now the memory of them filled her with despair, for she was convinced that she could not have passed, and it would be another two weeks before the results. Addie, in contrast, had exuded quiet confidence in the run-up to the exam, and concluded the paper with no sign of the blind panic that afflicted the others. It was not so much that Honor did not know the answers; the problem was extracting them from her disordered mind. The truth was that she had been unable to concentrate since Will had been posted to the Middle East. The fear that she might never see him again dominated her waking hours, and filled her with restless nightmares. What hope of achieving her SRN amongst all of that turmoil?

'East Grinstead,' the stationmaster called, and Honor jumped down from the carriage, amazed to have made it on time. She looked uncertainly around, to be hailed by a tall man in RAF uniform. It was not Matt, nor would she have recognised him if his face had been thus reconstructed. She swallowed quickly, and smiled.

'Are you Honor? I'm George, come to pick you up.' He gallantly took her small bag and gas mask, and waved her to a parked sports car, the hood up against the chill of late autumn. 'Matt's longing to see you!' he added, opening the door for her, and she slid into the low seat.

'How is he?' She looked round tentatively to take in more of the damaged face. It was the eyes that were most disconcerting, lacking lashes and brows, but she tried to ignore the rest as completely as she could. The nasal work was obviously only in the early stages, so there might be hope for a better outcome yet.

'Well, he's not allowed to brood on it, you know. None of us are, we just get on with it. Damn lucky to be alive!'

She noticed the drawn skin over his hands as he drove, and the fingers which were partially clawed in flexion. Was Matt going to be like this?

'How long have you been in hospital?' she asked, tentatively.

He changed gear expertly despite his damaged hands. 'Altogether, or in this one? Well, McIndoe's been working on me for about a year now, so I'm one of the original guinea pigs, you know.'

'Guinea pigs?' She looked across at him in the fading afternoon light.

'That's what we call ourselves, our club. You qualify by having the old man operate on you! It's not usually just the once, but heavens only knows where we'd all be without him. Take my hands, for instance. Some bright spark put tannic acid on them after they pulled me out of the kite – it forms a hard cement, meant to protect the skin. McIndoe reckons it's the worst thing to do: it gets infected under the crust and makes the fingers contract. He's put a stop to it now, but I was one of the early casualties. He got to me just in time, otherwise I'd have lost them both. Made them chip it off, use paraffin dressings instead. He's going to give me some new eyelids next week, and he's responsible for my rudimentary nose!'

Honor was puzzled by the matter-of-fact way in which he described his condition; it was almost flippant, and quite unlike any patients she had ever heard before. She assumed this was their coping strategy, the outward mood of the servicemen on these wards. Better that than self-pity, she reasoned, but she wondered how desperate they must feel in their darker moments. How many of them would fly again? Or feel that they could take part in normal society, bearing the scars of such disfigurement?

They drew up at the Queen Victoria Hospital. It comprised a traditional building of its period, reminding her of the Royal London, but surrounded by additional ward blocks and pleasant grounds.

'He's in Ward 3, I'll take you over after you've had a cup of tea.' George ushered her to a visitors' room, where a VAD nurse helped him with the kettle.

'Don't be silly, Rosalie, I can do it myself!'

The VAD wagged her finger at him. 'You'll just scald yourself, then what will the boss say?'

Honor raised her eyebrows. The wards she worked on were so strictly run, such fraternising with patients would never be allowed.

The long walk down the corridor to Ward 3 was overlain by the familiar smell of polish and disinfectant, but it did not quell her apprehension. She entered the high-ceilinged ward to find Matt's bed empty, the tidy sheets pulled back and objects neatly placed on his locker. One of the nurses stopped on her way past.

'He'll be back in a moment, he's being prepared for surgery tomorrow. He said he had a visitor today, a nurse, is that you?'

Honor having introduced herself, the nurse replied, 'I'm Jenny, the one who does all his dressings. He's doing really well, apart from feeling a bit sorry for himself. I'd like a word before you go, just a few things I need to find out. At least you won't be shocked, like some of the visitors who come here. Honestly, they just make things worse for the poor boys. You can sit and wait here.'

Nothing in her previous training had prepared her for Ward 3. The inmates were a noisy bunch, and she was certainly not expecting the low wolf whistle that came from the next bed. As for the facial injuries, no treatment could be more dramatic than the pedicle skin grafts which extended, proboscis-like, from mid-face to shoulder. The flap of skin, which had been formed into a tube, thus ensured the vital blood supply to the tissue until it could be grafted. She had never imagined such surgery, such intricate restoration of the human face. A group of men were playing cards around the stove, some in dressing gowns, others fully dressed, all bearing different scars but carrying the same trademark of a surgeon's devotion to duty. George clearly mirrored the prevailing spirit, which seemed more that of an unruly boys' school than a hospital. To cap it all, there was a keg of beer at the end of the ward which was dispensed to those who could not help themselves.

Two male orderlies were wheeling a trolley into the ward, and on it lay Matt. Not quite the old Matt, but mercifully recognisable despite a bandage over his left eye and ear and resolving pink scars on his left jaw.

She moved to meet him – 'Matt!' – and kissed his good cheek while he waved her away with bandaged hands.

'Steady on, babe! I'll never hear the last of it!'

Lifted with great gentleness on to his bed, she realised his injuries must be worst over his hands and thighs.

'I'm so glad to see you!' Matt rested back upon the pillows. 'Sorry I wasn't here, I'd just finished my saline bath and then they had to prep me for tomorrow. How are you?'

Honor smiled, swallowing away a sudden urge to cry. 'What do you mean, how am I?! Look, I brought you these.' She deposited four precious pears in a brown paper bag on his locker to hide her confusion. 'You look better than I thought you would…' she said, then faltered, thinking she had said the wrong thing.

'Do I really?' He was pleased, after all, and smiled that wide smile of his, just a little puckered by the pink lines on the left side. 'Yep, I've been lucky, all things considered – at least the boss hasn't had to make me a nose or eyelids!'

'What has he got to make for you, Matt?' she asked softly.

'Just some new hands, that's the first hurdle. I couldn't get the hood back, you see, bloody Hurricane! Just as well I was wearing my goggles and mask.' His voice tailed off.

'What happened?'

'Got cut off from the lads in formation, found myself in amongst some Dornier bombers. Next thing I know the bullets hit me and there's a spout of flame from the starboard wing root. I'm struggling to get out, pulling on the hood, thinking this is it, then suddenly I'm free, but burning as I fall. How the hell my parachute opened is a mystery to me, I blacked out, and here I am, or at least, here I ended up.'

'You're going to be all right, Matt.' She hoped her voice carried some conviction.

'Am I?' he answered, almost indulgently. 'Yes, of course, but what will I be able to do with these?' He held his bandaged hands in front of him. 'I want to fly again, you see. It'll be an age until I'm fit – bloody war'll be over by then!'

'Has Florence been to visit?'

He hesitated for an imperceptible moment before answering. 'Yes, of course. Bit tricky for her though, she's been posted up north,' he said, asserting as an afterthought, 'She's been an absolute brick about it all.'

'What op are you having tomorrow?'

'Skin grafting from my legs to my hands, tricky one, McIndoe says. Let's hope it takes this time.'

George ambled to the end of his bed. ''Course it will, old boy. We've laid bets on whether the gas man makes you sick, good sweepstake so far! We always do that, you know,' he added by way of explanation to Honor. 'Hunter says he'll buy him a drink if he vomits!'

'Hunter?'

'The chief anaesthetist, McIndoe's right-hand man. Now listen, Brown,' he sat down on the side of Matt's bed, 'is this pretty girl accounted for or not? There're one or two lads on the ward would like to know.'

Honor blushed, Matt coming to her rescue. 'Sorry, George, she's the property of my best friend!'

'Lucky chap!' George looked wistfully at her. 'Has he been here, I don't recall?'

'He's a Wellington pilot, Western Desert,' Honor said, to the quick rejoinder from George, 'Never mind, we can keep you company while he's away!'

'Bugger off, George.' Matt wanted the girl to himself, reminding him of the good times, when he faced the future with ignorance and optimism.

But their conversation became desultory. Honor could tell him little of Will's flying, for she knew nothing, the censor had seen to that. Sensing that Florence had become a delicate subject, their only recourse was to discuss Matt's condition, which she feared might depress him.

She was saved by Jenny. 'Not much longer now, you two, I don't want him tired before surgery.'

This time Matt submitted to her kiss. 'You'll come back, won't you?'

'Of course I will.' She put on her coat, and resisted the temptation to stroke his hair. He looked so much like a child, just the same as her small charges on the ward, his grave eyes following her every movement.

Outside the ward, she stopped in an effort to regain control, and Jenny called her back, ushering her into the sister's office. She closed the door.

'How do you find him?' Jenny had a tenacious, almost protective air.

'Pretty good, all things considered,' Honor replied. 'I'd been so frightened about his face.'

Jenny nodded. 'Yes, he's been comparatively lucky, but the boss doesn't know if he can save his hands. The last graft didn't take – strep infection.'

'That's why he's so low! What's happening with his girlfriend?'

Jenny answered brusquely: 'Oh, she was all over him at first, then the visits started to tail off. He says it's because she's been posted further away, but I rather doubt it. How long had they been together?'

Honor thought for a moment. It must have been since Desford, around February. 'Nearly a year, but I didn't know her well. Will, my boyfriend, used to say they were passionate about each other!'

Jenny's look said it all. 'Well, passion won't be on the cards for a bit. I hope she's not one of those girls who can't stay the course. After all, some of them stick by blokes who end up much worse than him, he's still a nice-looking lad!'

Honor thanked her and left the ward, glancing back to see if he was still watching her. The curtains were around his bed, so she made her way down the long corridor to the imposing front doors where George was outside, waiting in the car.

7

'Where to, gorgeous?' George said. 'You're surely not trying to get back tonight, it's nearly half past seven!'

Honor rummaged in her bag for the piece of paper Addie had given her with the address. Ever the organiser, Addie had realised that Beatie's parents lived close to East Grinstead and taken it upon herself to arrange for Honor to stay the night. Honor, none too keen upon the plan, had little option but to acquiesce.

'Of course they won't mind!' Addie said.

'But I don't know them!'

'Well I do, and it's what Beatie would expect. I've already rung them anyway, they're expecting you. Can't get hold of Beatie, but that's no surprise.'

The nurses had heard nothing from Beatie since her dramatic appearance after Ken's death. She had vanished into her work again, and they had not expected otherwise.

It was a short way to an imposing house on the outskirts of town, and as George motored up the drive Honor began to wish she had been more adamant in her refusal. However would she be received?

Polite as ever, George opened the car door for her and rang the bell, which was answered by the maid. Ushered in, they waited in the hall before Mrs Molesworth came down the stairs to meet them. She was younger than Honor had expected, and carefully dressed in a twinset and pleated plaid skirt. Her greeting was warm.

'You must be Honor! And this is…?' She turned to face the scarred airman without a shadow of reserve.

'George Falconer, Mrs Molesworth, just dropping this young lady off. I should get back to the hospital now.'

She was hearing none of it.

'Nonsense, you'll join us for a drink first.'

Honor was relieved to have his presence as she sat sipping her gin and tonic on the damask settee. Mrs Molesworth chatted effortlessly to George, to whom she was a picture of charm.

'I must have you boys round for an evening soon,' she said as he finished his second drink and stood to leave. 'I've been meaning to for some time.'

'It will be a pleasure, and thank you for the sundowners.' He turned his attention to Honor. 'Don't you worry about Matt, we'll keep him busy!'

After waving him goodbye, Honor washed her hands and face in the comfortable guest room. Brushing her hair, she hoped she looked presentable, but she need not have worried.

'We'll just have a light supper in the parlour, dear, my husband's away on business tonight. You're sweet to come so far hospital-visiting! I gather he's not your young man though, Addie told me as much. Those poor boys, what they've been through doesn't bear thinking about! You've reminded me I need to do my bit too. Anyway, we've lots of time for a nice chat and you can tell me all about the hospital.'

It was a surprisingly pleasant evening. Little mention was made of Beatie's unfortunate pregnancy, for which she had clearly been forgiven.

'She was such a headstrong girl, you know, we could never stop her doing anything. She was always in trouble at school! Anyway, I know you and Addie stood by her, and I'm grateful for that. Do you know what she's doing now? I hope she's not pushing herself too hard, after that dreadful illness! I never hear from her!'

'Well, I expect she's busy in the ATS,' Honor said.

'Do you think so? I keep wondering...' There was a pause. 'Did she tell you that her father is French? Bea never lets on she can speak it so well, keeps it to herself. When she said she wanted to be a nurse I suggested her languages might be of more use in the war effort, but she wouldn't hear of it! And now she'd rather drive motorcycles!'

'She looked pretty good at it when we saw her last!' Honor smiled at the memory of Beatie revving off down the Groby Road.

Retiring to bed some hours later, she sank gratefully into the pressed cotton sheets, yet closed her eyes to the image of a bandaged and immobile Matt. Praying she would never see Will suffer like that, she eventually drifted into an exhausted sleep.

2nd November 1941
Groby Road Hospital
Dear You,
I shouldn't really keep telling you how much I worry about you, but of course I do! Apart from anything, you are so far away, and I can't really imagine what it's like out there, never having travelled from the relative safety of these shores!

You will be pleased to hear that I went to visit Matt. He said to tell you he will be fine, but I'm afraid he has quite a bit more surgery to go through. Mercifully his face is not too badly burned, but his hands took the brunt of it. He is in a top-class unit there, so if anyone can work miracles, it is those doctors and nurses.

We're all shaken to hear that the Germans are so close to Moscow. Everyone is trying to do their bit to support the Soviets – even Mrs Churchill has set up a Russia fund, and Mr Stalin is now our favourite ally, Communist or no!

I don't know how quickly you receive these letters but I will go on writing them just the same, and hoping for the best.

Take great care of yourself in all that sand and heat.

From Me

8

The time lapse with their letters now was such that he felt completely out of touch with her life. Still waiting for her first missive to appear, he feared the crew would be sent to the advanced landing grounds before he could see her rounded handwriting again. It would be an age until he heard about her exam, or whether she had managed to visit Matt.

He shook the sand out of his bedding, not that it seemed to make much of a difference, as Don stuck his head round the tent flap.

'Come on, Fordham, we'll miss visiting hours!'

It was to be their first trip into Cairo, primarily to see Griff, who had survived with a neat appendicectomy scar.

'I told you it wasn't gyppy tummy!' Will said when they heard the news. Vic would be mightily relieved to have his navigator back, although the crew were on good terms with Reggie, and Griff was likely to be convalescing for a little while yet.

They hitched a lift on a truck destined for town, and as they drove along the dusty streets Will was amazed at the rank poverty of Arab life. The curious garb of the locals puzzled them all, clothed as they were in flowing robes against the desert sun. The ramshackle buildings looked pretty squalid, but it was the noise, the heat and the smells of Cairo which assailed them that first visit.

'We'll go to the flea market later,' Ted announced, but the others were more interested in the option of a cool drink in the bar of Shepheard's Hotel.

They were mobbed by ragged children as they drove past, running alongside the truck, holding out their hands; 'Baksheesh, mister, baksheesh!', but they ignored their cries.

There was even less respite when they descended outside the British General Hospital. 'Postcards, mister, good postcards', all of which they dismissed, as Ted put it, as unnecessary woppishness. Theirs was not a generation that had freed itself from the ties of Empire, or the attitudes it personified.

There were other reasons why they were so little engaged with the country in which they found themselves, apart from trying to survive its harsh climate and unyielding terrain. Egypt had become the battlefield in which they would fight for Europe, but was itself a neutral country, not one at war. It was just the scenery on the stage, as they were the actors who came and went. For the serviceman, the country was peripheral to the objective, which was to defeat Hitler, and the effort of so doing left them little reserve for anything other than a passing interest in its customs and history.

Inside the hospital, there existed a sense of order and tradition which prompted them to dust themselves off before they entered the ward. A QA nurse in a white buttoned dress and triangular veil looked up from adjusting a drip as they came in. Will took charge.

'Excuse me, Nurse, we've come to visit our navigator, Flying Officer Griffiths.'

She smiled at his diffidence. 'He's at the end of the ward, fluids only today so don't go giving him anything else! You've only about another half an hour for visiting time, you know.'

'Sorry, yes, we won't stay long.' He returned the smile. 'How's he doing?'

'Well, he's only third day post-op but the doctors are pleased with him. Should be off for convalescence soon.'

They heard Griff's voice first. 'Lads, down here!' followed by a 'Hush' from another nurse.

Seated around his bed, it soon became apparent that he was making a rapid recovery. Like all patients, he wished to spare them no details of his ordeal.

'The doc says if they'd waited any longer I'd be a goner. Abscess had burst inside me, it's a wonder I'm alive to tell the tale. I knew I was bloody sick, but thought it must be one of those wretched bugs. Never guessed it was my old appendix!'

'When are you getting out, you old skiver?' Don said.

'Not yet, old chap, got to be looked after by these pretty nurses a bit longer yet! Ouch, my scar!'

Once they had sampled his drinks and checked his observation chart they tired of the ward and decided to move on to the comparative luxury of the hotel.

'You're not going already!' Griff protested.

'Sorry, Rita Hayworth at the desk says visiting time is up and we've got a date with some cool beers.' Ted was ready for the off. 'You look great, old chum, see you soon!' He was down the ward while the others took more leisurely farewells.

'Watch yourselves in Cairo!' Griff called after them, but they did not heed his words, as Ted had already summoned a rickety taxi to their destination.

In a state of good humour at their friend's reprieve, they settled into the cool surroundings of the Shepheard's bar, ready to enjoy themselves. As they sipped their drinks, surrounded by the society girls and their attentive uniformed beaus, it was tempting to forget that tonight they would be back on base, in their tents in the sand, awaiting whatever mission tomorrow might bring.

9

It was Vic who brought them the news first, rousing them from their sleep in the early light of dawn.

'Come on, chaps, wakey-wakey, we're on for today, briefing at 0600!'

'What the hell's he talking about?' Arthur, still only half awake, drew his blanket around his head as though to exclude the unwelcome interruption.

Will took a long sip from his water bottle. It tasted no better than when he had arrived. 'I reckon we're on the move,' he replied, shaking out his boots before he put them on, 'up to one of the landing grounds, I expect. No peace for the wicked!'

Alternately yawning and grumbling as they assembled, the five crews were given a succinct briefing. It was November 16th, and Will was right, they would be taking off from Kabrit at 0800.

Squadron Leader Simpson came straight to the point. 'It's about a couple of hours' flying time west to LG 104. You'll be doing some local wireless testing there before we deploy you on ops, further inland at LG 75. Basically this takes you closer to the enemy,' he pointed to the map, 'and to the Libyan border. It's not going to be easy, and you'll find the landing grounds are pretty grim. Just remember what you're here for and who chose you for this job. I'll catch up with you at LG 75 before we commence ops.'

As the navigators clustered to check the maps again, Reggie included, Vic had a word with the rest of his crew.

'Sorry, Ted, day flying again so you'll need to have your eyes skinned. Will, you and I will go and check out the crate with the erks while the rest of you have a quick breakfast. And don't leave any of your kit behind here, you can be damn sure it'll have disappeared when we get back.'

Reggie, maps under his arms, looked less than cheery in the mess tent. 'I bloody hate those landing grounds,' he said, helping himself to fried eggs as though to fortify himself against the coming privations. 'Just when you think you couldn't possibly arrive at a worse one than you've just left, then there it is!' Nonetheless he now considered himself to be part of the crew, and whilst deeply sceptical about the feasibility of this operation, he had a sneaking desire to see it through with them.

Their Wellington, Z8948, R for Robert, had been passed as serviceable by the ground crew, who were used by now to working with much less promising planes. As for the Mark IIs, few of them believed that they would ever materialise in the desert, and deeply suspicious, reckoned it was just a rumour to boost morale.

The sandstorm started to gather about one hour into their flight, when Will was handing over to Vic. 'Christ, I don't like the look of that!' he said as the sky darkened ahead of them. 'Let's hope we can get her down while the visibility holds.'

It was as though they were becoming enveloped by a dark cloud, sweeping away the contours of the desert and sculpting them according to a new design. Rocked by the turbulent khamsin storm, Vic held the Wellington on course as they descended through deteriorating conditions to the barely visible landing strip below.

'I'm pretty sure that's 104, Skip,' Reggie called through his intercom. 'Bit tricky to be certain in this stuff. Make sure you cover your faces when we get out, or the ruddy sand'll choke you!'

Grateful for his advice, they ran with scarves held tightly over their faces through the stifling wind and dust to a cluster of tents nearby. They could make out the shapes of two other Wellingtons beside them, though were unable to see whether they included those of their fellow crews.

Dick was sitting inside one of them with his pilot, the infamous Screwball. He raised his hand in greeting but did not attempt to remove the handkerchief from his mouth and nose. The tent shook with each gust of wind, appearing likely to take off until two of the crew resorted to hanging on to the tent poles.

'How long does this go on for?' Will shouted at Reggie, who shook his head by way of reply.

There was little they could do but sit it out. The same question was in all of their minds: where were the other two planes? Arthur had not made it yet, and it was impossible to conceive of his plane continuing on course through such a storm. Vic forestalled Will's thoughts.

'He's always bloody late, is Wellesley, I bet he's been force-landed at one of the other landing grounds.'

Screwball drew a hip flask from his pocket, took a swig, wiped the top with a dusty hand, and passed it on. The whisky parched their throats as they gulped it, and Don made a mock-salute.

'Good man!'

Reggie rose to squint through the tightly closed tent flap. 'I think it's easing off!'

It was another hour before they considered that the wind had abated sufficiently to venture outside. The atmosphere was still full of dust, creeping up their noses and down their throats, making it difficult to breathe, and they kept their scarves up while they gazed at the havoc of the storm. Two of the tents were half-blown from their moorings, and one of the Wellingtons was almost submerged in sand. The landscape around them was gathered into drifts and silts among the dark rocks of the hills.

'How the hell are we going to get it out? That was my plane!' Screwball walked towards his bomber, which looked as though it had been beached upon a sandbank. He was joined by some of the ground crew, emerging slowly from the other tents.

'That's all right, Skip, it's always happening out here. We'll dig it out when it's over!' The chap who came to survey it with him was deeply bronzed, wearing nothing but shorts, desert boots and a small hat perched jauntily upon his head. 'Ruddy khamsin, at least you got down safe! We'll soon have it right for you!' He spoke in a broad cockney accent, in sharp contrast to Screwball's Canadian drawl.

'Won't all that sand foul up the engine?' The pilot was reasonably concerned, but the remark brought forth gales of laughter from the erks.

''E wants to know if the sand will bugger up the engine!' the fitter repeated amusedly. 'Listen, chieffy, if we couldn't stop sand buggering up a Wimpy engine, none of you lot would ever fly again!'

10

'So is this it?' Arthur landed his plane the following morning when the fog and dust of the previous day had given way to a steel-blue sky and relentless sun. Both of the last two Wellingtons had taken refuge overnight at LG 21 when the storm whipped up.

Fred was even less complimentary, looking around him at the straggle of dust-covered tents. Apart from those, the landing ground comprised nothing more than a large, compacted space of desert, a square marquee housing operations control, and a series of assorted vehicles, including caravan trailers and a sparse field kitchen.

'What a dive!' He pulled off his overalls. 'What's the tucker like here?'

'Sorry, old chap, bully beef and biscuits is all we've been offered so far.' Reggie was taking it all in his stride, however vociferous his complaints in advance. 'At least there's some beer!' he said.

'Lead on, that man! Just show me where the hell it is, and it better be cold! How long are we in this dump for?' Fred removed his trademark leather bush tucker hat from his head. It was perfect for the conditions, and allowed for his immediate identification.

'Not long enough, old chap,' Don said. 'A little bird's told me the balloon's about to go up, and that means no more wireless tests for us! You mark my words, it'll be the real thing tomorrow!'

'Bloody hell, not before I've downed a few beers! Simpson said we'd be on ops from LG 75!'

Vic was in charge of the situation. 'Well, you're both right, as it turns out. We move there tomorrow, and it's not time for your beer yet, Fred. We've already done our wireless testing for today – you lads'll have to get yours in ASAP.'

Looking resigned to his lot, Arthur passed a sweaty hand over his brow. 'OK, Skip, whatever you say. Can't say I'm that keen to unpack, anyway.'

Screwball's Wellington, Z8907, D for Dog, was landing from their morning sortie as they spoke. He was muttering crossly to Dick as they strolled over from the landing strip to the tent.

'How come I haven't got one?'

Dick shook his head, and looked helplessly at Will. 'They didn't issue him with a goolie chit,' he explained.

'It'll be in his RAF escape tin.' They had all been provided with such a tin, and had perused its contents with varied enthusiasm – Horlicks tablets, water purifying tablets, a small rubber bag, a tiny escape saw, and chalk and opium tablets, all of questionable use in a long, hot trek across an unforgiving desert.

'No it's not, he's already checked.' Arthur was finding it difficult to suppress a smile.

The chits, which explained in Arabic to the local tribes that they would be rewarded if they returned a downed airman to his own lines, were seen as near-essential travel documents. Stories as to their likely fate without one abounded, and most crew kept them in a safe place.

'I expect Vic can knock him one up! Hey, Skip!' Don called to the disappearing figure, bound for the ops tent. 'Screwball hasn't got a goolie chit!'

Vic turned and raised his eyebrows, squinting against the harsh desert sun. 'You don't say,' he returned coolly. 'Now what might that be worth, supposing I could muster one up?'

A lesser man than Screwball might have been tempted to plead, but he raised his hands to dispel any accompanying doubt.

'It's quite simple, chaps,' he announced, 'no goolie chit, no ops. I shall take to my camp bed until it appears.' He strode off majestically through the sand to his tent.

'I hope your Arabic is up to scratch,' Fred called. 'Don't fancy your chances without one!'

The sentiments of the nomadic Arabs towards bailed or crash-landed aircrew were unpredictable. Some tribes, including the Senussi Arabs, were pro-British and helped airman evade capture, particularly as they held little allegiance to the Italians, who had treated them badly. Others would be only too happy to hand them over to the Germans, with the added incentive of a bounty upon their heads. Each member of the crew was aware that survival in such a hostile terrain, particularly without water, would be extremely limited, quite apart from any possible injuries they might have sustained. It was all part of the folklore of the mess tent, the stories of those who had come down and survived, then made it back to British lines: each snippet of information could help save a man's life when it was his turn to face the odds.

11

As the tanks engaged on the first day of conflict, two Wellingtons flew slowly back and forth over enemy lines. It was November 18th 1941, the start of Operation Crusader. The British tank divisions had moved off at six that morning, crossed the 'wire', the Egyptian-Libyan border, some two hours later, and were positioning themselves in a pincer formation to relieve Tobruk, the strategic port, from the German siege. It was not going to be easy, and the tankies had worked long and hard to regain a level of military fitness for the challenge. There had been too many defeats in this theatre, and their commander, General Cunningham, wanted them to finish Rommel once and for all.

From the cockpit of R for Robert, it was tricky to tell one side from the other, but the crew knew that their flight from LG 75 had taken them well beyond the British lines. The seventh armoured division were throwing all they had against the Mark 3 Panzers, and the Wellington's jamming equipment was finally being put to its intended task, but this landscape was a far cry from the safe pastures of Salisbury Plain. The barren dustbowl beneath them was the backdrop to a mighty battle, as the M3 Stuart tanks hurtled headlong towards the armed might of the Deutsche Afrika Korps, their anti-tank guns firing endlessly and the sky punctuated by billowing clouds of smoke and fire.

Ted Baines had been dreading this moment from the start. Unable to swallow any breakfast, his thoughts since take-off had been concentrated on staying alive. Silhouetted as the Wellington was against the dazzling sun and sky, they could not have been more obvious to an enemy fighter, and as far as Ted was concerned, it was only a matter of time.

'Keep her steady, Will.' Vic's voice betrayed no loss of composure as he handed over the controls. It was the worst mission he had ever flown, this methodical to-and-froing over the battlefield while the jammer hissed beneath their fuselage, straining all of their nerves to breaking point, but he was determined to complete it. Like Ted, he had little hope of remaining unscathed in the attempt.

Checking all of the dials in front of him, Will felt better in charge. Vic was undoubtedly the best pilot he had ever flown with, but he preferred to be in the first pilot's seat; it was easier to forget their vulnerability while thus engrossed. They had been jamming for the best part of two hours when Ted's voice broke through the intercom.

'Macchis, Skip, on our tail, closing in!'

It was three of them, pouncing out of a cruel blue sky, leaving little time to react before the bullets hit. Will wrestled with the controls as the bomber jolted, then steered abruptly to port in evasive action, but not enough to shake them off. At such low altitude their usual tactic of corkscrewing was not an option.

There was a cry from Don: 'I'm hit, Skip!'

Vic, motioning to Will to carry on, made his way swiftly to the wireless operator's post.

'Everyone else all right? What's going on, Ted?' Will's voice came over the intercom, weaving the plane as he fought to assess the damage. All the controls were responding, fuel tanks still OK.

'Don's copped it, I'm trying to stop the bleeding!'

Vic's muffled response was all he heard until, 'Got one! Bastard!' from Ted, as a salvo of fire came from the rear turret. 'Get us out of here, Skip, before they come back!'

Baines watched the diving Macchi, smoke and flame pouring from its fuselage, without sympathy for its occupants. 'Serves them bloody right!'

he muttered under his breath, anxiously scanning the sky for the Italians' compatriots, who were nowhere to be seen.

'We gotta get out, Skip!' he repeated, as Will, taking the plane into a climb to give himself more manoeuvrability, asked, 'Can you find us a way out of here, Reg?'

'No prob, Skip, happy to oblige!' But Reggie knew it would be a long haul until they were out of danger. He had flown on some filthy missions, bombing Benghazi with 70 Squadron, dodging the flak, but none had taken more nerve than this. He reckoned the Macchis would return; the Wellington would be easy prey now.

'Is Don OK?' Will's voice came over the intercom, but it was a moment before Vic's reply.

'Not sure, he looks pretty shaky, lost a lot of blood... can you hold on there, Will?'

'Yes, but the oil pressure's dropping in the port engine.' He had been anxiously watching the needle fall – they were not losing height, but he could not make any more than he had already gained.

'We'd best swap places—' Vic was interrupted by Ted's urgent voice.

'Christ, Skip, they're back!' Never losing vigilance, Ted had spotted the two fighters coming back at them from the sun, the usual tactic to maximise surprise. They looked like angry homing hornets and he swivelled quickly in the Frazer Nash turret to try and pick one of them off before they were all done for. He'd never be able to get two in one day; the odds were stacked against them.

In front of them, Will saw a patch of cloud. If only they could make it, shake the Macchis off! Damn it, he needed to gain height, and the oil gauge was still dropping. All of his being was focused upon getting the lads and his plane out of this mess. Easing the throttle, he went for the best the Pegasus engines could offer, and they inched into cloud cover as the two Macchis closed in, Ted resolutely firing round after round of ammunition as they dodged for cover.

'We're in cloud, you lot, hold on!,' Will said. 'Where's the opposition, Ted?'

'Stymied!' Ted's relief was audible as Vic added, 'Good work, Will, I'll take over now, you come back and look after Don.'

Relinquishing the controls, Will made his way down the fuselage to the rest bed, where Don, ashen, was lying shivering.

'Tell Reggie to try the wireless,' he said faintly, but Reggie had already reported that it was out.

Taking the wounded man's pulse, Will wished he knew more about first aid. It did not feel very strong to him, so he checked the leg under the ripped, blood-soaked trousers to satisfy himself that Vic's tourniquet, his improvised leather belt, was working, which it appeared to be.

'Hold on, Don!' He knelt beside him, putting his hand on the clammy, cold brow. 'Skip, I don't like the look of him!'

They were the last words Don heard as he lapsed into unconsciousness, only the tourniquet between him and death as the stricken bomber limped its way slowly home.

12

Will collapsed in relief on his camp bed in the dusty tent. It was a miracle they had survived, though Don's condition was critical and the Red Cross plane had taken an age to reach them at LG 75. It was a tribute to Vic that he had somehow managed to land the plane in one piece, despite severe damage to R for Robert, and no wireless communications at all. Reggie had come up trumps too, navigating them back through difficult terrain, low over the battlefields, as the tanks waged war beneath them. At least their own side had not fired at them once they regained the British lines: unable as they were to give the signal of the day, they had relied on the troop's recognition of their own aircraft. That was another bonus of the Wellington: it was instantly recognisable, and went on flying no matter how many holes the enemy had put in it.

Arthur passed him a bottle of warm beer. 'Sounds crap to me,' he said uneasily. 'I don't fancy our chances tomorrow!' His Wellington had not been singled out for the first day's sortie, and Screwball was yet to return with D for Dog. It was turning out to be just as bad as he had feared, and he was not encouraged by the news from today's mission.

'Well, we're in the lap of the gods now!' Will replied, removing his fire-resistant ID disc from around his neck. Was that all that would be left of him, he pondered, as he looked at it lying in the palm of his hand? How close had they all been to death today? There was so much of life in front of him, not to be snuffed out in these shifting sands of eternity. He closed his eyes and sipped the beer. *Best not think about it, pretend it's never going to be me, stay focused, survive.*

'Worst thing is, we don't even know if the jamming works!' Arthur said bitterly. 'I'm not sure how they're going to find out, either.'

'Quite honestly, I'm beyond caring!' Will took another mouthful; it tasted good despite the temperature. 'Wake me up when Dick gets in.' He lay back, closing his eyes before lapsing into a dreamless doze.

When he awoke the tent was empty. He glanced at his watch; it was late afternoon. Where in hell were the others? Putting on his light shirt, he walked over to the landing strip. Several members of the ground crew were nearby, looking up at his Wellington.

'What's the damage?' Will assumed they would have the plane back in working order by now.

'She's a write-off, Skip!' The cockney erk shook his head. He hated to see a plane go U/S; it was as though they had all failed somehow. 'It's a bloody miracle you got back, look at this mess!'

The cloth-covered fuselage was riddled with bullet holes, and oil seeped slowly from the damaged tank.

'I thought you lot could patch up anything?' He looked up at the bold capital R on the side of his plane – surely they would not have to part with her so soon?

'Nah, not unless they send us a new engine sharpish!' The erk was equally depressed by this outcome. Wimpys were precious this far forward. 'You'll have to take one of the others tomorrow!'

'Tomorrow?' Will replied. His crew were not on jamming duty until the day after.

'Yes, haven't you heard? D for Dog's gone missing. As soon as it's light you lot are going out to look for the crew.' His voice was matter-of-fact, as though Will were being asked to drive a number ten bus around Piccadilly Circus, picking up passengers on the way.

There was no point questioning it; the ground crew always knew what was kicking off, especially on a small landing ground like this. Will turned away, swearing under his breath, hating the thought of Dick and Screwball out there in the desert, even assuming they were still alive, and went in search of further news.

Squadron Leader Simpson was feeling less than sanguine about the day's events. Whilst Crusader might have got off to a good start, he had only five Wellingtons for Operation Jostle: one had been damaged beyond repair and the other had gone missing. That left him only three at LG 75, so he would have to call in reinforcements, none of which would have the necessary jamming equipment ready for immediate use. In fact, the ground crew would have to salvage it from the other plane, and that would take valuable time. It was no surprise to him that his men had come under fighter attack, and he had personally campaigned for Spitfire backup for them, without success. They were, as the Australian navigator had succinctly put it, sitting ducks, and he wondered how long they could keep it up. Like all good campaigners, he baulked at sending his men to certain death, even if the authority for the operation came from the Prime Minister himself.

The light was fading as he took them through briefing, and the kerosene lamp on the table threw up flickering patterns on the darkening canvas of the tent. Despite his attempt to deliver the information with enthusiasm, they all knew it was bad news, and the tone amongst the crews was bereft of its usual flippancy.

'What's the gen on their whereabouts?' Reggie, who had spent more time in the desert than the others, held out little hope of finding them.

'We had wireless communication from them before they went down, signalling the port engine was on fire, so we know their location. We can't say if they bailed out or crash-landed, but if it was the latter, they won't have got far from their plane.' Simpson pointed to their likely location on the map. 'We think they're here, near Bir el Gubi, towards the line of deployment of the 22nd Armoured Brigade. We'd better get them out quickly, before they end up caught between them and the panzers.'

Vic drew a deep breath. It had been bad enough losing Don, who was fighting for his life when the Red Cross finally picked him up. He would soon have none of his original crew left, particularly since Fordham was about to be given his own command. To cap it all, they would be taking a different plane, F for Freddie, of which he had no experience and no sense of superstitious allegiance.

'Who'll be standing in as Wireless Operator?'

'Snowy Douglas.' They knew Snowy, another New Zealander, whose name derived from his shock of honey-blond hair.

Snowy should be up to the job, Vic reckoned, but having flown with Don for so long he felt a sharp sense of loss. He hoped to God the Scot would survive, but even if he did, there would be no chance of them ever crewing up together again, and he would miss his dependability and dry humour. Quite apart from his personal feelings, good wireless operators were hard to come by and if any task depended on them, then jamming enemy tanks was the one.

There was no room for emotion in the harsh world they inhabited: the next mission would be another struggle for survival, like the last.

'We reckon the whole operation should take about four to five hours,' Simpson added. He could not afford to lose Willis and his crew, and wanted them back in the shortest possible time. It would be worth the risk if there were any survivors out there, and with the return of the stranded crew there might be some hope for Jostle yet.

'What happens if we can't find them, sir?' Will asked. 'How long do you want us to go on looking?' Vic was not the only one to be struggling with the loss of a friend. It seemed a cruel act of fate to have met up with Dick again, only to lose him so soon.

'Unfortunately, we're expecting enemy fighters at this location, so I want you in and out pretty quickly. If they're not where we think they are, then you'll just have to call it a day – I need you back for the next jamming op.' Simpson knew it was going to be difficult for them to abandon the exercise, so wished to make his orders entirely clear. 'Your departure time is 0500, that means I expect you back at 0900, with a window of one more hour for the unexpected. Now unless there are any more questions, I suggest the pilot and navigator go over the course again, and I wish you all good luck.'

The usual terse RAF sign-off, thought Ted Baines as he left the tent; *they ask you to do the impossible and then wish you luck, as though that somehow makes it all right*. He doubted he would sleep much tonight; the thought of the Macchis coming for them again was enough to put paid to that.

13

The shadow of the plane fell across the sand as the two pilots, anxiously scanning the terrain below, looked out for signs of the missing Wellington.

'Not a dicky bird,' Will said, as the undulating amber landscape showed no sign of life, apart from the odd greyish clump of scrub.

'Reggie, how're we doing?' Vic had made good time on the run in and intended to perform a thorough sweep of the area, flying as low as he could.

'Spot on, that's Bir el Gubi down there,' Reg replied, but there was little to define the nomadic settlement other than a small stationary camel train. 'Sidi Rezegh airfield to the north, Skip, give it a wide berth!' For this was a key German base several miles south of the Tobruk perimeter. The 7th Armoured Brigade had made it the object of their first push, and Will could see the smoke on the horizon.

'Any signs of the 22nd?'

'They'll be south of us, Skip, moving up sharpish I should think.'

'OK, I'm turning for the next run. All quiet, Ted?'

Ted's voice over the intercom was cautious – 'So far so good, Skip' – knowing as he did that the devils could be on you before you had a chance to blink. His finger was on the trigger of the Browning gun, ready to blast at them the moment they did.

After several unrewarding criss-crossing flights over the location Vic became painfully aware that their time was nearly up. Where the hell was Screwball? Perhaps the crew had bailed out and taken cover, miles from the point of last radio contact. It was like looking for a needle in a proverbial haystack, and any moment now some Luftwaffe ace would descend from the skies and shoot F for Freddie to Kingdom Come. What was Simpson thinking of, sending them out when the chances of success were so slim?

Snowy added further to the uncertainty: 'I'm picking up some activity to the south, Skip, reckon it's our lot moving up. Hope they recognise us, I'm sending out today's signal.'

'Thanks, Snowy,' Vic said. The last thing they needed was friendly fire. 'I think we'd better call it a day, chaps. The balloon's about to go up around here, we've had our chance.'

Will frowned. 'Just give it one more go, Skip, they'd do it for us!'

'He's right, Skip,' Reggie said. 'The lads are done for down there!' Even Ted, ambivalent as he had been about the whole escapade, did not want to abandon the search.

And so it was that on the final traverse they spotted the grounded plane. It looked like a wounded beast, slewed on its side, but mercifully not burnt out.

'Christ! That's them!'

'As Vic flew lower, they made out a bunch of waving and shouting figures running crazily along a nearby ridge.

'Thank God, they're alive! How many can you see, Will?' Vic said.

'Not sure, difficult to say!'

'Let's get back – we'll ask the 22nd to pick them up, they should be close enough! Got their position, Snowy?'

'Got it, Skip!'

14

'We thought we were goners, you know.'

The dust on Dick's face was so thick his freckles were obscured. He, like the rest of the crew, was dirty, unkempt and thirsty.

'Thank God you stayed with the plane!' said Will.

'We didn't have much choice, the rear gunner had broken his leg. We couldn't leave him there.'

'Is he going to be all right?'

'Not sure, the bone was sticking out, that's not so good, is it? They got an army medic to him pretty quick once the Tank Corps picked us up.' Dick finished his biscuit, and took another deep draught of water.

Will shook his head. 'So what happened? Macchis get you?'

'Too bloody right they did! Nothing to stop them, is there? You know what it's like out there! The bandits were down on us like a ton of bricks! Next thing we know is, smoke is pouring from the port engine, Screwball's trying to get us home but we're in big trouble. I thought the whole plane was about to blow, we're getting ready to jump, then Screwball says, no, he'll bring her down.' Dick took a deep breath. 'Which he did – a bit bumpy, that's how the rear gunner got hurt. Bloody amazing we're alive! How the hell did you find us?'

'We had your position from the last radio signal. It was just luck, I reckon! Not ones to give up, you know.'

'What about you lot, why were you in F for Freddie?' Dick, ever observant, had not failed to notice.

'Had a dust-up with the Macchis too, they wrote off our plane. Vic managed to get us back, but Don's wounded, touch and go…'

Dick rose to his feet from his seat in the sand. 'If you ask me,' he said, 'this whole thing's a ruddy awful joke!'

The desert night was soundless, and only one of the tents emitted a dull light into the small hours.

Simpson, mulling over the events of the day, looked relieved, as well he might. His judgement had not been at fault, after all. How he would have rationalised the loss of F for Freddie if matters had turned out differently, he did not care to imagine. If Willis kept on pulling off stunts like that he would recommend him for the DFC, he thought, sipping his sweet tea and poring over the maps for tomorrow's mission.

Both of the Wellingtons on today's op had returned safely, but that did not allow for complacency, as at debriefing they had each reported enemy fighter interception. Simpson would have to send F for Freddie and D for Dog out again tomorrow, but he did not like to dwell on their chances. The attrition rate that was deemed acceptable by Bomber Command in Europe could be anything up to 12%, but his crews out here carried a much greater risk than that.

Eternally surprised by the acceptance of these young men, some barely out of their teens, that this was their lot in life, he was minded to find out if this particular op was effective. Not coming from 109 Squadron himself, he was chary of the boffins at TRE and wondered if they balanced their scientific enthusiasm against the mortal risks involved. Still, he was about to find out at first hand as Colonel Denman, a top War Office specialist in radio countermeasures, was joining them for the Fort Capuzzo sortie tomorrow, and expected to arrive at any time. *Best put on a good show*, he thought reluctantly, swatting away the bugs as he did so. That was it: he would double them up tomorrow, send four of them out instead of two and aim for eight hours of jamming. That should show the colonel how Winston's Wellingtons were doing.

15

The word had spread that there would be more sorties tomorrow; as usual the ground crew had let the information slip as they desperately worked to ready the planes. They knew about the 'boff' too, having watched him descend from the replacement Wellington late that afternoon.

''Ope 'e knows wot he's lettin' himself in for!' Len, the cockney, was not impressed at the prospect of a bigwig in one of his planes.

''Ave they told him how to bail out when the Macchis get 'im?' commented his mate, darkly. They shook their heads, and carried on cleaning the dust off the propeller blades.

Over in their tent, Will and Arthur were digesting the news. 'Who's going to take him up? I expect it'll be us,' Will said. He was tired, and there was a dull ache in the pit of his stomach. Hygiene was a constant problem, with such limited access to water, and one or two of the crew had already reported tummy problems, not that an attack of diarrhoea would necessarily stop you flying. There was always the Elsan in the plane, however much they tried to avoid using it. He winced and crouched over.

'You all right?' Arthur's words were barely out of his mouth before Will was off to the latrines.

Fortunately the spasms passed, and by the time for briefing he felt a little better. Dick had given him Screwball's remedy, a tot of whisky, and it certainly helped. Nonetheless he sat quietly throughout, listening to Simpson's detailed plan for the Fort Capuzzo sorties. It turned out that Denman had been assigned to Sergeant Nicholson in A for Able, much to Snowy's relief. None of them wanted an observer on their back, even if Denman gave the impression that he knew how to look after himself. Tall and imposing, with an air of quiet confidence, he had notched up time inside a Wellington at Boscombe Down, and was determined to see if the jamming was going according to plan.

Dick joined Will as they were leaving the tent. 'How are the guts, old fellow?'

'Give us a drop more of that whisky and I should get through the night!'

As dawn broke, Will faced the day with less than his usual fortitude. Apart from the niggly abdominal pain, he felt below par generally, and was unenthusiastic about his meagre breakfast.

'I told you at Kabrit it would be the last square meal we'd get!' Reggie was downing his tea. 'You all right, buster? Looking a bit pale today!'

Will forced himself to drink. 'Gyppy tummy. Lucky I haven't had it before.'

'Not a good day for it. Why don't you ask Vic to stand you down?' Reggie said. Truth was it took several months to build up your resistance to these bugs, which is why it was never a good idea to be put straight out to ops. Best to have a spell acclimatising, like he had been given when he first arrived.

'Not likely, they'll all think I'm LMF. I expect it'll pass.' Will, like most of his colleagues, would rather report for duty than go off sick, no matter how ill he felt. He did not care to imagine Vic's reaction, for who was to say that his symptoms were not those of anxiety, after all? He would not be the first airman to suffer a loosening of the bowels before take-off.

'You know best.' Reggie finished his biscuit. 'God, I'd die for some toast and marmalade!'

'Don't say that, you'll jinx us all!'

They were scheduled to be on the first sortie alongside A for Able, with about one hour's flying time to Fort Capuzzo, up past Sollum and the coast. The Italians had a habit of giving attractive names to desolate places, according to Reggie, who had a healthy disrespect for Mussolini and all he stood for. In contrast, the Allied servicemen looked up to Rommel, or the Desert Fox, as he was known. Now there was a general who knew how to lead his men, from the front!

Will glanced across at Nicholson's crew, who must have been feeling similarly indisposed, for there was little of the usual pre-flight banter. Perhaps they found the presence of the observer disconcerting, but if so, the colonel was blissfully unaware of it and solidly chewed his rations.

'Come on, you lot, we've got work to do! Everyone here?' Vic called them over, and they dusted off the crumbs, picked up their kit, and made their way over to their plane. At least there was less to carry; daytime flying in these temperatures meant that heat and dehydration were their enemies, rather than the bitter cold and frostbite afflicting the aircrews over the Ruhr.

Ted Baines was tired too, though not with gyppy tummy. He had not slept much, wondering if today would be his last. He had already written a farewell letter to his young wife, and left it with his personal effects in case he did not return. To think he might never see her again… He shook himself, and swung neatly into the rear turret. It would be better once they were airborne; he always hated the waiting.

The flight in started uneventfully, but as they neared the battle zone the activity of tanks and armoured columns was intense.

'How the hell do they know whose side they're on?' Vic said, but Will, like the rest of the crew, could not make head or tail of the scene. Far below them, tanks were firing sporadically at each other, red tracer following the bullet rounds, dust and mayhem, with 'brewed up' tanks emitting flame and smoke. Like trapped scorpions, the tanks would engage, withdraw and re-engage from a different angle, blasting each other with their mortar guns.

'Christ, I wouldn't like to get trapped in one of those!' Acutely aware that there could be worse places than the cockpit of a plane, Will wondered how the tank crews coped with the claustrophobia.

'How much further, Reggie?' Vic wanted to start jamming and get out as soon as possible.

'That'll do, Skip, Snowy should be able to go for it now, but you'll need to make some more height,' Reggie said. He could see the other Wellington above them on their port side, methodically starting the exercise.

'Keep your eyes skinned, Ted!' Vic knew that the rear gunner needed little encouragement.

Ted had not shared his premonitions with the crew, for after all, if he went for a burton, then so would they. He scanned the sky anxiously. Vic was flying low, trying to maximise the effectiveness of the jammer, but if he was not careful the enemy ground artillery would take them out. When Ted saw the fighter coming, as he had known it would, his first emotion was one of pure anger.

'Bastards! They're on us, Skip! Nine o'clock!'

Manhandling the control column, Vic climbed a lurching turn to starboard, as Ted fired the first salvo of bullets from the Browning guns. The Macchi dived underneath them: this pilot was a show-off, Ted felt intuitively; he would take the cocky Italian out on his next run-in. But as he pressed the trigger, there was no response, no barrage of ammunition to pepper him with, just an empty click.

'Christ, Skip, my guns are jammed!' Ted's voice was urgent; the fighter would have been within his sights, but he was impotent, exposed in his rear turret, powerless to respond. Wasting no time, Vic hauled the plane to port, just escaping the onslaught of bullets as the fighter screamed past them to home in upon A for Able.

'My God, I hope they've seen him,' Will said. Nicholson must be intent on his jamming, steadily flying to and fro, and seemingly oblivious to the attack.

In the split-second moment that followed, Will watched in disbelief as Able exploded in a ball of flame. Nothing remained of the bomber, just an orange blast and searing bright light. There would be no parachutes descending through the black smoke, and with a deft victory loop, the Macchi took to the hills.

There was a shocked silence over the intercom, before Vic collected himself.

'Ted, get out of there and into the ventral turret! Reg, we're going to have to abort the op, give me the bearings for 75, or anything closer. Everyone all right?'

The voices on the intercom were in the affirmative, but they all knew they would never be the same again.

29th November 1941

109 Squadron, Middle East

Dear You,

There's a bit of a flap on at the moment and I don't have a lot of time to write, but just wanted to let you know that I'm still in one piece! I never know if you are getting these letters, but I can't help hoping you do.

I can't truly say the desert improves with time, because it doesn't – if anything the winter storms and mud make it slightly worse! Not to mention the wretched flies!

I hope you are by now a fully credited SRN, and that I will have a letter with the good news soon.

You are always in my thoughts, you know, and I can't wait for the day I see you again.

From Me

16

'Addie, you must come with us!'

The group of young nurses stood waiting at the door, dressed up and ready to go out.

'It's only one evening, you can't miss the party!'

June was determined to bring her influence to bear on Addie, whom she considered far too saintly for her own good. Just because she had come top in the SRN finals, and was off to become a QA, there was no excuse for stand-offishness.

Even Honor did her best to persuade her. 'Please, Addie, it won't be any fun without you! Think how long we've been together, and all we've been through. It's our last chance, before we all go our separate ways…'

Finally, Addie relented and gathered her coat, making no attempt to improve her appearance before she did so.

'Lord, at least slap on a bit of lipstick!' June said. As far as she could see, Addie had gone into self-imposed purdah since Ken's death, never to emerge.

Addie sighed and rummaged in her bag. 'There, that better?' she retorted, as she applied the bright colour, in sharp contrast to her sombre mood, to her well-formed lips.

'Not much,' June replied, extracting her own hairbrush to improve Addie's coiffure. 'There, that'll have to do, or we'll be late!'

By the time they arrived at the pub, it was standing room only. It looked as though everyone had turned out for the celebration, and those early evacuees from the Lambeth were outnumbered by the local nurses. Most would be leaving for other hospitals, in Honor's case, the North Staffordshire Infirmary in Stoke-on-Trent.

'I'm glad you came!' Honor squeezed Addie's hand.

Addie smiled back. 'Me too. You were right, it's our last do!'

They raised their glasses in a mutual toast: 'To the Lambeth, and absent friends', gravely remembering those for whom there would be no more celebrations.

'And Beatie!'

'Of course! I wrote her a letter, care of her parents, just to let her know we're on our way,' Addie said.

'Where is she now?'

'Not sure, she hasn't said much about her new posting, it was her mother who told me.' Addie said. 'I'm sure she's all right – if anyone can come up smelling of roses, it has to be Beatie!'

'There you are!' They were interrupted by Molly, looking flushed. 'Where have you been?'

Honor was about to reply when she caught sight of Peter, close behind.

'Honor!' He took her hands warmly, oblivious to the company. 'I hear you're leaving us!'

He steered her away towards the bar. 'Let me get you a drink.' Then taking her to the relative solitude of a table in the corner, he looked earnestly at her.

'Why have you been avoiding me? I haven't seen you for ages!'

She shook her head. 'I haven't, honestly, it was just the exams, and night duty...'

He sipped his beer. 'OK, spit it out, where is he?' His eyes were gentle even though the question was not.

She returned his gaze before replying. 'Middle East, Desert Air Force.' Her voice was low, as though to protect Will in some way.

'Oh my God, that's why you've dropped off the radar!' Peter seemed genuinely concerned. 'When did he go?'

'Middle of October. Things aren't very good out there at the moment.' She took a mouthful of warm shandy, wondering what he would ask next.

'Don't I know it, the newspapers are full of it!' he said. 'Though I'm sure they make it out to be less of a failure than it really is! It must be hell out there.' He paused. 'When will you see him again?'

The question was always uppermost in her mind. For Honor, it was steadfastly 'when', and never 'if'. Of course he would come back to her, she would not allow herself to doubt it.

'I don't know, not for some time.' There was no other way to dress it up, for it was the harsh truth: she had no idea when Will's tour of duty would end. Until then, the flimsy, irregular airmail letters were all she could hope for.

The silence that ensued was not unfriendly. Peter did not attempt trite reassurances, and she was grateful for it.

'Let me drive you up to Stoke next week,' he suggested.

'No, I'll be fine on the train, I'm not the only one going.' She did not want to be beholden to him, or give him the slightest encouragement.

His voice was firm. 'Don't be silly, of course I will.' She had no time to reply before Molly was upon them again.

'I've been looking for you everywhere, come on, Honor,' she said, before dragging her away.

Peter sat thoughtfully by himself for a while, flicking aimlessly at a stained beer mat, hardly noticing when Addie sat down beside him.

'She told you, then?' Addie said.

He nodded. 'Yes, she told me. Bloody awful posting, I hope to God he makes it back!'

Addie's serene face did not betray what she already knew. She had seen the steadfastness of Peter's love for Honor, and did not underestimate its power. Who was to say how events would shape their lives?

'When do you start with the QAs?' In his opinion, she was thoroughly suited to be an army nurse; just what the forces needed. Her bereavement had lent her an extra maturity and poise, which would see her well in a theatre of war.

'Next week, Aldershot,' she replied. 'What will you do without us all?'

30th November 1941
Groby Road Hospital
Dear You,
I keep wondering how you are getting on, and I'm guessing you must be in danger because our newspapers are full of the Libyan Campaign. It doesn't sound as though the battle is anywhere near over yet, so please try and keep out of harm's way. Sometimes I think it's worse for those of us at home, just endlessly worrying about you and never knowing what's happening. It's very difficult to carry on with normal life, thinking what you must be going through.

Slightly better news on the Russian Front – let's hope the Germans are held up by the weather long enough for the Soviets to rally. Thank heavens for the Russian winter! They need all the help they can get.

I passed my exam, so am now a state registered nurse. My new job will be in the North Staffordshire Infirmary, Stoke-on-Trent, c/o Nurses' Home.

Please write to me there, however brief a letter, so I know that you are all right.

Missing you more than ever, and thinking of you constantly,
From Me

30th November 1941
Groby Road Hospital
Dear Beatie,
I trust this letter reaches you – I have sent it to your parents' home as Addie doesn't know where the FANYs have posted you. I hope you're still enjoying driving lorries and motorbikes!

I wanted to let you know that I'm moving on too – I just passed my SRN exams (don't ask me how!) and will be going to the North Staffs Infirmary, Stoke-on-Trent. If you have a chance, write to me there and let me know what you're up to.

Did you hear that I met your mother recently? One of Will's friends is in hospital in East Grinstead, so I stayed with her when I went to see him. It was funny being in your house when you weren't there! But your mother looked after me very well.

Will is in Egypt; heaven knows when I'll see him again.

Take care of yourself, Beatie, and keep in touch.

Love Honor

Part Eight:
The Cauldron

1

Through the small window at the side of the fuselage, Beatie could see the moon, a quarter full. She sat upright in the belly of the Halifax, as she had been taught during the exhaustive months of training, mentally checking her instructions as the small white bulb in the ceiling clicked off.

One of the dispatchers came to check on them. 'All right, miss?'

She nodded in reply. Her parachute course had been uneventful, and she had found it surprisingly easy to do as the grizzled RAF sergeant had told her. Like most of her instructors, he made no allowances for the fact that she was a woman. Beatie had forgotten what it was like to be treated any differently, although once or twice she had glimpsed a look of surprise, particularly amongst the pilots, as she had climbed into the plane. She did not recognise the ones who were dropping them tonight, but it was not the familiar ginger-haired navigator who gave her a shy smile each time he saw her.

It had never occurred to her to refuse the job, nor could she remember at precisely what point her FANY superiors had realised she was fluent in French. Even then, she had no idea why she had been sent to the imposing manor house in the country. It was some months before she was considered ready for her first mission, and she had been allowed to tell no one, not even her family, of the true nature of her work. As far as they were concerned, she was just driving lorries on despatch at RAF bases.

Fortunately, she had not needed to include Jim in her deception, for he had been posted to Malta, flying Spitfires from the island's beleaguered air bases. The odds would be stacked against them both, she reflected, remembering his look of bewilderment as they parted, as though he had not expected to mind so much. She was still not sufficiently emotionally intact to give him her heart, but then, in a curious way, neither was he. The arrangement had suited them both so far, and allowed her to detach herself from him as the job required.

As they crossed the Channel she could see the enemy flak, the irregular flashes lighting up the night sky. She took a sip of coffee from the thermos and passed it on to her partner, but there was no question of sleep for her, uncomfortable as she felt in the parachute and flying gear over her civilian French clothes. All of the labels had been scrutinised before she left, down to the last detail, for nothing must give her away. Her hand moved to check the revolver in her pocket: they had been taught to draw it on landing, just in case. She knew how to use it, too, but of course by then, the game would be well and truly up.

The pilot's voice came through the intercom. 'Twenty minutes to go, ready when I give the word!'

Beatie remembered the Loire valley from her childhood: the winding rivers and medieval towns. How much less welcoming would she find it tonight? She looked instinctively over to the packages that were to be dropped with them, for they would be adrift without them. Drawing her whisky flask from her pocket, she took a quick mouthful in the darkness. It burned her throat as she proffered it to her colleague, who shook his head. He was an old hand, unlike Beatie; he had made this drop before and knew the local resistance well. Not that it meant he would be able to help her, though – once they were down, she would be on her own.

The dispatcher was back, motioning her to the correct position over the aperture of the plane. A blast of cold air took her breath away as she gripped the sides. Looking down at the fleeting clouds in the night sky, and mindful of the fact that she had already escaped death once before, she readied herself for the jump.

2

'What the hell's that?' Arthur sat bolt upright in his camp bed. They had not been long asleep, after a miserable evening trying to keep the rain out of their tent during a heavy downpour that threatened to turn LG 75 into a quagmire of mud.

There could be no mistaking it, the sound of Jerry dive-bombers. The three men leapt from their beds and started running for the slit trench close by. It was a drill they had already rehearsed, but their first real raid was upon them, and they crouched down, covering their heads as the Stukas screeched overhead.

They could hear little but the incessant bombardment, the flashing lights spreading well beyond the landing ground to the encampment of the 4th Armoured Brigade to the east. Seeing at least one of their cherished Wimpys on fire, Will realised their operation must be in the balance.

The ground artillery of the 4th was taking its time to swing its guns into action.

'If only we had a few Spits to send after them!' Dick shouted.

Feeling equally impotent, Simpson looked on in dismay. He simply could not afford to lose any more planes. Apart from the fatal plight of Able, with Denman and the entire crew blown to Kingdom Come, another Wellington had been posted missing over the El Adem area. Miraculously, the remaining planes had managed to keep up jamming ops but the men were tired, under constant stress on every sortie.

He winced with every explosion, and prayed for it to end.

When the men finally emerged from the trenches, they were faced with a scene of destruction. Not one, but two Wellingtons were blazing uncontrollably. The dive-bombers had finished off what the rainstorm had started, and it was difficult to imagine any plane taking off from the craters and mud that were once a landing strip.

'Blimey!' Len was surveying the scene with the other erks. 'That was like Blackpool bloody illuminations! I thought we were all for it! They'll never put that fire out!'

As the fire tender consisted of only a sixty-gallon tank and a two-inch hosepipe, the blaze was set to drag on through the night. The onlookers, silhouetted against the light, looking for all the world like characters in some surreal puppet play, eventually made their way back to their tents.

By the time they gathered for briefing the next morning, still in cold and damp clothes, most of them had guessed that Simpson had run out of time.

'Well, chaps, it's been a terrible night. But let's not forget what a good show you've put up in the last three weeks. As you probably know, the 70th Tank Division has made it to Tobruk, and I for one have no doubt that they were greatly aided by your determined jamming of the enemy tanks. As always, Rommel had a surprise up his sleeve and drew off some of his forces from Sidi Rezegh to strike towards Egypt, but so far the panzers have been stymied by the 4th Indian, at least so my sources tell me. Likewise, the

South Africans are holding off the Italian Ariete division, but it's a bitter battle and neither side looks set to give up yet.

'We only need to look around us to see what Jerry is still capable of, but I'm having to draw you back to LG 104, then to Kabrit, while we wait for replacement planes. Flight Lieutenant Willis?'

'Yes, sir?'

'Do you think you can get your plane off the ground? It appears to be the only one left unscathed.'

'Of course, sir.' Vic looked his usual unflappable self, but as always, was probably the only pilot who could extricate a Wimpy from that mess.

'You'll take the other crews back with you, I want you all out of here before the Luftwaffe put in another call. Take-off at 0800, only essential kit, gentlemen. I'll see you in Kabrit, and don't forget, our work here has only just begun. I'm planning to resume ops as soon as we possibly can!'

They picked their way through the mud and debris back to their tents to salvage their meagre belongings.

'It could be worse, chaps,' said Reggie cheerfully. 'I'm looking forward to some decent nosh!'

3

Kabrit was heaven compared to the privations of the landing grounds. Their first objective on arrival was a swim in the lake, and as they threw off their dusty clothes and submerged themselves in the calm waters, they felt as though a million years of desert sand was being rinsed away.

Will struck off, in his strong front crawl across the lake, leaving the others far behind in the shallows. A frequent swimmer, he had never imagined such a pleasant contrast to the chilly waters of the North Yorkshire coast.

'Hey, wait for me!' Dick was trying to catch him up. They both lay on their backs, and floated, suspended in the inky water.

'This is absolute bliss!' They gazed up at the metallic blue sky, conscious of nothing but a sense of temporary deliverance.

'God, I've give my eye teeth not to have to go back!' Dick said. 'How much longer do you think we'll have to keep it up?'

'Haven't a clue! I reckon they'll try and find out whether there's any point in it first. Not that it stopped the Charge of the Light Brigade, if I remember my history correctly. Fact of the matter is, we're all expendable: you, me, the Wimpy – just about everyone including the camp mascot!'

It was a matter of amusement among the men that the Wing Co. had a pet dog, a rather mangy creature who had crept into camp one day and refused to leave. Widely accepted as more important to their commanding officer than any other being, the dog trotted obediently behind him and had been known to attend briefings.

'What does the dog think of today's target?' was the joke amongst No. 70 Squadron, or, more seditiously, 'Would the dog like to come with us on this one, sir?'

'Best not think about it!' Will continued, executing a lazy backstroke towards the shore. 'What shall we do later?'

'Reggie's organised a trip to Cairo. Says he wants to take us to the Gezira Club, whatever that is. Personally, I'd be just as happy with a decent sleep but he's very persuasive, is Reg.'

Will rolled over on to his front. 'Come on, race you to the shore!' The two swimmers gained momentum as they tried to outpace each other, finally struggling, exhausted and laughing, on to the sand.

As good as his word, Reggie, who was a member of the sporting club, wangled an entrance for his crewmates. Fred was unimpressed.

'What d' you call this, some pansies' paradise? Why are they knocking hell out of those horses?' His broad Australian accent carried across the subdued tones of the palm-fringed bar, causing one or two pretty girls to look up in amusement. They were immaculately clad, and could have stepped out from a Parisian couturier. Will supposed them to be members of the British expatriate community in the city, stolidly clinging to the pre-war customs of the upper classes.

'They're playing polo, Fred, and you'd better shut up, or you'll be thrown out!' Arthur said.

'OK, just line me up a beer and I'll go and see if any of these nice sheilas would like a chat!' Fred was undaunted, and to the mutual surprise of his friends, sat himself down beside the girls without ado. They were all soon sharing one of Fred's jokes, risqué as it was likely to be, and Arthur shook his head in amusement.

'Don't tell me Fred's going to have more luck in here than in his usual dives!'

'I wouldn't count it out!' Dick observed the pretty blonde incline her head towards Fred in a manner that suggested more than a passing interest.

'Whatever would a beauty like that see in an uncouth chappie like him?' Reggie said.

Will sighed. 'Best not ask, Reg. Now I've spied some nice little tennis courts out there, and I wouldn't mind a hit-around. Anyone join me?'

Kitted out in club whites, he and Arthur had a decent singles match. The ball pinged against the catgut, but the noise was so evocative of home that Will felt a constriction in his chest, that sudden wrench from all that was familiar and loved. Tennis had been a favourite of his at school, though he had never played it under such a dazzling sun. He beat Arthur 6-4, 7-5, before they abandoned it for the bar.

Fred was nowhere to be seen.

'He'll have to look after himself.' Reggie had no intention of waiting any longer. 'What say we go to the flicks? Anyone fancy *The Thin Man*?'

'Not personally, Reg, but lead on!'

4

'I thought I'd died and gone to heaven!' Fred said. 'What's more, she's going to see me again!'

'I shouldn't count your chickens, old chap,' Reggie cut in. 'Word has it we'll be back at the landing ground the day after tomorrow!'

Fred groaned loudly. 'Strewth, there's no peace for the wicked, is there? I'd rather be off to Benghazi with this lot, at least I might live to tell the tale!'

The few members of Number 70 Squadron left in the bar were making enough noise to compensate for their absent colleagues. The bombing raids had now extended beyond the mail run to include the transport and supply road from El Adem to Gazala, and there were constant sorties in direct support of the troops on the ground.

'What's that, not enjoying your special duties?' Max Norton joined them. 'I can't promise any more fun with us, I'm sorry to say!'

His navigator nodded in agreement. 'He's right, you should try mine laying in that harbour! God knows how we got out of that last op in one piece! Four of us Wimpys, flying in to drop the mines at five hundred feet, while another four stooge around low over the target to draw the searchlights and the ack-ack fire. Believe me, lads, it's no picnic out there, you're better off where you are!'

Vic said nothing, for they were all facing impossible odds. Despite the fact that the Eighth Army seemed to be inching its way forward, and Rommel retreating to a defensive position at Gazala, there would be no let-up for any of the Wellington squadrons in Egypt. Simpson had privately shared with him his misgivings over the jamming operations, but there was no saying how much longer they would have to keep them up.

There was a sudden commotion outside, causing them to put down their glasses and wander to the entrance.

'What's going on?' Dick asked an adjutant, whose colleague was running towards one of the Wellingtons parked at dispersal. It was pitch black outside, and very difficult to make out the shadowy figures.

'It's Flight Lieutenant Finlay, sir, we've orders to escort him from the turret of the plane!'

'What's he doing in there, all by himself?' Vic said. 'They're not on ops tonight, it's going nowhere!'

'I know, sir, it seems he's refusing to get out!'

'Why's he doing that?' Will said, but the adjutant seemed as nonplussed as they were.

'We'll come with you, make sure he's OK.' They both set out towards the plane, leaving the others to return to the bar.

Even in the dark, they knew every feature of the Wellington, and found Finlay sitting in the rear turret, hunched over, and seemingly oblivious to their presence.

'What's up, old chap?' Will's voice was calm. He sensed that this might take some time.

'I'm waiting for take-off!' Finlay sounded determined. 'I told the CO I'd be on ops tonight, detailed myself for this one. He hadn't crewed me up, silly bugger!'

Will looked out into the blackness beyond the Perspex. 'How long are you planning to wait?'

'As long as it takes! I'm all ready, the others'll be along in a bit!' Finlay resumed his position, checking the Browning guns with absorption.

Looking back at Vic with an expression of concern, Will continued, 'What say you come with us for a beer until they're ready?'

Finlay's voice was firm. 'I can't – they might go without me. I told the CO I'm staying here, he can take a running jump!' He tried to close the rear turret doors behind him.

Vic moved to stop him. 'Come on, old chap, let's get you out of here and sort it out later.'

'I don't trust any of you! Now piss off and leave me alone, I'm just waiting for the pilot!' Finlay's voice was starting to rise, and Will motioned to Vic to retreat. The adjutant was observing uneasily from the belly of the plane, holding on to one of the struts as though in need of support.

'We've orders to arrest him if he won't come quietly, sir,' he whispered.

Will shook his head. 'Would you all mind leaving the plane? I'm sure Finlay will come with me in a bit. He's just not ready yet, don't push him!'

'Look, see this.' Will moved closer to Finlay, and took Honor's picture out of his breast pocket, where it always lay. He could think of no other way to divert him. 'It's my girlfriend,' he added softly.

Finlay was quiet, scrutinising the little photograph of Honor, smiling in her nurse's uniform. 'She's pretty,' he pronounced. 'But I'd better just check the ammo…'

Will continued patiently, 'Her name's Honor. What about you, have you got a sweetheart back home?'

Behind the fixed eyes, there was a momentary flash of recognition, followed by a long pause.

'Well?' prompted Will.

Finlay drew a deep breath. 'I have, as a matter of fact.' He lapsed into himself once more.

'They'll be worrying about us, I suppose,' Will said, putting the photo safely away in his pocket once more. 'Pity we can't tell them what it's really like, they'd never stop fretting, would they?' It was his turn to pause. 'I hear you're a first-rate pilot, Finlay.'

The latter was true: the man was known for his bravery, and had extricated his crew from some tricky situations over Benghazi.

'That's a joke, isn't it! They trust me, you see, think I can bring them home! "We're all right with old Finlay, he's a lucky one!" Well I'm not, and we're all going to die.' Finlay polished the gun casing assiduously with his handkerchief while he spoke.

'At least they believe in you,' Will said, then he held the long silence that ensued.

'They bloody well shouldn't, that's why I'd be better off back here! Take a potshot at Jerry, not my fault if he blasts us out of the sky!'

Will removed Finlay's hand from the guns. 'Come on, old chap,' he said.

The flight lieutenant stood up, his expression truculent. 'All right, I'll come with you, but only for a bit.' He swung his way backwards through the rear turret doors. 'What are all these stupid buggers doing here?'

5

In the reeds at the side of the lake, a large white ibis poked its curved black beak into the mud. It was the sacred bird of Egypt, herald of the flood and symbol of the god Thoth, the master of time, but Arthur hardly noticed it. He sat on the jetty, watching the sun rise and turning over the flimsy telegram in his hands. There was little point in reading the stark message again; the capital letters had already spelled out the inevitable.

He gazed across the lake, remembering the soft touch of her cheek upon his, the anxious eyes which followed his every move, the enveloping certainty of his mother's love. How could it be that she had left his life, never to return?

His would be the second plane to take off, and there was no escaping the day. He rose, putting the telegram in his pocket, and turned towards dispersal, a solitary figure orphaned in time.

He did not come into view before Will was climbing the ladder with his crew in the early dawn, ready for the return flight to LG 104.

'So what happened to Finlay?' Vic sat down and began to check the controls before take-off. They would be first on the runway, which looked in better condition than of late.

'They sent him off to HQ Middle East, to go in front of a medical board,' Will answered, pulling down his seat. 'Waste of a damn good pilot, if you ask me. Who's to say he's barmy? If you ask me, he's probably the sanest bloke around. He just reckons we're all doomed, now that's not crazy, is it?'

'Hardly,' Vic replied, his usual guard down. He did not underestimate the challenge ahead: they would soon be back on an interminable jamming sortie while the Italian Regia Aeronautica threw all it could at them.

He continued mechanically, 'OK, all present and correct?' as the crew answered in turn. In fact, they were all unsettled by their stint away, which for Ted Baines, had merely felt like a stay of execution. Still, he had written to his wife again, telling her he loved her, and would be back as soon as he could. Best that she did not know how he really felt, and besides, such sentiments would not pass the censors.

Despite their joint sense of foreboding, the desert looked strangely beautiful that morning. The recent storms had settled, and the air was clear as they charted their way across a landscape of biblical design. The sand was dappled by the early morning sun, like gentle waves in a never-ending sea.

F for Freddie had been the first to take off, followed by the two replacement Wellingtons, Arthur in Q for Queenie and Screwball in T for Tommy. Quite how the ground crew had managed to refit them in time was beyond belief, but it had clearly involved some creative engineering, and of the three, only F for Freddie had the original jamming equipment. That meant that only two of the prototype Winston's Wellingtons could be put to their original use.

As he watched them land expertly on the barren desert landing strip, Simpson knew it would be their last effort in this operation. Unless they could be provided with newly kitted planes from England, the jamming would be off. It was a simple equation – two Wellingtons could not take on the retreating German tank army. Rommel looked set to dig himself in at El Agheila but that would merely allow him to regroup before his next offensive.

'Decent rest, Flight?' he asked Vic as he reported to his tent. Hardly waiting for a reply, he added, 'You'll not be here long, I'm afraid, I want you back at LG 75 tomorrow for ops.'

Vic nodded. 'How's it going, sir?' He could sense the exhaustion of the older man; a note of fatality had crept into his voice.

'Not too bad,' Simpson replied, 'unless you start counting the Army losses…'

'Do we know the scale of it?' Vic wished they had more regular briefings about the progress of Crusader; at least it would put their efforts in context.

Simpson wiped his brow. The daytime temperatures were still stifling, even in the winter, and the flies never let up. 'Thousands lost, I reckon, about the same on both sides. And what for, Willis? Some poxy bit of desert!'

Vic looked at the canvas matting on the floor while his superior collected himself. 'Sorry,' Simpson said, 'damn place gets to you!'

'Not at all, sir,' Vic replied. Then cautiously, 'Maybe you should have a spot of leave?'

'No can do, not while this show's still on the road.' His voice took on his usual authoritarian tone. 'I'll want to see the chaps at briefing, 1800 hours.' He turned to his maps.

As before, the crew were unimpressed by the accommodation.

'There's no bloody room in the tents!' Snowy was even more irritable than the others. 'I need a lie-down, Skip, got a bad headache.'

'He's just been on the binge, I bet,' Reggie said as Snowy left to sleep it off.

But when the man did not appear for briefing Will found him sweating on his bed, listlessly kicking off the clothes. After giving Snowy some water, and feeling his forehead, Will went to report to Vic.

'Not more sickness!' Vic began to wonder if the local diseases were more of a threat than the Luftwaffe. Hoping that the normally stalwart New Zealander would recover soon, he raided the medical supplies for some aspirin.

'What's it likely to be?' He conferred with Reggie, who knew more about the desert ailments than the rest of them.

'Oh, I shouldn't think it's anything too serious,' Reg said breezily. 'You know, the usual, sandfly fever or malaria!'

6th December 1941

Western Desert

Dear You,

I'm just taking a brief moment to write before we go back on ops. You are not to worry, I am perfectly well and seem to have avoided the local bugs apart from 'gyppy tummy', which everyone gets at some time or another. Our wireless operator has just gone down with something nasty, so we're giving him a wide berth!

I was so pleased to have your letter – well done to pass your SRN exams! I am very proud of you, and I hope you like your new job in the N. Staffs. I suppose you'll still be fever nursing there?

It looks as though I'm about to be given my own command, so we've both been promoted! Just finishing off an op here first, usual old stuff stooging around the desert looking for the opposition, who seem to spend most of their time stooging around looking for us!

I keep your photograph in my breast pocket all the time, and think of you endlessly. If I ever get out of this desert, I'll be back by your side in a shot and we'll never be parted again!

Take care of yourself, and write soon.

From Me

6

From the outside, it looked about as unwelcoming as any institution could. There was nothing of architectural note in its red brick facade, constructed by a wealthy benefactor in the last century, as though to emphasise that the relief of suffering would be no lavish undertaking.

Peter drew up in the car, which he had borrowed for the journey, but her first instinct was to stay inside.

'Here we are!' He leaned over as though to take a farewell kiss, but she ducked swiftly and was fumbling with the door.

'Thanks ever so for bringing me!' Honor had no idea where she was supposed to report, but felt that she had spent too much time with Peter already. Initially refusing his offer of a lift, she had conceded on the grounds of practicality but knew that it was wrong. What would Will think? With an unsettling feeling of disloyalty, she waited while Peter handed her the meagre suitcase containing her possessions.

He looked unperturbed by her sudden descent. 'Don't you want me to help you find out where you're meant to go?' he asked kindly. 'Look, you pop into the main office and I'll just draw up here. Let me just make sure you're in the right place.'

As ever, his reason prevailed and she knocked on the glass-windowed door, awkward and apprehensive.

'Yes?' The elderly woman was less than welcoming, looking at her through round pebble glasses.

'Please could you direct me to the nurses' home?' Honor asked politely. 'I have to report for my new job today.'

The woman drew a grey cardigan around her. 'Make-do and mend' was clearly popular in Staffordshire, for the garment looked as though it had been made from the unravelled wool of a previous garment.

'We're not expecting any domestic staff today,' she said censoriously, affecting to check a list on her desk.

Her type was familiar to Honor, who suspected that it would take more than a world war to change the embedded class prejudices of the day. She decided to ignore the remark, which represented something of a milestone given her assertive nature.

'No, I'm sure you're not. If you'd care to check the list of staff nurses, you will no doubt find me on it: Honor Newson.'

The woman sniffed before grudgingly issuing directions for the nurses' home around the corner. Honor thanked her with disarming politeness before going back to the car.

'I'll carry your case round,' Peter said, and was before her as she entered the three-storey building, crafted with the same lack of imagination as the one she had just left.

The nurses' home had the traditional smell of polish and disinfectant, conspiring to make her even more unsettled than before. She had become so accustomed to their Nissen hut, which despite its privations was an oasis of security compared to this. How would she ever make friends again, and in particular, how was she going to manage without Addie? She wished she shared Addie's quiet confidence about her future; perhaps she should have joined the QAs too. Anything would be better than this!

A tall, frizzy-haired girl was coming down the stairs, interested in the sight of Peter, as men were strictly forbidden in the home. She paused.

'Can I help?'

It would have been difficult to say whether her charm was laid on for Peter's benefit, but Honor was relieved to find that Rosie, having introduced herself, appeared willing to take her under her wing. Rosie watched interestedly as the newcomer said goodbye to the man, not very affectionately to her mind, then showed her up the wooden stairs to her room.

Once there, Rosie said. 'So who's he? Your sweetheart? Seems a nice bloke…'

'He's not – I mean, he is, well, he's a nice bloke but he's not my boyfriend.' Honor's confusion was highly entertaining to Rosie, who had been hoping for a diversion. She had arrived the previous day, and found the nurses' home a cheerless place.

'OK, you can tell me all about it later. That's your bed, I'm in the one over there. Tea is at six, and we all have to report to our wards at 7am sharp. The lists are downstairs.' Rosie flung herself upon the bed opposite. She looked a fraction too long for it, the sort of girl who would have been a good hockey player, cruising up and down the pitch with leggy ease. 'Where've you come from?'

They were soon deep in conversation, both pleased to find a kindred spirit. Honor learned that Rosie, also a newly qualified SRN, lived in Liverpool with a large and apparently exuberant family, of whom she spoke fondly. She was the eldest of five, and talked most about her brother Jack, who was in the Navy, a second lieutenant on the freezing Murmansk convoys.

'Isn't it awful, worrying that you might never see them again?' Rosie said, waiting for some confidences in return.

Not ready to share the details of her private life, Honor nodded in agreement. She had no intention of telling Rosie about Will yet, but Rosie was not one for giving up so easily.

'So, what about the chap who brought you?' She offered her an apple from her bag, which Honor took; she was hungry, as always, and it was a long time since her lunch of beef paste sandwiches and weak tea.

'He's not my boyfriend, you know,' Honor replied. 'That's Peter, one of the doctors in my last hospital. He's just a friend, honestly!'

'Sure he is, that's why he looks at you like that!' Rosie's mind was made up: there was a nice little romance going on, which was hardly surprising, given Honor's undeniably good looks.

'Come on then, your turn, who's the man in your life?' Honor said.

'There isn't one!' Rosie was firm. 'It's all everyone thinks about, but not me. I've got more sense, anyway, with four younger brothers I can tell you I've got no illusions about boys. Who needs them, anyway? I've enough bother worrying about Jack.' She crunched her apple core, before abruptly changing the subject.

'They say Russia's going to fall, you know.'

'Yes, I heard.' Honor had spent much of the journey discussing it with Peter. The German troops were agonisingly close to Moscow, and it seemed that nothing short of a miracle could stop them now. Even Peter, with his constant references to the historical resilience of the Russian race, was deeply pessimistic about the situation.

'Don't like to think where that'll leave us, do you? Come on, I think I heard the dinner bell, I only hope it's not as awful as last night!'

7

The table was a constant buzz of chatter. Rosie darted a smile at Honor, which she shyly returned, listening to the snippets of conversation around her. One of them, conducted by a uniformed staff nurse opposite, drew her attention.

'Sister thinks it might be a typhoid case, and we're barrier nursing as though it is.' Moira, whose information it was, looked self-important with her news, but one of the older nurses interrupted.

'I only hope it's a false alarm, Nurse. Perhaps you shouldn't spread rumours until you're sure of the facts. The last thing any of us want to see is a typhoid outbreak. I can remember the last one, and I assure you, it's no gossiping matter!'

Blushing, Moira sat back in her seat. 'I was only repeating what Sister said.'

'Maybe,' the nurse answered, her tone still one of reproof, 'but if I know Sister Duncan on Ward 2, she won't thank you for sharing it!'

Rosie raised her eyebrows. There was always the familiar hierarchy, no matter in which institution you arrived. She had long since decided that when she became a matron, as she fully intended to do, she would sweep it all away and introduce a more benevolent regime. Why should the younger nurses be treated with such disdain? Not to mention the poor probationers, whose lives seemed hardly worth living, worked to death for a paltry wage. Anyway, she was a staff nurse now, like her new friend Honor, both with distinctive uniforms and hopefully a little more standing.

They had already tried on the purple-striped fitted dresses, with starched collar and cuffs, and the white bibbed apron and cap. For her part, Honor could hardly believe she was allowed to wear it, but Rosie was more phlegmatic. She did not intend to stop there; it would be the dark blue sister's dress for her next.

Fatigued with the effort of this new environment, Honor longed for bed, however uncomfortable it might be. The rooms upstairs would be freezing, and she feared the return of her chilblains.

Rosie forestalled her. 'Want to pop out for a bit?' she suggested. 'I could do with a breather, and we can work out where we are.'

'We haven't got a pass,' Honor protested, but Rosie, with quiet authority, was having none of it.

'Come on, we're free agents until the morning, get your coat!' she ordered, instantly reminding Honor of Beatie when she had first met her, determined and rebellious.

It hardly proved worth the trouble, for the streets of Stoke adjacent to the hospital were deserted and dark. Even if there had been a pub within striking distance, Honor would have been reluctant to go in. Their footsteps slowed as their anticipation of the locality evaporated, and chatting desultorily, they soon found themselves outside the hospital again.

'Let's hope it's not all like that!' Rosie said, as at last, Honor turned in to her cold bed and wriggled her toes to keep the circulation moving.

The six o'clock alarm bell woke her with start, and the two young women negotiated their way around the glacial bedroom, readying themselves for a long day.

Honor had looked at the ward list the night before. She was down for Ward 2, men's medical, and it was there that she walked, after a breakfast of lukewarm porridge, to report to Sister Duncan. She smoothed down her white apron as she entered, and made sure her cap was on straight.

It would hardly have been fair to describe Sister Duncan as well upholstered, but her bosom seemed to merge imperceptibly with her waistline without any intervening zone. Her long white headdress completed the line as it flowed down her back, and her greying hair was primly parted.

Given long years of experience, she reckoned to sum up a nurse in the first few minutes. Looking Honor up and down, she settled on her face and saw the unmistakeable signs of an intelligent mind. Having trained at St Thomas' Hospital herself, she valued intelligence highly, though she was not about to let this young woman know that.

'Right, I want you specialling two of our patients in isolation,' Sister Duncan said. 'You'll need to gown up, strict barrier nursing, all soiled linen to the autoclave, and effluent in the metal drums. Nurse Kratz will show you the ropes.'

So Moira had been right: these must be the typhoid cases. Honor had not nursed the condition before, but had memorised all the facts for her exam. If she remembered rightly, this was the typical month for an outbreak and she wondered if the Medical Officer of Health had tracked down the source. Now what could it be: water supply, milk, carriers? She doubted it would be shellfish so far inland, and tried to remember the other possibilities as she entered the cubicle, swathed in a generous gown.

'Oh, good.' The nurse at the side of the bed greeted her. She spoke in a strange accent, which was difficult to place. 'We need to turn him, can you take the other side? Gently now, we have to do it very slowly.'

Honor leant to help her shift the feverish man towards her.

'Steady now, Charlie!' Honor registered the man's distended abdomen and extreme pallor.

'Let's get the bed bath done too,' the nurse continued. 'I'm Lotte, by the way. Who are you?'

Honor's experience of foreign languages was remote, or she would have recognised the German accent.

Their patient was clearly too ill to notice as Honor introduced herself, but they continued bathing him efficiently, working together well.

'Those are the rose spots.' Lotte pointed out a few light spots over Charlie's abdomen. 'We have to mark them, because they do not stay.' As soon as the bed bath was finished, she took a pen and drew around the edges of the spots.

'Have you nursed typhoid before?' Lotte asked, absorbed in her demarcation of the rash. Honor shook her head.

'Well.' She pronounced the word as 'Vell'. 'Strictly speaking, we are not sure yet, but Sister Duncan thinks it is, and that is good enough for me. Still, we wait for the results first. I'll look after you, don't look so worried!'

Lotte proved herself to be a competent, unfussy tutor. She could not have been much older than Honor, but seemed serious beyond her years, and her dark eyes were concentrated on her tasks. She took the temperature chart from the end of the bed.

'See, it is a stepladder, up and up,' she said, pointing out the line denoting the spiky rise during the first phase. 'He does not have diarrhoea yet,' she explained, and Honor remembered that the spots precede the copious 'pea soup' stools, which they would have to dispose of carefully in Izal drums. She looked at the chart again – that was it, day seven, he must be going into the second stage.

'Charlie works on a farm. Usually he is strong, but not so now, Charlie?'

The man shook his head weakly. He would have been a big chap, in health, but he lay inert and sleepy.

'Can you use the bottle for me, please?' Lotte raised the bedclothes. The young women were now no strangers to the male anatomy, and dealt with it as a matter of course. 'We have to check the urine, you know,' she said. She took the bottle and moved out of earshot. 'It is not so good from now on,' she whispered. 'That is when we lose them, in the second week.'

'How do you know so much about it?' Honor asked, and was met by a direct look from the deep eyes.

'I see it before, back home in Austria,' Lotte replied. 'That is when I was training to be a doctor.' Then, as quickly as she had divulged the confidence, she retreated into her discourse on the progress of the disease.

Honor held her peace. She would hear the full story by and by. Like many a wartime confidence, it would unravel in stages: the 'make-do and mend' of the mind.

8

Lotte Kratz, as she divulged during the course of that first week nursing the typhoid cases, was a Jewish refugee from Austria.

'I came as one of the nurses with the Kindertransport,' she said, as though Honor would understand. Knowing nothing about the trains taking children out of Nazi Germany, Honor learnt in silence of Lotte's journey via Berlin, with just a small leather case, looking after children separated from their parents, waving the long goodbye for security in another country. Lotte had been one of only three nurses accompanying the transport; her Aunt Metta had put her on the train the day after the Gestapo took her parents. Shocked by the spiralling downturn of events, and haunted by the sight of her distraught mother, she had done as Metta ordered her, and through the offices of the Society of Friends, she had finally finished up here, in Stoke.

'But first, I had to show I can learn English, well enough to work,' she added. Lotte had been in the third year of her medical training in Austria, but that would be out of the question in England: firstly, she, like most refugees, was penniless, and secondly few woman were gaining admission to medical school in 1939. Homeless and disorientated, she had settled for nurse training, though even then was not accepted by the London teaching hospitals. It was only the acute shortage of nurses in the deepening grip of war that led to an opening for her, at first in Birmingham, at the Children's Hospital.

Her fortitude astounded Honor. Lotte might never see her parents again, and had no clue what had become of them, but she strove to build a new life, always under the watchful eye of the authorities, who could class her as an enemy alien on a whim.

'You're so brave, Lotte.' They were sitting outside on a bench in the garden under the cold winter sun.

'No, not brave. The ones who are left behind are so much braver than I. You see, we know Hitler is a bad man, but now, I think, there is no hope, unless your country can defeat him. In Austria, our neighbours, who we had known so well, stood and watched as the Gestapo led my mother and father away. Just because they were Jews! Not one person tried to stop them, not one!'

Lotte's stoicism failed her, and she buried her head in her hands, allowing Honor to put her arm around her thin shoulders.

'Come on, you can't bottle it up all the time. I don't know how you keep going, after all that!'

The spasm of tears passed, and Lotte stood up, wiping her eyes. 'We have no choice in life, you know, but to carry on. Maybe I will see my mother and father again one day – what would they expect of me?'

The two women walked back to the ward, linking their arms down the cinder path.

If Sister Duncan knew of Lotte's past, she considered it irrelevant, for all that mattered to her was that the young woman was a hard-working nurse. She did not subscribe to the view that all Germans were the enemy, for as far as she was concerned, civilians were dragged into war against their will.

She noticed the two nurses coming in together from their morning break, and hoped that their future would not be blighted, like hers had been during the Great War. Sister Duncan had lost her young fiancé in the grim mud of Flanders, like so many of their generation. After the conflict was over, there were so few men around that she had given up hope of the joys of love and motherhood, and had become increasingly isolated in the world of nursing. Ironically, she had only trained in the first place in order to be sent to France, and thus a step closer to her young man. But that was when she was nineteen and handsome, a fiery girl of spirit, and not an ageing sister on a medical ward.

She called them into her office. 'The blood cultures have confirmed it's enteric fever. You must both be very vigilant of cross-infection, scrub your hands regularly and watch out for complications in your two patients. I fear we may have more, depending on the source, but let's hope it's localised. Have you been inoculated?'

Fortunately, Honor had received the new TAB vaccine when a supply had come into Groby Road that summer, but Lotte shook her head.

'I'll see what I can do.' Sister dismissed them with a nod.

Relying on Lotte's superior knowledge, and learning by her side, Honor gradually accustomed herself to the work. They both spent much of the day in the cubicles, stripping sheets, emptying bedpans filled with a pale yellow liquid stool streaked with blood and mucus, and administering as much glucose drink as their patients could be encouraged to take. The temperature responded to tepid sponging, and they were in the middle of this routine activity several days later when Charlie gasped.

'Oh, I've such a pain, Nurse!' His face was beaded with sweat.

'Where does it hurt?' Lotte took his pulse.

Charlie pointed to his tummy. 'Just here!'

Lotte drew back the bedclothes and gently palpated his abdomen, causing him to groan softly. That was traditionally the doctor's job, but Lotte's reaction was automatic.

'OK, try and breathe slowly, I'm going to see Sister.' She raised her eyebrows at Honor, washed her hands and de-gowned before leaving the cubicle.

Given the ashen appearance of her charge, Honor decided to take his blood pressure but was interrupted by the return of Lotte, not with Sister, but one of the house physicians who had been attending the morning round. He examined Charlie with no less care than Lotte, then drew the nurses to one side.

'You're right, it looks like a perf,' he said. 'How did you know?'

'She trained as a doctor before,' Honor put in, proud of her friend's accomplishments.

Dr Black looked at Lotte in surprise. He had noticed her odd accent but had never made further enquiries as to her background. Exhausted as he was by the constant work and lack of sleep, with his big round eyes, he resembled a nocturnal creature who has been startled by the light.

'Well, good for you,' he said. 'I'll go back and tell the consultant, then I expect one of the surgeons had better see him. Can you prepare a drip set for me?'

'At least they didn't all troop in!' Honor remembered those awful ward rounds, with poor Peter being hounded all the time. 'And what's a perf?'

Lotte was a model of clarity. 'We're safe, they don't like to come in the cubicle, for fear they all get it! And a perf,' she added, lowering her voice, 'is a little hole in the bowel, that will make Charlie very sick, until they find it and sew it up!'

9

During the course of the next week, two more cases were admitted, both from the same rural area, and Sister Duncan began to worry that this was the start of a full-blown epidemic. Thanks to prompt intervention by the surgeons, Charlie had survived one of the most serious complications, but one of the new admissions, a local farmer, was still in a critical state after a sudden bowel haemorrhage. Once again, Lotte's medical knowledge had come to the fore as she had immediately reacted to his collapse, sending Honor running for the doctor and putting up a drip herself when a doctor could not be immediately found.

Not that such an intervention by a nurse could be condoned, even if it was life-saving, and Sister Duncan took her to one side when the situation was under control, and the blood transfusion was flowing drop by precious drop into the vein.

'Nurse Kratz, it's not your job to put up a drip, you know.' Her voice was firm, but not unkind.

'I know, Sister, but Mr Cole was going to die! We could not find the doctor! I cannot stand and watch him bleed to death when I can save his life, it is against the Hippocratic oath!'

Sister Duncan shook her head. 'Nurses do not take the Hippocratic oath, and you must remember you are not a doctor here, nor will you ever be one.' She paused, registering the note of anguish on the girl's face. 'Still, I know what you did was motivated by the right reasons, and I won't be making a report. Just be careful!'

Whether it was this reprimand, or just her long struggle against the odds, Honor perceived a light had gone out in Lotte's world.

'What's the matter with her?' Dr Black said, as he checked Charlie's wound site. Lotte had left to collect some more dressings.

'She thinks you're telling her off,' Honor replied.

'Me? Not at all, I think she's jolly plucky – look how she saved that chap's life!' He was indignant, failing to appreciate the niceties of nursing rules and regulations. 'Just you tell her so from me!'

Dr Percival Black, Percy to his family and very few friends, thought he would never understand senior nurses. Here was a clever little refugee, already trained as a doctor, and all they could do was tear her off a strip when she took some initiative. The haemorrhage was such that every second counted, so she could hardly go and seek approval first. Perhaps they would have liked her to fill in a few forms while the man exsanguinated in front of her eyes!

'I'll try,' Honor said, 'but she just thinks everyone's against her.'

Lotte did not appear for supper that evening, and when Honor went to find her, she was lying on her bed gazing at the wall.

'Lotte, what's up?' Honor sat down on her bed. 'You mustn't take on so!' She reached for her hand, and noticed it was sweaty.

'It's not that,' Lotte replied softly. 'I don't feel so good.' Her normally animated dark eyes were dull.

Honor felt her forehead – there could be no doubt about it, Lotte was feverish.

'Did you have the vaccine, Lotte?' she asked quickly.

Lotte shook her head. 'They could not get it yet, I think Sister said it would be in later this week.'

'Drink some water, I'm going to fetch Home Sister.' As Honor ran down the stairs, there was only one thought in her mind.

Home Sister, who was in charge of their welfare, was equally worried, and before the evening was out, Lotte had been admitted to the women's medical ward.

'Can I come and see her?' Honor said, but the ward sister was adamant.

'Not until tomorrow, let's get her sorted out. It'll be strict barrier nursing until we know what she's got.'

Honor walked slowly back to the nursing home. The only consolation was that she had seen Dr Black on his way to the ward so she knew Lotte would be in sympathetic hands. The nurses were all used to the occupational hazards of their job, and at any one time, several might be in sickbay, but it would usually be with an infected finger or whitlow, or a nasty bout of flu.

Contracting typhoid was quite another matter, and all the worse for Lotte in a strange country with no family or friends to look out for her.

Despite Rosie's attempts at reassurance, Honor woke early the next morning and, with time to spare, hastened over to the ward. She met Percy on his way out.

'How is she?' she said.

Percy looked even more exhausted than ever, having spent much of the night working.

'Not so good,' he said grimly. 'She must have been feeling rotten for days, her temp is right up and she's already got rose spots. Why the hell didn't they make sure she was vaccinated? It's just not good enough, Honor!'

She started at the use of her Christian name, but Percy was past social niceties. As far as he was concerned, it was just another example of the incompetence of the nurses in charge – it was positively reckless to allow a nurse on to a typhoid ward without her TAB.

'Do you know anything about her family?' he said. 'Can they be contacted?'

Honor looked at him in dismay. 'Her close relatives were taken by the Gestapo – they're Jewish, you know. I think she has an aunt but goodness knows where! She's on her own, I'm afraid.'

Percy passed a hand over his brow. 'Poor little thing, I didn't know.' Then he added, without conviction, 'We must hope for the best then, mustn't we?'

10

She came off duty at eight o'clock, but after forcing down an unappetising meal of potato pie, Honor returned to Lotte's side. Ward Sister allowed her in this time, as there now seemed little doubt about the diagnosis, and she sat with her, fully gowned, while the night nurses tepid-sponged her. Lotte was almost unrousable, her cheeks were flushed, and she did not respond to Honor at all.

Percy looked in on his evening round.

'She looks dreadful!' Honor felt desperate for his opinion, for as far as she could see, Lotte was deteriorating in front of her eyes.

Percy looked at her charts, the night nurses fluttering around him like moths at a flame, Lotte's illness thus elevated by the arrival of a doctor. Having examined the prostrate girl carefully, he beckoned to them to withdraw.

'She's sinking into a typhoid state,' he said firmly. 'I'm going to see if I can get hold of some Felix's Vi-serum, I don't give much for her chances otherwise. She's not putting up any fight! Now listen, you two, I want you to push oral fluids, raise the foot of the bed, and I'll be back as soon as I can.

Honor, you can stay here for a bit but I don't want you nursing her, it's not your job tonight.'

He took off his gown, washed his hands, and strode out of the cubicle.

The night nurses looked at each other meaningfully and continued with their tasks, with perceptibly more energy than before.

Lotte was plucking at the bedclothes. 'Mutti!' she shouted, 'Mutti, *wo bist du*?'

'Shush, Lotte, please!' Honor held her hand helplessly, hearing the German accent thicken as the fever worsened. '*Vater, ich will an dich schauen*!'

One of the nurses shook her head. 'I didn't know we had Germans on the ward!'

It was nearly midnight when Percy returned, bearing a vial of the precious serum.

'Where did you get it?' Honor knew that it was like gold dust, and had never seen it used. She had learned all about it – the antibodies to the 'Vi' antigen of the bacillus, if she remembered rightly.

'I had to wake up the pharmacist, then bully him to death!' he replied. 'I told him she would die if he didn't give it to me!'

Honor's voice sounded small. 'Is that true?'

He did not meet her eyes, but his answer was direct. 'I'm afraid so.' He chivvied the nurses again, then turned back to Honor.

'You really must go and get some rest now, they'll look after her, and there's nothing you can do.' He raised his finger in anticipation of her reply. 'No, Honor, you must go, I insist!'

There was no repose for her in her cold bed that night, and she dreamt of pursuit, jackbooted Nazis in SS uniforms searching for her, with no hope of escape. Eventually dropping off to sleep at dawn, she awoke with a start, later than usual, to be told by Rosie that Lotte was alive and that Pearl Harbor had been bombed by the Japanese.

11

The wireless crackled as Matron fiddled with the tuning, eventually locating the BBC news. It was Monday morning, December 8th

1941, and she had made an unprecedented appearance in the nurses' home before breakfast, as though to emphasise the importance of the occasion. There could be no doubt about it: the Japanese navy had struck the main base of the United States Pacific Fleet the day before. Taking the Americans completely by surprise, waves of dive-bombers had strafed the port, battleships and airfields, leaving the burning wreckage of the fleet below.

'Does that mean the Americans will join the war now, Matron?' Rosie asked. She, like the other nurses, was muddled as to the geography, and they later took recourse to a world map to work out how the Japanese could have sailed across the Pacific Ocean to pull off such an audacious plan.

'I'm sure it will, Staff Nurse. President Roosevelt isn't going to like that one little bit. He's talking to the nation later on.' Matron looked smug – after all, it was what they had all been waiting for: a reason to bring the USA in as their allies, united in their struggle against Germany, and now Japan too.

'So, it's not just Europe anymore?'

'No, I'm afraid not, and I can tell you, the Japanese aren't likely to stop there. We will hear what Mr Churchill has to say at nine o'clock tonight. Now, that's enough delay, off to your wards!'

Honor was not there to hear Matron's views about the world situation. For her, Lotte took precedence, and she sped over to women's medical to find the night nurses in her cubicle going off duty.

One glance at Lotte was enough to tell her that she had survived the crisis. She was awake, lying flat on the raised bed, but squeezed her hand as Honor took it, and gave her a weak smile.

'Thank goodness you're all right!' Honor sat down beside her, and stroked Lotte's forehead, no longer hot and sweaty, but pleasantly cool to the touch.

'Have I been that ill?' Lotte's voice was no more than a whisper.

'You have, but you're getting better now.' Honor looked up as Percy entered the cubicle. He nodded appraisingly at Lotte, and looked at her chart before examining her carefully.

'I'll tell the nurses to keep going with the serum,' he concluded. 'She'll need it for the next two days. Looks as though it did the trick, anyway.'

'You saved her life,' Honor said, but he shrugged it off.

'That's my job, isn't it?'

They left the cubicle together, and she waited while he gave his instructions to the day staff.

'I must get off to Ward 2.' Honor was late for her shift, but for once, was prepared to face Sister Duncan's disapproval.

'OK, I'll be on the round later. Did anyone tell you the news?'

It was a day of curious twists and turns. Far from being cross, Sister Duncan seemed positively relieved to hear that Nurse Kratz was improving. Her conscience had been pricking her – that poor girl had reported for duty even when she was coming down with typhoid fever. Without friends and family, Kratz had just soldiered on. It was just as well Nurse Newson had taken the trouble to look after her, for no one else had bothered. According to Night Sister, Dr Black had risen to the challenge too, procuring the precious serum and refusing to let his patient die.

Sister Duncan was honest enough to admit when she was in the wrong. She should have made more of a fuss about the delayed vaccine, and she should have realised the girl was ill. She must not let compassion desert her, she resolved, as she readied herself for the morning ward round, running her finger along a bedrail to make sure not a speck of dust remained.

Too worried about Lotte to take in world events, it was not until the following evening that Honor had a chance to catch up on the news, though the hospital was buzzing with it. When she finally heard the Prime Minister's sonorous voice, reporting the sinking of the *Prince of Wales* and *Repulse* off Singapore by the Japs, she began to wonder if there was any arena of the war that was going their way. Avid for news from North Africa, she was disheartened that each advance was followed by a retreat, and wary of the recent Eighth Army push into Libya. Still, on another front, at least the Russians were fighting back, helped by a bitter winter for which the Germans were apparently unprepared.

The Giant Awakes! The newspaper headline summed it up for them: America was in the war at last. The question that now exercised them was how many more years it would last. For Honor, all that mattered was that as long as it took, Will would survive, and they would be together again.

Rosie smiled at her across the supper table. 'You look whacked! How's Lotte?'

Honor finished her mouthful of rabbit pie, which tasted rather better than usual. Imagine being able to eat proper food again, without rationing –

it was almost inconceivable! She had quite forgotten what an orange tasted like, it was so long since one passed her lips.

'She's looking much better, the serum's worked and she's managing a light diet!'

Lotte's progress appeared almost miraculous to Honor, and she was full of gratitude to Percy, who was frequently to be found at his patient's side. Much to the nurses' consternation, he would read to her from German books, his gentle voice surprisingly fluent.

'Where did you learn it?' Honor asked.

'My family have German friends in Heidelberg,' he said. 'I used to go youth hostelling in the Black Forest with them. In the *Jugendherberge*,' he added, for Lotte's benefit, as their eyes met.

'*Der Schwarzwald*!' Lotte said softly. '*Wann werde ich es wieder sehen*?'

12

The two men outside Ward 2 were wearing black homburg hats and dark overcoats. They knocked loudly, as though used to immediate attention.

Honor was in the sluice, separating the soiled linen into the containers of Izal. It was two weeks since Lotte had taken ill, and mercifully she had been the last case of the current epidemic. For her part, Honor never wanted to see another case of typhoid fever as long as she lived, nor ever again to lift those heavy wet sheets across into the strong-smelling caustic drums.

She could hear Sister Duncan's voice as she sealed the lid.

'What precisely is your business with her?' She sounded imperious, and the two men adjusted their posture accordingly. The taller one of the two stepped forward.

'We have reason to believe she is an enemy alien, listed to be interned on the Isle of Man,' he pronounced officiously.

Sister Duncan drew herself up to her full height. 'No nurse of mine is being sent to an internment camp!' She looked at them both with withering contempt. 'Haven't you got anything better to do than chase refugees around the country? Have you any idea what these people have been through? And take your hats off on my ward!'

His colleague removed his homburg before replying. 'It's orders – Miss Kratz has to go.'

'There's only one person gives orders on this ward, and that's me!' Sister Duncan said. 'Now I'll thank you to leave my ward immediately and don't bother to come back!' She strode to the door and held it open.

'This won't be the last you hear of this!'

But Sister slammed the door behind them.

Honor joined her as their figures receded down the corridor. 'Gosh, you gave them what for, Sister!'

'They'll get more than they bargained for if they try to come back!' Sister Duncan said. 'Now, there's no need to worry Nurse Kratz with any of this, she needs all her strength to get well.'

Honor was as good as her word, and Lotte was kept in the dark. Not so Percy, who had heard of it on the hospital grapevine.

'I hear Sister sent them packing!' he said to Honor on their way to women's medical. 'Still, I don't trust officialdom – maybe her convalescence has come at just the right time.'

Having formulated a plan, he broke it to Lotte later. She was sitting propped up on her cushions in bed, looking frail but determined, her dark eyes more striking than ever.

'Where are you sending me?' she asked. 'Can't I stay in sickbay until I'm well enough for work?'

He took her hand, and as if Honor needed any more proof of his growing regard, added, 'You know you can't, Lotte. You'll need some time to regain your strength. I've arranged for you to stay with my mother, she'll look after you.'

'With your mother?' Lotte said. 'Why would your mother want to do that?'

'Because I've asked her to, and she says she will. She's a member of the WVS, you know, runs the local branch, got fingers in all sorts of pies. You're to stay with her in Derbyshire for at least a month, then, when you're better and your tests are clear, you can come back.'

Without waiting for further discussion, he patted her on the shoulder and took his leave.

'Honor?' Lotte looked at her for support. 'Why is he doing this?'

'Dear Lotte, if you haven't worked it out, I'm certainly not going to tell you!' Honor hoped that the combination of the ward sister and the WVS centre organiser would be enough to keep the men in black hats at bay. 'It's all sorted anyway, you're going tomorrow!'

13

The newspaper lay open on a map of the Far East, with big black arrows showing the Japanese advance.

Honor looked at it in consternation, for as far as she could see, there was nothing stopping them. Gratefully accepting a cup of night-time cocoa from Rosie, she sat next to her and tried to fathom it out.

'It says we can't hold Hong Kong, General Maltby will have to surrender,' Rosie said, pointing to the historic British island at the southernmost tip of China. 'And the Japs are landing here, in the Philippines. It's a rout, if you ask me – they'll all be taken as prisoners of war.'

'Can't we fight back?' Honor could not believe that the Japanese army could sweep so conclusively through the peninsula. It was as bad as the German blitzkriegs, whole nations falling before the might of the enemy war machine.

'It doesn't look as though they're making much of a fist of it.' Rosie had friends on a rubber plantation near Singapore, and did not like to think what would become of Lavender, that childhood playmate of hers with the blonde curly hair.

It was a few days before Christmas, and both girls were on duty throughout the season. Not that Honor wanted to be anywhere without Will: her off-duty, once so precious to her, had become almost irrelevant in the absence of his company. Why did he have to be so far away? She envied the sweethearts of the bomber crews in Lincolnshire, returning to these shores in the cold light of dawn, able to spend time together in between ops. Still, she must remember the men who would not make it back, and wondered if Guy and Edek were still alive, or if they had perished, like so many of them, over the Ruhr. She pulled herself together; there was Matt to be visited in the New Year, and she should try and contact her sister Ruth.

'We'll be short-staffed next week, it's not going to be much fun!' Rosie continued. 'Will you be seeing that doctor chappie of yours over Christmas? Peter, that's the one!'

'He's not my "doctor chappie", as you so sweetly put it!' Honor felt she really must disabuse Rosie of such notions, and ventured to explain about Will.

Rosie pinched her cheek by way of reply. 'What, so you've got two sweethearts, have you?!' No amount of denials from Honor would persuade her otherwise. 'It's all right for some!' she teased. 'One overseas, and one at home for a spare!'

Honor shook her head, but gave up the unequal struggle. 'Come on.' She tried to change the subject instead. 'What about a trip to the cinema on our night off? I want to see *Mrs Miniver*, it's Greer Garson, you know.'

'Or maybe a carol service instead?' Rosie said. 'I like singing carols, it's about as close as we'll get to anything festive this year!'

Rosie had her way, and the next evening they took their place in the congregation at the Holy Trinity Church, well wrapped up against the cold, gazing at the beautiful Minton tiles on the floor and the arched stained glass windows. The choir was singing *Today on earth the angels sing* , but it felt as though peace was a long way away.

23rd December 1941
N. Staffs Infirmary, Stoke-on-Trent
Dear You,
I keep wondering how you will be spending Christmas, and I hope you get some time off and a decent meal! I am on duty for the next week but I don't really mind. Perhaps this time next year we'll be together again – who knows, the war might come to an end now the Americans are in it too?

I try to work out from the newspapers what's happening in the desert but it's rather muddling, it swings back and forth so. Still, it looks as though our side has the upper hand at the moment, and I only hope that's true! The papers are full of Libya, but no one here really understands the campaign. On the other hand we are reeling from the news that we are about to lose Hong Kong! Why can't our troops hold out?

I plan to visit Matt again when I have some off-duty. I wonder if you've heard from him at all?

Anyway, I can't send you a card or a present but enclose all my love instead, and hope for happier and safer times in 1942.

Take great care of yourself, I think of you always.
From Me
PS: Many happy returns on the 3rd!

14

Will looked up hopefully when the mail came in, but there was nothing for him. Even the flimsiest of letters would have helped, but he had not heard from her for weeks. Perhaps she was not receiving his letters either, and suffering the same sense of unease.

It would soon be time for briefing, though bad weather had disrupted operations so many times lately, grounding them with blinding rainstorms and reducing the airfields to glutinous mud. They had been abruptly pulled from Operation Jostle at the end of December, and incorporated into 162 Squadron at Shallufa. Still expected to take their part in radio countermeasures, they now carried bombs at the same time as they located and jammed enemy radio installations, but least they had finished with the tanks.

Dick put his head round the mess tent. 'How are y' doing, Skip?' To their joint satisfaction, Dick had ended up as his navigator when he took command of his own Wellington, T for Tommy, in January. 'I said I'd see you in a bloody great bomber one day!' he had reminded him good-naturedly, and their deep friendship grew into an easy working relationship. Screwball had been posted to Malta in the New Year, and Will had inherited a mix of men from other crews. Vic was still around, reliable as ever, usually on reconnaissance work in F for Freddie, which had been patched up more times than any of them could remember. Vic was happy enough, as Griff was back in the navigator's seat, right as rain once more.

'Arthur, you've got some post!' Dick said, taking the letter over to him, but Arthur hardly looked up from his book.

'Come on, show a bit more interest! You're lucky to have one!' Dick pulled up a camp chair next to him.

Arthur took the letter, but did not take his eyes off the book. 'I think I know what it's about.'

'Oh, sorry, old chap!'

Arthur had taken the news of his mother's death very hard. It was more than two months since he had received the telegram, but he felt no respite from her loss. He had confided to Will that his greatest worry now was his father, who was struggling to manage the farm without her.

'I hope to God he doesn't just jack it all in!' Arthur said on receiving the last hastily written note. 'It's my farm too! It's all I'm trained to do, apart from fly bombers, and that's not going to be much use in peacetime, is it?'

Will commiserated with him. It was bad enough trying to survive bombing raids along the enemy supply line, without the spectre of loss at home as well. Unintentionally Arthur's father was threatening his very stability, his home and his farm, at a time when he needed it most.

'Your father must be depressed, or he wouldn't be considering it!' Will said. 'Nobody would give up a farm!'

He privately shared Arthur's dream, the prospect of his own farm. When the war ended, he mused, if he was lucky enough to survive, he would go back to university, finish his course and then borrow the money from his father to buy a farm in Yorkshire.

The young man who entered the tent deferentially was not a member of His Majesty's Forces. He glanced at Dick and put down the water container he had carried in.

'*Grazie*, Carlo.' Dick nodded, bringing a fleeting smile from the dark-complexioned face.

'Can you speak Italian?' Will asked.

'Not really, just a few words, but it's like Latin, you know. Carlo's giving me some lessons when there's nothing better to do. You should join us, never know when it might come in handy!' Dick never lost an opportunity to improve his education, and the truth was that he had scooped all the school prizes in his year, not just in maths, for which he was renowned.

Carlo embarked upon some fast-flowing Italian, which made even Dick look puzzled.

'What's he saying?' Arthur stopped reading his book.

'Something about food, not sure exactly what!'

The Italian prisoners of war lived a contented existence at Shallufa, free to wander from their adjacent camp and to work as orderlies. They appeared to have no desire to escape, believing that the Axis forces would triumph and set them all free soon. They had a reputation for being excellent cooks, and as the men walked past their marquees towards the briefing tent a delicious smell of cooking assailed them.

'I wonder what they're having?' The food in RAF Shallufa was monotonous, despite its location at the top of the Suez Canal, close to fertile land.

'It'll be a damn sight better than we get,' Arthur replied. 'What's the Italian for "Can I come to supper?"'

Benghazi would be on the board again, they reckoned. The strategic supply port had spent only a short time in British hands after Christmas before Rommel had regrouped, surprised them all, and lifted it back. He was now dug in at El Agheila and likely to come up with a counter-strike soon. The pilots, endlessly bombing his supply lines, marvelled at his ability to bounce back from defeat.

'Why didn't we just go after him and finish him off?' Griff had asked. He had spent enough time out of action to follow events closely, and he could not for the life of him understand why the fall of Bardia, Sollum and Barce had not led to an Allied rout of the 'Desert Fox'.

Dick had the answer for him. 'It's all about supply lines, old boy. We go as far as we can in pursuit, like a piece of fully drawn elastic, then grind to a halt, which gives Rommel the opportunity to rearm and strike back. Then he does the same thing, just the other way round. Besides, his tanks are bigger than ours, and that's the truth of it!'

'We'll be going with 37 Squadron, then,' Dick said after briefing. 'To be frank, I'd rather be mine-laying with 221!'

They all reckoned that 221 Squadron, also based at Shallufa, had the plum job. One of three torpedo squadrons, they practised dropping dummy torpedoes in the Suez Bay, aiming for *HMS Abdiel*, which cruised at twenty-five knots in the calm waters below, turning on a sixpence to avoid them. It looked the perfect way to spend the day; even better when the crews were taken on board to see it from the other side.

Not so Benghazi, which would be defended by the usual fierce ack-ack guns and enemy fighters. It would be a flying time of about four hours to target, and they climbed up into the Wellington, Z8905, with a feeling of resignation. It was a freezing but clear night for a change, they were bombed up, and ready to go.

'Everyone OK?' Will's voice came down the intercom. He was the 'daddy' of the crew now, in charge of them all, and at the tender age of twenty-one years was already older then some of the new bods, including Ralph Wiggins, his rear gunner. Ralph was a Geordie, and his accent became almost unintelligible when excited. They had a new wireless operator too, Taffy, a reliable and thickset Welshman who had trained in 109 Squadron and was adept at picking up enemy radar. His second pilot was Arnie, notable in that he was one of the few black airmen in the Western Desert. He was part of the Dominion Air Force, from the Caribbean, and he was given to talk lovingly of his island in the sun, the wonderful women and the food – 'Oh my God, man, that is the place to be!' – so that Ralph planned to join him after the war, and never go back to dull and dark Newcastle, and the steelworks, again.

The crew bantered through take-off, and set course for target, Dick, with his usual precision, having left nothing to chance.

'What's that, Skip?' It was about three hours later when Arnie detected a change in the engine noise. Will glanced quickly at the dials: the port engine was stuttering, and without any further warning, died completely on him. He pressed the starter push switch without response, and cursed under his breath. Every pilot knew there was only one problem with a Wimpy, and that was its single-engine performance. Mercifully his perusal of the main instrument panel confirmed that all else was in working order, so now the overriding question was, could they get home?

'Jettison bombs?' Arnie said.

'Yes, let them go, we'll have to scrub!' Will reached for the bomb control panel. 'Calling all crew, we've a spot of bother with the port engine, I've had to shut it down and we're heading back. I'm about to let the bombs go, lads, and any other stuff we don't need. Taffy, I'll need you pumping oil. Bomb doors open!' Will knew what would happen from here on in. He would have to throttle back the starboard engine, or the Pegasus would overheat, resulting in a dramatic loss of height. They might just limp home, but it was a long way off.

'Dick, any landing grounds nearby?'

'We could try Sidi Barrani, Skip.'

'OK, ask them for a flare path. What's the flying time?'

'About an hour at this speed, it's worth a try!'

Despite their best efforts, and it was taking both pilots' joint strength to hold the aircraft on course, they were still losing height. Encapsulated in a pod of darkness, and listening intently to the engine noise, they flew low over the featureless, barren land.

'Not looking so good, lads, anyone want to bail out?' Will's voice came steadily over the intercom. Although he felt duty bound to stay at the controls, there was no reason to sacrifice his crew. If they wanted to jump, they might stand more chance than in some ropy crash-landing in No Man's Land.

'I'm staying put, Skip!' Ralph summed it up for them all. 'You'll get us back, and I don't fancy it out there! Never did trust those survival kits!'

Just as he was thinking they could hold the Wellington no longer, the landing lights came into view, their beacon in the darkness. His hands tightened around the control column.

'Here we go, lads, hold on tight!'

15

Dick was tucking into a plate of pasta as though his life depended on it. He resolved to visit Italy one day and do nothing else but eat spaghetti and drink Chianti. Where on earth did the Italian POWs find it?

Carlo helped him, and the other members of the crew, to some more. Ralph had given up trying to hold a conversation and chewed solidly, taking occasional swigs from his mug.

They had been stranded for two days at Sidi Barrani before the Wellington was serviceable again. The ground crew had worked on it round the clock, eventually concluding that there was a block in the oil filter. It would need a thorough going-over at Shallufa, but at least T for Tommy was flying on both engines again.

On their return, Carlo's effusive Italian welcome had finally been interpreted by Dick.

'He wants us to have a meal with the POWs,' he had informed the rest of the crew, causing Will to raise his eyebrows.

'When?' Arnie's attention was diverted at the thought of an alternative to the mess staple of bully beef. He spent much of his time fantasising about Caribbean delicacies, fried cassava and spicy chicken populating his dreams.

'Tonight,' Dick replied. 'That's right, isn't it, Carlo?'

'*Sì, sì, è stanotte!*' Carlo beamed at them all. He had given them up for lost, the gentle red-headed navigator and his friends, and wanted to welcome them back, to extend them true Italian hospitality.

And so he did, plying them with food and drink and introducing them to his fellow POWs in their marquee. They were short, shabby young men, appearing more naturally suited for peacetime than the lot of the common soldier. Unworldly by nature, they had been plucked from villages and farms to join Mussolini's glorious army. Not that they seemed to have much stomach for it anymore – they just wanted to go home.

'Carlo was a student before the war,' Dick translated, 'before he trained as a field gunner.' Carlo became even more animated as the evening continued, gesticulating about the prowess of the Australians, to whom he had surrendered at El Daba. He drew himself up to his full height, an imaginary gun at his shoulder, imitating them advancing relentlessly.

'He thinks they are superhuman, cigarette-smoking giants!' Dick laughed. 'He says he gave up straight away, no point resisting!'

Will had counted himself out of the entertainment. 'I'll pass on that one, lads!' It was too raw for him: all he could think of was the Macchi coming at them out of the sun, nearly killing Don into the bargain. He was not ready to share the Italians' meal, however delicious it might be, and doubted that they would make compassionate prison guards if the boot ever ended up on the other foot.

He had been planning to spend the evening reading, but Vic had other ideas. 'There's a concert in Cairo,' he said as they shared a cup of tea in the mess tent earlier that day. 'Fancy coming? We've got transport with the army – friend of mine in the 5th Tanks sorted it all out.'

And so it was, as his crew sampled the delights of Italian cuisine, that he sat listening to the Egyptian Symphony Orchestra's exquisite rendering of Tchaikovsky's *Pathétique Symphony*, grateful for the dim lighting in the concert hall, that obscured his face.

16

Lined up in front of the CO the next morning, the uniformed crew stood to attention in uneasy silence.

'Consorting with the enemy, that's what I call it! What the hell did you think you were all doing? Fordham, perhaps you'd like to explain yourself!'

The CO was a member of the old school, and had served in Iraq for many years before his current promotion. He was not overly impressed with the new recruits; after all, they came from all walks of life nowadays. Lacked the discipline, that was the trouble, never been drilled long and hard enough, in his opinion.

Will looked directly in front of him. 'The POWs wanted us to try their food, sir.'

'And you considered that acceptable behaviour for a member of His Majesty's Armed Forces?' The CO looked appalled; it was as though they had committed a heinous crime.

Unfortunately for them, the details of their feast had spread to the mess. It was Taffy who expanded upon the quality of their meal during a beer afterwards, overheard by an officious adjutant who promptly reported them.

'Well, sir, we thought it might make a welcome change,' was the best Will could manage by way of reply.

'And did it?' The CO looked thunderously at him.

Dick stepped forwards; he was not about to let Will take the rap any more. 'Excuse me, sir, the first pilot wasn't there, so he can't answer that question. I can – it was delicious and highly nourishing, I should think.'

'Not there?!' The CO looked as though he was about to explode. 'So where were you, Fordham?'

'At a concert, sir.'

'A concert?' He sounded like Oscar Wilde's Lady Bracknell – *A handbag?!* 'Was it good?'

'Yes, sir, it was.'

The comedy of the situation was becoming too much for Will. One look at Dick, and he would be finished.

The CO shook his head in despair. 'Well, I'm so glad you're all enjoying yourselves!' he said caustically. 'It may have escaped your notice, but there's a war on, and the Italians are the enemy. Fordham, the fact that you were not there is no defence – they are your crew and you should keep them in order. If they don't know how to behave, I would be grateful if you would tell them.'

He stood back and surveyed them all, from Will down to Ralph, pilot to rear gunner. In his eyes, they were a motley crew of half-trained civilians.

'I'm withdrawing your exit privileges for two weeks,' he added, 'as it would appear to me that you consider this whole set-up is for your entertainment. Good day, gentlemen!'

'Sir?' Dick could not resist the last word.

'Yes, Sinclair?'

'You don't suppose we might draft some of the Italian orderlies for kitchen duties? I'm sure our cooks are hard-pressed, it must be difficult churning out the same old food day after day! If we ate a better diet, we might be more efficient. You know what Julius Caesar said: an army marches on its stomach!'

'It wasn't Julius Caesar, it was Napoleon Bonaparte, you dimwit, and look what happened to him! Bugger off, the lot of you!'

He waited until they had gone before he called in his batman. 'Pearce!'

'Yes, sir?'

'It has come to my notice that some of the Italian POWs can rustle up a decent meal. Now, the C-in-C's visiting in a couple of days, so I wonder if you could locate the most promising ones and collar them to prepare us lunch. Nothing too elaborate you know, we don't want to show off, now do we? Perhaps we'll have a trial run the day before, just to make sure it's up to scratch!'

17

On each side of the landing strip, fields of asphodel had sprung up after the heavy rains. As they walked over the sweet-scented stocks, the heavy fragrance caught them unawares.

'I'd never have believed the desert could look like that.' Dick stooped to examine the spiky white flower. 'Completely out of nowhere!'

It was a clear day for their cross-country to Wadi Natrun, about halfway between Cairo and Alexandria. It would involve the usual oil consumption tests, but was a welcome respite from their nightly bombing raids. According to the latest briefing, the two opposing tank armies were lining up along a strip of land at Gazala, to the west of Tobruk, bringing in as much in the way of reinforcements as possible for the next stage of the battle. Meanwhile the job of the Desert Air Force was to sabotage Rommel's supply lines.

Arthur had looked gloomy. 'We'll never get out of here,' he had confided darkly to Will. 'No one's going to win, it's a classic stalemate.'

Privately, Will began to agree with him. Each time they were dispersed to another grim landing ground, and sent off on another hazardous raid to the Axis-controlled ports, he feared they would not return to tell the tale. Surviving a tour of duty out here would be little short of a miracle, and he would never see Honor again.

Unlike Arthur, he refused to voice such thoughts. He had a crew of men to rally, all facing their own private demons. Their only hope was to stick together like glue, form as tight a fighting unit as they could, drop the wretched bombs and get the hell out of whatever cauldron lay below.

'Right, steady as you go… left-left… steady… left-left… steady… bombs gone!' He and Dick were almost conjoined when it came to dropping bombs. By now, he could sense the precise moment when Dick would press the tit and the Wellington would surge upwards, relieved of its deadly burden. Only then would their chances improve, and he could turn the plane for home.

Arthur's state of mind was becoming more of a concern to him with each passing day. His friend seemed increasingly withdrawn, and nothing could jolt him out of it. Not that it affected Arthur's functionality, for he mechanically bombed his targets with accuracy and returned on schedule.

'He's completely lost his spark, that's what it is,' Dick said. 'It's as though he isn't really here at all!'

Feeling powerless to help, and out of his depth, Will could only attempt to keep Arthur interested in the minutiae of their lives, but he remained curiously remote, listening to their helpless laughter about the CO's rebuke without a shadow of amusement. It never crossed Will's mind to involve the MO, for that would bring into question Arthur's 'moral fibre', which was not at issue. The man was depressed, and with good reason.

'Wadi Natrun,' Dick informed them as the Wellington levelled out after take-off, 'is famous for its Coptic Christian monasteries, and its name means "Valley of the Salts". Guess what the salts are used for, Skip?'

'Haven't a clue!' Will and Arnie smiled at each other; Dick was a mine of useless information.

'Well, the salt, or natron, was used by the pharaohs for embalming! You need it for mummification, so to speak.'

Ralph's voice chipped in from the rear turret. 'What's mummification, Skip?'

Will looked down over the cockpit at the unfolding Nile Delta. 'Don't ask me, chaps, it sounds vaguely indecent!'

Over and above his efforts to learn Italian, Dick had immersed himself in Egyptian history, dragging his friends to the ancient Step Pyramid where they had ventured far down the narrow shafts to the spot where the Pharaoh had lain.

'So you mean the pyramids are just glorified death chambers?' Arnie felt sorry for the ancient Egyptians, having to lug all those stones into place for one dead king.

As the domed monastery buildings of the ancient settlement came into view, rosy-coloured cupolas in the morning light, there could be no doubting the beauty of the spot. The Wellington came in to land over the saline lakes, into an airfield populated by Tomahawks and Hurricanes.

No. 60 SAAF were part of the rear HQ at Wadi Natrun. Most of them were deployed on reconnaissance work, as the crew learned in the mess tent over lunch. Part of the diaspora of Colonial pilots who had volunteered to fight for the Old Country, the South Africans were tough and confident. They had trained under cloudless skies in the great open spaces of the Cape, Kenya or Rhodesia, and adapted well to the rigours of desert life.

'We're usually on Tac/R or photographic reconnaissance,' one of their pilots, Wits, explained. He was an Afrikaner, tall and strong, with the healthy demeanour of his Dutch forebears. 'It can get a bit lonely out there, flying low, finding out what troops are on the ground, what's on the roads, clueing up on the situation. Trouble is, Jerry's not too keen on us, are they, lads?'

His fellow aviators chipped in good-naturedly. 'If they don't get you with the ack-ack from the Bofors, then the 109s come after you, usually three at a time. Can be tricky, that one, the blighters are faster than us! Of course they're pretty keen to stop us getting back!'

'What do you make of the Tomahawks?' Arnie said.

'We hate them,' Wits replied succinctly. 'They're bloody dangerous unless you know what you're doing. If you open the throttle too fast on take-off, the engine cuts out when you're airborne! Give me a Hurricane any day!'

'At least the Tomahawks have got self-sealing fuel tanks,' one of the other pilots said. 'The Yanks got that right!'

Will thought of Matt, coming down in the blazing Hurricane – no such protection for him.

'I like the artwork!' Taffy spoke for them all, for one of the Tomahawks was decorated with a huge shark's mouth, making it look like a crazy fighting machine. By this stage of the war, crews were customising their planes with striking paintings, usually involving buxom blondes. Even the ground crews would adorn the bombs 'for Adolf', and the powers that be must have concluded it was all good for morale, for there were no attempts to stop them.

The crews lapsed into genial conversation; they were a friendly lot, the South Africans, and patriots to the core.

'Time to get cracking!' Will roused himself for the return leg, and they made their way across to their Wimpy, still chatting to Wits as they went.

Wits cocked his head on one side. He was listening intently to one of the Tomahawks taking off. 'Easy on the throttle, Jan…'

The crew watched in dismay as the jauntily painted single-engine plane took off, only making it to about a hundred feet before the engine cut out.

'Oh my Christ! I've told him before!' But Wits knew what would follow – the pilot tried to turn, flipped and spun into the ground, another young life in a heap of burning wreckage strewn across the sand.

18

The flak over the target was intense; showers of red tracer-shells streamed past them as Will, jockeying for position, took his turn to go in. Below him were the huge yellow flashes of bombs landing, and dazzling white flames of incendiaries lighting up the night sky.

'Jesus! All hell's broken loose down there!' Ralph's Geordie accent cut in from the rear turret. Each raid was worse than the one before; tonight they were part of a force of four Wellingtons attacking shipping and dock installations at Benghazi. Hence the wait, while underneath them the cauldron burned and seethed.

A shell burst below them, lifting the plane up in the air, and Will steadied the aircraft before descending to the target. The flak increased in intensity as Dick led them in. His steady monologue continued.

'Bomb doors open… OK, let's go down. Left-left… steady… right a bit… steady, left-left.' Then a pause. 'Bombs gone, Skip!'

The docks below had erupted into pyres of flame and black smoke, like a diabolical light show at the gates of Hell.

'Bang on target!' Dick shouted, and Will, needing no encouragement, swung away out to sea, the barrage from the jetties intensifying as they made for safety.

There was no refuge yet, instead Ralph's excited voice on the intercom: '109s, Skip, two of them, corkscrew!' The rear gunner was firing round after round from his Browning guns – maybe, just maybe, this was his chance to bring one of them down.

The pilot's response to the rear gunner's shout was split-second. Weaving the huge bomber on a path that swerved and twisted, until it seemed that the very fuselage was shuddering, Will jinked the plane around the sky, desperately trying to shake them off. One of the Messerschmitts was in Ralph's sights, just as he was climbing away. A murderous hail of bullets spouted from the Browning guns, and in a flash the fighter was spinning into a death dive.

'I got one, Skip!' Ralph shouted. 'I can't see his mate, you must have shaken him off in the turn!'

This time, thought Will.

'Keep your eyes peeled, in case he comes back for more. Good work, Ralph!' Will turned to Arnie. 'Let's get the hell out of here, lads!'

Their return was chalked up on the blackboard in the ops tent: *T for Tommy, pilot Flight Sergeant Fordham, return time 0400 hours*. Not all of the Wellingtons were back, and as he came out of a protracted session of debriefing with his crew, more than ready for his fried eggs and bacon, he glanced up at the board again. Q for Queenie was still out. That was Arthur's Wellington – he had been mine-laying in the docks, just beyond the Giuliana Mole.

Dick was at his side. 'He's taking his time,' he said.

Will just went on looking at the board; his desire for food and sleep had left him. 'I might just go and listen for him outside.'

They stood together for a long time, straining to hear the familiar noise of the Pegasus engine, drawing their flying jackets around them against the bitter cold.

It was not until dawn began to rise, streaks of pink light gathering along the horizon, that Will broke the silence. 'He's not coming back, is he, Dick?'

28th February 1942

Desert Air Force

Dear You,

I finally received your last letter, about two months after you sent it! I hope that you are keeping well and not finding the work too exhausting. And yes, please do visit Matt if you possibly can, I'm sure it would mean all the world to him.

My birthday rather passed me by this year but thank you for remembering! We have been on some pretty tough ops lately so not much time for celebrating. Still, it is good to be in charge of my own Wimpy and the lads are a great bunch.

Take care of yourself, too – I can promise I'm trying very hard to do the same and can't wait to see you too!

All my love.

From Me

Part Nine: The Other Enemy

1

Honor looked at the newspaper in disbelief. It was 21st June 1942 – the headline *Allies surrender at Tobruk* was accompanied by photographs of the burning, bombed-out port that Rommel had coveted for so long. It had all been so different last November, when the siege was lifted and the Eighth Army had sent the panzers retreating westward. Now, after a few short months the Desert Fox was back, forcing the South Africans to show the white flag, before he set off again on the chase into Egypt, reportedly pushing on towards Suez, his final trophy.

All she could think of was Will. If the British could not hold Cairo and Alexandria, it would all be over for him, either sacrificed in the final stages of battle or taken as a prisoner of war, like the thirty thousand men at Tobruk. Better a POW, she conceded; at least he might survive until it was all over. Reading that Churchill was to address the House of Commons, she felt sorry for the beleaguered Prime Minister, having to explain yet another defeat. It had been bad enough when Hong Kong fell in March, followed by the awful stories of Japanese atrocities, raping and bayoneting British prisoners. Would the Germans be more merciful in victory? Where were the Americans? She had thought that the tide would turn after Pearl Harbor, but as far as she could gather, the situation was worsening on every front.

It had been two long months since she received Will's last letter, revealing as it did so little of the truth. By the time the censors had finished with them, the letters were hardly worth the flimsy paper they were written on. Still, at least he was alive then, and she would not allow herself to believe otherwise now.

'What's up?' Rosie sat down beside her in the few minutes left before their shift. Honor silently passed her the paper, while Rosie swiftly skimmed the headlines.

'I don't get it!' she announced finally. 'When are we going to stand up and fight? With all respect to Mr Churchill, we're making a habit of surrendering, or as they like to call it, "strategic withdrawal"! It's time someone with a bit of guts took over out there, and gave Rommel some of his own medicine! I'm heartily sick of the news, it gets worse every day!'

She put her arm around Honor as they walked to the ward. It was an uncharacteristic gesture from the spirited girl, who enjoyed teasing more than sympathising.

'I expect he'll come back safe,' she said. 'He must be a good pilot, or he wouldn't have made it this far.'

The trouble with kindly gestures, as Honor knew only too well, was that they could reduce you to tears. She struggled to control herself as she entered Ward 2, for Sister Duncan would be having none of it, and there was work to do.

The summer sun was streaming in through the high windows of the men's medical ward, bathing it with a light that allowed Sister Duncan to identify dust in hitherto hidden nooks and crannies. Under her eagle eyes, the probationers were polishing the bedside tables fiercely, as though their very lives depended upon it.

Lotte, bearing urine bottles from the sluice, smiled broadly at Honor as she passed. After a protracted period of convalescence with Percy's mother, she had finally returned to the ward in early May, when her cultures were negative and she could be given a clean bill of health. Despite her loss of weight, which made her dark eyes look even deeper than before, she looked lively and cheerful.

There was a new admission on the ward, one of Honor's charges for the shift, and as she drew the curtains around his bed, Dr Percy Black himself came to join her.

'Morning, Mr Gibson, is your headache any better today?'

The burly middle-aged man in the bed shook his head. There was a tinge of jaundice in his skin, and his temperature was high.

'It's chronic, Doctor,' he said, 'and I feel as sick as a pig. Then me legs ache so…'

'He's been vomiting, according to the night staff, and I think he's jaundiced,' Honor added.

Percy nodded and examined the man carefully, palpating his liver edge and checking the conjunctivae of his eyes.

'We'd better check for bile in his urine, would you get a sample?' Then, to the patient, 'Are you a drinking man, Mr Gibson?'

'Who, me?' The patient screwed up his eyes. 'Well, I like me pint, if that's what you mean, but I'm not like some of them. I can stop when me time's up, you ask the missus!' He lay back upon the pillows, as though the effort of conversation was exhausting him.

Percy looked perplexed. 'We'll have to run a few tests, find out what's the matter. Try and keep your fluids up, and don't get out of bed. I'll take a drop of blood from you before I go.'

He motioned Honor away from the bedside.

'Will you check his urine for albumen and blood, as well as bile?' he asked. 'I'm not sure he's telling the truth about his drinking – maybe he's got acute alcoholic hepatitis. Try and find out a bit more before the round, would you? Dr Earnshaw is sure to ask some tricky questions!'

While Percy was not so much in awe of his consultant as Peter had been, the ward round was no place for humiliation if it could possibly be avoided. Honor hated to see the ritual hounding of the junior doctors, but there were not many specialists who could resist it.

Her desire to help Percy almost distracted her from her pressing concerns about Will, and as she tried to piece together the man's symptoms she wondered what information they had missed. There was usually a key to an obscure diagnosis; it was just a matter of unlocking it, or waiting for time to pass until the picture clicked into place.

Mr Gibson was uncommunicative as she gently washed him and changed his damp sheets, and he handed her the urine sample with a look of reproof.

'I'm not a boozer, if that's what he thinks, Nurse!'

'Of course you're not. Now just remind me, what job do you do?'

She had barely finished testing the urine in the sluice, before the ward round descended. Dr Earnshaw, sporting an immaculately cut navy suit, must have been popular with his women patients. He smiled disarmingly at Honor and Lotte, almost ignoring the medical staff.

'Well, Dr Black, what have we here?' Taking out his pocket watch, he listened to Percy's summary. Unimpressed, he examined the patient, looking thoughtful.

'How much do you drink, Mr Gibson?'

'They've already asked me, and I bet I don't drink any more than you do, sir!'

Dr Earnshaw smiled. 'I'm not sure how to take that! It can make you poorly, you know, too much alcohol, inflame your liver! Dr Black leans towards that diagnosis, as far as I can gather from his summary.'

The patient looked to Honor for support. 'I don't drink, do I, Nurse?'

The consultant's gaze flickered across at the staff nurse. *Pretty little thing*, he thought; *better-looking than the others, not likely to end up like Sister Duncan*.

'So, Nurse, are we all barking up the wrong tree?'

There was a silence before Honor replied, in a clear voice. 'I think so, sir.'

'You do, do you, Nurse? Now what leads you to that conclusion?'

'Well, sir, it's his occupation,' she said, rising to the challenge of the situation.

'Which is...?' Dr Earnshaw was amused by the interlude – what was she going to say next?

'He works in the sewers, sir.'

There was a further pause, but this time Dr Earnshaw quizzed her more gently.

'So you think he has...?'

Her voice was firm, but she did not dare look at Sister Duncan as she replied. 'Weil's disease, sir.'

Percy could hardly contain himself – 'Of course!' – and even Lotte was struggling to catch up.

Dr Earnshaw surveyed his audience. 'It's just as well we have an intelligent nurse on this ward. She asked the right question, didn't you, my dear? The key to the whole illness, hidden in his job! Of course he has Weil's disease, now tell us why.'

Sister Duncan stood impassively as Honor replied. 'He will have been infected by the rats in the sewers, sir – the Leptospira is excreted in their urine and gets in through the skin. It causes high temperature and jaundice, and haemorrhage too, in some cases.'

'Correct, my dear! Very observant of you. Dr Black will now tell us how we confirm it, if he can recall the facts correctly.'

Percy looked uncertain. 'You inoculate the patient's urine into a guinea pig, sir, or is it a rabbit?' he hazarded.

'I suggest the former of the two furry creatures, and on what day?'

A cloud fell over Percy's face. Both Honor and Lotte knew the answer, but would not say.

Dr Earnshaw looked at his watch again. 'Just ask the pretty staff nurse, she'll tell you, I've no doubt,' he sighed, before he swept majestically on to the next ward.

2

The letter waiting for her in the pigeonhole was not from Will. She recognised the erratic handwriting as Peter's, having tried so often to decipher it on patients' drug charts. Opening it reluctantly, she found that it was his intention to visit her.

I'll be driving up through Stoke on my way to the Lake District for a short holiday; when is your next off-duty? he wrote, as though she had no option but to agree. Her contact with Peter always made her feel uncomfortable, and undermined her steadfast preoccupation with Will.

Still, she had found no way of disengaging the friendship, and resigned herself to his arrival. Despite her misgivings, it would be a welcome escape from the hospital, even if only for a day. Added to which, Peter was always good company, and they were never short of conversation. Perhaps he might have news from Addie, who had been posted to Malta with the QAs. She looked at the date on the letter; his plans coincided exactly with her next break.

Rosie caught up with her as she folded the letter away. 'You've heard from Will!' By now, she had shared all Honor's confidences, and had ceased to doubt her love for the RAF pilot. In fact, she had added Will to her own worry list, watching the newsreels and comparing his lot to that of her cherished brother, Jack.

'No, it's from Peter, actually,' Honor replied.

'He's not one to give up, is he?' Rosie sounded amused, and continued relentlessly, 'So, what's the latest?'

Honor sighed. 'He's coming to see me next week.'

'It's all right for some!' Rosie teased. 'What will you do if he declares undying love?'

'He won't,' said Honor flatly.

'Why not?'

'Because he's done it before, and it didn't get him anywhere.'

'Ooh, you are a hard one, Honor Newson, and that's a fact!' Rosie rolled her eyes dramatically. 'Maybe he should try someone else for a change!'

Honor thought of Molly and wished it were so, for both their sakes.

They were blessed with some particularly balmy weather, and took to evening walks in a nearby park, where children shouted and played the same childhood games that they had hopped, and skipped and jumped themselves only a few years before. One evening, having managed to buy a bag of cherries, for 1/6d per pound, they lay on the grass eating the juicy fruit with reckless pleasure.

A scruffy urchin approached: 'Can we have one, miss?', before the two girls took pity on him and surrendered the rest of the treasured bag.

Lotte rarely joined them on these outings, as Percy took up most of her spare time. The pair were trying to conceal their relationship, behaving with utmost formality on the ward, but Honor could see his eyes light up for Lotte, and envied them the ever-present nature of their growing love.

Cloistered as they were on the wards, they were still exposed to the sharp realities of life. Britain was in the grip of rationing and hunger was a constant companion. Fantasies about food were never far from their minds, but their diet was unvarying: root vegetables, bread and potatoes stretched every possible way.

'What if they come back for her?' Rosie spat out her last cherry stone, far into the bushes.

'What, you mean the men in the hats?' The two girls were in the middle of a discussion about Lotte. 'Sister Duncan'll send them packing again, I should think!' Honor doubted that the officials would run the gamut of Sister's wrath for a second time. 'She doesn't want to lose her, too good a nurse to sit in an internment camp for the rest of the war!'

The weather held until the day of Peter's visit, and Honor, dressing in her best skirt and blouse, was looking forward to her freedom.

'You're looking pretty!' Rosie was lacing up her black regulation shoes. 'No wonder he fancies you!'

There was a knock at the door, and the two girl exchanged looks. Surely not Peter already – who would have let him in?

It was Home Sister, unusually grave-faced, pausing at the threshold for what seemed like an eternity.

'What is it, Sister?' Honor said.

'It's Staff Nurse Green I want.' She moved across towards Rosie uncertainly. 'Best sit down dear, I've got some bad news.'

Rosie waited until the end before letting out a low, animal scream. 'No!' she shouted. 'No, no, no!'

Her cries could be heard throughout the nurses' home, and Peter, arriving at the open front door, vaulted the stairs to find Honor next to her friend, hanging on to her, as distraught as if she had lost her own family.

'What the hell's happened?' He raised his voice above the shrieks. Rosie could not stop herself, and immediately in charge, he strode over and gripped her by the shoulders. 'Now stop it!'

She raised her face to his, her eyes unseeing, while he continued to hold her in a vice-like grip. 'Calm down,' he said. 'Now calm down!'

She stopped screaming and buckled, for her legs would not carry her, and he supported her gently to the bed.

'Hot tea, please, Sister, sugar in it.'

Home Sister scuttled from the room, relieved that someone had taken over. Really, Matron should have been with her – fancy having to tell the poor girl her entire family had been killed!

'What's happened?' He turned to Honor, who shook her head.

'Liverpool, a bomb… her family,' was all she could manage.

Rosie started to cry, the bitter, drooling sobs of those who have lost everything, and he took her in his arms. Patiently, he waited until she relapsed into the convulsive hiccups of grief.

'It's not true!' she repeated over and over again. 'It's not true!'

It was some time before Peter was able to piece together the facts. The family's house had taken a direct hit in the latest bombing raid – the port of Liverpool was never free from enemy attacks, although the Blitz in other cities was past its worst.

'Jack!' Rosie said. 'Who'll tell Jack?'

Peter learned about the brother in the Navy, on the Russian convoys. He might be all that was left for Rosie, if the cruel sea spared him.

'Come on, get up, I'm going to take you to Liverpool,' Peter said. 'We'll go in my car, Honor can come too. Then you can see for yourself what's been going on. You'll never rest otherwise!'

'Are you sure that's wise?' Home Sister did not approve. Had he thought what they might find?

'Quite sure. Come on, get yourselves ready! Sister, would you let her ward know? I believe Nurse Newson already has a pass. I'll bring them back tonight.'

His authority was undeniable, and Rosie responded to it. 'Let me wash my face first, and change,' she agreed, almost eagerly. Anything was better than inactivity. 'I don't believe it! Maybe they're still alive, in the rubble, just waiting to be dug out!'

3

Three small children were sitting in the pile of bricks on Virgil Street that had once been their home. The youngest, a girl, cradled a dusty doll and the boy looked expectantly up the street at the adults who were approaching, hoping to see a familiar face.

The whole row of the terrace had been bombed out, the fronts of the houses shored off, like a ruined dolls' house which had been opened by mistake. By now, the clean-up operation was beginning, with ARP wardens, nurses and volunteers picking their way amongst the demolished buildings. The scene was one of complete desolation.

Home Sister had been wrong: Rosie surveyed the street in disbelief but did not lose control. She walked halfway down, and looked up at the once-familiar skeleton of her home, treasured objects strewn among the ruins. Could anyone have come out of there alive?

'Rosie!' A burly fellow in workmen's clothes was heaving bricks from the house next door.

'Mr Baxter, where are they all?'

He stopped and wiped a dirty hand over his forehead. 'They didn't get to the shelter,' he answered simply, as though that was explanation in itself, then turned back to the rubble.

'But where are they?!' She was resolute, pulling at his arm until he faced her. Honor took her other hand, holding it tightly while they waited for his reply.

He swallowed. 'I'm sorry, love, they took the bodies to Smithdown Road Hospital. You'll find them all there.'

'All of them?'

'All of them.' He moved away, as if he could bear no more, and resumed his lonely, futile task.

Peter and Honor looked at each other in dismay. Like Rosie, they had harboured a glimmer of hope on the long drive to Liverpool, which was rapidly dispelled by the sight of the bomb damage as they made their way through the once-beautiful port. Whole areas were flattened near Cable Street and the docks and even the cathedral had been hit.

'You've got to take me there!' Rosie turned to Peter.

'Are you sure?' Even Peter had not bargained for identifying bomb victims. He suddenly wished they had waited in Stoke after all.

Rosie would have her way, of course. Peter and Honor sat silently side by side on a bench outside the makeshift morgue, the afternoon sunlight on their faces but far from their hearts.

Eventually, Rosie was returned to them by a solemn-faced Sister, but she was not the girl they knew.

'I'm so sorry,' Sister said, as the two figures closed around Rosie, locking her in their embrace, a living triptych to her mute despair.

Like so many return journeys, it took an age. It was past midnight, and Rosie lay fast asleep on the back seat, covered by a light rug. She looked peaceful, like the child she would never be again, buffered by her dreams.

'She'll never want to wake up,' Honor said quietly. They were all exhausted, and the motion of the car could easily have rocked her to sleep, but she strove to stay awake for Peter's sake.

'I got that one wrong.' His voice was defeated. Those images would be seared into Rosie's memory forever – he should have listened to Home Sister.

'No you didn't!' Honor replied, and he glanced into the back seat, fearful they had woken her. 'She had to see them,' she whispered. 'At least she could say goodbye! Imagine never glimpsing their faces again!'

He fell silent, negotiating the dark bends in the road. Then, 'Is that what you would want, if it were you?'

'Of course I would! She knows they're at peace.'

As a medical man, Peter doubted that an incendiary bomb was a peaceful way to meet one's end, but kept his counsel. He glanced across at her, wondering how she had stayed awake.

'So, what's the news from Egypt?' he said.

There was a pause.

'Not much, really,' she said. 'I haven't heard for some time. It doesn't help knowing about Tobruk – things are going from bad to worse out there…'

'Sounds one hell of a mess,' Peter replied softly. He wrestled with his thoughts: what if the young pilot never made it back? Would she have him then? It was immaterial to Peter that he was not her first choice, so sure was he of his own love.

Another silence fell.

'I'll always be waiting for you, you know.' At that moment, he vowed to wait an eternity for her. Never a betting man, he yearned to lay odds on the chance of having her as his own, marrying her when the war was over, and looking after her for the rest of her life.

She looked across at him, his profile clear against the moonlight.

'Peter—' But he would not let her finish.

'Don't.' He changed gear as they drew into the outskirts of Stoke. 'You see, I always know what you're going to say.'

N. Staffs Infirmary
10th July 1942
Dear You,
It is hard not to worry about you when the news is so bad. Mr Churchill says the Eighth Army will win through in the end, but I wish he'd mention the Desert Air Force a bit more! After all, they're not going to make it without your help, are they? I think of you constantly!

Very few of your letters are making it through but please go on writing. Sometimes I imagine they will arrive in a big sackful when the war is over, and we will read them together, holding hands, and remember all we have been through.

I, for one, will be very happy to lead a quiet life and exist without drama of any sort, or partings!

The Germans seem to be breaking through to the Volga, so we can only hope that the Russian Bear will hold them back. Fortunately for us, it doesn't seem to be in his nature to give up!

Hoping for better news soon, and please take care of yourself. Keep safe for my sake.

Love as always.
From Me

4

Arnie looked at the ops board with disgust.

'Enemy concentrations…' he muttered wearily, under his breath.

'Motorised transport…' Ralph chipped in. Will leant back on his chair, waiting for the inevitable briefing. They were all exhausted, having put in so many hours' night bombing since the beginning of July that he began to wonder how much more they could take. Rommel was advancing implacably into Egypt, while the Eighth Army and the RAF retreated in front of him. In the scramble back to the Canal Zone, the aircrews had found themselves taking off from one advanced landing ground after another, often minutes before the enemy arrived. Leapfrogging eastward to Alexandria, the only consolation was to be based at Shallufa, part of 40 Squadron, on a permanent station where they lived in huts, rather than tents.

The schedule had been relentless, either the long, nightly haul to Tobruk or the 'seek and destroy' missions of the mobile war, where their task was low-level bombing of Jerry convoys. As far as the crew were concerned, they might just as well have been bombing by day, as the flares from the Albacores lit up the desert like a stage, producing a night fighter's paradise. It was a miracle they were all still alive, Will reflected – except that they were not, for Q for Queenie had disappeared without trace, and all the crew were missing, believed killed. He had written to Arthur's father some weeks later, not that it would help, but Will wanted to express his own sense of loss. He could hardly imagine the man's grief, doubly bereft of both wife and son.

There could be no doubt about it – they were losing the Desert War. Even with the C-in-C flinging every available aircraft into the sky, night and day, even with the arrival of the USAAF and their long-range Liberators and Fortresses, there was no stopping the Desert Fox. It was rumoured that the evacuation plans for Cairo were already in place, and that Mussolini himself had arrived in Libya for his own triumphant march through the streets of Alexandria.

Neither Will, nor any of the others, could see what would stop him. Every time the crews bombed the enemy landing grounds that had once been their own – El Daba, Fuka, Gambut – the futility of the situation came home to them. They would never regain the territory, and most likely they would all end up POWs, like the compliant Italians on their base.

Honor was constantly in his mind. He was so sick of war; all he wanted was to see her again. Her last letter had taken two months to arrive, but at least it had given him hope. There could be no doubt that she would be waiting for him, if only he could make it back. He could never tell her what it was really like out here, or share his sense of desperation. He must keep all that to himself, and not let his crew see it either – they depended upon him, and were his responsibility.

So distracted was he by his own thoughts, he hardly listened to the CO's pep talk and the targets for tonight. He had heard it all before – maximum effort, backing up the Eighth, try and force Rommel to a halt on the Gazala road. He did not believe a word of it. Vic was in the row behind him, the same dependable Vic, outwardly solid as a rock, coping with the fact that Don, though still alive, had never returned – his injuries had proved too serious.

Arnie nudged him. 'Surprise, surprise,' he whispered, for they were on the board for Crete. He sat up and looked around – Dick was scrutinising the maps with fresh determination, and the CO was off again.

'So, gentlemen, T for Tommy and D for Dog are headed for Maleme airfield. Now, this is all a bit hush-hush, but the local resistance are taking a pop at it from the ground tonight and you'll be going in as backup. I don't need to remind you of the importance of Crete for the Luftwaffe – it's their main transit base for logistic support to the Afrika Korps. So I want you to give it all you've got, the more damage you can inflict, the better! Good luck, gentlemen!'

As they gathered their gear in the crewing-up room, Dick was more sanguine than the rest.

'Be a nice change, Skip,' he said; 'better than the enemy concentrations, anyway. Not that they're really concentrated, if you ask me: Jerry are stretched out for bloody miles of desert, it'd be much better to hit them on the coast road.'

'Well, it might be OK on the way back,' Will said. There would just be the problem of the Axis airfield to bomb first, as Taffy was quick to point out. As they walked out to their Wellington, bombed up and ready, Dick embarked upon a running commentary.

'They say the Cretans have been putting up one hell of a resistance, that's their tradition. Things are pretty bad there: talk of reprisals by the Germans, whole villages wiped out…'

'Let's hope we don't have to bail out,' said Arnie drily.

'Apparently the Germans blame them for their paratroop losses last year,' Dick continued blithely. 'They dropped their weapons in separate canisters, thinking the natives would be friendly, which they weren't.'

'What happened?' Ralph said.

'Well, they were sitting targets – couldn't get to their guns, just killed as they landed.'

'Christ, Jerry won't be doing that again in a hurry!' Ralph replied. It was a chilling prospect, floating unarmed through the sky to a hostile reception committee below.

Dick remembered the girl in the Halifax at Tempsford; even the SOE women carried revolvers in their pockets for the drop.

Their course took them out over the Med, north above the moonlit island to cross the White Mountains before swinging into Maleme airfield. Ack-ack tracers streamed around them, as they aligned towards the target. Ralph sat in his rear turret, watching the night sky for the deadly 109s – he was surprised they had not scrambled already.

'There's the river bed, to the left, vineyard ridge across to the right – the course is directly between.' Dick's voice was clear over the intercom. He moved to take up position in the bomb-aimer's station, lying prone above the Perspex panels, his thumb on the release button. 'Let's go down…'

Flying low, Will and Arnie could make out the dark silhouettes of the Junkers lined up on the airfield, some halfway in the hangars for repair.

'No sign of the resistance,' Arnie muttered as Will opened the bomb doors.

'Right a bit…left-left…right…steady…hold it…bombs gone, Skip!' Dick's signal was preceded by flashes of bright yellow flame from the perimeter of the field.

'Do you reckon that's the locals?' Arnie asked as their own bombs hurtled down to the runway below.

'That'll put the wind up them!' yelled Taffy, as the Wellington surged upwards, relieved of its four thousand-pound bomb load.

'Where in hell is the opposition?' Will did not like it; the Luftwaffe were surely not about to let them saunter in and out as they pleased? He suddenly wished they were back on the Gazala road – he felt trapped here, between the mountains and the sea.

Taking the bomber into a steep climb away from the action, he wheeled in a wide turn to the east, over vineyard ridge.

'Ralph, what's happening?'

'I can't see them, Skip!' Ralph's hand was on the Browning gun, ready for the onslaught. 'They must be out there somewhere!'

'Get me the course back, Dick, let's get the hell out of here!'

He had managed to reach the open sea before the lone fighter closed in. Knowing it would only be a matter of time, he was ready for evasive action even before he heard Ralph's urgent voice – 'Bandit, Skip – nine o'clock, corkscrew!' – and the stutter of the Brownings took over. Then, 'Bastard!'

'Where is he, Ralph?' The great bomber was weaving its way around the dark sky, pitching and falling like an unbroken stallion.

There was no reply.

'Get back there, Arnie, find out what's happened to him. I'll try and shake Jerry off…'

How many more times could they escape death, Will thought, the sweat breaking on his forehead. Damn fool mission – they were never going to make it home with a fighter on their tail and the rear gunner gone for a burton. Maybe they were all set to join him, in one catastrophic explosion as the 109 picked them off.

'Keep on this heading, Skip! Ralph must have nailed him – there's no trace!' Dick's voice came from the astrodome, and Will levelled out, on course low above the waves. He felt safer down there, nearer the sea; easier if they had to ditch.

Arnie made his way slowly down the fuselage. 'He's dead, Skip.'

They all kept silence as the Wellington flew on towards the dawn, the crystal waters unfolding beneath them as they neared the North African coast.

5

Will could not bear to look in the rear turret. As soon as they landed, he strode towards the debriefing tent, leaving Arnie to warn the ground crew. He did not care to think what would be left of Ralph – having stumbled upon the erks hosing out a turret only last week, Will had no illusions. The dogged bravery of those rear gunners had never failed to amaze him: isolated in their domains, ever watchful, terrified out of their wits more often than not. Ted Baines would take it hard, for despite his premonitions, he was one of the survivors, and about to complete a tour of duty.

Yet it was Ralph who had saved all of their lives, the young Geordie who would never feel the warm Caribbean sun on his face, or return to the cold industrial city of his youth. Fate was picking them off one by one – Arthur, now Ralph, who would be next? It was all so futile, for this war was as good as lost.

'You OK, Skip?' Dick did not expect a reply, and none was forthcoming.

They sat side by side during debrief, answering endless questions about the mission. Had they hit the target? What planes were the Luftwaffe deploying? How many did they take out? Had they seen any signs of the resistance? Were they sure the 109 had been downed?

Will answered in a monotone, supported by interjections from the crew. The photographs would give the reconnaissance bods all the gen they needed. He just wanted to sleep; breakfast first, then sleep.

'You can go now.' The intelligence officer had finished with them for today, his forms were filled in and operational records would be duly filed.

They rose.

'Flight Sergeant Fordham?'

Will waited while the others filed out. 'Yes, sir?'

'It's your job to write the letter, you know, the one that goes with the wingcos. Just add a bit of background for the family, nothing that would distress them.' He waved him out.

'Just a bit of background, sir, will do,' Will repeated mechanically. He could not conceive how his version of events could possibly soften the blow. Which bits did they want him to miss out? The abject fear, the pit in the stomach, the adrenaline surge, the searing pain of the bullet, the realisation of death?

'A plague on both your houses,' he muttered to himself, and headed for his bunk.

He awoke to see the padre waiting at the door. It was late afternoon, and he must have slept for hours, dirty and unshaven, in his shorts, with a hat over his face to keep off the flies. He was caked with sweat, and longed for a wash.

'Sorry, Fordham.' The padre looked embarrassed, 'I was told to bring you Wiggins' effects.' He handed Will a canvas bag.

'What do I do when I've finished with them?'

'You take out anything that might upset his family, you know what I mean, then give the rest back to the adjutant, and they send it back to his next of kin. Oh, and you write the letter, you know – *credit to HM forces, brave and loyal, steadfast in his duty…*'

Will took a sip of tepid water from his bottle. 'That bit won't be difficult – it's true. What about the rest?'

'They usually describe the op, and how he died, if it's at all possible.'

There was a pause. 'So, Padre, what does your God make of this senseless loss of life?' Will said quietly. For a moment, he really wanted to know. He was sure his mother would have had an answer.

'He's your God too, Fordham, and I haven't asked him,' the padre replied curtly, and left the room.

There was precious little in the bag to distinguish Ralph from any other nineteen-year-old. Will slowly turned over the contents: shaving stuff, wallet with an Egyptian pound note, a little photograph tucked in the side. He scrutinised it, smiling at the tousle-headed girl who looked out at him – was it from a fairground? Toothbrush, letter from his mother dated January 1942, exhorting him to take care of himself, and write more often.

No chance of that now, he thought, as he put back Ralph's meagre possessions. His bed would already have been taken by another, so transitory was their hold on each billet. Tomorrow another gunner would be sent to crew up with them, tomorrow they would all be sent on another op, and tonight, they would drink themselves to oblivion.

Despite his throbbing head the next morning, he arrived on time for his meeting with the CO. However relentless the schedule, each operation had been meticulously entered in his logbook, his neat handwriting unaltered by the course of events.

Warren looked at it closely. He was a tall, angular man in his thirties, clean-shaven, and not as casual about his appearance as some of his contemporaries.

'Seventy-four operational hours for July, sir,' Will said.

'So I see, around three quarters at night.' Warren countersigned the red-inked totals. 'That's a pretty gruelling month, Fordham.'

'Yes, sir, it's been like that for us all.'

Warren looked closely at the young flight sergeant. He had a reputation for reliability, Fordham, one of those pilots whom the crew trust to bring them home. There were dark shadows under his young eyes, and a look of resignation behind them.

'Bad business about your rear gunner,' the CO commented.

Will nodded, pursing his lips.

'I'm giving you and your crew a few weeks' leave,' Warren added. 'I'm sending you back to Kabrit to rest up.'

Hardly believing his ears, Will replied, 'But sir, I thought we needed every plane we could muster?'

Warren closed his logbook and handed it back. 'The Desert Air Force have put up a damn good show this month, you know. As a consequence, it looks as though the Eighth are finally managing to hold the line.' There was no triumphalism in his tone, just fatigue.

'Where, sir?'

'A place called Alamein.'

6

The open truck rumbled along the dusty, potholed road towards Cairo. The crew sat in the back, responding to each sideways lurch as the driver negotiated the chaotic transit of other vehicles; lorries, armoured cars, and on the side of the road, the Bedouin, high on their camels carrying heaped netfuls of melons bound for the city markets.

'Why didn't we bring the old crate down?' Arnie wanted to know, but the truth was, they were all exhilarated to escape from the endless pressure of flying. The day resembled nothing so much as a school outing, as far as Dick was concerned. They shouted across at one another, sharing chocolate bars and water, with no plans for the future other than a rest, and swim in the Great Bitter Lake.

Cairo looked little changed as they negotiated their way through, the same donkey carts with black-clad peasant women, interspersed with the odd American car. Life had been going on as usual, despite the threat of German occupation. Egypt, a neutral country, could switch allegiance to the victors with indifference, as long as it could reap the same profits. Not all the inhabitants of the ancient city were as optimistic, for outside the railway station was a scene of confusion, a massive conglomeration of Jews, Greeks and Armenians seeking passage to Palestine or the Sudan. They were not the only ones, Will realised, seeing the diplomatic cars bearing British and American flags.

'Looks like a bit of a flap!' Dick said. 'This lot must know Rommel's just around the corner!' Which, in fact, he was, straining against the Alamein line some sixty miles west of Alexandria.

'It's just another placeless name,' Dick had explained, in his usual fashion, the night before. 'There's nothing there, only a railway station. But it's a perfect defensive position for Auchinleck, with sea to the north and the Quattara Depression to the south – that's a marsh, Taffy, to you. So the Eighth are hardening their position, thank God, or we wouldn't be here enjoying ourselves, now would we?'

Arnie was not persuaded. 'We've heard it all before,' he said wearily, 'and whatever you say, the people here in Cairo are hedging their bets! We'll never beat Rommel, we never do, just hold him up for a bit.'

'Driver, pull in!' Dick shouted. 'That's Groppi's, the tea garden! Anyone fancy an ice cream?'

They sat under the awnings as though reality had been suspended, for nothing could be further from the desperate days of July. When the immaculate black-clad waiter brought their tea and ices, even Will was forced to smile.

'Who's paying?' he said, anticipating the answer.

'You are, Skip!'

It was as well that he had experienced a moment of release, for when he struck out across the lake that afternoon he could only think of Arthur, and Fred, and the rest of the crew of Q for Queenie. *Last time*, he thought, *last time, they were here*, and now every one of them was gone.

The mess that night was in exuberant mood.

'What's going on?' Will said. Surely there was no cause for celebration?

'The old man himself, that's what's going on!' said Dick, then seeing Will's blank look, 'Winston, that's who!'

'What are you on about, Dick?'

Dick clapped him on the back. 'He's here, in Cairo! I saw him getting out of his transport plane this afternoon! Who would have believed it?'

'Are you trying to tell me that the Prime Minister has flown into Kabrit?' Will shook his head.

'Too right, it's true, old chap! On his way to the British Embassy. They say he's come to shake things up! Apparently he's fed up with us losing all the time, a sentiment we can share!'

'I'll drink to that!' Arnie raised his glass, and downed it in one go.

'What can he do about it?' said Will. 'It's a stalemate, always has been.'

'Rumour has it that heads are going to roll! I wouldn't like to be one of the top brass out here, I might be looking for another job!'

'I don't see what difference it'll make – all commanders are the same, holed up making plans while the ordinary chaps cop it.' Will remembered the generals of the Great War, safe far behind the lines when the troops went over the top. 'Except, of course, Rommel, who's always in the thick of it, fighting with his men, that's why he wins.'

'Oh, cheer up, Skip!' Taffy had joined them. 'You can't underestimate old Winnie! Maybe the tide's about to change!'

'I'll believe it when it happens,' Will said.

Nonetheless, it was difficult not to be buoyed up by the arrival of the man himself. The following day, persuaded by Dick, he took a lift with them to Tel el-Kebir, an hour's drive along the coast. There Churchill was to inspect the 2nd New Zealand Division, and they watched as the Morris truck bearing Winston drove slowly past, the familiar figure erect, making his usual V for Victory sign. Clad in a pale linen suit, pith helmet and round sunglasses, cigar as ever in his mouth, he brought an air of solidity to the desert, a figure less transient than the shifting white sands on which he stood to shake the soldiers' hands.

'Who's that with him?' Arnie asked.

Dick, as always, had the answer. 'That's Sir Alan Brooke, Chief of General Staff.'

'So where's the Auk?'

It was 'the Auk', or General Auchinleck, commander of the Eighth Army, who had held the line at Alamein.

'Haven't you heard?' Dick replied promptly. 'He's been given the push. They say Strafer Gott's got the job.'

Will never failed to marvel at Dick's grasp of affairs. Like Guy, he was always in the know. General Gott sounded more like a German than a British commander, but Dick would be sure to have it right.

They watched as the truck bearing the stalwart Prime Minister drew slowly out of Tel el-Kebir.

'Where's he off to now?'

'Going to inspect the line at Alamein, take a shufti for himself,' Dick replied. 'You've got to hand it to the old man!'

7

As was the way with the ticking pendulum of events, the brief boost to morale brought about by Churchill's visit had been transitory. The RAF base in Kabrit was the first to know, for it was here that the Bombay Transport plane flying General Gott back from the tented HQ at Burg-el-Arab should have landed.

This time it was the ground crew who passed on the news. Will, tired from enforced inactivity, had joined the erks while they checked out one of the Liberators from 108 Squadron. The four-engine B-24 bombers were having an impact on the Desert Air Force, primarily because of the long distances they could fly, and it was acknowledged that as the campaign continued, so more and more Wellington Squadrons would be re-equipped with them.

'What do you reckon, Sid?' Will wanted the mechanic's view of the bomber.

'Well, guv, by and large I'm not a fan of the Yanks but once we've tinkered with the B-24s a bit, they should be OK.' Sid's attention was devoted to some wires he was soldering in the bomb bays.

'What's been the problem?' Will said.

'*Problems*, chieffy, not problem,' said Sid emphatically. 'The turrets were

U/S when the first lot arrived, so we had to fix that, now we're getting hang-ups from the electricals.'

Like all pilots, Will dreaded 'hang-ups', when the bombs failed to release from the bomb bay. There was no option but to fly back to base, heavily loaded and frequently harassed by fighters, before attempting to land with the lethal cargo intact.

'Not sure I like the sound of that!'

'I don't think you'll have much of a choice, chieffy, if what we hear is true.' Sid continued his painstaking work, only to be interrupted by a call from outside.

'Oi, Sid!' it was one of the other erks, delivering parts. 'Heard the latest?'

'Surprise me,' said Sid cynically, 'Rommel's given up and gone home to his missus?'

''Fraid not,' the erk replied. 'They say an Me-109 shot down General Gott's plane on its way back, they've all been killed! Poor bugger, just taking his place in an ordinary transport, taken out by a random fighter!'

'I thought he was the one who was going to turn things round!' said Will.

'Well, we never really believed that, did we, sir?' Sid went back to his electricals, concentrating his attention on the things that mattered.

'Nah, Sid, you're out of line there!' one of the other mechanics piped up. 'He was a pro, that bloke! My brother, he's in the 5th Tanks, says they bloody worshipped him – he was an old-timer, been here since '39.'

'I expect we'll get someone who knows damn all about the desert then!' Sid conceded. 'I won't be holding my breath to find out.'

Sid was not the only disillusioned one, and they would have forgotten about the replacement had not Dick kept up with events. In the canteen in mid-August, planning their afternoon, still unaccustomed to either being on leave or knowing how to enjoy it, he said, 'Name's Montgomery, that's the chap they've sent out to replace Gott.'

To the young aircrew, it seemed irrelevant who was commanding the Eighth Army, and they all ignored his remark.

'Anyone fancy a trip to Cairo? I want to try one of the markets,' Will said.

'What are you after buying, old boy?'

'Silk stockings.'

20th August 1942
RAF Kabrit
Dear You,
I hope you receive the enclosed and they are the right size. After much discussion, the lads reckoned 9 would be the safest, as I didn't have a clue! I had an interesting time bartering for them in the market – you have to pretend to walk away before the wogs finally accept your best offer. I don't know what my brother would make of it in the grocery shop in Guisborough, but it seems to work here.

Not much news – we are on leave for a few weeks after a hectic July. It's bliss to have some sleep even though the wretched flies don't let up, and the heat is unbearable. Anyway, I'm not complaining – as long as we're not on one of those infernal landing grounds, we're all happy.

Thank you for your letters – sometimes they come in a batch, then I have a great time reading them. It really means the world to know you're thinking of me, and you are in my thoughts all the time. One day, when we're together again, I can tell you how special you are, just in case you doubted it!

Don't worry about yours truly; I'm as careful as a pilot can be under the circumstances.

Take care of yourself too.

From me

8

'Matt wants us to meet him in town,' George said, as he took her small suitcase. He had been waiting for her at the entrance to the station, enjoying a cigarette, which he tossed away to shake her hand. She noticed there was still little movement in the flexed fingers, which felt cold and smooth despite the warm day.

'In town, where?' Honor took her place in the passenger seat as he opened the door.

George smiled, and she realised that McIndoe must have operated on his upper lip again. It was an improvement, however subtle. How many more attempts would the surgeon make to restore the young pilot's face?

'In the tea shop,' George replied. 'He wanted you to see him away from the ward, for a change. He's much better than he was…'

'How come? Did the grafts on his hands take?'

'Sort of.' George accelerated up the hill to the town. 'He's less depressed. Not banging on about getting back to flying anymore – as a matter of fact, he knows he can't, not with those hands. Once he accepted he wouldn't fly again – not fighters, not bombers, not any kite – he hit rock bottom, then came back up the other side.'

'Was it like that for you, George?' she asked gently.

'Me? Oh, I gave up hope long before Matt did. I had to, Honor, I was in too much of a mess. At least I was alive…'

'And the future, George?' she said.

'Oh my God, I'm nowhere near that one! Just live from day to day. Matt, now he's a different kettle of fish.'

He parked the sports car neatly outside the tea shop, and the bell jangled as they went in.

'Matt!'

As always, the sight of him made her want to cry. He put his arms around her, holding her to his uniformed chest.

He lifted her chin. 'Don't take on so, I'm fine!' But she knew it was not true; he was missing too many fingers for that.

Making the most of George's immaculately folded handkerchief, she sat down next to them, watching Matt's face intently all the time.

A trim waitress in white apron and black skirt approached for her order.

'Oh, just a cup of tea.'

'Nonsense,' said George, 'bring her one of those nice scones, Mabel, you know, the ones you could take out a chap at thirty paces with.'

Mabel smiled. She was used to the boys and their banter by now, even if it had been a bit of shock when they first came in.

'Certainly, sir.' She shot him her special smile.

'And don't forget that tasty rosehip jelly!'

'So.' Honor smoothed her summer dress down. It had pretty red sprigs on a cream background, and had used up twelve coupons, but she felt it was worth it to look nice for the boys. 'How are you really, Matt?'

'Never mind me, how about you? You're looking lovely isn't she, George? What's the news from Will?'

She took a deep breath. 'I don't hear much, you know, he can't tell me what it's really like. He's got his own Wellington, that I do know, and a first-rate crew. Honestly, I find out more from the newspapers than I do from him, and not much of that is good…'

George and Matt shot each other a covert glance. They had no illusions about the campaign he was embroiled in, nor the risks involved.

'Oh, he'll be all right!' Matt said breezily. 'You know Will, sensible to the last. He's got you to come back to, bound to be careful!'

'Do you really think so?'

''Course I do, babe, now here's your tea.'

As she tried to swallow the dry scone, she knew why he had wanted to meet her there. He looked more like the old Matt, despite his hands – he was dressed smartly in uniform and his head was high. The scars around his face were fading, and he was good-looking still. Could he see from his left eye? She did not like to think.

'Tell me about you!' she said, and Matt recounted his operations, and McIndoe's frustrations when his graft had become infected and failed to take.

'He had no choice you see, he had to take some of them off. I would have died otherwise.'

She took a long gulp of lukewarm tea. 'He's made a jolly good job of it!'

'Yes, he has, hasn't he? That's what Jenny says.'

Honor remembered Jenny, his watchful nurse. The bell at the door tinkled again.

'Talk of the devil…' said George, as Jenny came in. She smiled at Honor, and kissed Matt protectively on the cheek.

'You're not overdoing it, are you? Hello, Honor, it's nice to see you back.' She took off a light cardigan and settled comfortably in her seat.

Matt beamed across at them both. There was no preamble to his announcement. 'We've got some news for you, Jenny and I are engaged!'

It proved to be a day of surprises. Later that afternoon, George dropped her back to the Molesworths' house, but not before she could share in the general excitement about Matt and Jenny's wedding. The couple were wasting no time and planned to tie the knot in early September.

Unsurprisingly, Florence did not figure in the conversation, nor was she mentioned by anyone but George, in the car.

'She was quite something, that girl,' he said. 'Bit too hot for Matt to handle, though. She used to come down and see him at first, but obviously didn't fancy the long haul. He was heartbroken! My guess is she's found herself someone older, with a bit of cash – she knows which side her bread's buttered on!'

Unable to defend Florence, whom she hardly knew, Honor changed the subject.

'What about Jenny, is she in it for keeps?

'Too right she is, I don't believe she'd ever let him down. They plan to start a new life together after the war, in South Africa. Matt met some SAAF lads who are hoping to start a commercial airline there once this damned show is over. They want him to manage it, even though he won't be able to fly.'

Honor raised her eyebrows. Such rapid changes of fortune in these times, it was difficult to keep pace with any of her friends.

George did not stay to see Mrs Molesworth, but dropped her at the front door, as he was going to London to see a show, *Diamond Lil*. The guinea pigs had been given a row of the best seats, and he was looking forward to seeing the legendary Mae West. He kissed Honor's hand gallantly before driving off, his scarf waving in the breeze.

The maid answered the bell, and Honor was shown into the front room, to be rapidly followed by her hostess.

'Honor! You'll never guess what's happened!' Mrs Molesworth took her hand animatedly. 'It's Beatie, she's coming back later today! On leave! We weren't expecting it – her father isn't even here!'

'Good heavens! Just like that? Is anything the matter?'

'I don't think so, she just sent a wire to say she had a few days' break. She'll be on the eight o'clock train! I can't believe it, we haven't heard from her for ages! Imagine you being here too, she'll be thrilled!'

They spent the rest of the afternoon preparing for her arrival. Cook was to conjure up a special meal, and her room was aired.

Mrs Molesworth was too distracted to enquire at length about Matt, or the other inmates of Ward 3, but seemed delighted to hear about the wedding.

'Such whirlwind romances for you young people nowadays!' she said. 'When will it be your turn, dear?'

Even if Honor had wanted to mention Will, which she did not, Mrs Molesworth would not have listened. She was in a frenzy of anticipation until the car came to take her to the station.

'You wait here, dear, I won't be long.'

Honor walked around the well-appointed sitting room, looking desultorily at the framed photographs on a delicate inlaid table. Beatie as a baby, a chubby toddler, then a curly-haired girl, with that hint of determination already in her eyes.

The front door opened and she heard Beatie calling her name.

9

It was nearly midnight before they had some time to themselves. Mrs Molesworth had been at fever pitch all evening, fussing around her daughter, plying her with food and a stream of questions, most of which Beatie avoided answering. She looked thin, yet strangely elegant, with a poise that Honor could not recall. Tolerating her mother's attentions with amused restraint, exhaustion finally set in and the two girls excused themselves.

Beatie perched on Honor's bed in the comfortable guest room. 'I'm so pleased you're here! What an incredible coincidence! I was expecting a boring time resting up with the folks, and now look, I've got you too!'

They sipped their cocoa. 'FANYs treating you OK?' Honor said. Something about Beatie's account of events to date did not ring true. She purported to have been posted to Scotland, driving trucks, but divulged little more. Somehow, she did not look robust enough for heavy-duty transport.

'I've got you a present,' Beatie said by way of reply, and handed Honor a small package of tissue paper. 'It's all right, there's one for mother too – anyway, she has plenty of the stuff.'

Honor opened it in surprise. It was Chanel perfume, the sort of scent she would never have dreamt of wearing. Even the delicate wrapping looked expensive.

'Wherever did you get it?'

Beatie looked at her nails. 'Bond Street, when I was last in London,' she replied.

There was a pause. 'You've always been a rotten liar, Beatie Molesworth.'

Honor took her hands and turned them over. 'Look at these, they don't belong to a truck driver! What are you really up to?'

'I'm in the FANY Equipment Office.'

'Ah, yes, the Equipment Office,' Honor said. 'Well, you don't fool me, Beatie. If I had to guess, I'd say that perfume came from Paris, not London. It's all right, I know I can't ask any more. Just be careful!' She hugged her, and for the second time that day her eyes filled with tears.

Beatie wiped her nose on the back of her hand. She had learnt to keep her feelings under control, come what may, never to divulge her true situation, but for her, it was the hardest part. What if her parents only found out after she was captured, or even killed? She would never have the chance to say a proper goodbye.

Her last mission had been surprisingly straightforward, even though she felt sick with apprehension most of the time. Safely hidden by the local branch of the resistance in Saumur, she worked for them as a courier. According to her identity cards, she was Mademoiselle Annette Cormeau, but each time the German guards on the train scrutinised her papers, she doubted that she would make it through. Her French was impeccable, but her cover, that of a buyer for one of the Paris stores, seemed to her implausible. The documents she carried for the resistance were printed on rice paper, but it did not lessen her feeling of panic that they were in her possession.

Every encounter, no matter how trivial, carried risk. She took the utmost care to observe the way of life, and remain inconspicuous at all times. She had jettisoned her black leather shoes soon after arrival – the circuit organiser had commented that leather was now unobtainable in France, and she looked as though she had come straight from London.

Her last train journey was interminable, through the dark night to the capital. Some German officers had entered the compartment and sat down beside her. Affable to a man, they had engaged the pretty girl in endless conversation, and she had managed it, despite the sweat running down her back. There was always the pill, she told herself, the suicide pill sewn into the cuff of her shirt. She prayed that it would never come to that, and tried to keep cool.

The officers found her charming, and escorted her from the train, so that she avoided the customary exit checks. She had already anticipated their offer of a lift.

'Thank you, messieurs, my brother is coming to fetch me…'

It seemed a world away from the security of her family home, but Beatie knew it was only a matter of days before she would be back in the Halifax, waiting for the dispatcher to give her the signal, and jumping once more into the unknown.

The two girls observed each other gravely.

'You saved my life, you know,' Beatie said.

'Not for you to throw it away! How did you get involved?' Then, as no answer was forthcoming, 'Sorry, I promised not to ask. I wish you were still on that motorbike!'

'That makes two of us!'

'You should have seen June's face when you roared off down the road! It was worth it just for that!'

They both indulged in the humour of the memory.

'If only life was that simple!'

'It never is, Beatie. Anyway, your mother reckons you've got a bloke.'

'Does she?' Beatie was surprised. 'There's not much to tell – he's in Malta, flying Spitfires. Not sure which one of us is closer to death, actually!'

Honor looked shocked. 'Don't joke! Who is he, and where did you meet him? You're allowed to tell me that!'

'Well, I am, but I can't be bothered, it's too late and I'm tired! Anyway, that's where Addie is now – Malta, I saw her before she went. She looked so smart in her QA uniform, I almost wanted to change places with her there and then!'

They said goodnight, and Honor stroked Beatie's cheek. 'You don't have to sacrifice yourself, you know.'

'Don't I? Beatie shook her head. 'I'm in it too deep now, I've got to see it through.'

10

3rd September 1942
N. Staffs Infirmary
Dear You,

I can't believe it's three years since the war started – sometimes it feels as though life has been like this forever. I wish it was over and you were safely home, I'd never complain about anything again!

The Duke of Kent's funeral was only last week; dreadful to think of his poor wife and family. I expect you heard he was on active duty, crashed in a flying boat in Scotland.

I try to keep up with what is happening in the desert, but we only hear the half of it. I can't bear to think of you in the middle of all that fighting, so please watch out for yourself.

I went to see Matt, and guess what? He is engaged to be married, but not to Florence. His new sweetheart is a nurse on his ward called Jenny, who looked after him during his surgery. He will never be able to fly again, but is cheerful nonetheless.

I also bumped into one of my old friends from the Lambeth; she's in the FANYs now.

Please stay safe. I think of you every waking moment and sometimes dream of you too.

All my love.

From me

4th September 1942

Dear Addie,

I wanted to write although I've no idea if this letter will reach you. Apparently it takes more than two months for letters to get through to Malta now. We hear news about the siege and awful conditions you are all enduring, but I hope you are managing to keep your spirits up. I am sure you are a devoted QA and they are lucky to have you!

Beatie gave me your address. I saw her recently, which was such a surprise, when I went to visit Matt again at East Grinstead. She just happened to be on leave when I was there, so we had a chance to catch up. She is still with the FANYs, as you know.

Despite several operations, mostly on his hands, Matt will never fly again. He is cheerful enough, and planning to get married soon, to a nurse on the unit.

Will is flying Wellingtons in the Desert Air Force. I can't bear to think of his life constantly in danger. Still, I am always busy at work, which helps, and I feel more settled in Stoke now.

Take care of yourself, Addie – we know how dangerous it is out there and think of you always.

With love from Honor

11

The domes and towers of the ancient Maltese capital, Cita Vecchia, and the deep rocky valley between, were bathed in the radiant October heat. Addie stood on the stone balcony outside the ward, savouring the unexpected calm and the dazzling light. The long months of bomb damage could never extinguish the beauty of the island, as far as she was concerned, nor completely destroy its Mediterranean charm.

She glanced at her watch. It would soon be time for the midday raid, and she had work to finish. The Imtarfa Military Hospital was full to bursting, its 1,200 beds awash with casualties, none of whom could be evacuated during the year-long siege. By now, she was becoming resigned to the desperate lack of food, medical equipment, and supplies. The coal shortage meant that they only had steam for the autoclave twice a week, the Primus stoves were nearly unusable, and keeping theatres going when the temperatures dropped would be practically impossible. The Luftwaffe bombing raids were relentless, for Malta was ripe for invasion once the remaining airfields could be destroyed, and the remaining RAF Wellingtons, Gladiators and Spitfires had been all but decimated by the attacks. Still, they kept on flying and they kept on coming – a new squadron of Spitfires had arrived only last week, and the news had spread like wildfire on the hospital grapevine.

Everyone was at risk: the proximity of the hospital to the airfield meant that the Luftwaffe would have had difficulty avoiding the distinctive painted red crosses on the roofs, even if they had been so minded. Matron Buckingham, a doughty veteran of the first war, was convinced they were included in the targets. Only last week there had been extensive damage to the sisters' rooms, and one of her best nurses had died from her injuries. Undeterred, Matron had arranged their working day around the 7am, midday and 6pm raids. Addie had watched the first while she was getting dressed for breakfast, and was rewarded with the comforting sight of Spitfires attacking the Ju.88 formations.

The civilian population was near starving, and they were desperate for a convoy to make its way through. The minesweeper Manxman had been the last in, carrying limited supplies, but that was before the October blitz.

Addie carefully measured out a few drops of Dettol, which she diluted liberally before proceeding to the next bed. They were down to one gallon a month now, with a pint of spirit a week. As for medication, such as M and B, it was a distant dream, leading to many a lost life from septicaemia.

The young pilot was swathed with bandages over his head and eyes.

'How are you today?' she asked, putting the straw in his mouth, at which he drank eagerly from the water in the glass.

'Will these come off today, Nurse?' He motioned to his face. He had tried to be stoical since he crash-landed two weeks ago.

The doctors had told him that when the swelling subsided from his skull and orbital fractures, he might be able to see again, but as each day passed, his hope diminished. The thought of permanent blindness had devastated him – the once-confident young pilot was a shadow of his former self. He had become a passive and uncomplaining patient, asking for little, increasingly withdrawn.

'We'll have to wait for the surgeon, see what he says.' Addie made his bed, sheets as geometrical as ever; no siege would alter that. 'It won't be long now.'

'You always say that,' he replied. 'So cool and gentle, I often wonder what you look like, you know.'

'I hope you're not disappointed.'

'If I can see again, I shall propose on the spot!' Something of his old vigour resurfaced, then extinguished again.

She finished her tasks. 'The surgeon said he'd come up after his theatre list,' she added, 'so let's see what the afternoon brings.'

The distant drone of the Junkers interrupted them, and she knew she must be running late. It was only a matter of time before they would turn over the hospital for their dive on to the aerodrome, unless the Spitfires scattered them first.

'You'll be here, when they take the bandages off, won't you?'

'I'll be here.'

12

'He's on the run, Skip!'

Will looked up from his washing. Their current landing ground, behind the front line, was no better than the ones before, and they had been beset by electrical storms for most of October, which added to the misery of tented life. Still, at least the filthy weather had given them a brief lull before the Eighth Army kicked off again at Alamein, some ten days ago.

As always in the Desert War, it was well-nigh impossible to work out who was winning. They had heard the pounding barrage guns at the start of the offensive, thundering through the night while the flashes lit up the sky. It had gone on until dawn, when the five Wellingtons from his squadron, 162, had returned from their jamming operations. Their mission, flying backwards and forwards over the enemy tanks, mirrored almost a year to the day that of Operation Jostle, yet the two armies were still hammering hell out of each other. Whilst others in the squadron were buoyed up by the thought of a new general, more American tanks and long-distance bombers, and the latest strategy – 'No more retreats!' – he felt profoundly cynical about the outcome.

His most recent crate, B for Bertie, was not fitted up for radio countermeasures so he and the crew had been spared that first battle. There had been precious little let-up since, and the nightly briefing would send them back bombing enemy concentrations and motorised transport in the battle area. This time, they were not alone: the Bostons, Baltimores and Mitchells were out in formation during the day, eighteen at a time, in sufficient numbers to deter even the most resolute Luftwaffe ace.

It looked one hell of a mess down there, the Albacores lighting up clusters of vehicles and tanks already enveloped by black smoke. By the time they had dropped their own bombs, there were more bursts of green and white smoke, as the Tomahawks closed in, strafing vehicles which disintegrated into flying debris. Despite relentless ack-ack fire, B for Bertie had made it home so far, though he knew they must be on borrowed time.

Dick was not put off by his first pilot's indifference. 'Rommel – he's retreating!'

'How long for this time?'

'Honest, Skip, he's on the road – pulling back from El Daba to Fuka! We've got him!'

Will dried his hands, and draped the towel around his neck. He could not deny Dick his enthusiasm; after all, he was his staunchest friend as well as the best navigator in the business.

'So you think Monty's pulled it off?'

'It's beginning to look seriously like it, old chum. Word has it Rommel's down to about thirty-five tanks, and one of the Afrika Korps commanders has been taken prisoner! You wait, we'll be chasing them along the road tonight, as fast as they can go! It'll be a rout!'

Will pulled on his shirt. 'I'm not sure the words "Rommel" and "rout" go together, Dick, but let's go and see if you're right!'

On the way to the ops tent, Dick itemised the reasons for success.

'One – the Auk left Monty a static, strongly held front, with two firm ends, one at the sea and the other the Quattara Depression. Two – the Eighth Army's been reinforcing along short supply lines for months, we simply have better men and more weapons, thanks to the Yanks. Three – Monty breaks through with a good old-fashioned frontal attack, and four – the Germans spread their troops too evenly along the line, so they don't have a striking force in the rear, ready for a counter-attack. Outcome – the Germans are surprised by the central thrust, don't counter-attack in time, leaving Monty to push forward in a bulge into the German lines, which then leaves a classical enemy salient that they can nip off! Get it?'

Will shook his head, only half understanding and still sceptical about this change in fortunes.

By the time briefing had ended, it appeared Dick might have a point.

'Well, lads!' Even the normally morose squadron leader looked animated. 'Tonight, I'm pleased to say the Desert Fox has his tail between his legs! Operation Supercharge has finally broken through! We're going after him here,' he pointed to the board, 'between Fuka and Galal, and along the El Daba road. He's in retreat, not least because you lot have been bombing hell out of him for the last few weeks. Now it's not Guy Fawkes Night until tomorrow, but what say you go and light Rommel's fire in advance? Any questions?'

Suppressing a smile at the rallying call, Will nudged Arnie, who was sitting on the other side. Arnie raised his hand.

'Is it true that the Italians are surrendering?'

The squadron leader twirled his handlebar moustache. 'I wouldn't like to say, Flight Sergeant, except that they're usually among the first to do so! Of course, they'll be out on a limb if Rommel pulls back first, but I've no particular gen on that one. The planning officer will take you through the maps and the weather for tonight – bit clearer than of late, I'm pleased to say!'

The surreal air of hopefulness might have infected some of the crews, but it was not for Will. He still had a Wellington to fly, a crew to bring back safely, and a load of bombs to drop. His spirits would not lift until his tour of duty was over, and he could disembark from the North African coast forever, set for home.

The roads below them were jammed with enemy vehicles, closely packed targets offering little resistance. Navigation was almost superfluous, for the fires and explosions could be seen miles away, but Dick guided them into the fray.

'Let's go down, Skip, steady…left-left….right a bit…steady…hold it… bombs gone, Skip!'

For a split second Will felt sorry for the troops below, engulfed by the massed conflagration of 150 tons of bombs. The Wellington surged, and he turned for base, conscious only of a niggling headache, a pain behind his eyes, and an overwhelming desire to make it back as soon as possible.

'Aren't you coming over for some breakfast?' Dick asked solicitously after debrief. 'It's been a long night! Some of the lads from 70 Squadron fancy a party later!'

'I'd better go and lie down, I think, got a splitting headache…'

'Want some aspirin from the MO?'

He shook his head, and crawled into his camp bed without undressing, pulling the rough blanket over his face to keep the light from hurting his eyes. His muscles ached and he shivered feverishly, wanting nothing but the oblivion of sleep.

13

He had been dreaming about the waves breaking on the beach at Robin Hood's Bay, but as he surfaced from sleep the rhythmical sounds did not cease. Dimly conscious in the early dawn, he heard the noise of the machine as his chest rose and fell, and for a moment he thought he was a deep-sea diver floating immobile in the warm current of the sea.

Unable to surface from his trance, he looked across at a circle of yellow light. Lit by the dull beam was the white-clad figure of a nurse, writing at a small table. The wide triangular veil encircled her head, above a neatly buttoned white dress, making a tableau that was strangely angelic in the half-light.

'Nurse,' he whispered, hardly wanting to disturb her serenity, and constrained to speak by a thick collar around his neck. He seemed to have been placed in a coffin by mistake, or perhaps he had arrived in Heaven and no one had thought to let him out. If only he could move, there might be a handle on the inside for him to open.

She rose and came to his side. 'You've woken up,' she said softly.

'Where am I?' As the dream lifted, he began to panic.

She saw the alarm in his eyes. 'It's all right, you're quite safe – you're in hospital, you know. You've been delirious for days…'

'What with? And why can't I move?'

She did not meet his eyes. 'The doctor will be round later, he'll explain. Your muscles are weak, so the machine is helping you breathe. Can't you remember anything?' She proffered him a drink from a beaker with a spout.

Obscure visions of orderlies lifting him on to a stretcher, the pain in his back and neck as they did so, jolting in a hot ambulance. Was that here? Had he imagined the pounding headache, the army drilling on manoeuvres in his head? Or the hallucinations as he struggled to breathe? He frowned.

'Not really. How long have I been here?'

'A week now. You're in the 63rd British General Hospital, about ten miles out of Cairo. It's just as well they brought you here, where we have some iron lungs – you were in a bad way when you arrived.'

He dimly remembered Honor talking about iron lungs; surely that was for infantile paralysis? There must be some mistake – he was not a child, to succumb to a disease like that.

'When do I get out of this? They'll be needing me on ops.'

'I know,' she said, 'but we'll have to take it gently, one day at a time. First job today is to get you shaved and washed, then we have to move you, to stop you getting sore.'

'How will you do that?' What would happen if he could not breathe outside this contraption? He tried to move every muscle in his body, but only his arms and hands obeyed.

'We'll puff you on the hand ventilator, you'll see.'

It was thus that the orderlies and nurses bed-bathed and turned him, rubbing surgical spirit into his heels, changing his catheter, shifting the pillows that held him in position until they slid the drawer back and started the motor again. He could feel everything, motionless though he was, and the pain in his muscles was intense.

Feeling safer back inside, his chest heaved and subsided once again to the rhythm of the machine.

'There, time for your breakfast soon.' At least he could still swallow, disconcerting though it was to be fed like a baby. He looked up at the mirror above his head, which showed him the door to his cubicle and the corridor beyond. Two white-coated figures were on their way, walking with the confidence of those who have never had cause to doubt the basic gift of ambulation.

One of them was greying, with shrewd eyes and the look of an elder statesman, but it appeared to Will that the younger one was little older than himself.

'Good morning, Dr Garvin.' Nurse was looking spruce and ready, and he responded in like fashion.

'Good morning, Nurse, and how is our patient today?'

They moved to one side, where he could not hear their discussion, but reassembled at his head.

'Well, Sergeant, you've been very ill.' The older consultant spoke in a soft Scottish accent. 'I'm glad to hear you're improving today.'

'What's the matter with me?' Will knew that only one question was important now. He spoke as the iron lung filled with air, causing him to breathe out.

The two doctors exchanged a glance. 'You've got a temporary paralysis,' Dr Garvin replied. 'We did some tests, including a lumbar puncture, which you probably can't remember, so we're pretty sure about the diagnosis. Your respiratory muscles are involved, which is why we put you in an iron lung.'

'Involved with what?' Will suspected the jargon was an attempt to throw him off the scent.

'There are some nasty bugs around in this part of the world,' the physician continued, 'which you might not have been exposed to as a child. Where do you come from?'

'North Yorkshire,' Will said.

'Fit chap, I suppose, to get into the RAF. Sportsman?'

'Not bad at tennis. You still haven't answered my question.' Will was determined to extract the truth.

Dr Garvin paused. This was the worst part, having to tell the chap that he might not walk again. He would break that later, concentrate upon the here and now.

'I'm afraid you've got poliomyelitis.' That was it; the stark word was out, never to be retracted.

'What do you mean?' There was a time lapse built into the doctor's words, which Will's brain could not yet comprehend.

The physician continued more confidently now that the diagnosis had been divulged. 'You might know it as infantile paralysis. It's endemic out here in North Africa, you will have picked it up somewhere.'

More words he did not understand. Will felt curiously detached from reality, as though he had slipped back into the dream again.

'But I'm not a child, surely you've got it wrong.'

'I'm afraid not, old chap, IP is not confined to childhood, despite the name. That's why we have another name for it: poliomyelitis – it's a virus, we think, affecting the nerves in the spinal cord.'

'So when will I get better?'

His question hung in the air, suspended like his own inanimate self.

'Best not be thinking about that yet.' The physician turned to leave.

'Is that it?'

'For the moment, old chap. Dr Foyle will come back later, won't you?' He looked across at the younger man, who nodded, as though momentarily bereft of speech.

They stopped at the door, with the nurse, to talk amongst themselves. Like a debrief, Will thought, but he listened attentively, trying to catch the conversation. The young one must be Australian; he had heard that accent before and it reminded him of Fred. Not that he would be seeing Fred again.

'Have you heard of the Kenny method, sir?'

Dr Garvin's negative reply was peremptory – he had other patients to see.

The Australian voice continued, gently suggestive. 'I went to her clinic in Brisbane when I was a medical student. She's quite a lady – gets some great results.'

'What does she do?' Dr Garvin did not pretend to be an expert on the condition; he was a military man, more at home with the traumatic injuries of war.

'Well, she doesn't believe in immobilisation or splints. In fact she's not that keen on iron lungs except in severe cases of respiratory paralysis, like this one. She uses hot packs on the affected muscles, to stop the pain and spasm, then early passive movements, followed by physical therapy and hydrotherapy.'

'Well, we've not got that here. Shall we move on?'

But the young man was tenacious. He had seen the feisty Sister Kenny in action, removing the patients from the rigid frames, taking away the plaster casts and heavy callipers, and keeping the muscles moving with her own system of exercises. Originally derided by the medical establishment, she was now attracting favourable notice, and he, for one, believed in her.

'I could teach the nurses, sir – it's really quite straightforward, and worth a try. After all, he's got nothing to lose, has he?'

Dr Garvin looked at his watch. He was becoming restless; his theatre list would be starting soon. 'Oh, I suppose so, but don't waste too much of your time. Remember we're busy enough here with the casualties from Alamein. But you can give it a go if you must, just make sure all your other work comes first!'

Will watched them leave from the mirror above him. So he was a severe case, was he? When was someone going to tell him exactly what was going on?

The moving finger writ, and having writ, moved on. The ancient line sprang unbidden to his memory, as the day's slow routine began.

14

Hitler was not the enemy anymore – it was polio, and his body was the battleground.

Marty Foyle, for that was the young doctor's name, was one of the chief protagonists. Having always feared the disease himself, it took no leap of imagination for him to change places with the stricken airman. How would he want to be treated if that was him, lying there in an iron lung, unable to move?

Like all good generals, Marty needed to recruit an army. His good looks were his chief weapon as far as the nursing staff was concerned, but it was more than that; he possessed an irresistible energy.

'Come on, Sister, I'm going to show you how to make the Kenny packs.' He found that several of the QAs gathered round as he cut a heavy woollen blanket, purloined from the linen cupboard, into strips. He placed them in boiling water, then wrung them out as far as possible without scalding his own hands.

'Slide him out,' he ordered.

Will was wary. 'Don't I have any say in this?' But it was difficult not to respond to the Australian's enthusiasm. 'What's your name?' he asked, breathing in as the machine switched off. He was not as frightened as the first time, and could now tolerate short periods outside without the need for hand ventilation. It was as much a mental attitude, learning to breathe shallowly while exposed to the real world. In his musings, he was a large baby, born before his lungs had developed.

'Marty,' the Australian said, 'and Mrs Bossyboots is called Betty, in case you haven't already been introduced.'

His nurse, previously so self-possessed, blushed fiercely, but said nothing, despite a few curious looks from her assembled colleagues.

As Marty neatly wound the hot strips around his legs, so the pain diminished and Will could almost feel the muscles relax for the first time. Carefully supervised, Betty placed more hot packs on his chest, and the tightness relieved. He did not attempt to speak, but concentrated on his breathing.

Keeping a running commentary for his students, Marty started to move Will's limbs, now no longer in spasm, explaining as he did so the necessary stretching of the muscle groups. The nurses watched attentively; it was always a joy to be taught, however unconventional the treatment.

'Will, are you OK? I want you to think about this spot here, the quadriceps – right above the knee there, think of that. Think of pulling…' Marty instructed, and Will, not quite sure if he was doing it correctly, tried his best.

'Is that right?' Betty asked, performing an identical set of passive movements on his left leg.

'Spot on, couldn't make a better job of it myself! He has to think about the muscle while you do it, remind him of that at the same time.' Marty knew how to keep the troops on side. 'We'd better put him back, he's done very well!'

Back in the iron lung, when Will had pinked up, Marty asked, 'So what's it like, this Kenny treatment?'

Will smiled, with a flicker of his old sense of humour. 'If it means a lot of pretty nurses fussing over me, I'm all for it, Marty!'

From the outset, the fiercest skirmish of the conflict was being waged in his head. The two opposing armies, doubt and self-belief, were lining up and it was set to be a bitter struggle. Despite Dr Garvin's gloomy prognosis, Will refused to accept that he would never walk again, but in the darkest hours of the long night, to the monotonous fall and rise of the respirator, presentiments of disability crept unbidden into his mind. Surely he would not end up a cripple, like some of those children on Honor's ward? Worse than that was the fear of losing her, which could overwhelm him. He wanted to look after her, not the other way round, being pushed about in an invalid carriage while their young lives slipped away.

Despite his disinclination to communicate the true nature of his condition to anyone back home the hospital had insisted upon informing his parents. Not wanting Honor to be left out of the loop, he had asked them to include her too. Brief telegraphs had been sent to that effect, merely stating that he was in the 63rd BGH, in a stable condition, and that further correspondence would follow.

He could hardly bear to imagine the effect of the wire. Still, Honor would be relieved that he was in a British hospital, whatever had befallen him, and not missing, POW, or killed in action.

'What should I say in the letter, Betty?' he asked one day. He could tolerate longer periods outside the iron lung now, and his nurse, second in command of his troops, was administering the hot packs and supervising another QA as they performed the physiotherapy routine.

'Will, you must concentrate upon the muscle origin while we do this,' she said seriously. 'You know the score. Think of it, think of the tibialis anterior, just here – you have to, or it won't work. The way I see it is, if you don't exercise a muscle group, it will waste away. You have to work doubly hard to make sure your brain doesn't forget how to do it. Even a little flicker of muscle activity is a start, we can build on it.'

Betty was a trooper, there was no doubt about that. What had started as an attempt to please Marty, with whom she was deeply in love, had turned into a personal crusade. She was determined to get the young pilot back on his feet, no matter what it took, and her conviction outflanked the rest. On her off-duty, she would sometimes arrive on the ward and perform an extra session of treatment, cajoling the night staff to join her, so that they too would take the initiative.

'Has anyone ever told you you're a wonderful nurse?' He liked observing her quiet efficiency, and her absorption in her task.

She blushed, as she was wont to do. 'Don't be silly, I'm just doing my job.' She removed the packs and positioned him gently before sliding him back. 'Anyway, you should tell her the truth.' She flicked the switch of the respirator.

'I daren't,' Will said. 'What if she doesn't want me anymore? Why should she be tied to a cripple for the rest of her life?'

'William Fordham!' Betty looked shocked. He was usually so optimistic, this young chap. She had no intention of allowing doubt to creep in, not when they were doing so well. Like all good nurses, she knew the power of the mind in relation to disease, especially a debilitating one like this. No, she was not about to let that happen.

'Now you listen to me. If your sweetheart, Honor, is worth her salt she'll stand by you. Plus, she's a nurse, so even if you take a while to recover she'll understand. Secondly, and most importantly, you're not going to be a cripple, not if I have anything to do with it! Just look at the difference the treatment has made, even Dr Garvin had to admit that!'

It was true; the physician had spent some time examining him on the morning round, intrigued by the first signs of spontaneous muscle activity. He had reluctantly conceded that Dr Foyle might be on to something.

'So I don't want to hear any more talk like that! I'll help you write the letters – just come clean about it, and explain that you're making good progress. Anyway, you must let your parents know, your poor mother will be worried half to death!'

15

The truck drew up outside the hospital and Vic climbed out. 'Thanks, Sarge.' He made a half-salute to the driver as it drew away.

As he walked through the clean, cool building to the ward, he recalled the last time he had been there, to see Don, and prayed that he would find Will in better shape. Don, whose leg had been amputated below the knee, had long since been repatriated but he never ceased to miss him. *Best damn wireless operator I ever had!* he mused, wondering what course the Scotsman's life had taken since his return. If he ever made it back to Blighty himself he would look him up, whenever that might be.

In the three weeks since Will's dramatic departure in the ambulance, near death's door and unable to breathe, the German rout that Dick had predicted had not taken place. Rommel might have been beaten at Alamein but his withdrawal from Egypt into Libya had been conducted with skill and determination. The Eighth Army had lost their chance to cut off the German forces, and a break in the weather had brought driving rain and low cloud, such that the squadron had been grounded at a critical time. The Desert Fox was now holding a position at El Agheila, where the pursuing British outran their own supply lines, and both sides dug in, in time-hallowed fashion, to reinforce for the next stage. The Allies, though, were holding a trump card – Operation Torch, with major troop landings in Morocco, ready to confront Rommel on his west flank, and force him out of Africa.

205 Group was moving and changing too. While Vic was still in Kabrit, the rest of the squadron was either moving eastwards to LG 104, or being redeployed in Malta, where the long siege was over. He would soon be joining them on the island, flying from Luqa to attack targets in Tunisia.

Vic ran his fingers through his hair, hoping he looked tidy enough. As he neared the ward, the smell of disinfectant filled him with apprehension.

'I'm here to see Flight Sergeant Fordham,' he told the white-uniformed nurse nearest the door. She looked at him with interest, for Will had not received many visitors to date.

'I'll take you to his cubicle, he'll be pleased to see you.'

He followed her down the ward to a cluster of rooms at the end.

'You know he's in an iron lung, don't you?' she continued, in a matter-of-fact tone, giving Vic no time to reply.

'Visitor for you,' Betty announced, but Will knew – he had caught sight of the familiar figure in his mirror, causing his throat to constrict strangely.

Vic stood uncertain on the threshold, unaccustomed to the rhythmical noise of the motor. He was not expecting this, and had no idea what to do.

'Come in, old chap.'

It was a relief to hear Will's voice; at least he could still speak, whatever contraption they had put him in.

Betty pulled over a chair. 'Not too long now, we don't want him tired out. I'll be back in a bit.'

'How are you?' Vic sat down uneasily. 'What the hell have they put you in this for? It looks like a medieval torture chamber.'

'Spot of bother breathing, but I'm getting better.'

'When are you getting out of here? We could do with you back on ops, you know.'

Will smiled; the prospect of flying again, however dangerous it might be, seemed like heaven.

'No can do, they're going to send me home when I can breathe without it.'

Vic was alarmed. He felt completely in the dark – surely he should have been given a little more information?

'What's the diagnosis, Will?'

'Didn't they tell you? Infantile paralysis.' He spoke in short sentences in time with the machine, but it was enough for Vic.

'Christ Almighty, I had no idea! You'll be OK, though, won't you?'

''Course I will, just take a bit of time. Where are the others?'

'Arnie and the rest of your crew, including Dick, are in Malta. They didn't have time to visit before they left. Dick was very cut up about it, but I promised him I'd look in, make sure you were all right. I'm going there myself in a couple of days.'

Will felt the gulf opening between them. Vic and his friends were still in his old world, before polio. He longed to be back with them, getting kitted up for the next duty and easing the Wellington off the runway. So what if the enemy fighters came at you? At least you were part of the real world, taking your chances with the best of them. What sort of future could he expect now?

'You'll give them my regards?'

'Of course, old chap. Now is there anything I can do? Anything you want? Are they looking after you properly here?'

Betty reappeared. 'Time to go,' she said cheerfully, and Vic dutifully followed her from the room, looking back at his one-time second pilot with concern, and a wave of farewell.

'Just you hurry up and get better!'

In the corridor, he took Betty's hand. 'Tell me the truth!' he said urgently.

She paused, taking him in, the brown-limbed pilot, lines around his eyes from squinting at the sun: one of our best boys, like Will.

'The consultant says he'll never walk again.' Her back straightened, and her head was high, as though in defiance. 'But it's not true, I know it's not!'

30th November 1942
63rd British General Hospital
Cairo
Dear You,

I hope you haven't been worrying about me because I am much better. I didn't think you needed to know I was in hospital but the powers that be have their own rules.

Anyway, this is the story so far. Just as I was about to finish my tour of duty, and qualify for a decent spell of leave back home, I end up being brought in here on a stretcher. Bad timing! I thought it must be sandfly fever at first, but the docs ran a load of tests and tell me it's polio. Fortunately you are one of the few people I don't have to explain this to, for you know all about it.

I must have picked it up in this unclean country, and I'm sorry to say I'm not the only one. The paralysis is mainly legs and abdomen; my breathing is improving now. The nurses are doing a great job on me, some new method of treatment that the Australian doc knows all about. So you don't need to worry, I'll soon be right as rain and don't intend to let it set me back too much.

There is talk about evacuating me because I am aircrew but no dates yet. I'll send you a telegram if things change.

I am sorry not to have any more interesting news but not much happens here, as you can imagine! I hope you are keeping well, and think of you all the day and night.

With all my love.
From Me

16

'I have never promised anything but blood, tears, toil and sweat. Now, however, we have a new experience – we have victory.' Churchill's sonorous voice came over the crackling wireless, to the audience of attentive nurses. Not least Honor, who strained to catch every word.

'A bright beam has caught the helmets of our soldiers and warmed and cheered all our hearts. England always wins one battle – the last.'

As his words unfolded, there could be no doubt that the battle of Alamein had been the turning point. Could the Desert War really be over?

'This is not the end. It is not even the beginning of the end, but it is, perhaps, the end of the beginning.'

The broadcast of November 10th came to an end and the church bells started to ring, a sound that was by now unfamiliar. It was the first victory of the war, and the Prime Minister was making the most of it. Some could not join in the nation's thanksgiving: those whom the shifting desert sands had robbed of their husbands, sweethearts or sons.

Honor took Lotte's hand, conscious that even this turning of the tide would not stop her relatives dying in concentration camps. She sometimes wondered who would be left intact to celebrate at the end of this terrible war, whatever side they might be on.

'Is good news!' Lotte smiled back, but her eyes were full. 'Your boyfriend, maybe come home to you?'

Passing her a handkerchief, Honor shook her head. 'I'm afraid there's a lot of water to go under the bridge first!' It seemed most likely that the troops would be deployed elsewhere in the Mediterranean, and there was talk of an invasion of Italy. No, she was not counting upon seeing Will anytime soon.

Rosie was not with them to share the news. Her brother Jack was on shore leave, back from his last convoy, and she had gone to Scotland to see him. He was all she had left in the world now, and she lived for news of him. Honor hoped the meeting would give her some solace, for like Addie before her, Rosie had thrown herself into her work until she was almost extinguished by it.

The two girls walked over to the ward for the afternoon shift. It was bitterly cold, their breath lingering in the frosty air.

'Honor, I want to tell you something.' Lotte stopped on the path and turned to face her.

'What is it? You look ever so serious!'

Lotte paused. She had a secret and needed to share it.

'Come on, tell me what it is!'

'Is about Percy… he asked me to marry him!'

'But that's wonderful news!' Honor hugged her. 'I'm so pleased for you both!'

Her unreserved pleasure what not quite what Lotte had expected. 'So you think I should accept?'

'Of course you should, he's mad about you! Why ever wouldn't you?'

'What will happen to him if he marries enemy alien? It is not so good for him – his career, his family…'

Honor was having none of it. 'That is the most ridiculous thing I have ever heard! Of course you'll marry him – you love each other! Love can overcome all obstacles, you know, nothing can stand in its way!'

'You really think?' Lotte's pale cheeks looked flushed, despite the cold.

'I really think! There's one condition – that I'm there at the wedding!'

'Are you sure?' The girls hugged again, and Lotte whispered into her ear, 'It's on Friday, at the church down the road!'

The days that followed were infused with a hidden anticipation of the day. Lotte wanted no one to know, and even Percy had failed to inform his parents. Despite Honor's staunch support, he had an idea what his mother was going to say, and did not want to hear it. Mrs Black had been kindness itself to the young Austrian in her convalescence, but this was a different matter. An object for compassion was not the same thing as a prospective daughter-in-law. As for his father, he was abroad, in Geneva with the Red Cross. Honor would be one of the witnesses, but they needed another.

'Who do you think would do it?' Percy had caught up with her in the sluice after the ward round. She placed the instruments in the steriliser before answering.

'I think I know who you should ask,' Honor said.

'Who?'

'Sister Duncan.'

Percy's face registered near-horror. 'You must be joking!'

'I'm not – she's always been kind to Lotte. Look how she stopped those men taking her away to an internment camp. And if you think she hasn't worked out what's going on between you two, then you're not very observant!'

Eventually, Percy concurred, which was as well, for there was no time to look for an alternative. When he came out of Sister Duncan's office half an hour later, he looked as though he had been through the Spanish Inquisition, and immediately left the ward.

'Nurse Newson, my office!'

Honor's heart fell; perhaps she had given Percy the wrong advice?

'Yes, Sister Duncan?' She closed the door behind her, ready for the storm.

Sister Duncan took a deep breath. 'I've had some unusual requests in my life, but this one has to be the strangest. Dr Black tells me it was your idea to ask me to be a witness.' She fixed Honor with a steely gaze.

'Yes, it was, Sister,' Honor said. She had developed a great respect for the older woman, and sensed a spirit that was free. 'Lotte has no family, and I know you've looked out for her. We'd all like you to be there, if there's any chance.'

'You would, would you?' Sister Duncan was in full flow. 'Do you think he'll stand by her? She could hold him back – she's still an enemy alien, you know!'

'They love each other,' Honor said simply. 'I thought you'd understand.'

'Just a minute! I haven't finished!' Sister smoothed down her headdress. 'As it happens, I agree with you. What time is the ceremony?'

A smaller nuptial than the one in Holy Trinity church, that Saturday morning, would have been hard to find. Not for Lotte and Percy the crowd of relatives and friends, the carefully planned garments, the wedding organ ringing forth. Theirs was a simple plighting of troth, in front of the vicar, witnessed by only two nurses, one young and one old, but not too old to have forgotten the mystery of love.

As the couple sealed the knot with a kiss, Honor's efforts not to cry were undermined by Sister Duncan, who dabbed her eyes with a starched handkerchief, into which she then loudly blew her nose.

'Such a nice service, dear!' Sister said as they followed Percy and Lotte, both looking extraordinarily happy, from the church.

There was to be no reception. The newly-weds drove back to the nursing home to pick up Lotte's case: she only had one night off duty, and they were going to a hotel in the nearby countryside.

The two women walked slowly back through the streets of Stoke, the watery winter sun lightening the day, only breaking off their conversation when they reached the hospital.

A porter in the office hailed them as they went past.

'Telegram, Nurse Newson. Arrived just after you left!'

Honor clutched at Sister Duncan's arm. She thought she would faint, so Sister took the telegram and put it into her unwilling hands.

'I can't open it!'

'Yes, you can, dear, you have to. Do you want to sit down?' Sister Duncan nodded at the porter, who opened his door and motioned her to the chair.

Honor turned the telegram over in her hands, as if to delay the black printed words from entering her world.

'Shall I read it to you?' Sister said.

Honor nodded; nothing could stop it now.

> *Regret to inform you Sergeant William Fordham hospitalised 63rd British General Hospital Cairo stop Condition stable stop Sender Stuart Garvin MO Military Wing*

Part Ten: Liberators

1

The Liberator pulled smoothly off the runway at Kabrit, and rose over the North African coastline that had figured so often in his dreams of going home. Far from a vantage point in the cockpit, which he had once checked over so critically with his ground crew, Will lay encased in his iron lung. Betty smiled at him encouragingly, for it was she who had been detailed to accompany him for the eight-hour flight to Gibraltar, and thence to Hendon.

'I never thought I'd be going back like this,' Will said, but she could hardly hear him above the noise of the giant four engines.

He was one of twelve passengers, and it was the first time that the pilot, Flight Lieutenant Baker, had taken a patient in a respirator, but he liked the look of the pretty nurse. *Poor bugger*, he thought, *not a pleasant way to finish your tour of duty*, and gave a silent prayer of thanks for his own reprieve, and a spell of time at home, after nearly a year in the desert. A pilot with 160 Squadron, based at Shandur, he had been bombing the Axis forces in Tunisia, where Rommel was regrouping for a counter-offensive. It was 14th February 1943, and there was no sign of the Desert Fox giving up, despite the dual threat of the Eighth Army to the east, and the Allied forces from Algeria to the west. Operation Torch, mounted last November, had successfully brought American forces on to the North African coastline, to fight side by side with the Allies for the first time. The rain, sleet, hail and bitter cold had stopped the Allied advance through the mountains, and victory was not yet in sight, nor could it be counted upon, poised as Rommel was for a thrust against the American forces at Faïd Pass. Tripoli might now be in British hands, but the ports of Tunis and Bizerta, with their all-weather airfields, formed part of the strategic German supply line from Sicily, and these had been the targets for Baker and his crew.

The culmination of the battle for Tunisia, yet to be engaged, was not uppermost in Will's thoughts. His own enemy, polio, still had outposts in his muscles and his mind, and was proving as tricky an adversary as Rommel. How many times had he imagined seeing Honor again, when he had been fit and well: their happy reunion, a whirlwind marriage – the poet Marvell had the right words, centuries ago:

Let us roll all our strength and all
Our sweetness up into one ball,
And tear our pleasures with rough strife
Through the iron gates of life:
Thus, though we cannot make our sun
Stand still, yet we will make him run.

Neither he, nor their sun, would be running anymore. Still paralysed, unable to sweep her off her feet with his youthful strength, he faced a long road to recovery which she might not choose to travel.

It was a fact that his progress so far had been remarkable, according to Marty Foyle. Will was going to miss the confident Australian, who alongside Betty had badgered and cajoled successive teams of nurses and orderlies to continue his physical therapy. Able to tolerate most of the day, if not the night, outside the iron lung, he had even been taken to regular hydrotherapy in a local swimming pool. The sensation of swimming once again, however weak his legs, had induced a sense of near bliss as he felt the strength returning in his arms with each stroke. For his part, he would have stayed there for hours, buoyed up by the water, closing his eyes and thinking of the sea at Robin Hood's Bay.

'See what progress he's made, Dr Garvin,' Marty had said to his consultant at that last ward round in the 63rd BGH. 'I knew the Kenny treatment would work, I've seen it before!'

He was exultant, as only a young enthusiast can be, but Dr Garvin, after performing a detailed examination, was not so easily convinced.

'It's hardly a double-blind trial, Foyle,' he said. 'There could have been spontaneous recovery even without your intervention – that, after all, is the nature of the disease.'

Marty was undaunted, and winked at Will as they left. Later, coming back to make his farewell, he sat down by his bedside.

'I'll miss you, you're my prize patient!'

'Not according to your boss,' Will replied. 'Marty, do I really have to fly home in an iron lung? I'm out of it most of the time now.'

'Look, I know you don't want to, but it's safest that way. Your breathing won't be so good at altitude, and I don't want any problems. Best get you back safely, even at the expense of your dignity. Also, you'll need an escort, and that way Betty can get some leave.'

'I don't suppose I'll ever see you again.' Will frowned. 'I wish I didn't feel so dependent on you!'

Marty smiled. 'That, Skip, is also the nature of the disease. We've been in it together, haven't we? But I know you're going to be OK, just a bit more hard work on your part and you'll soon be on your feet, you'll see!'

'Do you think I'll ever fly again?'

'God knows, but I can't imagine why you'd want to after what you've been through! Anyway, it looks to me as though the Desert War is pretty near over, so we'll all be out of here. Rommel's going to be chucked out soon, the Yanks'll see to that!'

Will had felt vulnerable, leaving the hospital, and was glad to have Betty at his side. It was as though he was severing his bond with those who had kept faith with him, and he did not know from which biblical hills he would find his strength.

There had been one more important question he had to ask Marty before he left, but the young doctor had already anticipated it. The conversation had taken place late at night, the darkened ward giving an intimacy that was denied during the day.

'Are you going to marry Betty?' Will had asked abruptly, causing Marty to look up from the notebook in which he was recording Will's recovery.

'Oh, I don't know about that,' he said, taken off guard. 'I mean, she's a great girl, but I'm not really ready to settle down yet. I want to see the world, after this show is over, and I don't reckon a pretty English rose like that will wait for me.' Marty took up his pen again before asking, 'What about you? Betty says you've got a sweetheart at home.'

Will's voice was unsteady. 'I have, or had. I'm not sure she'll want me now. She's a nurse, but that doesn't mean she has to sacrifice her life to someone like me.'

'What do you mean, sacrifice? You're getting better, I'm expecting a full recovery, you know!'

''Course you are, Marty!' Will never doubted his conviction, and was grateful for it. 'Where would I have been without you? Anyway, life's not just about being able to walk, is it? What about sex? She has a right to expect that, like everyone else.' He lay back on the pillow, waiting for a reply.

Marty was his usual blunt self. 'Your sexual function will be normal, old chap – I suspect you know that already.'

Will nodded. He had first been aroused by the administrations of the nurses some time ago. But that still did not explain the mechanics of the act, especially in its conventional position.

Marty sighed. 'Do I have to spell it out? Once your leg muscles are stronger then you can do it any way you want, until then, she might have to go on top but most girls I know seem to like that. Got it? Your potency and fertility will be unaffected, so I don't see where the sacrifice comes in!'

Deep in the fuselage of the Liberator, Will mulled over Marty's words again as he let the respirator breathe for him. The young doctor clearly knew a great deal more about sex than he did, but there was plenty of time to learn. Betty had taken a break – the pilot seemed to have taken a fancy to her and was sharing his coffee with her. There were fewer night fighters around now, concentrated as they were upon the conflict zone in Tunisia, and the Liberator had passed beyond the Luftwaffe bases in Sicily some time ago. Malta was far behind them too – Dick and the squadron were still there, on bombing sorties to the ports of Sousse and Sfax whenever the weather allowed. It had been a cruel winter, according to the reports, but at least the convoys were now landing again in Malta and the siege had been relieved.

There had been no chance to say goodbye to any of his crew, and Vic had been his last visitor, before his posting to Malta with the rest. Wondering if he would ever see them again, and wishing he was in the cockpit of the B24, back at the controls, Will fell into an uneasy sleep.

He woke in the early dawn. Betty was back, ministering to him through the portholes of the iron lung.

'Not long now!' she said. She sat beside him, making sure his fluid intake was adequate, as the Rock came into view. 'I'm off to take a look!' Of course she was, but then, he had seen it before, as second pilot, from the Wellington, on his way out, nearly a year and a half before.

2

As the ambulance that bore them both to the British Military Hospital jolted its way up the hill, Betty sat up front, excited to be back in Gibraltar where she had first been posted as a QA, and hoping to find some of her old friends. The historic naval base, in British hands since 1704, had allowed domination of the sea lanes into the Mediterranean, and proved to be an ever-present thorn in Hitler's side. Even from the stretcher on which he was carried into the imposing, porticoed building, Will could see the wide vista of the sea, naval ships at anchor in the bay, and the Rock towering above.

'How long are we going to be here?' He was impatient to be home, come what may, rather than speculate endlessly about his future.

'Just a few days.' Betty, loyal and efficient as ever, was unwilling to pass on his care to the resident nurses without briefing them fully as to his needs.

'Why couldn't we have stopped at Malta? I could have seen my crew!' But Will knew only too well the dangers of the runway at Luqa; difficult enough for a Wellington, let alone a Liberator, quite apart from the distance they needed to cover on this first leg of the journey. It was a rhetorical question, to which Betty gave a half-hearted answer.

'Will, don't be daft, it's nicer here, no rationing, and no chance of them trying to hang on to you until you're better – that's what they'd do in Malta.'

He suspected she was right, and allowed himself to be fussed over. His room looked over the bay, and for the moment he was content to rest and regain his strength.

Betty left him after giving detailed instructions to two of her new colleagues about his muscle exercises.

It was not until the next morning that a trim little nurse, bringing his breakfast, held up a letter on the tray.

'This is for you, I think – you're Flight Sergeant William Fordham, aren't you?'

He looked puzzled, for who would know he was there? He had been allowed to send two telegrams from Cairo advising of his return, one to his parents and one to Honor, but that had been only two days ago.

The handwriting looked familiar, and the envelope uncensored.

RAF Luqa
10th February 1943
Dear Will,

I hope this reaches you, for I've been told you'll end up in Gib en route for home. A chap from the base is flying back there today so I thought it would be worth a chance. Anyway, it makes a change to write a letter without the censors poring over it, and having their little laugh.

As it happens, I'm in dock myself – the Imtarfa Military, but nothing half as bad as you; just a nasty case of 'Malta dog' (the vilest tummy bug I have ever had). I should be out soon, just recuperating for another couple of days before they have me back with the crew, fully bombed up and set for Bizerta, or whichever Tunisian port takes their fancy.

We have all been so worried about you – it was awful seeing you carted off like that and then not being able to visit before we were all sent here. None of us knew you had infantile paralysis until Vic visited you. He was very cut up about it, seeing you in an iron lung like that. One of the nurses told him you were going to be all right so we're all hoping that's true and you're well back on the road to recovery.

I must be honest, it's not been the same since you left – you were our skipper, and we all trusted you to bring us home. Teams like that take a long time in the making, and yours was one of the best.

I was wrong about Rommel wasn't I, when I said it would be a rout? Rather regretting that now, as we set off each night in filthy weather to try and stop him. Quite a few of our lads aren't making it back, and the show is far from over. We still don't know which of us will be at the breakfast table on any given morning, not that there's much to eat when we're there!

At least you have the comfort of knowing Honor will be waiting for you, and I hate to say it, but it could be worse. The very moment I finish my tour of duty and get back home, I'll come and visit you wherever you are.

I'll be sorry to leave these pretty nurses, but some of the chaps in here are in a bad way, and I certainly wouldn't like to change places with any of them. Most of them would give their eye teeth to be evacuated, so I hope the gen I had from the 63rd BGH is right, and you are safely on your way.

You know what Winston says: keep buggering on! And best of luck from us all.

Dick

3

Another hospital, another ward. Except this time he was home at last, or at least on British soil. On landing at Hendon, he had no idea where he would be sent until Betty, having filled in numerous documents, managed to find out.

'It's good news, Will, you're going to the Princess Mary Hospital in Halton!' Then, responding to his blank look, 'You must have heard of it, it's one of the best RAF hospitals in the country!' Betty was a QA herself, but that did not alter her respect for another force's medical services. 'You'll be well looked after there, they probably have the latest in polio treatment!'

'Where is it?'

'Not sure, somewhere in Buckinghamshire. I'll be coming with you in the ambulance, don't worry!'

'Somewhere in Buckinghamshire' proved to be Aylesbury, which by coincidence was close to Grendon Underwood, the village where Honor had grown up. His spirits lifted; perhaps she was there even now, on a spell of off-duty with her parents, and could just look in and see him as soon as he arrived. Except of course, he did not really want her to see him carted in like this, on a stretcher. Better to wait until he was settled in.

The grey skies looked positively welcoming after the harsh desert sun, and the cool, damp air, peculiar to his own country, pleasantly familiar. It seemed as though he had been away from these shores for a lifetime, as though his old life had been burnt out of him in the desert, leaving him raw and defenceless for the one that lay ahead.

'Right, sir, we'll soon have you on the way.' The orderly's voice was competent and brisk, and even if the ambulance design was no better than before, he was jolted along the country roads at a decent pace. He remembered Florence and her perilous driving that first time on the way to Groby Road. Where would she be now?

It was nearly dusk when the ambulance stopped and the back doors were opened. His stretcher was carried swiftly through the red-brick, pavilioned hospital, and into the main hall. More paperwork for Betty, who seemed undaunted by the challenges. In fact, she was enjoying herself – it would be interesting to see the hospital and be updated on the latest treatments. She had spent so long in field hospitals that the smell of polish was intoxicating. Added to which, there was the matter of a rendezvous with the B24 pilot back in London once her charge was safely delivered. Flight Lieutenant Baker was handsome, and very keen, and although she was mad about Marty she had a feeling he would let her down one day.

First of all, though, she had to make sure the staff knew what they were doing, but it was with no little deference that she approached the ward sister. The Princess Mary RAF nurse uniform was different to her own, and rather inferior, she thought, despite the wide white veil and starched collar above the white dress. However, there was little doubt about their respective positions, and each allowed for immediate recognition.

Betty withdrew with Sister to her office, while Will waited on his stretcher in the airy ward, surrounded by aircrew in various states of ill-health and incapacity.

'Evening, old chap!' a voice hailed him from a nearby bed. 'Come to join the few?'

Despite raising his head from the stretcher, Will was unable to see the occupant, who was obscured by a large bed frame under the sheets.

'Hope not,' he replied. 'I'm just passing through, with any luck!'

'That's what they all say, isn't it, Boz?' the voice came back. But Boz, whoever he might be, made no reply. 'What are you in for?'

Before Will had time to answer, Betty was back with Sister and he was being carried to a cubicle at the end of the ward, where he was manoeuvred back into an iron lung, despite his protests.

'It's only for tonight, Will,' Betty said. 'They just want to make sure you're stable after the journey.'

Sister Curtis raised her eyebrows at the obvious familiarity between the two, but kept her counsel. She was an experienced RAF nurse, having entered the service after her SRN training, but had never served abroad as her husband was not keen upon them being parted. She had missed a good posting to Bermuda as a consequence, and felt a little envious of girls like this one, who had nursed in the thick of it, where Sister conceded normal barriers might be down.

It was another hour before he was settled, and Betty departed for the nurses' home.

'I'll be back in the morning.' She waved, leaving him once more to his thoughts and a longer, darker night than he was used to. Would the sun never rise? Rather the rose-infused dawns of the desert, when the sun brought the sands to life before he was ready to wake.

The day staff were as efficient as their night-time colleagues, and he was soon out of the respirator, washed, changed and breakfasted before the morning round. This comprised an unfamiliar hierarchy – the consultant was a squadron leader as well as a medical man and the nurses all bore RAF ranks. Betty had taken her place among them and looked her usual confident self.

'So,' Dr McWhirter began, 'who's going to give me the history?'

Betty stepped forward, and embarked upon a concise summary of Will's condition, including details of his treatment to date.

'Thank you, Nurse. That's interesting, I've heard of the Kenny technique, of course, but we use it in a modified form here. Results look promising so far, it has to be said. They reckon she has the ear of Roosevelt himself.'

The degree of disability suffered by the President of the United States of America was a closely guarded secret. He was rarely seen in a standing position, except in carefully taken photographs, and it appeared likely that he had been more or less wheelchair-bound since contracting poliomyelitis in his late thirties. Despite that, he had gone on to high office and no one doubted his exceptional qualities, not least as an important ally and friend to Winston himself. Will pricked up his ears, for he knew little of the story.

'So how are you today, Flight Sergeant Fordham?'

'Glad to be home, sir. My breathing's much better, I don't think I need the iron lung anymore.'

'I think I'll be the judge of that.' The consultant examined him thoroughly, testing his muscle power and checking his lung volumes, asking him to blow into a calibrated tube. He took his time before pronouncing his verdict.

'There's no doubt you're making a steady recovery,' he said finally, 'but you've a way to go yet. Firstly, I want you kept in the respirator at night for the next week, then I'll review your oxygenation. Secondly, you'll be starting on intensive exercises, we've got to get more power back in these legs. Fortunately, you're in the right place – there isn't a better physical therapy department in the country. You'll need hydrotherapy as well, and massage, that's the norm. Tell me something: are you hoping to fly again?'

However unlikely it might seem, there could only be one reply. 'Of course I am, sir.'

'Well, I'm not ruling it out, but it won't be this year, and possibly not even next. But don't lose sight of it, if that's your goal – you never can tell with this disease.'

Will looked across at Betty, who appeared to be holding her breath.

'That's it then, any questions?'

Of course there was, the big one. 'Yes, sir, when will I be able to walk?'

'I can't say precisely, but I think you will walk again. There is definite evidence of functional recovery in your quadriceps, and the flexors and extensors of your lower limbs. With intensive therapy, we can build on that. Your legs will never be as strong as your arms, but they should be good enough to get by.'

He turned to leave, followed by all on the round except Betty, who came and sat by Will's side. She lowered her head to his shoulder, where she rested it quietly. When she looked up, her eyes were bright with tears.

'I told you so, all along!'

4

First Marty, and now Betty. When she said goodbye later that morning, he was nearly overwhelmed with emotion. Only the fortitude instilled through months of service allowed him to keep control.

'You'll write, won't you?' She stroked his cheek, as a lover would. Their physical intimacy had been in some ways closer, but his heart was already taken, and he had to let her go.

'Of course I will. Now get off, won't you, before I make a fool of myself!' He blew his nose on the sheet.

'Will?' She turned back at the door to the cubicle.

'Yes, old thing?'

'I'll never forget you.'

With that, she was suddenly gone, hurrying down through the ward, hardly stopping even to take her leave from Sister.

He felt bereft, his lowest point so far. There had been so many things he should have said, and now he would never see her again. He looked at the bare trees, framed by cloud outside his window, and wondered how many more farewells he would have to make before this war was over.

There would be no time for contemplation. A well-built orderly appeared with his wheelchair. 'Ready, sir? Time for your trip to the gym!'

'I'm not quite ready for that, am I?' said Will as he was lifted across from the bed, proving the man to be as strong as he looked.

'The "gym" is where you'll be spending most of the day. The old hands have another name for it, as you'll soon find out!'

On his progress down the ward he took in his surroundings. It was a twelve-bedded Nightingale ward, spacious and airy, and half the beds were currently vacated by their residents who he presumed to be at the same destination. As he passed the last bed, the friendly voice hailed him again.

'Ah, you're up, are you? Off to the torture chamber, I suppose? Hope you've got your shorts on!'

The orderly wheeled him to the bedside, to reveal a moustachioed man with wavy dark hair, reading a copy of *Tee Emm* magazine.

'Pleased to meet you,' the man added. 'Rhodri Llewellyn, 76 Squadron.'

'Blimey, Rod, you sound posh today,' the orderly said.

'Don't want standards to slip, now do we? Boz, wake up, we've a sprog!'

Will frowned, that being the term for newly qualified aircrew, but the orderly interceded once again.

'Don't take any notice of Rod, he calls all the new admissions that. He's been here too long, poor bugger, likes to have a little joke. Won't be leaving us for a while yet, will you, Rod?'

The airman looked hurt. 'Only if the process of ambulation does not require legs,' he answered. 'Boz, wake up and be sociable!'

But Boz was no more inclined to answer than he had been the previous night, and pulled the sheets over his head.

'I'm Fordham.' Will extended his hand, but he was already being wheeled into the long corridor before there was a chance for further conversation.

On the way to the gym, he learnt that Rod was a bilateral amputee.

'Got shot up in a raid over Cologne,' the orderly said. 'He managed to get them back to Manston but crash-landed in the fog. He was trapped on the cockpit of the Lanc! As for Boz, the second pilot, he nearly copped it too. Funnily enough, Boz has one good leg, but is in a worse way than his skipper. Rod's the one who keeps him going – they were on their last op of the tour. Boz was going to get married but his sweetheart's gone off with another bloke, so no wonder he's in a mess!'

Will wanted to ask more, but the door was opened to a huge and airy room. If some of the equipment was familiar, those using it were definitely not traditional sportsmen. Every injury dreamt up by the great god Mars, bringer of war, was represented there – amputations, fractures, leg wounds, nerve damage, spinal injury. Tending to the afflicted in an atmosphere of surprising calm were members of the Massage Corps, mostly women physiotherapists and male orderlies. In charge of proceedings was Sergeant Forbes, a dour and exacting Scotsman whose personal mission was to threaten or cajole the serviceman back to mobility, depending upon his mood.

'Let's be having him!' Forbes instructed the orderly to move Will to a bed underneath a metal-framed contraption that looked like a climbing apparatus. There were various slings and pulleys attached to the bars at the top. Will was beginning to understand why Rod had called it a torture chamber. After an exacting half an hour putting him through his paces Forbes stood up.

'Did the MO ask you if you hoped to fly again, laddie?'

Will nodded.

'He always asks that,' Forbes replied disparagingly. 'He thinks it's important for your morale. Personally I think it's a bloody stupid question – we'll have our work cut out getting you on your feet again, let alone flying a Wellington! Still, I'm minded to think that the hospital in Cairo did all right, with that Kenny treatment, but that's a breeze compared to what I've got in store for you. I'll have no slacking, there's no place for that in RAF Halton. No retreating either, you have to fight it, every day. I don't want you in here any longer than needs be, so we'll be trying our best to get you out, on two feet! Today we'll be kicking off quietly with some massage and graduated exercise, then tomorrow it starts in earnest. Any questions?'

The pep talk reminded Will of that first evening in Desford. What had the CO said – something about hard work and no slacking or dodging of the rules? Odd to think that he now had to master the art of walking, as exacting a challenge as flying had seemed then.

'Is it worth asking how long it'll take?'

'No, it's not – the answer to that lies within you, not me. You can take over now, Barbour!'

The white-uniformed young woman thus summoned looked even younger than him, a shy girl who would not meet Will's eyes. Once again he saw Rod's point, this time about the shorts.

'Soap and water first, then oil,' she announced. 'It'll revive your skin.'

He watched as she prepared to massage each leg in turn. 'What's your name?'

'Barbour,' she said, deftly commencing on his left calf. It was a pleasant sensation, altogether more professional than he had experienced before.

'I meant your Christian name.'

She was not to be drawn. 'Sergeant Forbes doesn't allow first names,' she replied, concentrating on her work.

He lay back, relaxing for the first time since his admission. Perhaps they really did know what they were doing here. As for Forbes, he suspected his bark would be worse than his bite. Prepared to go along with any treatment that meant he could walk out of here sooner rather than later, Will resolved to write to Honor once he was back on the ward.

Ward 15
PMRAF Hospital, nr Aylesbury, Bucks
24th February 1943
Dearest You,
As you should know from the telegram I have finally arrived. I certainly didn't anticipate coming home on a stretcher, but then I had no idea how long it would take me to recover.

Still, it's reassuring to be back in an RAF hospital, though I can't complain about the military one in Cairo. I was the first polio case to be evacuated, aircrew category One, so I can't grumble. I'm gradually getting better, and they seem to know what they're doing here.

All the time I was out there I kept planning what we would do and what I would say to you when I got back. It was so difficult to write any of my true feelings, knowing that the censors were reading my letters. I'd just finished my tour of operations and was due to come home for a long rest, so you can see how I couldn't have picked a worse time!

You know, the expression 'dying to see you' should really be revised to 'living to see you', because when things haven't seemed too good, that is what kept me going, and still does.

I have an overwhelming desire to see you again, and tell you what I feel for you. Please come as soon as you can – I've also sent a short note to you at your home address, just in case you happen to be there.

Not long now, can hardly wait to see you.

All my love from Me

5

Honor stood in Matron's office, waiting for her decision. She had not been invited to sit down, nor did she want to, resolute as she felt in her request.

'Compassionate leave, is it, Nurse Newson?' The elderly woman looked over the top of her round glasses at the young woman in front of her.

'Yes, Matron, Sister Duncan suggested I ask for it. I have been saving up my off-duty, just in case.'

'Could you remind me of the circumstances?' Matron was making her work for it, as Honor had anticipated she would.

'My boyfriend is in the RAF, Matron. He's just been invalided back after contracting polio in the desert. He's been over there for nearly eighteen months in all, flying Wellingtons.'

'And?'

'And I want to visit him at the Princess Mary Hospital in Halton. I've just had a letter to say that's where he is.'

'Can't you wait until your next scheduled off-duty? If every nurse in my hospital went running off like this, I'd have no one left to look after the patients.'

Honor's back straightened. She had already determined to go, whatever Matron said. She felt as if she would burst, having to beg for leave while Will lay waiting for her, not so very far away. She had read behind his letter to all his hopes and fears, and she had no intention of letting him down.

'I'm sorry, Matron, but if someone you loved had been risking their life for their country, I think you'd want to see them, especially if they ended up in hospital. Quite apart from anything else, if it wasn't for the RAF, Hitler would already have invaded this country and I doubt we'd be having this conversation at all.'

Matron raised her eyebrows. She was not used to such frankness in her staff nurses, but in truth, the girl was right. The Battle of Alamein had been the first victory of the war, and it was reasonable to suppose that this young man had played some part in it. Until that turning point, they had known nothing but defeat.

Reaching for her pen, Matron signed the chit. 'I'll give you a week, no more,' she said. 'And make sure you're back on time!'

'I will be! Thank you, Matron!' Honor could have kissed her, but managed a dignified exit from the room, before running down the corridor as though she had been blown by the wind.

She hardly knew which train she would catch, but sped to the nurses' home and packed. It was still early afternoon; she would set off as soon as she could. Scribbling a note for Rosie, she picked up her case and made her way to the porter's lodge, calling in on Ward 2 as she went.

Lotte was directly inside, so she called to her.

'Lotte, tell Sister I'm on my way! Matron's given me a week!'

Lotte wiped her hands. 'Where will you stay? It's miles away!'

'I'll make my peace with my parents and stay there! I'll be fine!'

'Be careful, and good luck!'

Honor just made it on to the 2.30pm train to Birmingham, her first connection. She struggled to find a seat, for all the trains were packed. Fortunately, the weather had been a little milder of late, so she would not have to endure a freezing journey. At least she would be in familiar territory at her destination, Aylesbury. After weeks of inactivity, she could hardly believe that she was on her way to see him. The three months since she had first received the telegram about his hospitalisation had been punctuated with such conflicting news that she had no idea what to expect.

Peter had been the least optimistic about Will's prognosis. He had visited Honor and Rosie after a dismal Christmas, ostensibly to cheer them both up, but had radically failed in the attempt. Rosie was living in her own private world, still grieving for her family each moment of the day, and only kept going by her brother Jack. Peter had taken the two girls to a nearby pub, but Rosie had excused herself early, leaving the two together. The conversation had inevitably drifted to Will.

'So what have you managed to find out?' Peter had asked, sipping his beer.

'Not much,' Honor admitted, 'but I think he was in an iron lung for a bit. It's his legs, mostly, but he says he should be better soon.'

'And you believe that?' Peter replied.

'I don't know what to believe!' She looked at him beseechingly. Why could he not just leave her in peace? She would find out soon enough.

'For God's sake, Honor, you trained on polio wards!' Peter said. 'If his respiratory muscles are affected then it's a severe case, you know that! What makes you think he's going to walk again? Has anyone said that's likely?'

She was silenced, forced to face her own doubts. Peter had said nothing that she had not anticipated, in the dark, lonely hours of the night.

He reached for her hand, sensing that he was overdoing it.

'Look, I'm sorry, I didn't mean to upset you. I just think you should be prepared for the worst. And you must keep your options open.'

'Options?' Honor asked quietly. 'What do you mean?'

'Just don't go thinking you've got to sacrifice your life to some lofty notion of caring for him! You don't know what you could be taking on!'

He had gone too far this time, and she rose to leave.

'I'll be waiting for you!' he had called after her. Then, alone with his thoughts, he had downed his pint in one. 'Damn and blast it!'

The train, slow at the best of times, ground to a halt outside New Street Station. Honor hoped it was not another bomb scare, in which she could be delayed for hours. Birmingham was a prime target for the Luftwaffe, and now that the RAF was taking nightly bombing raids to German cities, including Berlin, retaliatory strikes were bound to happen. She glanced at a newspaper that had been left behind on her seat. *Russians step up the fight!* The Soviet Army was making a remarkable comeback since their victory in Stalingrad in early February. The Nazis were being driven out of Russian cities one by one – Rostov, Kharkov, Kursk. Peter had been right about that, she remembered – he had predicted the Russians would never surrender. She could only hope that he would be proved wrong about Will.

Her eyes drifted down the page to an article about Malta. The convoys were now making their way through, and conditions beginning to improve. The islanders had shown extraordinary fortitude – it was hardly surprising that the king had awarded them all the George Cross.

She had written to Addie in a tumult of anxiety after receiving Will's letter from the hospital.

N. Staffs Infirmary
15th December 1942
Dear Addie,
I hear from the wireless that the siege has been lifted and I hope life is easier now in Malta. I miss you terribly and often wish we were all back in Groby Road!

I'm really proud of you, working under such dangerous conditions. Who'd ever have thought it when we started nursing?

I'm afraid I've had some bad news: Will is in hospital in Cairo – 63rd BGH, with polio. He has been in an iron lung so must have had it badly. He's still there and I don't know where he'll be evacuated to – maybe Malta, then you might nurse him too! I can't bear to think of him in a strange place with such an awful disease. I expect polio must be rife out there, and wonder if you have seen a lot of cases? Anyway, it's agonising because I know so little, and just have to keep waiting for news. Look out for him, though, won't you? I think I'd feel better if he was in your hospital, though I don't suppose there's much chance of that happening!

Not much news of my own. Very busy on the wards after a bad influenza outbreak, nasty cases of pneumonia and wish we had more M and B.

Keep safe, Addie, I'll write again when I know more!

Love Honor

6

The hospital garden below the balcony, a profusion of pastel-blue leadwort and pink geranium the summer before, was whipped by wind and rains. Nights of thunder and lightning, ferocious gales sweeping the sea, had transformed Malta from a honey-coloured island into a grey, embattled outpost of rock. The shutters on the ward blew open, letting in an icy blast of wind and rain, and Addie struggled to close them.

'Let me help you.' The red-headed navigator was not asleep – he too had been awakened by the storms. They pushed at the shutters together, finally forcing them closed.

'Thanks!' she said gratefully. 'Would you like a cup of tea?'

Dick would, for he was feeling much better and the profuse diarrhoea which had afflicted him for days seemed to be easing. He felt weak, but at least could contemplate recovery now the cramps had ceased.

The ward was quiet as she came back to his bed with the mugs. It was a luxury to have decent tea again, after the desperate lack of food they had endured towards the end of the siege. There had been times when she had wondered if she would ever leave the island alive – it was not until she stood among the waving crowds on the bastions as the *SS Ohio* had limped its way into port on the Feast Day of Santa Maria last August that she allowed herself to hope for deliverance. Up until then, there had been the constant fear of German invasion. Now, life was gradually beginning to improve; she was not perpetually starving and the hospital had coal, water, bandages and light.

There had been more injuries, though, since the Spitfire Squadrons had arrived. There were five in all now, taking the fight back to the Luftwaffe, using the same determination that had prevailed during the Battle of Britain. After months of relentless bombing by the Germans, who had all but razed the island to the ground, the tide was turning. It was not just Spitfires taking off from Luqa – they saw Wellingtons and Beaufighters setting out to bomb Rommel's supply lines and sink his tankers. The Royal Navy subs were tracking them too; nearly every week the *Malta Times* had encouraging news of torpedoes hitting the mark.

Addie had witnessed casualties beyond her imagining. Too many cases, despite the best efforts of the doctors and nurses, had ended with a Union Jack flag being draped over another coffin. She had become quietly resigned to it, just attempting to do her best, and ever conscious that the boy on the stretcher could have been Ken.

As winter closed its grip upon the island she yearned for the balmy summer days, the dazzling light and azure seas. Malta would always have a place in her heart, for it was here that she had found a degree of peace, despite the daily ravages of conflict. What was it Nelson had said, centuries before? 'Malta is in my thoughts, waking and sleeping.'

'Glad I'm not flying in this!' Dick took a mouthful of his tea – there was sugar in it, for a change.

'I think you'll be in for a few days yet,' Addie said. 'It usually takes a week or so to recover.'

'What's it caused by?' Dick must be feeling better; for up to now he'd been beyond caring as to the aetiology of his complaint.

'Malta dog? Probably bad sanitation and contaminated water supplies. It's some type of enteric fever, peculiar to this place.' Addie supposed that in a well-equipped hospital the pathologists would already have isolated the organism.

A restless moan came from a nearby cubicle. Addie rose to her feet, but it stopped.

'Who's that?' Dick asked. He looked across at her – she had an unusual serenity, this girl, which he could discern even in the dim light of the ward.

She shook her head. 'It's one of the Spitfire pilots. He's been in for ages – had a bad prang, might have been engine failure. He had multiple face and skull fractures, and he's lost his sight. We hoped it would come back as the swelling subsided, but it hasn't yet. He's due for surgery tomorrow. There's a naval surgeon who specialises in his type of injury, going to try and realign the bones. With any luck, it'll do the trick, but the poor boy doesn't believe that he'll ever see again.' She rose and took Dick's mug. 'Maybe you might have time for a chat with him in the morning, cheer him up a bit. He's not going to theatre until noon.'

7

Some presentiment, the airman's warning sign, had trickled into Dick's consciousness. When he entered the cubicle the following morning, he realised he had known all along. The man in front of him was bandaged over his forehead and eyes, but Dick recognised him in an instant.

'Oh my God! Jim! Jim Alderdice! It's Dick!'

'Who?' The face turned towards him, a note of confusion in his voice.

Dick strode over to the bed and took his hand. 'It's me, Sinclair! You remember, we were at Desford together!'

There was a pause. 'Were you the ginger-haired chappie who got thrown off the course?'

'That's me! One and the same! I can't believe it!'

'What the hell are you doing here?'

'I'm with 40 Squadron here, Wellington navigator. Had a nasty bout of Malta dog, hope to be out soon.'

Jim lay back on the bed. 'Well, I'll be damned! For a moment I thought you were a figment of my imagination!' He paused, the recollections streaming in. 'Desford – those were the days, weren't they? All we wanted to do was fly! We didn't have a clue…' His wide mouth formed into a smile, the memories bringing him to life again, then clouded over.

Dick sat down on the bed. 'I'm awfully sorry about your prang, old chap. I hear the surgeons are going to fix you up today.'

Jim nodded. 'So they say. I've a feeling it won't work. Do you remember when we went out on ops, some bloke or another would always know when his time was up? Say something like, "I won't be in the pub tomorrow, have a drink on me"? Well that's how I feel – I don't think I'm going to make it back, whatever they say.'

''Course you are, Jim! I hear the surgeon's a pro, one of the nurses told me about him. You'll be right as rain, able to see again too, you bet!'

'Hmm, I rather doubt it. I've had too much time to think, in here.' He held his hands up to his bandaged face. 'You see, I don't reckon I'm cut out for being blind for the rest of my life. I never was that brave, despite all of my talk!'

'You've been one hell of a plucky pilot, if what I hear is true!'

Jim shook his head. 'That's a different type of bravery, it's just spur-of-the-moment stuff. The real heroes are the ones who can live with the consequences, build their lives again, hang on to what's left. I'm not sure I have that type of courage.'

Dick thought of Will, still battling his disease, but said nothing. He did not think that would help Jim now.

'Look, chum, I'll be rooting for you, whatever happens. You've got to stay positive. I'll be here, waiting for you when you come back from theatre – that nice nurse won't mind.'

'Oh, Addie, do you mean?' Jim smiled again. 'She's not a nurse, she's a saint, if you ask me. I just wish I could have seen her face, just once.'

'You will, don't be silly!' Dick, seeing another nurse approaching, rose to leave.

'Dick! One more thing – please, you have to humour me,' Jim said. 'There was a girl, in the FANYs – if anything happens to me, you must let her know. Her address is in my notebook, in my locker.' He fumbled towards it, eventually feeling his way into the small cupboard where it lay. He handed it across. 'First page, read it out, make sure you've got it right.'

Dick looked at the firm black handwriting; did it belong to Jim, or the girl? He read out the name.

'That's her.' Jim clasped the book shut as he took it back. 'Yes, that's her.'

Dick watched as they wheeled Jim's trolley down to theatre. Once the pre-op sedatives had taken effect, he had glided into oblivion. Dick was too experienced an airman to discount another's premonitions, and he spent the afternoon uneasily, lying on his bed or pacing the ward.

When the night staff arrived, Jim was still not back.

'Where is he?' Dick asked Addie as soon as she appeared.

She hesitated, searching for the words. It was too personal a grief for her; she should have stopped herself becoming so involved.

'He never came round from the anaesthetic. I'm sorry, it just didn't work out.' Addie looked at him, her expression at once troubled and hurt. 'They did the best they could, you know.'

Imtarfa Military Hospital, Malta

28th February 1943

Dear Miss Molesworth,

I apologise if this news comes as a shock, but I regret to tell you that Jim Alderdice died during surgery yesterday. The doctors had hoped to restore his sight but he never came round from the operation. As you can imagine, brain surgery is very risky, even under the most favourable of conditions, which in all truth, is not the case here.

Jim asked me to write to you because he reckoned that he might not pull through and wanted to make sure you knew. I first met him at our flying training school at Desford – he was a fearless airman and an experienced Spitfire pilot by the time he came here. Malta is a tricky posting, as I'm sure you know. When he had the prang last summer it looked as though he might recover, but it was not to be.

He was courageous to the end, and it is an honour to have been his friend. If you want to find out more when I get home (not sure when that will be), then I would be happy to meet you.

Until then, good luck and please accept my sincere condolences.

Yours truly,

Dick Sinclair

8

'At the double! Keep up, laddie!'

He was there again, running through muddy fields near Desford, harangued by the drill sergeant. Guy was at his side, and Jim out in front, uncharacteristically sprinting ahead towards the gate. They would never make it back for breakfast unless he speeded up, but his legs just would not go any faster.

'Wait, lads, I'm coming…'

The cramps in his muscles jolted him from the dream. It had been so vivid, for a moment Will thought he was running still.

As he came to, it seemed that his entire body was aching. Sergeant Forbes had long since stopped humouring him in the gym, and reverted to his role as in-house despot. There was no let-up to the schedule now, just hours of agony and self-doubt.

'If I tell you to take your weight on your legs, do it!' Forbes had yelled as he stood unsteadily between the parallel bars. He had tried, and fallen, as he knew he would. 'Pull yourself up!' Forbes had commanded.

'I can't!'

'Look, laddie, unless you want to spend the rest of your life in a wheelchair, you'd better bloody try!'

It took a supreme effort for him to haul himself back on to the bars; just as well his arms were becoming stronger day by day. Forbes would no doubt be having him do press-ups soon, on some ingeniously modified piece of equipment.

'I hate that bastard,' Boz had muttered under his breath. He was on the set of bars next to Will. 'Honest to God, I'm going to kill him as soon as I can walk!'

Boz's disgust extended far beyond Forbes and included all the staff in the hospital, if not in the entire RAF. For his first few days on the ward, Will had thought that Boz would never emerge from the bedclothes, and his attendance at the gym was sporadic. Unlike Will, he had no motivation for recovery.

'Quite frankly, Fordham, I wish I was dead, then no one would shout at me and I could get a decent sleep!' Boz pronounced at lunch on the ward that day.

Rod dipped his bread in his soup. 'Don't bind on so! You know we're both lucky to be alive!'

'Says who?' But Boz was momentarily silenced and finished his soup.

Boz would never forget the raid – the searchlights trapping them in a barrage of flak, the deadly conflagration of light from the city below. The explosion had rocked the Lancaster, tearing a great hole in the port fin. Rod had ordered the crew to bail as the bomber made the coast, but the two of them had stayed at the broken controls so the lads might make it out of the front escape hatch. Then the looming runway, the back-breaking crash...

Despite reassurance that his leg would mend, it was Boz who had fallen into a deep depression on the ward. Most days he just wanted to stay under the sheets, in a private white world where no one could touch him. He could not bear to think about Viv; why had she left him? They had first met at a dance in Lincoln – she was a looker, Viv, as mad about him as he was about her. Now she wanted no more of him, cut him off with hardly a proper goodbye. He had told her he would soon be out, back at Scampton once he was walking again. She did not want to know, and in losing her he had lost his will to recover.

The closer Boz came to being certified LMF, the more Rod was determined to save him. While he himself might not be able to fly again, Boz certainly could. He was a dependable second pilot, just the bloke you needed over the Ruhr when things looked dicey. Rod decided on shock action.

'There's no point you crawling back in your pit,' he said as Boz, exhausted after breakfast, tried to take to his bed. 'She's not worth it!'

'How do you know?' Boz's voice was muffled by the sheets, barely engaging.

Rod was determined. Even a relapse would be better than this. 'One of the crew told me something when he visited yesterday.'

'What?' Boz peered over the sheet reluctantly. 'What did he say, then?'

'That Viv had been seen holding hands with a Yank,' Rod replied. It was cruel, but he had no choice.

Boz sat up in bed, drawing back the sheet. 'A Yank?' he said incredulously.

'Yes, sorry, mate, I wasn't going to tell you, but I think it's better you know. One of the USAAF blokes, you know, all uniform and talk, took her fancy – she's not the only one, they can sweet-talk them into anything. Best let her go if that's the way it is – you'd never be able to trust her. You know what those Yanks are after, only one thing on their minds!'

'Bastard! Taking my girl while I'm laid up here. I'll throttle him when I find him!' Boz called for an orderly. 'Get me my crutches! I'm damned if I'm not going to that bloody gym after all!'

Will's progress was measured in tiny achievements, each one building on the one before. Sometimes at the end of the day he saw no headway, so drained was he by the routine. He concentrated upon improving as much as he could before Honor saw him. It would not be long now; with any luck his letter would have arrived.

He was resting on his bed in the early afternoon before the next session, his eyes half-closed as he dozed off.

'Visitor for you!'

Will sat up with a start – could it be Honor at last?

Standing at the end of his bed, looking as uncomfortable as only a hospital visitor can, stood the old man. He was wearing a warm overcoat over his suit, his hat still firmly on his head.

'Hello, son.'

'Father, I wasn't expecting you so soon!' This was the truth, for Will knew that the journey, a long way from Guisborough on the train, would have involved going through London, a city the old man had never cared to visit.

'Aye, it's been a bit of a mission, but your mother wouldn't rest until I'd come. She's that worried, doesn't know where to put herself. I said you'd be all right, but she's been niggling away. I thought I'd just get on down, see for myself. Mind if I have a seat?'

Will motioned to the chairs and his father drew one up.

'By, lad, I'd never thought you'd be coming back like this!' He took of his hat, but did not dispense with his overcoat.

'That makes two of us,' Will said.

'What's the latest then, about your infantile paralysis? Are you going to be able to walk again?' It was typical of his father to come straight to the point, no need to beat about the bush.

'The doctor says so,' Will replied. 'I just don't know how long it'll take.'

'It's a bad business! How did you pick it up?'

Will tried as best he could to fill him in with the details, wishing Betty was here to give one of her concise summaries – they sounded so much more substantial, unlike the flimsy details he could impart.

'Eh, lad! And you'd finished your tour of duty, had you?'

'I had, Father.'

He knew not to expect warm sentiments from the old man; it was not his style. There would be no effusive comments about his contribution to the war effort, the risks he had run, or the country in which he had been called upon to fight. It was as though that was superfluous to requirements, an unnecessary accompaniment to the here and now.

'Your mother sent you this.' The old man reached in his bag, and produced a fruit cake, rich and firm, the sort he had not seen for months. 'She's been saving her coupons to make it for you,' he added.

Will looked at the cake, suddenly overwhelmed. 'I don't like to eat it, thinking of her going hungry.'

'Don't be silly, lad, you need to build up your strength. I'll make sure your mother's fed. Not that it makes much difference, she's always running around after everyone else.'

'You'll give her my love?'

'I will that, but I'm not going yet. Your mother said I had to speak to the doctor, find out what's going on. I'm off to ask that ward sister to find him for me, I'll be back later.'

His father walked purposefully up the ward and knocked on Sister's door. He must have succeeded in his task, for a little while later Dr McWhirter entered the ward and joined them. Will was not included in the conversation, which took some time. He lay back on his bed and watched the skies clear – a good day for flying now the cloud cover had lifted. One day, he would be able to stop appraising the weather as though he were due to go on ops, but not yet.

It must have been a good hour before the old man reappeared.

'You've taken your time! I wasn't sure they could see you.'

But he had forgotten the authority of the man, a frequent mistake of the young, too intimately associated with their parents not to harbour a shadow of contempt.

'They'd see me, I knew that. Your mother was right, best to get it from the horse's mouth. It looks as though you'll be in here a while yet, son.'

'How long? Did they say?' Will was unsettled – had they told his father more than they had told him?

The old man sat down again. 'They say you'll walk again, that's all that matters to me. You'll just have to be patient, son, and work hard at it. At least you're out of that iron lung, your mother didn't like to think of that.'

He gathered up his coat and hat. 'I'll be on my way now. I've to stay in London tonight, catch an early train up north tomorrow. At least I can put your mother's mind at rest.'

Will took his hand, not a usual gesture between them. 'Thank you for coming, Father.'

'Of course I would, son. Happen you'll be on your feet next time I'm here.'

Like the others before him, he was gone, his figure receding through the ward doors into the world beyond.

9

Spring had come surprisingly early and the daffodils were in bloom. The clear sunlight of early March shone through the high windows of the ward, reminding him that the lambing season would soon be upon the farmers in the Dales.

Will sat on the side of his bed and pulled his crutches towards him. He was able to make his own way to the gym now, as long as he took his time. Keeping his balance could prove tricky, but at last his legs were beginning to hold firm.

One of the nurses opened the ward door for him and he made his way down the long corridor. There was a slight figure coming in the opposite direction, and something in the swing of her hips caused him to slow his pace. He watched as she came closer, finally stopping altogether as she ran towards him.

'Will!'

He was nearly knocked to his feet as Honor threw her arms around his neck.

'It's you, it's really you!' She drew back and touched his face, thinner and older, but still the same Will.

'I thought I'd lost you!' He bent to kiss her, nearly toppling them both, until they steadied as one; her small frame supporting his. 'I've been living to see you!'

There were others making their way up and down the corridor that morning, but for Will and Honor, they did not exist. They were in their own world, and time held them close in his hand.

Epilogue

'Saint Leonard, you see, was the patron saint of those afflicted by disease, and of prisoners and captives – in short, all those who need to be unchained.'

Dick had arrived early at the church, as befitted his role, and the vicar was showing him the stained glass window in the north aisle. They looked up at the laying on of hands; the bright Victorian artistry depicting the healing of a lame boy and blind man. Illuminated by the summer light, the window came to life as surely as the miracle it depicted.

The church door opened. There were to be few guests, apart from the families of the bride and groom, but those men that arrived were mostly in RAF uniform, and one or two in wheelchairs or on crutches. The young women were dressed in short frocks or trim suits, the fashion of 1943 allowing them to show off their figures and economise upon material at the same time.

'You all right?' Dick asked.

Will nodded. How could he not be?

'Pity Vic's not here!'

40 Squadron had moved on to the Italian campaign, and Vic was with them, part of the Desert Air Force bombardment of Sicily. Once the Allies had secured their foothold, the fighting would move up through Italy, so Vic was not expected back any time soon.

Though not all of the faces were familiar, Dick could pick out some of them. He caught a glimpse of a woman at the back of the church, a fleeting image like the one at the hatch of the Halifax, ready to jump. He shook himself; most of the girls here would be nurses from Groby Road or Stoke.

Will glanced across at one of the pews filling up, and recognised Matt. That must be Jenny with him; looked like a nice girl. Apart from Dick, Matt would be the only one from the Desford days – Guy's Wellington had been shot down last spring over Germany on a night raid to Berlin. He was a POW, like so many of the bomber crews, facing a period of incarceration until the war's end. Andrew had died in India, from the complications of cerebral malaria, as Will had found out when he contacted Dr Farrington for news.

'Andrew would want you to keep the car,' the doctor had added at the end of the conversation, but Will was too cut up to reply.

He said a silent farewell to the gentle fair-haired pacifist, and the countless other comrades he had lost. Some, like Arthur, were still posted missing, presumed dead, but what hope now that they would ever return? Dick had been right: Will was one of the lucky ones.

She would be here soon. As the organist started to play, a couple hurried in, ushering two dark-haired children, too old to be their own. Edek and Alice, but who was with them?

He would have to find out later, for Honor was walking down the aisle towards him, dressed in white, on her father's arm. Will put aside his stick, and stepped forward to meet her.